### MARK BROWNING
He knew nothing of his mother, except that his future lay in her birthplace—if only he could uncover Savannah's secrets.

### ROBERT MACKAY
He was a simple, honest man, and from the moment he took Mark into his home, the older man was Mark's friend and mentor. He was the one man Mark never wanted to hurt, and the one man Mark could hurt most deeply.

### ELIZA MCQUEEN MACKAY
She was the queen of Robert's home, the mother of his children, his perfect helpmate—and the winner of Mark's heart.

### CAROLINE CAMERON
The secret of her grandparents' fifty-year-old hatred could destroy her reputation; her love for Mark could destroy her happiness.

### OSMUND KOTT
Driven by hatred and jealousy, he knew the scandal that jeopardized Mark's future in Savannah. How could Mark fight an enemy he did not know existed?

## Novels by Eugenia Price

### St. Simons Trilogy

LIGHTHOUSE
NEW MOON RISING
THE BELOVED INVADER

### Florida Trilogy

DON JUAN MCQUEEN
MARIA
MARGARET'S STORY

### Savannah Quartet

SAVANNAH
TO SEE YOUR FACE AGAIN
BEFORE THE DARKNESS FALLS
STRANGER IN SAVANNAH

### Georgia Trilogy

BRIGHT CAPTIVITY
WHERE SHADOWS GO
BEAUTY FROM ASHES

# Savannah

## Eugenia Price

St. Martin's Paperbacks

Published by arrangement with Doubleday

SAVANNAH

ISBN: 0-312-96232-0

Printed in the United States of America

Doubleday hardcover edition published 1983
Berkley edition/August 1984
Jove edition/February 1990
St. Martin's Paperbacks edition/April 1997

St. Martin's Paperbacks are published by St. Martin's Press, 175 Fifth Avenue, New York, NY 10010.

10  9  8  7  6  5  4

For *Easter Straker*

# Savannah

*Part I*

# 1812–1813

# ONE

HANDS gripping the rail of the plunging schooner *Eliza*, young
Mark Browning, his well-tailored clothes wet and rumpled,
stood on deck alone, determined not to be sick. From beneath
a fashionable slouch cap, strands of damp chestnut hair clung
to his lean face as he struggled for balance against the sea.

Except for trips by boat to and from his Philadelphia home
and Yale College, Mark had never sailed. His late father's
tales of storms at sea, however graphic, in no way prepared
him for this. Even so, his resolve held. Mark was headed for
Savannah to build a life, to make his own way. He meant
someday to create his own family because the last two other
members of the small one into which he was born twenty years
ago were now dead. There were friends and connections, but
no one mattered anymore back in Philadelphia.

Bearing south, the schooner slid down, then vaulted up and
over gray walls of towering Atlantic waves. Mark's slender,
strong body, more than adequate to any test he'd ever given it,
was no match for this power. The *Eliza* floundered helplessly,
inching forward, then seeming to rush back—getting nowhere.
There was no visible storm, no rain, no wind, but the sea raged
and hurled its weight over the deck—not in a regular motion
so that a man might anticipate the next dousing—but with
quixotic, uneven force, as though designed to take him off
guard, to catch him with his hands momentarily loosed on the
railing. There were no women or children aboard and most
men were below, as were his cabin mates, too ill to move from
their berths. Now and then during the turbulent morning, a

3

few passengers braved the deck in desperation, unable to endure the smell of sickness in the stuffy staterooms and half-
ashamed, as was Mark, that their stomachs churned when, in
truth, there was no recognizable storm.

"Mind over matter," he imagined he heard dead Aunt
Nassie's voice chide. "You've a strong mind, Mark—a
Browning mind. Use it! Just concentrate. You won't be ill.
*Concentrate.*"

On what? The sleek, handsome schooner *Eliza*—his only
protection from the flailing sea? In fair weather, he was sure
she rode high in the water, her bow proud and sharp, cleanly
severing the waves, gliding, cradling passengers in safety for
sun- and moonlight strolls on her deck, for sound sleep in her
small, but adequate, cabins and staterooms.

May 22, 1812, the date of Mark's high-spirited departure
from Philadelphia—only two days ago—had been a storybook
day for sailing. A spring blue sky, with just the right amount
of wind moving white, puffy clouds about, seemed suited to
the *Eliza*. Her passengers read on deck; a few played flutes
and fiddles brought along to while away the hours. The mainly
prosperous gentlemen aboard cooked their meals in relative
comfort on their own charcoal stoves or good-naturedly
waited their turn in the ship's galley.

On the first day, Mark was drawn to one passenger—a
stocky, but graceful, gentleman with a short Brutus haircut,
who seemed to enjoy himself immensely. His name, Mark
learned, was Robert Mackay, a prosperous merchant from
Savannah. The Savannah mercantile world held Mark's interest, but it was the easy charm of Mackay himself that drew
him. The moment his two somewhat dull cabin mates announced that they were dining with friends in another part of
the ship, Mark invited Robert Mackay to share his meal of salt
fish and hominy, which he would prepare himself. Mackay
refused with regret because he was dining with the captain;
unexpectedly, Mark felt rebuffed. "Thin skin because you're
frightened and nervous about going to a strange place," Aunt
Nassie would have said. He supposed so. In spite of his excitement and anticipation, he was more nervous than lonely.
After all, dining by himself would be no new experience. He
had taken his meals alone almost every night of the long year
since Aunt Nassie and his father died. He simply wanted to

know Robert Mackay of Savannah and he vowed to find a way.

A gigantic wave swept his feet from under him so that, momentarily, only the frantic grip of his hands kept him from pitching overboard. When the wave sucked back into the sea and his boots were once more firmly on deck, he swallowed a flood of hot fluid forced up by his queasy stomach and shut his eyes against the sting of salt spray.

Without warning, a wall of leaden water struck him with such force that in nightmare tempo he felt his hands wrenched from the ship's rail and his body borne back and down until his head struck a hard object.

Then, nothing.

Sometime later, when Mark regained consciousness, he noticed the quiet first, the heavy water rushing by the ship's hull, then the lulling motion of being safely rocked, then the pain in his head and shoulder. The merest movement of his head on what seemed to be a pillow made him wince.

"Not so fast, son. Take your time. Take all the time you need."

Through the pain, the man's calm, almost musical voice, very close by, lessened some of the tension in his body. Mark took a deep breath and then, as though he'd been asleep for a long time, forced open his eyes. The pleasant, open-featured, middle-aged gentleman smiled at him. A smile Mark could only recognize at first as beautiful: strong, even teeth, a well-formed mouth and dark eyes so large and kind, they seemed to embrace him. It was Robert Mackay of Savannah.

"I apologize for my ship's uncouth treatment, young man," Mackay said. "The *Eliza* is seldom so rough with her passengers. Notice how gently she carries you now?"

"Yes, sir," Mark half whispered. "Has the wind died?"

Mackay chuckled. "On the contrary. The wind rose soon after we carried you down those narrow, steep steps. Lack of wind was our problem. The good ship *Eliza* just needed wind to fill her sails. We're lifted to the tops of the waves now, buoyed along. The wind is going around the clock—steadily."

"I—see."

"Actually, the ship's normally rather like the dear lady for whom I named her—full of charm, agreeable, welcoming. The

*Eliza* and I deeply regret the uncivil treatment, son."

Mark tried a smile and then, to hide his distress at the pain in his right shoulder, closed his eyes again. "It's—all right, sir. I'm—not a good sailor."

Only when he felt it taken away and a fresh, cool cloth laid gently on his forehead did Mark realize that a compress had been there at all. He sighed. "Thank you, sir. That's—good of you."

"Well, my ship and I have much to make up for," Mackay said.

His eyes still closed, Mark asked, "You own this beautiful schooner?"

"Yes. She's named for my wife. And, as a rule, she is just what you called her—beautiful. As is my wife. Actually, both Elizas are more than merely beautiful. They're kind, constant, poised." Mackay's smile was in his voice. "Are you headed for Charleston or all the way to my home city of Savannah?"

Mark opened his eyes. "Oh, all the way to Savannah, sir. From now on, Savannah is my home city, too."

"Is that so?"

Looking around the stateroom, larger than his own, Mark frowned. "How long have I—been here, Mr. Mackay? And, where am I?"

"You're in my stateroom, son, and you've been here for over two hours. I've learned about the conditions in your cabin. If you and I had met before you signed on, I'd have seen to better quarters for you. How you managed in the same crowded space with those two obnoxious fellows, I can't imagine."

"They were pleasant enough, until today." He smiled weakly. "I remember one of them said that just looking at the table swinging on its gimbals made him feel ill."

Mackay made a face. "Ugh. Well, I've ordered the place cleaned up. They'd been sick over every inch of it. But for the remainder of the voyage, you'll be right here where I can look after you."

"Where will you sleep?"

"The captain has an extra berth. Your effects are here already. Most of your trunks were moved to the captain's stateroom along with mine. I took the liberty of selecting what I thought you'd need for the next five days or so until we reach Savannah."

"I'll never be able to thank you."

"The only thanks I need will be a good report after a thorough examination now that you're conscious again."

"There's a doctor aboard?"

Mackay grinned. "Indeed so. The most unusual of doctors. George Jones is president of the Georgia Medical Society, a full-fledged judge and currently the mayor of Savannah."

Mark managed a smile. "Sounds impressive. I'll be glad to have him check me over. But"—the smile came a bit more easily now—"do I address him as Doctor or Judge or—Your Honor?"

Mackay's laugh was as musical as his speech. "Since he'll be checking mainly on what I'm afraid might be a broken collarbone, why not try Doctor? I'll go for him now." At the narrow wooden door of the stateroom, Mackay turned back. "Incidentally, you and I will make it fine as friends. I like your cheerful disposition."

When Mackay's longtime friend, Savannah's mayor, Dr. George Jones, had come and gone—his sartorial elegance as impressive as his careful examination—Mark swung his legs out of Mackay's bunk and sat up. "I think I'll live, sir. Thanks to you."

"At least we know your collarbone is still in one piece, but should you be sitting up yet?"

Mark grinned. "Well, the doctor, the judge *and* his honor, all three, suggested that I might do what I feel like doing. What I feel up to is some common courtesy to you. When Dr. Jones recommended that I take it easy for several days, you tricked me, you know, by asking me before him to stay indefinitely at your home in Savannah."

Mackay laughed. "Of course I tricked you. You're far too well-bred to start an argument with a stranger present. You had no choice but to agree."

"If you think back, sir, I didn't actually agree. I didn't say anything one way or the other. I really can't presume upon you. A good night's sleep and I'll be fit again. But I would appreciate your recommending lodgings in Savannah. Just something clean and reasonably comfortable."

Mackay turned a straight chair backward and straddled it. "Well, now, that gives me as good an excuse as any to talk about the peculiar and partly delightful little city of Savannah.

Once the threat of another war with Britain is past or once the war is over—whichever eventuality may occur—Savannah will indeed have one or two good hotels. Not yet. So, since doctor's orders are for rest and care, your address will be—for as long as you need us—the Mackay house on Broughton Street."

"Surely, there's some sort of inn or tavern—a respectable boardinghouse."

"Well, there is one shabby inn. President Washington stayed there during his memorable visit to Savannah in 1791. And, perhaps because the citizens so exhausted the great man with their celebration of him, he may have slept well. That was more than twenty years ago. As it is today, it will not supply your early impression of Savannah. I forbid it."

A slow smile spread over Mark's lean, even features.

"Did I say something funny?" Mackay asked.

"That phrase 'forbid it' has a history with me."

"Oh?"

"My Aunt Nassie, who reared me, always said to forbid me was the surest way to be sure I did a thing."

"And does that still apply with you?"

Mark was silent for a time. "I don't know. You see, there's so much I don't know about myself. More and more it seems to me that those who presume to—to being cultivated say a lot of things they don't really mean."

"Bull's-eye," Mackay laughed. "So-called cultivated folk seldom say what they mean if anyone of consequence is listening." He laid his hand on Mark's knee. "I did mean it when I said you're more than welcome at my home, son."

"Oh, I wasn't referring to you, sir. I meant—myself. You see, in my anxiety not to impose, I refused your kindness point-blank. And that isn't what I really meant at all. The truth is, I'd give almost anything for a few days with a—real family." He studied his slender, smooth hands. "Family life is one experience I've missed. But you don't know me at all. Are you always so openhearted?"

"No, I'm not. In fact, I'm boringly protective of Mrs. Mackay and our children. Still, I seem to know all I need to know about you."

"How can you?"

"I suppose, in part, because I'm forty years old and have

met numbers of men both here and abroad. Have, in my business as a merchant, had to make quick judgments. For now, I simply know all I need to know about you." To Mark, Mackay's laugh had a safe sound. "After all, Browning, I had a look at your wardrobe, your trunks, your brushes, your razor. You're a gentleman. Your manners, and especially those straightforward gray eyes of yours, are to me most revealing. You're not only a gentleman by birth and breeding, you're good and trusting in your heart. Now, does that answer your question?"

Mark felt himself redden. "You haven't asked about my family—not once."

"I know you're from Philadelphia. I figure you'll tell me more when you're ready."

"My mother died when I was three." He frowned slightly. "I—don't think I really remember her at all. Father's spinster sister, Aunt Nassie, reared me."

"You and your aunt and your father lived together?"

"Not my father. Aunt Nassie and I lived in what is still called the old Browning mansion on Locust Street. Father traveled the world from the day after my mother's funeral. I suppose you'd say he didn't really live anywhere." Mark smiled a little. "Unlike his only child, he was a fine sailor. Spent much of his life traveling at sea. He inherited the family business from my grandfather, who died before I was born. I guess Papa and Grandfather didn't exactly get along, but there was only one son." Mackay, he thought, knows how to listen and for some reason Mark needed to talk. "I don't actually know that they didn't get along, but when he visited me, I could never get my father to talk about Grandfather Browning except to say that they were not at all alike."

"And does it bother you somehow—not knowing about your grandfather?"

The characteristic small frown appeared again and vanished. "I'd have liked knowing what made him so successful. Funny thing, my aunt, who was my best friend, wouldn't talk about him either. Except to say that Grandfather had no time for anything but the business." Mark's eyes filled. "I know this makes us sound like a family of pretty cold fish. That isn't true. Aunt Nassie loved my father as though he'd been her own son. She loved me, too." Blinking back tears, he added,

"I guess it's obvious how much I loved her. Except for my four years at Yale, she was just about my world. I always had more fun with her than with friends my age. I—loved her very much. My father was devoted to her, too."

Mackay was silent for a time, then said, "You speak of your father and aunt in the past tense."

"Yes, sir. Papa died a little over a year ago. Died where he spent so much of his life—on the high seas. He was drowned in a storm off the Bahamas. Aunt Nassie died, too, a month later. As a result of the shock, our doctor said."

Slowly, Robert Mackay got up from his chair and sat beside Mark on the bunk. "I'm sorry, son. I'm truly sorry. But, I'm also *here*. And I will be, from now on."

An unbidden sob shook Mark's body. He was sure Mackay heard it, but equally sure that his new friend would give him time to compose himself.

As months, even years, can unroll with the speed of lightning in the memory, Mark was back in Philadelphia again, a twelve-year-old boy standing beside his father on the corner of Front and German streets, his young heart pounding as it always did during Mark Browning, Sr.'s rare visits. The boy knew that at any moment the tall, golden-haired man beside him would lean down, shake his hand, give him the flashing smile that always seemed to belong to someone else, then swing once more into a rented carriage and vanish for another year or two or three. That day the boy longed so painfully for his father to stay with him that on a public street corner, the longing spilled out in tears. Pretending not to notice, Mark Browning, Sr., mussed his son's thick, dark hair, shook his hand, smiled and was gone.

There had been three more visits but no more tears.

Mackay, still sitting beside him, was waiting with quiet patience and no sense of either haste or idle curiosity. Mark tried to think of something appropriate to explain his long silence, but he could think of nothing. Why had that one visit when he had let his father see him cry come so clearly now, of all times? Why hadn't he remembered the last hours spent with his father? Why not their last good-bye—the theatrical last doff of the fine brushed top hat? Why not any of the earlier visits in which Mark had so reveled as a boy? He had adored every sight of his dashing, golden father, had so enjoyed himself every moment of each visit that at age seven he had felt sympathy for his young friends who had the same dull father about the house every day giving orders. "I'd rather have my father just once in a while," he'd declare, "than your old-fogy fathers every day! My father tells me by the hour about his travels to the Far East, to Africa, to England, to France and Spain and Italy! China, too, and Japan. My father and I have more real fun in two weeks together than you'll ever know about!"

At this moment, in the creaking stateroom in the company of his new friend, suddenly Mark knew why the unexpected memory had been of that earlier farewell to his parent rather than the last one. What his father had confessed to him on that last visit had been so securely locked away, so firmly pushed to the back of his mind, that not once during the long year alone in the big house, grieving for both his father and Aunt Nassie, had he dared dwell on it. He could tell no one and so he had pushed it aside. Buried it.

Oh, he had accepted what his father had confessed as truth. Facts were facts. What he had buried, he realized, was his own response at the moment his father had confessed. Mark had not doubted that his troubled parent was telling him the truth. Even his imaginative father would never have made up such a thing. The torment—alive to this day—lay in not being able to remember *how* he himself had responded, in having lost forever the chance to ask. His father seemed to have vanished from his life more surely than had Aunt Nassie, because he had been able to visit her grave. Mark Browning, Sr., had no grave. Drowned at sea, the shining, tormented man had simply vanished in all ways.

With his whole heart, once he had been told, Mark had understood why his father had lived his restless life as he did. Once the words were out of the elder Browning's mouth—in a flash following the initial pain at having been so deceived—Mark had understood, had known, deep inside himself, *why* his father had deliberately misled him. With the knowing had come a different pain: His father had needed him at the moment of confession and Mark could not remember one word he himself had said. He could recall—even this minute in the *Eliza*'s stateroom—every word his father had spoken, but *not one word of his own*.

He turned his head slightly to look at Mackay, whose brown eyes were calm and expectant. The friendly silence brought an impulse so strong that Mark got quickly to his feet to quell it: If I dared tell Mackay what Papa confessed to me, he thought, maybe I could remember what it was that I said to him that last day. Instead, he stood, silent, his back to Mackay. To babble would show his anxious youth, and more than anything, he wanted Robert Mackay's respect—as a *man* able to make his own way in a strange city.

When the silence grew awkwardly long, Mackay spoke in a quiet, firm voice. "Life has certainly handed you a double blow, son. You've been handed the kind of double blow few mature men are asked by the Almighty to endure. You have my sympathy. Most of all, you have my deepest respect."

Mark stared at him. "Your—respect? How did you know I wanted that above everything?"

"I didn't. But you have it." Mackay stood, too. "And don't forget, I'm here when and if you need to talk more later. Right now, doctor's orders are for you to rest. I have business with the captain, but his stateroom adjoins this one. When you've had a nap and want company again, just knock on the wall. I'll come right back with a pot of tea and some biscuits." With that, Mackay eased Mark down onto the bed, lifted both legs onto it and pulled up the sheet. "Go on and laugh at my mother-hen behavior. But I know even a forty-year-old likes to be fussed over when he's not well. My wife is superb at the art of spoiling me. You can do with a bit of the same medicine."

He gave Mark a smiling salute and strode toward the door. Then he turned abruptly back, his high forehead creased in concentration as though he'd just remembered something. "Was your father's name Mark Browning, too? And did he own the vast Browning World Shipping Company?"

Mark frowned. "Why, yes, sir. You—didn't know him, did you?"

"I've suddenly remembered. We dined together once in Liverpool! And that had to be less than two years ago."

Mark felt as though he couldn't breathe. "Then—you saw him after I did. . . ."

"I recall it was just before I moved my family back to Savannah. We intended to stay in England. My firm has an office there, but with the trouble pending between our two countries, I felt I had to get my wife and children back here while we could still find safe passage." Mackay spread his hands in amazement. "Now, why didn't I make the connection with the name Browning? I'll never forget the man I dined with that night. Never."

"Why? Why won't you ever forget him?"

Mackay was again seated on the side of Mark's berth. "I'm not quite sure. His appearance, for one thing. A stunningly handsome gentleman—that shock of golden hair, physique like a Greek god. So important in the world of commerce— the owner of the giant among shipping firms—" Mackay frowned. "And yet, he seemed—lost in a way. Oh, nothing he said. Highly entertaining conversationalist, widely read— brilliant, in fact. But—"

"But what?"

"You're not much like him, are you?"

"No, sir. I'm not like him. We looked nothing alike. He always said I was a lot like my Savannah-born mother."

Mackay clapped a hand to his forehead. "Savannah! You go right on startling me! Your mother was born in Savannah? What was her maiden name? I've certainly heard of her family!"

"Cotting."

Robert Mackay thought a minute. "Cotting? Funny, I don't recall hearing that name—ever. Were your parents married in Savannah?"

"Philadelphia. And except to talk endlessly about how lovely she was, how right for him, I now realize that my father told me almost nothing about her. All I know about their courtship is that he vowed he couldn't wait for all the Savannah wedding folderol, so when she came to the ship to say good-bye the day he was to sail back to Philadelphia, he took her by the hand right then and there and stole her away."

"When was that?" Mackay asked. "I didn't come to Savannah myself until 1790."

"I think they left Savannah about three years earlier. My Aunt Nassie, who loved my mother very much, always said she spent the first two years of their married life teaching my mother how to be Mrs. Mark Browning—in Philadelphia."

Mackay grinned. "Not an easy job to be Mrs. Mark Browning anywhere, I'd think. Least of all in fashionable Philadelphia.''

"Papa always told me that my mother was considered the loveliest, most charming young matron in town."

"But surely, he spoke of her Savannah family."

"No. Only about my mother herself. You see, he did begin to travel right after she died. I was only three. I really don't remember actually living with my father. All my life as I was growing up, I just lived for his visits. Aunt Nassie and I didn't dare travel abroad, although she adored Europe. We could never be sure when Papa might visit us. Neither of us would have missed a visit for anything on this earth."

"I see. But your Aunt Nassie must have stayed in touch with your mother's family in Savannah."

Tears stung Mark's eyes. "For a whole year, Mr. Mackay—alone in that big house—I've kicked myself because I never seemed to ask the right questions of anyone. Now, I can't. Mother, it seems, was an orphan when she married my father. If she had brothers and sisters, I was never told."

"Cotting, Cotting . . ." Mackay muttered, scratching his head, trying to make the Savannah connection.

"I probably shouldn't even mention any of this. It only makes me seem dumber, without a shred of normal curiosity all those years."

"Don't kick yourself for not asking. Children are romantics at heart. You just didn't think to ask the hard questions. And evidently they didn't give you any facts—beyond her charm, her beauty."

"That's right. And until the last time I saw Papa, what they did tell me seemed enough." He thought a minute and then, deciding that he had nothing to lose, went on. "There was one night—I was about six years old—when I was roused from a sound sleep by Aunt Nassie's voice downstairs. Ordinarily, she never raised her voice. That night, shaking like a leaf, I crawled out of bed and listened at the top of the big stair because I could tell she was livid with rage at someone. A man. I couldn't see him because the stairway curved. I remember only that I was scared at the way Aunt Nassie sounded. The man kind of mumbled. Looking back, I think he must have been drunk."

"Could you hear what he said at all?"

"No. But I could hear Aunt Nassie. For once, she forgot about waking me. She was almost shrieking that he'd better hie himself back to Savannah, Georgia, and stay there or she'd have him put in jail. Then, she shouted for him to get out, and I heard the door slam. For a long time I lay in my bed trembling, but even then I didn't know why I was scared. In about half an hour, pretending to be asleep, I heard Aunt Nassie look in on me, then close my door softly and walk down the upstairs hall to her own room."

"You didn't ask her about it the next day?"

"I'm ashamed to say I didn't."

"Do you know why you didn't?"

Mark frowned. "Who understands something he did or did not do when he was six?"

"You're right, of course."

"I didn't mean to sound rude, sir. It's just that I've tried for so long to understand—even about myself."

"Do you think that man had a connection with your mother?"

"That night such a thought never crossed my mind. The fact that he was obviously from Savannah has made me wonder since. I do know what I have to do, though."

"Make it a point to find out when you reach the city?"

"No. Put the whole thing out of my mind forever." Mark looked straight at Mackay. "I've spent a solid year, almost all of it alone, groping my way toward the conclusion that because I can't make heads or tails of my early life, I need a brand new one. Oh, I had social friends in Philadelphia, but no one I'd talk to even as freely as I'm talking to you. You see, my life has always appeared more mysterious to my friends than to me—if that makes any sense. To me, it was just—my life. I never knew what it would be like to have my parents living in the same house with me. Aunt Nassie was my world, and except for the excitement of Papa's visits, she filled it. I don't remember when my parents were both there. Having only Aunt Nassie seemed natural to me. After she and my father were gone, no one mattered anymore." He smiled a little. "Oh, I broke down and cried when the carriage rolled down our long drive for the last time, but except for our old driver, I was alone. No one saw me cry. That's all past. I'm free now. Footloose and fancy-free and once I set foot on that dock in Savannah, a whole new life begins."

Mackay thought for a moment. Then he said, "You don't sound as though you're bluffing, either. I'm almost convinced that you have—somehow—settled all this in your mind. Put it behind you. In only a year, too. And at your age!"

"Once I decided to head for Savannah, sir, that settled it."

"Well," Mackay said, "I'm honored that I could be with you during this shipboard interlude. It's probably an important time—before you get to Savannah."

The small frown, which came often if Mark was deep in thought, appeared and as quickly vanished. "I—I hope I haven't given you the impression that I'm bitter about any of this. Did I, sir?"

"No. No, you didn't. And I'm surprised. It seems to me you've just been stating facts."

"The way I see it, starting a new life doesn't mean discarding any of the old. It won't be possible to put the memory of my father and Aunt Nassie behind me. I don't want to. Aunt Nassie will always be my real friend. I did almost worship my father. But one of the few things I brought along is a large portrait of my mother, which always hung above our drawing room fireplace. Aunt Nassie and I used to sit before the fire and look up at her. She was as beautiful as my father was handsome. I have her coloring—brown, wavy hair, gray eyes. When I was a boy, I imagined that I could tell by the portrait that I looked something like her." He laughed softly. "Now, she seems far too ethereal, too lovely, even to have been mere flesh and blood—like me."

"I'm glad you brought the portrait. I'll look forward to seeing it."

"It's here, on board, in a wooden crate in the hold. A few pieces of furniture I especially liked will come later if I decide I need them. I put them in one of the Browning warehouses before I left. You see, I won't need the furniture and the silver and so on until much later, when I plan to build my own house in Savannah. But the portrait goes right up on the wall of whatever rooms I find now." He went on matter-of-factly. "I sold the old Browning mansion, the adjoining land and the buildings, almost all the furniture, silver, crystal, linens—just about everything. I'm really beginning my own life."

He felt Mackay studying him. "That must have been terribly hard for you—getting rid of so much.''

"Yes, sir, it was. But I'm more certain every day that I did the right thing. You see, I knew—well, almost the way a man knows about his faith in God—that Savannah is where I belong. I've known for most of the past year.''

Robert Mackay took a deep breath and let it out noisily. "You are, to say the very least, a surprising and impressive young man. How old are you, Mark?''

"Twenty. I had a birthday last week.''

Mackay whistled. "I guess it's just dawned on me—a year from now you'll be a fabulously wealthy young man! My partner, William Mein, and I are proud of owning this ship and two others. Our holdings pale beside what will soon be your firm, son. I bow to you.'' He laughed. "With wealth such as yours, I guarantee you a wide welcome in Savannah! Nothing gains entrée to Savannah business and society circles more swiftly than wealth. You'll have the young ladies lining up, straining their dainty ears for the jingle of your coins. I can picture it now—''

"Sir,'' Mark interrupted, almost curtly. "I beg you to promise that you will *not* tell anyone about my—connection with Browning World Shipping. *Not anyone*. You caught me in a weak moment when you told me you'd actually met my father, or I wouldn't have told even you. You see, I haven't made up my mind yet whether or not I want the Browning fortune. More accurately, whether or not I'm entitled to it.''

"*What?* You're the sole heir, aren't you?''

Mark nodded. "And next year, when I reach my majority, it will be for me to decide. But I want to make my own way. In the mercantile field. I graduated from Yale in business. I want to find out what I can do for myself. And Aunt Nassie always said, 'Too much money can be a hindrance.' She'd always had plenty, but she tried to live as though she didn't. Which meant, as she saw it, that she tried hard not to miss the small joys no amount of money can bring to anyone.''

"She sounds like my wife.''

"I've already signed away to charity everything my aunt left me,'' Mark went on. "That's all settled. At least I've signed papers of intent until I'm twenty-one next year. I—I just haven't decided yet about Browning World Shipping.''

Mackay stared at him for a moment. "And what does your

family lawyer say about all this—indecision?''

"He thinks I'm quite crazy. Believes I'll come to my senses.'' Mark grinned. "Aunt Nassie warned me about old Woolsey, though, long before we learned of my father's death. 'Woolsey's a good man,' she'd say, 'smart as they come. But after I'm gone, if you find you ever want to leave Philadelphia, don't let him stop you. A big chunk of his income would go with you, don't forget.' ''

"And did Woolsey try to stop you?''

"Yes, sir.''

"I see he didn't succeed. Well, you have my reluctant promise not to spread this amazing story around Savannah. I don't understand you, either, but I do promise. It's certainly your business.'' Then, "By the way, does that promise include my wife? I share confidences with her regularly. She's my conscience.''

"I hope you won't tell—anyone, please, sir. Not until I've had a chance to earn my acceptance.''

Mackay sighed, then extended his hand. "I hereby solemnly swear. With my wife, Eliza, it won't be easy, but I do promise.''

"Thank you.''

"I'll make you a wager, though. That this enormous decision will be so much on your mind, within no time you'll tell her yourself. She's that kind of lady.'' Slapping both palms down on his sturdy thighs, Robert Mackay stood up. "I have to say again I'm glad we'll be together out here on the briny deep for a few more days before we dock in Savannah. I need time to get my own sea legs with a surprising young fellow like you.''

Abruptly, Mark said, "I do mean to pay room and board at your house, Mr. Mackay.''

"That I will not agree to!''

"But Mr. Woolsey will be sending me a monthly income. No more, no less, than I need to be comfortable. Quite enough. I set the figure myself.''

"You set the allowance yourself—and it's modest?''

"I hope that doesn't make you think less of me.''

"Do you really want to know how it does make me feel?''

"Yes, sir,'' Mark said, squirming in the bed to find a position less painful to his shoulder.

"It makes me feel foolish to have offered advice and friendship to you. I doubt that you need anyone."

"That's not true! I'm determined, but I need someone to bolster my courage. More than anything, I want your friendship, sir. I beg you to believe that!"

Mackay rubbed his chin thoughtfully. "Undoubtedly, what I meant to say was that with your unique slant of mind, I wonder if I'll be *able* to advise you. I came to Savannah when I was seventeen and made use of every hand up anyone offered me. If I'd had the wealth my widowed mother lost during the Revolution, I'd have wanted everyone in town to know it. Do you consider me less of a man for that?"

"Oh, no, sir. That's what most people would want. And I don't disagree. It's just that I—well, I'd like to dig around, maybe inside myself, in the hope of finding, of finding—" He broke off.

"Of finding what?"

"I guess I don't know what to call it yet. I think more than anything else right now, I want to discover who I really am." Mark laughed a bit sheepishly. "That's a disease of all young people, I suppose."

"Wouldn't finding out some facts about your mother's family help?"

Mark thought a moment. "I'm sure it would. But honestly, that isn't the reason I chose Savannah."

"Of course I'm teeming to know why you did choose my city."

"My father. Every single time he visited me as I was growing up, he spoke so glowingly of the town; without knowing it, he convinced me that it would be the one place on earth for me to spend my life."

"He came to Savannah often on business?"

"When he was young, yes. He loved the city. He even kept some sketches and paintings he'd made at the time he met my mother. You know how colorfully he could describe the places he'd been."

"Indeed I do. I feel I never need stir myself to visit Shanghai. Not after your father described it."

"Then, you can imagine what a roseate glow he gave Savannah for me. Of course, unless another war breaks out with Britain, I'm also well aware that prospects for Savannah's mercantile future are enormous. I'm sure I can locate the kind of work I want. But, mainly, I need to find out what matters most to me in life.''

Mackay raised an eyebrow. "And you need to be poor in order to do that?"

"No. I just feel that men unencumbered with much money have more time to think—and to learn. To be friends."

"I see. Well, I'm getting out of here before you hand me still another surprise. I've tired you with too much talk as it is. Knock on that wall, now, when you want tea and company."

"I will. Thank you."

"And don't lie there thinking. Those squeaking blocks on the sheets tell me the crew is trimming the *Eliza*'s fores'l and mains'l. The wind is gradually changing. Take a nap."

"I'll try."

# TWO

MARK did try to sleep; tried holding his eyes shut, his aching body still. But the jammed shoulder hurt, his head ached, and as through almost every night during the long year past, too many thoughts crowded his mind.

He had meant to ask Robert Mackay more questions about Savannah, about Mackay's chance meeting with his father two years ago. The questions, half-formed now, jumbled into each other. Each path down which his mind rushed ended invariably with the now familiar, fragmented, haunting images of his golden-haired, poignantly handsome father struggling for life against an angry sea and losing the struggle in what must have been a similar dark-varnished stateroom.

*"Mind over matter, Mark."*

Why could he still almost hear Aunt Nassie's voice when the memory of his father's voice had vanished? He squeezed his eyes shut again. How do you manage mind over matter, Aunt Nassie, his heart cried, when your mind is so full of so many things? Who can stop thoughts from happening?

Mark had been so sure, on the bright Philadelphia spring day as he strode along the wharf toward the *Eliza,* that prospects of a new city and a new life would stop such thoughts, would put an end to the one dagger question that always left him feeling as helpless as a child: the tearing, clawing question he had spoken aloud again and again as he paced the high-ceilinged, spacious parlor of the old Browning mansion night after night, alone, during the first months after Aunt Nassie's death.

Until now, his vow never again to form the words of that question aloud had held. It was barely holding now as he lay in

21

Mackay's berth, struggling to rest. He hadn't formed the words, but how did a man hold back a thought?

If only there had been one more visit before Papa died!

If only Papa's confession had not come during our last visit . . . if only I had let him know that I understood why he had been running away all that time, trying to escape his pain at losing my mother. Even as a young boy, if I'd known, surely I would have told him that I understood. And it might have helped. Did Aunt Nassie understand why her beloved brother had spent the years fleeing his own heartbreak?

*Did Aunt Nassie know that her brother was not away handling the vast international business of the family shipping company?*

Mark pulled himself up onto an elbow, feeling that his head would split if he tried one minute longer to lie still.

He struck the mattress with his fist. "I can't ask her if she understood," he said aloud. "I can't ask Aunt Nassie anything! She's—dead. As dead as Papa. I can't ask either of them—anything."

The low voices of Robert Mackay and the captain, just on the other side of the tongue-and-groove partition, hummed pleasantly. Mark could stop his thoughts by tapping on the wall. Instead, he decided to try once more to remember his last meeting with his father—to try again to recall one small, so far forgotten word that might free him from the exhausting self-blame he still carried. The shock had been so great when his father had at last confessed he had been running away all those years—handling no family business whatever—that for the life of him Mark could not remember his own response. He did not know that he *had* understood, had actually begun, at the moment of Papa's confession, to feel his father's agony through all those lonely years without the beloved Melissa. Mark had begun to see his mother far more clearly as the lovely, laughing young woman Mark Browning, Sr., had loved. He might now be free forever of the guilt if he could only remember that on their last visit, he had let his father *know* of his understanding.

Every visit from his father through all those years as Mark was growing up had brought joy. The brief times together had fulfilled his own boyish need to see, to listen, to adore his parent, but with no thought of his father's need. A man who had suffered as he now knew Mark, Sr., had suffered, desperately needed a friend who understood. Did his father have such a friend?

Mark could not even remember a time when he had actually been forced to accept the fact that his father didn't live with him in the same house. That the elder Browning had a good reason for being away, the boy had never questioned. Some fathers were doctors or lawyers or ministers. His father headed a huge shipping enterprise that kept him traveling across the world and that was that. It still puzzled him that at Yale his classmates had made cutting remarks because Mark Browning, Sr., did not live at home in Philadelphia. "A man as rich as your father could hire twenty men to do his traveling for him," one friend invariably jibed each time he'd had too much to drink. Their taunts had not even angered Mark. His friends didn't understand, and maybe no one would ever understand, that Mark simply loved his parent exactly as he was.

Leaning on his elbow made the shoulder ache more. He eased down onto the pillows again. His father had seemed to give him so much. He was on the schooner Eliza bound for Savannah now because of his father's influence. In a way he wouldn't attempt to explain, he owed all the bright prospects of his new Savannah adventure to the man whose very name and family connections had brought such awesome respect to Robert Mackay's eyes.

Mark Browning, Sr., on every visit back to Philadelphia, had indeed spoken at length of his own love for Savannah: as beautiful, he believed, in its way as Philadelphia and like Philadelphia, still more British than American. "The only spot of its kind in the country," he'd declare. "Savannah has the congenial warmth of a village, but with the elegance and charm of a lovely English city. And the sky, Mark? I'll never, never forget the changing Savannah sky. Often floating with coastal clouds, often clear blue, often low and gray in the rain—but always the Savannah sky seems to be embracing the city. I've seen cities in the world whose skies appear remote. Not so Savannah." And then, his father would sigh and his eyes would fill with the familiar pain young Mark assumed had always been there. "Your mother could not have been born anywhere else on the face of the earth," he would say slowly, his mind seeming to recall in an instant each exotic foreign city he'd visited. "She could only have been born in Savannah."

Through the years, Mark had come to wait eagerly for the inevitable praise of his mother. "I never want you to forget her, son. She and Savannah will always be one to me. Beautiful, gentle, strong, warm of heart, graceful of manner."

Growing up, he had struggled to recall something real about his mother. He did think at times that he remembered her laughter, the tilt of her head, a scent on the air when she passed by; but only the portrait brought any hint of her features, and even there, the artist had shrouded her beauty in mist. The young woman herself had become shrouded in mist to her only child.

During visits from his father, the boy had merely sat listening, spellbound, nodding, eager, trying to take in and keep every word spoken about his mother and Savannah, but asking almost no questions.

Their final time together was different. As they had done on the last day of each visit since Mark's fifteenth birthday, father and son sat together at the City Tavern. They had just been served their claret when Mark asked a question that five seconds earlier he had no thought of asking: "You've traveled the world, Papa, ever since Mama died. But you've never gone back to Savannah. Why?"

Seated across the narrow, heavy oak table, Mark, Sr., said nothing. He didn't even look at his son. He sat motionless except to move the wine about in his glass in slow circles.

"I've been wondering about Savannah ever since you were here a year and a half ago," Mark went on. "I don't mean to pry, but with Savannah's fine deep-water port, I've never figured out why your business doesn't take you there often. You love the city so much." Still his father said nothing, went on watching the wine move round and round. "Mightn't it be good to see Savannah again? To take me with you? We've never taken a trip together. Maybe I could even meet some of my mother's family. I didn't want to ask in a letter, but I suddenly got irked at myself that I've never found out who my Savannah grandparents were."

"I had my reasons for not telling you—for not ever going back there. I still have them."

His father's voice was suddenly so strange, the suffering in the deep-set eyes so sharp, Mark felt quickly ashamed. "I'm—sorry, Papa."

"Sorry, Mark? For what? For finally acquiring a son's normal curiosity? For years I've expected—and dreaded—a barrage of questions from you!"

"I care more about you, sir, than about finding out anything. Please, just forget I even asked."

Mark, Sr., now looked straight at him. "You may be one of the few men on earth who will never have to worry about hurting anyone, son. Sometimes I've felt you weren't related to me at all. Sometimes you appear to be—too good. Too forgiving to be true. Are you, Mark? Are you too good to be true?"

Mark could still remember how his own face burned, how awkward and ill at ease he felt. He remembered, too, that all he could think to say was feeble: a clumsy, young, unconvincing attempt to bridge the sudden barrier by telling his father how his fist had itched to smack itself against the faces of not one but two overbearing Yale professors who had given him a lower grade than he expected . . . how he had indeed flattened a man almost twice his size in a town-and-gown brawl one night. The boyish spiel had at least brought a crooked smile to his father's face.

"Good for you," Mark, Sr., said. "That relieves me a little. At least you're not—perfect." The crooked smile vanished. "I haven't gone back to Savannah because I *couldn't* go. I still can't bear to be anywhere—*she* lived." the rich voice faltered. "I'm—a very weak man." In one gulp he emptied his glass.

"You mean—my mother," Mark said softly.

"Yes. Your mother. And I thank you, son, for not making that a question. You could so easily have gasped, 'Do you mean my mother—*after fifteen long years?*' "

"I'd never say a thing like that."

"Why not?"

"Well, because it would never occur to me, I guess. I—I'm just not surprised that you—still grieve for her."

The man, his face white and taut, studied his son for a long time. "You're really *not* surprised, are you?"

"No, sir. I'm just sad for you."

"Aha! Good. Not sorry for me. Sad for me, eh?"

Mark nodded.

"Well, son, you finally got around to asking your question

about why I've never been back to Savannah except in my tortured memories, so this may be as good a time as any to ask you a question that's haunted me." His father took a deep breath. "Year after year, especially when I'm on the other side of the world from you, I've wondered how a boy could just go on seeming to be so happy to see me wander into Philadelphia at *my* convenience—for spasmodic visits whose length *I* selfishly decide." He leaned across the narrow table. "Mark, are you old enough yet to know why it is that you evidently don't despise me for having deserted you all these years?"

"Papa, you haven't *deserted* me! You—you've been traveling because of the business."

His father struck the table. "I have *not* been in touch with any part of Browning Shipping since your mother—went away! Except to extract money from the firm, I've had no connection with it whatever." Glancing about him, he lowered his voice to a biting whisper. "I've avoided my father's business like the plague! I've—been running from my pain. *Don't ever be so stupid.* A man can't run from pain. It goes right along with him. Do you hear me?"

Again, Mark only nodded. No words formed.

"I deserted you, son. *I deserted you* the day after we buried your mother. I dumped you in my blessed sister's lap and began to run." He lowered his head. "I'm still running."

Alone now in the stateroom, as though the blow had just come, Mark covered his face with his hands.

"Why don't you despise me, son? *Why don't you despise me?*"

To that point, the memory had been clear. It was clear now. Mark knew he had answered his father's painful question with a question of his own: "Who *has* managed the business, Papa?"

"A man named Parsons. James Parsons."

"James Parsons?"

"Don't ask me about James Parsons until you answer my question about *you!* Why don't you despise me for deserting you?"

Abruptly, Mark uncovered his face and opened his eyes wide. Forgetting for the moment that Robert Mackay might hear him on the other side of the thin stateroom wall, he said aloud in a surprisingly strong and steady voice exactly what he knew he'd said to his father that day:

*"I couldn't despise you, Papa. I love you too much. I understand too well about your pain. Don't blame yourself for what you couldn't help."*

In that instant, he knew beyond the shadow of any doubt that he *had spoken* those very words to his father!

The relief was so great, he found himself sitting up in bed, as though listening. What he seemed to hear was his own voice again as on that day: "I'd rather be with you thirteen times in fifteen years, Papa, than to spend every day with any other father on earth!"

Even the reeling in his head had lessened. Every muscle in his body went slack, easy. He had spoken only what he had always felt in his heart toward the man whose name he bore. Had the shock of learning that another man had made the giant company succeed blocked his memory of what he had really said to Papa that last time? Blocked his memory for all that time? Could grief—double grief for his father and for Aunt Nassie—cause a man to *forget* the very thing that might have lessened the pain? He had carried the heavy burden of false guilt all that time just because, until now, he could not remember anything he had said to his father except to ask who had been operating the business.

He breathed deeply, yawned, slid back down in the bed and was sound asleep when Robert Mackay returned three hours later bringing biscuits, tea, soup and cooked dried apples from the captain's stateroom.

Their light meal finished, Mark, still in bed but dressed for sleep in a clean nightshirt Mackay had brought, said, "I'd like you to stay, Mr. Mackay, but shouldn't you get some rest too now?"

Wiping his hands after stacking their used utensils for the steward, Mackay laughed. "You think I need rest, but you hope I'll stay and talk awhile, eh? Well, I'm not one bit sleepy, so if you feel like talking, I'd be delighted to stay for a cigar. Do you smoke?"

"Not yet."

Tilted back in the one straight chair, his boots on one of Mark's smaller trunks, Mackay clipped and lighted his cigar from their one candle. "You're a lifesaver to me, actually," he said, puffing contentedly. "I so loathe being away from my wife and children and I find the usual shipboard company so deadly, I'll stay as long as you feel ready for conversation."

"You don't like to travel, sir? I mean, you leave Savannah only when business forces you to leave? You'd rather be in Savannah than any other place?"

Mackay laughed a little. "As long as my family is there, yes. For sure, I'd rather be in Savannah than any other city in backward Georgia—even any other city in the United States. We travel often to Newport, on occasion to your city of Philadelphia, but when I have to go on business alone, my children plague me every minute I'm away. There are nights in strange beds in Liverpool, in Paris, in Bonn, in The Hague, even here in this country, when I think I'll die if I can't find out *that minute* how each child is faring. How each has changed, grown, bumped his or her head, skinned which knee—" He broke off, his open, even features suddenly pained. "You see, I was in London back in 1804 when my partner, William Mein, had to write me that my firstborn son, my namesake, had died. Robert was four."

"Oh, sir, that must have been a terrible ordeal for you— making that long voyage home alone with your grief, not knowing how your wife was managing. . . ."

Mackay gave him a grateful smile. "For any age, you're a sensitive man. For twenty, you're hard to believe." Mackay smoked for a time in silence. "But then, you've already had experiences many older men never have. I hope you and I are still friends—even better friends—by the time you're my age. At forty, I predict you'll be a truly remarkable gentleman."

Mark grinned. "How many children do you have?"

Mackay returned the grin. "I'll tell you gladly. There are four. Jack, eight, William, seven, Eliza Anne is four and little Kate, two."

"I'm eager to know them all."

"To have a guest like you in the house will send them bounding—out of control."

"I can't picture Mrs. Mackay's children out of control. Not from what you've told me of her."

"Oh, she's very human. But perhaps the world's most unselfish lady, and the most understanding. Actually, we're apart more than either of us would choose. She visits relatives in England and Jamaica for months at a time; I travel on business. We despise being apart—manage to sink a ship or two loading them down with love letters—but she actually urges me to enjoy myself when we're not together. When she's abroad, for instance, I live a Savannah bachelor's life and soon you'll find out that such is not the life of a recluse. I dine out, attend balls—squire the ladies. But they're all friends of ours." Mackay tapped the ashes from his cigar, then said abruptly, "You must get that rest the doctor ordered, Mark."

"Could I ask one more question?"

"What is it?"

"My father didn't mention me the night you dined with him in Liverpool, did he?"

Robert Mackay's warm, brown eyes clouded. He got slowly to his feet and stood looking down at Mark. "If we're to be friends, as I hope and pray, there must always be some honesty between us, do you agree?"

"Oh, yes, sir." A half smile turned up one side of Mark's mouth. "My father didn't mention me, I'm sure. And you're not going to believe that it's all right that he didn't."

"My first thought was to lie to you, to say he had boasted of his fine son back in Philadelphia."

"If you'd said that, I might not feel as secure with you as I'm beginning to feel, sir. You see, that wouldn't have sounded a bit like Papa."

Mackay frowned, studying the young, expressive face. "You're really not hurt that he didn't bring up your name, are you? You're really quite calm and collected about the whole thing. Am I too forward to ask—how that can be?"

"No, sir. Not at all. You see, I'm accustomed to being misunderstood where my father is concerned." He sighed, waited a moment. When he spoke again, his voice had a quiet certainty. "But as I told my father the last time we were together, I'd rather have had him for thirteen glorious visits than to have had any other father on earth—every day."

Mackay shook his head. "How could the man have appeared to be so lost—when he had a son like you waiting for him?"

"Because he was lost, I think. Lost in grief, over the death of my mother. He didn't find himself in all those years."

"I see. Poor man. Tell me, Mark, did he know how well you understood?"

Mark closed his eyes a moment and then looked straight at

Mackay. "Yes. I began to understand—just in time to let him know."

"And did it help him?"

"I don't know. He left within a few minutes. I didn't see him again. But he's—with my mother now. I'm sure he's fine for the first time since she left him all those years ago. They *are* together again, you know."

"Uh—yes, yes. Of course." Mackay sighed. "At least, I have to believe my four-year-old son, Robert, is—is living somewhere."

"He is, sir. I'm sorry our conversation brought your little boy back to mind. I hope it doesn't cause you to sleep poorly."

"I'll sleep. That's one thing at which I'm expert. Pleasant dreams to you, son. Pleasant dreams of your new life—in *our* city."

"Oh, yes!"

At the door, Mackay turned back and saluted. "See you in the morning a little after eight. We'll scratch up some breakfast together."

"I'll look forward to that."

Mark had never saluted a person before—only the flag. He saluted Mackay now. And he liked the feeling. It brought a brand new sense of comfort and real camaraderie with someone besides Aunt Nassie.

# THREE

FOR breakfast they boiled eggs, dunked Mark's slightly stale Philadelphia buns in hot coffee brewed over the coals of Mackay's portable stove, and all morning, as Mark watched, his new friend tended the pot of lobscouse he had concocted.

"So, you've never eaten lobscouse," Mackay said when Mark, bathed and dressed in a fresh white shirt and trim, gray trousers, stretched himself again on the bunk.

"I've heard of it, but I've never eaten it."

"Then, you haven't lived. The good sailor's friend is lobscouse."

Mark laughed. "Remember yesterday, sir. I'm not a good sailor."

"Nonsense. Anyway, the *Eliza* is going to show us consideration today. I had a good talk with her just after dawn this morning."

A gentleman had no need to cook except when at sea without wife or servant, and since Mark had never been at sea, cooking was a mystery to him. Mackay, on the other hand, was obviously practiced and enjoyed the process. As he fitted a lid on his sterno pot, he explained that he'd hung a chunk of salt beef all night over the side of the ship so that, when he cut it into thin, small pieces, it looked rather fresh. Then, into the stew pot he chopped potatoes and onions, added water and plenty of pepper. By 10 A.M. the stateroom truly smelled as aromatic as Aunt Nassie and Mark used to play-pretend theirs did on cook's day off.

"You are better today," Mackay said, settling himself again after tending the pot. "You look better. Good color in your

31

cheeks. How does the shoulder feel after the exertion of a bath?"

Mark flexed it. "Still sore, but mending. I still think I could have washed my hair, too."

"Why bother until you reach my house?"

"Feels stringy after being doused with all that salt spray yesterday. I don't want you to be ashamed of me when I meet your family."

Mackay pulled at his own Brutus haircut, brushed to the front over his forehead, no strand more than two inches in length. "I recommend my hairstyle, son. I can keep it clean in less time than it takes to shave. But then, young men like you—extremely clean-cut, exceedingly handsome young men like you—must needs be a bit vain."

"You mean you're not vain at all?"

Mackay laughed. "I hope I have sense enough never to try to fool you. And I wish I could make all of life right for you"—Mackay snapped his fingers—"like that. Of course I can't, and of course that would be bad for you. But let me tell you something. I'm a farily prosperous merchant and often I'm accosted by young men boasting or wheedling—trying one way or another to impress me so that I'll put them to work to learn my business. I think on the whole I'm generally patient with them. After all, I came to Savannah at seventeen and a fine gentleman took me in until I could make it on my own. But I tell you honestly, no one else has interested or perplexed or drawn me as you do. Now, have I a right to expect you to believe that?"

Mark's quick frown came and vanished. Looking straight at Robert Mackay, he said in his forthright manner, "I guess I'd believe whatever you told me. I grew up among gentlemen who were kind and generous to me as a favor to Aunt Nassie, I always thought. You've shown me a personal kindness that I feel is somehow—just for me."

"You're right. It is."

"You really know very little about me as a person except that I can't keep my footing in a rough sea and that I'm on my way, with no letters of introduction, to make a life for myself in the wonderful city of Savannah."

Mackay raised one dark, even eyebrow. "You have a fairly idealistic concept of Savannah, I fear. You *can* believe me, but don't make believing everybody you meet—a habit."

"When you first came to Savannah, sir, did you find a lot of people tricking you because you were young?"

Mackay laughed. "No. I can't honestly say that I did. But I doubt that even then I'd ever have told anyone I believed *anything* he said."

"Aunt Nassie always said I was too quick to believe people."

Mackay got up to stir the lobscouse again. "I do wish I could have known your Aunt Nassie."

"So do I! She was a real sleuth when it came to ferreting out hypocrites, but I'm positive she wouldn't have found one hypocritical bone in your body."

Back in his chair, feet propped once more on Mark's trunk, Mackay laughed. "Then the lady wasn't as smart as I thought."

"Talk some more about your wife, will you?"

Mackay's laughter dwindled to a smile that filled his large, brown eyes. For a long moment there was only the smile. Not prideful. Rather, a look of certainty, as though to say: *Mrs. Mackay and I have well settled it. We are one. It is forever. And it is all—good.*

Finally, Robert Mackay spoke softly. "My wife? Son, I do not exaggerate when I say that I married one of the most perceptive, gentlest, strongest women God ever created."

"Is she very beautiful?"

"To me, she is. A near perfect figure—not too tall, so as to cause me to appear of even more average height than I am. Soft, light-brown hair, hazel eyes that can calm me with a glance. A natural mother. Our children are indeed blessed. Perhaps she's fooled considerably by me—she always calls me her 'dearest friend.' But in the main, she keeps me sensible by her talent for seeming to see all of life with God's eyes."

Mark was listening intently. "I think I know something of what you mean by that, but would you tell me what it is to *you*—to see with God's eyes?"

"A good question. One I've wondered about for almost all of the twelve years in which Eliza and I have belonged to each other. What I think I mean is that unlike most people, she is a realist. My theory is that God sees things and people exactly as they are. He can and does—at the same instant—see both the good and the evil in us all. He still loves us. As nearly as a human being can do that, my wife does." He chuckled. "She sees me as I am—and loves me anyway."

"I hope she goes on loving you after you arrive home with a stranger in tow."

"If that were all I had to worry about, my life would indeed be simple." He paused. "Mark, how much thought did you give to the possibility of war with Britain before you decided to move to Savannah?"

"I thought a lot about it. Are you worried about war?"

"Any man whose work is connected with shipping is deeply worried. Nothing the United States has tried has worked out. Jefferson's attempts to solve the maritime problem failed; now it looks as though Madison will be no more fortunate. It seems to me our only hope of avoiding war is Britain's economy."

"Their economy, sir?"

Mackay nodded. "You see, with my business connections in England, I manage to keep abreast of things. They're in bad shape, mostly because of the enormous expense of fighting Napoleon. In my opinion, if our government can hold steady a bit longer, Britain may be forced to give in—cancel those infernal orders-in-council that so disrupt our shipping, impress our sailors, cut us off from vital ports."

They were silent for a moment. Then Mark said, "I don't see how we can sit still while they go on boarding our vessels—jerking our sailors off United States ships—forcing them to serve in the British Navy."

In answer, Mackay merely commented that he was amazed the *Eliza* had so far escaped on her voyage south.

"Would they board us on this route so close to our own shores, sir?"

"Well, perhaps such an event is less likely now that we're in southern waters, but not long ago, an American vessel was boarded nearer to the coast of New England than we are right now to the coast of North Carolina. I don't worry, but for one reason only. Worrying would perturb me." He grinned impishly. "I'm very opposed to anything or anyone who makes me uncomfortable." Stirring the pot again, he glanced over his shoulder. "You know, son, I can't help wondering how many young men your age would have dared give up that easy

life in Philadelphia—fine home, servants, all the money you
could want to spend, no business worries—in order to dive
headlong into a new career at an uncertain time like this. And
in a strange port city, of all places."

"I know this sounds peculiar, sir, but Savannah doesn't
seem like a strange place to me because of my father's love for
it."

"It is, though. And its main business—shipping and trade—
will be heavily damaged, if not wiped out, in the event of a war
with Britain on the high seas. You're a remarkably courageous
lad."

Mark laughed. "Or perhaps a bit crazy?"

"Perhaps. All adventurers are, I suppose."

"Funny, I've never thought of myself in any way as an
adventurer."

"How do you think of yourself?"

Mark shrugged. "Just as—Mark Browning."

"That may be your secret. Do you like business?"

"Yes sir. I was second in my class at Yale. I'm not sure I'll
go into shipping, though. I'm just not very interested in owning ships."

"Oh, ho! The most deliriously happy time of my life was
the launching of a brand new ship of my own—the *General
Oglethorpe.*"

"You've built a ship yourself?"

"Had one built at St. Mary's, Georgia." He shuddered.
"St. Mary's is an uncivil, primitive, mosquito-infested town
on the Georgia-Florida border, but the day the *General Oglethorpe* slid into the water there was a glorious one for me.
Fellow by the name of John Patterson, a skilled shipwright
from your home city, built her. Five hundred thirty tons
burden—the most exquisite form I ever beheld!" He chuckled
to himself. "I remember how hard I worked on one letter to
Mrs. Mackay from St. Mary's, trying to convince her that my
ugly, exhausting journey had been worth it. I'd have made six
such journeys just to see that ship launched. Mrs. Mackay and
I had only been married something over a year at the time. But
quite long enough for her to be well aware of my love of personal comfort. She had worried herself half-sick over my
rough journey to the Florida border."

"Do you still own the *General Oglethorpe?*"

"No. Perhaps I laid too much stock in her. She was wrecked the next year—I was aboard—near one of the Bahama Keys. Twenty-three men died. My darling ship was destroyed. Captain Patterson, nine sailors, two slaves and I were miraculously saved in a lifeboat. After twelve days of total discomfort on the seas, a Charleston schooner picked us up."

"You must have been ill after such an ordeal."

"Felt rotten for a day, but after a brandy rub and dry clothes, I went straight to a dance the next night in New Providence."

His eyes teasing, Mark said, "Dancing must mean almost as much to you as your ships."

Mackay laughed. "I love to dance! But I never take social life seriously. That's my secret. You'll meet some ladies and gentlemen in Savannah, believe me, who take it far more seriously than church. One lady in particular, my good friend and favorite hostess, Julia Scarbrough. The countess, I call her, right to her face. She isn't one bit insulted. Quite the contrary. Her husband, William Scarbrough, is a wealthy merchant, and a blessing that he is. Only a wealthy man could keep the countess afloat socially."

"Does Mrs. Mackay enjoy Savannah social life?"

Mackay smiled the proud, contented smile that seemed always prompted by any mention of his wife. "Yes, but her life wouldn't end abruptly if Savannah society ceased. I think sometimes she pretends a bit for my sake. Unlike the countess, and fortunately for me, Eliza is not obliged to buy a new gown for each occasion. Savannah society is not at the center of her life—it is merely a part of it." After another comfortable silence, he added, "One thing I know, Mark—you and my Eliza are going to be friends."

"I hope so."

"I know it. Now and then, I have almost a womanly hunch. I distinctly have one of my hunches about the two of you."

"You'll make me nervous about meeting her. I do want to please you after all this kindness."

"Rubbish. You already please me. And although the British have vastly diminished my supply of dollars by disrupting our trade, I'll make you any kind of wager you like on the certainty that you and Mrs. Mackay are somehow cut from the same bolt. Why, I find I'm already counting on her helping me to learn how *not* to let you surprise me quite so often!"

"You mean my indecision about my inheritance, don't you?"

"In the main, yes. And that's a fine example of my prediction about you and Eliza. She would not find it at all difficult—as I do—to believe that next year you might really turn down all that money!"

# FOUR

ON a date he would never forget, May 31, 1812, at sunrise, Mark stood beside Robert Mackay on the *Eliza*'s deck, waiting for his first glimpse of Savannah. So that Mark would miss nothing, Mackay had positioned them near the bow as the schooner, crusty with salt from battling the sea, moved regally through the waters of Tybee Roads toward the bar pilot's bobbing dinghy.

"Good, that's old Thompson waiting for us," Mackay said, waving at the white-haired man standing straight in the tiny boat. "We're fortunate. He must be in his seventies, but Thompson's still the best pilot on the coast."

After a moment's hesitation, Mark yielded to the impulse to wave at old Thompson, too. Thompson waved back.

"Glad you greeted him," Mackay laughed. "He'll be in my office first thing tomorrow to find out who you are. He keeps close track of every new face in town. Your illustrious Dr. George Jones is the mayor, but Thompson acknowledges no superior."

"Does he stay out there on that big harbor boat night and day?"

"That's right. The four bar pilots work in month-long shifts. Now, watch Thompson shinny up the side of our ship and over. He knows we're watching."

Mark, his face shining, said, "He takes that rope ladder like a monkey!"

Even with the good tide, Mackay allowed that the slow entrance would take four to five hours.

"That strip of green over there," Mackay pointed to portside sometime later, "is Tybee Island with its light tower.

We're at the mouth of the Savannah River. Over there is Long Island. An hour or so up ahead on the right, you'll see Jones, then Elba.''

So many thoughts crowded Mark's mind as he listened and looked that he said nothing for a time. There was no need to talk. He could tell how much Mackay was relishing his friend's first glimpse of the Savannah and Chatham County environs. A stiff, clean sea breeze parted and reparted Mark's heavy brown hair. Without thinking, he had removed his cap, as a man does upon entering a church. The breeze lifted and then flattened his hair, seemed to refresh his soul as he reveled in the panorama of greening marsh at St. Augustine Creek, partially flooded rice fields, patches of dense woods and glinting water. Slowly, slowly, he was nearing his mother's birthplace—his father's remembered dream—but most of all, he was nearing his own chosen city. *His own place to be.*

He looked at Robert Mackay and beamed. Mackay beamed back. For an hour or more, they sat in silence on a huge coil of rope.

"Over there to our left, now, you can see Fort Jackson," Mackay shouted above the wind in the sails, which seemed noisier now that they were slowly, almost imperceptibly, navigating the curves in the river. "Not much of a fort, but—" He peered more closely. "Well! There seems to be some real activity at last! Look!"

"Yes, sir," Mark said, making no effort to conceal his excitement. "I'd say they're pushing hard. Must be fifty or sixty Negroes working. Are they slaves?"

Mackay gave him a surprised look. "Oh, I'm sure they are. The uniformed officer overseeing the job could be that young William McRee, United States Department of Engineers. My wife wrote me at the North that his assignment here to build Fort Jackson has finally stirred Savannahians to some sense of danger from the war threat. McRee must be quite a fellow. Only eighteen or nineteen, I'm told, when he began this work several years ago."

The young officer saluted them as they passed, but at once turned back to supervising the slaves at their work. Two triangular derricks and a crane moved steadily, hoisting loads of brick, mortar and men as caulking and new bricklaying progressed on the small battery, which stood in a semicircle just above the edge of a rice field. A barracks building had been completed above the revetted earthwork, and Mackay said that it was at least an improvement over the last time he had seen it.

"Fort Jackson was a mud fort back during our Revolution," Mackay explained. "Nicknamed Fort Mud. Now, it's Savannah's first masonry fort. Have you given any thought to the military company you'll join, Mark?"

"Not really." He smiled. "The Chatham Artillery sounds fine to me, sir, since you belong to it."

"Splendid! None better and I'll be proud to recommend you. We'll sign you up tomorrow. You'll be right at home with the men in the Chatham Artillery. Our best people. The kind of gentlemen you'll need to know." Mackay's intelligent face grew suddenly solemn as he looked squarely at Mark. "I'm sure it's evident how glad I am to be coming home, but I want this to be a homecoming for you, too. No lonely rooms at a boardinghouse. You have a real family waiting for you—as surely as they wait for me. And for as long as you'll stay, home for you is our place on Broughton Street. A big, rambling, friendly house, plenty of room. Do you have the children straight in your mind now?"

"I think so. William is eight, Jack seven, Eliza Anne four, and little Kate is two."

Four hundred yards or so upstream from Fort Jackson, the *Eliza* inched past a sizable row of wharves above which sat a wooden building with a large sign reading Turnbull's Tavern. The whole shoreline was backed with waving fields of rice as far as the eye could see.

"By the way," Mackay said, "if we had a lesser bar pilot than old Thompson, a slightly larger ship and a bit less influence in the city, we'd have to unload some of our cargo over there, then take it on into town in smaller boats. With care, the *Eliza* will do fine, though, and—"

"And you do have influence in the city."

"A measure of it. My partner, William Mein, and I have our own wharf. We'll nose our bow right into it after a while. Thank heaven the tide's favorable." He sighed heavily. "This slow, tacking creep into Savannah is always the longest part of a sea journey for me. I think each time I return that my old heart won't stand the suspense until I can see my family again. And, Mark?"

"Yes, sir?"

"Even if you did manage to slip quietly away from Philadelphia, I guarantee your arrival in Savannah, once we see my family, will be cordial and noisy."

After a long pause, Mark said, "I've always wanted to be a part of a real family with children. That's one of the reasons I've agreed to impose on you and Mrs. Mackay for a few days."

Mackay snapped his fingers. "And here I thought it was my charm as a host. Well, so be it. Now, Mark—now, look up ahead!"

Leaning out over the rail, just before noon, Mark caught his first glimpse of the east end of town—not exactly what anyone would call charming, but it was Savannah. The schooner glided slowly up the river past the crumbling ruins of old Fort Wayne, the land around it strewn with patched wooden shacks and a dumping ground. Not a single church spire rose above the tiny, tree-choked city, but there did rise the tower of the City Exchange on the waterfront; the houses appeared hidden among green trees, and as his father had declared, the cloudless, blue May sky seemed to be embracing it all.

At the ship's railing, docking whistles filling the air, Mackay shouted, "Not very romantic from here, is it?"

Mark didn't answer at once. He was too busy looking. Then, he said simply, "But it *is* Savannah, sir."

So near the town, the river now swarmed with every kind of small boat, even dugouts. The junky waterfront, its wharves stacked with crates and barrels and bags of rice, was strewn with broken glass and refuse and teemed with half-clothed Negroes and whites at work. Stevedores shouted and cursed. Some sang. Horses strained to move overloaded carts and wagons along the river road and up the steep, sandy bluff, inching along, then sliding back, raising clouds of dust that settled on the sweaty men. A few rather sturdy buildings stood among others neglected and vacant. Mackay explained that the long row of warehouses and offices was called Factor's Row.

"One day we'll rebuild our waterfront," Mackay went on. "You definitely won't find the charm your father spoke of until we climb above all this, across the Strand, up to Bay Street—rid our nostrils and eyes of these dusty doings and the stench of those dripping human beings out here. My office is

Number One Commerce Row." He pointed toward the frame
and stone structures along the east end of the high bluff.
"Mein and I have a good, sound warehouse there on the lower
level. Our store and offices are on top. I know we plan to
rebuild. If only we can stay out of another war with Britain,
Savannah's waterfront may be quite respectable someday."

"The people of Savannah must be very nervous about a
war—being so close to the Atlantic," Mark said.

"My wife wrote that it's almost all they've talked about this
past month. But Savannahians tend to talk a lot about political subjects and expend all their efforts on dancing, drinking
and making money. I was really surprised to see that frenzied
activity at Fort Jackson when we passed." Mackay threw an
arm around Mark's shoulder. "You may well be the only
gentleman in town not intent upon money."

"I'm going to be a good businessman, even so," he said
with a sly smile. "I promise you won't be embarrassed by
me."

The schooner had eased upriver until Hutchinson and Fig
islands were directly across on their right. The river, between
the two islands and the steep, sandy bluff, seemed narrower
now so near the wooden wharves. Mark had no intention of
judging Savannah by its trashy, patched-together waterfront.
He'd yet to see a waterfront appear welcoming. The ugliness
and shouting and confusion into which they headed was, after
all, the lifeline of any port city. Here, as it had been back
home.

"Will your family be at the wharf to meet you?" he asked.

"No. Absolutely not. It's too rough down here. The children are too young. Mrs. Mackay never comes unless we're
sailing somewhere. But you can be sure they know our ship's
about to dock. One of my clerks will have seen us from the
upstairs balcony. He's already been to Broughton Street to
spread the word."

"I think you should go on ahead," Mark said as Bar Pilot
Thompson eased the *Eliza* into the slip at the Mein and
Mackay wharf. "Just as soon as the dockhands pull us in, you
go ashore—straight home to your family. I'll see to our baggage and find my own way to your house."

"Nonsense! You could find it, of course. It's only a short
walk. But my man, Hero, is on his way by now with a wagon
to handle our boxes and trunks." His eyes dancing with an-

ticipation, Mackay rubbed his square, strong hands together. "You and I will head right for Broughton Street together."

"But, sir, you've been away since March. I'll feel like an intruder being there when you first see your children and Mrs.—"

"If you do, you'll get over it within two minutes. I promise."

So eager was Robert Mackay to see his family that he didn't slow his pace as he and Mark hurried along the Strand, straight past the entrance to his office on Commerce Row.

"Business comes second to my family. Time enough tomorrow for me to show you our establishment," he said.

Across Bay Street, they walked the few steps to Bull, turned left into it, and Mark saw for the first time the wide, sandy thoroughfare that bisected the city from the river on the north to South Broad at the far limits.

"That must be Johnson Square up ahead," Mark said, slowing his pace involuntarily.

Mackay gave him a surprised look. "Indeed it is, but how did you know?"

"My father talked a lot about all of Bull Street. He met my mother right there in Johnson Square. It's—lovely—isn't it?"

"We're proud of all our squares now. The city fathers planted the chinaberry trees and put up those white cedar posts and chain fences just before my family and I got back from England last year. Those little tended footpaths help, too. Not too many years ago, our squares were unsightly wagon stops—the places where country folk spent the night when they came to town. James Oglethorpe, founder of the colony of Georgia, did a tasteful job of laying out our squares. It's past time we beautified them." Mackay pointed down Bull Street—tree-lined, spacious, ending less than a mile to the south in the narrow road that led straight through a pine forest to Vernonburg. "I envision Bull Street someday becoming a world-renowned boulevard. Over there on the corner is your still unfinished Episcopal Church, Mark. Not ready for worship yet, of course. But they say patience is a Christian virtue."

"Christ Church, eh?"

"Right. The most conservative, the wealthiest church in town. I'm pleased to add that my Independent Presbyterian

Church is ranked second. Over there on the other side of Bull is perhaps our finest emporium, owned by a leading citizen, Andrew Low." He took Mark's arm and hurried him along. "Time for sight-seeing tomorrow. Our homecoming must rank even above Savannah right now."

They crossed Congress and hurried one more block south to Broughton. No sooner had they turned left on Broughton when two boys literally tumbled out from behind a high oleander hedge and began to leap toward them shouting, "Papa! Papa!" at the top of their voices.

His face flushed with happiness, Robert Mackay fell to one knee in the sand, both arms stretched wide.

The boys—one a curly towhead, the other with straight, black hair flying—tackled their father, hugging and kissing his neck and face, knocking his fawn-colored top hat into the street.

Mark, standing back a bit from the noisy group, went to pick up the hat. He brushed it off and stood holding it, waiting—and enjoying.

Still on his knees, Mackay embraced his sons again and again, mussing both heads, kissing them each noisily on the mouth. Then, the boys, still attempting to shout all the news at once, clung to him as Mackay stood, dusted off his trousers and presented his son Jack, of the tumbled, dark hair, and William, of the yellow curls, to "my new friend, our house-guest, Mr. Mark Browning of Philadelphia." The boys shook hands politely, William in silence, but giving Mark a wide, large-toothed smile, while Jack said pertly, "You'll be awfully glad you decided to visit Savannah, Mr. Browning. We're about to be a thriving city any day now. Just as soon as the United States whips the British again."

"Here now," his father laughed. "What's that, Jack? Do you know for a fact that we're going to war?"

"Uncle John McQueen says so," William offered. "Jack doesn't know except for what Uncle John said. Uncle John went to the meeting today at the courthouse."

"They met at high noon and 'in a state of high patriotism,' " Jack piped. "Uncle John said so. Alderman T.U.P. Charlton read a resolution that said everybody there was to say whatever he thought about going to war against Britain. I guess every man at the meeting was bustin' with patriotism—except Uncle John."

Mackay gave Jack a playful spank. "Your Uncle John is as much a patriot as anyone anywhere!"

"But you know how he is," Jack insisted. "I heard him tell Mama he's just not much interested in governments. Doesn't trust 'em. He was in school over there through a lot of the French Revolution—and with Grandfather McQueen in Spanish Florida. Uncle John is pretty much a man of the world, and *he* thinks there will be a war."

"How about you, William?" Mark asked. "Do you think war is coming?"

William gave him a look of surprised delight. "Do you really want to know what I think, Mr. Browning?"

"I certainly do. Why wouldn't I?"

"Aw, I don't know. I'm just used to old Jack getting his two cents' worth in first. He thinks he's so smart."

"Well," Jack said, twisting a heel into the sandy street. "It's just that I always have an opinion. After all, I'm eight and he's only seven."

"I, too, have an opinion," Mackay broke in. "I want to see your mother — and your little sisters. Come along, both of you."

"I'd still like to know William's thoughts on the matter," Mark said as they hurried along tree-lined Broughton Street, past mostly frame houses, some with large, shady yards. "Do you think we'll go to war against Britain, William?"

"Yes, sir. And maybe East Florida, too. Going to war against Florida always bothers Uncle John McQueen."

"Uncle John, by the way, Mark, is my wife's brother," Mackay explained. "He's a planter here now. But lived in East Florida with his father, John McQueen, Sr., when he was a young man. He liked it down there, as did his father—a most colorful old gentleman, adored by his family, still gossiped about in Savannah. Known during his later years as Don Juan McQueen, so prominent did he become in Spanish Florida. My wife's brother loves this country well enough. He's just been caught in the cross fire between Georgia and Florida for a good part of his life. To try to conquer St. Augustine has long been a Georgia habit, as I'm sure you know."

"Yes. Former President Jefferson would relish his declining years if we could finally get Florida," Mark said.

"I wouldn't be surprised if Jefferson and President Madison aren't still in touch on the whole matter." Mackay smiled.

"Do you know Thomas Jefferson, Mr. Browning?" William asked.

"No, son," Mark said with a wide grin. "I'm not quite old enough to know a famous gentleman like Jefferson, but I do know he tried hard to get the Florida land for the United States."

"How old are you?" Jack asked.

"I'm twenty."

The boy whistled. "That's pretty old, but not too."

"I'm glad. You and William are both so well informed, I don't feel a lot older than either one of you."

"There they are!" Mackay shouted, breaking into a run at the sight of a slender, brown-haired woman, who carried a little girl in one arm and held tightly to the hand of another incredibly lovely, dark-haired child.

In one swoop, Robert Mackay embraced all three of his girls and, taking the baby, brought Eliza to meet Mark.

"My friend," he said proudly, "here she is! This is my beloved wife, Eliza McQueen Mackay. Observe her well, son. This lady will change your life—for the better, as she has changed mine!"

Mackay continued his flowery introductions, something about having adopted Mark, but Mark was staring at Eliza Mackay—and trying not to. Her expression told him that she paid no mind to her husband's exaggerated presentation, but understood and adored him exactly as he was. She was not what a portrait painter would call beautiful, but there was a deeply tender light in her intelligent hazel eyes, a welcoming, graceful tilt to her slender shoulders, an almost familiar quality about her smile that drew Mark to her as though he had waited a lifetime for this moment.

"We're all glad—more than glad you're here, Mr. Browning," she was saying, her hand extended. "We wouldn't think of allowing you to stay anywhere in town but with us." After Mark's lips had brushed her hand, she turned to her husband with a direct, unflirtatious but wonderfully woman look of love. She was still addressing Mark, but her look was for Mackay. "If my husband has decided to adopt you, then, so have I."

"You're not a bit too old to be our brother," Jack shouted, and William, without a word, gave Mark a warm, adoring glance that said far more than Jack's noisy approval.

Mark could only look from one to the other, searching for something adequate to say. His boyish smile came first; then, as his whole being was swept with a sense of having come home, finding words was suddenly not so difficult. "I had planned to stay a few days," he said. "And surely, you've made me feel welcome, Mrs. Mackay. Maybe more welcome than—ever in my life. You and your sons. But"—the smile widened—"what about these other two young ladies?" He stooped until his face was at eye level with the four-year-old. "How about you, Eliza Anne? Do you want me to visit at your house?"

Still holding her father's hand, the little girl appeared to think a moment; then, laughing aloud, she hurled herself into Mark's arms and hugged him hard around the neck.

"That settles it," Mackay said, beaming, "because I haven't heard one word of objection from baby Kate, either."

"Kate's only two," Eliza Anne whispered loudly in Mark's ear.

Their feet sank into the deep, soft sand of Broughton Street as they walked together toward the rambling three-storied white frame house on its big lot, but Mark felt as though he were flying.

That evening, after good food, laughter, checkers and horseplay with the children, everyone retired early, Mark to a large, airy corner room on the second floor.

When he had said good night and closed the door, he fully intended to lie awake for a long time to enjoy his thoughts. Thoughts of what he'd see tomorrow morning when he opened the shutters to his first sunrise in Savannah. This day, his arrival day, had been like a dream. A warm, merry, family dream to which he longed to cling, a dream in which he felt he could hide forever among these easy, beautifully natural yet cultivated people.

Stretched on the bed in his last clean nightshirt, he allowed himself to dwell on the security it would bring to be a member of such a family. "I'd stay with them forever, if I could," he whispered to no one, a habit formed during the long year in which there had been no one to listen. Already, he loved the children—thoughtful, reserved William in particular, although he had fallen under the spell of Jack's precocious charm and Eliza Anne's dark, irresistible beauty. On the voyage down, Robert Mackay had certainly become the most important man in the world to him. The characteristic quick frown creased Mark's forehead. Why do I even feel better about myself since I've known Robert Mackay? he wondered. Not just about my future. I don't intend to lean on him ever. I guess I feel better about being me, because he makes me feel his equal.

He stretched his lean, muscular body between the cool sheets. He was comfortable in far more than his body. Interested, aware of himself as—himself. He knew nothing at all about marketing rice or cotton or timber or skins. He'd learned only the basic principles of business at Yale. And yet, he felt somehow safe and unperturbed in Mackay's house—comfortable in himself.

This night, when he wanted to stay awake, to savor even this temporary security, his eyes grew heavy too soon. His thoughts drifted. He drifted. Not once did he have to fight off the haunting vision of his father struggling for breath in a lonely stateroom, the ancient weight of the sea pressing down upon him. Not once did he imagine he heard Aunt Nassie's familiar dry cough from her room down the hall. Neither beloved person troubled him. Rather, for the first time they seemed to be undergirding him, to be all they now could ever be to him—blessed, strong, colorful presences from his boyhood. They were gone. Boyhood was gone.

As Savannah would replace Philadelphia, he prayed that the Mackays would become his family. The children, Mackay himself. But at the thought of Mackay's wife, a still deeper peace spread through him, as though it moved along in his blood. It was not a passive, numbing peace. There was action in it, even excitement. But it was peace and with a purpose, all new, magnetic, inescapable. He had no desire to escape it. Only a desire to hold, to dwell on each still brief, but vivid, memory of the ease and strength and inner beauty of Eliza Mackay.

Sleep came as he heard her low laughter behind the closed door of the Mackays' bedroom door down the wide upstairs hall.

*       *       *

"I've missed your laughter," Mackay murmured, her head in its accustomed place on his shoulder. "The miracle happened again, didn't it? I made it home safely. I'm here once more—in our bed, with you. I hate every absence."

"And having Mark somehow makes it all—even better, doesn't it, dearest friend?"

"I knew you'd like the boy," he said. "I wouldn't have invited him to stay awhile with us if I hadn't been sure you would."

"I don't know when I've met a more appealingly charming young man. And yet, charming doesn't really describe him. He's—well, I know absolutely nothing about him, Robert, and yet with seemingly no effort whatever, he's—close to me. Almost a part of our family."

Mackay chuckled but said nothing.

"I know why you're laughing. My usual reticence is missing. It just isn't like me to open my heart so quickly. I'm a bit puzzled, frankly, at myself."

"Good!"

"Good?"

"Makes me feel better. I puzzle myself far too often for a man my age. You almost never puzzle yourself."

"That makes me sound like a self-complacent simpleton."

"Kiss me."

After a long, slow kiss that caused her to cling to him when he'd taken his mouth away, he whispered, "There. Would an attractive gentleman such as I kiss a self-complacent simpleton?"

"No," she said with a sigh. "I hope I'm never self-complacent. You deserve none of that. It's just that normally, I need time to judge a person. I simply loved that boy—on sight, right in the middle of Broughton Street."

"As did I, helping to carry him down that narrow ship's stair to my stateroom when the sea laid him low."

"Is Dr. Jones perfectly sure he'll be all right?"

"His shoulder will be painful for a time, but he's all right." Mackay sighed. "The boy's had a strange life, Eliza. Unnatural in many ways. He should be scarred by it; he doesn't seem to be. There appears to be no self-pity, not even a shred of affectation anywhere in him. He's vulnerable, in fact. As are most people without artifice—if one can find them."

"Did he tell you very much about himself?"

"He seemed to be most open with me. Not trying to impress me. Not once. You know how I hate that. But, yes, he told me quite a lot, I'd say. At least, I feel I know him better than I should in such a short time." He settled himself closer to her. "His mother died when he was three—as did my father. I don't remember Papa at all except what Mother told me about him when I was older. Sometimes I think I remember him at the time her stories took place. I don't. It's the same with Mark."

"He's—never known what it's like to have a mother. Robert, how sad!"

"Of course it's sad, but this seems not to have occurred to Mark. At least not in any disturbing way. You see, he had Aunt Nassie, his father's sister, Natalie Browning, with whom he lived—alone—from the day after they buried his mother."

"But what about his father?"

"Absent. Always absent. I can see the Philadelphia census reports: 'Natalie Browning, spinster; Mark Browning, Jr., minor; Mark Browning, Sr., absent.' According to what I gather from Mark, his father never lived in Philadelphia again after the death of his lovely young wife."

"Robert, do you mean that Mark, through all his boyhood, lived with neither parent in the house?"

"Not after his first three years. Just Aunt Nassie. He adored her. Calls her his best friend. She must have been a remarkable lady. Tutored him as a boy. Then he was sent to Yale, but her influence seems to have been indelible. Frankly, I doubt that he would ever have left Philadelphia had she lived."

"Oh, don't tell me she died, too!"

"A year ago. One month after his father drowned at sea."

She reached for his hand. "Two deaths—so close together!"

"He lost the two people he loved most in all the world—just a year ago."

"But the way he is with our children—lighthearted, full of play. Robert, I'd never have guessed!"

"Nor would I. He's a rarely sensitive young man, too. All I can figure is that he has managed, in that year spent alone after their deaths, to accept things as they are—without bitterness. He's evidently made peace with his tragedies. Eliza, the boy is a strange mixture of determination and what seems to me to be almost a weak acquiescence.''

"Weak? Never! You watch him. If there's a weak bone in Mark Browning's body, I'll be the most surprised person on earth.''

He chuckled softly. "Well, now the boy's managed to bring out an impetuous side of my wife even I hadn't seen! How do you know so much so soon, Mrs. Mackay?''

She waited. "I—don't know. I only know I do.''

"And you don't know a fraction of what I know about him!''

"True. But I know Mark. I also know how silly that sounds. He *isn't* weak.''

"He's unlike any other young man I've ever met.''

"Because he isn't fighting what he can do nothing about?''

"Perhaps. He isn't afraid; I know that. Here he is in Savannah with no letters of introduction and no intention whatever of making use of any family connections to help himself along in business.''

"That's refreshing.''

"It's jarring! He's extremely well informed, his principles are steely strong, his values almost too high for me.''

"Whatever do you mean by that?''

He took a deep breath and exhaled noisily. "I can't tell you what I mean. I promised. It has to do with a—financial decision he must make when he's twenty-one next year, and unless I'm mistaken, he's going to make a foolish decision. Foolish by my standards, which well may be far lower than his.''

"Robert, you're talking in riddles!''

"I know I am. But I promised Mark not to tell anyone a single thing about his finances. I gave him my word.''

"Not even your wife?''

"Not even you. I asked him about that, in fact. Told him you're my conscience. He begged me to keep his confidence, at least until he's made his own way in Savannah.''

Eliza said nothing for a time. Then, "Good for Mark! I don't blame him one bit. If there's something I need to know eventually, I'm sure he'll tell me.''

Mackay pulled her to him. "If I know Mark *and* you, he'll be confiding in you in no time. As I did even when you were only beautiful—not more beautiful as you are now. Eliza, I missed you dreadfully this time.''

"Dearest friend, I wonder how I manage to—breathe when you're out of my sight. . . ."

They kissed long and deeply. "I not only have trouble breathing, I do almost nothing well without you, it seems. Oh, Eliza . . . my dearest, dearest Eliza, who loves me." His hands and mouth began to speak to her as words could not.

They lay motionless in the sweet silence that followed their loving. Then Eliza asked, "Will there be—a war, Robert?"

He began to laugh softly. "What a question at what a time! Only my lovely, pragmatic, *thinking* wife would ask it. Can't you control that busy mind of yours, for my pride's sake, at a time like this?"

"Don't tease. Tell me. What did you hear at the North? Will the coastal cities up there agree to a declaration of war with Britain?"

"Yes, I think they will. For the same reasons the citizens of Savannah will agree. Shipping. Our lifeline. Britain is choking our shipping. You and I will be paupers if they don't lift those orders-in-council—stop kidnapping our sailors, open up the sea-lanes. The interior states will fight them in order to stop Britain's Indian agitation. All our reasons are selfish, but I predict war with the old mother country, which we both love, within three months or less."

"John thinks so, too. He hates the whole idea."

"So do I. Is your brother all right? Has his bride learned how to settle down and give the man the love he offered her for so long?"

"They're fine. Oh, Margaret will always be—Margaret. But, in a way, maybe that's good. After all, John did wait for eighteen years for her to tire of being an international belle. He deserves an exciting wife. She's matured, but Margaret will always be exciting. Actually, much of John's loathing of the idea of war with Britain is because Margaret would be cut off from our family there and in Jamaica. He lives his life for her. Robert?"

"Hm?"

"Do you think Britain *will* rescind the orders-in-council? In time?"

"My dear wife, only God in heaven knows. And that is the end of our political discussion for this night. Your husband is just plain sleepy. I promised Mark I'd give him my whole day tomorrow—show him our city. That means I arise at dawn and hie me to my countinghouse for an hour or two before breakfast.''

"Do you sometimes wish I didn't try to think through anything political?''

"You mean turn into a mental bore as do most other ladies in your social class? The answer is no. I'm not a bookish intellectual, as you well know. If you didn't hold serious converse with me, I'd turn into a bore!''

She hit him affectionately on the chest. "I'm serious. I pick such peculiar times to bring things up. You know I do.''

"But you always take my word as gospel when I explain my profound opinions. What more can a man ask?''

"I see you can't be serious tonight.''

"No,'' he said, settling his warm, eager body into a comfortable place in the familiar curve of hers. "I'm too happy to be serious except about being madly in love with you.''

# FIVE

"WHAT a pleasant sight after the confusion of Commerce Row," Mackay said as he strode into the large, sunlit dining room the next morning just as the Exchange clock struck half after eight. To Eliza and Mark, still at the breakfast table, he boomed good morning, kissed his wife, shook his guest's hand and seated himself in his chair at the head of the table. "Sleep well, Mark?"

"Better than in a year, sir, thank you. I hope you did."

"Like an old, fallen log. Am I too late to see the children, Eliza?"

"Afraid so. The boys have gone to school and Hannah is bathing the girls. I'll ring for your breakfast. You must be starved."

"No, no. I ate an enormous breakfast with Mein at the Exchange Coffee Shop." He patted his slightly thickening waistline. "Too much, in fact. But you know how I tend to overeat when someone's badgering me. Mein was very badgerish today. That poor devil, Osmund Kott, has been haranguing him most of the time I was away." He shook his head. "Poor Kott."

"What was he after this time?" Eliza asked.

"A job, which is out of the question. And Kott knows full well it is. The man hasn't been sober enough to hold a job in years. Mostly, he refuses to believe that we have no more ships going to Philadelphia in the foreseeable future. Probably too soused to realize how imminent war is, or doesn't care. Insists he has to get to Philadelphia. A matter of life and death."

She passed more grits to Mark. "Whose death this time?"

Mackay shrugged. "Kott is never that definite, my dear. It

54

seems Alexander Mein let him make the journey to Philadelphia some fourteen years ago on one of their ships." He turned to-Mark. "That was before I went with Mein and Mein, or perhaps the year I joined the firm; we can't quite remember. At any rate, Kott was allowed to go north then. He insists he should be given free passage again."

"He doesn't even offer to work for his passage?" Mark asked.

"Yes; I believe he did do some rough work on that first trip. Any kind of work would be out of the question for him now."

"How old is Osmund Kott, Robert?"

"I doubt that he's more than forty-five, my dear. He looks sixty most of the time. Once a rather handsome man. His habit has all but canceled that." Mackay's eyes smiled amusement. "I find it hard to take Mein's frustration too seriously, though. Kott's harmless, I'm sure, but somehow he threatens my associate. Oh, Osmund's a nuisance at times, but he's more than a nuisance to Mein. He actually seems to be frightened by the man."

"That makes no sense whatever, does it?" Eliza asked.

"Not to me. Look here, Mark can't be interested in Osmund Kott. What's this you two have been doing?" Mackay pulled a long sheet of foolscap toward him. "Aha! A map of Savannah."

"Oh, I've been trying to draw our squares—the layout of the city for Mark," she said, pouring more coffee. "Eliza Anne, at four, is a better artist than her mother."

"I don't agree," Mark said eagerly. "I'm sure I could see the city on my own just by following your map, ma'am. There are twelve squares laid out like a grid; the town is bounded by Bay Street on the north at the waterfront, by South Broad on the south end of town adjoining the Common, and by East and West Broad on each side. Actually, the plan is as logical as Philadelphia's."

"Right you are," Mackay agreed. "Like Philadelphia, Savannah began as a planned city. It didn't just grow because it happened to be near a river, or because a battle was fought here and a few soldiers stayed. The colony's Trustees, through Georgia's progressive founder, Oglethorpe, kept a firm hand on it from the start. Penn did that with your home city. There's some sense to the plan. A cause for pride, I've always felt—and for criticism as well. When our city fathers falter, they can't fall back on the alibi that Savannah is still turning into a city. It's been a city since 1733. I'm sure your father told you all about our history, though.''

"In a manner, yes. But always draped over in romance."

"Well," Eliza said, "we are romantic, I think. In part, a beautiful and romantic city. And if our commerce is given a chance to continue, we'll be even more beautiful."

"*If* we don't go to war. But, my dearest wife, today is June first, and after talking with Mein, if the United States and Britain are not at war by the end of June, I'll eat—Sheftall Sheftall's leather tricorn!"

"Sheftall Sheftall? What a wonderful name," Mark said. "Who's he?"

"Ah, Sheftall Sheftall, affectionately known as Cocked Hat Sheftall. A gentleman you must meet," Mackay informed him. "In fact, if we don't encounter him on the streets today—Bay Street especially—I might have to eat his cocked hat a second time."

"Does he really still wear a cocked hat?" Mark asked.

"Knickerbockers, too," Mackay declared. "And, of course, silver buckles on his slippers."

"Why is that, sir?"

"Savannah's most eccentric citizen, Revolutionary War hero, learned lawyer, is quite happily still locked in the eighteenth century. His true identity remains with the years of the American Revolution. Cocked Hat Sheftall is among our most beloved citizens, but he doesn't like our 1812 era and so keeps himself in the time of which he does approve. That of General George Washington."

"I'd love to know more about him," Mark said. "Certainly I want to meet the gentleman."

"Both will occur at one and the same time, I have no doubt—that is, if you have the time. One meets Sheftall Sheftall, and if he is in the mood, which is almost always, one learns about Sheftall Sheftall's valor, patriotism and military achievements at one and the same instant."

Eliza laughed. "Now, Robert, don't prejudice Mark before he meets him. Mr. Sheftall is a real experience, Mark. A brilliant mind, I've always thought."

"So brilliant, it glints like his shoe buckles in the sun, Eliza, my dear. I meant no disparagement. Cocked Hat Sheftall has no greater devotee in all Savannah than your husband. I've no doubt that if indeed we are at war with Britain again by the end of the month, Sheftall Sheftall will be firing off letters of instruction to President James Madison by every possible conveyance."

"Is this gentleman taken seriously in town?" Mark asked.

"How would you answer that, Eliza?"

"Mr. Sheftall is not a buffoon, if that's what you mean, Mark. He makes people smile, but he's very, very loved. The name Sheftall is an honored name. His grandfather, Benjamin Sheftall, an Ashkenazy Jew from Germany, reached Savannah almost as early as General Oglethorpe. His father, Mordecai, stood well enough in our social scale to be one of the five incorporators of the philanthropic Union Society. The Sheftalls have always been substantial in our city."

Mackay handed the empty cup at his place to Eliza. "Maybe I will have a drop of coffee, my dear." Eliza filled the cup and smiled as Mackay reached also for one of Emphie's biscuits and the honey pot. "You and I will undoubtedly see Sheftall Sheftall this very day, Mark, as we walk the town. One thing is certain: If indeed we do fight the British again, it will bring a youthful gleam to his eyes."

"I've been thinking about what you said of Britain's crumbling economy," Mark said. "Maybe that really will cause her to weaken and change her ways with us."

"That could happen," Mackay said, wiping honey from his hands on a freshly laundered napkin. "But, Britain's economy has been bad for months and—"

"Oh, we've had enough of war with Britain," Eliza interrupted. "Mark, my husband and I have been scarred in one way or another by trouble with the British for most of our lives, haven't we, dear?"

Mackay shook his head. "Indeed we have. Even though we didn't meet until some years after I came to Savannah, our lives were already running down parallel roads. Our childhoods were affected by mixed loyalties of families divided by the Revolution." He laid his hand over Eliza's. "The Grange, the plantation where this lovely lady was born on the Savannah River, was raided by soldiers from both sides. My own father's wealth as an Indian merchant was dissipated during the Revolution because he was a Patriot; my mother's Malbone family from Newport were Tories. Eliza's father, Don Juan McQueen, was a rabid American Patriot, as were her grandparents on her mother's side, but her mother's sisters married Tories. They and their families had to leave America. They're still in England and Jamaica because of trouble between our two countries." He shrugged. "We're Savannahians, loyal Americans, but still with strong ties in Britain. We prefer British society, feel easier with it. My business partner's brother, Alexander Mein, has a lucrative firm over there; our company works hand in glove with his when politics and the threat of war allow."

Mackay stood abruptly. "Time is going by, Mark. You and I have a busy day. I'm determined to strip away the romantic notions you have of this town. You're one of us now and I want you to see Savannah as she really is: bawdy and poor and half-drunk on either end of town; respectable, family-conscious, elegant, money-mad and highfalutin in the middle; potentially lovely throughout."

Mark stood, too, and bowed to Eliza. "Thank you, Mrs. Mackay. Breakfast was delicious and I'm going to surprise your husband by how much you've already taught me about the city." He turned to Mackay. "I even know that the original trust lots were laid out in equal parcels sixty by ninety feet—and that the plan holds to this day." He smiled admiringly at Eliza. "And I quite agree with Mrs. Mackay that it is fortunate that General Oglethorpe named the town for the river and not for himself. I can't imagine the city being called anything but—Savannah."

Mackay feigned a pout. "I don't think you two missed me at all during breakfast. But, didn't I tell you she's a remarkable lady, son? As intelligent as she is lovely to look at?"

"You did, sir. But, if you'll excuse me, you really didn't do her justice."

Retracing yesterday's route back toward Johnson Square, Mark asked the population of Savannah.

"Six thousand, more or less, I'd say," Mackay answered. "About half of that number colored."

"All slaves?"

"No. Most are, of course, but we have perhaps two or three hundred free people of color." After a pause, Mackay said enthusiastically, "We can take a closer look now at your Episcopal Church up here in Johnson Square. The first Christ Church burned many years ago. This new one will be grand if they ever finish it. Actually, it was going very well until the hurricane of 1804 flattened it. A Frenchman by the name of Boucher was the designer. He had to leave town," Mackay laughed, "for having a mind of his own. You see, he insisted upon entertaining free people of color in his own dining room!"

They strolled into Johnson Square and stood looking at Christ Church, a rather handsome red brick building, Mark thought, with some trim in place, freshly painted white, but with no steeple yet.

"I understand the steeple will be sixty or sixty-five feet tall," Mackay said.

"Mr. Mackay? Does your firm deal in slaves?"

"We did until such trade was outlawed some four years ago. Mein and Mackay try not to miss a trick in business." He chuckled. "But we don't break the law—knowingly."

"Do other Savannah firms also comply with that law? Or are you free to say?"

"No, Mark. I'm not free to say. By the way, you're not one of those Philadelphia Abolitionists, are you?"

"I've never joined them, no, but Aunt Nassie was an active Abolitionist right up until her death."

"I see."

Mark stopped walking and looked at him. "Does that—bother you, sir?"

"That your aunt held antislavery sentiments? Not at all. Slavery's a ghastly institution, but it is an institution. How does one dispense with it?"

"I—don't know."

"Might as well tell you that law-breaking slaves are whipped publicly here in Savannah." Mackay glanced at Mark, who was frowning but said nothing. "Every so often someone brings up the matter in Council. A few of us highly disapprove of such public punishment. I do my best to keep my children from watching. Perhaps someday we'll get a law forbidding it. Mark?"

"Yes, sir?"

"Savannah isn't a—perfect town."

"I—I'm not that young and idealistic." He gave Mackay a tight smile. "Don't worry about my embarrassing you with my aunt's views, or mine, on the slavery issue."

Mackay threw his arm about Mark's shoulder. "Understood. Now, you and I are headed, of course, for Commerce Row, at the east end of Factor's Row. I want you to meet my partner, William Mein, *if* he didn't change his mind and leave for one of his plantations today. He's as fine a gentleman as you could imagine, but he's unpredictable, except for his integrity."

"You put a lot of stock in integrity, don't you?"

"I do. By the way, I should have mentioned before that when someone calls Johnson Square Church Square, think nothing of it. Your Christ Church is just that important. Old South Carolinian Robert Johnson, for whom it was named, is often forgotten. The same is true of Courthouse Square, back a ways. Its real name is Wright Square."

Standing at the corner of Bull and Bay streets, Mackay looked east on Bay and then west. "I visualize all this being rebuilt someday. All these wooden buildings will be torn down, new brick and stucco buildings put up." His shoulders slumped a bit. "After we win the war with Britain, of course. Hang that war! Its very potential is a dream-blocker, isn't it? So close to the sea, we could be attacked here, you know."

"Yes, sir. I thought about all that, too, before I decided to become a Savannahian. But I made up my mind that if I took the plunge, I'd stick with the town through good times and bad."

Mackay smiled approval as they started across Bay Street toward the grassy Strand that separated Bay from Factor's Row. "If you don't mind a suggestion, Mark, keep your opinions on slavery to yourself and you'll be one of the most respected citizens we have in no time. Of course, we all have to keep something to ourselves, no matter where we live."

Grabbing Mark's arm, Mackay pulled him back a step to avoid a careening horse and cart. "Watch yourself, young fellow," Mackay shouted at the driver. "There's a five-dollar fine for driving a light, unloaded cart beyond a walk!" Mackay shook his head. "Why does youth demand to move so fast?"

"I don't know, sir. I guess we just like it." Almost across Bay Street, Mark, chancing to look back, stopped short. "Mr. Mackay, look!"

"What is it? We're out of order, too, stopping in the middle of a street."

"I know; let's go back."

On the flagstone sidewalk again, Mackay whispered, "What's wrong?"

"There, sir."

His face buried in a newspaper, so that only the top of his brown tricorn showed above it, silver buckles gleaming in the sun, Sheftall Sheftall ambled toward them, looking neither to the right nor to the left.

Mackay nodded. "It's old Cocked Hat all right," he said softly. "I'll introduce you. Ah, good morning, Mr. Sheftall! Wouldn't it be fine if we could keep this pleasant breeze straight through the hot summer months?"

Ever so slightly, just enough so that he could give them one quick glance through his tiny gold spectacles, Sheftall Sheftall lowered his paper, then reburied his face in it.

"Mr. Sheftall," Mackay went on, shouting a bit in deference, Mark supposed, to the somewhat older man's hearing. "There's a splendid newcomer to town and he's most eager to meet you, sir."

Once more, even less noticeably, the paper was lowered a fraction, just long enough for the bright-eyed man to say, "Sorry, Mr. Mackay. Another time. I'm very busy with the latest news of the impending war with Britain. Another time, sir."

The round, intent face vanished again behind the newspaper, and Sheftall Sheftall shuffled away toward his house on Broughton.

Mackay, grinning, shrugged. "Not today, Mark. And that's that."

They crossed Bay Street, all the way this time, both still smiling at the abrupt encounter.

"I really can't wait to get to know Mr. Sheftall, now. He's magnificent," Mark said.

"I had a hunch you'd appreciate him thoroughly." Mackay straightened his white cravat. "Well, here we are at what I loosely call 'famous Commerce Row.'" Mackay pointed to a splendid new brick building, the only one sporting a watchtower. "That belongs to Joseph Habersham, Jr. He's just about to take baby brother Robert into the business with him. Come to think of it, June first is when Robert is to begin, and that's today. Let's go congratulate them both. The Habersham factorage and commission business is one of our best. I'm sure Joseph would be interested in interviewing you, Mark."

"Whatever you say, sir. But I know so little about his business, I promise to keep still."

"Nonsense."

They strode across the Strand and onto the wooden bridge that spanned the bluff and led to the entrances of the offices and warehouses. Inside Habersham's office, the walls paneled in dark wood, Mackay was greeted cordially by Joseph. After introductions, Habersham apologized for the din from the wharf below—shouts, ships' bells, bang and clatter as wagons were loaded and unloaded—and for the absence of his new partner, young brother Robert.

"The day is too pleasant to close a window," Habersham explained, "and Mackay, you, of all men, know the after-effects of a true Savannah celebration. We had one last night at my house, and today, which was to start his commercial career, found poor Robert unable to leave his bed."

Mackay laughed. "I do know indeed. And this is as good an introduction as any for my friend Browning to the waterfront *and* the social chaos of Commerce Row. There is never a silent moment through which to work, Mark, and we do play hard in Savannah. We're good at it, too! Our ladies are the prettiest, our food and wine the best—our spirits already high when each celebration begins, in fact. Even on those infernal summer evenings when our temperature hovers around ninety-six degrees, Savannahians have been known to give balls. But, seriously, we do work here on Commerce Row in the noise —work as hard as we play. Right, Habersham?"

"Absolutely, and one good effort deserves another. The world of commerce has never been stable for long. We plunge up and then down, but always up again—and then we celebrate. Will you be in town long, Mr. Browning?"

"Yes, sir. I'm here to stay."

"I see."

"My new friend holds a degree in business from Yale," Mackay said, "He's interested in joining one of our counting-houses in some capacity. I'm honoring him, dear Joseph, with his first introduction to a business giant—yóu."

Mark looked from one to the other, a fleeting question pricking his mind: Didn't Robert Mackay want him with *his*

firm—even as a clerk until he learned? He had allowed himself
to hope for that more surely than he'd realized until this
minute.

"I'd enjoy a talk with you, Browning." Habersham was obviously interested. "How about this afternoon?"

"No reason why not," Mackay agreed. "I want to show
him our city, but I can have him back here promptly at two
P.M. Will that do?"

"I'll be delighted to see you then, young man. By the way,
are you spoken for by one of our local military regiments?"

"Yes, he most certainly is," Mackay retorted.

"Chatham Artillery, eh? Splendid."

"We're stopping at my office, then straight by the adjutant's house to sign him on."

"You mean to tell me you brought him here before he's
even seen your establishment, Mackay?"

"I did. All in the name of wishing young Robert well.
You'll do that for us when he's recovered enough to care
about our well-wishing, won't you?"

"I will. See you at two, Browning."

Of far more interest to Mark were the somewhat less elegant, but equally busy, offices of Mein and Mackay at Number One Commerce Row. He liked William Mein, a few years
older than Robert Mackay, he supposed, affable, unpreten-
tious and obviously accustomed to success.

"This is all well and good, Mackay, to be showing Mr.
Browning our city, to sign him up with the Chatham Artillery—but why in the name of common sense let Habersham
have the first chance to hire him?"

Mark liked tall, sandy-haired William Mein more than ever.

"Don't worry, partner, I have first divvies on the boy,
haven't I, Mark?"

"Yes, sir!"

"But, as much as I'd like him to work with us, I want him to
know enough firsthand to make his own decision."

Mein stretched his long legs and leaned back in his chair.
"Mackay's infernal fairness is, I swear it, sometimes my
heaviest burden, Browning."

Mark grinned, but said nothing.

Mackay winked at Mark. "I'm his Scottish Presbyterian
conscience. You might just as well know what a really bad

man he is. Mean Mein, he's called—all over town.''

Mark liked both men—liked them together, felt easy with their mutual trust and ribbing. "I certainly am fortunate to find out the truth about you two—right off," he said. "I'll know *not* to let Mr. Mackay find out when I have my first questionable idea.''

"Come straight to me," Mein said. "Mackay's too trustworthy to be trusted."

Taking Mark by the arm, Mackay led him toward the door. "Let's continue our trip around the city, friend. This man's no good to us."

William Mein leaned forward, his face abruptly troubled. "Before you go, Mackay—Osmund Kott was here again right after you left for home this morning."

"Time to collect his monthly stipend from your client, Jonathan Cameron?"

"No. Cameron sends his money at midmonth, regularly as a clock strikes. Mackay, I know you're not close to Mr. Cameron as I've been all these years, but could you possibly take him on as a client? You're a far better factor than I. Better suited personally."

"Never! I have enough problems of my own, thank you. No one respects the planter Jonathan Cameron more deeply than I, but he's always been your client; you've handled his factoring business at Knightsford since before the turn of the century. I have no desire whatever to help you rid yourself of his blackmailer, Osmund Kott, Esquire."

"*Esquire?* That—that no good drunk?"

"He may not own a square inch of property, but he's an educated man. I doff my hat to any man—sober or not—who educates himself by reading, as Kott always has. I don't find him too repulsive, but I'll keep it that way, thank you. Intimacy with Kott, I suspect, *could* breed contempt. Was he back insisting that we are sending another of our ships to Philadelphia?"

"Yes, he hasn't dropped that, but—he now demands that I give poor old Cameron the word that Kott will leave Savannah forever for the sum of five thousand dollars!"

Mackay turned to Mark. "Son, we apologize for exposing you to what appears to be—and is—a totally irrational matter."

"Oh, that's quite all right, sir," Mark said. "Why don't I

just wait in the next room until you've finished talking?"

Mein stood. "Perhaps that would be more pleasant for you, Browning. We won't be long."

Mark left the office, closing the door behind him, and sat on a wooden bench in the outer room, but the single wooden partition did not prevent his hearing their conversation.

"You've got to refuse to see Kott the next time he shows up here," Mackay said, his voice curt. "I'm sick of the same old complaint, William, and I'm distressed at seeing you so upset by it."

"I did refuse to see him today, but he pushed my clerk aside and strode right into this office—stood where you're standing now. He's the vilest of men, Mackay. He should be so beholden to Jonathan Cameron, he'd fall on his knees in gratitude at the mention of his name. Ever since Osmund Kott was let out of Bethesda Orphanage thirty years ago, old Cameron has supported him—with no questions asked. In return, he despises my client."

"But why?"

"By some means, he found out that it was Cameron who took pity on him as a fatherless six-year-old boy. Kott's mother was apparently a low type of woman. I don't know all the facts, but Cameron made adequate contribution to Bethesda until the boy was fifteen and could leave the orphanage. He's lived ever since on Cameron's largesse. Why Jonathan allows it, I don't know. I don't understand it—not any of it. When I'm at my Coleraine plantation, I spend three or four evenings a week with Cameron at Knightsford. I've loved the old gentleman as though he were my own father ever since I bought my acreage adjoining his. I wouldn't see him hurt for all the diamonds in Africa!" Mark heard Mein's loud sigh. "He is hurt, though, hourly—not only by Kott but by living under the same roof with his wife, Ethel. He's as good as she is evil. A godly, respectable, kindhearted gentleman, if ever one lived. Why he doesn't wash his hands of Kott, I'll never know. He risks losing me as his factor, I can tell you."

After a pause, Mackay said, "Jonathan Cameron's afraid of Kott, William. Deathly afraid of him."

There was another silence and then Mein said softly, "Yes. He must be. We're both reasonably generous men, Mackay, but I can't picture either of us handing out money to a worthless animal like Osmund Kott."

Desperately, Mark wanted to move out of hearing, while at the same time curiosity forced him to stay.

"Of course, on his sober days, Kott can be good company," Mackay mused. "I don't think our town's young literary giant, William Thorne Williams, enjoys an occasional conversation with anyone more than with Osmund Kott."

"I wonder, Mackay, if Kott ever tried to get money out of Williams?"

"He claims not. I'm far from literary, but I do visit now and then at Williams's bookshop. We've spoken of Kott. Williams believes him to have inherited what money he has."

"Ha!"

"Look here, I don't intend to keep my new friend waiting, partner. Mark and I have a full day. I wish I could help you; I can't. There isn't any help until someone can get Cameron to admit what it is Kott holds over his head."

Mark heard someone—Mein, he was sure—slap the desk. "No one could have *anything* to hold over Jonathan Cameron's head! He's as fine a—"

"I know, I know," Mackay interrupted. "But Kott has leverage of some kind unless Cameron is the biggest fool in Georgia. Now, be a gentleman yourself and say good-bye to young Browning. He may turn out to be very important to us."

After a friendly parting with Mein, Mackay and Mark stood again outside on the Strand while Mackay pointed out the offices of other merchants and factors—Sturges and Burroughs, Maher and Norris, Mars and Fahm and, especially, the narrow building belonging to a Frenchman to whom Mackay was obviously devoted.

"Over there, three doors from the end of Commerce Row, labors François-Didier Petit de Villers—known to some not impressed with French blood as 'Monsieur Petit Devil Ears.' Nothing could be further from the truth. Petit is an entirely guileless creature and my good friend. Lost his adored wife, who had just reached her twenty-sixth birthday, while visiting in your home city less than three years ago. Old Petit has been crushed by Maria's death. She left him two young children. My Eliza is godmother to one. You will like Petit, who, by the way, left a month ago for Philadelphia to visit Maria's grave. Perhaps doing that will help the man."

They walked west along Bay and turned on Drayton, past the rear of Christ Church and the Bank of the State of Georgia. Abruptly, Mark stopped walking. "Mr. Mackay?"

"Yes?"

"I'll never be able to thank you."

Mackay gave him his slow, merry smile. "You already have, Mark, by *responding* to my beloved little sand hill called Savannah. Not an elegant city yet—not Charleston by the wildest stretch of anyone's imaginings. But give us time here on the bluff above the river. Give us time."

"Oh, yes, sir! All the time I have left on earth belongs to—Savannah." He felt his face flush. "I know this sounds improbable, but I belonged to Savannah—even before we docked yesterday."

They walked on. "I believe that. When I returned from school in Scotland as a boy and could find no work in my home city of Augusta, I hied me here. Savannah was certainly not beautiful at all in those days." Mackay chuckled. "As I told you, poor folk drove their wagons and carts in from the country to sell their wares. They parked horses, chickens to cook, bedding—everything, including themselves—in our poor squares. But, the squares and carefully laid out streets and lots were there. Old wooden buildings tumbled about among the squares, but the essence of what the city can be was visible to me even then. Young men do have very good vision, you know."

Until noon, when they promised Eliza to be home for an early meal, they walked and Mackay talked steadily, evaluating property, explaining the numerous vacant, weed-choked lots where almost no new buildings had been erected since the disastrous fire of 1796 and the hurricane of 1804. In fact, they enjoyed themselves for such a long time, they would now have to wait until after Mark's appointment with Joseph Habersham for the all-important visit to the house of the adjutant of the Chatham Artillery.

A few minutes before two, when Mark went off alone to keep his appointment with Habersham, Robert and Eliza lingered at table in the square high-ceilinged dining room.

"I thought he went reluctantly," Eliza said. "I must say this is one of those rare times when I don't understand you."

"Why shouldn't the boy get to know a prominent gentleman like Joseph Habersham?" Mackay asked pleasantly. "I thought I was being kind."

"My dear, I know your motives, but can't you see Mark is longing to learn your profession straight from *you?* In the firm of Mein and Mackay?"

He gave her his sunny smile. "And I'm longing to have him. I'm even planning how many voyages he can take in my place—leaving me here with my beloveds."

"Then, why are you—"

"—stalling for an entire half day before I make him a proposition?" He was laughing now. "Dear, serious Eliza, Mark just arrived! Habersham is the only other firm he might consider joining. I want him to see what a sobersides Joseph can be where business is concerned. No one is more charming at a party, but in business Habersham just never learned how to enjoy the risks. Mark will be happier than he can now imagine to be working with our firm once he's heard Joseph expound on the market. And the danger of war. The boy needs to find out that life isn't all earnest, even when a man's minding his business."

"But what if Mr. Habersham's seriousness appeals to Mark?"

He took her hand. "I have every intention of leaving them together exactly one-half hour, before I whisk Mark away to sign him on with the Chatham Artillery." He took out his watch and opened it. "Allowing time for me to walk briskly to Commerce Row, I estimate that forty minutes from now, Mark will be so relieved to see me, he'll offer his services to Mein and Mackay on the spot."

"He strikes me as a naturally serious young man."

"Mark Browning is an undiscovered young man—even to himself, he believes. He's still haunted by, though not rebellious over, the deaths in his family."

"Before you came home from the office this morning, Mark told me about losing Aunt Nassie and his father."

"I knew he would. I knew it! I'm relieved that he did, Eliza. I need you to know all he'll tell you about himself, too. I don't want to make decisions about him on my own. He seems fine, but the boy must still be in grief."

"Of course he is and that's part of what I mean. Are you sure you aren't rushing him just a little?"

"Quite sure." Mackay got up, kissed her hair and then her mouth. "All my flurrying around is just part of Mark's big welcome to Savannah."

She touched his cheek. "I know, dearest friend. I do trust you to do all that's best for him. It's just that I'm already so attached to him, I need to be sure that he works for you and that he stays with us here a long, long time."

"Thank you for saying that."

"Why thank me? I mean every word."

He grinned. "After twelve years as your husband, don't you think I know you always mean every word you say? I have plans for Mark. Plans that I'd find troublesome only if I thought you didn't cotton to the boy as I have from the minute I set eyes on him."

"No need to be troubled." She looked up at him, a smile crinkling the corners of her eyes. "Just go now and rescue Mark."

# SIX

STRIDING up Bay after they had again left Habersham's office, Mackay noticed that Mark said little; seemed too quiet, in fact. Not exactly glum, but surely not responsive as Mackay wanted everyone to be.

"You don't need to tell me," he said, "that you found Habersham likable, fully abreast of the imminent danger of war—fully determined, as is almost every American, not to allow British domination to go on. You also found him a talking record book of markets worldwide."

"You summed up the interview better than I could have, sir," Mark answered. "Mr. Habersham is certainly informed. I liked him fine."

"Is that all?"

"Well, yes."

If the boy doesn't want to express himself further, Mackay thought, let it be. I'll change the subject, try to cheer him up a bit. "Before this year is over, Mark," he went on, "the city will own this fine edifice we're passing—the Exchange building. You see, little by little through the years, the City Council has added to its shares of stock in Savannah's Exchange. We've almost stopped using the place as an exchange, anyway." After a beat he asked, "Mark? Are you listening to my erudite account of events in this town?"

"Oh, yes, sir, I'm listening. Will the Exchange building then be used as a city hall—the seat of government?"

"You're a courteous young man, but right now, you don't care a fig about an answer to that question. Nor does it seem of very much importance that we're on our way to enlist you

70

in the city's most prestigious military company. What's worrying you, son?''

"I—I guess I'm not quite sure how to tell you."

"Did Habersham offer you a position with his firm?''

"Yes, sir.''

"And what did you tell him?''

"That I need time.''

"Of course you do. Tomorrow, I intend to set up interviews
with still other factors and merchants.''

"But, Mr. Mackay—why?''

Mackay stopped walking, laid both hands on Mark's shoulders and said, "So that when I offer you a position with Mein
and Mackay, you'll be even more certain than you think you
are right now that working with me is what you want.''

"Working with you, if you need me, is exactly what I want,
sir! I already know that.''

"Then why are you so—unsmiling? Solemn? If, after your
remaining interviews, you still want to work with my firm,
you're hired!''

The change in Mark's expression was so swift, so like the
sun breaking above a storm cloud, that Mackay laughed. "I'm
not laughing at you. I'm laughing because of you. Your face is
as interesting as a coastal sky. As sudden, as changeable. You
actually had me worried after we left Joseph Habersham's office.''

"I'm sorry. I was just thinking hard. I guess I've been alone
so much this past year, I forget how I must look to other
people.''

They turned off Bay onto Whitaker and crossed an alley
before Mackay spoke again. "That's an interesting thought. I
wonder if we change expression much when we're alone—
when there's no need to impress or comfort or amuse or calm
anyone by the way we look. I hadn't thought about that.''

"I used to smile a lot just to make Aunt Nassie happy.
I know how I felt every time my father smiled at me—or
laughed. You have a gift for making people happy, Mr. Mackay.''

"I do? How is that?''

"You're welcoming. I've already noticed how Mrs. Mackay
responds when you laugh or smile. At the dinner table last
night, it was you who set our mood.''

"Nonsense. Or, if it isn't nonsense, it's simply good fortune. I act as I feel—most of the time. And with my family, I'm at my best. Speaking of Mrs. Mackay, the last thing she said to me when I left the house to meet you at Habersham's was that I am to insist that you stay with us for a long, long time. May we count on that?"

"I guess I'd hoped she felt that way. I'm honored that she wants me."

"One thing you'll learn, Mark, is that when she says something, she means it with all her heart." He chuckled. "Why, last night in our room, she told me she thinks you're beautiful."

"I know I'm blushing."

"Yes, you are—a little. But why should women have a corner on the market of beauty?" He pointed at a two-storied frame house on the opposite side of Whitaker Street. "That's where our adjutant lives. In no time now, you'll be among the lofty ranks of the Chatham Artillery, and"—he laughed—"just wait until our Savannah girls see you in your blue cutaway and plumed chapeau de bras!"

Enthusiastically, Mackay steered him across the street and, as they waited for the adjutant to answer their knock, said warmly, "This is a big moment for you, son, but I honestly think bringing you into the ranks of my company means even more to me."

In midafternoon on June 3, Eliza sat waiting on the front steps of the Mackay house when Mark and Robert returned from a citizens' meeting in Courthouse Square. A meeting Robert would otherwise have attended alone because John McQueen still showed mainly cynicism over the trouble with Britain.

I'm glad Robert has Mark, she thought, jumping to her feet and running toward them as they swung up the brick walkway. "What happened? I've been out here watching for you two for over half an hour."

"A lot of talk," Mackay said, encircling her waist. "Oh, a resolution passed, of course." He turned to Mark. "You tell her, son. You're a Savannah citizen now."

"Yes," Eliza said. "I'd love to hear your opinion, Mark. How did our prominent gentlemen strike you—in action?"

"Well, Alderman Charlton's resolution was certainly—uh—"

"Pontifical," Mackay supplied the word.

Mark grinned. "Correct. But eloquent. It called for the United States to erect new works at old Fort Wayne on the site the federal government evidently just bought."

"That's in town," Eliza said. "Are they really worried about the city itself?"

"Yes, ma'am, they are. You see, Fort Jackson is to protect the river, Fort Wayne the people in case the British get past Fort Jackson."

Eliza frowned. "Robert, what Mark says sounds so—threatening."

"It does. But Savannah has blown hot and cold on the danger of war with Britain since the year we left to live in London, remember? I judge by the facts, not by Judge Charlton's pontification. They were moving gunpowder to and from the town magazine six or seven years ago. Depending upon which party one attended, even then, war was either imminent—or not even discussed. The city is blowing hot at the moment. If Britain lifts the infamous orders-in-council and shipping eases, we'll all blow cold again. As I've told you, Mark, coin of the realm rules us. If coin of the realm is readily available, all is well; if not, patriotism mounts, fortifications hum with activity, spirits rise to battle. Coin of the realm *alone* regulates the temperature in this town."

"I know how these long, wordy meetings bore you, Robert," Eliza said when he'd finished his spiel, "but what do you really think?"

"That the United States Congress will declare war on Britain before the end of the month," he said quietly, leading them up the walk to the house. "And with all the talk we heard today about calling up the Republican Blues and the Volunteer Guards for active duty, I'm downright relieved to have Mark all but in uniform. He and I, your brother and, of course, the other men in the Chatham Artillery are to protect you here in town."

"That suits me," Eliza said as they walked through the open doorway into the cool, wide front hall.

"When did Remick, the tailor, promise to have your uniform finished?" Mackay asked Mark, when Eliza left to get tea.

"Next week, sir. I'll be proud to wear it."

"Oh, I guarantee that. I've never donned my uniform once

without pride. About all we've done is our stints at Fort Jackson, drill, parade and fire salutes on special days, but it's the best company of the lot."

For the rest of that week, Mark faithfully kept the remaining interviews Mackay had set for him, and listened patiently as each man boasted of his business as it was before Jefferson's embargo and Madison's bungling of the trouble with the British. All but one, who could not afford a new man, offered Mark a position. Then, when the last appointment had been met, Mackay hired him.

"You know this is what I wanted," Mark said, beaming as he and Mackay headed for his first day of work on Thursday morning, June 11. "I already knew I wanted to work with you, sir, even before we reached Savannah."

"But now I can boast that even after all those interviews, you chose the firm of Mein and Mackay!"

Mark laughed. "Magnificent day, isn't it?"

"A nearly perfect day, Mark. Except for the British cloud up ahead."

They were silent a moment; then Mark said, "You know, sir, if what we read in the newspapers about Britain's failing economy is correct, and if Congress could hold off just a little with that declaration of war, I still think Britain might well rescind those orders-in-council."

"That would calm us here—and people in New York, Philadelphia, Boston—but it wouldn't calm the frontier states. The British would go right on keeping the Indians there riled up."

"Complicated, isn't it?"

"Causes for war always are." Mackay sighed. "One thing we do know: Savannah—so close to the sea, so mired in her own selfish interests—is *not* prepared for attack and can't be soon." He took Mark's arm as they crossed Bay Street and walked toward the entrance of Number One Commerce Row. "But we're not at war now so far as you and I know. Today is today; the day on which you begin your big Savannah dream. War or no war, Mein and Mackay is the lucky firm with Mark Browning as its new clerk in charge of shipping."

Mark grinned. "My Aunt Nassie always said that God uses everything—the good and the bad. Might be just as well that shipping is curtailed a bit. At least, until I learn something about it."

\*      \*      \*

Seated on the high stool at his narrow desk in the back of Mein and Mackay later that day, Mark had spotted a gunboat moving into an open slip on the Savannah waterfront. With his long glass, he could see that it was gunboat number 168. He had not stopped work to investigate it, for there was too much to learn about the intricacies of shipping orders and bills of lading. But when Mackay read aloud the *Republican and Savannah Evening Ledger* at home early the following week, all the speculation along Factor's Walk as to why the gunboat had come in from the sea was clarified.

" 'Colonel Cuthbert, aide-de-camp to Georgia Governor David B. Mitchell, and commander of the Corps of Republican Blues of this city,' " Mackay read, " 'arrived here last week in gunboat number one hundred sixty-eight for the purpose of procuring one hundred men to proceed to East Florida.' "

Mackay banged the paper with the back of his hand. "Here it goes again," he said. "Even if the United States Government does not declare war on Britain, I do believe Governor Mitchell won't rest until Georgia declares still another futile war on East Florida. Heaven knows, Eliza, I hated that mosquito-ridden province in all those months of trying to settle your father's estate for John, but I swear I'm also sick of Georgia's bungling attempts to conquer it."

"Grandfather Don Juan McQueen would be really worried if he were still alive, wouldn't he, Mama?" William wanted to know.

"Yes, dear, he would be." She sighed, smoothing a child's sock around her darning egg.

Jack piped, "Mark, Mama says he really loved living in East Florida. She used to visit him there and go to Government House balls with Grandfather when she was a girl. That was a long, long, *long* time ago, of course."

"It was no such thing," his mother flared. "I'm only thirty-four now, I'll have you know." She turned to Mark. "We're rude with all this family talk when you don't know about my father. Someday I'll tell you. The children's strange name for him—Grandfather Don Juan McQueen—is simply because they like the way it sounds." She smiled tenderly. "Father liked the way it sounded, too. My poor mother hated it."

"Grandmother McQueen would never live down there with him," Jack said importantly. "It broke her heart and his too,

I guess. But, he became a Catholic and Grandmother Mc-Queen thought that was evil.''

"That's enough, Jack," Eliza said. "Your father is reading the newspaper to us. Let's finish all the war talk before the girls come home from the neighbors. Go on, dear.''

"Let me see, where was I? Actually, Mark and I knew Cuthbert had arrived. You saw his gunboat dock, didn't you, Mark?''

"Yes, sir, I did."

"You saw the gunboat, Mark?" both boys chorused. "And you didn't go down to find out what it was doing there?''

"Quiet, both of you," their father said and continued to read: " 'A call was made on the patriotism of the young men of this place, which was so promptly attended that the number of volunteers soon exceeded that required. The Republican Blues and the Savannah Volunteer Guards were accepted for service in East Florida and were shortly after encamped on the South Common, where they remain until Friday, when they will strike their tents, march to the bluff and embark. They will be escorted to the place of embarkation by the Chatham Artillery and the Chatham Rangers.' There we are, Mark! You can don that new uniform and see your first typically Savannah military action.''

"William and I are going to follow the parade," Jack declared.

"Of course you are," Mackay agreed. "Mark is going to need a good, strong supporting audience. You can both cheer every time he marches by. That is, if you keep running ahead as you usually do.''

"Oh, sure we will," Jack said. "But why did they choose the Blues and the Volunteer Guards to go to conquer East Florida? How come you and Mark can't go?''

"Someone has to stay behind to protect the city," Mackay said. "The Chatham Artillery and the Chatham Rangers will do that.''

"That isn't what I heard the other day," Jack said. "We were playing hunter-hunt-the-hare-o with the Johnson boys, and they said only the high-society Southern gentlemen like our father belong to the Chatham Artillery. High-society companies don't get the dirty duty. Are we high society?''

"We are nothing of the kind. We are—just us," Eliza said firmly. "Your father is a merchant, our friends are all respectable folk—but we are simply Mackays and it so happens your father chose the Chatham Artillery."

Mackay laughed. "I could not have given a better explanation, my dear. Thank you. Listen to this, Jack. It says right here in the paper that only the Blues and the Guards will go to Florida because 'it is deemed necessary to leave the two other uniformed corps to assist in the protection of the city in case of danger.' "

"Danger from what?"

"You know perfectly well, Jack, that while nothing definite is known, there is a strong possibility we may have to go to war again against Britain."

"Why? William and I liked living over there. We were just making some good friends when we had to leave. We don't hate the British."

"Hating the British is beside the point. But if you had lived through the first war with Britain, you might have a lingering prejudice or two. Lots of older Savannahians have, you know."

"Tell me again why the Blues and the Guards are going to conquer East Florida."

"Jack, I'll be the most surprised man in Georgia if anyone conquers anything. But, well, there's just always been a lot of trouble between Florida and the state of Georgia," Mackay explained. "It would seem just so much better in all ways if the United States owned Florida, too. Spain has never been friendly toward us. They keep the Indians riled up. Georgia colored who cross the St. Mary's River at the border are free at once; Spain has never cooperated in returning them to their owners. And Spain *is* an ally of Britain's."

"Why don't you try on your uniform, Mark?" William interrupted pointedly.

"I tried it on last night," Mark said. "In my room."

"But we wanta see it, too!"

"Mark, do," Eliza urged. "I may need to move a button or take in a seam for you."

Mark stole a glance at Mackay, who nodded firmly.

"All right. I'll go upstairs and put it on." He grinned. "I really would like the family's approval."

In a few minutes a tall, beaming young man descended the stair in full-dress summer uniform, his hand on the handle of a new shiny short sword—a hanger—in its black leather scabbard. The deep-blue wool jacket and white trousers were stiffly new, the black, plumed chapeau was held under his arm proudly. "Well," he asked, "how do I look?"

Both boys whistled their admiration, Mackay applauded, and Eliza went to him and gave him a long, approving, affectionate hug—and a kiss.

# SEVEN

WORD didn't reach Savannah for almost a week, but on June 18 both houses of Congress voted to declare another war on Britain. No one was surprised.

Without waiting for word from the federal government, the Savannah City Council had, only a few days earlier, acted on its own to begin strengthening the works at Fort Wayne on the east edge of town by the river. As an "act of patriotism by our fellow citizens," the Council's appeal urged the loan of "all male slaves whose labors can be dispensed with; those from the city will be returned to their owners for meals and lodging, and those from the country will be furnished with provisions and lodgings."

"We'll all comply to the extent possible," Mackay told Mark as they hurried to a citizens' meeting in Courthouse Square in early July, "but I confess I'm delighted that at least one thousand dollars will simply be billed to the federal government. We don't have that kind of cash here right now."

"Do you think we'll find out at this meeting what General Thomas Pinckney plans for Savannah's defense? The poor man has only been here two days. That's not long enough for a real inspection, is it? Do you think the subject of his plans will even come up today?"

"What I expect to hear," Mackay declared, "is about forty-five minutes of highly patriotic talk. My lawyer, T.U.P. Charlton, will be his handsomely rakish self and in fine voice. The gentleman never fails us. Otherwise, we'll wait to know needed details until the *Georgian* or the *Ledger* is in our hands next week."

Mackay was right on all counts. And this time, Mark read the war news aloud to the family: " 'General Thomas Pinckney of the Southern Division of the Army, who arrived in the city on the twenty-second, and was received with honors, including a salute by the Chatham Artillery and the Rangers, left immediately—' "

"Is that the way the Chatham Artillery protects the city, Papa? By firing salutes?"

Mackay laughed. "It does seem so, doesn't it, Jack? But don't interrupt Mark while he's reading."

Mark grinned and went on. " '—left immediately, having suggested plans for fortifying the place. The work will be carried on by a committee of council composed of Alderman J. B. Read, G. V. Proctor and T.U.P. Charlton.' "

"Mr. Charlton's initials spell *tup,*" Jack mused.

"Son!"

"Yes, sir."

"I won't read what seems to be a lot of repetition," Mark said, scanning ahead. " 'Whereas Major General Thomas Pinckney has determined to cause to be built immediately on the site of Fort Wayne'—and so on and on and on—'and whereas the major general has recommended that the City Council direct their attention to the erection of such works on the South Common agreeable to the plan explained as of great importance to the protection of the city.' Well," Mark interrupted the account, "new works on the South Common is *not* more of the same. That means they're going to build earthworks all around the city! The remainder of the article is pretty much repetition—the citizens to supply labor and so forth."

"Our dashing Judge T.U.P. Charlton inserted that notice, I have no doubt," Mackay joked. "If it's too magnificently wordy to cover it all when you read it aloud, that's Charlton. Good man, though, Mark. A state legislator at twenty-one, attorney general at twenty-five, judge on the bench of the Eastern Circuit at twenty-seven. Truly a mental giant—and a hot-tempered, eloquent Regency buck of whom I'm extremely fond. The judge has served me well as my attorney for years. I know his writing style. He inserted that notice."

"Well, after all, dear," Eliza said, "Judge Charlton is the chairman of our Committee on Public Safety."

"And he will serve tirelessly," Mackay agreed.

"Is there anything in the paper, Mark, about the soldiers we saluted off to East Florida?" William asked.

"Not a word, my friend."

Mackay snorted. "Mitchell and his men are undoubtedly sitting down there by the St. Mary's River swatting mosquitoes, trying to decide what to do next."

"Things might turn out better for them this time," Eliza offered.

"Don't count on it, my dear. The conquest of East Florida is simply a favorite Georgia diversion now, as in the past, and I predict, for the future as well. Oh, by the way, Mark and I found out today that our company, the 'high-society' boys in the Chatham Artillery, will by next week be a part of the First Regiment of Georgia Militia. Nothing short of a miracle could have forced those companies to unite. And since one miracle has taken place, are you in the market for another, Mark?"

"A—miracle, sir?"

"According to my experience, it would be. I worked hard for nearly three years before the Mein brothers offered me a working interest in the firm. I'm offering you one as of right now—within a month of your first day of work."

Eliza sat straight in her chair. "Robert, that's wonderful!"

"Whoop-ee!" Jack yelled. "Will it be Mein and Mackay and Browning from now on, Papa?"

Ignoring his son, Mackay watched Mark's face. "You don't exactly look like a man who's just been offered—even a small miracle," he said softly.

"You're offering me a *working interest?*"

"Will it be Mein and Mackay and—"

"No, son. It won't be Mein and Mackay and Browning—just yet. You see, Mark, I'm offering you a share in my part of the company. I'm sure you're wondering why I've brought it up in front of the family. The answer is simple. We consider you one of us now. My boys are both young yet. If something should happen to me, there would be a bright, industrious, extremely well educated young man to handle my interests."

"Papa," William gasped. "Are you old enough to—*die?*"

"Certainly not! But a good businessman covers all possible contingencies. I travel a lot, when the country isn't at war. There are shipwrecks, epidemics, accidents."

After a long, weighted silence, Mark spoke just above a whisper. "This—is a miracle, sir. Nothing short of one. But, I just don't know enough yet about the business even to make a decision on something so—so tremendous."

"I don't see why not," Mackay said easily.

Mark sat looking helplessly from one to another in the family group.

Without a word, Eliza crossed the room and stood beside him, her hand on his shoulder. Finally, she said, "My husband means you only well, Mark. He isn't rushing you. I know his heart. He loves you like a son. So do I."

"I—love you—like a brother." William's voice squeaked with emotion and shyness.

"Me, too," Jack said.

"There is no hurry about anything," Eliza went on, her husband nodding assent. "We'll just go on enjoying each other the same as always. Only more so."

Mark's tender smile, directed at Eliza and the boys, vanished as his eyes went back to Mackay. "I—I've only been here such a short time, sir. Caring about me—like a member of the family? In such a short time?"

Mackay was in no hurry to answer the question, which he knew came from Mark's emotions, not his head. Finally, leaning comfortably back in his big chair, he said, "I don't really think you're overly surprised at the offer, son. You know how superior your work has been, how fast you've caught on." He raised his hand. "Now, don't argue that point. I know that you know and you know that I know you know." Jack giggled, but Mackay went on almost casually. "It may be a bit hard to believe how we feel about you. Take your time on that. We'll simply prove it as the days go by." He thought a moment, then leaned abruptly toward Mark. "Tell you what I'll do. I'll go on paying you the exact same salary, even as my working partner. That will prevent your feeling any urgency to prove yourself for a time. Of course, I'd planned on giving you a raise. That can wait for the present, since the firm has precious little money, anyway. Somehow I think that will help convince you."

No one spoke as Mark looked at Mackay for a long time. The look said, Thank you, for remembering my seeming idiosyncrasy about money. Aloud, a big smile lighting his face, Mark said, "You do know me pretty well, don't you, Mr. Mackay? I'll do whatever you need me to do at the office, but I just don't need a raise. Thank you, for understanding."

\*    \*    \*

That night, as Eliza and Robert lay talking in their bedroom, Eliza surprised him by asking, "What prompted you to offer Mark so much—so soon?"

"You don't agree?"

"Oh, yes. I'm happy about it, but what made you come to such an abrupt decision? You're not—ill, are you?"

He kissed her with total authority. "There . . . does that answer your question? I've never been better. My offer has only to do with Mark himself. The boy has inordinate learning ability. I can't yet believe—and I watch him every day—how thoroughly he's learned the basics of being a merchant. Why, with him handling the shipping end of my business, I'd be rich in no time—except for the infernal war with Britain. Mark is a born decision maker. Oh, he always consults me first—or Mein—but the boy has invariably made the right choices on his own."

After a silence, she asked, "What did you mean, Robert, and what did he mean when you passed some secret knowledge between you about *not* giving him his deserved raise in salary?"

Never in the years of their marriage had he so longed to break a promise and confide in her. Why not tell her that in a matter of months, this singular young man, whom they all loved as though he had always belonged in their home, could be—if he chose—one of America's richest men? There was still no reason at all to tell her—no reason for the conflict between his promise to Mark and his need to tell Eliza—except that Eliza was Eliza and he had always told her everything.

"Eliza?"

"Hm?"

"Does my keeping Mark's confidence about his financial decision create any sort of—barrier between us?"

"Oh, no! I just feel so close to Mark, it seems almost strange that he's keeping something from me. But, my darling, it's all right. It's perfectly all right."

Mackay sighed. "Yes," he said, sounding almost let down. "Yes, I'm sure that it is. You see, dearest, I'm really longing to tell you."

"Should I know? Is it something I need to know in order to be right for Mark?"

"No. I can't honestly say that it is. And I'm sure, although I don't understand it, that it's far easier for Mark to be himself with you as matters stand now."

"Now, that *does* make me curious. I want you to keep your promise, though. Mark trusts you utterly. Robert, do you suppose he grieves alone in his room at night over his father and aunt?"

"I'm sure he does at times. I'm also sure that the Mackays are easing the loneliness. He revels in being a part of a real family after all these years. And the lad seems to have been born with a mind blessed with uncommon balance." He drew a deep breath. "I can't help comparing myself in my grief when we lost our little boy. I didn't fare as well as Mark has."

"Does Mark know about our Robert?"

"I told him. I don't remember his exact words, but whatever he said helped me. Maybe it was just the way he looked at me when I told him. His face says so much! He's far stronger than I am in my grief—even though almost eight years have passed."

"Does Mark ever seem strange to you, Robert?"

"No. Not strange. But he's a very, very different young man from any I've ever known. He's almost guileless . . . too good for his own welfare. I detected no shred of self-pity in the lad—not a minute's worth during our hours and hours of conversation on the voyage down. He's always had every material advantage, but except for his aunt, he really had no one in his family to love or need him. No memory of a mother, helter-skelter visits from a father away constantly on business. Then, within one month, no one. Most young men would be drowning in self-pity. He isn't. Oh, he admits to the pain it all caused him, but to Mark, his life is simply his life and he accepts it. By some means, he just goes on with things as they are and expects good to come of it. At twenty, he has learned, or was born knowing, how to spend his energies only on what he can handle. He doesn't waste either time or energy in moiling or regretting or pitying himself. The boy gains strength from being as he is. I know he does! More strength than I have—eight years after we lost our son." His voice broke. "Eliza, I'm still full of self-pity at times because I don't have Robert to watch, to guide, to laugh with—to experience. When I give in to those times, I feel old and weak and indecisive. Mark is simply a strong, puzzling young man."

"But, he's also vulnerable."

For a long time, neither spoke. Then, Eliza whispered, "Do you suppose God sent Mark to us because our little Robert is with Him now? Does that sound overly sentimental? Too much the way a woman would think?"

He smoothed her hair. "It sounds like you. Eliza, I think Mark longs to tell you so many things. Perhaps even the secret he asked me to keep. Perhaps more than he's told me. He just hasn't had a chance to be alone with you. Have you thought of that?"

"No. I suppose you could be right."

"Right? Mrs. Mackay, this is your husband! How often have you found him to be wrong?" He was teasing, his voice low, full of love, meaning to cheer her after bringing up their own boy's death.

She snuggled closer but did not let him change the subject. "It's true, Robert. When you and Mark are home, the children are usually with us. They're harder and harder to get to bed now that Mark's here."

"And when they have turned in, there I sit. I think he needs to be alone with you. The boy's never had a mother to talk to, you know."

"Was she a Philadelphian?"

"You mean he hasn't told you his mother was born right here in Savannah?"

"Heavens, no! Why haven't you told me?"

"I—I don't know. I guess I just assumed he had. He didn't swear me to secrecy on that. But he knew so little to tell me about her on the voyage down, I wonder if she really was a Savannahian."

"What was her family name?"

"Cotting. And for the life of me, I can't make a connection. I never heard the name Cotting, did you?"

"No. But my family knew everyone in town—in town and out of town—from the Revolution on. Surely Cousin Margaret or John will know if there were Cottings."

"Mark knows next to nothing about his mother or her family. Only that she was an orphan—and beautiful—when Mark Browning, Sr., fell in love with her and stole her away. I suppose he could have the town confused with another. His father traveled so much."

Eliza kissed him and turned over. "Hurry, Robert. We've got to sleep fast. I need to talk to Mark and he may very well need to talk to me."

Curving his body against hers, his arm about her, Mackay said in an unaccustomed solemn voice: "He does need you. He needs you as a separate friend from me. He needs the two of us together as his friends. He needs me as his friend at work. But no one person—or even two—can ever give Mark all he needs, in my opinion."

"Is he—that unusual?"

"Far more than he knows. Actually, he seems to consider himself quite uncomplicated, transparent. And, Eliza, he may be." For a time he was quiet, holding her. Then, "Do you think most of us are so full of confused motives, quirks, selfish twists and suspicions that when a truly undesigning, well-intentioned person comes among us, we jump to the conclusion that *he* is the mystery—not us?"

# EIGHT

BEFORE nine o'clock the next morning, Eliza and Mark waved good-bye to Mackay and the children, who were heading, picnic basket in hand, toward the Mein and Mackay wharf; there they would board the company skiff and sail downriver to newly renovated Fort Jackson.

"You were dear to choose to stay and help me mulch my shrubbery, Mark," Eliza said as they walked together toward the big magnolia- and oak-shaded side yard, where a pile of winter pine straw had been dumped. "I'm sure you'd much rather see what's been done at Fort Jackson."

He gave her his sunny smile. "You're wrong, Miss Eliza. I'm too new in the Chatham Artillery to pull any duty there. Helping you is what I want to do. After all, your husband and I don't take many days away from work."

"I'm both flattered and pleased. But not one bit sorry that you won't be able to serve at Jackson yet. In fact, I'm glad." She handed him a large basket to fill with straw. "I don't care how quiet our city seems, I've grown accustomed to the security of men in the house now. I like it. I'd hate being here alone with the children in all the uncertainty about the war. Oh, toss another forkful of straw right over here, please, Mark—under those big azaleas."

The thermometer had reached eighty-five degrees by late morning, but the two worked easily and calmly, both in straw hats, both dressed as lightly as custom allowed, determined to mulch Eliza's roses, oleanders and azaleas against the searing Savannah summer heat.

"I still think I should be the one on my knees doing what you're doing, Miss Eliza."

"No one has ever mulched to suit me. Men are too much in a hurry to do it right. I like to work a little straw into the top layer of soil—like that, see?" In a moment she stopped, balanced herself back on her heels and looked up at Mark. "On second thought, you just might be the one man who *could* learn. You aren't a bit impatient, are you?"

"Except when I'm hungry."

"Here, try it. I'm curious now. See if you can do it properly around this rosebush."

Perspiration beaded his forehead as he dropped to his knees beside her and began to work carefully, mixing the straw and the top soil, then piling other straw high and loosely around the trunk of a fragrant, large double-pink rose.

Eliza stood watching, surprised and yet not surprised that he was doing it to perfection. He worked swiftly—glancing up at her now and then—his face glowing with the heat and effort, absorbed and happy to be succeeding at the simple task.

When he had finished, in one graceful movement he stood up, quite near her, beaming. She could feel the heat from his young, agile body.

"Well?" he asked.

"I intend to announce at supper this very evening, when everyone is present, that at long last I have found a truly expert mulcher! You've done it often, haven't you?"

"No, ma'am. As your husband would say, I'm just talented."

"I wish you'd talk to me about yourself and my husband, Mark."

She had stopped smiling. His smile faded, too. "I—I'd like to, but I don't quite know what you mean me to—talk about."

"Then, back to your knees, young man. You work far faster than I. I'll fork out the straw for you. We can finish these last ten bushes in no time and then we'll have lemonade on the porch and I'll tell you what I mean."

Seated together in wooden rocking chairs on the side veranda, cool glasses of lemonade in hand, straw hats tossed aside, the two smiled at each other for a time and then Eliza said, "What comes to your mind first when you think of my husband, Mark?"

The somehow lovable frown, to which Eliza had grown accustomed, creased the generous space between his eyes, then was gone. "When I think of Mr. Mackay? The best friend I ever had and—a completely happy man."

She leaned toward him. "Oh, thank you. I have to thank you because wives can determine a man's happiness."

"You determine his, I know that."

"Mark, he maneuvered the children on that picnic today, you know."

"He did?"

"Robert realized that you and I had never had a chance to get acquainted—alone. It's important to him that we are friends for our own sakes."

He laughed. "Then I'm doubly glad I passed the mulching test."

"You've picked up a touch of Robert's good humor, I do believe."

"I'd like that. But all of you have made me feel so wanted, so at home, I think I've also gotten back some of my own. My Aunt Nassie and I used to laugh at the dumbest things. I remember one Thanksgiving Day, we decided to let cook stay home with her family. I was about ten, I guess. And there we were—just the two of us—in our big kitchen, both awkward, both giggling, struggling to butter the bird before we slid him into the fireplace oven."

"Was your Aunt Nassie a good cook?"

"No! She was a terrible cook! We'd always had servants. She could work a fine piece of needlepoint and write magnificently blistering letters to the editors of the local papers, but Aunt Nassie was no more at home in a kitchen than I."

Eliza began to fan vigorously with her hat. "So, what happened to the turkey?"

"Well," he laughed, "I was holding him and her job was to smear the butter around—under his wings, legs—all over."

"Yes?"

"We'd forgotten to get the butter out of the cellar so it could soften, and poor Aunt Nassie—grease almost to her elbows—was struggling. She tried; how she tried! 'Hold him higher, Mark,' she'd shout. And every time I lifted all twenty pounds of turkey in the air, I'd giggle harder and another chunk of butter would slip out of her hand and fall on the kitchen floor. Just when she'd managed to grease him under both wings, I somehow took a short step. My feet hit a hunk of butter and across the floor I went, skidding all the way into the butler's pantry hot on the trail of the half-greased bird, which had jumped out ahead of me!''

Sharing his amusement, Eliza asked, "Then, what happened? Did you pick the turkey up and bake it anyway?''

"We did indeed. And if we'd known how long to let him bake, he might have been delicious. I really don't remember that we got control of our laughter all day long." He wiped his forehead with the back of his hand. "Then, when we finally sat down to eat—just the two of us—we broke into fresh giggles because who would serve whom? She'd never carved a turkey and neither had I.''

"So, who did carve?''

"After sharpening the knife three times, I managed to chop up the bird. It really wasn't carved; it was chopped. The meal was awful, but we loved it. We took turns serving each other.''

Eliza leaned toward him. "Oh, I wish I'd known Aunt Nassie. I've never been very gay or funny myself, but I've always loved colorful, free, laughing people. My father was like that.''

Unashamed, Mark wiped away tears—whether from laughter or sorrow at the mention of his aunt, he seemed not to care. "Aunt Nassie was colorful, all right. A rebel in what she termed 'the social set from which there is no escape.' A very handsome lady, who seemed to me to have everything sorted out. She was born to money, but didn't think about it. With her, living came first. Live every second, every minute, she believed, then the hours and the years would take care of themselves. I remember many times she'd feign a headache in order to get out of attending a silver tea. Then, she'd put on comfortable shoes, an old dress and a shawl, take me by the hand and head for Washington Square to see how far the buds were out on the trees. She adored old, comfortable clothes —and everything that had life in it. I loved her with all my heart. I miss her every day." The tiny frown came and went. "But somehow, since I've been here with all of you, so much of the pain is gone. Do you think it's really gone? I mean, I do have to get my own place. I'm ashamed to have been here this long. I've stayed for a very selfish reason. I feel almost like myself again. Since I've been here, I don't sicken inside quite so often that I'll never have another visit from my father. Aunt Nassie was the center of my life. A visit from Papa was

my excitement. It was strange, losing them both within a
month."

"Your father was Aunt Nassie's only brother?"

"That's right."

"She must have died of a broken heart."

"I think so."

"And did you want to die too then, Mark?"

He gave her a startled look. "That's a funny question."

"Is it?"

He thought a moment, then said, "You might be the only
person on earth who would think to ask a question like that,
Miss Eliza."

"I don't know about that, but without my husband and our
children, I'd have wanted to die when I lost both my parents
within two years. My mother was my Aunt Nassie. My adven-
turous father was—my excitement, too."

Mark's smile was warm. "Don Juan McQueen?"

"Yes. I adored him. The high point in my young life was to
be squired to balls at St. Augustine's Government House with
Don Juan McQueen, my father—always the handsomest gentleman present, always spreading charm and cheer. My
mother hated it when he began to be called Don Juan Mc-
Queen. She never called him anything but John. Was your
father wonderful-looking, too?"

"Oh, yes, ma'am. The few times he visited me after I grew
older, I realized that he was. His face was strong, masculine—
like Mr. Mackay's—evenly featured. He had dark-browed,
deep-set blue eyes and his thick hair was—like gold." He
laughed softly. "I still remember the puzzled looks on the
faces of certain people when, as a small boy, I'd walk up to
them on the street, holding Papa's hand, and say, 'This is my
father!' Of course, they didn't have any way of knowing I
only saw him every few years when he came to visit us." He
paused, a bit indecisively, then went on. "You see, Miss Eliza,
my mother died when I was three. It broke my father's heart.
He left the next day after she was buried and never lived at our
house again. He only visited. Thirteen visits in fifteen years."

He had been staring into the shade-and-sun-streaked yard as
he talked. Now, Eliza could feel him looking at her. Not
knowing quite what to say, she waited, aware that Mark saw
her cheeks wet with tears.

"Thank you," he said. "I'm sorry to make you cry, but seeing you care like that almost wipes out the last of my pain. Not the missing—the pain.''

She sighed. ''Mark, Mark . . . I'm crying for you, but also for myself. We've had some remarkably similar experiences. You see, I was only eleven when my father left for Spanish Florida. He never lived with us again, either. My mother loved him, but she could never bring herself to take us to live in a Catholic land. Savannah people, especially some of the older ones, still gossip about Papa, blame him for—deserting us.'' She took a deep breath. ''If he hadn't fled Georgia, he'd have gone to debtors' prison. They both suffered because, you see, they never stopped loving each other.''

Mark set down his empty glass on a table between their chairs and looked away again—into the shadows under the magnolia trees. ''Your mother was strong, wasn't she?''

''I—don't know. I honestly don't know about that. I know I had a strong-willed grandmother—her mother. The things about which I'm sure, contradict each other at times. I know Mama loved Papa. I know he loved her. I know we all eventually tired of trying to be close with so many miles separating us.''

He turned his eyes back to her and smiled. ''Things were simply the way they were.''

She returned his smile. ''Yes. Things were—the way they were.''

''I'm sure your mother was beautiful,'' he said after a time.

''Oh, yes. Far prettier than I.''

''I don't believe that.''

''I'll show you her picture sometime. You'll see.''

''I wish I could be sure I remember my mother. There are times when I'm positive that I am remembering a gesture, a look—a living expression in her eyes. Her laughter. I'm sure I remember her scent. I thought of her when I smelled that big pink rose we mulched a while ago. I guess I'm really not sure about anything except that my memory of what she must have been like is—*beautiful.*'' He breathed the word. ''Delicate, slender. Dark hair, quite like mine. I have her eyes, Aunt Nassie always said.''

He fell silent. Eliza waited, longing for him to tell her more.

''Miss Eliza, I brought her portrait with me. That's what's in the square, flat crate out in your carriage house.''

''Oh, Mark, we must have Hero unpack it right away! Your

mother's portrait should hang in your room upstairs—or anywhere in the house you'd like.''

Her heart moved toward him as it always did when he gave her his sudden, open smile. "Thank you. I—I've put off unpacking the painting, I think.''

"Do you know why?''

"I didn't intend to stay here very long, for one thing. I—I guess I also thought that maybe if I didn't see my mother's face for a while, it might help me jump more surely into this new life with all of you.''

"You decide,'' she said softly. "We all want whatever is right for you.''

"Miss Eliza?''

"Hm?''

"Did Mr. Mackay tell you that my mother was born here?''

"Yes, Mark. He told me just last night. Her name was Cotting.''

"That's right. Melissa Cotting.'' He was looking straight at her now. "Did you—ever know her family?''

"My husband told me that you are only fairly sure your mother was a Savannah girl.''

"Oh, I'm positive.''

"You are? I got the idea somehow that—''

"Well, Mr. Mackay may have thought I could be confused because I know so little about her, actually, but she was born here.''

"I see. Since last night, I have thought and thought about it, trying to make some connection. I simply can't do it.'' She leaned toward him. "I know how deeply you must want to know about her family here. I'm sure it bothers you every day, especially when you're alone.''

The sunny smile came again. "No. It interests me, but it doesn't really bother me. And my mother's family isn't the reason I chose Savannah. Undoubtedly, they just aren't here anymore. Mr. Mackay didn't understand when I told him, but it's true that I came to Savannah for the city itself.'' He paused. "There was one time when I begged Papa to tell me about my maternal grandparents, even to bring me here. He did neither, for reasons of his own.''

"When was that?''

"The last time I saw him.'' They sat in silence for a time. Then Mark said, "I'd like you to know, Miss Eliza, that on our last visit, my father told me something else, which seemed to blot out what curiosity I'd had about my mother's family. It seemed to blot out—a lot, in fact.'' He stopped, studied his hands, then looked back at her intently. ''I haven't even told Mr. Mackay this yet.''

''And you don't need to tell me, unless you really want to.''

''I do want to. I still try to protect my father, I think, especially with other businessmen. Maybe that's why I haven't told your husband. I really want Mr. Mackay to know everything about me. So, maybe you'll tell him for me.''

''If it will help in any way, of course I'll tell him.''

In a surprisingly quiet voice, he began: ''That last day with him, I learned from Papa for the first time that he had *not* been away all those years on business as I'd always thought. He'd inherited a successful company and I always took for granted that he traveled the world on the firm's business. That day he told me that, except to draw money from the company, he'd had no connection with it since my mother died. None at all! He traveled only because he dared not stop.''

''Mark! Oh, Mark . . .''

''I don't remember the day he left—the day after my mother's burial. I was too young. I—just grew up with him gone. It didn't even seem to anger me when my boyhood friends and later my Yale classmates made remarks. Their fathers came home every day from an office or a store. Mine simply didn't. If their fathers took a trip, they came home. My father visited me when he could.'' A smile lighted his face. ''And, Miss Eliza, it was like the days leading up to Christmas for Aunt Nassie and me when we knew he was coming! But, well, how could I miss what I'd never experienced? I don't remember having both a father and a mother at home. I had everything else I needed and most of what I wanted and I had Aunt Nassie and that was the way my life was.''

''You never resented once—his not living with you?''

''No, ma'am,'' he said simply and Eliza knew he was telling the truth.

''You see, what hurt me so much—when he drowned—was that for a whole year after he was gone, I couldn't be sure that I had *been* what Papa needed me to be the last time we were together, when he confessed all this.'' He stood abruptly. ''Miss Eliza, he had been running from his grief all those years! He could never face coming back to Savannah because he had found Melissa Cotting here. He could never live in our house in Philadelphia because he had lived there with her. He was running all that time! Running from country to country, back and forth across mountains and oceans—trying to get relief from that awful sorrow. He never did learn to live without my mother. And all that time, I didn't have any idea how he hurt!"

"Mark, you were a child! How could you have known? What had your Aunt Nassie told you about his trips?"

"I—I don't remember that she told me much of anything. She just pitched in and helped me make a wonderful game out of each visit."

"Oh, I think I understand your aunt so well! I know she meant to be making it all easier for you—growing up. I can almost feel how she struggled with herself—"

"Aunt Nassie?"

"Yes! How she must have vowed, each time he left, to tell you that the poor man was suffering." She took a deep breath. "Then, each time, she'd think—next time he comes. Mark, Mark . . . you're very brave."

He tried to laugh. "I don't see anything brave about me. When I was thirteen or fourteen, I remember thinking about the terrible sadness in Papa's eyes. But he was such a magnificent storyteller, such a superb conversationalist, he made me forget it. He could make me laugh, could make my eyes pop out in wonder, cause me to sit on the edge of my chair with suspense at the sea tales he'd heard, the strange, faraway places he'd been. Oh, sometimes I'd catch him staring at me, his eyes clouded." He sat back down. "Miss Eliza, I could be more sensitive to him now. I wish I had the chance. He always talked a lot about my mother to me."

"What did he tell you about her?"

"Oh, that he'd met her here in Savannah. in Johnson Square, that she was gentle, full of fun and play, more beautiful than—" He stopped. "Miss Eliza, I feel as foolish as I must seem to you right now that I didn't think to ask Papa any practical questions about her. I just didn't think to inquire about grandparents because I'd never had any. Grandfather and Grandmother Browning died before I was born. Mostly, I wish I'd asked Papa about my mother. I just didn't *think* to ask. He mesmerized me with his poetic talk of her. That seemed to be enough for me then. I really had planned to find out lots more. He stunned me so by telling me that another man had run my grandfather's business all those years, I let him go without asking. I feel pretty dumb about a lot of things, I guess. But—'' The smile came. "It's too late for any of that now. I'm glad I told you, and I would like to hang my mother's portrait in my room.''

"We'll do it today! Mark, you don't know anything about your mother's family here—where they lived, their business?''

"Nothing. Miss Eliza, I hope I don't sound too peculiar when I say that by now it doesn't seem to have any connection with me. It does have, I know, but—'' He shrugged. "Mr. Mackay never heard of the Cottings and neither did you. I guess I'm lucky not to be bothered about it when there's no way to find out.''

"You're right, of course, but what a mature viewpoint. Human nature generally flies in the face—even of the impossible. Especially young human nature." She leaned her head against the high back of her chair. "I admit I was terribly curious when my husband told me she was born here. Thanks to you, I'm not so curious now. More mystified, I think. After all, I was born out on the Savannah River at a plantation called The Grange. My family knew everyone—certainly, everyone of means.''

"Oh, I have no way of knowing that the Cottings were people of means. They may have just been too poor for you to have heard of them.''

Eliza sat up, looked at him. "That doesn't bother you either, does it?''

He grinned. "What good would it do?''

"Mark, do you realize how—different you are? How unique?''

She saw the tiny frown come and go, but he said nothing. "Has anyone else told you that?''

He sighed deeply. "Yes. My father, certainly. Even Aunt Nassie at times. Mr. Mackay. Other people. I don't ask why anymore.''

"I'll tell you why. Because there isn't one trace of bitterness in you. How can that be? Has God protected you from it?''

"I guess He has. Bitterness would be—a waste, wouldn't it?''

She thought that through. "Yes. Yes, of course it would be. Mark?''

"Ma'am?"

"Has this talk meant half as much to you as it has meant to me?"

Abruptly, he reached for her hand. For a long time, he held it so tightly, his knuckles whitened. Eliza gripped his hand in return.

"All right," she said at last. "That tells me more than if you'd been foolish enough to try with words. Stay with us as long as you need to stay. As long as it helps you at all to be under this roof, please stay, Mark. I—need you, too. We all need you."

Just before dark that evening, to catch a rising breeze, Eliza and Robert went for a walk around Johnson Square.

"Do you think he will stay with us, Eliza?"

"Yes. Yes, I do."

"And what about accepting my offer of an interest in the firm? Did he discuss that with you today?"

"He didn't mention it. I'm sure he would want to give you his decision on that."

"Did he tell you about his inheritance?"

"Inheritance? No. Not a word. Robert, is that what you promised Mark not to discuss with anyone?"

He sighed. "I wish he'd told you! I must say you don't seem one bit surprised that he didn't. Or disappointed."

"No. Actually, I think he was just so deep in what he did tell me about his parents and Aunt Nassie that he may have forgotten the inheritance, or whatever it is you're guarding so carefully."

"Forgotten!" He clapped a hand to his forehead. "Well, did he even tell you the name of the shipping company his father owned?"

"Not that I remember. I'm sure not. We only spoke of the things that seemed to matter to Mark himself."

"I suppose what you say really shouldn't surprise me. Knowing Mark—knowing you." He took her arm. "You both make me feel like a dirty old money-grubber at times."

"That's a silly thing to say."

"I suppose so."

"Elaborate, then."

"Do I have to? Can't we just be glad we have the boy with us? Can't I get by with contending that it's you and Mark who are—just different from the rest of the human race?"

"And you are very fond of us both."

"I am, indeed. And we're blessed to have him. Our sons talked about him all day. Jack, in fact, is most inquisitive about Mark's family."

"Our Jack is?"

"I take it you didn't find out about his mother," he went on, "who she was."

"No."

"I'd stake my reputation on the fact that he's already told us everything he knows about her. Mark Browning would never invent a lie—even a deception. He asked me to keep—a certain financial secret for a time, but there isn't real deception in it. He just wants to win his way here on his own merit—not on his family's—"

"His family's *what*, Robert?"

"Eliza, haven't you guessed the secret I'm straining to tell you?"

"Oh, I suppose when he's twenty-one, he inherits some money. He seems to be the last living member of his immediate family."

Mackay sighed noisily. "That's part of it. I'd be ever so relieved if you'd guess it all! What did he tell you today?"

"Deep, personal things that he needed to share." She stopped walking and looked up at him. "His father wasn't away handling the firm's business all those years. The very last time Mark saw him, he confessed to the boy that he'd had *no connection whatever* with the family business since the day they buried Mark's mother."

Mackay stared at her. "Then, why did the man travel?"

"He was—running, Mark says. From his grief. The only connection he had with the family firm was to collect his money in order to keep traveling and, I assume, to support Mark and Aunt Nassie."

"Eliza, why didn't Mark tell me that?"

"I'm sure it would have embarrassed him for his father, to have told a hard-working businessman like you. He asked me to tell you."

They walked on slowly for a long time before Mackay finally said, "I'll be a son of a gun! How could a fine boy like Mark have such a self-centered weakling for a father? Who ran the enormous company all that time?"

"Mark didn't say. Just that someone else handled it entirely."

Mackay took another deep breath. "I'm so seldom at a loss for words, I find it downright embarrassing." He turned her abruptly to him. "This whole thing twirls me up like a dancing bear, but I suppose you just accepted the story of his father's ignominy—as calmly as Mark does."

"I did not. I was—flabbergasted. But, darling, I know Mark far better now. And I like what I know even more."

# NINE

WHEN the Fourth of July arrived, bright and hot and windy, offices and stores and warehouses closed their doors for a full day of celebration. Bells all over town began to ring at dawn, and every man who owned a uniform was up early and dressed for what Mackay called "our annual soldierly display under the waving standard of our company."

Mark and the entire Mackay family, except little Kate, spent the long day out in the city. The two men, dressed proudly in their Chatham Artillery uniforms, marched, fired salutes and performed drills, while the boys ran after the parade and lustily joined in patriotic songs. In great, good humor, everyone listened endlessly to orations that were, in Mackay's words, "so flowery they put my wife's garden to shame!"

When it was time for dinner to be served at the Exchange Coffee Shop for "Respectable Republican Citizens," Hannah and Hero found the family in the crowd and took the children home to eat; Mark went with the Mackays to dine, to listen to more patriotic orations and to partake of toasts. Toasts that began with the first President, George Washington, and covered them all up to and including President Madison—then veered to prominent Georgians. When the still enthusiastic diners began to raise glasses to eminent men of the city, ward by ward, Mackay deftly steered Eliza and Mark outside and headed them home.

"They would have been toasting you next, Mr. Mackay," Mark laughed. "We might have waited at least for that."

"And I would have, by then, been sound asleep," Mackay said. "Don't forget, young man, I spent the night on what amounted to a board at Fort Jackson so I'd be on hand before dawn to represent you and other lazy members of the Chatham Artillery."

Mark grinned. "I know, sir, and I commend you. Your salutes were fired in perfect form."

"How does Fort Jackson look these days?" Eliza wanted to know as they turned into Broughton Street. "What would Major Pinckney think of it now?"

"If he gave no warning of his arrival, he might faint to see it. Oh, work has been done. Young McRee did all anyone could do with limited funds, but I never spent a night in such unmitigated discomfort." He linked his arms through theirs. "Still, it's been a buoyant day, hasn't it? The war has at least fired up the town's patriotism."

"It's been the best day I've ever spent," Mark said, with the quick sincerity they'd both come to expect. "I thought Philadelphia knew how to celebrate the Fourth. It didn't compare with Savannah today—for me."

"That's because you're hopelessly in love with the city," Eliza said. "How I hope you stay that way."

"And how I hope he never becomes an alderman," Mackay laughed. "Alderman Browning might never find anything wrong with his town. Or, if he did, I swear he'd find a way to gloss it over."

"You can joke about it if you like, sir. I intend to be in love with Savannah until the day I die. I never take a walk alone that I don't dream of the time when her streets will be lined with great houses, stores, churches, libraries."

"Banks," Mackay joked. "For heaven's sake, don't forget our 'great' banks!"

At the house, after Eliza went to hear the children's prayers, Mackay and Mark, their chapeaus carefully hung in the back hall on high hooks out of the reach of small hands, stopped in the parlor for one more toast to the festive day.

"You did enjoy yourself, didn't you?" Mackay asked, splashing a bit of brandy into large-bowled crystal snifters.

"Every minute," Mark said, swirling the amber liquid about in his glass as his father used to do.

"I hope you know, son, how deeply we all want you to stay right here on Broughton Street with us until—" he winked, "until you find the beautiful young lady for whom you'll want to build a fine house of your own."

Mark grinned. "I dream about that, too, sir. And I know it's rude of me not even to mention when I'll be moving—"

Mackay raised his hand to stop him. "Nothing of the sort! The very roots of your life have been torn up, Mark. You've made a noble leap, but time, time, time is important. Take all you need."

"It looks as though that's what I'm doing."

"When you're my age—twice yours—a month is far shorter than it seems to you now. A month is nothing at all."

"This month has begun my life for me again." He fell into a characteristic silence while he thought what he would say next. Mackay waited.

"I haven't stopped thinking about your most generous offer of a working interest in your share of the business, either," Mark said at last, looking at Mackay in his disarmingly direct way. "I haven't been at all businesslike about it. I should have given you an answer. I haven't been businesslike about that or my staying on here."

"You're not supposed to be businesslike except on Commerce Row," Mackay said lightly. "But once you step into my countinghouse down by the river, you're all business."

The tiny frown flickered and vanished. "Am I?"

"Do you think that I'd have made an offer like that to just any—callow boy? Scarcely. Mark, you're a born businessman and, wonder of wonders, without one discernible bit of sophistry. At the same time, you cleverly influence William Mein without his suspecting."

"I do? How?"

"You know how fond I am of him, but he's the most maddening business partner anyone ever endured. If he didn't have so much insurance stock and property, he'd be a pauper now simply because he can't keep his mind made up. Do you know that back in 1809, while my family was still in England, Mein and I ran a notice in the *Republican* that we were, by mutual and cordial consent, dissolving our partnership?"

"Yes, sir. I refiled all those papers the other day."

"So you did. I'd forgotten. Mark, that notice ran three years ago! Mein's been changing his mind or forgetting to wind up this or that or arguing with our attorneys ever since. We're not really partners now at all, but we both still go to work at Number One Commerce Row. That is, when Mein remembers to arrive. I excused it for two years because he was a newlywed. Now, I've run out of excuses. But I've observed that when you're in the office with him, he becomes decisive, even efficient. Can't believe my eyes. Mein and Mackay have a confusing relationship to say the least—as confusing as it is pleasant, actually—but none of it has seemed to disturb you. You've been exceedingly courteous to him, and yet you've almost got him to the point of coming to grips with our future."

Mark was smiling. "Mr. Mein has too many irons in the fire."

"Exactly! My hope is that when you give me your answer and I can inform him that you hold an interest in my share of the company, he will make up his mind once and for all to have our mutual holdings legally divided."

Mark sipped the last of his brandy, then looked straight at Mackay. "Speaking of business, I do have a request."

"Anything I can do for you, son, I'll do."

"Good. I want to begin paying room and board here as of July first."

Surprised, Mackay laughed. "You tricked me! So help me, that's the first tiny streak of guile I've seen in you. But, if you feel you must pay, I agree."

Mark slid down in his chair, relieved. "I'll feel a lot better about wolfing down so many of Emphie's biscuits. You see, I do want to—stay on here for a time. Unless I become an inconvenience."

"That doesn't deserve a comment." Mackay drained his glass. "Mark? Have you made up your mind about your inheritance yet?"

"Truthfully, I haven't given it much thought. I've just been enjoying all of you. Is that because I'm immature?"

For once, Mackay didn't answer immediately. "Immature? Son, with you, I honestly don't know. Sometimes I feel you're my senior. The other day at the office when you sensed—and rightly—that Bob Harrold was telling me the truth about those billings, you seemed far older and wiser than I. Without your intercession for him, I would have fired one of the best wharf supervisors I've ever had."

"I made a lucky guess."

"No. You wouldn't have stuck in your heels with me as you did on a mere guess. Somehow, you *knew*."

"I felt as though I knew, sir." As though to give himself

courage, he sat up straight in his chair, leaned forward and asked bluntly: "Mr. Mackay, why did you offer me an interest in your business so soon after I began to work for you? Is that an impertinent question?"

"No, it isn't. I had two reasons. First, as I said, we never know what might happen. I'm in excellent health now, but no man can know about tomorrow or the next day. Should something happen to me, my business affairs, because of good old Mein's procrastination, would not be in order so that my wife could sell. You're the only capable person I've felt I trusted."

"But, I'm not yet twenty-one! What about Mrs. Mackay's brother, John McQueen?"

Mackay smiled a little sadly. "I'm as fond of John as a brother-in-law could be. I've always like him. I've tried to prove it by spending months in that godforsaken East Florida colony attempting to salvage even a fraction of his father's enormous Spanish landholdings. But, likable gentleman that he is, John is not a strong man. He's brilliant at times—he was the first planter to discover that oil can be produced from our common benne seed—but he has no ambition. Seems to lack faith in the future of—any country. As a boy, he was in school in Paris during their Revolution. Then he lived here, followed by years in Spanish Florida with his father. He's hopped from one rented plantation to another since, never quite making a go of planting. Of anything. He's buying his place at Causton's Bluff now. Maybe that will work. Who knows? This is confidential, but your question deserved an answer. That's it."

"I see. That won't prejudice me against him, I promise. I'm so attached to Miss Eliza, I'm eager to meet her brother."

"I'm glad to hear you say that. Now, my second reason for making you the offer is just between us. You will be a rich man soon and—"

"But, sir, I—"

"I know. Still, even if you take only a portion of what's coming to you by economic standards in Savannah, you'll still be extremely well off. Someday you'll own your own mercantile brokerage. Someday, if I live, I'll be too old to work. You and my sons are friends. Why not have a ready-made firm at hand when you're ready for it? One you know. One you've helped build."

Mark gave him an open, wholehearted smile of gratitude. "I will have to say you've thought it through, sir. I need you to help guide my thinking. It's true that I've just been having a good time *living* here. Oh, I think about business during the day at the countinghouse, but once I'm back here in the evening, I—well, I—"

"You become as young as you really are. And that's as it should be."

Mark looked at him for a moment, then got abruptly to his feet and walked to the front window. "Mr. Mackay, the truth is, this minute, I'm fairly sure I've made up my mind on both issues. Actually, deep inside, since last year, I've known that I had no right to inherit all the Browning fortune. I'm sure Miss Eliza told you that my father did nothing to build it for all those years."

"Yes, she told me. But legally, you're still your father's only heir. You do have a right to it—to all of it!"

His back to Mackay, still looking out into the soft darkness, Mark said, "No, I don't. A man named James Parsons, of New York, should have most of the company. I knew that the day I first told you that I had questions about inheriting all the assets. Parsons increased the company's worth by over a hundred percent during those years my father was—running from his grief. Our attorney, Woolsey, told me that. Showed me proof of it. I really knew then that I could *not* take the whole inheritance. You see, Woolsey just made such a fuss about it, for a time—the shape I was in—I wavered. I knew then that I should take one fourth of it. No more." He turned to face Mackay. "I'm only taking a quarter share."

"Will that be enough to build your own fortune, Mark?"

He was smiling his easy smile. "All told, it will be a million dollars more than you had, sir."

Mackay whistled. "Even with a quarter interest, you'll be the richest man in Savannah, son!"

"But only the two of us will know it. Right?"

Mackay sighed. "If you insist."

"I do. Someday I mean to tell Mrs. Mackay. She knows everything already except the name and the size of Browning World Shipping. I want her to know that, too, sometime. But I guess I want her to care about me for myself first."

"You must know she does!"

"I also know that keeping my secret is very hard for you."

"Mark, she already assumes you'll have an inheritance. I don't see—"

"I'm sure she does. I just don't want anyone to know the size of it. As for the working interest you offered me—yes. It's an honor. But I have one stipulation."

Mackay raised a quizzical eyebrow.

"No raise in salary because of it. You promised. I just don't want you to change your mind. I know how tight things are now and I'm fine." He held out his hands in a helpless gesture. "I—I think I know what's going through your mind. I understand how odd I must seem to you, sir. But I just don't care about a lot of money. I care about learning all I can from *you.*" The fluttering candles blazed up long enough for Mackay to see that Mark was deeply moved. "I honestly don't think I could face living now—without being close to you and Miss Eliza and the children."

After a meaningful silence in which both men showed in their eyes what no words could express, Mackay got up, walked to where Mark stood, snapped to attention and saluted.

Mark returned the salute and then fell into Mackay's outstretched arms for the first bear hug of his life.

# TEN

THE heavy, sultry summer days flew by for Mark. His new responsibilities at the countinghouse absorbed him, and life with the Mackays still seemed too happy to be real. Saying good night and good morning to a whole family went on bracketing his days with a kind of joy he felt foolish even trying to explain.

Savannah itself seemed to languish in a hammock of suspended waiting. The country was at war with Britain again, and yet, aside from the sometimes harried and sometimes halfhearted work on the city's fortifications, a pervasive restlessness held almost everyone but Mark. He was there and for him that was enough. Listening to Mackay and Mein explain why things were so dull merely amused him.

"We're just not accustomed to being in town during this infernal hot weather," Mein grumbled. "Everyone who is anyone always goes north. At least for July and August. This summer the town's swarming with people!"

"And no social life," Mackay complained. "Not that I mind having a legitimate excuse to avoid balls in ninety-eight-degree heat."

At breakfast with Eliza and Mackay on a stuffy, still morning, Mark accused Mackay of missing the social whirl, and Eliza agreed.

"You know him better than he thinks, Mark. He's always fussed about Savannah's lavish society affairs, but he really thrives on them. And the reason he does is that no party or ball or dinner is quite the same without Robert N. Mackay, Esquire. Why, in the past, Julia Scarbrough, no less, has postponed an event simply because he was away on business."

"That, dear wife, is not true. If forced to choose, Countess Julia would rather give an elaborate entertainment than receive a new emerald lavaliere from husband William. She postpones for no one. I'm surprised she doesn't give something, war or no war."

"Actually, I expect it any day now that September's here," Eliza said.

"You and I should give a small something, in fact," Mackay said. "We should at least have the Scarbroughs for dinner."

"Oh, Robert, entertaining Julia makes me so nervous!"

"Nonsense. Mark needs to know them both. Scarbrough's one of our most important citizens, Mark. A financial wizard as a merchant, a genius in things mechanical—he's even designed a machine that is supposed to fly! We could have Petit de Villers and the Meins and Joseph and Robert Habersham and their ladies. And your brother, John, and his wife, Delilah."

Mark glanced at Mackay. "Delilah? Isn't Mrs. McQueen's name Margaret?"

"Of course it is," Eliza interjected. "Mark's a member of the family now, Robert, I think he deserves to understand your scandalous nickname for Cousin Margaret. Not everyone finds it funny."

Mackay bowed, a Cheshire cat grin on his face. "Then, you explain, my dear. I'll enjoy listening."

Eliza gave Robert a look that both adored and reprimanded him. "All right," she said. "My brother, John, married our cousin—but only after a long, long period of patient, devoted waiting. He's thirty-seven now and Margaret is thirty-four."

"You see," Mackay broke in, "Margaret had a veritable string of hearts to break first. There was William Mein, a half dozen other gentlemen of note here in Savannah, including *the* William Scarbrough, now married to Countess Julia, a host of men in Jamaica and England—and finally, our patient, persevering John won out. They married two years ago." Realizing he had cut off Eliza's story, Mackay laughed, reached to pat her hand. "There, my dear, don't you feel better now that *you've* explained Cousin Margaret to Mark?"

"Yes, dearest friend, I do. But then, I always feel better when I obey you."

Delighted by their sparring, Mark laughed, then pushed

back his chair and stood. "Sorry to interrupt this breakfast party, but I'm due at the office."

On his feet, too, bursting as usual with energy, Mackay bent to kiss Eliza. "How about next Wednesday evening, Mrs. Mackay? Is that too soon for our dinner plans?"

"Too soon and too hot. Let's think in terms of at least mid-October. After all, I don't intend to embarrass you before Julia Scarbrough with a less than elegant meal. We do have shortages, Robert. I'll have to do some sleuthing to see what I'll be able to serve."

"Don't jump to any wild conclusions about our friend the countess Julia, Mark," Mackay chuckled as they strode through Johnson Square toward Bay. "She's, first of all, a strikingly beautiful young lady. About twenty-five or -six, I'd say. Raven hair, violet eyes, white, white skin—truly lovely, if a touch buxom. But, just a touch." He laid a hand on Mark's arm. "And speak of the devil—here she comes out of Andrew Low's Emporium!" Mackay doffed his hat and bowed deeply. "Good morning, dear, *dear* countess. Minus twenty or thirty degrees, it's a glorious morning!"

Mark stood to one side as Julia Scarbrough spewed forth a stream of honeyed words by which he gathered that she absolutely reveled in every chance meeting with Robert Mackay.

"And this, dear Julia, is our new and cherished friend, my business associate and houseguest, Mr. Mark Browning—lately of Philadelphia, now, forever, of Savannah. Mark, may I present Savannah's reigning queen, Mrs. William Scarbrough?"

Bowing, Mark lifted his hat, too. "I'm honored, Mrs. Scarbrough. I've already heard so much about you."

"Have you really, dear boy? How exciting! Robert, you fox, what have you been saying about me? Except, of course, that my parties are the best in town." She overlaughed. "He is a wicked flatterer, you know, Mr. Browning. But I wouldn't think of giving one of my blowouts without him. His lovely Eliza is so serenely decorative, and Robert the catalyst that keeps everyone pleasured. Actually, having Robert Mackay on one's side is the first essential to making it in this snooty town, right, Robert?"

"We all need as many folk on our side as possible, lovely lady."

"There, you see, Mr. Browning? He didn't really say anything in that pretty speech, but didn't it sound profound?"

"You're out early, Julia."

"An early fitting for some new gowns. But mainly, I'm off to pay a call on Eliza."

"She'll be delighted."

"I'm never quite sure of that, but I go anyway. She's the perfect, reserved complement for you, Robert. I have told you that, haven't I?"

"Many times."

"Frankly, I timed my call today so I'd miss you. I have private business with Eliza. Woman business." She gave Mark a sly glance. Not the glance of a thoroughly refined lady, but attractive nevertheless. "Everyone in town knows you're here, Mr. Browning, and that our generous Mr. Mackay has taken you under his wing, but I, for one, feel we've neglected you horribly. All because of this dreadfully inconvenient war about which we hear nothing. So, I'm off to speak with Eliza concerning your need for some female wings to protect you!" She laughed a raucous, though downright likable, laugh.

The Exchange clock began to strike nine. Mackay bowed again. "Dear countess, you must excuse me. We're due at the office at this very minute."

"Of course, you dear, hardworking merchants. Run along and make simply pots of money today, do you hear? Oh, by the way, Mr. Browning. My husband wondered at breakfast— as I believe many men in the mercantile world are wondering these days—if by any chance you could be related to *the* Brownings of the world-famed Browning World Shipping Company?"

Mackay saw the dismay in his eyes. But all Mark said was, "I'm—just Mark Browning, Mrs. Scarbrough. And so happy to be Mark Browning of Savannah."

Her smile faded a bit as she peered at him, then at Mackay. "He has your knack, too, hasn't he, Robert? What a pretty speech, which told me nothing, really."

After they had bid her good-bye and hurried across Bay Street in silence, Mackay slowed his pace. "Mark? You mustn't give the countess a serious thought—as she would say, 'really.' She's downright coarse at times. Her North Carolina background, undoubtedly. I keep hoping she'll outgrow it at some point. For the moment, she seems unable not to say exactly what she thinks. But, believe me, we're fond of her. She truly wants to buoy our spirits. Wants first, of course, to buoy her own social standing in town, but she's generous of heart, too. William, her husband, is of fine *South* Carolina stock— son of a well-known physician there, wealthy in his own right —and has a finger in many prosperous pies. He's a valuable connection for you, as is Julia."

"Did she just guess about Browning World Shipping because of my last name?"

"I'm sure she did. The fact that her guess happens to be correct is of no consequence whatever now. And, Mark, as important as families are—as prominent as yours has been for all these years—you can't expect people not to inquire."

Mark looked troubled. "I know, but I do so want to make my way as plain Mark Browning—me."

"I know and you will. But you must be reasonable about it, too. Browning's a famous name in any seaport town—almost anywhere in the world. And certainly, you can be proud of owning it." When Mark said nothing, Mackay added as they reached the door of Number One Commerce Row, "I doubt that anyone will ever think of you as 'plain Mark Browning,' but never mind. After all, you have the whole Mackay clan right with you to protect you from Savannah."

Mark grinned uneasily. "Do I need protection from Savannah?"

"Everyone does—everyone, every day. The town's a world unto itself—elegant, mostly pleasant, invariably nosy. The ladies are generally bored, the men competitive at every turn. Except for a few who, like Petit, would walk a plank for a friend, I stay on guard. It's second nature by now. And it's not bad, actually. Don't worry at all about dear Julia. Eliza can handle her. Whatever she's up to, Eliza will be there looking after your interests."


"On second thought, Eliza, my dear, I believe I will take another scone. William and I did have such an early breakfast."

In the Mackay parlor, Eliza passed the scones again and poured more coffee.

"Give my best compliments to your faithful Hannah," Julia spoke through a mouthful. "These are delicious! Full of currants. Good for the blood. Now, Eliza, I have another call to make, so I must get to the point.''

"All right, Julia. I'm listening.'

Julia Scarbrough swallowed another large bite of buttered scone, made an effort to lick her fingers gracefully, unfolded her lace fan, leaned back in her chair and said, "Do you ever madden Robert by that—everlasting calm of yours? You do madden me at times, you know."

"No, I didn't know that. I meant no harm."

"Naturally. Now, what of that absolutely devastating young man you have living here with you? Tell me all about him. *All* . . .''

"Well, Mark has come to be like one of us; he *is* one of us. My husband met him on his last voyage down from Philadelphia before the war. The boy's fulfilling a longtime dream of living in Savannah. He's sensitive, tender, beautifully mannered, delightful company—the children love him to distraction. As do Robert and I."

"But what's his background? His family? Who are his parents?" She fanned furiously.

"Mark's an orphan. His mother died when he was three. A year ago he lost his one beloved aunt, who reared him, and his father—both within a month. He has no family. I'm sure he had friends at Yale and in Philadelphia from his childhood— but he speaks of no one. He's truly making a new, fresh start."

"Haven't you pressed him for—family connections?"

"No."

"Why not?"

"We don't care. We simply like Mark for himself."

"That's all very noble, my dear, but aren't you worried about him? I am!"

"Why?"

"Well, he's been here since early summer and—Eliza, has the boy been invited anywhere? Is he meeting our young ladies in town? Oh, I know this dreary war is limiting entertainment—it isn't considered good form and all—still the boy is so appealing! So attractive, so fine-featured—could he be a poet? He has a poet's profile!"

"I don't think he writes, but he loves books. Robert is going to take him to meet William Thorne Williams down at his new bookshop soon. We feel Mark will really enjoy Mr. Williams."

"Oh, upon my word! Bookish William Thorne Williams? He's dusty, like his shop. Surely you can think up livelier contacts."

"We haven't felt we should push Mark in any direction. It was such a short time ago that he lost the two people dearest to him on earth. Moving away from his home was a wrench, even though he had so completely made up his mind to come here. Julia?"

"My dear?"

"Mark is fine, just as he is. He loves working with Robert, he seems fond of our children. Especially my usually shy, reserved William, who adores him. Mark is—all right. You needn't worry."

"But the young ladies in town are panting to meet him!"

"They will. In fact, Robert and I are giving a dinner party later when it isn't quite so stifling."

Julia propped one hand on a hip, tapped her chin with her fan. "I've just decided. I'm not waiting. Good taste in wartime or not, I'm giving a ball—a dress ball just as soon as I can arrange it!"

"In this weather, Julia? It's even too hot for Robert to think of dancing, and you know how he loves it."

"Most of us, because of this *phantom* war, have stayed in town, so why not ignore the weather and give all our spirits a lift?"

"We feel we can't—because of the war and the slow shipping—afford anything lavish," Eliza said firmly.

"Oh, well, I'm sure my husband will be of that mind, too, until I've had a chance to talk him out of it. I'll see to hiring the musicians right away. Do you think five pieces would be enough? Say, a pianoforte, two violins, a flute and, well, either a harp or a cello? And I've just decided I'm going to have all our beds taken down for that night so we can dance over the entire house! I want it gay and yeasty and—enchanting—for that lovely young Mark Browning."

Eliza sighed, but she was smiling. "I don't know what to say, Julia. Mark does seem to have more serious, far simpler things on his mind."

"More serious than romance? How can that be?" She rattled Eliza's thin china perilously as she put down her cup. "Eliza Mackay? Is it true that this young man is the fabulously wealthy heir to that rich, rich Mark Browning who owned Browning World Shipping?"

Eliza sat straight in her chair. "I've never discussed that with him."

"My dear, Browning, probably the largest, most powerful shipping firm in the world, was based in Philadelphia, although the main office is now in New York. The boy comes from Philadelphia. The firm was owned by the late Mark Browning, Sr. Your young man's father died a year ago. Your young man's name is Mark Browning, too. Long ago my husband heard some scandal about Browning Senior. Something about his having sired a son by a—not very savory Savannah woman. Beautiful, I believe, but not at all from good stock. Why, Eliza! You're clinching your hands together so hard they're white! It's true, isn't it? I've hit it smack in the middle, haven't I?"

"No, Julia, you have not! You have hit nothing smack in the middle." Her voice was knife-edged. "And I demand that you not repeat any of this ludicrous story—ever again—to anyone! Do you hear me?"

"But the facts add up. Your young man must be the scion of that world-renowned Browning family!"

"Before God, that's the first I've heard that firm mentioned in connection with our Mark."

"But, Eliza, haven't you asked him about his family? His mother?"

"I've asked only if he remembers her. He's not sure. She died when he was three."

"His father?"

"It seems he traveled for most of Mark's young life. Mark has told us how he admired and loved him—also how he depended on his rather amazing aunt, Natalié Browning, who reared him. How she died of heartbreak—leaving Mark alone —shortly after the news came of his father's drowning in a storm off the Bahamas."

"Is—that all?"

"That's all."

"And you're not curious? You don't really want to help the boy get off on the right foot here in Savannah?"

"No, I'm not curious and I'm perfectly certain he *is* getting off on the right foot here."

"Doesn't he mention his mother's people?"

"No. Not to me."

"And you haven't asked? You're not dying to know? Surely, if she's from any worthwhile Savannah family, you'd know of them. You've lived here—except for your time in England—most of your life, Eliza."

"Yes, I have. And no, I'm not dying to know one thing more than Mark is ready to tell us—of his own accord."

"I mean the boy well, Eliza. I mean him—so well."

"I know you do, Julia. I do know that. I just hate to see him become the subject of gossip—so soon. He's a very vulnerable young man."

"And so incredibly handsome! Why, when Robert introduced me to him on my way here, I found myself thinking, his features must be nearly perfect. Are they? His straight, poet's nose, those deep-set, expression-filled gray eyes. White, white teeth—a smile that literally made my knees buckle. I do hope he doesn't cut his hair in that fashionable short, brushed-forward Brutus style just to be like Robert. I adore the young man's flowing, heavy, dark hair—cut just right—only partially covering his ears."

"Julia, please don't gossip about Mark."

"But he has to be from the Philadelphia Brownings! His father has to be the one who scandalized the whole city by siring his son by that woman, then brought him right into the house in Philadelphia for his poor wife to rear!"

"That is the most fallacious story I've ever heard and I could prove it!"

"How, *how?*"

Eliza's voice trembled with fury. "Only a short time ago, when he decided to pay us room and board and stay here for a time, he unpacked and hung in his room a magnificent oil portrait of Mrs. Mark Browning, Sr. Mark is the living picture of her!"

"Show it to me at once."

"Only Mark should do that, Julia," Eliza answered coldly. Then, a pleading note in her voice, she urged, "Why not drop the speculation and just be your true, warmhearted self with him, Julia? A ball if you must, but what he needs now more than anything on earth is friends. I assure you there's no truth to that story. Become his friend and he'll gladly show you his mother's portrait."

"You're sure you won't let me see it now?"

"I'm sure."

Julia stood. "All right, I'll become his friend. Heaven knows, that will be easy on my part. I promise to seal my lips, too. But I am going to give a blowout and see to it that he meets Savannah's best. That is, unless you think I should wait until we know for sure about—his mother's family."

Eliza stood too. "There's no need for that. Enjoy planning your ball, Julia."

"Oh, I intend to." She folded the fan, promptly unfolded it and fanned herself again rapidly. "It's a real mystery. No matter what you say, Eliza, we have a bona fide mystery on our hands! I promise you, though, not to breathe a word to anyone. Only, mind you, because of my deep regard for you and Robert. But be prepared, Eliza, for the truth to come to light eventually. Savannah has never been a healthy climate for secrets."

# ELEVEN

MARK groomed himself with great care in preparation for his first social appearance in Savannah. He had shaved, patted his face with eau de cologne and trimmed his hair slightly. The portable copper tub where he'd soaked in a leisurely bath still stood in his room. Hero and a helper would empty and remove it while he and the Mackays were at the Scarbroughs for what Mackay assured him would be a "blowout to end all blowouts." At a meeting of the Chatham Artillery that afternoon, the men had, because of the September heat, decided against wearing military uniforms.

Wrapped in a long, blue silk robe, Mark studied his dress clothes, purchased before he left Philadelphia and never worn. Across the high tester bed lay the gray-blue claw-hammer tailcoat—the cut of which he liked—and a pair of fitted pearl-gray trousers. He had selected for tonight a yellow waistcoat with vertical stripes, and tossing the robe aside, he examined the fine, white shirt with its fresh front frill. Satisfied, he slipped into it and fastened the high, stiff collar with a gold button. He hoped Miss Eliza would approve of the way he looked. Of course, this first appearance was important in all ways. He would surely meet everyone who was considered prominent in Savannah and he dearly cared about Mackay's approval. Yet, somehow, tonight he was dressing to please Miss Eliza.

Wrapping a white stock twice around the high collar, he wondered what she would be wearing. No matter. To him, she would be the loveliest lady at the ball. Her gown would not

cause people to turn and stare. It would be just right. A thrill
of anticipation coursed through him. Everything Eliza Mackay said or did was in the most exact taste. And natural. Her
poise, her beauty, the warmth of her personality, were never
contrived. In a thin everyday dress, on the hottest day, she
seemed cool, in control, lovely. Never detached. Mark had
never told her anything—even casually—when she had not
been attentive and caring. Tonight ladies would undoubtedly
be overdressed, conscious of themselves, flirting, demanding
attention. Miss Eliza would not. She would be herself, and for
Mark, that was beginning to be—everything.

Before a long pier glass in the corner of the room nearest
the large window, he pulled on the trousers, adjusted the new
coat to his wide youthful shoulders, then slipped his feet into
plain black pumps and wondered if ever there had been a
more suitable couple than the Mackays. He sighed, sizing himself up in the glass. Would he ever be a part of a marriage like
theirs?

Aunt Nassie would approve his appearance this evening, he
thought, turning this way and that to be sure each article of his
costume was just right. He frowned. His stock looked all
right, but would Aunt Nassie approve the bulky knot? He un-
tied the cravat and tried again. Better.

"Mark? You're handsome enough," Mackay called from
downstairs. "Time to go. Our carriage waits."

Hurriedly, he straightened his room and put his folded
dressing gown in the clothespress; he remembered with delight
that he would meet Miss Eliza's brother, John McQueen, and
his Margaret. They must already be downstairs, in fact. A
sense of total well-being engulfed him.

"I'm part of a family," he whispered to himself. "I'm a
part of a real family—with in-laws and cousins!"

In the wide downstairs front hall when Mark made his appearance, Robert Mackay was sharing a private laugh with a
tall, stunning, dark-haired woman in bright-green silk.

"I hope I'm not interrupting," he said, at the foot of the
stair.

"Never!" Mackay rushed to him, launching into an elaborate introduction. "And, Cousin Margaret McQueen, the
handsome apparition you now see bowing over your hand is

our treasured houseguest, my new business associate, Mr. Mark Browning!''

"I'm delighted, Mr. Browning, and, Robert, if he is half as brilliant at business as he is—arresting—you have indeed found a treasure."

"I've looked forward to this moment with much excitement, Mrs. McQueen," Mark said.

"Have you? Why?"

He already liked her. Her candid question sealed it. "Mainly, because Mr. Mackay did his usual excellent job of describing your beauty."

"And, my reputation as Savannah's Delilah, I've no doubt." She laughed. "I'm a settled old married lady of thirty-four now, sir. Have no fear. All of you young Samsons are quite safe in my company."

At that moment Eliza joined them, holding affectionately to the arm of a thin-faced, black-eyed gentleman with sideburns, who came at once to shake Mark's hand.

"Don't trouble yourself with still another introduction, brother-in-law," he said to Mackay. "I'm John McQueen, the unamusing member of the family, Mr. Browning. This is a pleasure."

"For me, too, sir."

"He's not at all unamusing," Margaret chided. "He simply adores acting the cynic when there's a stranger around, and it's time to drop whatever serious discussion you and your sister have been having, John. We're off to Julia's 'blowout,' and heaven knows that's no place for solemnity."

Mark had been half-listening, but his eyes were fixed on Eliza, who stood smiling at them as though they were all beloved children. To him, she had never looked so beautiful. Her yellow Chinese silk dress—simple, hanging straight to the floor below its empire waist—was just right for her coloring. About her light-brown hair she had tied a matching yellow band, and on either side of her face fell two loose curls. As she moved to Robert's side, Mark glimpsed the heavy white satin underskirt, embroidered with blue forget-me-nots. Maybe the McQueens noticed and maybe not, but Mark saw Robert Mackay's hands linger lovingly as he draped Eliza's shoulders with a thin three-cornered stole of Mechlin lace, which had been tossed over the hall bench.

Mackay's barouche was in mint condition, and Hero, splen-did in somewhat faded blue livery, drove them proudly along Broughton toward the west side of the city where the Scar-broughs' large, all-frame house stood on the corner of Broughton and Pine. "A scenic spot," Mackay declared, "surrounded by woodlands and marsh and cooled by breezes off two tidal creeks."

"I've attended some interesting parties, here and abroad," said Margaret, seated with John in the seat opposite Mark and the Mackays, "but none to equal the countess's affairs. I hope you're hungry, Mr. Browning. I daresay Philadelphia spreads no more lavish feast than you'll see tonight."

"Pay her no mind," John said in his clipped speech. "My charming wife chooses to ignore the fact that there's a war on."

"I guarantee nothing so irrelevant as a war will stop Julia Scarbrough."

"Correct, cousin," Mackay said, wiping his perspiring forehead. "And watch all invited guests gorge themselves as though she'd waited, as any sensible woman would have, for November to toss her blowout."

"I certainly don't intend to overeat," John said.

To change the subject, Mark asked, "Will you have good crops this year, Mr. McQueen?"

"Rotten, thank you. I jinx the weather. Too much sun. No rain to speak of in two months."

"John, I forbid one more word of gloomy talk," Margaret ordered. "This is a night for revelry and if you two McQueens insist upon being staid and proper, you'll simply drive Robert and me to all sorts of excesses to compensate."

Eliza laughed. "Except for this smothering heat, I'm in a most festive mood."

"Look, who is that gentleman ambling along out there?" Margaret wanted to know. "He's dressed for a party. Do you suppose he's headed for the Scarbroughs' on foot?"

"I'll be a son of a gun," Mackay muttered. "That looks for all the world like Osmund Kott!"

"It can't be!" Margaret exclaimed. "Julia would never—"

"But, he's Thorne Williams's assistant at the bookshop

now, I heard," Eliza interrupted. "I suppose Osmund could be invited."

"Never, my dear. Julia acts democratic but isn't a bit," Mackay said. "Still, old Osmund is dressed to the teeth, isn't he?"

Mark turned to look back at the man making his way through the deep sand, his features blurred now by the dust from their carriage. "Is that the gentleman who annoys Mr. Mein, sir?" Mark asked. "He looks presentable enough."

"It is. And he can appear as gentlemanly as anyone in town when he has a mind to. Where Kott learned manners, no one knows. But he did. A lot of us are worried that William Thorne Williams has taken him on in the shop."

"But if someone like Mr. Williams shows confidence in him, Robert, how do we know Osmund Kott won't respond to it? Maybe he'll reform and—"

Mackay laughed. "Our streets may turn to gold dust, too, any day, Eliza, my dear."

"But no one is hopeless."

"That's where Osmund Kott is different," John said dryly. "He is hopeless. You don't think that good and trusting young Williams would invite Kott without the Scarbroughs' knowledge, do you?"

"Not in a million years, John. Our native intellectual is a trusting man—a good man, none better—but he's also courteous. He wouldn't risk Julia's wrath."

"No one but William Thorne Williams would risk hiring him in the first place," John said.

"Oh, well, it's none of our affair. Maybe Osmund Kott is merely on his way to pay a clandestine call on a prominent lady. We must notice carefully who *isn't* at Julia's ball."

"Margaret, you're impossible."

Mark smiled at Eliza. She returned his smile. "I'm flattered to be escorted by two such handsome gentlemen," she said.

"This torturous collar is already chafing my neck," Mackay grumbled. "I may just sit on the sidelines and watch the poor young girls faint and come to and faint again at the sight of our Mr. Browning. As the countess would say, 'You're going to be a knockout at the blowout,' Mark."

"Don't believe him, Mr. Browning," Margaret said, "even you can't bewitch our pretty young things enough to keep

Robert Mackay on the sidelines. Julia won't permit it! Robert is her favorite dancing partner. She'll lead off the dancing with her fairly adroit husband, but you watch—she'll be in Robert's graceful company for the second."

The carriage creaks and rattles lessened and their ride smoothed out as Hero turned off Broughton into the long, semicircular drive to the Scarbrough house. Light blazed from every window and the open front door.

"Julia's had a lot of pine straw spread on this drive," John said to no one in particular. "Rides like a down pillow."

At the entrance, because Eliza had been seated in the middle, it fell to Mark's happy lot to lift her down from the carriage step.

"I'm going to be so proud of you, Mark," she whispered, squeezing his hand.

The sprightly measures of a gavotte erupted from somewhere deep inside the imposing house, and Mark, in response to Eliza, could only beam his joy to be there in her company —in Savannah.

On the ample front veranda, Mackay, wiping dust from the toes of his slippers, muttered that he prayed the countess was going to ease up a bit on her beloved formalities in deference to everyone's misery from the heat. "But I'm not hopeful," he added. "Anyway, I always survive heat better when I'm dancing at a good clip. Minuets and pavanes are deadly; they stir up no breeze whatever."

"Hush, Robert," Eliza said. "You've never failed to love every minute of Julia's parties. Look, the house is already crowded."

"I'm dying to see how she's decorated," Margaret whispered loudly. "What's blooming now?"

Julia herself, sparkling with sapphires to match her blue gown, swept toward them down the wide front hall, and two steps behind, smiling graciously, as always, came William Scarbrough.

"Now the ball can begin," Julia caroled, extending her hand first to Robert. "How marvelous that you could come, dear Robert, dear Eliza, dear Margaret, dear John—and dear, dear Mr. Browning!" Grabbing Mark's lapel, she pulled him slightly to one side and whispered, "Look over there—a whole bevy of trembling young belles absolutely titillated at the thought of meeting you." In her normal, carrying voice, she boomed, "And I've called you Mr. Browning for the last time! I've adopted you, too. You're Mark from this moment on—to me, of course."

"I'm delighted," he said, bowing over her surprisingly strong, wide hand.

When the music came to an end, Julia, with her husband beside her, took a commanding position about five steps up the front stair and clapped her hands. "Good evening, dear friends and neighbors," she projected, gesturing widely. The crowd applauded her. "My husband and I welcome you all with open arms and it is my pleasure, my distinct pleasure, to announce a small variation in our usual procedure. In order to give our party just the right tone for such a chilly evening—" she waited for the laughter, which dutifully came, "I am instigating a somewhat more dignified first dance."

Mackay groaned. Eliza shushed him.

"So as to bring on our company in the most ceremonious fashion possible, my husband and I will open the ball by leading you onto the floor with the swaying grace of a stately pavane!"

The smattering of polite applause masked most of Mackay's second groan, but gritting his teeth, he took Eliza's hand, waited for the Scarbroughs to lead out, and sweltered with the others as gracefully as possible through the slow, formal dance. Mark, with no partner, stood watching.

"It does look as though she might have taken time to introduce poor Mark to at least one young lady before we began to perform," John muttered to Margaret as they met, bowed, swayed and stepped.

"But, look at him—he's loving this. After all, at his age, he probably hates a pavane, too. I will say Julia's done splendidly as usual with her decor," Margaret went on. "Her magnolia trees must be naked of leaves. But she's certainly done the most with them. Daisies, all white oleanders. And where do you suppose she found those miles of white satin ribbon draping every green swag? Green and white give the illusion of coolness, anyway."

"I know what Robert would say to that: 'It is no illusion, my dear cousin, that my shirt is already dripping wet.' "

"Who ever heard of dancing before we even have a drink of something cool?"

"No one," John replied.

When the pavane ended at last, the small orchestra, almost hidden behind a wall of magnolia leaves wired on a trellis, slid into an Irish jig and, sure enough, Robert and Julia leaped into action. Popular tunes of the day—"The British Grenadier," "Derry Down," "Robin Adair" and "Hail Columbia"—followed. Having imbibed cooling drinks, the dancers conversed in louder and louder voices as they whirled and swept about the polished floors of the downstairs room.

After an hour of dancing, Mark had met at least eleven young ladies and had politely asked so many to write his name in their books, he worried that he would miss dancing even once with Eliza.

Cousin Margaret McQueen had seen to it that she and Mark had a dance scheduled, and when the orchestra struck up again, she hurried him upstairs.

"I had to see for myself that it's really true," she panted at the top of the stair.

Mark laughed. "What, Miss Margaret?"

"That Julia actually had the beds taken down up here for more dancing room! Look, it's true. She did it. Only that one door is closed."

"Glad you thought of this," he said, swooping her lightly across the floor of the first empty bedroom. "It's hotter up here, but roomier. Undoubtedly that's why we seem to be alone." Pleased that this lady, fourteen years his senior, was so unabashedly flirting with him, Mark felt he'd never danced so well.

"You're graceful as a fawn," she said. "I might have made poor, darling John wait still longer if you hadn't been hiding up in Philadelphia in your cradle! You're handsome, Mark, you're graceful and you've enough charm to stop every heart here. Welcome to the family!"

"Thank you, Cousin Margaret. I feel welcome. I do hope Miss Eliza has saved a dance for me, though."

"You adore her, don't you? So do I. Eliza was always my favorite cousin." Smiling up at him, obviously teasing, she asked, "Why do you adore her? She isn't as pretty as I. What does she have about her that makes her so irresistible to all of us?"

He slowed a bit, felt his face flush, then said simply, "She has—herself."

Abruptly, he whirled Margaret so that she faced the open bedroom doorway. Startled, he whispered, "Who is that?"

Margaret gasped, stopped dancing, but did not move a step nearer the man in the doorway. His striking face was lined, dissipated, the wide-set, pale-blue eyes amused at her surprise.

"Osmund Kott, what on earth are *you* doing here?" she demanded.

"Attending the Scarbrough ball," he replied in a husky, but somehow cultivated, voice.

"Without invitation," she snapped. "I'm sure you're not welcome!"

"No one tried to stop me downstairs," he said. "I was told, in fact, by a servant that I'd find Mr. Jonathan Cameron up here."

"You're drunk as usual," Margaret's voice crackled. "You and everyone else knows Mr. Cameron is too old to come all the way into the city—least of all to attend an affair such as this." She stamped her foot. "Oh, why am I even talking with you? Get out!"

"I'd like an introduction to your gentleman friend first," Kott said, his speech slurred, but compelling. "The new man in town."

"Mark, let's go back downstairs."

At the doorway, his hands pressed against the frame on each side, Kott blocked them with his body. "I'm a gentleman, Mrs. McQueen," he said. "I have no intention of causing trouble, but I do desire to meet this young man."

Unsure of just what to do, Mark's instinct prompted him to say, "My name is Mark—"

"No!"

"But, Cousin Margaret, I don't see the harm in—"

"You don't know this scoundrel. Whatever his reason for wanting to meet you, it's an evil one. Please step aside and let us pass!"

Osmund Kott didn't move a muscle.

Angry, Margaret began to beat on Kott's chest and when he grabbed her hands in both of his, Mark knocked him sprawling backward into the upstairs hall.

For a long moment, he and Margaret stood there—Mark

rubbing his knuckles—looking down at Kott.

"I apologize, sir," Mark said. "But I couldn't allow you to lay hands on the lady."

The door across the hall, which had been closed, was jerked open and Mark looked straight into the eyes of an elderly man, immaculately dressed in white. His thick, wavy hair was as silver as moonlight, but he was ruddy-cheeked and, although he grasped an ebony cane, did not seem to be leaning on it for support. For what seemed a long time, the man peered at Mark, then at Osmund Kott—still on the floor.

"Mr. Cameron!" Margaret gasped. "I—I didn't dream you were here, sir." Her poise wavered. "May I—present Mark Browning, associated with Robert Mackay. Mark, this is Mr. Jonathan Cameron of Knightsford plantation, one of Savannah's beloved and illustrious citizens."

Mark extended his hand, but Cameron made no move. He just stared at him in an awkward silence. Then, as though quickly recovered from some buried thought of his own, and still ignoring Kott, he shook Mark's hand warmly. "This is my pleasure, Mr.—Browning. I'm honored to meet you."

"I'm the one who's honored, sir. I've already heard how respected you are in town. Your place adjoins Mr. Mein's Coleraine plantation out on the Savannah River, doesn't it?" He glanced down at Kott. "I—hope we didn't disturb you too much."

Cameron shook his head, brushing off the apology. Then he turned his attention fully to Osmund Kott, who was pulling himself to his knees. "Whatever it is you want, Osmund, in order to leave town, you may have." Cameron's voice was strangely resigned, neither kind nor unkind. "You've only to let my factor, William Mein, know. Now, get up and get out of this house." To Mark and Margaret, he added, "I deeply regret all of this, Mrs. McQueen, Mr. Browning."

Kott struggled to his feet, adjusted his cravat and waistcoat, smoothed his long, light hair, bowed to Mark and said coldly, "I apologize to you, *Mr. Browning.*"

"And to the lady, I hope," Mark said.

Osmund Kott bowed unsteadily. "Of course, to the lady, too."

When Kott had moved slowly down the stairs and out of sight, the old man hung his head. "This is most embarrassing.

The poor fellow is—has always been—an embarrassment to the entire city. I've failed to help him. I doubt that anyone ever can. I hope and pray that you will both forget that any of this happened at all. I—wish I could."

Mark felt moved by the dignity and suffering of Jonathan Cameron. Whatever caused the suffering, he probably would never know, would never need to know. But that the gentle, aristocratic man suffered, no one could doubt.

"Is your wife with you in town, Mr. Cameron?" Margaret asked.

He smiled a little and, to Mark, the sad beauty in the aging face was almost too poignant to bear. "No, Mrs. McQueen, she isn't."

"Who came with you, sir?"

"Who came with me, Miss Margaret? Why, my pride and joy—my granddaughter, Caroline. Nothing would do but that she come to this ball tonight. The young ladies all up and down the Savannah River are setting their beribboned bonnets for you, Mr. Browning."

"Oh! Oh, yes. Thanks for the warning," Mark smiled. "I'm sure I danced with Miss Caroline Cameron just a short while ago."

"She'll be stricken if you've forgotten." Cameron was smiling too.

"I haven't forgotten. She's too engaging to forget. Dark hair? Eyes violet-blue, like yours, sir. Light as a feather on the dance floor."

"I'll be sure to tell her. She'll live on that for weeks out there at Knightsford. A lonely place for a young lady. Is John well, Miss Margaret?"

"Yes, he is. Aren't you coming downstairs? I know he'd love to see you."

"I've known John McQueen since he was a toddler. I never lost my regard—and sympathy—for his father." He shook his head, looked away for a moment, his eyes dimmed with what in an older person can be a sudden confusion of time and events—past and present. "I still find it difficult to think of that vital gentleman, John McQueen of Savannah, dying alone as Don Juan McQueen, in that backward Spanish province—his friends and family all here."

"Would you care to join the others downstairs with us, sir?" Mark asked.

"I'd planned to, yes," Cameron said. "Just needed a short rest from the boat trip to the city. Is—is my factor, William Mein, here?"

"Yes," Margaret said, taking Cameron's arm. "But this is not the time for business. You're going to dance—with me."

Smiling, Cameron glanced at his cane. "All right. Let me take this back to my room. A ball's no place for it."

When Julia Scarbrough caught sight of Jonathan Cameron descending the stair with Mark and Margaret, she rushed to meet him. "Jonathan! You come so seldom to the city, we never get to talk! You simply must dance with me this minute, so that we can catch up!"

Watching them move off together, Margaret moved into her husband's arms. "Well," she said, "I'll have to wait my turn with the old darling. See you later, Mark."

A somewhat lumpish young lady, gowned in bilious pink organza, which added greatly to her girth, curtsied before Mark, reminding him that this dance was hers. He bowed, encircled her soft, damp back with a somewhat unwilling arm and moved her—it amounted to that—across the floor, his eyes, at every turn, searching for Eliza. He had not yet danced with her and he had thought about it, wondered where she was, even in the midst of the altercation upstairs.

"I've been looking forward to our dance, Mr. Browning," the girl in his arms cooed. "I guess you're just about the talk of the whole city these days. Are you enjoying yourself here in Savannah?"

He forced himself to look and then to smile at his partner. "Oh—yes, oh, yes. Being in Savannah is a dream come true for me." Lame enough response, he thought, but he hoped adequate. "I foresee big things for the city. I hope to be a part of it."

"But, you're already the center of it, sir!" She giggled. "Didn't you hear me say that with all the young ladies in town, you're the one topic of conversation?"

Completing what he hoped was a fairly graceful whirl on the polished floor of Julia Scarbrough's huge dining room—also stripped of its furniture for the night—he managed another smile and a nod. "Thank you, but I'm sure you're exaggerating," he muttered, still looking for Eliza and Robert.

"Oh, but I'm not! I'm not exaggerating one bit—not one single bit, Mr. Browning. I didn't have to, since I'm a born dancer, but I know of at least six other girls who took special dancing classes just to be *able* to impress you tonight."

The music came mercifully to a halt and the drummer rolled for attention.

"The next dance will be the last before we dine," Julia called out, "so be forewarned. Our musicians will render one more number, but you have a choice. You may dance, especially if one more dance matters to some of our young folk—" she winked broadly. "Or, you may begin now, as the orchestra plays, to make your way outside to the back terrace, where there just might be a wartime bite or two to eat."

As Julia was making her little speech, Mark saw Eliza slip quietly around the edge of the crowd and walk directly toward him. He bowed to his plump partner, who, pouting, turned on her heel and left. Mark held out his hands to Eliza.

"I've found you just in time," she laughed. "Here." She showed him his name in her dance book. "I wrote it in myself. Robert has already decided to make his way outside to sample Julia's 'bite or two' of wartime fare. I think William Mein wants to talk business. Can you imagine, on a festive night like this?"

In what he hoped was a convincingly teasing voice, Mark said, "What I can't imagine is how Mr. Mackay could allow you one minute alone. No one here is as lovely as you are tonight, Miss Eliza."

"Actually, Robert had little choice. Mr. Mein seemed quite agitated about something."

The music was Aunt Nassie's favorite, "Drink to Me Only with Thine Eyes." Mark loved it, too, and always he'd rather dance than eat. With Eliza Mackay in his arms for the first time, he couldn't think of one thing to say to her as they moved with the music. He rejected telling her about the incident upstairs with Cameron and Osmund Kott. That was no subject for such a moment. She was silent, too, but she didn't stop smiling and now and then, when Mark executed a particularly graceful turn, their eyes met. And love passed between them. No more love than before, but a kind of love Mark had never experienced. His body was not responding to her as a man responds to a desirable woman. Rather, his whole being experienced joy. Fleetingly, he wondered why Mein was agitated, hoped that his friend Mackay was not having a difficult time of it—and then, the awareness of Eliza again. Her responses to his every step seemed to be there almost before he moved. Maybe, he thought, no two people had ever been so in harmony. Even beautiful Caroline Cameron, dancing nearby now with M. de Villers, seemed young and inconsequential beside Eliza. He would fall in love someday, he was sure. But romance between a man and a woman held inevitable complications—complications blessedly absent between himself and Eliza Mackay.

The orchestra repeated a chorus. He was grateful.

Robert Mackay cast an avid eye toward the rows of long, damask-covered tables set up in the back garden of the Scarbrough house. William Mein hurried him away from the crowd already gathering to watch the pink, juicy slices of four hams peel away under the servants' sharp knives. Mackay was relieved to see that Julia had indeed come through with his favorite—four enormous silver bowls of her delicious marinated shrimp. There were chickens, too, baked whole, and just as Mein pulled him off to one side, at the far end of the tables he saw more high, enticing cakes than he had time to count. And, of course, there were pitchers of tea, Julia's bottomless punch bowl, and bottles and bottles of wine from Scarbrough's superb cellar.

"This had better be important, William," Mackay said as they stopped in a secluded corner of the garden beside a stone bench.

"It is, Robert. I've come to the end of my rope with Osmund Kott—*and* Jonathan Cameron!"

"Oh, I thought you'd been dangling there for years."

"I am in no mood for your humor, sir."

Mein's voice was unnaturally icy and forceful. Mackay, a foot propped on the bench, gave him a quizzical look. "So I see. What on earth's the matter—beyond the usual blackmailing by Kott?"

"He was here tonight!"

"Osmund Kott really was—here?"

"He was. And by some means, he got upstairs where a few guests were dancing. Our Mr. Browning and your wife's Cousin Margaret McQueen among them. I don't know what happened, but Mark knocked Kott down. Flattened him in the upstairs hall."

Mackay's hands dropped to his sides. "Mark hit Kott? *Why?*"

"How do I know why? I applaud him for it, though. I wish I'd had the pleasure myself. God knows I've wanted to often enough over the years. But that has all come to an end. I told Cameron so just now. It—it hurt me to have to tell him. I love the old gentleman, but since he won't tell me why Kott has such a stranglehold on him, I'm through."

"You mean—you are no longer Jonathan Cameron's factor?"

"After twenty years, I am no longer Jonathan Cameron's factor."

Mackay sank down on the bench. "You're upset, William," he said. "Rest here a minute and let's try to think this out."

"I don't need to rest and I've already thought it out. I'm simply telling you as my partner that the account of Jonathan Cameron is no longer with our firm. I've put up with this mysterious, nerve-racking business as long as I can. I'm through."

Mackay got to his feet. "The music's stopped. My wife and Mark will be looking for me. I don't blame you for dropping the account." He laid his hand on Mein's shoulder. "We'll get along without it. Far more harmoniously, I have no doubt. By the way, are old Cameron and his granddaughter guests of the Scarbroughs? Frankly, I was surprised to see him here."

"Julia's doing. Cameron told me she wouldn't take no for an answer. She's determined that Mark is going to meet eligible young ladies. Heaven knows we don't have a girl in town as beautiful as Jonathan's granddaughter, Caroline. Cameron sent word for me to arrange lodgings. My wife's relatives have us crowded out. Julia welcomed them here with open arms. I'm sure she's already got the match all worked out in her fertile mind. Caroline Cameron's a remarkable young lady."

Mackay agreed. "But the countess will find out that unless Mark is interested, even her best-laid plans can falter. The boy has a mind of his own. How did Cameron take it when you told him you were no longer his factor?"

"Not well. In fact, I still feel ashamed of myself for doing it. Not for quitting, but for quitting such a fine old man. He seems in good health, certainly for his age, but he doesn't get to the city often anymore. He needs a reliable factor if anyone does."

"I know," Mackay said. "He does need someone to look after his affairs. But he needs more than a reliable factor; with Kott on his back, he needs a saint."

# TWELVE

AFTER the ball, Margaret and John McQueen, whose plantation, Causton's Bluff, was on the river two miles south of the city, spent the night in town at the Mackays. Breakfast the next morning was lighthearted with talk of the countess's triumph, but for Mark there was a shadow of anxiety. He had not asked Margaret McQueen to say nothing of the strange episode with Osmund Kott upstairs at the Scarbrough house. There had been no chance to let her know that he wanted to tell both Mackays himself.

He had slept little. Whether anyone would believe it or not, Mark Browning had never struck another human being except at that one town-and-gown brawl in his sophomore year at Yale. This time he had protected a lady. His unease was not exactly guilt. Still, it was there and would be, he knew, until Eliza and Mackay knew the whole story. The whole story? Mark himself certainly didn't know it. And, oddly, he disliked not knowing.

They had finished eating. Second cups of coffee were served. Margaret had said nothing of the incident. Mark even thought that at one point she had given him a reassuring look, but he couldn't be certain.

Finally, Mackay got up, announced that it was time for work, kissed Eliza, then Cousin Margaret and shook John's hand. "Don't wait to visit us again until the countess gives another blowout, you two."

As Mark bowed to Margaret and shook John's hand, Eliza complained gently that they were leaving for work almost an hour early.

"I want to stop by William Thorne Williams's bookshop," Mackay explained, quickly adding that he was not turning intellectual, but wanted Mark to know Williams better, since Chatham Artillery eating and drinking bouts were not exactly conducive to the exchange of ideas.

"You haven't ridden your horse to work since I've been here, sir," Mark said as he and Mackay walked out Broughton. "Don't you miss it?"

"Not especially. I rode because I had no walking companion. Besides, my middle is expanding. Our daily trips are good for me, especially the brisk way we stride right along."

"I was wondering if we could slow down a little today, since we're early. There's something I need to tell you."

Carefully, Mark told him everything that had happened with Osmund Kott the night before.

After a moment, Mackay said, "I guess old Cameron must have passed the word to Mein. Mein told me all he knew about it last night. I'm glad you hit Kott. I'm also glad to know the details. There've been times when I'd have relished connecting with that mean face myself."

"I'd hit him before I realized."

"Any man would have stopped him just as you did."

"Thank you."

"I don't know why you're thanking me! There's scarcely a man in the city—gentleman or not—who wouldn't welcome the chance." Mackay thought a minute. "I take it old Mr. Cameron didn't bat an eye over it. Did he seem glad you'd hit Osmund? Did he seem surprised? Did he show concern for him?"

"No, sir. I lay awake trying to figure that out, too. He—he just told him to tell Mr. Mein what he needed in order to get out of town. From then on, while Kott staggered back downstairs, Mr. Cameron was charming and pleasant to Miss Margaret and me. As though nothing untoward had happened at all."

"You're an associate in the firm now, Mark; you might as well know. Mein quit last night as Cameron's factor. After two decades. I don't blame him, but I feel sorry for the old gentleman. He needs a factor in the worst way. Mein simply had his fill. He's through. I hope it doesn't damage his friendship with Cameron. They're practically neighbors, you know, out on the Savannah River."

"Will your friend Monsieur Petit de Villers or Mr. Habersham or one of the other factors take Mr. Cameron on?"

"That I can't say. I'm inclined to doubt it. Cameron was once a vastly wealthy man. He still owns hundreds of acres of valuable Knightsford land, but something has drained his cash during the years. Planters generally operate on credit from their factors. Cameron more than most. My guess is that it's Kott draining away his money."

"But how? I mean, is Osmund Kott related to him in some way? Or—"

"No one knows. If Jonathan Cameron weren't so highly respected, didn't have such a flawless reputation, I'd assume Kott was blackmailing him."

"Didn't I hear you use that word with Mr. Mein once? In connection with Kott?"

Mackay laughed a little. "Yes. But I just get so sick of hearing Mein complain, I tend to ride him a bit hard. What could any man hold over the head of an untainted human being like Jonathan Cameron?"

Mark thought a moment. "Why do you suppose Kott was so determined to be introduced to me last night?"

"Say! That was what caused the flare-up, wasn't it?" Mackay pushed his top hat to one side and scratched his head. "I'll be hanged if I know, Mark. You're so new in town. You'd never even met Mr. Cameron until after you sent Kott sprawling; why would he demand to meet you? Look, we can't let Osmund Kott bother us. I'm glad you told me about last night, though. Will you tell Eliza?"

"Oh, yes, sir. I tell her just about everything these days."

Mackay threw an arm around him. "Tell her, Mark. She's far wiser than I."

They had turned onto Bay and were within a few steps of the narrow shop of William Thorne Williams.

"If Kott's in the shop, we'll say good morning and get right out. If not, I may leave you to visit awhile with Williams. He's a truly brainy gentleman." Mackay chuckled. "My Scottish tutors did their best with me, but somehow I never cottoned to the classics. I think you need a friend like young Williams. I'm fond of him, although why he hired Osmund, I'll never know."

"Kott may like books. Maybe Mr. Williams thinks he can help him by giving him a chance to be around them."

"Rubbish. Just plain rubbish. People have been trying to help Osmund Kott for all of his forty-five years! Old Cameron made huge contributions to Bethesda Orphanage when Kott was a boy there, I'm told, just so they'd take good care of the brat. He's hopeless."

"Is—is he only forty-five years old?"

"I think no more. Looks sixty at times. Still, as my kind wife insists, he isn't really a bad-looking man. Those large, pale, wide-spaced eyes and flashy smile. To me, a strange, flat face. But then, I see him through the eyes of trouble. He's seldom caused anything else."

"I guess if he grew up in an orphanage, no one knows anything about his family."

"That's right. Hard to believe he ever had a mother, in fact." Mackay opened the bottom of Williams's Dutch door and a little bell jangled. The room appeared empty. "Williams?" Mackay called out. "Is *the* William Thorne Williams on the premises?"

From the back of the shop, out of sight, they heard a light clatter. Then, dressed in a neat white shirt and tan waistcoat, wiping perspiration from his high forehead, Osmund Kott stepped through the swinging door that separated the shop from the workroom in back, his hand extended, a gracious smile on his face.

"Good morning, Mr. Mackay," he said warmly.

Mackay ignored the outstretched hand, mumbled a greeting, but did not return Kott's smile.

"And good morning to you, Mr. Browning. I'm sure you both want to see my employer, Mr. Williams. I'm sorry to have to tell you, but he's laid up with a pesky summer cold. I could tell he didn't feel well yesterday, so I went by his house to look in on him early today. Sneezing, coughing—I urged him to stay in bed. After all, why pay me if I can't tend shop as well as unpack shipments of books?"

When neither man found anything to say, Kott went on: "By the way, I apologize for keeping you waiting, but I'm in the process of unpacking a crate of *gems* from England! I'd really just begun to sort them, but already I've discovered two of the most handsomely bound volumes I've ever seen. Do you care for the poems of Coleridge, Mr. Browning?"

"Why, yes. Yes, I do."

"Then, you'll surely want to see at least one of these new books—*The Collected Poems* of both Coleridge and Wordsworth. Brand new edition and it does contain *The Rime of the Ancient Mariner,* in case you're wondering."

"No," Mackay said flatly. "No, Osmund, we weren't wondering. So, Williams won't be in the shop at all today?"

"He certainly shouldn't be." Kott smiled and Mark noticed his strong white teeth. Unusual in a man his age. "But you know, Mr. Mackay, how he loves this bookshop. Is there a message?"

"No," Mackay said tersely. "Nothing important."

"Just a visit?"

"Just a visit."

"You're both welcome to spend time upstairs in our reading room."

"I'll bet it's a hundred and ten up there today," Mackay said.

"Then, how about you, Mr. Browning? It would be my pleasure to take you up—show you around, acquaint you with the content of our shelves."

"Mr. Browning and I both need to get to the office," Mackay said, taking Mark's arm and heading for the door.

"Too bad, sir. I'll tell Mr. Williams that you came by."

"You do that," Mackay called back. He jerked open the half door; the cheerful bell tinkled and Mackay banged the door behind them.

Outside, they crossed Bay and hurried east toward Number One Commerce Row before Mark wondered aloud: "That fellow could earn a good living on the stage, sir! I never saw such a change in anyone. Why, today, he's a gentleman!"

"That," Mackay said, "depends upon your definition of a gentleman. He enrages me so, I'm going to pray all day long—and I'm ashamed to say I seldom pray in the countinghouse. But today I'm going to beg the Almighty to lock Mein's mouth if he even considers mentioning either Osmund Kott *or* dear old helpless Jonathan Cameron!"

"Do you think Mr. Cameron is really helpless, sir?"

"I don't know what I think. Let's pretend we just walked straight to Commerce Row and didn't even slow our stride at the establishment of William Thorne Williams. There's work to be done—in our own behalf. I have a family to support and someday so will you!"

# THIRTEEN

IN early November, when, as Robert said, "a man can breathe Savannah air without fear of suffocation," the Mackays gave their dinner party. John and Margaret McQueen came to town from Causton's Bluff, and along with Petit de Villers, the Meins, the Scarbroughs, the Habersham brothers and their wives, William Thorne Williams and his new wife, Wilhelmina, Eliza invited Caroline Cameron as Mark's dinner partner.

Since all the men present were members of the Chatham Artillery, they wore dress uniforms, and when Mark presented himself in the front hall for Eliza's approval, she gave him an admiring hug.

"You couldn't be handsomer," she said. "You and Caroline will make a picture! I'll tell you a secret. There isn't a city girl to compare with her."

He beamed. "I agree she's lovely to look at, and she's a marvelous dancer. Beyond that, I don't know much about her; but I trust you, Miss Eliza."

"You *can* trust me. Caroline's only seventeen, but she's highly intelligent, mature for her age—and strong-minded, like you. Not stubborn—strong-minded. There's a difference." Her eyes grew serious. "But unless I'm wrong, Mark, this pairing off for the evening with you could mean far more to her than to you."

His tiny frown flickered.

"I saw that little frown," she went on. "Don't worry, but do be completely honest with her always."

He laughed a bit nervously. "You mean, don't flirt with her?"

"I mean exactly that! Her grandfather's plantation is a lonely place for a young girl to live. Just—be careful of her."

"But I remember her as being so self-assured. The other young ladies I danced with at the Scarbroughs'—smothered me. Miss Caroline didn't even flirt."

"That's just more of what I mean. Knightsford is lonely and it's isolated from everything that usually fills a young girl's life. Every trip to Savannah is a big event. Jonathan must know how lonely it is out there for her. He would never have let her come without him this time if she hadn't let him know how much it meant to her. She adores her grandfather. You see, her own parents died within a week of each other in a yellow fever epidemic when the child was less than a year old. Mr. Cameron has been both father and mother to her all these years."

"But, doesn't she have a grandmother?"

Eliza's look was guarded. "Yes, she has a grandmother —Ethel Cameron. That's all I'll say right now."

Mark thought a minute; then, in his direct, open way, he said, "Miss Eliza, you're not a matchmaker, are you?"

She hugged him again and gave his shoulder a reassuring pat. "No, I'm not. I don't believe in that. I simply care about Caroline, and I care so deeply about you." She adjusted his leather stock. "Mark? Am I letting my imagination run away when I say that Caroline—in some manner—reminds me of your mother's portrait?"

He showed no surprise whatever. "No, ma'am, you're not. I thought about it the first time I saw her."

Dinner conversation ranged from Mackay's unwillingness to run for alderman because he coveted every hour with his family, and hated attending meetings, to the mounting victories at sea over the British. When the ladies had left the men to cigars and brandy, Mackay and the others drank to Captain Isaac Hull, for his capture of the British frigate *Guerrière;* to Captain Jacob Jones, who took the sloop of war *Frolic,* a ship far superior to his own; and to Commodore Stephen Decatur, of the frigate *United States,* for his signal triumph over the British frigate *Macedonian*. When they rejoined the ladies a half hour or so before time to say good night, everyone predicted a citywide victory celebration early in the new year 1813. "After all," Petit de Villers joked, "the city is far from prepared for a war that still goes on. We have to do something to make ourselves feel patriotic!'' They all agreed. The war was not over and Savannah was definitely not prepared for possible British attack. Much of the refurbishing had been finished at Fort Wayne, but the earthworks that were to surround the city weren't half completed. In the face of such laxness, Savannahians felt the need to overcelebrate victories at sea.

Mark listened to every joke, every admission that Savannah would always prefer to celebrate rather than to prepare. He and Caroline still stood with the Mackays at the front door as the last of their guests left by carriage. William Mein's barouche waited for Caroline in the street. She thanked the Mackays graciously, Mark thought. One would never have guessed that she had attended so few social functions in her seventeen years.

After Eliza had kissed her good night, Caroline turned to Mark: "It's such a cool, beautiful night, Mr. Browning, why don't we dismiss the carriage and walk to Mr. Mein's house on Bay Street? I need the exercise. I ate too much!''

He agreed at once, but did not miss Eliza's look when she reminded him to be careful. Mackay, for an entirely different reason, warned him, too; Mackay's warning had to do with the worsening climate of Savannah streets at night.

"There has been a lot of trouble lately,'' Mark said to Caroline as, alone for the first time, they began walking west on Broughton. "We'll go as far on Broughton as we can before cutting out to Bay. Our street seems safe enough.''

She laughed. "I'm not one bit afraid. All the drunken sailors and local ne'er-do-wells have their brawls much farther over toward Yamacraw Bluff, don't they?''

"I think they rather spill out almost anywhere once it's dark,'' Mark said. "I probably should have brought a pine torch, but I think we have enough moonlight, don't you?''

Caroline didn't answer at once. "Yes,'' she finally agreed, just above a whisper. "Yes. I think—we do have enough moonlight, Mr. Browning.''

Mark remembered Eliza's parting look. What should he say next? They had exhausted war talk at dinner, had also exhausted their pleasant teasing of good-natured Julia Scarbrough. He doubted that Caroline would be much interested in the mercantile business. He decided to walk along in silence for a time. Then, quite unexpectedly, he heard himself say, "Miss Caroline, sometime when you're at the Mackays' house again, I'd like to show you a portrait of my mother."

"Oh, I'd be honored, sir," she said. Her words did not gush out. She simply stated what he believed to be a fact. She would be genuinely interested in knowing what his mother looked like. "Your—mother isn't living, is she." It wasn't a question. Someone had obviously told her that he had no parents.

"No. She died when I was three. I guess that's why her portrait means so much. You—you make me think of the way she must have been. I don't remember her. At least, I'm pretty sure I don't. You know how it is when relatives talk a lot about someone, you're never quite sure whether it's something they've told you or—"

"Or whether you're actually remembering. Yes, I know. I—I'm an orphan, too."

"Miss Eliza told me."

An almost round, full moon stood directly overhead. His eyes grown accustomed to the night, Mark could see her face plainly when, after a time, she looked directly up at him and asked in her straightforward manner: "Do you expect to marry and have a family of your own someday, Mr. Browning?"

"Oh, yes," he said. "And you?"

"I hope to, but not as long as my grandfather lives."

"Would he object?"

"No, no. He's the most generous man who ever drew breath, but I love him too much to leave him at the mercy of my—grandmother."

Mark couldn't guess what she meant by that, but she settled his confusion at once.

"In case you think I'm being facetious, I'm not. My grandmother is well born, better educated than most women in what she calls her 'aristocratic class,' and she's still quite handsome looking—was probably pretty once—but she's a born tyrant. Do you think there are some people who are all meanness and spite? All evil?"

"I don't know. My Aunt Nassie, who brought me up, always said there must be some good in everyone, but she also added that with some it seldom shows up."

They laughed.

"At least, Osmund Kott couldn't crash the Mackays' dinner

party tonight," she said abruptly. "He's in jail again."

"I'm sorry to hear that."

"Well, I'm not. If there's any good in him, I've never seen it."

"But one morning when Mr. Mackay and I stopped by William Thorne Williams's shop, Mr. Kott was there alone and he was most gentlemanly. He knows books, too, and loves them. Don't you think that indicates some sort of—virtue?" Mark laughed a little. "In my opinion, no one can be all bad and still love books."

"How gentlemanly was he when you knocked him down at the Scarbroughs' that night?"

"Oh. Your grandfather told you."

She took a deep breath. "He tells me everything, *except* why he goes on year in and year out allowing Osmund—I even hate his name—to take his money and scare him until he's half sick!"

"Kott scares your grandfather?"

"I don't know what else to call it."

"How could he? Oh, I know he's loose-tongued. I know he can be menacing when he's drunk, but why would he be able to frighten a man like your grandfather?"

Caroline sighed. "Mr. Browning, if I knew that—aside from my grandmother's hateful disposition—I wouldn't have a care in the world."

For nearly a block they walked in silence, Mark feeling both revulsion and attraction toward the entire Kott-Cameron affair. In his private thoughts since the night he'd struck Kott, and especially since meeting him in the bookshop, he had somehow begun to pity the man. Such feelings had, in fact, annoyed him at times. Robert Mackay and William Mein would enjoy seeing Kott drop off the edge of the earth. That, Mark knew well. What had Miss Eliza said about him when Mark had told her that he'd struck Kott? She had been the only person who understood Mark's shame for having lost control, but she had also reminded him that for all his life, Osmund Kott had brought out the worst in everyone. "Everyone," she had added, "except Jonathan Cameron, who has serenely borne the brunt of Osmund's cruelty."

Serenely? Caroline had just said that her grandfather lived in fear. Fear and serenity cancel each other. Miss Eliza had said, too, that she tried—often in vain—to remember that

God loves Osmund Kott as much as He loves each of the Mackays—and Mark.

The revulsion Mark felt—and the attraction—seemed to go even beyond Kott himself. Keep clear of him—of them all— one part of his nature warned. Find out about Kott, try to understand, urged another part.

"If you ever hear *anything*—anything at all about Osmund Kott that might help me to help my grandfather, will you tell me, Mr. Browning?" Caroline asked the surprising question in a clear, firm voice.

For a moment he hesitated. Then, he heard himself say, "Yes, Miss Caroline. I will."

They had reached the Mein house on Bay. She extended her hand and Mark kissed it, perhaps, he thought, too tenderly in view of Miss Eliza's warning. For reasons that went far beyond her fresh, natural beauty, he was drawn to Caroline Cameron. He longed to help her. She had not treated him as the eligible new man in town as they'd walked along in the moonlight. She had needed to talk, to reach, somehow, for help. The firm smooth skin on her hand was cool and yielding. He waited as long as he dared to take his lips away.

Striding back to the Mackay house, he felt an urge to tell Miss Eliza that—that what? That, of course, he wasn't in love with Caroline, but that he did feel drawn to her. She was so alone, with no one her age to help in her strange family trouble.

He grinned. No trouble at all imagining Mackay's skeptical laugh should he hear Mark say such a thing. Miss Eliza wouldn't laugh. She would look at him with those melting hazel eyes and she would understand.

It seemed quite understandable to him, too, that when an independent young woman such as Caroline Cameron even hinted that he might help her, it made a man feel good. Why not?

All the way home, he whistled "Drink to Me Only with Thine Eyes."

# FOURTEEN

MONTH-LONG preparations for Christmas—Mark's first in Savannah—made the dark, early December days seem bright. He was glad to see that war shortages in no way dampened spirits at the Mackays'. For as long as Mark could remember, he and Aunt Nassie had made the most of the whole month of December. No boy could have had a more adaptable, livelier playmate than Aunt Nassie, and only now and then had he asked why his father never joined their Christmas celebrations.

"And what did Aunt Nassie answer when you asked?" Mackay wanted to know as the three adults lingered at the Christmas table that first year together.

"Robert," Eliza scolded. "That's too personal."

"No, it isn't, Miss Eliza," Mark said easily. "I'm trying to remember. I guess she'd just hug me and remind me that even a fine traveler like Papa couldn't make it across the world in time for Christmas. Something like that. She satisfied me, anyway. I don't remember any bad times over it. Papa always sent us wonderful presents. He never failed."

"A lot more, I'm sure, than we could manage for our offspring this year," Mackay said. "This frazzlin' war is getting on my nerves. Oh, I know we're planning a citywide New Year's celebration of all our naval victories, but naval victories don't enable a father to buy his children a proper Christmas."

"They didn't seem to notice," Mark said. "And when I went out to Knightsford with them to cut greens to decorate the house, William assured me that we were doing the very thing that made Christmas merry at the Mackay house."

145

"Did William say that?" Eliza asked.

"Yes, ma'am. And with big old tears in his eyes."

Mackay looked surprised. "Tears?"

"He missed you, sir. They all told me that this year was the first time you hadn't gone with them."

"And here I thought I was doing them a favor to let them go alone with you, Mark!"

"Oh, I think William's tears were tears of meaning, too. Gathering those Christmas greens is a deeply poignant experience for the children. That's a tribute to their parents, I'd say."

"Tell me," Mackay changed the subject. "Did you see the beauteous Caroline Cameron at her grandfather's place?"

"Oh, she helped us!"

Mackay's eyes twinkled. "Did she now! What a surprise."

"Robert!"

"Don't reprimand me, dear Eliza. Participants in a purely platonic friendship don't always race through the woods together at the slightest opportunity. Especially not on a cold, rainy December day. Do they?"

Mark grinned but said nothing.

"You two have it your way, I'll have it mine," Mackay teased. "I've been in love—I am in love. Who's a better authority on romance than I? I recognize the signs."

"Name one, please, husband dear."

"Didn't Mark ask if we could persuade the Meins to invite Caroline and her grandfather for the town's big New Year's celebration?"

"Well, certainly I did," Mark laughed. "I just thought coming to the city at such a colorful time would be good for—"

"—for the poor old man," Mackay finished. "Of course. I have an idea. Why not invite Jonathan Cameron alone?"

"Robert, you're going too far now," Eliza said firmly. "And, I think a bit heavy-handed. You know Mr. Cameron never comes to town without Caroline."

Mackay poked Mark affectionately with his fist. "Oh, very well. The truth is, I've spoken to Mein, and Mrs. Mein has already written inviting them both."

"Not Mrs. Cameron?" Mark asked.

"Anytime he's invited, Ethel Cameron is always included, son," Mackay said. "But I'll wager any amount of money that the old dragon won't set foot within the city limits of Savannah until she comes to bury Jonathan in the town cemetery. If, indeed, then.''

Mark thought for a minute. "Was there ever a time when the Camerons—got along? I mean, were they fond of each other during the early years of their marriage? I know you're both too young to remember, but—"

"It was arranged, that marriage," Eliza said sadly. "I remember my own grandmother talking about how Ethel Cameron's parents—steely folk, evidently—set it all up with the rigidity of a business deal. Usually, families try to make an arranged marriage seem—of the heart. They didn't bother."

"But Mr. Cameron is such a gentle, warm man," Mark said. "I can't imagine his allowing himself to be married off to anyone he didn't love."

"In those days there was a lot of such arranging, Mark," Mackay explained. "It was strictly business. Mein knows something of the terms. It seems there were two medium-sized family plantations—one owned by Ethel's family, the other by Cameron's. The present Knightsford is made up of those two tracts."

"Mark, Ethel Cameron is a handsome lady," Eliza said. "Well bred, quite well educated."

"Oh, I know all about her superior education," Mackay snorted. "Old Cameron visits Thorne Williams's shop to buy her books. He told Williams once that his wife was even better-read than Williams himself! Said she hated being married to him so intensely that she's spent her adult life educating herself—reading—to avoid Cameron."

"Do you suppose Mr. Cameron persuaded William Thorne Williams to hire Osmund Kott?" Mark asked.

Mackay grunted. "I'll bet you're right, son. Hadn't thought of that. I supposed young do-gooder Williams simply thought he could give the poor disadvantaged Kott a hand up. And *that* no one could do. No matter who tries, Kott will end up giving a boot to the seat of the trousers."

"Robert!"

"Sorry, my dear. But you know I speak the truth. Anyway, I heard yesterday that they're going to keep Kott in jail on that disorderly conduct charge until after our New Year's celebration. He taught himself some French, so Mayor George Jones is sure it's Kott inciting that gang of hard-drinking French sailors to their spurts of violence at the Yamacraw waterfront.''

"Has anyone ever—liked Osmund Kott?''

"Mark," Mackay declared, "you have asked the unanswerable. I never heard Jonathan Cameron say one word against him, but it would take a lot more than that to convince me that he likes him. That anyone really liked him, for that matter. Even his mother! If he ever had one.''

"You see, Mark," Eliza said carefully, "if Osmund were merely a loiterer, a drunk, he'd be simpler to figure out. Sometimes, he does seem to be only a—''

"Bum," Mackay supplied the word.

"Well, yes," she agreed. "But then he changes into that quite polished gentleman you met in Mr. Williams's shop, and we don't know what to think.''

The January 1 celebration, at which the whole city welcomed the new year 1813 in what Mackay called "colorful, pretentious, joyful fashion," was such a success that the mayor and the aldermen tendered their thanks "to every citizen who constructively aided in the celebration of the triumphant naval exploits at sea." Mackay noted that the Council's resolution was careful to use the word "constructively" so as not to include the free-for-all that killed two and injured five habitués of the waterfront.

"At least, Osmund Kott can't be blamed," Mark said.

"That's right, son. They managed to keep him locked up through the whole thing. But even Kott, had he broken out of jail, as he's done more than once, could not have tarnished the magnificence of our military parade. Did you notice the mayor's statement that the Chatham Artillery formations were 'the most brilliant in military appearance ever witnessed in the city'?''

Mark grinned. "I do think Mayor Jones included the Hussars and the Republican Blues in that appraisal, along with us, don't you?''

"Mm," Mackay mused, "perhaps.''

"I know one person who was unstinting in her praise of the Chatham Artillery," Eliza said.

"Caroline?''

"Caroline. She and I stayed together all day and she just couldn't stop repeating how thrilling all of you were—marching in such flawless lines, coat sleeves barely touching."

"Especially one fairly new member." Mackay winked. "The young corporal from Philadelphia. Why wouldn't he stand out? His uniform is the newest."

"Caroline's staying over for the opening of Chatham Academy," Mark said, his face glowing. "We're taking a boat ride tomorrow afternoon."

"Just the two of you?" Mackay wanted to know.

"Yes, sir! I haven't rowed a boat in more than two years. I hope I haven't forgotten how."

"I hope our mild weather holds," Eliza said.

"And I haven't been asked, but I hereby dismiss you from work at the countinghouse."

"I'm ahead of you, Mr. Mackay. My billings are up to date through day after tomorrow."

"Then, I'll supply the boat."

"I've already rented one at Ancioux's pier."

"Well, I declare," Mackay said, a mock scowl on his face. "I declare, I just don't know that mere friends went to so much bother to be together. I hate to tell you this, but Black Terpin down at our dock predicts temperatures near freezing tonight."

The temperature next day was not freezing, but it was in the mid-thirties at 2 P.M. when Mark called for Caroline at the Meins' house on Bay.

"Is it too cold?" he asked. "I don't want you to get sick. It could be really chilly on the river."

"Afraid someone will call us crazy?" she responded. "I want to take a boat ride with you."

Mark, shivering in his fur-collared greatcoat, laughed. "I'm game if you are. But we could talk in more comfort at the Mackays'. The children are shopping for new clothes with their father and Mrs. Mackay's working on the decorations for the Chatham Academy's grand opening day after tomorrow."

Without a word, she took his arm and matched his long strides along Bay in the direction of Ancioux's pier. They had not gone one full block before Mark, then Caroline, spotted Sheftall Sheftall, his face and part of his cocked hat buried as usual in a newspaper.

"Mr. Sheftall," she cried. "Good afternoon, sir. I'm so

glad to see you! You remember me, don't you? I'm Caroline
Cameron, Jonathan's granddaughter.''

Cocked Hat Sheftall, dressed as usual in knee breeches and
his well-mended Revolutionary jacket, bowed and swept his
old leather tricorn almost to the sidewalk. "Indeed, I do
remember you, lovely lady,'' he said, "but more as a child.
After I address myself in apology to your young man here for
snubbing him and Robert Mackay several months ago, I shall
inquire after my client, Jonathan Cameron.'' Still holding his
hat, he turned squarely to Mark. "My sincere apologies for
not pausing to converse with you and Mackay that day, sir. I
was very busy. I have, of course, since learned that you are
young Mark Browning, lately of Philadelphia. I am Sheftall
Sheftall, at age fifteen a Savannah merchant, then war hero
and now attorney-at-law—Jonathan Cameron being my only
client.''

Mark shook his hand. "Yes, sir, I've heard a lot about you,
but I didn't know you were Mr. Cameron's attorney.''

"Few know it anymore," Sheftall said casually. "Still fewer
remember. Cameron is an ideal client. His attorney, because
of Cameron's sterling character and love of his plantation, is
seldom bothered. Tell me, Browning, how is the ebullient Mr.
Mackay these days? You see, I've been away in Charleston for
several months. I visit there now and then, since it's still more
or less the social and religious center for respectable Jews. My
heart lies here in Savannah, alas.''

"Alas?'' Caroline asked pleasantly. "I thought you loved
Savannah, Mr. Sheftall.''

"I do love Savannah. After all, my father, Mordecai Sheftall, was born here but two years after Oglethorpe settled the
city.''

"I'm sure Grandfather will be glad you're back," she said.
"He always says the streets of Savannah lack ornamentation
when you're not about.''

"Jonathan is correct, I suppose," Sheftall agreed. "I'm a
fixture, at least, if not an ornament. How is that good man
your grandfather, Miss Caroline?''

"He's well, thank you.''

"Enjoying the brief respite, I'm sure, while that scalawag
Osmund Kott is in jail.''

Mark was embarrassed for Caroline, but her expression

showed that she was either accustomed to such talk of her grandfather and Kott or accustomed to Sheftall Sheftall's bluntness, or both. She merely smiled knowingly.

"You've heard about Kott, I'm sure, Browning."

"Yes, sir. A little."

"Too bad you didn't hit him harder when you had the chance." After a brief pause, Sheftall went on: "So, you're slated to be a rich man, Browning."

It wasn't a question. It was a statement. "I—well, I do reach my majority in the spring of this year, sir." He saw Caroline's quick frown. "I—I don't think of myself as—rich."

"Splendid," Sheftall said. "That would indeed be dull. Treat him with care, Caroline Cameron. He's not only a fine-appearing young gentleman, he could well be the key to your —riddle."

"I'm too old for riddles, sir. What you just said makes no sense whatever and you know it!"

Sheftall raised a finger and quoted: " 'Time will discover everything to posterity; it, Time, is a babbler and speaks even when no question is put.' Euripides." He rubbed his hands. "Now, it is too cold for an old man of fifty-one to stand longer in the wind off the river. And since young love must flower, I bid you both good day."

"I'll be sure to tell Grandfather that I saw you. He's staying at the Meins', if you'd like to visit," Caroline called after him. But Sheftall Sheftall had finished his various speeches, was on his way to the newspaper office and did not look back.

Mark pulled his fur collar over his chin and waited for her to speak first.

"You really don't think of yourself as rich, do you?" she asked in a quiet voice. "You don't have to answer. I know you don't. I'm glad."

"It is awfully cold," he said lamely. "Are you sure you want to take a boat ride on that windy river?"

Her sudden, lighthearted smile answered his question. "Yes! My cape is lined and it's pure wool. The water and the wind will do us good." She took his arm. "Come on. Let's walk fast. Forget what I said about your being rich. It's none of my business, anyway. And I do want our boat ride. I'm alone so much at Knightsford, I need to be crazy once in a while." She laughed up at him. "And you, poor man, have been chosen. No serious talk on the river. Let's just be—crazy and *ourselves*."

The tiny rowboat was waiting at Ancioux's wharf, and as they headed downriver toward Fort Jackson, Mark shouted: "We're crazy all right. Why didn't I go *up*river?"

"What difference does it make?" she laughed back at him, the wind pushing her voice away.

"I'm out of practice at rowing, that's the difference. I'm tired already! The return trip would have been easier *down*river." He was laughing, too, his arms feeling heavy and awkward against the weight of the oars. "But we don't care, do we? I didn't promise you an expert oarsman."

"And I didn't ask for one. I just wanted to take a boat ride with you—when no one else in their right mind would dare try it! Will we be able to see John McQueen's Causton's Bluff plantation on St. Augustine Creek as we go by?"

"I don't know," Mark called back. "I don't even know if I can make it to St. Augustine Creek."

"Stop belittling your prowess. You're wonderful!"

Pulling on the heavy oars did not prevent his looking and looking at her as she sat facing him on the board seat, her cheeks and eyes glowing, her thick, dark hair whipping under the brim of a blue bonnet tied beneath her chin.

"Caroline? You're wonderful, too."

"Crazy wonderful?"

"Crazy wonderful."

Compared with the activity on warmer days, the river was almost empty. He was beginning to realize what a fine idea she'd had, when, from the corner of his eye, he saw an old dugout almost leap from the riverbank and head toward them. The two men aboard, paddling canoe fashion, worked at double speed. Caroline, who hadn't noticed, was saying something about how few people could just let go and be spontaneously foolish now and then. And that he would be surprised at how ugly life could be at a picturesque spot like Knightsford. Mark, watching the dugout, could now see that both occupants were white—one in a ragged French naval uniform, the other wearing a heavy, brown hooded jacket. Until now, he hadn't been sure where they were heading. He was sure now, and the man in the hooded jacket was Osmund Kott!

"Caroline, hold on!" Mark shouted.

"Why?"

"Look—they're coming right for us!"

"Pull!" She pointed toward the bank. "Pull faster! They're going to hit us!"

With every ounce of strength, Mark dragged on the left oar, vainly trying to turn them quickly toward land to avoid what appeared a deliberate collision. Kott, unshaven from the weeks in jail, looked like a wild man.

"Caroline! Please, hold on as tight as you can!"

"We ram them?" The Frenchman's voice came clearly on the wind.

Kott laughed now and shouted: "No! Hold to!"

By scant inches, the battered dugout veered away and then pulled alongside.

*"Bon jour,"* Kott called. "Rather a rough day for romance, eh?"

"Osmund Kott," Caroline shouted, "you're as insane as people say you are!"

Standing in the dugout, his paddle feathering the water, Kott bowed. "No, Mademoiselle Caroline, I am not insane. Far from it." Even projecting against the wind, he was using his gentleman's voice now, his gentleman's diction. "I've merely come with a message. A very, very important message. *Il est très important.*"

"What's the message?" Mark yelled. "What's so important that you would risk our lives in this current?"

"Osmund! Is something wrong with Grandfather?"

Kott shrugged. "How would I know? I've just been set free from prison, dear Caroline. My word, can you both forgive me for not introducing my cohort, Monsieur Jean Genêt? Monsieur Jean is a stalwart, loyal friend."

The Frenchman grinned a silly grin, showing only yellowed lower teeth.

"Thought we were going to ram you broadside, eh?" Osmund asked pleasantly. "My friend Jean is like a big boy. He was just having a little fun—if at your expense, Lady Caroline. We both ask your pardon. *Nous demandons votre pardon.*"

"Start rowing, Mark, please!" Caroline begged. "I've had enough of this."

Kott pulled a pistol. "I would not advise that you make one stroke with an oar until I have delivered my message."

"Then, deliver it," Mark snapped.

"In time. In *my* time, Browning. Actually, I have a message for each of you. For Miss Caroline to her grandfather—her *beloved* grandfather. Tell him I must have one thousand dollars before he returns to Knightsford following the social event marking the opening of Chatham Academy!"

Mark saw Caroline's face crumple. She seemed on the verge of tears. "Osmund," she wailed, "how did you find out about our plans to go *there?*"

Kott smiled. "Just tell him I will be at the back entrance of the new academy building promptly at three o'clock, January fifth, to receive the money."

"I won't tell him any such thing!"

He shoved the gun at her. "Oh, yes you will, dear child."

"Don't call me 'dear child'!"

Osmund laughed at her. "As for you, Browning, the wealthy young gentleman with the quick fist—keep your own counsel!"

"About what?"

"About any of this—incident on the river—about everything! Just stay clear of Jonathan Cameron's affairs. I know more than you know about yourself, fancy man, and I'll use it!"

"You make no sense, Kott!"

"I make all the sense in the world to myself. Through the coastal grapevine, I have just learned that both your father and your haughty aunt, Natalie Browning, are dead. You are the Browning who counts now, so watch your p's and q's."

Mark could only stare at him.

"Let's go, Mark, *now*," Caroline begged. "Just start rowing."

Kott bowed again and replaced the pistol in his belt. "Go anytime." He signaled the Frenchman, and their dugout eased slowly away. "The rear entrance, dear Caroline," Kott called back. "Chatham Academy, three P.M., January fifth."

Mark pulled mightily on both oars. Neither spoke until Kott and the Frenchman were out of hearing, heading back to shore.

"They're gone." Caroline's voice and body trembled. "And I think we should turn around and go back to Ancioux's wharf. As usual, he's spoiled everything." She began to cry softly. "Forget what he said to you; he's bluffing."

"But where did he learn Aunt Nassie's name? Her name *was* Natalie!"

"Who knows? I'm—sorry," she sobbed. "I hate weeping women! But he always has *spoiled everything!*"

After seeing Caroline safely to William Mein's house, Mark hurried home to the Mackays, his brain whirling with questions, eager, as he'd never been before, to confide in them both. He thought of no possible way that Osmund Kott could know anything of his family, and yet, daily, he realized—now with growing anxiety—how little he himself knew.

Mackay would be at home by now with Miss Eliza and the children, but Mark prayed that, by some means, he could speak to the parents alone. Jack's overactive curiosity would never allow discussion of such madness as Osmund Kott's assault on the river, without a million questions.

He had just reached the front walkway when Robert Mackay ran excitedly out to meet him.

"Good, you're here, Mark! I want you with me when I tell her. I've just done a ridiculous thing financially, but something that will make Eliza the happiest woman in Savannah. She and the children are waiting in the parlor. I saw you from the corner window swinging up Broughton. Been waiting for you. They know something's up and they're all as noisy as blue jays after a hawk! I'm the hawk."

Frustrated, but glad for anything that so elated his friend, Mark asked, "What about me? Do I have to join the blue jays? Or will you tell me first what's up?"

"I think I'll have to tell you out here. You can help me heighten their suspense."

Gleefully, Mackay told Mark that he had just closed the deal for the purchase of The Grange, the Savannah River plantation where Eliza was born in 1778 when her father, John McQueen, was a British prisoner of war.

"Having The Grange back in the family will not only make Eliza lyrical," he said, "it will really please Cousin Margaret. She was born there, too, you know. In colonial times The Grange belonged to Margaret's father, Basil Cowper. Mary

Cowper, Margaret's mother, is Miss Eliza's aunt. The Cowpers, unfortunate people, had to flee at the end of the Revolution." He grinned. "Their British loyalty never waned."

"Mr. Cowper's dead now, isn't he?"

"Yes. And Aunt Mary will never come back here. She's still ensconced at his place in Jamaica. Well, what do you think of my surprise?"

"I think it's fine, sir. Miss Eliza will be happy, I know."

"Mark, is something wrong?"

"Uh—no, sir. Not really."

"Something go wrong between you and Caroline?"

He smiled. "Far from it. She's an amazing girl. At seventeen, she goes on surprising me with her maturity."

"She's had to grow up. If you knew her grandmother, you'd understand why." Mackay steered Mark up the steps. "Then, shall we go in and spring our surprise on the waiting jay birds?"

There was so much joy, so much downright hilarity at the Mackay house that night, that Mark found no chance whatever to bring up the eerie encounter on the river. Even if there'd been a chance to speak alone with the Mackays, he wouldn't have shattered their merriment with a mention of Osmund Kott. Anyway, what right did he have to discuss something that seemed so personal and hurtful to Caroline without her permission? He could wait.

In bed that night, Mark lay thinking, wondering . . . Was Kott deranged? Was he really blackmailing Jonathan Cameron? It seemed so. Still, there has to be a reason for blackmail. Everyone so revered Cameron, what possible reason could Kott have? As Mark had walked Caroline back to the Meins', she vowed a second time that she had never been able to find out how her grandfather even met Kott. "When I used to ask him," she'd said, "he would pat my head, give me that melting look and assure me that he just cared about Osmund as a human being and felt obligated to help him all he could."

"Obligated? Why?"

There seemed to be no answers to anyone's questions about Cameron, and surely, Mark told himself, Kott was lying when he said he knew about Aunt Nassie and Mark's father! Oh, the Browning Company was so vast, Kott might have heard that

Papa died, he reasoned, but to imply that he knew more about me than I know had to be pure bluff. Because I'm in Savannah now, he could easily have guessed that Aunt Nassie died, too, but how did he even know she existed? How did he find out that her name was—Natalie Browning?

He sat up in bed suddenly—staring into the darkness.

Could it be that Osmund Kott knew Mark's mother before his father took her to Philadelphia? Kott is about forty-five, Mackay had said. Melissa Browning would be forty now, had she lived. A kind of fear possessed him. Why? He shivered. It was cold in the room, but that was not what he felt. He felt—something like a presence.

He swung his legs out of the warm covers; his hand shaking, he groped his way from one familiar piece of furniture to another, all the way across the room to the fireplace, and lit a candle.

Of course, there was no one else in the room. Shivering now from the pressing cold, he stood in his nightshirt, holding the candle so that it threw a wavering, yellow light over his mother's face in the portrait that hung above the mantel.

"Mama?" he whispered. "Mama, you look so much like—*her*. You look enough like Caroline to be her sister! But, you'd be too old. . . ."

He held the candle closer to light up the face with the hint of a smile. The smile that always caused Mark to feel cheated. She seemed almost ready to laugh. But she never laughed. She couldn't.

"Caroline laughs a lot," he whispered into the icy room.

The thought of Caroline's laughter made him feel a little foolish standing in his nightshirt. His mother's face had always quieted his fears; now there was Caroline, so like her. He would give anything to be able to look at Caroline this minute or to talk with Aunt Nassie, who had never failed him. He was a man now. Surely, if he could ask, Aunt Nassie would tell him all she knew about his mother. Caroline, by being Caroline, making her way alone through the mystery in her own family, would give him courage, too—quiet his fears. Why did he need courage? What if Osmund Kott had known his mother—her family? Someone had known them. They had lived somewhere in or near Savannah. Another surge of longing for Aunt Nassie engulfed him.

He raised the candle for one more glimpse of his mother's

face, and for the first time he realized that he had never longed for her. Because he'd never known her, the portrait had seemed enough. That Caroline, at times, so resembled this face gave even more meaning to the painting and a growing delight.

He moved closer to the portrait, and like the soft swell of first light, long before the sun appears, something new and nearly tangible seemed to pass between him and his mother . . . something beyond the heartmoving, misty beauty that, until now, had been enough.

He had held Caroline in his arms, dancing, had admired her grace, as much when she walked beside him as when they danced. At night, alone, he could call up her fresh, flower scent, the cadence of her low voice, the soft, oddly British rhythm of her speech. He did not imagine himself in love with her, but from the start he had been drawn—to Caroline whole. To all of her.

His mother had once been whole, too—animated and alive and warm and fragrant and full of laughter. He blew out the candle and felt his way back to bed.

He had plans to see Caroline at least three more times before she and her grandfather returned to Knightsford. And now that Robert Mackay had bought The Grange—not five miles from Knightsford—they would be going out there often. Soon, perhaps. He was escorting her, of course, to the ceremonies at the new Chatham Academy day after tomorrow, and because he knew she'd be nervous about Osmund Kott's demand, Mark meant to stay close to her. She had, she had said, no choice but to give the old man Osmund's message. Peculiarly, Mark thought, everyone seemed to stay as far outside the strange, destructive relationship between the two men as possible. Even Caroline, whose devotion to Cameron no one could question.

Curling his body for warmth, he still felt chilled. Could he be falling in love with Caroline? How did a man know these things? He had been attracted to other young ladies, none seriously. Caroline was unlike them all. Unlike anyone he'd ever known. She was a dizzying alchemy of healthy, sun-and-wind-kissed tomboy; a devastatingly beautiful, grace-filled woman—as comfortable, he was sure, astride a horse or climbing a giant oak as she was gliding across a ballroom. In his arms among the swirl of music and dancers, he could almost feel her in tight control of the passion that had swept him, too, he now realized, at the moment of their first dance at the Scarbroughs' ball. But was he falling in love with her? He thought not. He enjoyed being with her. Certainly a new, strong bond had formed between them after the episode on the river. She had been both terrified and bold. She had pleaded with him to help her, and yet she had stayed in almost complete command. From deep within him there stirred a new desire to protect her from whatever ugliness Kott might cause. Had the icy fear of a few moments ago sprung from that? Had the fear that Osmund Kott might have known his mother in some troublesome way been related only to Caroline? Hadn't it seemed related to himself, too?

He turned over and pulled the covers up over his ear. Whatever the cause, the fear had passed. Since boyhood, alone in the big house with Aunt Nassie, he had tried to drift off to sleep counting the good things in his life. There had been so many—the good things always overshadowing the bad. There was an endless list of good things to mull over now, tonight. His mind was fully at ease over his inheritance. He had done the right thing—for him, the comfortable, natural thing. Old Woolsey would have his letter any day now, in which Mark had instructed the family lawyer to draw up whatever papers were necessary so that James Parsons, who had managed the enormous growth of Browning Shipping for most of Mark's life, would receive three fourths of the holdings. Mark, as sole heir, would retain one fourth. Even with restricted shipping during the war, he would still have a yearly income of something like seventy-five thousand dollars—more money than he could comprehend. That was all settled, and tonight his peace of mind was one of the good things.

The fine prospects of seeing Caroline more often in the future, his highly stimulating work, his secure, close relationship with the Mackay family, his continuing joy at waking each day to the still exciting realization that he was, at last, in Savannah—good. All good.

If ever someday he could make a woman as happy as Robert Mackay had made Miss Eliza tonight when he told her of his purchase of her birthplace, life would be complete. In the dark he smiled, remembering Miss Eliza's childlike delight. At times, he loved Miss Eliza so much, he marveled that there was room for any other woman. There was room—there had to be—but Eliza Mackay was a part of that, too. "Be sure you have enough covers, Mark," she had said when she hugged him good night an hour or so ago.

He got up, found another quilt and spread it over the bed. Miss Eliza would ask tomorrow if he'd done that.

Under the covers again, he found his warm place and tried to settle himself in it for sleep. The extra cover helped. Miss Eliza's reminder was warming him for the long night. A cold wind scraped a magnolia branch back and forth against the corner of the frame house. He could feel the chill of it on his forehead.

The Mackays were warming each other down the hall.

The thought made Mark happy. And lonely. In the Mein house, just a few blocks away, Caroline lay alone in another bed, warm, he hoped.

A long time passed before he fell asleep, but he was no longer thinking of Osmund Kott's madness on the river. He ached too painfully to be warming someone himself. To be warmed.

# FIFTEEN

AT the rear entrance of Chatham Academy, Mark and Caroline, safely out of sight, watched her grandfather hand Osmund Kott the money just as the Exchange clock struck three times. No words passed between the two men. Only money. That night, Caroline made Mark promise that he would say nothing at all to the Mackays—to anyone—about what had happened on the river. When he asked why, she would say only that if he cared about her, he would keep it between the two of them. After that, on each trip to The Grange, she thanked him. He needed no thanks. His first impulse, of course, had been to tell the Mackays. He was glad now that Mackay's surprise of The Grange had kept him silent. That was the least he could do for Caroline.

The Grange, surveyed at 470 acres, was not what could be termed a productive plantation; but Mackay had made Eliza happy by buying it, and the family went often in their roomy private sloop for picnics beside the river and under the great trees. A previous owner had sold off the small acreage suitable for growing rice, but Mackay didn't mind that. His work as a merchant and a factor had taught him that corn and cotton were now the dependable crops. Of course, it would require years to bring the land back to productivity, but Mackay's enthusiasm knew no bounds because The Grange made Eliza happy. "And part of my merriment," he confessed to her, "is that our owning The Grange brings Mark and Caroline together far more often. Did you know I'm promoting that romance?"

She knew it and felt the same inclination. But Eliza was, as always, less inclined than her husband to push things along.

"Better to let nature take its course," she told him. "I'm just glad for right now that our visits seem to cheer Mr. Cameron. He's really heartbroken that William Mein is no longer his factor."

"No one knows that better than I," Mackay said. "I've almost run out of excuses as to why I can't take on his account. I may have to come right out and tell the dear old man that I will have nothing whatever to do with any dealings that put me in contact with Osmund Kott. The fact remains, though—he has to find someone."

Early in the spring of 1813, Mackay's French friend, Petit de Villers, did enter into a trial arrangement with Cameron, but within a month Kott, along with a mob of French cronies from the waterfront, landed once more in jail. Rather than obey Cameron by trying to free Osmund, even patient Petit severed the arrangement.

"That Kott is going to be the death of Monsieur Cameron," Petit told Mackay in his thick French accent. "And as much as my heart dictates that I help the venerable gentleman, I can be no part of it. I am on shaky ground myself still, from my own grief." Then, he had given Robert a look that Mackay would never forget. *"Mon ami*, give thanks to God every day of your life that your wife is still—every night in your bed."

By special assessment of the City Council, just before Mark's birthday on May 20, 1813, the sum of four thousand dollars was raised for the purpose of more effectively defending the city against British attack, expected now by almost everyone. Work was still unfinished on the earthworks that were to surround the city, and the arch marauder, Sir George Cockburn, in command of the British fleet in southern waters, plundered at will in the vicinity. He carried on a petty, troublesome slave trade from his headquarters at Dungeness House on Cumberland Island to the south, and his marauders spread along the Georgia coast, causing destruction and alarm. Rumors were rife in town that Cockburn's men had landed on St. Simons Island, a mere seventy water miles south of Savannah.

Even Mackay wearied of the mounting anxieties, which he continually minimized with his family. "Fear only makes everything worse," he told Mark on their way to work one sultry summer day. "The war will be over one way or another before Savannah can possibly be properly defended. All this worry isn't going to change that one iota. The Mackays, at least, have a place to go if Cockburn attacks here. The Grange. So, we might as well stop looking for a British sailor behind every piling at the wharf and enjoy ourselves while we wait and see."

But anxiety and extreme patriotism went on quickening the pulse of the city. To give vent to their rising patriotic fervor and, Mackay believed, to distract them from their fears, Savannah citizens celebrated at every opportunity. A British brig, the *Epervier*, eighteen guns, was captured by the United States sloop of war *Peacock*, and when Captain Lewis Warrington proudly brought his prize into the Savannah harbor, the town went wild. When news of the victory of Captain David Porter of the *Essex* over two British warships, the *Phoebe* and the *Cherub*, reached Savannah, the mayor and the aldermen made plans for still another celebration.

Mark, of course, marched proudly with the Chatham Artillery on every occasion, and except to slip away to deposit his first inherited monies in the new Merchants' National Bank, he lived his every waking hour with the Mackays. And, when possible, with Caroline. Should Mackay ask about the inheritance, he would gladly tell him. There was no longer any need for secrecy. He went to the bank alone simply because, except for some future use if ever he needed money or if Mackay should need it, the large sum of seventy-five thousand dollars in an account bearing his name changed nothing. Nothing at all.

The year 1813, Mark's first full year in Savannah, had been for the city an exhausting time of both panic and ceremony. Few minded that the year would soon be ending. As Christmas neared, there was even more frustration because by now, entertaining was almost out of the question.

"We'll just have to enjoy each other in our separate families," Mackay said at dinner one mild December night, some two weeks before Christmas. "That won't do anyone harm. Of course my own holiday prospects, considering the attractiveness of my family"—he glanced proudly about the table—"will be superior as always."

"I'll be glad if you and Mama and Mark have to stay home every night," Eliza Anne said.

"Me too," Jack agreed. "Mark can teach me how to play chess."

"But what if Mama and Papa and Mark wish that there were some parties to go to?" William wanted to know.

"We'll like it fine, just being with all of you, William." Eliza reached to pat her older son's hand. "But you're thoughtful to consider what we might like."

"Leave it to old William to come up with a way to make Eliza Anne and me look selfish," Jack grumbled.

"I don't think he meant it that way," Mark said.

"Then, what did he mean?"

"Whatever," Mark said, grinning, "I like it that you and Eliza Anne want us here and I also like it that William cares how we feel about it."

Mackay thrust his folded napkin in its ivory ring and plunked it down on the table. "If the President had Mark to negotiate for him, we might be finished with the rotten war by now!"

"We'll still go to Knightsford to cut our Christmas greens, won't we?" Jack asked.

"Of course, son. You've got The Grange land now, too, don't forget!"

"Can Mark get time off from work to go with us, Papa?"

"Mark's his own boss. A full partner with me. He can cut greens anytime he wants to."

"It might take a long, long time this year," Eliza Anne said, her excitement growing. "Twice as long. Hunting holly and mistletoe at both Knightsford and The Grange! I might even get a blister!"

"That's not going to work this year," Jack said firmly. "You had me pulling you around in that cart because of your silly blister last year. Christmas greens are heavy enough to pull."

"Sister really had a blister last year," William said. "It even rubbed off!"

"Aw, pipe down, William!"

"That's enough, boys. I have an announcement. It should interest all of you. Osmund Kott is—gone!"

Besieged with questions from them all, Mackay explained that although Kott had been back in jail only once during the summer for starting a tavern fight, no one had to give the man another thought for a while, at least.

"Why do you think he left?" Eliza asked.

"My theory is that when Cameron heard the rumors that

we're forming a Vigilance Committee in town to try to stop the infiltration of British spies at the waterfront—along with the brawls—he paid Kott off again to leave town. Probably the biggest amount yet—to get him away."

"To protect Osmund, do you think, Robert?"

"I wouldn't be at all surprised." He sighed. "Why in heaven's name the man would want to protect him, I don't know, but at any rate, Kott's gone."

"How do you know he really went, Papa?" Jack wanted to know.

"I saw him leave. He left on the first ship of ours to make the run north in months."

"Do you know where Kott's heading?" Mark asked.

"Our ship's bound for New York and he's on it. That's all I know. At least Savannah's rid of him for a time. Cameron and Caroline can both breathe easier." Mackay grinned at Mark. "And don't ask me how I know your lovely lady was worried. I could tell by watching your moods.'"

"I'm that transparent, eh?"

"What does being transparent mean?" William asked.

"It means what I'm thinking is no secret, William. It means your father can see right through me. That he knew I worried when Miss Caroline worried."

William gave Mark his customary adoring look. "I bet I'm the gladdest of all that old Kott's gone."

"And why is that, son?" Mackay asked.

"Because—well, I care a lot that Mark doesn't have much to worry about. I'm afraid he might leave if he has to worry a lot."

"Aw, you're not even thinking about going anywhere, are you, Mark?" Jack was confident.

"Of course he isn't," Eliza Anne said. "Mark lives here with us."

"Eliza Anne and Jack are right on the money," Mark said. "This last year and a half have been the happiest time of my whole life. William, I can't think of anything—ever—that might rid you of me."

William beamed, then frowned. "Well, people do funny things. If you married Miss Caroline, I bet you'd leave us in a minute."

Mackay saw color rise in Mark's face. "What makes you think that might be in the offing, son? Is there something afoot here about which I'm not aware? Mark?''

"No, sir. Maybe no one but Miss Eliza will believe me when I say this, but fond as I am of Caroline, the thought of marriage hasn't crossed my mind.''

"Do you think that's true, Mama?'' William asked.

Mackay saw Eliza give Mark her irresistible, sunny smile, drawing a smile in return.

"Yes, William,'' she said in a quiet voice. "If Mark says he hasn't thought of marriage yet, then it's true. He hasn't. I hope nothing dreadful happens to poor Osmund, but I'm as glad as everyone else that he's gone.''

"I know what let's do!'' Jack shrilled. "Let's go to The Grange and have a picnic to celebrate the dirty dog's departure!''

"Jack!'' Mackay's tone was stern. "You will never call anyone a 'dirty dog' again, do you hear me?''

"Well, isn't he?''

Mackay sighed. "Eliza, you may answer that one.''

"We don't know, Jack,'' she said. "No one seems to know much of anything about Osmund Kott, but calling him names certainly won't help matters.''

"I'm sorry,'' Jack said, briefly repentant. Then, "How about just a plain picnic, Papa, at The Grange?''

"Not now, son.''

"Why?''

"Because no one can be absolutely sure just where Cockburn and his men are plundering the Georgia coast these days.''

"They—Cockburn and his men—wouldn't be likely to land up near The Grange or Knightsford or Coleraine before they'd strike us here, would they, sir?''

"No, Mark, but you and I can keep better posted by being here.''

"If your father says so,'' Eliza backed him up, "we're staying in town.''

"Whillikers!'' Jack jumped to his feet, his eyes lighted with excitement. "You mean, Papa, we might have a real *battle* smack-dab in town?''

Mackay didn't answer at once. The boys are as different as day and night, he thought. Jack's ready to do battle and William turns pale with terror. He cleared his throat. "Now, listen, both of you boys. Just because the citizens of Savannah—however late they were to start—are working from dawn to dark, scraping up money, recruiting laborers in order to defend our city, it does not mean there is going to be a pitched battle on Bull Street! It means only that any wise man prepares for the worst. Then, if it doesn't happen''—he gave William a reassuring smile—"the job's been done and there never again needs to be all this flurry and uncertainty over our fortifications. No one in Savannah knows that we will be attacked. No one knows that we won't be. It's simply important to be ready, either way.''

He could see William's pinched features soften a little. "I—I guess,'' the boy said, "that now that you're sergeant orderly of the Chatham Artillery, I really don't need to worry anyway, do I, Papa?''

## Part II

# 1814–1816

# *SIXTEEN*

By late spring 1814, more work had been done on the fortifications that would surround the city. Earthworks and wooden gun mountings had gone up from Fort Wayne southwest to Liberty Street, across Bull to Spring Hill, and were moving north to Farm. The city appeared somewhat more secure against British attack, but Savannahians were far from peaceful. At least once a week, citizens were terrorized by outbreaks of violence among foreign sailors and waterfront derelicts. When the third fire was set in one week, so much panic seized the city that the Council took action. Fires frightened everyone far more than the possibility of a British attack, so the long-discussed Vigilance Committee was finally appointed. Mackay was a member and his lawyer and friend, Judge T.U.P. Charlton, was made its chairman.

At the close of a business conference in Mackay's office on a steaming afternoon in August, Charlton lighted an expensive cigar, crossed his elegantly clad legs, exhaled a billow of smoke and asked, "Sure you won't join me in a cigar?"

"Thank you, no," Mackay replied, wiping his face on his handkerchief. "Even your smoke makes me hotter."

"Sorry, but I enjoy the taste. By the way, Robert, there's no doubt in my mind that you will be elected alderman this fall."

"It looks that way, in spite of the fact that I really don't want the job. Before we leave the subject of my tangled legal affairs here at the firm, Judge, are you quite certain that since the partnership between Mein and me is not yet finally dissolved, I am not obliged to handle a former client of his?"

"You don't normally doubt my legal expertise," Charlton said casually. "Of course, you mean Jonathan Cameron.

Once and for all, Mackay, you are in no way obligated because papers showing the intent of both you and Mein to dissolve have been in the court files for so long, they're undoubtedly yellowing with age. Why do you continue to ask?"

"Because of that rascal Kott. I'll sleep better at night if I'm dead certain I have no obligation to Cameron."

"Put the matter out of your mind." Charlton took another deep drag on the cigar and changed the subject. "Now, as chairman of the Vigilance Committee, I need a responsible young man to collect records of the whereabouts of all ne'er-do-wells in every tavern, boardinghouse and ship. Someone totally responsible, but not afraid and not squeamish about collecting from the often low-class tavern owners and foreign ship captains. Our committee needs records from each ward in the city so as to apprehend all idle and disorderly persons having no visible estate or lawful employment. Would young Browning help us out in your ward? We need someone with his reliability."

"Why not walk around the corner to Mark's office and ask him yourself?"

"Because he isn't in his office. He's down on your steaming, filthy wharf." He brushed at his linen vest. "I'm obviously not dressed for a visit to the wharf!"

Mackay grinned. "You do indeed resemble a Regency gentleman of high fashion."

"On my way to take tea with the Telfair sisters. A matter of raising money for our library, I believe. Will you ask Browning?"

"No." Mackay looked at Charlton for a time, then said, "Judge, that boy needs a lawyer. I know you're too successful, too proud, too busy, even to hint that you might like a new client. But while you make your proposition for the committee, couldn't you put aside your vanity long enough to offer your services as Mark's attorney?"

"Why can't you suggest me?"

"I have."

"And Browning rejected the idea?"

"Not exactly. He just feels he has no need of a lawyer right now. But he does need one! He's—he's going to be a success."

"What you mean is that he's already enormously wealthy. What a naïve young man he must be to think that he could keep such wealth a secret in a city like Savannah! We all know he's the heir to the Browning fortune.''

"And I'm relieved you do. Hiding good fortune or wealth comes about as naturally to me as flying. For two long years, I've kept Mark's secret. I promised, though, on the voyage down." Mackay shook his head. "He's just not like other young men. He honestly didn't want it known for a time."

"And do you feel he needs financial advice right now?"

"I—I'm not sure."

"Has he appeared worried, troubled?"

"No."

"Then, why fret about it?"

"Consarn it, Judge, I don't know that either. But doesn't it stand to reason that a young man of twenty-two who has just come into a fortune needs legal counsel? That's just common sense, isn't it?"

"It would seem so. I'm really not sure, beyond speaking to him about serving the committee, what I can say. He is aware of my reputation, of course. That I handle your affairs."

"In a way, I feel a bit silly, frankly, even bringing up his need of a lawyer. He seems simply to enjoy his days, his work, my family, and although my wife disagrees, my guess is that he's in love with Jonathan Cameron's granddaughter."

"I wouldn't encourage that if I were you."

"Why not? Caroline's just right for Mark. She's as bright as he is. How many women can claim that?"

Charlton snuffed out his cigar and stood to go. "But, Mackay, you know as well as I that when Cameron dies, his heirs will be left with that despicable Kott on their hands. And only Sheftall Sheftall to handle legal matters. If Cocked Hat gives no more time to Cameron's estate than he gives to Cameron—"

"Wait a minute," Mackay interrupted. "What do you mean by Kott and Cameron's heirs?"

"No need to look so incredulous. Whatever Kott holds over Cameron during his lifetime, he can still hold over his memory."

Mackay frowned. "Blackmail his memory, eh?"

"Of course. Well, the Telfair sisters do not like to be kept waiting. Uh—do you know for certain that Browning has received his inheritance?"

"I do not. It hasn't been easy, but I have not brought it up once. I just don't speak of money with the boy. He—he has no passion for it whatever. He's mastered it, but business seems almost secondary. I simply refuse to pry."

Charlton settled his top hat in place. "You mystify me almost as much as does your protégé, sir. Robert Mackay the gregarious—suddenly, Robert Mackay the reticent."

Mark, happy to be of service to the Vigilance Committee, was relieved that he wouldn't find Kott's name on the vagrancy reports he delivered regularly to Judge Charlton's rather elaborate law offices in Hogg's Tenement. No one had ever so repelled him as did Kott, and yet, lately, his curiosity about the man had grown. He had kept his promise to Caroline not to tell even the Mackays about that cold, wild day on the river when Osmund had nearly rammed their boat, but Mark had not forgotten it. For the most part, his days were good beyond his dreams of what life in Savannah might be. Now and then, he felt ashamed to be so happy in the midst of war. But so far, Savannah had not been attacked and the tide of battle on the seas was turning toward the United States. The work of the Vigilance Committee had been effective, so that even the mood of the city had lightened. The continuing celebrations in town allowed Mark to feel a bit less guilty that his own spirit seemed so free.

If only Woodrow Woolsey back in Philadelphia would stop stalling with the final papers, which would deed the lion's share of the Browning Company to James Parsons, Mark's private, personal world would be free, too. Obviously, Woolsey still hoped that he would change his mind, come to his senses—keep the entire fortune for himself. Perhaps only time could convince him that Mark's mind was made up once and for all. Actually, he found himself forgetting about the whole inheritance for days at a time. The sum of seventy-five thousand dollars—only one quarter of the profits for the first year after his father's death—was safely in the bank. Profits for the second year would come soon. Woolsey would surely wind it all up when Mark accepted only seventy-five thousand a second time. When he thought about the inheritance at all, his mind went more and more to Parsons. At times, alone in his bed at night, Mark tried to imagine what Parsons might be like. With Woolsey still stalling, Mark had no way of knowing that James Parsons even knew of the so-called generous settlement. How old was Parsons? In his fifties, Mark supposed.

Was he married? Did he have a wife and children?

On the porch, one pleasant fall evening shortly after Mackay had been elected alderman, Mark laid aside his section of the *Republican and Savannah Evening Ledger* and asked, "Why do you suppose I've begun to think so much about James Parsons these days, sir?"

Mackay looked at him over the paper and said, "Well, Parsons is the man responsible, in a measure at least, for your wealth."

"That's been true for most of my life, though. And I've known about it for over three years. Lately, I find myself wondering what he's like, how well he knew my father. I—I've even thought that maybe he knew my mother, too."

Mackay tossed his paper to the floor. "Well, now, you may have hit on something! The Browning World Shipping headquarters was moved to New York from Philadelphia only ten or twelve years ago, wasn't it?"

"I think so."

"Since Parsons evidently ran the company from the time your mother died, he undoubtedly knew her, at least. Mark, are you beginning to be troubled that *you* know so little of her? You've been so occupied with getting settled here, but you're a bona fide Savannahian now. Should we make some effort to find her family? At least find out something about them?"

Mark didn't answer at once. If only he could talk about the nightmare day on the river when Osmund Kott mentioned the name Natalie Browning and disclosed that he knew both she and Mark, Sr., were dead. But Mark couldn't tell Mackay. He had promised Caroline never to tell anyone.

"I don't think there's any point in trying here in town, sir," he said at last. "I have thought about writing to Parsons, though. I'm sure he knows by now that he owns most of the company. Old Woolsey finally gave up trying to change my mind. Mr. Parsons should have heard from him a month ago. The papers are all signed."

Mackay stared at him. "And you haven't had so much as a line of thanks from Parsons? Of course, the man may have had a heart seizure."

Mark laughed. "I don't need to be thanked. It's just that lately I've wondered how much he knows about my parents."

"But I should think a lengthy expression of gratitude would

be the least he could do for you!"

"Sir, James Parsons earned the money. He kept the company not just afloat but prospering. You know something? I'm going to write to Parsons tonight. This little talk has helped me make up my mind. If he'll let me, I might even travel to New York when it's safe, to talk to Parsons. That is, when I've finished with my duties for the Vigilance Committee."

"Oh, by the way, Mark, I almost forgot to tell you. I learned last night at Council meeting that the word is that Brigadier General Floyd is bringing us what seems to be an ample force of federal troops to protect the city. We hope to be able to discontinue the Vigilance Committee at the end of this year. Does that relieve you?"

"It would free me to go to New York, if Parsons agrees to see me."

"He'd better fall on his knees to you!"

Ignoring this, Mark said, "I've had an interesting time working for the committee. I've gotten better acquainted with Judge Charlton. I like him. If he'll have me as a client, I've decided to retain him someday—when I have need of a lawyer."

Mackay, smiling broadly, said nothing.

"Why the big smile, sir? Did I say something funny?"

"No. Wise and solid. Something I should have known you'd say when the time came. Has the time come for you to speak out to Miss Caroline, Mark?"

"No, sir, it hasn't. I care too much for her to do anything rash."

"Rash? Selling everything you owned to settle in Savannah was as rash as even a young man could imagine. You don't agree that was—rash?"

"No, sir," Mark disagreed pleasantly. "Not to me, it wasn't. Mr. Mackay, you don't seem to realize that Savannah is the woman I love. I'll thank you not to criticize her. Someday I'm going to build my own good house to add to her beauty. I think about it a lot. Sometimes in my room, I even make sketches. I don't want anything palatial. I want simple, good lines, very well constructed of the best materials—maybe three stories. Brick. Better brick than the kind Mr. Mein makes at Coleraine." He laughed softly. "I even think of what the front stair might look like."

"And do you like what you see?"

"Oh, yes, sir. I wish I understood more about architecture. William Thorne Williams says he can order a book of plans from New York, but if I go up there to talk to Parsons, I could buy one myself."

They sat deep in their own thoughts for a time. Fall jar flies buzzed in the quiet. Eliza's azalea bushes, thick and shadowy near the veranda, brushed the wooden railing in a rising breeze.

"Mark?"

"Yes, sir?"

"Has your heart ever been so full of so many important, lasting things that you wish someone would think of a few new words to describe the feeling?"

"Oh, yes. I feel that way most of the time."

Mackay leaned his head against the high-backed porch chair. "Well, I just thought I'd ask. So do I. So do I."

Later that night, at the kneehole desk beside the big front window in his room, Mark sharpened a quill and began to write to James Parsons.

20 September, 1814

Dear Mr. Parsons,

I am certain that you have heard by now from Mr. Woodrow Woolsey, my attorney in Philadelphia, and that you must be aware of at least some of my gratitude for your years of excellent and faithful work in behalf of my father's firm. It is my hope and prayer that you have accepted my settlement, which gives me a practical means of showing my thanks.

That, however, is not my reason for writing. I am now well settled in Savannah, a city my father loved, and the city in which my mother was born.

My situation here is superb. I hold a working partnership with Mr. Robert Mackay of the firm of Mein and Mackay, Savannah merchants. I enjoy my work to the fullest, and am devoted to all the Mackays. I am now, in all ways, a Savannahian. I have made the right decision and am at peace and happy, except for the increasingly troublesome fact that I know so little about either my father or my mother, as people. Somehow,

this curiosity grows as my other affairs settle
themselves. Perhaps only now I have time to dwell on
my own unanswered questions. It is my impression that
you have been closely associated with my family's company through all the years of my life. I was born in
1792. I do not remember my mother, since she died
when I was three. My father never again lived at the
old Browning mansion, but, of course, he visited me as
often as he could.

My request of you is this: Could I come to see you in
New York or, at my expense, would you visit me here
so that you may perhaps put my mind at ease? I am so
eager to know who my mother was. Do you know? Is
there any chance that my father, who so obviously
trusted you, also confided in you?

My mother's maiden name was Melissa Cotting and I
know her only from the oil portrait that hangs now in
my room here at the Mackay house. If my request appears overly young, I pray you will indulge me anyway.
In most ways, I feel I am maturing, but this mass of
unanswered questions seems somehow to keep me tied
to a past about which I know so little. It is strange,
isn't it, how much children accept on blind faith? Even
Mrs. Mackay, who has lived much of her life in and
near Savannah, does not know of my mother's family.
No one seems to know.

Did you ever hear of a rather strange man named Osmund Kott? He has left Savannah, it is hoped by
everyone here, for good. But before he left, in a most
troubling way, he let me know that he somehow knew
of my father's death and the death of my father's
sister, my aunt, Natalie Browning. Forgive my burden-
ing you with all this, but if you could inform me, I will
be even more in your debt.

You may write in care of Mein and Mackay, Number
One Commerce Row, Savannah, Georgia.

> My sincere and deep respect to you,
> MARK BROWNING, JR.

The next day Mark handed his letter to the captain of the
same boat that brought a letter for him from James Parsons.

Standing on the windy dock, he opened it and read the short message:

New York City
September 14, 1814

My dear Mr. Browning,

I was overwhelmed by your act of fairness and generosity. The Browning Company has been my life for many years. It will continue to be. If ever I can be of service, you have but to advise me.

Yr Obed'nt Servant,
JAMES PARSONS

The letter was so short, so to the point, Mark laughed. He had, he realized, expected a rather more exuberant response to his decision to sign over three fourths of the Browning Company to Parsons. Still, he mused, if anyone had asked me if I expected a flowery outpouring of gratitude, I'd have said a resounding no. It just shows how we can hide our motives even from ourselves, I suppose. Climbing up the steep wooden steps that led from the wharf to his office, he was still laughing. Not at Parsons, at himself. The brief, terse note would make Mackay laugh too, he was sure.

A few minutes later, in Mackay's office, his friend did not laugh. "The least the scoundrel could have done was to write you a page or two of appreciation!"

Mark felt his face flush. He looked straight at Mackay. "That's why the letter struck me funny. I hadn't realized it—at least, I hadn't admitted it—but I think I did expect a somewhat exaggerated gratitude."

"Exaggerated? Mark, any other young man in the whole United States would have taken every cent of that inheritance!"

"I'm not accountable for anyone but me, sir. Mr. Woolsey agreed with you, but he did tell me the truth about all Parsons did through those years. He deserves every dollar he'll ever get. You know my father paid no attention whatever to the business after—"

"I know, I know, I know! But, half of the firm would have been more than enough. Even a quarter of it."

"I'm satisfied with my decision, sir. Could we just leave it there?"

A smile began to light Mackay's face. "Aunt Nassie was right about you, son. Remember when you told me she always said that to forbid you to do something was a guarantee you'll do it?"

"I remember."

"You are stubborn, aren't you?"

Mark only grinned.

"Drat the whole thing, anyway! You have a knack of acting in your quiet, controlled manner that mixes me up considerably. I admit to that. You're either stubborn as a Georgia mule in this case, or you're absolutely right. Right, in a way I don't think I'd dare try. I'd take the company. Owning the whole thing would make me as certain as you seem to be— right now. Did you send that letter to Parsons asking to see him?"

"Yes, sir. It went out on the same ship that brought his note to me. I asked a lot of questions, too."

Within a scant two weeks, Mark received a letter from the head clerk in Parsons's New York office. Because of shipping problems caused by the war, James Parsons would be abroad until spring of next year. The letter closed with the promise that immediately upon his return, Mark's letter would be called to Parsons's attention.

That someone besides Parsons had read his highly personal questions made him uneasy, but Mark hoped he sounded convincing when he told Mackay that he could adjust to the delay. "After all," he said, "I've been in ignorance about my family for my whole life. I can wait another six months."

# SEVENTEEN

THROUGHOUT September rumors flew about the town squares, in the shops, at church on Sundays, in every counting-house along the waterfront, that British Admiral Cockburn was indeed heading for Savannah—that, in fact, he had landed briefly at Bonaventure, on the outskirts of the city.

To Mackay it seemed that the City Council spent its time thinking up reasons to call emergency meetings. The city's fortifications, in progress for so long, were still not completed across the last gap in the line between the magazine and the river. "With more faith in example than precept," he told Eliza when he came home from an emergency meeting on September 25, "the mayor and every single alderman will report at eight o'clock tomorrow morning, equipped with hoes, axes and spades. The contention is that if Cockburn is so near, then let us finish the earthworks ourselves." He added, "Most of us dressed, I have no doubt, in top hat, stiff collars and gloves."

The Council urged all other citizens to join the effort, and, of course, Mark went with Mackay. This burst of defensive effort did not stop with the aldermen's blistered hands. Late in January of the new year 1815, the Council urgently requested Commodore Hugh G. Campbell, in command of the United States flotilla stationed off the coast of Savannah, to sink vessels at any points he might deem expedient for the obstruction of the river to marauding British vessels. Even the Vigilance Committee was hurriedly reappointed, and Mark promised Judge Charlton that he would gladly resume his old duties.

Then, the fortifications completed at last, civic activity suddenly slowed when word finally reached Savannah that in January General Andrew Jackson had soundly defeated the British at New Orleans. It was not until February 28 that the city learned of President Madison's actual proclamation of peace with Britain which brought it all to an end.

In bed the night they learned of the peace, Mackay began to laugh softly.

"All right," Eliza said, "what's so funny?"

"Savannah. God bless us all, I say. Almost on the day we learned that the war is over, our little town finally completed its defense preparations. At our next Council meeting there will be such a storm of ornate resolves and heartfelt votes of thanks that we may well find our next crisis to be a paper shortage."

"But, it's over."

"Yes, it's over."

"You're enjoying being an alderman, after all, aren't you, dear?"

"Except for all those emergency meetings that keep your face out of my sight." He touched her cheek. "That face I love," he murmured. "That wonderful face I love . . ."

"I marvel every day that you do," she said simply.

In response, because there were no words, Mackay held her closer, his hand stroking her shoulder. They were blessed as husband and wife. Their family was blessed. Savannah had escaped the war almost entirely. The city, too, was blessed. He sighed.

"Any reason for that sigh, Robert?"

"Relief, I guess. We had such a flurry of effort there at the end, peace almost saps my energy."

"Wasn't it a strange war? It all seemed so close and yet it wasn't." She pressed her face against his shoulder. "I think you're sleepy."

"I am."

"Good night, dearest friend. I'm going to try to thank God a little before I drift off. I'm sleepy, too, though. I may not get far." She kissed him tenderly before turning away.

He began to thank God, too, silently. Then, unexpectedly, James Parsons interrupted his prayer. Reverence vanished. Since Mark's short note of gratitude from Parsons, now almost six months ago, every thought of him made Mackay snort. He would wager with anyone for any amount of money that in all the history of estate settling, no man ever came out as well as Parsons—simply for having done his job!

Forcing his thoughts back to prayer, he asked the Almighty to bless Mark and the children. He prayed for each by name; Jack and William and Eliza Anne and little Kate—and Mark—had become one and the same to him. He prayed for his children to stay healthy, to learn well. He prayed that waiting six long months for Parsons to return had not harmed Mark. He prayed also that James Parsons would share all he knew to put the boy's mind at rest about his family.

Praying for the young people he loved sent him off to sleep feeling contented and quite a bit more spiritual.

Within a fortnight the city seemed to return almost to daily, peaceful occupation. Savannah society appeared bent on compensating for the dearth of parties, and in the two weeks following the end of the war, balls and dinners galore were planned, even though supplies were still scarce. Mackay and Mark, along with every other merchant, spent longer hours at their countinghouses because more and more ships could once again be dispatched safely.

The two, walking home one crisp March evening, reveled in the clear spring air and a crimson sunset that stained the frame houses and the Spanish moss that hung from the trees lining the streets.

"My father loved Savannah's waving moss," Mark said. "He used to tell me—and I thought he was exaggerating—that plain gray moss turned the color of Savannah sunsets. He was right."

"I'm sure I don't need to remind you that it's been over six months since your friend and business associate, James Parsons, went abroad. He should be back—at least this month. I doubt there's any trouble now booking passage."

"You don't think I'm watching too soon for a letter?"

"You're worried more than you've shown, aren't you, son?"

"No, sir," Mark answered in a quiet voice. "I really don't think I worry; it's just that after all these years, I want to know some of the answers." Then, as though dismissing the whole thing, he added: "By the way, I finished allotting all the cargo space on the *Eliza* for her first voyage north."

"You finished? Already?"

"Yes, sir. The *Eliza* always gets my best attention. She introduced us."

"So she did. The luckiest day of my life, too, except for the day my wife made her foolish leap into my heart." They strode along without talk for a time. Then Mackay asked, "You still don't want Eliza to question her old friends a little about your mother's family? When women talk together, one thing reminds of another. She cares about you as much as I do, you know."

"Oh, I know that. But she's so busy now. Jack and Kate both sick with colds. I'd rather wait to see what I find out from Mr. Parsons."

"There's that independent streak again. I've lost count of how many times that suddenly authoritative tone in your voice has silenced me. You may grow up to be governor someday."

"Are you teasing?"

"About your being governor? Yes. I'd hate to think you'd waste yourself in politics. About your independent streak? No. I'm not teasing."

"Mr. Mackay, there's no way Miss Eliza could find out anything without talking to several other people."

"And you've learned that Savannah is a city with a relentlessly wagging tongue."

"Yes, sir. I'll just keep watching for Parsons's letter."

The letter came during the first week in April, but it was addressed not to Mark but to Mackay himself. Mackay seldom met a boat, but this time he was on his dock inspecting some new bolts of silk before ordering them to be unloaded and so found the letter.

When he reached his private office, he quickly closed the door and broke the sealing wax, which bore the imprint of an elaborate J.P.

27 March, 1815

Dear Mr. Mackay,

I returned from abroad to find a letter written in September last year by Mr. Mark Browning. I'm sure he awaits a reply. I have thought much and decided that since the answers to the questions regarding his parents, especially his Savannah-born mother, may be upsetting, I would inform you first and let you use your judgment about telling Browning.

Over a year ago, I allowed myself to be blackmailed by a despicable fellow about whom young Browning also asked. He threatened to spread his own ugly history in Savannah, thereby causing trouble for Mark Browning, if I did not make an opening for him in the firm. I succumbed to his threats because I know his story to be true. This person is called Osmund Kott, but that is not his real name, since he bore the same name as Browning's mother, Melissa Cotting. Kott was Cotting and he and she were brother and sister. Osmund Kott is young Browning's uncle on his mother's side.

Mackay stared out his office window at the thicket of ships' masts and dazzling water. That Osmund Kott could be Mark's uncle was more than he could take in. The lovely, mist-shrouded young face in the portrait that hung in Mark's room could not be Kott's own sister! *Could not be*.

Drawn, in spite of his revulsion, Mackay went back to the long letter:

Born to the mistress of a married planter named Jonathan Cameron, the Cotting children, after their mother, Mary Cotting, died from consumption, were separated. Kott was raised at Savannah's Bethesda Orphanage and supported by Cameron. Where she spent her childhood I am not sure, but by the age of ten, little Melissa Cotting, Browning's mother, lived in the house of a Savannah seamstress, who taught her manners and how to sew. Melissa was bright, a good student and very pretty, evidently happy as a girl. Her brother, Osmund, at the orphanage, was bitter; but he is, I can tell you, also bright and swift to learn new work and was once rather handsome, I should think. He is also, so far as I can tell, bizarre—perhaps even mean.

Wealthy, prominent Mark Browning, Sr., met Melissa Cotting selling vegetables from the seamstress's garden in Savannah's Johnson Square. He fell in love with her, stole her away to Philadelphia and married her after his sister, Natalie Browning, trained the girl for a time. Melissa died when their only child, your young man there, was but three.

With your permission, I will, of course, pass this information along to young Browning, or you may hand him this letter. But, from what I have pieced together from Kott himself, he undoubtedly still blackmails Mr. Jonathan Cameron because of his and his dead sister's illegitimate births. Cameron must still guard his secret well.

Sir, I hesitate to make all this known to young Browning without your advice. The boy seems contented there and although I fully understand his desire to learn of his mother's Savannah connections, so far as I know, only Osmund Kott and his father, Jonathan Cameron, remain. Would it not be better to let sleeping dogs lie? Browning has asked to visit me. I await your opinion.

Y$^{rs}$ obediently,
JAMES PARSONS

Slowly, numbly, Mackay folded the letter and placed it deep inside his coat pocket. Only one thought came clear: He would have to show the letter to Eliza. It would, of course, be far better to let sleeping dogs lie! That was not possible. Mark waited daily for an answer from Parsons. He sighed heavily. Even Eliza will have to weigh this in her mind for a long time.

He sat staring out beyond the tall ships to the open river, bustling with minor traffic—sailing skiffs, dinghies, dugouts. He sighed again. "Parsons must not be such a hard fellow after all," he said aloud in a rough whisper.

The letter showed that he seemed, at least, to care about Mark.

# EIGHTEEN

THROUGH the evening at home with Eliza, Mark and the children, Mackay managed not to show his anxiety. It wasn't easy. Mounting the stair with Eliza, after the others were in bed, he wondered how in the name of common sense he could go on pretending, should he and Eliza decide on that course for now.

In their room he surprised her by asking that they sit up yet awhile. "I have something so important to talk over with you," he said, "that I need to see your face when I tell you."

Seated across from her beside the open window, he handed her Parsons's letter. Without a word, she began to read, never once taking her eyes from the pages. A rain so soft it was almost a mist dripped from the big oak beyond their corner of the house. Mackay waited, his heart racing. He could feel it.

Finally, Eliza looked at him, her eyes dark with shock and pain. "Oh, Robert! Poor Mark," she murmured. "Poor, *poor* old Jonathan Cameron!"

"Eliza, I cannot—I will not—make this decision alone."

She laid the letter on the table between their chairs. For a long moment, she stared at it, saying nothing.

"For God's sake, Eliza, tell me *something* of what you're thinking!"

"My darling, I'm having exactly the same thoughts and questions—all muddled—that you must have had when you first read this." She rubbed her forehead. "Give me time. The only thing I see at all clearly right now is that we must not make a hasty decision."

"Oh, I agree. If Mark weren't waiting for an answer to his letter from Parsons, I'd say we should make a pact between us never to mention a word of it.''

"He is waiting."

"Rather well, too, actually. He doesn't strike me as having a tortured, private, unshared world of anxiety that he holds to himself—away from us. Now and then, he seems almost to be observing himself as he waits."

"But, he is waiting. And, oh, Robert, that distresses me so!''

"Me, too. If he weren't so frazzlin' *good* about it, I'd be better able to handle the sorry affair. Eliza, I can't bear to see that boy hurt!''

"You and I have to go on as though we know nothing at all about any of it, until we decide how to tell him.''

"Hide the way we feel? Can we do that?''

"We have to," she said firmly. "And pray that not a breath of this gets loose in the city. Thank heaven, Julia Scarbrough is visiting her relatives in North Carolina for the summer.''

"Why single out poor Julia? Oh, I know she blabs and sputters, but why did you mention Julia in particular?''

"Way back when Mark first came to town, she tossed off some wild story about Mark's father having sired a son by a servant girl or some such idiocy. I silenced her."

"You must have put the fear of God into her. I've never heard a word about anything so outrageous.''

"Well, Julia isn't mean. She's just horribly curious." Eliza leaned toward him. "But, Robert, where there's smoke, there's fire, we now know. Julia's distorted story was just a generation off. Mark isn't illegitimate. His lovely mother evidently was."

"Yes." Mackay's eyes filled with tears. "I wish the Almighty had not chosen to trust *us* with all this!''

"Be glad for Mark's sake that He did.''

Mackay began to pace the room. "It's just that I can't help fighting what I can't change. I can't help the boy—and Lord, how I want to!''

"Sit down, dear. The floor creaks.''

Back in his chair, he whispered, "Can you think straight?''

"No, and I think we'd better stop trying.''

"If the story gets abroad in the town, it could ruin Mark's life.''

"If he allows it, yes.''

"But what could he do about wagging tongues?''

"*He* has done nothing wrong."

"He doesn't need to have sinned to start the tongues in this town."

"Savannah's no worse than Charleston or any other place its size. We're getting nowhere, darling. Let's turn it over to God and go to bed."

"That doesn't sound too practical, but—all right. You do it."

They bowed their heads. In a moment, Eliza prayed: "Father, here it is—all of it. Please let us know what to do. And please, please watch over Mark!"

Neither spoke for a time; then Mackay asked, "Is that all there is to it? Is that all we have to say to the Almighty?"

"That's all, dearest. He knows about it, anyway. He knows how helpless we are." She marched him toward the bed. "Out of your dressing gown and under the covers. The Lord also knows we're both too stunned and too tired to think tonight."

In bed, Mackay held out his arm. Her head nestled into its usual place. "Eliza, shall we just go along for a few days— until something comes to one of us?"

"Yes. One day at a time."

He groaned, settling himself. "Not easy for me."

"I know. But promise?"

"Promise."

Every day for a week, during which the Mackays came to no decision, Robert watched Mark check every boat for a letter from Parsons.

"I can't endure this much longer," he told Eliza, alone with her at the breakfast table. "Mark hurries down to the wharf to meet every ship from the north. Just yesterday, he asked again if I was sure it would be all right if Parsons stayed here with us when and if he comes to Savannah. He also asked if I could get along without him should Parsons want him to go to New York. I feel almost as though I'm lying to the boy. I hate it. Hasn't anything at all come to you?"

"Only that we can't go on this way. And maybe we're doing the wrong thing to try to protect him. Won't he find out about his mother's being Cameron's daughter—about his Uncle Osmund—sooner or later?"

Mackay drained his coffee cup and banged it in the saucer. "Sorry, my dear. Hard on china, I know. Yes. He's bound to find out, but if he would only settle things with Caroline first.''

Her look was incredulous. "Robert, you are an incurable romantic! We have no way of knowing that Mark loves Caroline in the way a man should love a wife. No way at all."

"Oh, he's just shy. His strange, lonely boyhood robbed him of love. He's desperate for love."

"Nonsense. The boy truly loved his aunt. And his feelings for his father were the most unselfish I've ever heard of. He also had the usual young boy crushes on his dancing partners. He had lots of friends."

"How do you know?"

"Mark talks to me, too, dear."

Mackay pushed back his plate and tossed his rumpled napkin aside. "I still say that we should wait until he's proposed to Caroline. My hunch about that is strong. He'll need a brave, devoted, loyal woman to share the blow—once he knows. Good friends are fine, but a man needs a woman at a really bad time."

"Fold your napkin, dear, and put it back in the ring, please."

"Oh, oh, yes." As he obeyed, he went on fervently, "We must make ways, Eliza, for those two young people to see more of each other—right away."

"Robert, Mark and Caroline are—the same as first cousins."

"I know, I know that. But look at the satisfactory cousin marriages we know about. Look at Delilah and John Mc-Queen! I could name others. My hunch is very, very strong that before Mark finds out, he should have a good, long time with Caroline!"

"Would you want to trick Mark into marrying Caroline Cameron and then find out that he's her cousin? Would you want to trick him into marrying right into the Osmund Kott mess?"

He frowned, thought a minute and then began to smile. "That *is* what I was suggesting, isn't it? Eliza, I swear, I hadn't thought that far ahead. I was just so intent upon Mark's having Caroline—when he'll need her so much."

She laid her hand on his. "That's because you *are* an incurable romantic."

He reached into his jacket pocket. "I am indeed—just what you call me." He handed her a thin lacquered box. "This came in a cargo from Shanghai yesterday. I saw at once that no other woman deserved it. Only you, dear Eliza, will ever wear it now—to remind you of your incurable romantic, who loves you with all his blundering heart."

She opened the box and held up a small jade heart on its gold chain. "It's beautiful, Robert, and it must have cost a lot of money!"

He beamed. "It did."

"But, oh, dearest friend, I adore it. How can I thank you?"

He thought a minute. "By agreeing to leave the children here with Hannah and Hero for a week while you and I visit The Grange—just the two of us. And Mark, of course."

She laughed. "And Mark, too? I wonder why."

"Eliza Mackay, that boy *is* moving toward a real romance with Caroline. I can see all the signs. In fact, he informed me that he'd cleared time for himself away from the counting-house this coming week. Mark's *going* to The Grange. The renovations on our cottage there should be finished by now. Are we going with him?"

"Of course we're going! The children are all well. They mind Hannah better most of the time, anyway." She paused. "So, Mark had already made his plans to leave town for a week. Maybe he isn't as nervous about hearing from Parsons as we think."

"He is nervous, but in his anxiety, his mind went to Caroline. I tell you, the boy's in love with her. He only needs a push. He hasn't seen her in two months or more. He needs to be with her."

She kissed his hand. "Robert, Robert, I need to be with you—forever. I was thinking last night, isn't it wonderful that God worked it out so that life doesn't end here?"

"Hm? Oh, yes, yes, of course," he said, his mind on more earthly matters. "I leave heaven to you and the Lord, Eliza, but your husband has the gift of pretending that even one glorious day right here is an eternity. When we step from our boat onto Grange land, that moment will begin a week-long eternity and it will have no end at all. I promise. I promise both heaven and eternity—every day we're out there."

"I know all your powers, sir."

"And for that week, we won't give Mark's trouble a thought, either, will we? For his sake, naturally. He'll be in heaven with Caroline, too."

"We're stalling about telling him, aren't we?"

He got up from the table. "Of course we're stalling. But can one more week make much difference? Who knows what might happen out there in that glorious spot by the river?" Eliza followed him to the front hall. "Mark may come back from this week so fortified in his heart, that—"

"You're incorrigible."

"That's why you married me. Opposites attract."

"Robert?"

"Is what you're about to say of a serious nature? If it is, don't say it."

"Wouldn't you hate to see Mark marry into the Cameron trouble?"

"He's in it anyway, even though he doesn't know it yet."

"I know, but *Ethel* Cameron!"

He brushed vigorously at his top hat with his sleeve. "Listen, Eliza, Mark can handle Ethel. She's like fifty other Philadelphia *grandes dames* he's encountered."

"That's not true and you know it. I know he's met her, but she's so cultivated and charming outwardly, Mark has no notion yet of what she's really like. Robert, that woman doesn't even like her own granddaughter!"

"Caroline?"

"Yes, Caroline."

"Now you're being overly serious like your own dear mother, looking for trouble."

"No, I'm not. My woman's instinct tells me that Caroline's deep devotion to her grandfather seethes like a caldron inside Ethel."

Gently, but firmly, Mackay kissed her hands, then her mouth. "You've forgotten already, dearest. For a whole week—and it's beginning as of right now—we aren't going to entertain one unpleasant thought. You're going on a holiday with me, remember?"

He peered down at her until she began to smile.

"Yes, sir," she said. "And—wearing a jade heart!"

# NINETEEN

WHEN Mackay and Mark eased the family sloop into Cameron's dock a few miles upriver, Caroline and her grandfather were waiting with three of their servants on hand to help secure the boat and handle baggage.

"Ahoy!" Mackay called. "What a splendid welcoming committee!"

Assisted out of the sloop by Mark into the strong hands of Jonathan Cameron, Eliza greeted him, then embraced Caroline. "What fine neighbors you are," she said, "not only allowing us to use your dock until ours is repaired, but meeting us. Thank you."

Mackay, after shaking hands with Cameron, gave him a big wink as they both stood watching Mark bow over Caroline's hand and kiss it—not once, but three times.

"You look lovelier than ever," Mark murmured.

"I'm so glad you're here," Caroline said directly to Mark. "And"—she whispered in his ear—"the surprise is waiting!"

"What's all this?" Mackay wanted to know. "Whispering secrets?"

"The children have a surprise for you, Robert and Eliza," Cameron said. "Thanks to Mark. It arrived this morning."

"Just in the nick of time," Caroline cried. "Mark, I didn't sleep all night, wondering if *it* would really get here!"

"What on earth?" Eliza asked. "Robert, are you sure you're not behind all this?"

"On my honor, I swear it. I'm as innocent as a rose."

Caroline hurried them across the dock, up the narrow, sandy river path and around to the other side of a stand of myrtle trees, where waited a handsome new green carriage hitched to a team of Cameron bays.

"Hurray!" Mark was shouting. "It did get here, didn't it?"

"Caroline, Mark, a new carriage?" The Mackays were dumbfounded.

"For the two of you," Mark was beaming.

"It's all Mark's doing," Caroline said. "When he found out you were coming too this week, he picked it out in town and hired two of your stevedores, Mr. Mackay, to raft it out. They rode back on your dock horses Mark borrowed for the big event. They haven't been gone an hour! Isn't it a splendid carriage, Miss Eliza?"

"My, yes, but Mark, why such a fine one for out here in the country?"

"Why not, Miss Eliza? I knew you and Mr. Mackay were on a kind of second honeymoon this week, and—"

"Indeed we are, son!"

"—and for so long, I've wanted to do something for you both."

"It's a love gift," Cameron said, his silver hair lighted by the sun, his face glowing. "The boy is merely showing his gratitude."

"But such an expensive way to show it," Mackay marveled, walking around the carriage, running his hand over the smooth lacquered doors, the fine brass fittings. "It's a beauty! A real beauty." He glanced at Mark. "The merchant in me wants to know how much?"

"Robert!" Eliza scolded.

Mark's face flushed, he grinned. "I—I don't know, sir."

"You don't know? You didn't ask?"

"Afraid not. It was just what I wanted. I felt lucky to find it."

"No matter," Caroline laughed. "It's here, it's the new Mackay carriage for use at The Grange, we're all together, your restored cottage is a dream—so let's go inspect it. You, too, Grandfather."

"Thank you, child," he said, the first touch of sadness in his voice. "Prince promised your grandmother I'd come right back to the house."

"Whatever for?" Caroline wanted to know.

The old man shrugged. "I just take the easy way," he said, not at all self-pitying, stating a fact. "You go on to the cottage. I know how excited you are, Caroline, about the way it looks now." He smiled. "My granddaughter's been working on your cottage, Mackays, all week."

After a happy tour of the remodeled house—Caroline even had geraniums blooming on the wide, low windowsills—the Mackays freshened up from their river trip and headed for the new carriage.

"You rushed things a bit, I think," Eliza said as Robert hurried her along. "You really mustn't be so obvious about maneuvering time alone for those two, darling."

"I couldn't have been obvious," he said, handing her into the carriage. "Such a thought never crossed my mind! I simply couldn't wait for *us* to be alone." In the seat beside her, he picked up the reins and signaled the horses. "Here we are in heaven, Mrs. Mackay. How do you like it?"

"Robert, Robert," she said, clinging to his arm, "you and I live in heaven—every day!"

"Even when I'm cross and tired at the end of a workday? Even when the boys fight and the girls show how spoiled they are?"

"Even heaven would get boring if the climate stayed the same every day." After a moment, she asked, "Isn't Mark the limit? What a truly luxurious, comfortable carriage! I couldn't think of anything proper to say to him."

Mackay laughed. "You hugged him three times. No better thanks on earth than a hug from you."

"I hope he didn't go into a lot of debt."

*"Debt?"*

"Yes, it was such a sweet, extravagant thing for him to do."

"You really *do* forget about it, don't you?"

"Forget what?"

"Eliza, dear Eliza, Mark is an extremely wealthy young man!"

"Oh, oh, yes. But he wasn't when I first met him. He isn't any different for me now."

"Nothing could make him happier than to hear you say that."

"He knows it."

They rode for a time in silence, broken only by the iron-tired carriage grinding through the sand, the rattle of the harness, and the exuberant spring singing of cardinals, wrens and towhees. Eliza held tightly to his right hand, the reins lay loosely in his left.

"Afraid you might lose me?" he teased.

"Always."

"I wish I were a towhee. I'd like to make that kind of music when I call you."

"You do. No music compares with your voice calling to me from downstairs."

"Where do you suppose Mark and Caroline are?" he asked.

"Hearing the birds, too, I hope."


"I found this spot when I was out here last time," Mark said, helping Caroline over a giant live oak root, around to the other side of an ancient tree. "See? Instead of humping up, the roots on this side are sort of scooped out. Try it. Doesn't that make a perfect seat?"

Holding firmly to his hand for balance, she sat down in the hollow of the gnarled root and straightened the long skirt of her blue cotton, tucking one side under so that Mark could share the same comfortable root.

"Thank you, ma'am," he said, settling himself beneath the wide, low branch. "Isn't this cozy? Look how far that branch over us grows out before it turns up. Must be twenty-five feet. Are these big oaks hundreds of years old?"

She laughed a little. "I doubt it. Live oaks grow rather fast."

"I'd like to climb up that limb, would you?"

"Not when I'm so comfortable."

"Oh, I don't mean right now. But if we did climb it, I'd promise to get you back down."

She merely smiled.

"Don't feel crazy today, eh?" he asked.

"Not very."

"Is anything wrong?"

"Why do you ask that?"

"Well, I did have to wait ten minutes or so while you and your grandfather had a somewhat—intense—conversation on the Knightsford veranda before we left a while ago. I don't need to know—I really don't. But I hope nothing's wrong."

"I can see why you'd think so," she answered in her always direct, honest manner. "I did give him a consoling hug before

I joined you. I'm sure you saw it. He needed that hug."

"He's feeling all right, isn't he?"

"Yes. In his body, if that's what you mean." She turned to him. "Mark, my darling grandfather is never—all right. No man could be, married to my grandmother."

Mark said nothing.

After a moment she drew her breath deeply, as though to nerve herself, and said, "What Grandfather was telling me was that my grandmother is—*demanding* that you have tea alone with her tomorrow."

"Well, I'll be delighted to accept. She was most courteous to me the one time I saw her."

"She can be the world's most charmingly courteous lady," Caroline said, her voice suddenly sharp-edged. "She *is* a lady, you know. There's no way in which any of us could ever forget that. She wouldn't permit it." Then, "Mark, I've been too ashamed to tell you much, but neither do I think I've tried to hide from you—how things are. My grandparents never talk to each other. Never. Except through the servants or through me."

"Oh, I'm so sorry."

"Don't ask why they don't."

"I wouldn't."

She laid her hand affectionately on his. He grasped it tightly. "Of course you wouldn't. You don't have ugly thoughts."

"Everyone has some."

"Not like theirs." She pushed back the dark curly lock that often fell forward when she was thinking or trying to explain. "Oh, I shouldn't include Grandfather. I have no reason to believe he hates her. I know she hates him, though."

"Caroline, that's really—"

"Yes," she snapped. "That's really—horrible. No one has to tell me. I've grown up with it. I guess I was about seven when Grandfather stopped trying to talk with her. For years he did everything a man could do to keep her in—in something resembling acceptable humor."

Mark slipped his arm around her.

"I wish sometimes you hadn't met me," she went on, "but now, I don't know how I managed without you. Even when we're not together, which is most of the time, I still know— you're somewhere. And that you're you. I do thank you."

"Caroline, if you'd marry me, I could take you away! We could stay with the Mackays until I could build us a town house, and—"

Her fingers were over his lips, stopping him. "Hush! Please don't mention such a thing again! I don't want you to marry me out of sympathy."

"But I wouldn't be, Caroline! Listen to me—"

"No! You listen to me. *I will not leave Grandfather in that house alone with her.*"

"You're upset now. Why don't we wait until later and talk some more? Please, can't we—wait? Don't say anything else now."

She pushed him away and struggled to her feet. "Let's walk. It will all be better if we just walk—*fast.*"

He led her back to the path by the river and they strode along as fast as her thin slippers allowed.

"I said too much," she gasped. "I just get—*so angry.* My grandfather is such a kind, good man. Too tenderhearted for his own best interests. Everyone says that about him. He hurts all the time. Every minute of his life, he's in mental anguish. Don't say anything, Mark. Just let me talk. If only I had some idea of *why* she hates him so. Some idea of why her heart—if she has one—is so hardened to him."

Mark went on supporting her, his arm about her waist, but he waited.

"They had one child, my father. She did allow Grandfather to come near her—that once, those years ago. But, Mark, I'll never forget the cold loathing in her eyes all those times Grandfather sent me to her through the years to beg her—to beg her just to talk to him. All that was a long time ago. I was just a little girl when it started. At least, I guess that's when it began. She refused to speak to him way back then—for weeks at a time. Grandfather would cry and beg me to plead with her, for him. He was desperate. Men get desperate, too." She sighed heavily again. "Somehow, with the passing of the years, he's learned how to live with what I've always thought of as—*the trouble.* What started it, I can't tell you because I honestly don't know. It's always been just—the trouble."

She slowed her brisk pace, tried to smile at him.

"I really care—so much," he said simply.

"I know you do. And it infuriates me that she's demanding to see you alone!"

"Why?"

"She's so tricky. I'm just terribly worried about what she might tell you!"

"What could she tell me that would worry you?"

"I don't know. I just know that her seeing you alone terrifies Grandfather."

"Whatever she says can't make any difference between us." She stopped to look straight at him. "Or between you and my grandfather?"

"How could it?"

"I don't know, Mark! I just know I have a sense of foreboding, and I'm sorry you have to—see her alone. . . ."

# TWENTY

At the allotted time, a few minutes before four o'clock, Mark waited in the small, but well-appointed, front parlor of the Cameron house. Old Prince, whom Mark already knew and liked, had admitted him with quiet courtesy.

"Settle yourself in that high-backed chair, Master Mark," Prince had said. "Miss Ethel, she be right down. She say thank you for coming to take tea with her."

Mark had slept little last night, dreading the encounter. Yet, sitting now in the stiff, brocaded wing chair, he felt an odd sense of expectation. He had thought a lot about how he must try to be fair-minded, must not prejudge this woman to whom no one seemed drawn. Her loneliness must be almost total, although Prince had spoken of her with more than usual respect.

Caroline had convinced Mark at lunch today with the Mackays that she supposed she once loved Ethel Cameron—"the way young grandchildren just naturally love their grandparents." When Mackay jokingly asked what kind of love that was exactly, no one had a very satisfactory answer. During the interview with the old lady, Mark meant to defend Caroline, if there arose a need for it. He felt warmly toward Mr. Cameron, but he decided to say little or nothing about him to his wife. Of course, Ethel Cameron might not mention either her husband or her granddaughter. Who had the faintest idea why she had demanded to see Mark? No one. Not the Mackays, not Caroline. Not even Cameron himself when he rode to the Mackay cottage this morning.

Ethel Cameron's demand to see Mark could, of course, concern his intentions toward Caroline. Even that seemed remote, since no one but Caroline herself—since yesterday—had any idea that Mark had a thought of marrying into the Cameron family. Indeed, such a thing had never seriously occurred to him before.

The afternoon was mild, neither warm nor cool. He felt as though he'd dressed properly. Correct attire, he knew, mattered to the lady for whom he waited. His light-gray trousers fitted well. He had purposely chosen a soft, calm green waistcoat. Aunt Nassie had always like him in green because it set off his dark hair. Was he trying to impress Ethel Cameron? He was certainly hoping not to antagonize her.

He heard one creak, then two creaks from the direction of the wide, graceful stair that swept down from the second story into the entrance hall. She was coming. Light, swift footfalls crossed the hall, and when the woman appeared in the open double doorway, Mark leaped to his feet.

Ethel Cameron did not immediately enter the room. This small, odd lack of movement put Mark even more on guard. She was wearing a costly beige silk fitted dress, three wide rows of pleated ruffles barely touching the floor. About her narrow, erect shoulders, she had thrown a thin cloud-white shawl, the fringe of which she stood twisting in her aging, graceful jewel-laden hands.

For an instant, she reminded him of a shy child. Ridiculous, of course. This was Ethel Cameron, the self-willed, isolated lady who for years had kept even her gentle husband tiptoeing around her personality.

Mark smiled. They had met. There would be no introductions. On the one occasion when he had seen her at the Meins' Coleraine, the adjoining plantation, she had shown him every courtesy. The transparent skin of her even-featured face shrank into folds of age beneath her chin. She returned his smile, but only with her narrow lips. Her eyes remained unreadable. He did not know their color.

"You are kind to take tea with me," she said, extending her hand.

Mark bowed over it; the delicate bones and cotton-soft flesh belied the strength he felt as her fingertips unexpectedly pressed his. "I'm honored, Mrs. Cameron," he said. "A truly beautiful spring day outside. Your white wisteria in the big oak out front is the loveliest I've seen since I've been south."

"Be seated, young man." She gestured toward the chair

where Mark had waited, and took a seat directly opposite on the edge of a blue-striped love seat near the tea table. Mark had scarcely noticed the handsome, low table, spread with fine linen and set with an ornately embossed silver teapot steaming over its spirit lamp. A squat silver sugar bowl and cream jug and other accoutrements necessary to a properly served tea reminded him of the silver he had sold back in Philadelphia.

"I am aware that you have far better things to do with your time during your visit out here," she said, "and so, as soon as our tea is served, I shall come right to the point. I'm sure my servants heard me come down the stair. Tea will be here directly."

"I'm in no hurry, Mrs. Cameron," he said in what he hoped was a cordial voice. "No hurry whatever."

She merely nodded, then fell completely silent. After a time, Mark cleared his throat. Ethel Cameron gave him a somewhat hopeful look as though she would welcome a comment, but he thought of nothing to say and the thick stillness engulfed them again. Dogs barking down at the quarters, some distance from the big house, sounded loud and nearby.

One hound began to yelp, and the yelping became so raucous that Mark ventured, "One of the dogs must have something treed."

"Undoubtedly."

He had never been known to lack for social pleasantries, but somehow he felt unsure now. It was she who had invited him to tea. If she wanted small talk, wouldn't she be about the business of making it? Caroline's grandmother made him nervous in a way he couldn't have explained, but she also touched him. He cleared his throat again. Once more, she gave him the somewhat hopeful look.

"Sitting here with you reminds me of teas my aunt and I had together as I was growing up in Philadelphia," he said. "Usually, they were quite informal, but now and then, she would have a yen to get out the family silver and serve a proper tea."

"Go on."

"Well, you see, Aunt Nassie and I played a lot of games. When we had our tea table set with the good silver, she called it—playing aristocrats." He laughed a little.

Ethel Cameron did not laugh. "I don't understand what

that means," she said in her refined, papery voice. "Either one is an aristocrat or one isn't, I should think."

"Yes, of course, but—"

Blessedly, two light-skinned servant girls in matching dresses entered the room, bearing hot buttered muffins, biscuits, slices of ham so thin you could see through them, jams and jellies. Not one word passed between the servants and their lady. The girls quickly finished, bowed and left.

"Muffins?" Mrs. Cameron asked, passing a cutwork silver breadbasket, its lifted linen cover revealing delicately browned, real English muffins.

"Yes, thank you. Those look delicious."

"I assume they are." She continued passing food until Mark's china plate was piled high. Then, for herself, she took one single biscuit and began to pour their tea. "Cream and sugar, Mr. Browning?"

"Please."

"Now then," she said, setting her untouched cup of tea on the small table beside her. So that Mark would begin, she took one bite of her own biscuit. "Now then," she repeated, "I hope you will enjoy your tea and that you will listen to me. I should say, I hope you will *hear* me. There's a vast difference, you know, between merely listening and hearing."

"Yes, ma'am. Mr. Mackay and I were discussing that difference just the other day."

"You could have done far worse than to associate yourself with the Mackay family. Both husband and wife are from good stock. Mr. Mackay's father, I understand, was a successful Scottish merchant before his early death in Augusta. His mother's people, the distinguished Malbones of Newport, of course, are above reproach. Speaking of fine silver, there is a large chest of Malbone silver, a chest left locked for all these years since the death nearly half a century ago of Godfrey Malbone, Mackay's grandfather. I daresay it will be opened one day and countless treasures will be found in it. A most distinguished family. Mrs. Mackay's mother's line is also excellent, as was her father's, I believe."

Why, Mark wondered, couldn't she have brought up these subjects during the long, tense quiet before tea came? He fully intended to listen—to hear what she had to tell him—fairmindedly. As fair-mindedly as all the talk of her would allow.

The hot breads were delicious, but suddenly, he wasn't hungry. "I'm ready to listen, and to hear, Mrs. Cameron," he said earnestly.

Before she responded, almost as though to give herself strength, he thought, she sipped her tea once, twice, three times, then replaced the cup on the table and began.

"You have been told, I'm sure, Mr. Browning, that I am a spiteful, hate-filled woman." She raised her hand. "Please don't interrupt, no matter what I say. Thank you. What I really am, will be for you to decide, if you care one way or another. Just before my seventeenth birthday, my marriage to Mr. Cameron was arranged by his family and mine in compliance with the need to enlarge both family plantations." She stiffened almost imperceptibly. "My—romance was guided, not by a lover's star, but by two sets of boundary lines. I was not against the marriage. As with any young girl, I felt my destiny was marriage to a gentleman from an acceptable family, and the Camerons were certainly more than acceptable. Mr. Cameron and I had known each other as children. Then schooling abroad for him separated us for all our maturing years, so that when we were brought together following the family decision, we were strangers. But, deeply rooted in the tradition of good families marrying into other good families, we acquiesced, do you see?"

She expected no answer. He said nothing. She continued. "As I told you, I was not quite seventeen." She swept her arm about the parlor. "This house was built for us, the productive plantations were joined, and life began." She laughed. The sound was as dry as powder. "Our only child came within two years—our sturdy, spirited, quite handsome son, named by custom for his father. Young Jon brought me the only real joy I've known in the long, long eternity of my marriage to his father." Her lips tightened. "His father, the gentle, kindly, revered man you know—and undoubtedly like tremendously —Mr. Jonathan Cameron, with whom everyone sympathizes."

Mark thought it best—especially when he studied her eyes— to allow his face to show nothing.

"The chubby, laughing boy, our son, did bring me untold joy. So much joy that foolishly—stupidly—I allowed it to spill over into my relationship with his father, which until then had never been anything but formal and, to me, quite dead." Her graceful blue-veined hands fluttered. "Oh, my husband pretended, in his way, to feel warmly toward me as I pretended, in mine, during the early years. We did have a child together. Jonathan Cameron was considered handsome." Her shoulders straightened, her sharply honed chin lifted. "And—I was considered beautiful, do you see? 'The perfect couple,' neighbors said. 'What a good marriage in all ways!' In all ways, except that in time, we began to loathe each other." She shuddered. "For me, the thought of him clad only in a nightshirt —beside me on a bed—came to be something to dread and avoid. I did avoid it by demanding my own room, do you see?"

Already, Mark dreaded each new revelation, and yet, he could not take his eyes off her face.

"When our son was old enough to play with other children on the plantation, age four or five, perhaps, I—I—" She broke off, her mouth trembling, her hands clenching and unclenching in her lap. Mark could see her battle for composure. Her shoulders stiffened, she sat even more erect on the love seat. The dark, colorless eyes searched the ceiling once, then darted to the floor.

"When our son was four or five," she went on, "quite by accident, I—found—out—about—it—*all*. Little Jon had been playing with the small son of an English indentured servant, my seamstress, procured by my husband in Charleston." Her words were coming in a strangely measured tempo now: one—at—a—time. "The indentured servant was a fine seamstress. I found her more than acceptable. Certainly, she was pretty, in a working-class sort of way. Dark, curly hair, gray-blue eyes, her speech remarkably correct for one with her lower-class background. She read incessantly. So much so that I had to put a stop to it when possible or I'd never have received my finished sewing, do you see? I—rather sympathized with her reading, actually." The aging voice softened a little. "I have lived my life, kept my sanity, in fact, through books. They continue to be my escape from the—ugliness of each hour, do you see? But, she *was* a servant and I was her mistress." The refined chin lifted. "In fact, I found out about it all by attempting to curtail her reading. One spring afternoon, not unlike this one, as I recall, I went to her cottage, where she lived with her small son, born illegitimately a year after she began serving her indenture. My husband agreed with me that she had undoubtedly been with a certain man who saw to timbering for Mr. Cameron on occasion.

"As I said, I went to her cottage, peeped through an open window in order to satisfy myself that she was sewing and not reading a book. I—I was, by then, foolishly warming a bit toward Mr. Cameron, you see. I so wanted to look my best at all times. I had no intention of scolding her. I merely wanted to satisfy myself that she was sewing."

Mark saw Ethel Cameron's shoulders sag almost imperceptibly and her eyes glaze over in such a way that he couldn't decide whether or not they had filled with tears.

"I—satisfied myself all right!" She almost barked the words. "Brazenly, before an open window, my husband stood with this—hussy in his arms, kissing her and kissing her. I stepped back and waited. And listened . . ."

" 'I'll take care of everything,' he was saying to her in a voice so full of love and caring that it was, to me, not his voice at all. I'd never heard him speak that way before. 'We've done fine with Osmund, haven't we, my dearest? We can manage with our new child, too. You'll see. Above all, beautiful Mary, you must not worry. You—must—not—worry!' "

Mark stared at the old lady, grateful that she was not looking at him. The opaque eyes were riveted on the carpet under the tea table.

"Mrs. Cameron," he breathed, "did you say that this woman's son was named—*Osmund?*"

She nodded vigorously, her thin lips twitching, but she said nothing.

From some dark need in her, this wretchedly proud woman had chosen to tell Mark what no one in Savannah seemed to know—even Caroline! What, dear God, was he expected to say? She had told *him* and no one else that Osmund Kott was Jonathan Cameron's own son—born out of wedlock to a servant girl. Suddenly, Mark was on his feet.

"I am not finished," she said in an abruptly quiet voice. "Be seated, please."

Once more, he sat on the edge of the big, hard chair. What else *could* she have to tell him? And why—why out of the whole of Chatham County—had she chosen him to know the truth about why Osmund had the power to cause her husband a lifetime of anguish and trouble? Why had she told Mark anything at all? What could she expect of him?

"To show you, Mr. Browning, that my husband's love for

this woman was no passing affair, mind you, this second child by her was sired five years after Osmund was born." A sick smile pulled at the corners of her mouth. "Actually, although I wouldn't give him the satisfaction of knowing, I believe that he *tried* to stay away from the seamstress, Mary, during that five-year period. Perhaps I was not suspicious enough. But, as I recall those five years between his children by her, he was away often. When he did stay here, he was kinder, almost understanding with me. I'll go so far as to say that he may have tried to break away from her. He was helpless, evidently, against his love, his desire for Mary Cotting."

The name Cotting struck like a blow. Mark slumped back against the unyielding chair. Ethel Cameron was looking directly at him now. He tried to sit up straight, as a gentleman should. He could not. "Mrs. Cameron"—his voice was hoarse—"did you say her name was—*Mary Cotting?*"

"I did. The same as your mother's name before she was fortunate enough to have captured her aristocratic gentleman, your father. Your mother's name was Melissa, was it not?"

He nodded. "Yes, ma'am. Melissa—Cotting."

She looked away, rubbed her forehead. Then, with a jerk, she straightened her shoulders and looked back at Mark. "Would you believe, young man, that after my seamstress, Mary Cotting, died from consumption when Melissa was but four, little Melissa and I—grew to be quite fond of each other?"

"She—my mother lived here—with you after her own mother died?" He had managed only a whisper.

"Until it seemed best that she leave. The sight of her—with me—turned your grandfather into a raging lion."

"My—grandfather!"

"Dear Mr. Browning, I'm sure this has been a dreadful shock to you, but Jonathan Cameron, through an illegitimate daughter, *is*, after all, your grandfather. Your respected, revered, so-called *gentle* grandfather! The sight of little Melissa, prettier every day she lived, clinging to my hand, laughing up at me, changed my husband into a—monster toward me! I could never tell whether he hated himself more than he hated me or the other way around. It didn't matter. I had already suffered too much to endure the further disgrace of a divorce. I dared not allow myself to grow more attached to the child. I demanded that he send her to the city to be brought up by a reputable Scottish widow, who, for a fee, could teach Melissa to sew and bring her up in the fear of God."

Mark could only go on staring at her. There was no mistaking it now—Ethel Cameron's eyes were brimming with tears. She dabbed at them with a handkerchief.

"You see, Mr. Browning, I had come to love this indescribably pretty little waif, Melissa." She struck her hands together sharply. "I *hated* who she was, but I couldn't resist *her.*" Tears were coursing now down the thin, powdered cheeks. "If my weeping puzzles you, it needn't. Caroline told me that your mother, little Melissa, died when you were three. In one of our rare talks, Caroline told me—just last night, as a matter of fact. Strange as this may sound to you, I'm grieving today that your mother is dead. That she died so young."

She fell silent and, for what seemed a full minute, looked so deeply into Mark's eyes, he wanted to run from the room.

"I longed, oh, God, how I longed for Melissa to have been my daughter! Do you believe I can still, at times, feel her small arms tight around my neck? Do you believe I can still, at times, hear her laughter? I hated her mother—" Ethel Cameron's voice became almost a growl. "I loathed her father even more. I still loathe him, but I loved Melissa."

All Mark could think to say when she fell suddenly silent was, "Then, why did you send her away to Savannah to live with the widow?"

Like a marionette manipulated by strings, she got up—one section of her body seeming to move at a time—and walked woodenly across the room to stand by a window that looked out onto the Savannah River.

Mark stood, too, but he did not follow her.

After a long time, she turned slowly to face him. "I will answer your question now." Her voice was low. "I loved Melissa, but I hated *him* more than I loved the child. I did have a moment of choice. There was a time, perhaps a month of time, when once more I could sense his struggling to care about me in some way. That's when my choice came, do you see? Had I chosen to help Jonathan learn to love me, Melissa could have stayed with us, could have become our little daughter. We could have legally adopted her. People would have thought us noble to have taken in the orphaned daughter of a dead servant girl." Her thin shoulders stiffened. "I couldn't make myself choose to do that. I longed to, but it would have given him too much satisfaction! I—sent her away.''

The width of the room lay between them. Mark didn't move, nor did she.

"You're very like her," Ethel said. "You're so like her, I long at this moment to—take you in my arms, Mark Browning. . . .''

He saw her sway slightly, then steady herself. A rush of pity seemed to drain away his strength. Perhaps, he thought wildly, he and Ethel Cameron needed at this moment to steady each other. In his mind, he rushed across the room and took the old woman in his arms. Her thin arms slid gratefully about his neck and they held each other.

In reality, he hadn't moved. Had made no move toward her. Had said not one word. And then, this came: "Someday, Mrs. Cameron, I hope you'll agree to explain to me why you have burdened me with knowing all this.''

She stared at him. Then, her hand flew to her mouth. "I—*have* burdened you, haven't I? Oh, what a ghastly burden I've given you! What will you do?''

"I'm not sure," he said. "My mother died when I was too young to grieve, or even to realize her death. I don't understand what you've gained by telling me. I assume you had some reason. And, I suppose I should thank you. I've wanted to know about my mother for a long time. I didn't know anything, really, except that she was born in Savannah and—that she was beautiful." He was staring at the ornate handle of the teapot, which had reminded him of Aunt Nassie's silver service. "Living with what you've told me won't be easy. I—hope to manage it. You see, I don't know much about the measure of my own courage yet.''

She clutched her head for an instant with both hands, then dropped them—clasped loosely in a ladylike posture. "Mark Browning, you're very like your mother in appearance, coloring, personality, beauty. But I only knew Melissa as a child. That last statement of yours, about courage, made me think of the woman I hated—Mary Cotting herself. I'm growing old now. I can look back with some sense of disinterest, enough to realize that indeed Mary Cotting was a woman of high courage—perhaps even humility. She never flaunted her courage, nor have you. I forced her to *find* courage. I made life most difficult for her every minute I could. But, in a manner, I did admire her." She took a step toward him. "Can you possibly believe that when your grandmother, Mary Cotting, died, I was glad for her? I see your frown. But think of it this way. She escaped *me* when she died. Even in heaven, if she repented, Mary Cotting will have my husband in a way I'll never have him. Do you see? In a way I'll never have him—not on earth, not through all eternity." She lifted her chin again. "They're all perfectly right about me, you know. I am a very mean-spirited woman. Twisted love, you might say. Isn't hate—twisted love?"

Unconsciously, Mark had taken a few steps toward her. "Will I tire you too much if I ask you—again—why you told me this today, Mrs. Cameron?"

"For—your own sake. I can sense your attachment to my granddaughter. I thought you deserved to know that she's your half first cousin."

Until that moment, Caroline had not entered Mark's mind. His frown came, lingered, then vanished.

"Your mother, Melissa, had that tiny, fleeting frown," Ethel said softly. "She had it when she was still a baby. I wonder if you did." Abruptly, she held out her hand to him. "Mr. Browning, mainly, I told you because I wanted to warn you!"

He made no move toward her extended hand.

"To warn you about Jonathan. About that unpredictable Osmund Kott. People are ugly. *Ugly.* All people."

"I don't happen to believe that."

"Well, they are. Osmund Kott and I may be the ugliest of all. I understand Osmund, do you see? I watched him as a child. I watched from my window upstairs the morning my husband drove away with him as a small boy—to Bethesda Orphanage. Osmund *hated* his father that day. The years at the orphanage deepened his hatred."

"I—I can't take it in that Osmund Kott is—my uncle."

"Just don't allow Caroline to drag you into the dark shadows of her grandfather's life!"

"I'm—already a part of his life," he said. "I'm—his grandson."

"But if you marry into another family, no one need know that. You at least have a chance to escape, that way."

"Mrs. Cameron, what will I be escaping?"

"The ruinous Savannah tongues, should they find out! Jonathan and Osmund!"

"I haven't heard one word against Mr. Cameron and I've been here more than two years. The Mackays know nothing of his relationship with Osmund Kott except that Kott blackmails him. No one knows why. No one here knows this story. I've had to write to the gentleman in New York who operates my father's company—hoping he can tell me something about my mother's Savannah family. No one in Savannah knows."

"Mr. Cameron's lawyer, Mr. Sheftall Sheftall, knows."

"If he does, he keeps it to himself." Mark went toward her. "I'm not afraid. I'm—stunned at what you've told me, but I find I'm not afraid."

She looked so exhausted, his earlier thought of embracing her rushed back.

"I've told you all this—for your own sake. Perhaps for mine. I loved little Melissa."

Except for the slight, perfumed warmth, the thin, old body he held in his arms the next moment might have been lifeless.

In his earlier fantasy of embracing her, she had slipped her arms about his neck. Now, she did not. She was standing stiff as a ramrod, but not pulling away, his arms still about her, when a horse galloped up outside and they heard running footsteps on the veranda.

Ethel Cameron gave him two brisk pats on the shoulder and stepped back just as Caroline burst into the room.

"Mark!" she cried. "Come quickly! Hurry! Something terrible's happened to Mr. Mackay! Hurry!"

# TWENTY-ONE

THERE was scarcely time for words as Caroline and Mark raced out of the house and swung bareback onto her waiting horse.

"The Mackays were taking a pleasure ride in the new carriage—" She held on to Mark's waist as they galloped along. "Mr. Mackay just—stiffened, grabbed his chest, Miss Eliza said, and fainted."

"How did she get him back to the cottage?"

"She drove the team and held him at the same time! How she kept him from falling out, I'll never know. I happened to be at their cottage, working on those curtains that won't hang right."

Her thoughts, as they pounded along the sandy shortcut, were fragmented and frantic. A snatch of breathed prayer: "Dear God don't let Mr. Mackay die! She loves him so much, Mark loves him so much!" Then a stab of dread at what her grandmother might have said to Mark. Then a prayer of gratitude that Mark was there to ride with her, that they would meet together whatever they'd find when they reached the Mackay cottage. How Eliza loved her Robert! How I love Mark! . . . What does a woman do when the man she loves—dies?

They rounded the last bend in the sandy lane that led to the clearing around The Grange cottage. Mark slowed the horse and jumped off, the animal still trotting. He reached for Caroline. For an instant she was in his arms, then they were both running toward the front porch.

As they hurtled up the steep front steps, Eliza Mackay appeared at the door, a finger to her lips. "He's asleep," she whispered. "God is looking after him. Do you know that Dr. George Jones was visiting at the Meins—saw me drive by— saw Robert lying against me in a faint—followed us here? He's with him now." Eliza fell weeping into Mark's arms. "Oh, Mark, he—didn't die," she gasped. "Robert—didn't die. I—I couldn't tell. All the way here in the carriage, I—just held him. He was so—gray. I—couldn't—tell."

"Not many women could have done what you did," Caroline said.

"She's strong," Mark whispered, still holding Eliza—holding her, stroking her back, holding her.

"I think she needs to sit down, Mark. Don't you want to rest a little, Miss Eliza?"

"No!" Mark's voice was so sharp, Caroline felt as though he'd struck her. She said nothing. He went on holding Eliza Mackay in his arms as he might hold an injured child.

"Caroline's right," Eliza said after a time, trying to smile. "I'd better sit down like a lady." She stepped away from his embrace. "After all, I can't just go on letting you keep me upright, Mark. We can all wait here in the porch chairs."

Caroline didn't move at once. She was too intent on Mark's face when Eliza pulled away. He looked bereft, as though he had just suffered a loss too painful to bear. He, too, stood rooted where he had held Eliza, his arms still half extended, accentuating their emptiness. Then, his smile included them both. Caroline's heart squeezed with love for him and dismay at the intensity with which he had held Eliza Mackay. Since their first meeting at the Scarbrough ball, now so long ago, Mark's smile had always brought out the sun for Caroline, no matter how heavy the cloud. She returned the smile now. "I don't think you and I are acting very intelligently, Mark, do you? We're not as strong as Miss Eliza."

"Nonsense," Eliza said. "You're both scared. I've had a few more minutes to take it all in. I've been with him. You're still not quite able to believe it, I'm sure."

Mark led Caroline to a chair that stood a bit apart from the two in which the Mackays always sat. His concern for her was real, but it was the concern of a brother for his sister. Caroline watched him take the chair beside Eliza Mackay and reach at once for her hand.

"I'm here now, Miss Eliza," he said tenderly. "With Dr. Jones's help, you and I will pull him through just fine. We won't *let* anything happen to him. We love him too much."

Eliza held tightly to Mark, nodding agreement, tears on her cheeks.

Deliberately looking away, out over the greening marsh that bordered the river, Caroline told herself, I'm a third leg! Who needs a third leg?

"I guess God knew we just couldn't get along without him," Mark was saying. Those and other intimate, comforting words, still holding Eliza Mackay's hand. "You don't need to try to answer," he whispered. "Just rest, rest."

Caroline began to recognize shame rising in her like a fever. Here they were, faced with the near tragedy of a wonderful man's death, and she was hurt because Mark was trying to comfort a sweet-natured lady whose life had almost been torn apart.

A childlike desire possessed her: She wanted her grandfather, always the safe, comforting presence against any danger that loomed to hurt or frighten her.

Miss Eliza's head lay back against the slats of the tall wooden chair. Mark still held her hand, leaning toward her, watching her intently. Caroline knew the feel of Mark's hand, the young strength of it, the assurance. Any touch from him seemed to spring straight out of his heart. His generous, good heart. Dear God, she prayed, in the strange silence of the spring afternoon, don't let *his* heart stop—ever. He isn't mine, the way Robert Mackay belongs to Miss Eliza, but please, please, never take him from me.

Except for the tension crackling in the Cameron parlor when she had rushed in to drag Mark away, he had shown not one ill effect of his time with her grandmother. Looking at him now, lost in his moment with Eliza Mackay, anyone could see that he had forgotten about Ethel Cameron.

Without opening her eyes, Eliza said, "Dr. Jones is sure it was only a mild heart seizure. He won't die, will he, Mark? You said we won't let him, didn't you?"

"That's right," he murmured. "And we won't!"

Caroline jumped to her feet. "I think I'll ride to Mr. Mein's place. Grandfather's with him there today. They'll both be so worried about Mr. Mackay."

"Good idea." Mark glanced briefly at Caroline.

"I'm so grateful to you, Caroline, my dear, for bringing Mark to me."

All Caroline could think of to say was, "You're welcome."

Mark hurried after her to help her mount, but with a burst of effort, she leaped astride the horse herself and galloped off.

For nearly an hour, seated in Mackay's chair beside Eliza, Mark held her hand in silence, aware of his own pulse. His thoughts careened wildly. They contrasted so utterly with his nearly motionless body, he felt as though he might explode. For those moments in which he had held Eliza in his arms, trying to absorb the ghastly truth that his friend Mackay could die, he had almost forgotten what Ethel Cameron had told him. Within a matter of minutes, his life had been split down the middle; the sharp, pitiless axe of her tale had cleaved his identity—even to himself—as surely as an axe cleaves a pine log. A slender, stiff old lady had splintered almost everything, except his place in the lives of both Mackays and the children.

Sitting there, trying to be perfectly quiet, he felt conscious of his own arms. His own arms, which had felt the strangely scented, unyielding body of Ethel Cameron—and Eliza. What a price to pay—Mackay's frightening illness—but at long last he had, for those pain-filled, ecstatic moments, held Eliza in his arms. Eliza, willingly in his arms because she needed him.

Ethel Cameron told me the whole story.

Eliza clung to me, let me hold her, needed me.

Too much. Too much, too fast. *I am Osmund Kott's nephew. . . . Jonathan Cameron is my grandfather. . . .*

Mrs. Cameron told me the whole story. Too much. Mackay is so ill. Eliza is so afraid of losing him. I'm afraid, too. Of losing Mr. Mackay and of knowing about poor, dead Mary Cotting's love for Jonathan Cameron. Of Cameron's helpless love for dead Mary Cotting, my grandmother . . .

If only he could be beside Mackay, he thought crazily, matching his energetic steps, the two friends walking to work together as though nothing unusual had happened. As though Mackay were not deathly ill and Ethel Cameron had never broken her silence.

He longed to draw in a deep, deep breath of spring air. He dared not. Eliza's eyes were closed, but she would surely hear and want to know if she could help him in any way. Yes, dear Eliza, you can help me by being here, by touching. He thought the words so earnestly, he marveled that she did not respond. Her closed eyelids fluttered. She was not sleeping. He must ask nothing of her from now on, demand no time that she did not offer. If his own world fell entirely apart because of who he now knew himself to be, *Eliza must not know*. Not anytime soon.

*Was* he still himself? Did knowing that his mother was the blood sister of Osmund Kott change Mark himself? How different might he have been had little Melissa Cotting been allowed to live out her childhood at Knightsford in the same house with the Camerons? Would she even have met Mark Browning, Sr.? Would he, Mark, be in the world at all?

The nightmare tea party in the Cameron parlor had seemed even to wipe Aunt Nassie from his life. His father, now more than ever, was a stranger. The spacious Philadelphia house had been part of a safe dream from which he had suddenly been jarred awake. He thought of the old wooden fence at Yale, but the faces of his classmates who had carved their names there had dimmed and blurred. Even Savannah and the comfortable, rambling Mackay house seemed far, far away.

There appeared to be no present to which he could return, except Eliza resting in the next chair. Nothing could induce him to drop her firm, square little hand, but his own strength was gone. He was tired to the marrow of his bones. He was holding Eliza's hand for his own sake.

A door at the back of the cottage opened softly and closed. Steady, quiet footsteps moved along the bare floor of the back hall and across the parlor carpet to the front door. Eliza leaped to her feet.

"Doctor!"

George Jones, as stylishly dressed and as impressive as he had been at that long-ago first meeting on the *Eliza,* came out onto the tiny porch. "Calm yourself," he said, his voice firm. "Your husband is sleeping quite naturally now. His pulse is almost back to normal. The rhythm good and strong."

A good, strong heart rhythm suited Robert Mackay, Mark thought irrelevantly, steadying Eliza as she slumped, relieved, against him.

"Thank you," she whispered. "Oh, Dr. Jones, how can I ever thank you? You're—leaving now?"

The intelligent, piercing eyes seemed to stab at her. "Listen to me, Eliza Mackay. Your husband came very close to his grave today. Leaving? Even if I didn't know and revere the man, I wouldn't leave him! He's a critically sick patient. My place is here." Wearily, he removed his small, round, gold-framed spectacles and rubbed his eyes. "The trouble is, we don't know much about what to do for the human heart when it's in trouble." He replaced the spectacles and peered at Mark. "I'm glad you're here, Browning. Watch over this dear and loyal lady. She probably saved her husband's life getting him back here as she did."

"I don't know how she managed," Mark said. "Except that there's no one on earth like her."

"Nonsense. What about feeding my husband, Doctor? Will he be able to have some gruel—or tea—anything this evening?"

"Not a bite. Let him sleep. That's God's medicine and He knows all there is to know about hearts. He should. He created them. I notice Mackay has a bit of a roll around his waistline, anyway. Be good if he lost ten or fifteen pounds."

The sun, lowering slowly behind the cottage, cast—not the usual coppery red glow on the pines in front, but a soft, pale-golden sheen that picked out, Mark thought, every long, dark-green needle. A mockingbird chose a quiet-voiced warbler to imitate. The trio on the porch spoke almost in whispers.

"I have a prescription for *you*, Mrs. Mackay," Jones said.

"For me? If he's all right, so am I."

"Don't be too sure. You had a traumatic experience driving your husband here, alone and terrified. You may well find when you try to sleep, your body won't lie still." He laid a hand on Mark's shoulder. "You have this fine, strong young man now while you're up and about. You have him to lean on. Loneliness and anxiety may come once you try to sleep. I plan to mix you a light dose of laudanum."

"I refuse it!"

"Miss Eliza . . ."

"You heard me, both of you. I'll be just fine. If Robert isn't going to leave me, I'll be fine." She was staring out toward the lighted pines. Mark tightened his grip on her arm. "Robert's —my life," she said to no one in particular.

"Browning, I hope you didn't have an engagement with your young lady over at the Camerons'," Dr. Jones said as Mark led Eliza back to the chair and eased her into it.

"What, sir?" He glanced absently at Jones, then went back to watching Eliza. Her dear face seemed suddenly drained of all its blood. "Might she faint, Doctor?"

"I think not, now that you've made her sit down again. Fetch a basin of cool water and keep her forehead and face refreshed for a time."

"Oh, yes, sir!" He hurried into the house.

"Don't give the boy a bad time, Eliza," Jones said when Mark had gone inside.

She stared at him. "I wouldn't think of doing that!"

"You will if you try to do more than you're able. Don't forget that you and I know a secret no one else has any idea about. You'll harm yourself if you don't rest, and you could also harm your baby."

She nodded, a weak smile softening her face. "I'd planned to tell Robert on the carriage ride today. I'll wait now until he's much better to tell him. It will help him get well. He's always so happy when a child is coming."

"You'll know the right time to tell him."

Mark returned with a basin of cool water and a linen towel. On his knees beside her, he wrung out the towel and laid it on her forehead, first brushing back the light-brown curls he loved.

"Thank you, Mark, dear."

"That'll help," the doctor said. "But, son, if I were you, I'd just cool the towels, lay them on her head—but then take your own hand away. It warms the towel too quickly. You don't need to hold the compress in place."

Embarrassed, Mark jerked back his hand. "I'm sorry, Miss Eliza. I guess I didn't realize."

"Your hand feels good on my head." She leaned back against the chair. "Let's go against the doctor's orders. You can change the towel more often. I—like your hand just where it was."

Jones chuckled. "All right, pamper her, Browning. She deserves it. Say, you didn't answer my question about the Cameron girl. Were you planning to call on her this evening? If so, I can stop at Knightsford on my way back to Mein's and explain why you won't be there. I'm sure she and her grandfather are at home by now."

For the life of him, Mark couldn't remember whether or not he had told Caroline that she could expect him this evening. "Uh, well, if you don't mind, sir. It couldn't do any harm for you to stop. I'd be ever so grateful. But I thought you weren't leaving Mr. Mackay anytime soon."

"I'm not. Not for an hour or two." He smiled. "Granted, I may be a little late delivering your message to pretty Miss Caroline, but it will be delivered sooner or later. Don't worry about her. She's a strong young lady. She's had to be. If you'll excuse me now, Mrs. Mackay, I'll go back to my patient."

Still on his knees beside her, Mark removed the towel, redipped it in the cool water and, after giving her his best smile, placed it again over her eyes and forehead. "We're going to be just fine, Miss Eliza," he said. "We're all going to be just fine."

"Mark? What did Ethel Cameron want?"

This was the last question he had expected at a time like this. Desperately, he tried to think what to say.

"Did she have a special reason for demanding that you have tea with her? Or was it just one of her—peculiar quirks?"

"It—it must have been one of her quirks," he said lamely.

"Well, what did you talk about all that time?"

"Oh, she—she told me about how her marriage to Jonathan Cameron had been arranged by their two families in order to enlarge the plantation holdings. I—I guess she hasn't always been so cold to him as she is now."

Eliza waited to answer, then she said, "I see. I shouldn't have been nosy. I was, wasn't I?"

"Oh, Miss Eliza, you have a right to know anything about anything I do!"

She whisked the towel away so she could look at him. "Mark Browning, I have not. That's ridiculous. Poor Ethel." She smiled at him. "I think I know why she wanted to be with you."

"You do?"

She shook her head yes. "You impressed her. And—" The smile faded. "Any woman who has so isolated herself from life as she has, might literally grab at the chance for an hour alone with you. You're a very appealing young man, you know."

"You said that, I didn't," he teased.

"And I should know. You've been like a rock to me this afternoon. I couldn't have—held up at all without you."

He dipped the towel again, wrung it out and placed it quickly over her eyes. It was better that she not see his face. More than anything, he wanted to be a rock for Eliza. His heart reached toward her in gratitude. Even in the midst of her own fright and anxiety, she had given him a way out of any more talk about his visit with Ethel Cameron. He was far from ready to discuss it with anyone. Until he could sort things out, until his own heart felt quieter, he preferred to carry the new burden alone.

He was still kneeling beside her, and his eyes never left her face. She must be exerting a tremendous effort right now not to show too much worry—for his sake. For love of her, he would find the strength to carry his new burden with enough grace and courage so that she would not have to give him an added thought. He would find a way to pretend that, except for Mackay's critical illness, things were as hopeful and happy for him as they had been when everyone woke up that morning.

God knew he longed to tell her. His need for Eliza's understanding and counsel rose every few minutes in his throat like thirst. Even more, he longed to be able to tell Mackay, who would take it all as seriously as would Miss Eliza, who would care as deeply, but who could also be counted on to set the whole ugly matter into perspective. Mackay would be able to calm the new, strange fear Mark had experienced since the moment he'd known that from now on, he would be the vortex of the mystery that had surrounded Jonathan Cameron for more than forty years.

He freshened the towel again and they exchanged reassuring smiles. For a long moment, he waited even to return to his thoughts, for fear she'd sense the turmoil. Her grip on his hand loosened. He hoped she'd fallen into a light sleep.

Mark allowed his gaze to leave her face, to move out over the almost mirror-quiet river. Since he had known Eliza Mackay, less time had been spent in his room back in town looking —when he needed added peace—at his mother's face in the misty portrait. Now, without warning, he longed to see it. A new desolation engulfed him. How could he ever again be calmed by that face? For the first time since Ethel Cameron had told her story, he was struck with the tragedy of Mary Cotting and Jonathan Cameron. Melissa's young, heart-lifting features had for far too long meant only wistful happiness. If he could see her face this minute, would it help? Would the portrait ever help again?

He had gone to tea with Ethel Cameron at four o'clock. The gold watch his father had given him during their last visit showed that nearly four hours had passed. Hours in which his personal universe had been jolted apart—by Mackay's illness and by Ethel Cameron's tragic story. Story? *Fact.*

My mother was illegitimate. Not unheard of among the working class, and my grandmother was an indentured servant. . . . A working-class woman. He tried the phrase and could honestly say that it had no effect whatever. He felt no sting. Truthfully, until now, he had not given that part of the story a thought. Mary Cotting was probably better educated from her wide reading than the typical society lady. "She read incessantly," Ethel Cameron had said. "So much so that I had to put a stop to it when possible or I'd never have received my finished sewing, do you see? I—rather sympathized with her reading, actually. I have . . . kept my sanity, in fact, through books."

His heart moved toward the brittle woman in her fine dress and her empty life. What was the real difference between her need to read in order to keep her sanity and Mary Cotting's need to escape the lonely anguish of her life? The young, pretty English girl whom Jonathan Cameron loved, Mark supposed, would always be, to him, merely a person named Mary Cotting. Not his own grandmother. He had lived his life without grandparents. The stern face of Grandfather Browning, dead before Mark was born, had merely been a reminder that there was a prosperous business in the family because the old man had lived. Oddly, he'd never seen a portrait of Grandmother Browning, and neither his father nor Aunt Nassie spoke of her except to say that she had come from a long line of ministers.

Could the appealing face in the portrait hanging now in his Savannah room ever be, to him, Mary Cotting's daughter? Jonathan Cameron's daughter?

Would he ever again be able to spend an easy, social time with Jonathan Cameron, the beloved gentleman who had lived all these years with the agonizing truth locked inside? How had Mr. Cameron managed what must have been life-shattering grief when spirited Mary Cotting died of consumption? Who had comforted him?

The sky over the longleaf pines was darkening now, was almost colorless. He could no longer see Eliza's features clearly, but into the depth of his being *somewhere*—his heart? his mind? his spirit?—a clear, quiet light slowly began to beam. Eliza's eyes, which could always comfort him, buoy him, were still closed. Yet, an untroubled, definite quiet, a light-filled quiet, was moving steadily through him. Light was leaving the sky and slowly entering him, leading his thoughts into new places: If Aunt Nassie had been right about God, she and Mark's father were together again right now, perhaps talking it all over. If Aunt Nassie and her brother were together, then Mary Cotting and her child Melissa were reunited, too. Jonathan Cameron's old age was now blessed by Caroline.

Were the only two real victims Ethel Cameron and Osmund Kott?

Both had been unable not to allow bitterness to twist their souls out of shape.

*"Isn't hate—twisted love?"*

Osmund Kott was to be pitied, too, Mark was sure, but even in this new, unexpected clarity, Mark still found Kott easier to fear, to dread, than to pity. Not so Ethel Cameron. Somehow, in a way he didn't understand, he knew that he could be with her again. Could, at least, let the strange, stiff, admittedly mean woman see by his manner and his smile, perhaps even by his words, that what she had told him was *not* going to destroy his life.

He could almost hear Aunt Nassie say, "Mark, go right on! That was all in the past. Your life is now—and in the future."

As he tested himself on geography and arithmetic and history as a boy, before Aunt Nassie was to give him an examination, he now silently tried himself out on several tough facts: Osmund Kott's mother was my grandmother. *All right.* Osmund Kott is my uncle. *All right.* Jonathan Cameron is not only Caroline's grandfather, he is my grandfather, as well. By some means, which he didn't need to know at this moment, that would be all right, too.

Darkness had filled the sky. The pines had vanished into it. He touched Eliza's hand. "Should we go inside?" he whispered. "It might be damp for you out here. Grange Annie has lighted candles in the back parlor. I can see their reflection from here. I could spread a pallet for you on the sofa."

She took the towel from her eyes. "You sound so grown up, Mark. So in charge of me. I like it. I—think I must have slept a little."

"Dr. Jones is still with him. I'm sure that's a good sign," he said.

"You are? Why?"

"If anything had changed for the worse, he'd have told us. Would you like for me to tiptoe back to your bedroom and ask?"

"No." She squeezed his hand. "No, we're going to be obedient. George Jones says Robert needs sleep. I've been able to sit out here, like a lump, for that reason. We'll stay here. It's all I can do for him. Mark?"

"Yes, ma'am?"

"I do think I'd like a cup of tea."

His heart singing, as though by asking she'd given him a gift, he hurried softly to the kitchen, where big-boned Grange Annie sat waiting, too. He asked for the tea.

"You go back to her," Annie whispered, her small brown eyes swelled from weeping. "My heart bleed for Miss Eliza. I done work for the Mackays no more'n a few months, but they got their hands round my heart. Both of 'em got their hands round my heart! I be thankin' the Lord that sweet lady got you to be with her, Master Mark. Her own is too young. I been talkin' to the Lord."

Mark gave her a hug. "You know, I believe you have been praying, Annie. And do you know why I believe it? Because in the last twenty minutes or so, I've begun to feel that whatever comes, we're all going to be all right. You'll bring her tea when it's brewed?"

"An' some for you. Biscuits an' my jelly, too."

Tiptoeing back down the hall toward the porch, Mark marveled at how calm he felt. The tide of turmoil was subsiding. Beyond the curiously timed sense of calm, there was also a new goal at hand: being all both Mackays needed him to be. In their separate ways, the Mackays had their hands around his heart, too, needing him, while also giving him strength.

# TWENTY-TWO

FROM the window of his planter's office downstairs in the Knightsford big house, Jonathan watched for Caroline every afternoon when she returned from her daily trips to The Grange. Dr. Jones had stayed on at Mein's for two extra days, but was now back in Savannah. A week had passed since Mackay's attack and Cameron felt embarrassed that he had not paid him a visit. He had not gone because Caroline thought it best that she ride the daily four miles or so without him. The girl was the apple of his eye, and he had long been convinced that the best way an older person could show love to a younger was to work at remembering what it had been like to be young.

"You know Mrs. Mackay will be sitting beside his bed," Caroline had explained, almost too carefully. "Dr. Jones told us that no other visitors are allowed in Mr. Mackay's room. And, oh, Grandfather, you know she wouldn't *want* to leave him to be polite—even to you! Not even for a few minutes. I can go every day. Mark will tell me exactly how the patient's getting along and I can report straight to you."

He glanced at the clock. A quarter past five. Caroline usually rode up around five. Today she'd taken a dewberry cobbler from the Knightsford kitchen. Perhaps she'd stayed to have some with Mark and Miss Eliza.

Still at his office window, Cameron saw his granddaughter break through the thicket at the north end of the big house and hand over her horse to the groomsman. But instead of flying inside to tell him of her visit, he watched her walk away slowly, head down, toward the river.

His first impulse was to hurry outside after her, to find out

if Mackay was worse. He curbed the impulse. The first thing
Caroline would have done, if Robert's condition had wors-
ened, would have been to rush indoors to tell him. It's something to do with Caroline herself, he thought. If she isn't
seriously in love with the Browning boy, then I know nothing
of love—and something is giving her pain. He sighed. After all
the years, Jonathan Cameron still loved. He ran a hand
through his thick, silver hair. Time did seem to be going by
faster now, though. He was glad. They had asked God's forgiveness together right after little Melissa was born. Mary Cotting would be waiting for him in the next world.

From the window he kept Caroline in sight. She was
standing now on the dock, her wide-brimmed yellow straw hat
hanging from one hand, its green ribbons as limp as her lovely
shoulders.

It was still warm and humid outside, but from habit,
Jonathan slipped into his white linen jacket. I know I'm not
just imagining that the child is troubled, he told himself as he
walked across the wide lawn, carrying his cane. Of course,
Mackay could be worse or, God forbid, dead. Caroline, were
that true, would be devastated for Mrs. Mackay. He quick-
ened his step.

"I might have known you'd come out," Caroline said when
he reached the dock. "You're a fussbudget." She kissed him
lightly on the forehead.

"Is Mackay worse, my dear? I guess not, since you called
me a fussbudget. I'm relieved." He breathed deeply, inhaling
the scent of the river and its black marsh mud. "An enormous
quantity of joy would go out of life for everyone who knows
Robert Mackay, should he die."

"Mark all but worships him."

"I know. Mackay's been good to the young man. I'm sure
he's like a father to Mark." His dimming eyes moved out
across the water. "Eliza, I hope, is like a mother to him."

He could feel her eyes on him.

"If you're so sure Mr. Mackay is like a father to Mark, why
is it that you only *hope* Miss Eliza is like a mother?"

"I do declare, Caroline, if you were a young gentleman, I'd
urge you to become a lawyer!"

"That's no answer."

She had completely misunderstood. He had been remembering Mark's real mother, little Melissa. What Caroline imag-

ined he meant, he had no idea. "My comment, my dear, has been blown all out of shape. If I used the word 'hope' regarding Eliza, I was merely thinking of her responsibility all day long to her own children. Women often don't have time to be a mother to anyone outside their own brood, you know."

"Oh," she said.

He vowed to be more prudent. Old age was bringing carelessness. She seemed surprisingly relieved. "You haven't told me how Mackay feels today, young lady."

"I didn't see him and I wouldn't allow Miss Eliza to leave him. Mark says he's much, much better, though. He and Miss Eliza have taken turns sitting beside his bed the last few nights. Just in case. Mark says he takes light food. And sends his apologies to us all—and to the Meins—for 'turning up his toes,' as he put it. He'd looked forward to the Meins' dinner party last night. Mark says Mr. Mackay was furious when he learned that the party had been canceled because of him."

"Mackay should not allow himself to be upset. To fret."

"That's why Mark's going back to Savannah. You see, the children are expecting their parents to come home sometime Saturday."

"They haven't been told, I suppose."

"No. Mark's going to explain it all to them himself. The Mackay children adore Mark."

The old man smiled at her, slipped an arm around her waist. "And they aren't alone in that, are they?"

Without warning, she began to sob, her face buried in the white linen of his jacket. He said nothing, but stood holding her, soothing her, waiting until the weeping slowed.

"There," he murmured, handing her his large white handkerchief. "Do we know what brought that on?"

"Yes," she gasped. "Yes, Grandfather. We know. You know as well as I—how I love Mark! And don't talk to me as though I were ten years old. I'm a woman. I'm—nineteen now." She stepped back. "With your shoulder so nearby, it makes it too easy for me to be a weeping female. Mark doesn't need one of those."

Cameron took her arm and led her off the dock and onto the tree-shaded lane that ran for a distance along the river, away from the big house. "No, he doesn't need a typical weeping female, but then, you could never be that."

"I don't want to be! Oh, I never want to be. Eliza Mackay is so strong. I can *feel* the pain in her heart. I've never known another woman who loved her husband as she loves Robert Mackay. Her eyes follow every move he makes—even lying in his bed, Mark says. She never lets Mr. Mackay see her weep, but Mark says she cries at night.''

"The shock of a thing like that is dreadful for a woman." Jonathan shook his head. "Dreadful for a man, for that matter. I imagine Mackay would be beside himself were she in that bed instead of him." He paused, struggling to control his own emotions. "They—truly love. Believe me, I know how Mackay would feel were Eliza dangerously ill."

"You do, Grandfather?"

He would have to watch himself! Not once before had he come that close to divulging his secret to Caroline. But suddenly, he was living his own panic again as Mary Cotting lay dying in her little cottage—alone except for the few times he could sneak away from Ethel and hurry to her. Both his legs seemed made of wood then. They were like wood now, this minute. The memory engulfed him: He was once more pushing himself laborious step after laborious step, getting to her even for a few stolen moments—one more frantic attempt to assure her of his love. In the memory, Mary lay dying again, leaving him again! Of all times, during a talk with Caroline . . .

"How do you know the way Mr. Mackay would feel were Miss Eliza in danger of dying?"

The answer was so important, he took the needed time to compose himself. "I've never had reason to say this before, my dear," he spoke at last, hoping to keep his voice steady, "but Mackay loves her the way I have always wished that I—could love your grandmother, Ethel."

She stopped to face him. "I—I didn't know that. I didn't know it—at all." When he said nothing, she took his arm and they began to walk again, more slowly. After a while, she asked, "Do you have any idea why Grandmother demanded that Mark have tea with her?"

He sighed. "I wish I did. As always, I have no ideas about her. Except, at times, almost to pity her."

"I don't even think I pity her."

"I understand."

"You do, don't you? Do you suppose you understand everything?"

He laughed weakly. "I understand—almost nothing. But, Caroline, my dear, try very hard to be patient with Mark."

"What do you mean—patient?"

"So much has happened to the boy in such a few years—ghastly loss, grief, vast financial gain, new work, new city, new friends. He's a remarkably mature young man. Mackay believes he could succeed at anything he put his hand to. But as well as Mackay knows him, he is also very puzzled that Mark seems almost devoid of ambition. Ambition, as we planters and merchants recognize it. Perhaps in time—"

"Oh, that," she said casually. "Just because Mark doesn't go about grubbing for money, striving to be a still bigger financial success, Mr. Mackay and the other men on Factor's Row think he's—peculiar. Well, he isn't. He wants to succeed. He is succeeding. He just isn't bewitched by money or what it can buy. If Mark were poor and I rich, he wouldn't be influenced either way. He wouldn't be after my money and he wouldn't be in awe of me because of it. Mark respects people for their true worth."

"I wonder if—his mother was—like that." Jonathan mused, as to himself.

"His *mother?*"

"Uh—is that what I said, my dear? I meant to say, I wonder if his father was like that."

"Oh, Mark's father was shattered by grief. Who knows what the poor man was really like? Mark told me that his father never once stopped running from his grief. He may not have cared once during all those years that he had inherited the largest shipping firm in the world! He only cared about—love."

"The boy's told you quite a lot about himself, hasn't he?"

"Yes. But I didn't ask. He just told me."

"That's a high compliment."

"Grandfather, I don't want compliments! I want him to love me!"

"He sees you at every opportunity, it seems to me."

"Except—when Miss Eliza needs him."

"Has Mark mentioned marriage, Caroline?"

"Yes." Her answer came at once, with her usual directness. "He asked me once to marry him, at a moment when he was feeling genuinely sorry for me because of Grandmother's meanness."

"And you turned him down."

"Of course I did. I don't want him—that way. I don't need to be rescued. I have you."

"I go back to that word 'patience,' Caroline. Mark Browning spent all his formative years with an aunt. A wonderful lady, according to Mackay, but he never knew, never experienced, a home with a good marriage. Never knew, except from the agony of watching his father grieve, how much the man loved—Melissa."

"Did Mark tell you his mother's name was—Melissa?"

He caught his breath. "I—I guess he must have told me. At any rate, the boy needs time." Their talk had made him unusually tired. "Would you mind if we began to walk back toward the house, my dear? The old legs are a bit stubborn today."

"Fine," she said absently as they turned to retrace their steps. "Grandfather? I've never known what it's like to grow up in a house where there was a good marriage, either."

What strength he had left seemed to drain away. "True," he said softly. "Very true. Your parents did love each other, though."

"But I don't remember them."

"You and Mark have a lot in common, haven't you?"

They walked along for a time in silence, then Caroline said, "Mark took me, along with Miss Eliza, of course, upstairs to see his mother's portrait hanging in his room on Broughton Street. He's so proud—so touched by her beauty, even now. And, Grandfather, she was—lovely!"

"I—I should like very much to see the portrait."

"I'm sure Mark would be glad to show you. But I'm really puzzled that he makes no effort to find out, now that he lives in Savannah, who she really was. Do you realize that he doesn't know his own maternal grandparents' first names? That he just knows his mother's maiden name was Cotting?"

Jonathan felt his heart constrict. "That—that's very sad."

Impulsively, she hugged his arm. "Well, we can't help any of it. Thank you, because I feel lots better now that we've talked—about Mark. You really like him, don't you?"

"My dear, I've never met a young man I liked more. I'm trying to recall when you met Mark."

"Don't you remember, that night at the Scarbroughs' when Mark flattened Osmund Kott with one blow?" She laughed a little. "No wonder we both like him. And isn't it marvelous that Osmund is finally gone? Maybe, if we pray hard, he'll never, never come back to torment you, ever again!"

"Who knows?" He sighed with relief. At least this time, Caroline wasn't going to scold him for having given money to Osmund that last time at the back door of Chatham Academy. Long ago she had given up pleading with him to tell her *why* he bothered with Osmund Kott at all. "As for Mark," he went on, feeling on safer ground, "I not only like him, I'm downright proud of him. Proud to be counted among his Savannah friends. If, indeed, he does so count me."

"Isn't it about time you tended to some business in town?" she asked abruptly.

"Why?"

"I asked first. Isn't there something that needs your attention there?"

Her smile gave him his clue. "Well, as a matter of fact, I'm still plagued by having no factor to handle my affairs. I guess I keep putting off the inevitable. Tired of being turned down."

"You're only turned down because everyone's afraid Osmund might come back again."

He had no strength to hold up his end of an argument about Kott. Obviously she wanted to make a trip to the city. He would keep the emphasis there. "Why do you want to go to town, Caroline, my dear?"

"Well, I'm told Mr. Mackay suggested that I would be far better than Mark at selecting the dresses and shoes and things Miss Eliza will need since they have to stay longer in the country. Mark's going to tell the children about their father tomorrow, but Miss Eliza agrees with her husband that I would—"

Cameron interrupted her with soft laughter. "And I agree with them both. It's downright callous to allow poor Mark to make the trip alone anyway," he teased. "We'll go, too, if you'll promise to remember the word 'patience.' "

Her arms were around him, hugging him. Jonathan felt so glad to see her happy that he forgot his shame at having given in mainly to keep her from saying another word about Osmund.

About midafternoon the next day, after they took the Camerons to Mein's house on Bay in Mark's carriage, he and

Hero rode side by side in the driver's seat toward Broughton Street.

"I know what a jolt it was for you, Hero," Mark said, "finding only me when you expected both Mackays. But I feel Mr. Mackay's going to be all right."

Hero, unashamedly, wiped tears with the back of his hand. "You—you sure, Mister Mark?"

"As sure as anyone could be right now. And I need you to help me keep the children's spirits up. Try to get hold of yourself before we get there, Hero. I don't look forward to telling them. I'll need you and Emphie and Hannah—now, more than ever."

"Yes, sir," Hero said, struggling to assure Mark with a not very convincing smile. "Could we take our time getting there, sir? It give me a chance to settle my heart. There ain't nobody anywhere—like Master Robert." Tears still wet his brown cheeks. "They come—just one in a box, sir, like him."

At the house, Hero took Mark's valises to his room, and at Mark's suggestion, Hannah brought lemonade and ginger cookies to the porch for him and the children. Abnormally quiet, from the moment he told them why their parents did not come home, the four tried at once to cling to him.

"Sit down, all of you," he ordered, trying to sound as casual as possible, but determined to tell them the truth, even five-year-old Kate. "We need a family conference. Gather round."

There was no need to tell them to do that. All eyes were riveted on him: William, even paler than usual; Jack, the picture of Mackay, frowning his worry; Eliza Anne, clinging to Mark's hand; Kate, on his lap before he was quite settled, both arms around his neck.

"Is Mama all right?" William asked first.

"Is Papa going to—die?" Jack demanded.

At that, Kate began to cry and Eliza Anne's large, dark eyes filled with tears.

"No, no, no," he said quickly. "That's the good news I have for you. Your mother is all right, but your father did have a heart seizure."

"What's that?" Eliza Anne wanted to know. "Did Papa's heart—hurt?"

"I expect it did for a few seconds, but he fainted in the carriage while he was driving, fell over against your mother—deadweight—and she proceeded to grab the reins and gallop the horses nearly four miles back to the cottage. The servants helped her get him in the house."

"Could he walk by then?" William asked.

"No, two servants carried him. But Dr. Jones just happened to be visiting the Meins and he came at once. By the time I got there, your father was better and sound asleep."

"Where were you?" William asked.

"Uh—well, I had the honor of being invited to tea that afternoon by Mrs. Cameron."

Jack whistled. "And you went? You weren't scared of her?"

"Scared? No. Why should I be?"

"She's so mean!"

"Well, let's say she's—unusual."

"I didn't think she ever invited anybody," Eliza Anne said, tears still slipping down her cheeks. "Even Mama says Mrs. Cameron's a mystery."

"Who cares about her?" William snapped. "Is our papa still real sick—in bed? Can he walk yet?"

"He can sit up in a chair for a few minutes at a time. Your mother, of course, never leaves him. He's well enough for her to sleep in bed beside him now. Until yesterday, she and I took turns sitting up in his room all night."

"Papa wasn't sick when they went away," Kate said, half to herself. "Will he still be sick when they come home?"

"When are they coming?"

"Well, that's hard to say right now. Dr. Jones says your father will have to rest for a long time before he can come back to the city."

"Maybe another whole week?" Jack asked.

"Oh, longer than that. All summer, I'd think."

A heavy moment passed before William turned and ran from the room and Kate began screaming her protest. Jack, always the brave, manly son, reached for Mark's hand and held it tight.

"William's kind of a sissy," he explained, his own mouth trembling. "He'll go off by himself and cry, probably."

As though not to miss anything important, Kate lowered her crying a bit.

Eliza Anne, still clinging to Mark's other hand, dropped it, marched to the center of the floor and announced with seven-year-old superiority: "Hush, Kate! Mark will be here with us. He'll run our papa's business and—he'll be our—papa. Won't you, Mark?"

Kate was quiet now. "You're absolutely right, honey. I'll certainly be here. I'll do all I can to keep the business going. I can never be—your papa. No one could be. But what do you say to this? I'll be here, I'll work hard, we'll play a lot and read books together—and I'll be your real friend."

Eliza Anne looked straight at him. "But you're already our real friend. Don't you think you could—be just a little more?"

"I'll sure help," Jack said hoarsely.

"I count on you, Jack. William, too."

"You'll have to know sooner or later," Jack said, "if you don't already, that William sort of crumbles when anybody mentions the word—death. Even dead ducks. He's funny that way. Otherwise, he's all right."

"He certainly is," Mark agreed. "After we've had some lemonade and cookies, I'll go upstairs and have a man-to-man talk with William."

Eliza Anne sighed heavily. "It might help some, Mark."

"Yeah. Some," Jack said.

"You won't need to do that." William was back standing in the doorway. "I won't need Mark to do anything special. I'll help as much as anybody."

Eliza Anne passed the cookies, William poured the lemonade, and then the full impact of what had happened seemed to strike them all. For as long as they needed to cry, Mark sat with them and cried too.

Finally, Jack blew his nose hard and noisily. "I never did understand why there have to be—tears."

"Sometimes they just have to come," Mark said as matter-of-factly as he could manage. "They even help."

"I don't make tears very often," William said. "They get kind of locked up behind my eyes."

Eliza Anne held out her hand for Mark's handkerchief, blew, not too daintily, then handed it back to him. "We've cried now," she said. "We won't have to do that again."

Mark could find no words to tell them what their brave acceptance meant to him. Of course they had all cried. No father had ever been a more attractive playmate, no father had ever shown more love, more openhearted attention, more care,

than Robert Mackay had shown his children. Every moment
he had been able to spend with them, he had spent truly with
them, entering into their separate childhood worlds. He would
be the hardest possible father to lose.

But Mark's thoughts, as the children rallied, were of Eliza,
the one woman he could ever love *wholly*. Desperately, he
hoped that she was all right this minute. With Mark, for her
sake, almost every breath had become a prayer for Mackay's
complete recovery. Mark had been so close to Eliza through
the first week of watching the sickroom, of listening for each
dry cough, each groan, he ached now—not knowing how
things were for her. For Mackay, his friend. One thing he
knew: If Mackay was still making progress, Eliza would be all
right.

It gave him pain but also joy to picture her sitting by that
bed, watching. The picture gave him joy because Eliza could
not bear to be any other place. His own feelings seemed almost
beside the point. What did matter was—Eliza.

"When can we go to The Grange to see Mama and Papa?"
Eliza Anne wanted to know.

"Dr. Jones suggested that in about a month—sometime in
late May or early June—seeing all of you might be just what
your father will need."

"I expect it would make him feel better," William said
solemnly.

"If Katie doesn't pull one of her screaming fits," Jack said.

"I stopped pretty soon," Kate said, again almost to herself.

Mark took a deep breath. "You know what? We should all
think about bed early tonight. I have to admit I'm tired. Does
that sound all right?"

"I don't want to go to sleep," Kate said. "I'm afraid something might happen to Papa and I wouldn't know about it!"

"But, Katie, you forget about me," Mark teased. "I've had
a long day and tomorrow will be even longer. You see, Miss
Caroline and her grandfather came to town with me and we're
all going to spread a whopping picnic in our side yard tomorrow afternoon. That means I get up at dawn in order to leave
work early."

Eliza Anne cried, "Oh, I love Miss Caroline!"

"Who doesn't?" Jack wanted to know. "And I guess Mr.
Cameron's a pretty good old fellow, too, in his way."

"I like him especially." William was still solemn. "I'd give almost anything if we had a grandfather with white hair like his. We never did have a grandfather. Did you, Mark?"

The dry scent of Ethel Cameron's potpourri came from nowhere. It was still possible to forget—especially in the face of Mackay's illness—that Jonathan Cameron *was* Mark's grandfather. "I—I never knew my grandfather," he said.

"Did you only have one?"

"No. There were two. But like all of you, I never knew them."

"Does Mr. Cameron always wear white clothes?"

"Why, I don't know, Jack. I guess I've never seen him in anything but white, now that you mention it."

"Papa says it's great that dirty old Osmund Kott's left town," Jack said. "For poor Mr. Cameron's sake. Sometime I think I might just up and ask Mr. Cameron why he lets dirty old Osmund worry him."

"You could ask him tomorrow," Eliza Anne suggested.

"No, no, no," Mark said quickly. "Not tomorrow, not ever. That would be prying. Nosiness. Your mother definitely does not approve of your being nosy. And, Jack, do you really think it's gentlemanly or Christian of you to call Mr. Kott—dirty?"

Jack shrugged. "Aw, I don't mean his face is dirty, except after he's been in jail for a while. Mark? Now that our mother and father are not here, are you our boss?"

He laughed. "I'm your partner. Partners do offer each other advice and help, don't they?"

Jack's bright, sudden smile was beguiling as usual. "I like being your partner." He stuck out his hand. "Shake."

William shook Mark's hand, too, still solemn, then Eliza Anne, and with a loud "me too," Kate grabbed his other hand and pumped so hard they made themselves laugh.

So far, Mark thought, so good.

It helped to know that through the day, even the wakeful hours of the night, Eliza would be praying for them all.

# TWENTY-THREE

ALMOST daily during the next fortnight, Eliza found a way to send a letter to Mark and the children. The best hour of Mark's day had come to be letter-sharing time just before supper.

"Papa is doing better than anyone expected," she wrote in mid-May. "Dr. Jones makes a special trip out here once a week and he is most pleased. He says your father is a true iron man. I never knew a man of iron to be so tender and dear and loving, did you? I have to scold him for wanting to talk too much. He hates having to rest. And vows that it helps him to brag about his children. No visitors are allowed yet, and so he does his bragging to me, which is always likely to make us both laugh, since he agrees that—next to him—I am well acquainted with all four of you, too."

"Boy, I think he's lots better," Jack said. "When he's bragging about us, he's better. That sounds like he's his old self all right."

"I wrote to Mama and Papa today," William said in what for him was a boastful manner. "Miss Caroline sent it for me by one of Mein's servants taking supplies."

"Aw, rats," Jack sputtered. "Now, why didn't I think of doin' that first? After all, you're only one year older."

"Good for you, William." Mark mussed his curly, light hair. "Have you any idea how happy that will make them? Hearing right from you? Is what you wrote a secret?"

"Not especially. I just told them about all of us—"

"Yeah," Jack interrupted, "but I wonder what?"

"None of your business. And I told them how fine it was that Miss Caroline and her grandfather are visiting in Savannah right now because they spend a lot of time here at our house and that I like them both."

"I'll bet you wrote about Miss Caroline, all right," Jack scoffed. "I like her fine, too, but I don't sit around mooning at her the way you do, William."

"Who asked you!"

"I can see, can't I?"

"I also told them that if Mark ever had to get married, I'd agree in a way, so long as he married Miss Caroline Cameron."

"You'd marry her yourself if you weren't only eleven," Jack sneered. "Moony, moony, moony."

Mark laughed, a bit nervously. "That's enough, both of you. I'm not marrying anyone. I do think it was good of you to write, though, William. And I have a surprise. I met Dr. Jones on Bay Street today and he says it will be fine if we all go out to The Grange the first week in June!"

One warm, rainy afternoon, a letter came from Eliza and with it a package. At his desk in the office next to Mackay's empty one, Mark's hands trembled as he broke the seal.

The Grange
26 May, 1815

Dear Mark,

I still miss you. And my heart still overflows with gratitude for your sustaining love and support during that dreadful first week. I am enclosing a letter that you can read to the children, but this is for you only.

I had an unexpected visitor this morning. In fact, the last person I'd *ever* expect—Ethel Cameron. She came in their bright green gig, driving the horse herself. Dressed in a fashionable gray driving suit, she sat sedately on the edge of one of our old parlor chairs and refused refreshment of any kind. As usual, she wasted no words. Of course, she asked after Robert, gave me her best wishes for his recovery and directly inquired after you. I scarcely knew what to say because I didn't know what she wanted to hear. So, I told her how dear you are to us all, how we depend upon you in every way, especially now, that you are handling the business

with your usual excellence. She rose, nodded her thanks
and handed me a book for you—quite an old book—of
Shakespeare's sonnets. I have wrapped it and am sending it with this letter. I could not resist leafing
through, but found nothing but the inscription, *For
Mary*, on the flyleaf. Who Mary was, I have no idea.

Something in Ethel's manner touched me so that I
wanted very much to do as she asked. It is a very pretty
little volume—white vellum with gold lettering. At
least, I know you love the Shakespeare sonnets. I love
them, too.

> Thank you, dear Mark,
> Y<sup>r</sup> afft
> ELIZA MACKAY

Mark had unsealed the package, but had not yet looked at
the small book, when a soft knock came at his office door. He
was annoyed for a moment and did not call out as he sat running his fingers over the smooth curve of the volume's vellum
spine. The knock was repeated. Quickly, he turned to the flyleaf and saw in a pale, slanting script: *For Mary*.

He sank back in his chair. The Mary of the inscription had
to be Mary Cotting! *How* did Ethel Cameron come by Mary
Cotting's book?

When the knock was repeated, still soft, but more insistent,
he called out, "Yes, come in."

He laid the book on the corner of his desk, the door opened
quietly and Jonathan Cameron said, "Good morning, son."

Mark stood to welcome him. "I'm honored, sir. Do sit
down. We needed the rain we're having today."

"Correct," Cameron said, easing himself into the chair on
the other side of Mark's sturdy desk. "Just hope it doesn't
rain too long. A rice planter always has to pray for enough dry
days to bake out the mud for the June planting. There's nothing so aggravating as our marsh mud turned to glue on the bit
of a seed drill."

"I'd like to watch you plant your rice seed sometime.
Caroline tells me it's quite exciting. Rice is temperamental, I
take it?"

"It is, indeed." Cameron smiled proudly. "And that granddaughter of mine is a born planter!"

"I know she stays right with you and your field hands through the whole process, but I assumed it was because she's so devoted to her grandfather."

Had Jonathan Cameron come merely for a visit? To tell him something about Caroline? This was his first time to see Cameron face to face knowing that he was his grandfather. Mark's heart pounded. Can a man pray two ways at once? he wondered. Can he beg God to find out nothing more and, at the same time, to find out—everything? The relationship with Cameron—as it had been since Mark began to see Caroline— was comfortable. With all his heart, he longed to keep it that way. Yet he also longed to tell this long-suffering, good man that Mark Browning would be proud to have it known that he was Jonathan Cameron's grandson.

"Caroline and I are as close as can be," Cameron was saying, "but it's more than her liking to be with me that causes her to wade about the fields at planting time. Why, she's been known to get out of her bed in the black of night to be on hand when a newly planted field is flooded for the first time by the tide." He shook his head in proud approval. "I marvel that one so young and beautiful could be satisfied out in the country as she is."

"You bring her to town often, though," Mark said, his high, stiff collar feeling tight in the damp heat.

"As much as I enjoy discussing my granddaughter, I came here on another matter," Cameron said. "To me, a highly important one."

Mark felt suddenly afraid.

"Could you spare half an hour or so for me?" Cameron asked.

"Of course, sir."

"My mission is business, strictly business. I don't want your response to what I have to say to be influenced in any way by your—friendship with Caroline or with me."

Instant relief flooded Mark's mind.

"As you know," Cameron went on, "my longtime friend William Mein grew weary, lost his patience entirely with the steady flow of trouble he was forced to share with me because of—the man known as Osmund Kott."

He makes no bones about that part of the truth, Mark thought.

"I am in need, rather desperate need, of a new factor. I'll be honest with you. I've talked, since Caroline and I have been in town, with both Habershams, with Scarbrough, with Petit de Villers—and others." The hint of a helpless smile creased his tanned, kind face. "No one wants me as a client. It has nothing, I'm sure, to do with my being difficult to work with. My business reputation is sound. I pay my debts as well as the next man. I do consider my factor's unique problems. No one wants—Osmund. Purposely, I tried to persuade all the others to take me on as a client—before asking you. Mackay has told me that you have no experience as a factor. He also has no doubt that you would be first-rate at the work. But he did beg me not to ask you. I had a long talk with him the afternoon before he fell ill. I know why he is against your doing it. He loves you like a son. He knows Osmund. But, Mark, please help me. I need you. My crop will be ready one of these days. If you don't help me, what will I do?"

Becoming his grandfather's factor had never once crossed Mark's mind. Quite unexpectedly, he heard himself ask, "Did—Caroline urge you to ask me, sir?"

The sadness that filled the old man's eyes caused Mark to despise what he'd just done. He had not only posed an ungallant question where Caroline was concerned, implying incorrectly that she was pushing for a closer relationship; he had also insulted Jonathan Cameron's business acumen. Cameron had been a successful planter for far too many years to allow the romantic whim of a granddaughter, even such a beloved granddaughter, to influence a business decision.

"Don't answer my question, sir," Mark blurted. "I apologize for it. I beg you to forget I even asked it. I know she would not do that and I know you would not be swayed by such a thing." In the stifling warmth of his office, Mark felt sick. He took out his handkerchief and wiped his forehead. The linen, too, was warm from the heat of his body. If he, at his age, felt ill living through this tense moment, how must the old gentleman feel?

Mark reached for the aging, though elegant, hand that lay quietly on the desk. "Yes, Mr. Cameron. Yes, I'll be your factor. In fact, I want to be. I know you'll be patient with my inexperience, but helping you is—is—the least I can do!"

A quick, anticipatory smile played about the beautiful old face. Cameron grasped Mark's hand, evidently reading nothing into what Mark had said.

In a lightning flash, Mark saw the semblance of the same anticipatory smile that graced the portrait of his mother. In another flicker of time, he was feeling at home with that half smile. Familiar with it. He had seen it since he was a little boy, every day, every night.

"You've no way of knowing—no way at all,". Cameron said with feeling, "what you've just done for me, son. Caroline and I were going back home tomorrow should you have turned me down. I'll stay now and if you can see me, will bring my records to you." He got slowly to his feet. "I've taken too much of your time. And frankly, at my age, a man can tolerate only so much—emotion. Undoubtedly, that sounds like the statement of someone losing his grip." The bent shoulders straightened. "I assure you, I'm not losing it. I—I just—" He broke off. He had seen the white book.

Mark, now standing, too, followed Jonathan Cameron's gaze to the corner of the desk. The smile had vanished from the elderly man's face. In its place, a blank stare of disbelief.

The frail hand, trembling noticeably, reached across to pick up the volume. He opened it at once to the flyleaf. In a moment he closed the book, held it ever so briefly, then laid it down.

Desperately wanting to help, Mark said lamely, "I see you're fond of Shakespeare, too. My Aunt Nassie reared me on him."

When Cameron looked at Mark again, his eyes were brimming. "Yes," he said, with surprising firmness. "I've always been a devotee of the Bard's work. I—I was just interested in seeing—that particular edition."

Is he going to ask me where I got it? Mark wondered, the stuffy room closing in still more.

"I've seen and—read from that same edition," Cameron said, "a long time ago. A very long time ago."

It was all Mark could manage not to throw his arms around Jonathan Cameron and cry: "I know, Grandfather! I know—about all of it! I know—about you and me. I've come to love you, sir. I have, I have. *Today*."

When the schooner from New York docked that afternoon, there was a letter for Mackay with the return address of Mr. James Parsons. Mark stood on the Mein and Mackay wharf in the rain for a long time, trying to decide what to do.

Why would Parsons be writing to Mackay? It had been so long since he had sent his own letter to Parsons asking to see him. What possible reason would he have for writing Robert Mackay now? Not a business reason. Mark knew there had been no contracts with Browning World Shipping since the war ended.

The purple ink was blurring in the drizzle. He hurried inside. In his office, the door closed, he sat for a long time—uncomfortable in his damp clothes—staring at the unopened letter. One flick of his thumb would break the seal. That was out of the question. The letter was for Mackay. Parsons could have nothing to say to Robert Mackay that would matter seriously, anyway.

He grinned to himself. The temptation had been very slight, actually. He would simply enclose the letter when he made his next report to the Mackays concerning the business and the children.

Dr. Jones brought Mark's letter to The Grange when he made his weekly medical call. "He's doing fine," the doctor assured Eliza, "but let him rest for an hour or so after I've gone before you read young Browning's letter to him. He'll revel in it. He tells me every word in those letters. I want his periods of excitement to be well spaced."

Twice, after Dr. Jones left, she peeked in at Robert. He was sleeping, but to give herself something to anticipate, she purposely did not open the letter until he called to her.

"Coming, darling," she said, and hurried into his sunny room. "The rain's stopped. We could even have a sunset after a while." He held out his arms. "You're a sleepyhead . . . a beautiful sleepyhead," she said, kissing him. "I love you today, dearest friend."

He was pale, his large, dark eyes blue-circled; his normally square, muscular hands felt weak and dry when she held them, but he was better. He was joking more every day.

"I'm kissing more expertly, don't you think?" he asked.

"Oh, every time! But then, you've kissed me more expertly for nearly sixteen years, sir." She held out the letter. "Look what Dr. Jones brought from town."

"Aha! A letter from Mark! What would we do without that boy? I'm longing to see our children, but I don't worry about them at all, do you? I worry about Mark, though. He must be so tired. Handling both his work and mine, climbed over every night by four wildcats whom he takes on countless picnics, fishing expeditions, hikes—even for swimming lessons. How does he keep up with it all? *And*—Caroline.''

''He's young and his motives are so truly good, he never wastes any energy feeling sorry for himself. That's his secret, remember? You said so once.'' She grew suddenly serious. ''Mark has had so much thrown at him in such a short time.''

''Yes,'' he teased. ''Like seventy-five thousand dollars a year.''

She smacked his arm. ''Shame on you.''

''Read the letter. I love the boy as much as you love him. I'm just more penurious. But you adore me anyway. Read, woman!''

The seal broken, she unfolded the page bearing Mark's familiar, clear handwriting. When she did, the Parsons letter fell to the floor. ''What's this?''

''What, what, what?''

''A letter for you, dear, from James Parsons!''

He groaned. ''Oh, Eliza, now you have to let me talk about that whole thing. I've tried half a dozen times since I've been dumped here like a—sack of rice. I'm fine today. Perfectly well enough to reach our decision. I feel like a heel keeping Parsons waiting for my answer all this time.''

''Sh! Try to be a little quiet. Let me read his letter to you before we discuss anything about what we know about Mark's mother and the whole Cameron affair.'' She broke the seal on Parsons's letter and began to read: '' 'My dear Mr. Mackay, Since I have not heard from you in reply to my letter concerning the somewhat strange story of your associate, Mr. Mark Browning, I thought it best to write this brief note to let you know I have been called at once to Liverpool, then the West Indies for perhaps as long as seven or eight months. Our offices there face some new problems still connected with the resumption of shipping since the war with Britain. In recent days, with more time to think it through, it comes to me that perhaps there is no need to rush to tell young Browning the whole disturbing story. He may take it well, he may not, but might it not be best to give him more time to settle himself as a citizen of Savannah? I tend strongly toward this decision. If you disagree, because of my absence from the country, you will have to tell him. As long as Kott is here, why not leave well enough alone? You may reach me at Browning World Shipping, Liverpool, until the end of this year. I should be back in the United States by late spring of the new year 1816. The Liverpool office will know my whereabouts. I do not sail for three days and will write to young Mr. Browning before I go. I feel some guilt that so much time has passed since his letter asking to meet with me. Your obedient servant, James Parsons.' ''

Mackay shook his head. "Parsons, who doesn't even know Mark, may just be wiser than we are. Is there really any urgency, Eliza, to tell the boy all this? He certainly has his hands full enough with me laid up."

"I'd give anything if he *never* had to know," she said. "But, dearest, we have to be sure we're not still stalling."

"Of course we've been stalling! Except for a few weeks there when I didn't feel so well—"

"Didn't feel so well! Robert, you—you were terribly ill. I have no guilt at all for not bringing it up during that dreadful time."

"As long as Kott's not here, people do tend to forget about him. Maybe we should wait until Parsons comes back next year. After all, except for Jonathan Cameron, who in the whole city knows the story but us?"

"Ethel Cameron must know it. Robert, how could she *not* know?"

He shrugged. "Say, I'd forgotten that the very hour I turned up my toes that day, old Ethel and Mark were having tea! Did you ever find out why she did that?"

"I asked Mark. He said she just talked about how she hadn't always been so cold to her husband. About their arranged marriage."

"Funny thing to tell a young man she scarcely knows. What else?"

"That's about all. I didn't press him. I think she's just lonely. Mark certainly hasn't acted as though she told him anything disturbing."

"No, he hasn't. Listen, let's keep it to ourselves until we hear again from Parsons. When I'm back to writing letters again, I'll let him know at his Liverpool office that we decided to take his advice."

"You're sure?"

"I'm very sure. Retelling tales like this can so often cause more trouble."

"All right. There's no advice I value more than yours, dearest."

"And you can be peaceful about it?"

"Yes. I can be. But, Robert, don't you owe Mark some sort of explanation of the letter he enclosed from Parsons? You know he saw James Parsons's name on it before he sent it here."

He scratched his head. "I hadn't thought that far," he said, frowning. "You're right, of course. When he and the children visit us, I'll just mention that Parsons is a fine businessman, that I had a letter urging our firm to think in terms of Browning Shipping the next time we send goods to a foreign port."

"But that won't be quite true, will it?"

"Not quite." He grinned. "I think it will do for the present, though." He pulled himself up on his elbow. "Right now, I want to hear Mark's letter about offspring one, offspring two, offspring three and offspring four. And, Eliza, don't you think it's time to tell the children and Mark that there will be offspring number five early next year?"

"Should I write it in a letter? Or wait to tell them all face to face? They should be visiting us soon."

"Write it! By all means, write it—in today's letter! They need to feel a part of things in our family. Mark's done a magnificent job, but I'm sure taking the children into our confidence on something so important as a new member will help enormously. Now, read Mark's letter to me."

He beamed as she read, picturing it all. They were fine, Mark wrote. Eliza Anne was drawing some quite interesting pictures, William was turning into a bookworm, Jack could now dive quite expertly and Kate—with the forbearance of Emphie in the kitchen—had baked raisin cookies. Best of all, they would be coming soon for a visit.

News of the baby to be born next year did indeed excite the children, especially Kate, who kept insisting that Mark promise to do all he could to capture the stork when the big bird flew down from the sky with the infant in its long bill. Mark uneasily tried to steer Kate onto a different subject, not only for her sake but for his own. Of course he was glad for Miss

*Eugenia Price*

Eliza and for Mackay and the children that there would be a new member in the family. Still, the birth of a baby would mean pain for Eliza, and, daily, Mark's dread of that grew. It had been hard enough watching his friend Mackay suffer. The thought of pain for Eliza was more than he could endure. Women died in childbirth, too. He had never been exposed to the mysterious, frightening experience, but he had heard stories. A classmate at Yale had lost a sister during the birth of her first child. Even the baby had died.

Most of the time he found it possible to keep his two personal worlds apart—almost never touching. In his room at night or in the early morning as he bathed and dressed, he thought often about his client Jonathan Cameron—as his grandfather. To God, when he prayed for the kindly old gentleman, he called him Grandfather Cameron. In that private world he also thought about his grandmother, Mary Cotting, and even about his uncle, Osmund Kott. And in the same secret world, long ago, he had admitted that he loved Eliza Mackay too well. That he went on feeling almost content in loving her as he did, amazed even Mark. With all his young heart and body, he longed to be in Mackay's place, but his devotion to Mackay, his gratitude that the happy, good man was getting well, went on undiminished. If the child Eliza carried now could have been Mark's child—there, inevitably, he chopped off the thought. Thoughts, if nurtured, even if permitted to run their course, could, Aunt Nassie had always told him, begin a destructive life of their own.

He did not have to stop *loving* Eliza Mackay. On Broughton Street or at The Grange, he lived under the same roof with her. So deeply did he treasure his secret attachment, he had no inclination to open the door between the two worlds. He felt as blessed in his outer world—filled with the children and his work and helping the Mackays—as in his private world of thoughts that he could not share with anyone but God.

Only Savannah joined the two. The city itself kept him steady. His two worlds met in this place. Somehow, he did not feel divided.

# TWENTY-FOUR

WHEN Mark took the children for their fourth visit to The Grange in early September, there was double cause for celebration. In the interim since their August trip, Hero had taught William how to handle the sheet on the family boat. At the Cameron dock when William himself eased the boat toward shore, there stood his father, waving both hands high in the air.

"Sir, it's better than Christmas having you up and about again," Mark said as he and Mackay took chairs on the small porch that afternoon. "I thought Jack and Kate might actually jump overboard and swim when they saw you waiting for us today."

"Made them happy, did it? Well, think how it made me feel."

"It certainly didn't seem to do you any harm."

"Of course it didn't. Except for that infernally cautious Doc Jones, I'd have been back at work six weeks ago."

Mark laughed. "I'm glad he made you behave. You look wonderful. And I've never seen anyone as happy as Miss Eliza. She's happier than ever—and more beautiful."

"Mark, she's been a marvel. Carrying a child, too, through it all. I knew her, I thought, before. Not the way I know her now. She's far finer than gold." Mackay scooted his chair, the better to look at Mark's face. "Now, we've covered the children, we've dispensed with me, we've shared our total admiration for my wife. What about you?"

"Oh, working hard, playing hard with the children, learning a lot."

"You'll know so much about our business when I finally get

back in harness, I'll have to hire you as a tutor."

"I seem to learn something new every day. Especially how much I don't know about being Mr. Cameron's factor. I like factoring, though. It's more personal, somehow, than straight merchandising." He paused. "I think I've found out a lot about myself, too."

"Oh?"

He laughed. "I now know that I can do a pretty fair job with four lonely children."

"We'll never be able to thank you for that. They're absolutely devoted to you."

"I—may have children of my own someday, but I don't see how I could love them any more." Then, "Mr. Mackay, is Miss Eliza—getting along all right with the new baby on its way?"

"Spendidly! Everything normal. Say, Mark, you and Jonathan Cameron seem to be doing well together. Any problems there at all? Any badgering from Kott?"

"None. I don't even know where he is."

"Jonathan still hasn't explained a word to you, eh?"

"No, sir. Oh, he makes no bones about the trouble Kott caused his other factors. He told me point-blank that he came to me because he couldn't persuade anyone else to take his account. That's all he's ever said. I've grown so fond of Mr. Cameron personally, I don't ask questions. I just try to spare him when I can. It looks as though he may have a fairly good year. I certainly hope so. He is very short of cash."

"Who isn't? But I'm sure Kott drained him before he left."

Mark didn't comment. Both men sat for a time, watching a heavy, gray thunderhead begin to form out over the river.

"I hope that cloud means rain," Mark said. "Mr. Cameron needs it on his late corn. I've learned, though, that we can have a lot of coastal thunder without a drop of rain."

Mackay reached to give him two brisk pats on the forearm. "Son—I say it again—you're too good to be true. You've been completely unselfish with my family and me. I wish I could find a way to thank you, but maybe it's all for the best, even for you." Mackay's eyes twinkled with mischief. "Aren't you getting invaluable experience both in running a business by yourself and in heading a household? How's the big romance progressing? My children are in love with Caroline, too, they tell me. They're all together right now, in fact, down by the river.''

.''I know. They invited me. Caroline's been wonderful with them. She and her grandfather were in town over a month, you know. We saw them often. She's gay and lighthearted. The children need that. She has a fine sense of play, and yet she's the one teaching Eliza Anne how to draw so well.''

"So I understand. But, no wedding plans yet?"

"No, sir."

Mark meant to say no more because there was simply no more to tell. He hadn't even tried to imagine how Caroline might accept the tangled story Ethel Cameron had told him. And even if it made no difference to her, there were now no marriage plans in Mark's future.

"After an illness such as mine," Mackay was saying, "a man thinks about many things. I may live for several years. I may not. I want you to know how much I care, Mark. I care about every remaining year of your life. I want life for you to be as fine and full and rich as you deserve. You deserve far more than you'll probably find, of course. But from now on I want you to conduct yourself with me exactly as we've been from the start. I'm all but well. And if anything—anything at all—bothers you, I'm here. If you need to try out any secret thoughts on someone, just remember, I'm here. And perhaps—" he tapped his chest over his heart, "perhaps I have a bit more understanding than before."

Mark sat, biting his lower lip, struggling with a sudden, almost overpowering desire to pour out the whole truth. He dared not. Mackay was not entirely well yet. "Thank you," he said. "Those two words sound so far short of what I mean. Of what I feel toward you, sir. But I hope you believe me when I swear that inside, where it counts, I seem to be managing rather well."

That night, beside Eliza, Mackay said, "I had a fine talk with Mark this evening just before the storm hit."

"Oh, I'm glad."

"Do you know, at one point in our conversation, I had a strange feeling that he already knows. He doesn't, I'm sure. Since Ethel Cameron apparently told him nothing that day, there's no way he could know, but he took such pains to assure me that he was managing well—'inside,' as he said, 'where it counts.' What else could he have meant by that?''

"Maybe he meant all he's had to handle for us these past months. Now that William Mein is away, his load is even heavier.''

"Maybe." He was quiet a moment, then asked, "Do you want to know what I think?''

"Of course I do.''

"I've had time to do some deep thinking this evening since my talk with him. While I was supposed to be resting. He and Cameron are quite evidently coming along well in their business dealings. Mark likes being a factor. He's involved in Cameron's rice planting, his corn fields—everything at Knightsford. Somehow, it strikes me as more than a mere business involvement. Mark cares about the old fellow.''

"And you think Jonathan Cameron, Mark's grandfather, should be the one to tell him.''

"I do indeed! That would be far better for Mark and far better for Jonathan. If the old gentleman unburdened himself of that heavy load just once, he might live a lot longer.''

She touched his face tenderly. "Robert, dear Robert, we put the whole thing in God's hands, remember?''

"I know. But I keep wanting to take it back—fix it. Fix everything, for Mark's sake.''

Eliza had been forced to lay down the law to her husband in order to keep him on doctor's orders, away from Savannah until November. The damaged heart had not responded steadily enough to suit Jones. "Some days, it's fine," he explained to her. "At other times, the beat is weak and irregular. More rest. Lots more rest, Eliza, even after you're back in the city.''

With William Mein and his wife away at Newport on holiday, Mark's work load had become enormous. Mackay worried.

"The only thing I know to do to keep him from being so agitated about the office," Mark told Eliza one evening before Christmas, after the Mackays had returned, "is for me to brace up, act less tired when I do finally get home at night. We can't let him go on worrying.''

"You'll do no such thing," she scolded. "You're doing all anyone could do to handle things by yourself. I won't have you falling ill, too. Don't try to joke or entertain him unless you feel like it. That's an order. This is your home, too, Mark."

"At least I have good news for him tonight. Our last shipment of rice to Liverpool netted enough for him to pay off all but a few hundred dollars of The Grange mortgage. Is anyone upstairs with him now?"

"Yes. Judge Charlton's been up there too long. Robert was determined to catch up on all that took place at Council meetings after Mr. McAllister resigned and Judge Charlton took over as interim mayor."

Mark gave her a puzzled look. "But, Miss Eliza, we've had an election since then. T.U.P. Charlton has now been *elected* mayor. A whole new term is under way."

She covered her eyes with her hands. "Of course. What's the matter with me? I knew that!"

"You're exhausted, too." He took away her mending and led her to the parlor sofa. Mark had not yet grown accustomed to seeing Eliza huge with child. It frightened him. He felt both fear and gladness. Mackay was lyrical, of course. That part was good. For the first time in so long, sure signs of the happy man Mackay had always been showed plainly. Mark watched daily for the signs. When he found Mackay's expectations high, his humor in full flower, Mark's own spirits lifted. The melancholy that struck every time he saw Eliza lumber across the floor, her graceful, swinging walk distorted by the child she carried, came, Mark knew, from jealousy. Admitting it had not been easy, devoted as he was to Mackay.

For more than a month, so intense had been his struggle to balance the warring emotions, it had become a necessity each night to try to offer to God his growing love for the woman whose very life revolved around her love for Mark's best friend. So earnestly did he perform this act of relinquishment, on his knees each night beside his bed, that he had been able to go on mainly without guilt. He refused to be thrown off balance by false guilt. As strong as his love for Eliza, was his eagerness to keep Mackay's affairs in order at the office. With all his heart he wanted his friend to be well again, and along with his prayers for Mackay's recovery, Mark could contribute his own efforts at work. False guilt could damage his judgment. His own damaged judgment could cause Mackay harm. Carrying the weight of a hopeless love was hard enough. Any man fool enough to fall in love with another man's wife bore a hopeless burden. He meant to bear his without resentment. Certainly, without false guilt, because he could no more stop loving Eliza Mackay than he could stop breathing.

"When your load seems too heavy, take out a blessing and examine it well," Aunt Nassie used to say. Mark's life, at times, seemed top-heavy with blessings. He was a part of the city he loved, a part of the family he loved, a success in the work he chose. He did not feel bitter at the sight of Eliza bearing another man's child. The child, when it came, would simply enlarge Mark's own world. A world that almost always was so secure and right, he couldn't have picked out just one blessing to examine had he tried.

At the same time his affection for Caroline seemed to deepen. At night he talked to God about her, too. It was surely no secret to the Almighty that Mark felt drawn to the vitality and grace of her glorious young body as he'd never been drawn to any other woman. A good thing the Lord can encompass our contradictions, he thought, one night when he couldn't sleep for thinking of Caroline Cameron's mouth on his.

Each time she came to town, Mark's pulse leaped, his heart soared. He and Caroline, in spite of his added work load, had taken in three concerts and a touring exhibit of wax figures and had joked and laughed through countless picnics on the Strand—just the two of them. At first he had been annoyed when Caroline insisted upon leaving the Mackay children behind. Now, he preferred being alone with her.

So much—all around him—was good. And he *was* managing. He would always manage, as long as Eliza was there for him to love. The sight of her distended body these days, the thought of her pain ahead when the infant would, at last, be born, pained him. But once the child was there, even that would be better. He would love the new baby—boy or girl—because he loved the child's parents in a way he had never before understood love.

# TWENTY-FIVE

ELIZA'S time came in the late evening of January 7, in the new year 1816. Mark ran the three blocks to get Dr. Jones.

"It might be a few hours yet," he heard Jones tell Mackay as he urged him to stay quietly in bed and wait.

A few hours to Mark was longer than eternity. Through the night, in his room, he listened to the low bustling sounds coming from behind the closed door of the Mackays' room down the hall as Dr. Jones and Hannah worked over Eliza. Mark had not undressed. He wouldn't sleep anyway and maybe—just maybe—he might be needed.

He had managed to help Emphie get the children to bed, and Dr. Jones checked now and then in the spare room to make certain that Mackay stayed, as ordered, in bed there.

"Couldn't I sit with him?" Mark had asked Jones.

"No, sir, you may not. He'll talk if there's anyone to listen. He's improving and I want him to continue to improve. Mrs. Mackay does well at times like this. I've delivered her other children. You'd better rest, too, Browning. You're pale as a ghost. Ever been present at a birth before?"

"No, sir."

"It's a part of life. As is death."

About eleven o'clock, William crept out of his own bed and into Mark's room. "Will Mama—be close to death the way Papa was?" he asked.

"No, of course not," Mark heard himself say firmly. "Your mother isn't really sick, William. She's giving you a new brother or sister. Which do you want?"

"A sister, I think. I have my hands full as it is with Jack."

253

"Want to crawl in my bed, William? I'm staying dressed in case I'm needed. But I can turn down the covers for you, and I'll be right here."

"No, thank you. I just wanted to be sure Mama wouldn't —die." They hugged each other.

Stretched across the bed again after William had tiptoed back to his own room, Mark wished the boy had stayed. He had helped himself, somewhat, by assuring William that his mother wasn't really ill, but women did die in childbirth.

The fact that Eliza might die was so unbearable, he forced himself to think about William. What a valued man William Mackay could turn out to be, he thought, and wondered what he really meant by that. William, the shy, almost solemn, Mackay boy. Oh, maybe he's daring and cheerful enough except when compared with Jack, who thrives on risk and adventure and jokes and riddles and hunting and any boy's pastimes. William joined his brother in all of it, as best he could, except for hunting. "I don't like fishing too much, either," he'd once confided to Mark. "It seems kind of cruel, if fish have any feelings, to hook the inside of their mouths. I kind of dream about it sometimes after I've done it. I only go with Jack so he won't call me a sissy. But"—the thin, pointed chin had jutted—"I won't go hunting! I know people have to eat, but I don't hate rabbits or anything like that. I couldn't kill them the way people killed the British."

Mark propped his head on his clasped hands and stared at the white ceiling. If William ever falls in love, he thought, he'll love with every ounce of his being. And how he could be hurt!

Every muscle in Mark's body ached. "You'd better rest, too, Browning," Dr. Jones had warned. Mark laughed aloud without smiling. His muscles ached because of the tense waiting. Turned on his side, in hopes of easing the ache, he listened. There were almost no sounds in the big house now except from the night outside, which was January cold and windy. The house, with more fires burning than usual, creaked and groaned, protesting the wind that pushed against it. A word or two of instruction from Dr. Jones to Hannah or Eliza could not really be understood. Once, Hannah laughed softly. Eliza must be all right. They must just be—waiting.

As Mark waited.

He struck the bed with his fist. Why, when a man gained momentary pleasure from the act of lovemaking, did a woman have to endure such long hours of pain and torment? Earnestly, he prayed for Eliza and begged God to let it be easy for her.

Then, from behind the closed door down the hall, he heard quick footsteps, scraps of hurried talk. He sat bolt upright, scarcely daring to breathe because Eliza had begun to groan and then to whimper—struggling, he knew, for all their sakes, to let her agony out quietly.

A bucket banged against something in the closed room. He heard Hannah's running steps and then Eliza screamed.

Mark leaped from the bed. Standing stock-still in the middle of the room, he heard her scream again. He jerked open his door and in three long strides stood outside the closed room where she was, his heart pounding so that he fought to pull in the next breath.

The spare room door opened and Mackay appeared in the candle-lit doorway, his short hair mussed, his face pale, expectant.

Mackay's hand was out to Mark, who went toward him.

Dr. Jones was giving Eliza orders now, his brusque voice *ordering* her!

"Don't worry, Mark! Don't worry, it's all right," Mackay whispered hoarsely. "She's—she's—"

The final scream—a shriek of pain and victory—died away.

"Eliza's—all right now," Mackay finished his sentence. "It's bad the first time a man goes through this. I was alone with the servants when our son Robert came. The little fellow who only lived to be four." He gripped Mark's hand tightly. "She's fine. I'm not lying to you, son. And I'm not being callous about this. Feel my hand; I'm in a cold sweat. Who does get used to it? Ever. Only God knows why the woman has to pay the whole price."

A series of sharp slaps was followed by the wailing cry of an infant. Mark saw Mackay's face light up.

"Listen! Did you hear that, Mark? I'm a father again!"

He pumped Mark's hand. Mark tried to respond. He was too weak.

In a moment the closed door opened just enough for Dr. Jones to stick his head into the hall and say sharply, "Mrs. Mackay said to tell Mr. Mackay it's a girl and that he is to get right back into bed!"

After Mark left Mackay, well tucked in, he lighted a fresh

candle in his own room and stood looking for a long time at his mother's portrait, the wavering flame caressing the face that to Mark was still all enchantment. Until now, he had never once thought about the agony he'd caused her all those years ago. She had sat for the portrait after he was born, Aunt Nassie said. Even after all the pain he'd caused her, she could smile that anticipatory smile. *I hope I gave her some happiness, too,* he thought. *I hope I did.*

Wearily, he began to undress, then stopped when he remembered William. Poor boy would be terrified surely at his mother's screams. Mark slipped out of his room again and along the shadowy corridor, to listen outside the door of the boys' room. Two levels of snoring came from inside. William and Jack were both asleep.

On his way back to his own room, he managed a weak smile. They had been through this before—William three times. Once they had heard the baby cry, Mark realized, they knew it was all over and had gone right to sleep.

Before breakfast, as soon as Mackay had seen her and the new baby, Eliza sent for Mark. Until she motioned for him to come in, he stood in the doorway, looking at her tired, haunting face. *It's only natural that she'd be tired,* he told himself, and even the shadows around her eyes were beautiful.

"I don't bear such close inspection, Mark," she said with a weak smile, "but *she* does. Over there in the crib—tell me what you think of my new daughter."

The youngest baby he'd ever seen lay squirming, wrinkled and quite red—eyes tightly shut, fat, dimpled hands reaching, drawing back, fingers curling and uncurling. "She's—she's a busy little thing already," he said, feeling utterly helpless.

"Maybe that's a good sign," Eliza said. "Mark?"

He rushed to the bedside. "You're—all right, aren't you?" he whispered. "I'm so relieved!"

"Me, too. Do take care of yourself, now," she warned. "Try to come home early tonight from work. I kept everyone up so late."

"Oh, don't worry about me," he said. "You take care of yourself. That's what matters."

"It is only part of what matters." Her voice was firm now. "Watch after Robert. Try to keep him calm. He's so excited." Briefly, her hand touched his. "I'll be up to help you with everything—in just a few days, I promise."

"William wants very much to go to work with me today," he said. "Will it be all right with you if I take him along?"

"I'd be ever so relieved if you did. Everything that happens is somehow always harder on poor William. Yes. By all means, take him."

Striding through the crisp, January sunshine with William, Mark thought for the first time in months of the word "contentment." I love her so much, he thought, as they reached the entrance to Number One Commerce Row, I can honestly be almost content just knowing that she needs me sometimes. He gave William a big smile. It was always good to be with William.

"Would you like to run down to the wharf and bring up the mail?" he asked the boy.

William hung back a little. "Yes, sir. But then, can I just come and sit in your office with you after that?"

Mark gave the bill of William's cap a tug. "I want you to! I'll be going over the Liverpool Cotton Exchange figures first thing today—not very interesting for you, but we'll be together."

When William smiled, which was far rarer than with Jack, Mark always noticed. The boy's eyes seemed to be offering a gift with the smile. His obvious adoration both cheered and concerned Mark. Because of it, his obligation to William was somehow deeper.

Within half an hour, William was back with the Philadelphia and New York papers and a bundle of letters. Shuffling through the mail, Mark stopped at one thin letter from Browning Shipping.

"Is that a letter you wanted?" William asked.

"Yes," he said absently. "Yes, it is."

"The one with your company's name on it?"

"You don't miss much, do you?" Mark broke the seal and began to read. With no apology for the long, long delay, James Parsons informed him in a few lines that when he returned from abroad in the spring, he would hope for a meeting with Mark in New York.

"Good or bad news?" William asked.

He shrugged. "Neither, I guess."

Tossing the single sheet into the trash basket, Mark looked

out and down the river where it wound its glistening way to the
sea. He felt no particular disappointment. For months he tried
to figure out why Parsons appeared to be avoiding him, but he
knew now, after his visit with Ethel Cameron, that the man
must know the whole story and had simply dreaded telling him
the truth. Not once had Mark doubted that all of Ethel
Cameron's story was true—every word. He still longed to
know more of what his father was really like. The only hope of
that still lay in Parsons, but he could wait now. Things were
somehow—shifting.

Things? His own priorities? Undoubtedly. His memories of
Aunt Nassie remained clear and helpful. Always helpful. But
thoughts of his father were no longer so tragic, no longer so
disturbed by his own need to change his memory of the
golden, sorrowing stranger into a man for whom he could
honestly grieve. What had become real about Mark Browning,
Sr., was—the city itself. In an almost palpable sense, his
father had given him Savannah. His own roots were down to
stay now, deep in the sandy soil of the city he meant to help
build. The slowly emerging little city where he would live for
all the remaining years of his life. Mark and the city would
grow together.

The Savannah Free School would be established this year,
along with the new Bank of the State of Georgia. Wesley
Chapel would be completed sometime soon, and most important to him, his own Christ Church would in the near future be
finished at last.

When Eliza was up again, he'd go back to his evening walks
during which he'd been studying Savannah properties with the
idea of investing some of his capital. More absorbing, though,
than possible investments for making still more money, was
searching out the spot where he would someday build his own
home. To live in alone? As a bachelor? Invariably, he pushed
the question aside, because there was no answer.

He would not build what Savannahians called a mansion.
The talk around town now of proposed new houses, to be built
on a grand scale as the wealth of the merchant class increased,
didn't particularly interest Mark except that he hoped, for the
city's sake, they would be well designed. His own home would
be, first of all, excellently built, roomy, suitable for entertaining, but there would also be an air of simplicity about it.
People would notice its real worth on second glance, not first.

It would be built of imported English bricks. His house would have a slate roof and white shutters and trim. He might consider building a row of good houses for income property, but his own house would stand alone—perhaps on two trust lots.

There was certainly no hurry about any of it. In fact, there was plenty of time. And plenty to do now, especially until Miss Eliza was up and about again. He smiled at William, who smiled back but said nothing. The boy seemed content, too. It was good to be sure that in his future there would be William's future and Jack's—and the girls'. Mackay was getting well. His friend Mackay would always be a part of everything that concerned Mark as a businessman and as a human being.

And, there would be Miss Eliza—to love.

Yes, there had been a definite shift. The present and the future, he supposed, were moving the past few years into history, where they belonged.

The future? Deliberately, he rejected the sense of dread that came every time he reminded himself that his uncle, Osmund Kott, could someday also be in his future. Through the long months of Mackay's illness, Mark had kept a pact with himself. A pact to refuse worry over trouble that had not yet surfaced. "Our Lord took the time to remind us, Mark," Aunt Nassie used to say, "that today's trouble is all we have the capacity to cope with. 'Sufficient unto the day is the evil thereof.' Borrowing what might or might not be tomorrow's trouble is sheer waste of time and energy." On that truth, he had made his vow to reject all dread of Kott. Anyone could give dread room to flourish by twisting a predicament this way and that, by dwelling on what might happen.

Was his gradual, but very real, sense of developing adequacy a commonplace for a man his age? Was it merely a part of growing up? Or a sign that he was still young? No matter. Ethel Cameron's story had not lessened his feeling of security. His security still lay where it had been since he lost his father and Aunt Nassie—in himself. Jonathan Cameron and Osmund Kott and Mary Cotting had never been a part of his life. Kott could cause him trouble. Still, the Bible also said that "man is born to trouble as the sparks fly upward." Osmund Kott could make sparks all right. No one doubted that, but Mark meant to add no fuel of his own by worrying now about something that might never happen.

He glanced again at the quiet boy sitting almost motionless

on a straight chair in the corner of the office. He smiled at William and the boy smiled back again, another gift.

"Don't you dare let me catch you growing up to be as rude as I've been for the past ten minutes, young man, do you hear me?"

William swung his legs a couple of times and the smile deepened. "You're not rude, Mark. I know there's a lot on your mind. I just like to be here with you."

"And I with you." He took out the Liverpool Cotton Exchange report, tapped the pages into an even stack on his desk and began to look at them. He wasn't concentrating. One more thing needed to be said to William.

"Do you think there's anything better in all the world, son, than to be friends as you and I are?"

Throughout the steamy summer, Mackay did not spend a single full day at the countinghouse. On a still, close evening in September, he and Mark sat together in their favorite spot— the big side porch—hoping to catch a breeze. They had said nothing for quite some time, but Mark sensed that his friend was busy with a plan.

Finally, Mackay said, "That tyrant, George Jones, has declared that I will be allowed to return full time to work before Christmas—*if* I'm a good boy."

Mark laughed. "And what constitutes being a good boy?"

"Making a voyage to the North for a month at Newport, where the air isn't ninety percent water. Actually, Mark, I can obey the old coot and handle some personal business up there at the same time." Mackay uncrossed his legs and eagerly leaned forward. "You see, for fifty years, since the death of my mother's father, Godfrey Malbone of Newport, there has been a large, very heavy, unopened chest stored there in a warehouse."

"Oh, yes, sir," Mark said. "I know about the Malbone chest."

"You know about it? Who told you?"

"Mrs. Cameron. The day she invited me to tea. The day you got sick."

"Hm. Savannah's grapevine never fails to amaze me. Well, be that as it may, the old chest has been there all this time, the descendants—myself among them—only guessing at its probable contents. One rumor has it full of invaluable silver. You know how Americans are—heirs scattered all over. No one felt obliged or authorized to open it. Of course, it could be stuffed with old newspapers!" He laughed. "Eliza's been curious about the whole thing for years. And finally, it is to be opened late this month at Newport. I still have friends and relatives there. Before the recent trouble with Britain, we traveled every summer to Newport. And will again, certainly, next year. All the surviving members of the Malbone family are to be present and assist in the division of the contents of the old chest. Then there's another matter. Eliza and I think that Jack and William should be in the hands of a good Northern teacher. I've learned of a gentleman, a scholar by the name of Mc-Culloch in New York, who is opening a school. What would you think if you and I booked passage for ourselves and the boys in about a week?"

Mark's surprise gave way to delight. "Me, too, sir? You really want me to go with you? Will Mein be on hand to handle our affairs here?"

"He will be. And since I live the life of a slave who only follows orders, my wife has *ordered* me to take you along. She doesn't trust me, as you know."

"You won't worry about Miss Eliza here without either of us?"

"Of course I'll worry. I've always worried about her and the children when I've been forced to travel. But, how about it, Mark? Will you go with me?"

"Why, yes, sir. I can take care of some personal business, too. I had another letter from James Parsons just yesterday. He's back in New York for several months now. I'd like to catch him while I can."

Mackay frowned. "I see. Well, fine, fine." He was grinning now. "By the way, as you might already have guessed, I booked passage for you and the boys and me on the *Eliza*. It worked out just right. Once at sea, you and I can hoist a few to commemorate the scene of our meeting."

"I'll like that, sir. If you're allowed wine by then."

Mackay waved both hands at him in disgust. "Not you, too, Mark! I'm perfectly well. I could go back to work tomorrow morning. Look at the color in my face, the sparkle in my eyes. I'm going north only to pacify Eliza and her medical tyrant." He stretched his legs and leaned back in the porch chair. "So, you heard from the phantom Parsons, eh?"

"Yes, sir. Truthfully, my need to talk to him isn't as pressing as it used to be. Oh, I'd still like to know some details. But
I'm—I'm at home here now, with all of you. I'm afraid I
don't even worry anymore about having outstayed my welcome." He looked about the thickly planted, shady yard.
"This now seems like—my first real home. I guess I actually
did start a new life in Savannah."

"You know how that pleases me. But, never allow anything
to dim the splendid memories you have of the years with Aunt
Nassie. I wish she could draw up in her fine carriage right now
and join us here on the porch, don't you?"

"I'd like nothing better. And, don't worry. She stays with
me always. I was thinking this morning, on my way to work,
that she seems close by in a new way these days. We don't have
any way of proving it, but it must be that our loved ones who
have left us know about us as they did here on earth. Maybe
they're more aware of what we do, what we think, what we
feel. Do you believe that?"

Mackay sighed. "I certainly want to believe it. Even heaven
wouldn't satisfy me if I couldn't know the smallest things
about Eliza and the children." He sat up with a smile and
banged Mark on the knee. "And, of course, when I go to my
long home, I'll want to know all about you, son. You are
young enough, you know, to be my son." He laughed. "Or,
more accurately, at forty-four, I'm old enough to be your
father!"

In his room that night, Mark wrote separate letters to
Jonathan Cameron and to Caroline, telling them of his
planned trip to the North. To Jonathan, he wrote reassuringly, promising to handle the sale of his crops before leaving.
To Caroline, he wrote: "Please ask your grandfather to bring
you to the city at the end of next week, if possible. I suddenly
find I can't bear the thought of making an ocean voyage
without seeing you—being with you again—before I go. I beg
you to come. Miss Eliza will need you, I'm sure. The Mc-
Queens are preparing to sail for Jamaica to visit Cousin
Margaret's mother for several months; the boys will leave with
us for school—not to return, perhaps, for several years. I can
think of no one who would cheer and comfort Miss Eliza as
you can. I am attempting to arrange your visit as a surprise for
her. Undoubtedly, your grandfather will prefer his old room

at the Meins, but you might consider stopping here, offering to stay with Miss Eliza when we are gone. She and the girls will be rattling about in this big house alone. I know in my heart that she will welcome you with open arms. As will I, if only you will come."

The letters, written and sealed, relieved him. Mackay's business would be all right for a month. Mark would see to that, but he had to put Jonathan Cameron's mind at rest over his crops. And he needed to know that Caroline would be with Eliza.

He caught himself once more thinking of Miss Eliza as—Eliza. He brushed the thought aside, certain that he had done the right thing to invite Caroline to stay with her. Mark could already feel Eliza's loneliness for "her boys," the gnawing uneasiness that her beloved Robert might overdo. Caroline's sunny disposition, her humor, would help the days pass.

He would miss knowing that Eliza was all right. It no longer seemed strange to him that he would also miss the feel of Caroline's arms about him. This minute, at his desk, he closed his eyes and the memory of her smooth, young skin set his blood racing. The fresh fragrance of her black curls could be called up at will these days—was called up more and more often. As exhausted as he'd been through most of Mackay's illness, he had made the trip again and again to Knightsford, unable to get enough of Caroline's nearness. Each time they were together, he forced himself not to kiss her responsive mouth too often. The experience, each time he did kiss her, was so perfect, he meant to keep it that way.

Surely, he was madly in love with her slender but fulsome body. Whether he truly loved *her*, in the way he loved Eliza Mackay, even he didn't know. He felt that he did, in some way, revere Caroline Cameron. Even in the gale of his passion for her, there must be reverence. Without it, he would kiss her far more often.

# TWENTY-SIX

CAROLINE had been with Eliza for more than a week when they both received letters from Mark, delivered to the house on Broughton by his junior clerk. When the letters came, the two women sat on the shady side porch—a pitcher of cool tea on a wrought-iron table between them and the infant, Sallie, asleep in her cradle beside Eliza.

Caroline, about to jump out of her sprigged voile dress with excitement, cried, "Oh, Miss Eliza, how like Mark to give his clerk instructions to watch every ship and then hurry straight here with our letters!"

"It's exactly like him," Eliza said, breaking the seal on hers. "Excuse me, but I need to know why my husband didn't write, too. He's usually the most prolific letter writer."

For a time they sat absorbed in their separate letters, both brief, on single pages.

10 September, 1816
Aboard the *Eliza*

Dearest Miss Eliza,

I know you're wondering why you are hearing from me first. Don't worry. Mr. Mackay is fine. Can you believe that he obeyed me when I forbade him to write to you tonight—our first night at sea? I thought our departure excitement, etc., was enough for one day. He went to bed, as he says, "like a good boy."

Of course, there isn't much to write so early in our voyage, but the sea is smooth, the wind steady, and we lifted a very small glass of port (the boys had tea) to the happy memory of my first voyage aboard this same

*Eliza*. Somehow, there is special meaning in the coincidence that the boat which took me safely to my beloved Savannah bears your name. I promise your husband is in good hands, mine. At least, I will try valiantly to watch over him. Give hugs to all three girls, Eliza Anne, Kate and Baby Sallie. I send my love and my devotion to you.

Y<sup>r</sup> faithful
MARK BROWNING

"Well," she said, relieved. "So far, so good. My husband didn't get a chance to write that first night at sea because Mark wouldn't let him! Good for Mark, I say."

Caroline smiled absently in Eliza's direction and began her own letter from Mark—for the second time, but not aloud.

10 September, 1816
Aboard the *Eliza*

Dear Caroline,

Was it impertinent of me to kiss you good-bye before the world at the Savannah waterfront? I hope not. Honestly, I didn't intend to kiss your mouth—only your hand. I must have lost my head. And at age twenty-four, too. If forgiveness is in order, I beg you to forgive me.

Not much to write about yet. Mr. Mackay is already in bed for the night and the boys with him. Since he owns the boat, cots were brought into his stateroom for them. They don't want him out of their sight for a minute. I wonder if they'll ever grow accustomed to being away from their parents and Broughton Street. My heart goes out to them. I trust you are enjoying your visit in town. Give the dear old place my love and I will write again soon. Mail will reach us after next week at Browning World Shipping, New York. Miss Eliza, of course, knows the Newport address. We go there first so that Mr. Mackay can be on hand for the opening of the famous heirloom chest said to be filled with silver. I will watch by every opportunity for your letters.

Afft'ly,
MARK BROWNING

Eliza smiled. "I see Mark's letter made you happy, too."

"Yes! Oh, yes. He seems to want me to write to him in New York after next week." She sighed. "Browning World Shipping. Just think!"

"One of the world's largest firms."

"But it always surprises me when I remember that Mark's so—rich."

"I'm glad to hear that."

"Miss Eliza? You know I'm in love with Mark, don't you?"

"Yes, Caroline. I've known for some time."

"Of course, practically every girl in Savannah not spoken for is also in love with him. Even some who are spoken for, Mrs. Mein declares. They're marrying their gentlemen as second best." She folded her letter carefully. "I also hope you know that Mark is—not very much in love with me."

"I know nothing of the kind!"

"Oh, you don't need to be careful. Remember, I'm Caroline Cameron. I know about sadness and second-best living. I've been reared by my grandparents, don't forget. In a way, that's been fortunate. I know better than to expect life to be perfect. I do believe in facing facts. Mark is—well, he's deeply fond of me. He likes my company—we laugh a lot. He likes very much to kiss me. To hold me. He freely admits that. But—" Her voice wavered for the first time. "But only Grandfather and you know that I'm quite aware that his love for me isn't—like mine for him."

Eliza reached for her hand. She jerked it back. "No, don't comfort me. It's all right. Thank you for understanding, but I think I understand Mark, too." She gave a little laugh. "You see, Miss Eliza, I like you so much, if you comforted me, I might cry. I hate weeping women!"

"It's very important that you understand Mark, my dear. The boy has already made such strides since he's been a Savannahian."

"He'd like your calling him that!"

"I know. I sometimes think those of us who've lived here most of our lives don't really see the city as Mark sees it. I pray he always loves Savannah as much as right now. But, Caroline, be patient with him where his feelings for you are concerned."

"You sound like Grandfather."

"He's right. Mark's heart has been very scarred. I'm convinced they're all salutary scars—the kind that have toughened him where he needed it. He's found the city he dreamed about, the work; he has a family for as long as he needs us. He'll let his heart settle, too, one day. If you can wait."

Her look was incredulous. "Oh, I'll wait! What else could I do—but wait for Mark? If I have to wait for years while he marries someone else, I will. What else can I do? This is *Mark* we're talking about! I—I love him—the way you love Mr. Mackay."

Eliza looked at the young, earnest face for a long time, then said, "If that's true, you're right to wait. There could never be another man for you. Not ever."

The Tontine Coffee House
New York
September 17, 1816

My dearest Eliza,

Mark, the boys and I arrived here last evening at six o'clock, after one of the sweetest voyages I ever experienced. Only five passengers besides ourselves and everything good to eat and drink, and the new beds on the *Eliza* will, I predict, enhance her reputation. I long for you to be with us. The views surpass most I have met with and the beauty of the New York countryside is delightful. This is more of a summer climate than Newport, where we go next. Alas, though, crowded city conditions forced us to stay at the Tontine Coffee House being just by the vessel. Bugs? I swear to you beds were never so copiously inhabited. Cervantes describes some of the beds that Sancho occupied, but he never slept or attempted to sleep at The Tontine in New York. If he had, he would have told his story far more vividly.

I spoke at length last evening with Mr. McCulloch, who I am certain will make gentlemen and scholars of our two sons. He is the very man I wish the boys to tutor under. He is all we could wish for and has only fifteen pupils and will not exceed that number. His scholars are kept to themselves, and their principal playmate will be McCulloch himself. French is most commonly spoken. By the time our sons return home, they will outshine us in their cultivated intellects. I hope to have them well settled by next week, and Mark will then accompany me to Newport for the opening of the famous chest. Our trunks have been shipped ahead.

Now, my best beloved, do not worry about me. I think you can tell by the chipper tone of this letter that I am feeling pert, brilliant, witty and more fascinating than ever. Do give my dearest love to our three daughters, remember me to Caroline, and all deepest love and devotion to my beautiful wife.

Your ROBERT MACKAY

The clerk from Mark's office made almost daily trips with letters from both men for Eliza and Caroline.

"I wonder," Eliza said, when they'd read those dated September 25, "if ever God created a sweeter, more thoughtful young man than Mark. He doesn't need to write me every time he writes to you!"

In a surprisingly solemn voice, Caroline answered, "No, God never created *anyone* like Mark." All she said about his regular letters to Eliza was, "I suppose he just wants you to be sure Mr. Mackay is really all right."

"And not just fooling me with his buoyant letters? Well, Robert isn't fooling me. He's never pretended to be well when he isn't. The dear man loves sympathy too much. I feel quite peaceful about him. And he does seem to like the new school. If Mr. McCulloch is half as expert as Robert makes him out, Jack and William will get accustomed to being away from all of us. They'll take the change far better, I'm sure, than will their mother."

Remembering, as she did each day, that Mark expected her to be cheerful with Miss Eliza, Caroline said brightly, "Mr. Mackay might be at the opening of the old silver chest in Newport today!"

"If he got the boys settled, he could be. I've reminded him in a letter that if it is silver, we need compotes and pitchers, should he have a choice. I get goose bumps at the thought of that old chest! I've known about it for years, but I'd almost given up hope that it would ever be opened."

A letter from Mackay, dated September 28, came on October 5 from—of all unexpected places—Philadelphia.

Dearest Eliza,

We were able to book passage here and since Mark
longed to visit his aunt's grave, he and I came to
Philadelphia on impulse. The dividing of the silver was
both harrowing and rewarding and I think you will be
pleased with my choices. I yearned to get my hands on
a seventeenth-century posset pot and cover, but it
would have meant a carefully worded quarrel with a
distant cousin and I am too happy for quarrels. I did
fall heir to two pitchers and one handsome compote.
Mark literally grieves that he did not know you when
he disposed of much of the Browning silver. He loves
you deeply, Eliza. The old Browning mansion is one of
the most magnificent houses I've seen anywhere, but
time is limited and I must keep my description of it
until we are once more together.

The boys said good-bye to us in a show of courage
and satisfaction with their new schoolmaster and with
their living quarters. There is so much to tell you when
I get back, which I shall make as soon as possible—undoubtedly, mid-October, when the good ship *Eliza* is
due to return.

Tomorrow we go again to New York, where Mark
will attempt to see Parsons. Finding out that he is factor to his own grandfather will surely be a blow, but
the least of the blow, I should think.

We dined today at the Washington Hotel, and after
dinner went to visit the United States ship *Franklin*
—one of the finest. I hope to find a letter from you
when we reach New York and in it, the glorious news
that my four charming women are missing me and
adoring me. Mark's Philadelphia is a growing city, the
handsomest I have ever visited in America. But all
Mark can think of is our return to Savannah.
Remember me to everyone and kisses to all of you.
God bless you, my very dear and most beloved Eliza.

Yours ever and sincerely,<br>
ROBERT MACKAY

P.S. If Captain Nance holds to his schedule, weather
permitting, I could be with you, my darling, on 14 October.

Eliza felt selfish not sharing her letter with Caroline, who received none that day, but Robert had said too much about Mark and his interview with James Parsons. Eliza was certain now that Caroline knew nothing of the heartbreak her grandfather had hidden for so many years—but only that, for some mysterious reason, Osmund Kott was trouble for the old man. Well, Mark would know the whole story soon. James Parsons would tell him once they were back in New York. If Mark wants Caroline to know, it must be his decision.

She fell asleep that night, praying for Mark, thanking God that Robert would be with him when he found out.

Today was October 5. Nine more days and Robert would be beside her again. Together, they would do everything possible to help Mark.

At dinner in New York on the evening of October 5, Mark noticed that Mackay was even more talkative than usual and he understood why. Tomorrow, at long last, Mark would see James Parsons. The possibility of finding answers to the questions that had for so long gone unanswered should have made this an anxious evening. Kind, protective Mackay was trying his best to keep him entertained.

As soon as they'd ordered dinner, Mackay began to rave about the old Browning mansion, telling Mark for the third or fourth time how much he appreciated the chance to see it.

"How did the old house look to you, son?"

"All right. But with all the remodeling, not very familiar. I liked showing it to you, though."

"And do you really believe that seeing it helped cut the last tie to Philadelphia?"

Mark smiled. "I was already free. What do I have to do or say to convince you, my friend? You must know by now that *I am a Savannahian*. My home—my real home now—is on Broughton." He passed a napkin-covered basket of hot bread to Mackay. "That is, until the Mackay family grows tired of having me underfoot."

Mackay's face went abruptly solemn. "I know that was supposed to be a joke. I'm not laughing. Do you think I'll ever live long enough to grow tired of having Jack underfoot? Or William?"

"Not if the look on your face when you told them good-bye was any indication. I felt sorrier for you than for the boys."

"So did I. Oh, my, so did I." Mackay lifted the napkin and examined the steaming bread. "You're not a bit nervous about seeing Parsons tomorrow, are you?"

"No. I would have been—once. I'm not expecting any great revelations. Nothing I don't already know."

His friend appeared puzzled, Mark thought, seemed about to ask a question, then thought better of it.

Mackay buttered a chunk of hot bread and took an enormous bite. "Just baked," he said, chewing. "Have some. Annoys Eliza when I talk while chewing. Funny thing, I never do it when I'm with her. But then, she brings out the best in me. Always has."

"Me, too," Mark said, buttering a piece of bread for himself.

"Can you believe we'll actually be on our way back to her day after tomorrow? After sixteen years, I still get prickles when it comes time to see her again. Do you think she really knows how deeply I love her? How I—depend upon her love for me?"

"Yes, sir, I do. I—I certainly do know how deeply she loves you."

"Your little frown flickered there between your eyes for a few seconds. Why?"

"Oh, did it? I don't know, unless I was wondering what another man's chances might be—ever to find a love like yours."

"Your chances to find it are far better than with most men," Mackay said sincerely. "Far better." When Mark didn't answer, he asked, "Don't you want to know why?"

"Yes, sir."

"Because you don't seem to have a selfish bone in your body, son. You wouldn't be sitting here with me at this dinner table right now if you had."

Mark's baffled expression was his response.

"I mean that," Mackay went on. "You made this voyage just so you could look after me—be sure I took care of myself. So that Eliza wouldn't worry about me. Your work load, when we get back, will be doubled. You'll be tired from the voyage and—"

"That's enough," Mark laughed. "I'm seeing Parsons tomorrow. I needed to come, too."

"I thought you did, but now I'm not so sure. Seeing Parsons was all you talked about for a time—not lately. Tonight, you don't even seem normally curious."

"I'm still looking forward to meeting the man who did so much for my father and for me, but if something happened that I didn't see him, I'd live happily ever after. Seeing Parsons isn't going to change anything—from the way it is right now. Please don't worry about it."

"Worry? Who's worrying? I don't believe in worry."

"Mr. Mackay, do you remember when I told you not long ago that I'm all right inside—where it counts?"

"Yes, yes, of course I remember."

"Well, it's still true."

As they ate their meal of jellied consommé, fish, baked chicken, beans, English peas and boiled custard—Mark's favorite since childhood—Mackay teased him unmercifully about Caroline. Reminded him that from his, Mackay's, wise, older viewpoint, Mark had at his beck and call the ideal woman. "Natural, poised, steady, mature for her years—incredibly beautiful."

Mackay's romantic proddings no longer embarrassed Mark. In spite of his love for Eliza, his feeling toward Caroline had taken a compelling turn that even he did not understand.

Mark drained his after-dinner brandy.

"Say, watch that," Mackay said. "I never saw you down a glass of brandy so fast before, young man. Are you sure you're not worried about your interview with Parsons tomorrow?"

"Yes!" For a moment, the question grated. Ridiculous, of course. Why wouldn't Mackay assume he would be worried? Mark's head felt heavy, thick. From the brandy, yes, but also because he couldn't bear pretending with this man who was so deeply a part of every facet of his own life. "Mr. Mackay," he blurted, "I still don't know myself very well. If I did, I'd know why I haven't told you something before. I thought I was proving my independence, I guess, by handling it all myself. Then, your illness and the new baby—"

"Mark, what are you trying to tell me?"

For nearly an hour, seated across from his friend in the almost empty hotel dining room, he talked—almost without interruption from Mackay. As the words flowed, his voice steadied. Before long, he was aware that he sounded like a man telling Ethel Cameron's strange story about a third party.

Mackay's dark eyes mirrored the deep, unfaltering loyalty on which Mark counted. At the end of the story, he waited for Mackay to speak. When Mackay only laid his hand over his, Mark said, "You—don't seem very surprised."

"I'm not. You see, I also kept from you that Parsons wrote the whole story to me long ago."

Mark stared at him. "To *you?*".

"That's right. A caring act on his part, as I see it. He wanted my advice, and Eliza's, as to how much damage the truth might do you personally." Mackay sighed. "He gave us a chance to tell you first. Together, we decided to wait until after our short holiday at The Grange, to give ourselves time to weigh everything. We love you like a son, Mark. It was an enormous responsibility."

"I see that."

"You knew all along, too, unbeknown to us. End result? Three people, devoted to one another, played a game for all those rotten weeks while I was demanding so much attention. I may know one thing you don't. Kott landed in New York. He's working for the Browning Company."

"Kott works for—Mr. Parsons now?"

"He does. Parsons wrote that, too. He despises Osmund, but evidently Osmund is doing a fine job. Seems to have completely reformed. He's sober—another person. Extraordinarily able. Parsons wrote also that he thought maybe Eliza and I should let it all ride awhile."

Mark gave Mackay his warm smile. "Let's stop trying to explain anything. No one has to pretend any longer. I certainly didn't want to have to pretend that I was hearing it from Parsons tomorrow for the first time."

"You look as relieved as I feel," Mackay said, returning the smile. "Eliza will be, too, but she'll grieve that you carried it all this time alone." For a while he sat looking at Mark. "You are—a curious mixture of youth and maturity, son. But, as Eliza always says, you're vulnerable. You may still be vulnerable where your heart is concerned, even when you're an old, old man. I won't tease about Caroline anymore. I promise. I think she's right for you, but be careful to whom you give that vulnerable heart. I won't play Cupid again. I do promise."

"I don't mind. I really don't mind now, sir."

"We should get to bed," Mackay said, "but somehow I—hate to say good night. This minute I just had a not very helpful thought. I wonder if in all the world there *is* another woman I'd personally be willing to trust with your heart, but Eliza!''

Mackay was grinning broadly when he said that, trying almost too hard to be his usual, light-hand-on-the-rein self. Mark would have to find a similar response that would be truthful. He thought of nothing.

"So, what will we do?" Mackay, still smiling, went on. "If Eliza is the only woman good enough for you—perceptive enough, trustworthy enough—what will we do? The lady's taken!"

"Yes, sir, she certainly is—taken." He struggled to smile, but tears stung his eyes and his throat tightened.

"Jonathan Cameron hasn't told you one word, has he?"

"No, sir. Maybe someday, when he gets to know me better. I hope so. I've always wanted a grandfather."

"What stumps me is why old Ethel was the one to inform you! If Cameron himself had told you, it would have been an act of kindness. From her, it's out-and-out cruelty." Mackay shook his head. "I don't know how you managed to go on as though nothing had happened. Of course, she seldom comes to town, and even if she did, I somehow don't think she'd tell anyone else. She must have had some twisted reason of her own for telling you. Jonathan certainly has kept his secret all these years. . . ."

"Even from Caroline."

"Will you tell her, Mark?"

"I don't know."

"At any rate, no one else in all Savannah knows the story. I can swear to that. I think you're fairly safe from gossip."

"I'm not afraid of that."

Mackay gave him a long, searching look. "I don't think you are. Could you marry Caroline, knowing that she may never find out?"

Mark grinned. "I thought you weren't going to play Cupid anymore."

"I asked a straightforward question."

"Yes, if that was the only reason not to marry her, I could."

"You—don't love her, do you?"

The tiny frown was barely noticeable. "I—love her in many ways. I'd give almost anything to make love to her. But, I—I guess I've watched Miss Eliza too long now. God only made one woman like her."

Mackay gave him a keen, quizzical look. The dark eyes narrowed. Mark's heart pounded. Then, the older man slapped the table with his open hand, the expansive smile back abruptly. "You're dead right about my wife, son! There's only one. Keep your sights high, though. If a fun-loving Regency buck like me can find a lady like Eliza, just think what the good Lord might have in store for *you!*"

Arm in arm—both, Mark thought, distinctly relieved—they made their way across the hotel lobby and up the stairs. Searching through his pockets for his room key, Mackay mentioned that while Mark saw Parsons tomorrow, he would be shopping for gifts for Eliza and the girls.

At Mackay's door they shook hands, then hugged good night—the second bear hug of Mark's life.

After a sound night's sleep, Mark rose early for breakfast with Mackay, who always vowed that his stomach gave him no peace after the sun rose. When Mark opened his door to bring in the pail of hot water for his bath, he saw Mackay's pail of water still in the hall outside his room; so he went about bathing and dressing himself in a leisurely fashion. Miss Eliza would be glad to know Mackay had slept late. He would write to her tonight, after he saw Parsons.

What, he wondered, as he rubbed up a lather on his shaving brush, would Parsons think of him as a man? He meant to select his clothes even more carefully than usual, in case James Parsons expected him to dress according to his means. Moving the razor along his angular jaw, Mark decided upon the new brown waistcoat and light-tan trousers he'd bought when he and Mackay went shopping in Philadelphia. Maybe, with a yellow cravat.

In the looking glass, before which he shaved, he saw the small frown crease his forehead. A habit he scarcely remembered, until Mackay mentioned it. Even Ethel Cameron had mentioned the frown, telling him that his mother had had the same habit. Had Mrs. Cameron called it endearing? Many of the details of his time with the inscrutable woman were gone. He'd purposely tried to wipe out the memory, he supposed. This morning, though, he liked knowing that even as a child, his mother had had the little frowning habit. Did she do it when something perplexed her? When she was trying to figure out what an adult meant? He didn't even know why he did it. The shock of what Ethel Cameron had told him that day locked so many questions inside. Question he wished now he had asked.

I should be making notes of some specific questions for Parsons, he thought, as he toweled his face. Since he got up, his mind had been mostly on the somehow satisfying conversation with Mackay last night. A conversation that could so easily have ended in disaster. Instead, he felt unusually lighthearted this morning, and more grateful to Robert Mackay than even Mark himself could have put into words. Grateful to his friend and close to him.

After cleaning his razor in a bowl of clear water, he put it in its leather case and began to dress. He was whistling a made-up tune. In just two more days they'd be back on the *Eliza,* headed for—home.

A pier glass in the corner of his room showed him that he had chosen well in Philadelphia. His old tailor seemed glad to see Mark and certainly, from the cut of the new coat, hadn't lost his touch.

The reflected image in the pier glass—a dark-haired, prosperous-looking, well-groomed young man—smiled. Not at his own good looks. He had just remembered the half hour he'd spent in the walnut-paneled office of Woodrow Woolsey, no longer the Browning family attorney. "I still think you're foolish, Mark, for having turned your back on a fortune," Woolsey had said, peering over his gold-rimmed spectacles. "But, you appear on your way toward making another in Georgia. I wish you well."

Mackay's earnings in the firm would be increased by almost 60 percent this year. Mark would share in it. He was on his way.

At Mackay's door—the pail of water still standing in the hall but no longer steaming—Mark knocked lightly. And waited. There was no answer.

He knocked again, more sharply. It was already eight-thirty. His appointment with Parsons was at ten o'clock.

He rapped still harder and called, "Mr. Mackay? Mr. Mackay, it's Mark. Time to get up!"

Still there was not a sound to be heard from inside the room. He tried the doorknob. Locked, of course.

For an instant he stood, wondering what to do. Then he was running down the two flights of stairs to the hotel desk to ask for an extra key to Mackay's door.

"Room two-fifteen, sir. The extra key, please!" he demanded of the fat, bald man behind the counter. "My friend, Mr. Robert Mackay of Savannah, doesn't answer my knock. His door is locked. It's past time he was up."

The rotund gentleman stood slowly, shaking his head from side to side. "Sorry, Mr. Browning. Against house rules to give out the spare key except to the guest occupying the room."

"But, sir, I've got to get in! He's not been well. Can't you make an exception this once? Mr. Mackay and I are traveling together."

The round, shiny head shook with agitation. "Sorry, sir. Rules of the house, but if you can wait until I inform the manager, I can go up with you and unlock Mr. Mackay's door."

The man was gone into an inner office for long, long minutes, but finally they were climbing the stair, and at Mackay's door the clerk inserted a huge master key and swung it open. The curtains were still drawn. Mackay lay sprawled face down across the fully made bed.

Mark rushed to him, calling his name.

As the clerk drew one set of curtains to let in the bright, autumn light, Mark turned Mackay on his back. The large, warm, brown eyes stared unseeing at the ceiling.

He was dead.

# TWENTY-SEVEN

THE six-day voyage south had been smooth, "sweet," Mackay would have called it. After the initial shock, Mark's grief had seemed to mount in stages. The Episcopal service at Trinity Church in New York—odd for Scottish Robert Mackay, the Presbyterian—was the earliest possible service Mark could arrange if he was to see the boys back to their school and board the *Eliza* himself on October 7. William and Jack had been good soldiers. Jack first, then William, had agreed that their father would not want them to leave school. William, his thin face pinched with the struggle not to weep, had clung to Mark at their good-bye in the parlor of McCulloch's house. Jack, tears streaming, had saluted bravely. "Please tell Mama to be all right," Jack had whispered. It was William who let Mark know how glad he was that their mother would have Mark beside her.

The three had stood, Mark between the boys, holding hands, while Robert Mackay was buried beneath Trinity's Gothic spire in New York, such a long way from Savannah.

On the *Eliza*, traveling alone now, Mark had rejected Captain Nance's offer of Mackay's more spacious stateroom. Instead, he took a cramped, single cabin he'd never seen before. The strange surroundings did not help. The "sweet" voyage—light winds, smooth sea—did not match the storm of grief and dread inside him. Twice, he dined with Captain Nance. Sharing their memories of Mackay had helped some. Mostly, day after heavy day—under a sunny sky or low, gray clouds—he struggled to prepare himself, by some means, to face what lay ahead.

On the morning of the last day, just as the *Eliza* was leaving the open sea to begin her slow movement up the Savannah River, he stood in the prow in almost the exact spot where Robert Mackay had first shown him Savannah. This time he scarcely noticed the Tybee light tower; the yellowing rice fields bent by the wind, alive with workers at harvest; Fort Jackson, where his friend had pulled his duty so often for the Chatham Artillery. From the moment he'd looked at those unseeing brown eyes, Mark's thoughts, no matter what task or duty was at hand, had seemed to crash into the inevitable moment when he would have to tell Eliza.

Please, God, he prayed, let the tide hold so that we can go right on into our wharf. He was exhausted. Sleep, since Mackay's death, had been measurable in spans of two or three hours at best. The wind burned his eyes, raw from his own weeping, from lack of sleep.

His hands gripped the railing until his fingers hurt. He was going home to Eliza, but how would he find words to tell her that the strong, laughing man—the shining center of her world —would never come home again? Would not even be buried in Savannah soil. That she would have no grave to visit, to honor, to remember with flowers through the years. That she could not even be buried beside him. In a way, Mark supposed, she might have been better able to accept it all had he died during the long illness at The Grange. But Robert Mackay, the last time Mark saw him, had seemed more alive than Mark himself: his infectiously buoyant, tender, energetic self.

He let his hands go slack on the railing. I should be praying for a docking delay, he thought. *I* haven't accepted it yet. It's still not real to *me* that he's gone! The clatter and shouts and rumble that drifted out from Turnbull's wharves as the *Eliza* eased past did not blot out the memories of the sound of the boys' weeping and his own, the minister's sonorous voice, the clods thudding the lid of a coffin that unbelievably confined Robert Mackay.

"Won't be too long now, Mr. Browning," Captain Nance called from somewhere just above where he stood.

"That's right," he tried to shout back. His voice split and the foreign sound of it seemed to begin the worst nightmare thought of all. In the midst of his own deep grief for Mackay, he began to long, as never before, to hold Eliza in his arms. To comfort her, to ease her heart—even a little. "Unless she falls into my arms," he said aloud roughly, "I cannot do that! I dare not."

Thank God, she wouldn't be on the dock waiting.

*"Too uncivil, our waterfront,"* Mackay had said that first day. *"My man, Hero, will be there to take care of our luggage. Someone from my office will have run to the house to tell my family that we're moving in toward the wharf. Hero will be there."*

Hero would be there today. Telling the gentle-mannered servant, who all but worshiped Mackay, would be hard enough. In spite of that, Mark was comforted some. Hero had become a friend, too. Caroline, he felt sure, would still be at the Broughton Street house. That would also help.

The *Eliza*, Mackay's pride and joy, under the hand of old Thompson, the bar pilot, had moved majestically past the stacked wharves at Turnbull's Tavern, where ordinary cargoes were unloaded. Her owner was not aboard, but the *Eliza* still carried the privilege of Mackay's high standing on Commerce Row. There was no reprieve from the tide. Too soon, the sleek schooner made her way past Fort Wayne and, slowing still more, moved perfectly into the Mein and Mackay slip, her prow extending proudly out over River Street.

Mark was not ready.

Tears had begun to flow down his cheeks. With an already damp handkerchief, he wiped his burning eyes and began to scan the crowd. Hero's fine, dark head should be easily visible above the throng of people meeting the boat, of stevedores clearing wharf space for the *Eliza*'s cargo. Fresh tears came in such a rush that seeing was difficult. At last, he glimpsed the long, waving arm. Hero was there, eager as always, to welcome his master home. Eliza, Mark knew, would be calling the two older girls, so they could meet Papa together. In a few minutes, once Mark had begun the solitary walk to Broughton Street, he would meet them—Eliza as childlike in her anticipation as her girls. Undoubtedly, they would meet him halfway to the house, hurrying. . . .

"Dear God," he breathed, "when they see only—me—what will happen?"

Hero's arm still waved above the heads of the others on the wharf and Mark forced himself to wave back.

And then . . . far below Hero's broad shoulders, he saw her . . . waving, too, pushing her way through the crowd. She was

dressed in soft green, her happy, eager face framed by a bonnet of the same shade.

Church bells were ringing; Mark remembered it was Sunday. Eliza had obviously sent the girls to church with Caroline
so that, with Hero to look after her on the waterfront, she
could meet her husband alone.

He tried later to remember leaving the ship. He couldn't. He
could only remember moving toward her along the noisy,
crowded dock. She had seen him. She had seen Mark *alone*
and had stopped hurrying. He would always remember that
much. She had stopped dead in her tracks. A burly stevedore
tossed an enormous bag of rice so near her, Mark gasped. A
running child struck her—hard enough to turn her almost
around. She seemed not to notice. Clutching her green beaded
purse—Mark knew the purse well—she stood staring at him
with almost no expression on her face. He was moving toward
her as slowly as he could walk and not lose his balance—the
awful dread upon him—the emptiness causing his head to
swim. No words formed. There would have to be words eventually. Now, only four or five steps away from Eliza, nothing
came but an unspoken cry: God! Oh, God, help us both!

Her small, square hand reached toward him—not in greeting—reaching. About her neck, she was wearing the green
jade heart. He saw her lips form his name, but no sound came.

The hazel eyes held only the question he dreaded. No! No,
he thought abruptly. *She knows.* It isn't a question. Eliza
knows. I don't have to tell her.

Grasping both her hands, he looked down at her and shook
his head yes.

Yes. Yes, Eliza Mackay, he's gone. He won't ever come
home again. Your life has been broken apart. We can't nurse
him back to health this time. He's—gone.

Mark felt himself sway as he caught her. Hero's strong arm
shot out to steady them both momentarily. Then, she pulled
away. Something about the set of her head, the unnatural glint
in her eyes, seemed to slam shut a door. Mark stepped back.

*This moment belonged only to her.* Realization was freezing
her heart, turning it from flesh and blood to an icy mass that
would somehow protect her until something—God knew what
—could be done.

Mark heard his own voice, hoarse, asking a commonplace
question of Hero. "Did you come over in the carriage?"

"No, sir. Miss Eliza, she say she wanted to walk."

She was too excited to ride; Mark reconstructed the moment before she and Hero left the house. He could even hear her eager voice: "Yes, Hero, I'm going to walk! In fact, I may even—fly! I'm on my way to meet my husband—*alone*. I may fly apart, actually, if I don't get in a good walk first."

Now she stood, pine-straight, her chin high, her eyes dry, looking at the elegantly formed prow of the *Eliza* above her head. Looking and looking at the proud ship he'd named for her. Looking and looking, her lips drained of color, but suggesting almost a secret smile over something only the two of them would ever know. On her face was a kind of desperate victory, Mark thought. An intimately shared secret knowledge displayed in the midst of the traffic and noise and bedlam of the wharf.

She seemed so drawn into herself that Mark took still another step back—away from her.

Hero stood with his head bowed. Both men felt unnecessary, out of place in this moment that awesomely appeared to be—*shared*.

Then, she turned to Mark, her hand out again—still not in greeting—but in firm recognition of what lay ahead for her, for the children, for him.

"I—sent Eliza Anne and Kate with Caroline to church," she said; so softly that Mark had to lean down to hear. "I felt—a bit selfish. Now, I think it was best. Do the boys know?"

"Yes. They were with me in New York—at the church."

She nodded. Mark tucked her hand under his arm and they started across the crowded wharf toward the steep steps that led up to the Strand. Holding her hand helped him. Painfully aware that he had not yet spoken one word of comfort, he tightened his fingers over hers. Hers squeezed back.

Hero, without even asking, had gone for Mark's trunks—and Mackay's. Mark felt enormous gratitude. Not only for help with the luggage but because Hero, whose devotion to both Mackays ran so deep, seemed confident that Miss Eliza would be all right with Mark.

For a week Mark kept the offices of Mein and Mackay closed. Because Mark and Mackay were due back, Mein was away again at the North, but would, Mark knew, want the honor done in memory of his longtime partner.

The days of that week both dragged and flew by. They flew because his attention was focused on Eliza. They dragged because all of life was so foreign without Mackay. For hours at a time, Mark and Caroline simply sat with Eliza on the side porch or, through two stormy days, in the big, familiar parlor. The house was tomb-quiet. Even Eliza Anne and Kate tiptoed wherever they went, their eyes never dry long enough to lose the red swelling. Often, Caroline took them for walks and then Mark sat alone with Eliza, his heart a mass of pain as he watched her struggle to control a grief he knew he couldn't fathom. At the close of each day, he found himself loving her even more, longing more intensely to be able somehow to make her life good again.

The two stormy days early in the week, the air dark and heavy, had seemed worse for her. Each night, alone in his bed, he began to pray for sunshine tomorrow.

On Thursday of that first week, the sun came out after a noon shower and Mark hurried to dry off her favorite porch chair and arrange cushions in it. He took the chair beside her.

"Things look fresh, don't they?" she asked tonelessly.

"Yes, they do." His voice sounded overeager. "I love the way the gray moss swags turn pale green when it rains."

She turned her head slightly to look at him. "You're dearer to me than ever, Mark. Will I ever be able to thank you?"

"I hope you never try. When you need to be by yourself, you will tell me, won't you? I'd be honored if you felt that free with me."

"Yes, I will. The hours alone in my room at night seem enough. More than enough. Mark, there is something I have to know. It's been stabbing in and out of my mind ever since —ever since you came back. Did you see Mr. Parsons in New York?"

For a moment, he couldn't answer. An unexpected lump rose in his throat at the thought of her even bothering to care at a time like this.

"No. No, there wasn't time."

"I've reread Robert's last letter to me a hundred times. You were to see Parsons the day he—" A dry sob tore from her. "—the day he *died*." She drew a deep breath. "There, I've made myself say it. I had to use the word sooner or later."

Mark prayed for the right thing to say. Nothing came.

"You and I are going to make our way alone now," she went on. "We mustn't have any cloudy areas between us. There is—something Robert and I should have told you. I'll—have to tell you since you had no time to see Parsons."

He could help her. He could at least put her mind at ease over the Cameron story. "I know," he said. "I know—the whole thing!"

"You know?"

"I've known since Mrs. Cameron invited me to tea the afternoon Mr. Mackay fell ill at The Grange. She told me then."

Incredulous, Eliza turned to him and reached for his hand. He took hers in both of his. "You knew all through—Robert's illness in the country? You knew the whole story—and didn't say one word to us?"

"Not with him so sick."

"But, how did you—manage—all that time, alone?"

"It wasn't too bad, I guess, because what mattered most right then was—you. You and Mr. Mackay. I don't think anyone can really concentrate on but one thing at a time. Caring so much about—you—helped me put things in perspective."

She sat staring out into the yard, over the tops of her azalea bushes. Drops of rain glistened on their dark leaves. He waited, still holding her hand.

Then, on her drawn face, he saw a hint of a smile. "It's as though I can hear him say right now, 'Mark is different, Eliza. Mark's not like other young men his age.' " She looked at him. "You are, you know. As close as we've been, as close as we were that afternoon at The Grange, the natural thing would have been for you to tell me right off what Ethel Cameron spewed out to you."

He patted her hand. "Excuse me, but she really didn't—spew it out. Telling me was hard for her, too. I think she needed to tell someone that during the time Jonathan Cameron was—with my grandmother, Mary Cotting, Ethel Cameron—loved him."

"Do you believe that?"

"Yes, ma'am, I do."

"But it was cruel for her, a stranger, to tell you after all those years!"

"Miss Eliza, I don't think she's—quite logical. I don't think we can judge her by what anyone else might have done. It bothered me that day, but it just doesn't seem very important anymore—why she told me."

"Mark, don't you wonder how I know the story?"

"No. Mr. Mackay told me that Parsons had written it. It was decent of Parsons to want to be careful in case it might harm me. Mr. Mackay told me, after I'd poured out the whole story to him that night. Telling him—that night—seemed to settle the whole thing for me once and for all."

"Which night, Mark?"

"The night—"

"—*he died.*" She finished for him.

"Yes." Then, "Miss Eliza, Osmund Kott is in New York."

"How did you find that out?"

"Mr. Mackay told me. Kott has a good paying job with the Browning Company. Since I didn't get to ask Parsons, I don't know anything more about it. Apparently, Kott's doing his work. I think he's capable of it." Realizing that he had been gripping her hand, Mark loosened his fingers. "Say, if I go along, don't you think it might be good for you to walk around the yard a little? I'm going to be right here, Miss Eliza, for as long as you need me. We'll have lots of time to talk."

*Part III*

# 1816–1818

# TWENTY-EIGHT

CAROLINE stayed at the Broughton Street house until just before Christmas. Feeling that she could help Miss Eliza more by keeping the two older girls occupied than in any other way, she spent as much time as possible with them. They all wrote often to the boys in New York, and in the evenings Caroline tried to fill the house with music. She played the old harpsichord Eliza's father had given her as a girl, Kate strummed her very own dulcimer—a present from Mark—and Eliza Anne could now play Cousin Margaret's old violin rather well. Mark and Eliza played audience, listened attentively for the most part and never failed to applaud even the most uneven rendition of Mark's favorite song, "Drink to Me Only with Thine Eyes."

When the girls had been sent to bed, Caroline would go on playing the harpsichord—mostly Bach or Scarlatti because Eliza loved both composers' work.

Often, in the deep of night, Mark and Caroline would meet in their dressing gowns in the upstairs hall, both too worried about Eliza for sleep. After a time, neither was surprised to see the other tiptoeing toward Eliza's room or listening at their respective doors to the sound of her weeping.

"Why do we keep getting up, creeping about, Mark? What do we think we can do for her?"

He would shake his head, smile a little and go back to his room.

One clear, early December morning, she and Mark walked together toward Johnson Square, Mark escorting her on a shopping errand for Eliza. Caroline repeated the question: "What *do* we think we can do for her by getting up at night, just to listen to her weeping?''

"Nothing," he said. "Sometimes I feel guilty about hearing her weep. At least today, we're doing something definite. It's good of you to select some dress styles for her. Maybe wanting even new mourning dresses means she's actually thinking of going out—to church, anyway."

"She is," Caroline said. "But not because she wants to. Because she knows people will start talking if she doesn't. It's been two months now. Of course she has to wear black for a long time, yet. I hate the thought of Miss Eliza in black. I don't think Mr. Mackay would like it, either."

"Do you think she really liked the black silk and cotton goods I picked out the other day?"

"Oh, yes, Mark. You have splendid taste. I don't know—I honestly don't know what Miss Eliza would have done without you."

"Without *you*," he said, linking his arm with hers. "I don't know what I would have done if you hadn't been—with us."

She waited before answering. "I wouldn't be leaving, even for Christmas, if it weren't for Grandfather. In the letter I got from him yesterday, he's refusing to hold the 'Christmas gif' party for his people without me. I've never left him alone—with her—this long, you know." She sighed. "He's seventy-three now. He could—be gone, too, by next Christmas." When he said nothing, she asked, "You do believe I'd stay through the holidays and help with Miss Eliza and the children if I could, don't you, Mark? Christmas is such a terrible time to be sad."

He smiled down at her. "Of course I believe you. I care about—your grandfather, too. You must both come back early in the new year. Miss Eliza needs you with her, and your grandfather and I will have to plan his spring ordering from London."

"I don't think Miss Eliza needs anyone but you. The girls try so hard, and at eight and six, they can be quite a lot of comfort. But Miss Eliza needs—a man coming home from work every day with news of the town and with an appetite. She told me the other day that one of the things that frightened her most about the future was the day you begin to think about building your own house."

Caroline noticed that he kept his eyes straight ahead when he asked, "She really said that? I guess I did mention to her the other day how much I admired Isaiah Davenport's plans for the new home he's building for himself on State. Did she really say that?"

"Do you think I'd make it up?"

He gave her a sideways glance, which told her nothing. They were nearing Andrew Low's store. Caroline slowed their pace, needing a last minute alone with him. "If the black crepe veiling has come in, she might even go to church with you this Sunday," she said.

"I'd like that. Otherwise, with you gone, I'd have to sit in my solitary Browning pew alone."

"Before we go in the store, there's something else Miss Eliza's both dreading and anticipating." *I'm purposely detaining him,* she thought—*and didn't care.* "She's dreading—*and* looking forward to—the first time you take her to Mr. Mackay's church when the building is finally finished. You know how proud he was of it. The Mackays were going to have the architect, John Holden Greene, to dinner on his next visit from Rhode Island to inspect the church. Miss Eliza can't talk much about it—she cries—but she dreads it."

"She tells you a lot, doesn't she?"

"Yes. I'm devoted to her, too."

He sighed, his hand on the brass knob of the tall door to Andrew Low's Emporium. "Caroline, Miss Eliza depends on you. I've also come to depend on you. Maybe—too much."

She smiled—casually, she hoped. *"You*—depend on me, Mr. Browning?"

His tiny frown flickered. "Yes, I do."

For an instant she let her gloved hand fall over his on the doorknob. "Well, you *can* depend on me." She made herself smile more broadly. "Until you're a very old man and I'm a very old lady."

Having Caroline in the house so often was, for Eliza, like a breath of fresh air let into her suffocating grief. She had always believed a wife and mother to be responsible in large part for the atmosphere in any home. No one felt well and cheerful every day, but from the first week of her married life, she had tried her best to create the kind of environment in which the family could flourish. She was still trying, for the children's sake and for Mark's, but oh, grieving was work— hard work. Caroline and her grandfather were in town for the laying of the cornerstone of Mackay's Presbyterian Church on January 13, 1817, and they came again in the late spring.

Jonathan Cameron still preferred his room at Mein's house, but Caroline now was a regular guest on Broughton Street.

"What a difference it makes, having you with us, Caroline," Eliza said as they unfolded yards of new green-and-white-striped cotton on the sewing table Hero had set up for them on the sunny side porch. "If I had to make the girls' new everyday dresses by myself today, I'd be dreading it."

"No one would ever guess," Caroline answered, smoothing a length of yardage so that Eliza could do the cutting. "I think you've been so plucky—and cheerful."

Eliza made only a small scoffing sound.

"But it's true, you have been. Mark thinks so, too. And the girls tell me all about how you are when I'm not here."

Eliza looked up, scissors in hand. "They report to you on my behavior?"

"And both of them tell me over and over that lots of times when one or the other of them has been about to have a crying spell, you say something cheerful, which turns off the tears."

"I don't feel cheerful. I'm putting it on."

"Only because you're trying to make it easier for them. It isn't hard for people to be cheerful if they feel that way already. What you do is—like a love gift to them."

Eliza, her eyes brimming, smiled at her. "Thank you. I'm doing my best, which, to me, most of the time seems pretty feeble. Hand me the pincushion, please?"

For several minutes Caroline held the ripped-apart pieces of an old dress of Kate's firmly on the material while Eliza schemed and pinned. "They don't like being dressed alike any longer," she said, "so I'm trying to get cushion covers for The Grange porch chairs, too, out of this one piece of goods."

A towhee called "sweet, sweet" from somewhere close to the porch railing.

Eliza stopped to listen. "Robert liked the towhee's song best of all."

When Caroline only smiled, Eliza felt a rush of gratitude toward her for knowing when and when not to try to say something. There were times, after all, as when she stopped to listen to Robert's favorite birdcall, when there was nothing that could be said.

The bird gave its bright spring call again and Eliza went back to her pinning.

"I wish you could have seen Grandfather's face on that steamboat trip into town this time," Caroline mused after a while. "He loved it! He stood on the little deck the whole time and said over and over, 'Just think, Caroline, we're moving right along by means of—steam! Not a sail in sight.' He was like a child."

"How did you like it?"

"All right, I guess. Noisy. I think I like sailing better, but Grandfather loved the speed of it. Did you hear that regular steamboat service will begin sometime this year between Savannah and Charleston?"

Holding a skirt panel in place, Eliza looked up. "No, I hadn't heard. Was it in the paper?"

Caroline nodded. "Grandfather read it aloud to me. They even printed a schedule, although no one knows yet when it will start. But a boat will arrive here each Monday and depart for Charleston each Tuesday. Just think about that! No waiting on the wind or the weather or the tide with a steam engine. Grandfather is lyrical."

Tears were blurring Eliza's vision again, but she managed a small laugh. "My oh my, wouldn't my husband have loved that! The regular schedule and the speed of such a river trip would be just his meat!" A glimpse of the tender, caring look in Caroline's eyes brought still more tears.

"I'm so proud of you, Miss Eliza."

She sighed. "In spite of my never-ending tears and all the trouble I've caused you and Mark?" She tried another laugh.

"Don't you know that when someone is loved the way Mark and I love you, there just is no such thing as trouble?"

Not trusting herself to answer, Eliza smiled her gratitude.

"Besides, Mark's so busy these days, if you didn't make me feel welcome here, I—I'd never see him."

"Oh, that boy *is* busy. He vows my husband's affairs were not in bad order, but everything was so sudden." She secured a square of material with pins and stood looking out at the sharp, clean shadow of the nearest oak tree patterned on the grass. "The firm of Mein and Mackay is finally dissolved. Death—is so final, even William Mein couldn't delay breaking the partnership any longer. Mark says I now own all of

Robert's share of the firm, clear and free. Mark and I think we'll sell it. You see, since he took on your grandfather's factoring account, he's discovered that he likes being a factor far more than he liked being a merchant. Oh, I suppose he'll do some of both, but after we've had a little more time to think about it, I expect we'll decide it's best for me to sell my interest in the firm.''

"Isn't it—wonderful that you have Mark, Miss Eliza?"

"Oh, Caroline! I can't even think what my life might be like now without him!''

After a time, Caroline asked, ''You're—not going to sell The Grange, are you?''

"No, I most certainly am not. The land is not productive yet, but no, my dear. I'm far too sentimental about The Grange. He bought it to please me, to give me back some of my happy childhood memories there." Hurriedly, she returned to her cutting. "And soon, I'm sure I'll be able to go to The Grange again, as usual.''

"Do you suppose—if you do sell the business—that you and the girls might move to The Grange?"

"No, I don't think I could. I loved it as my grandparents' plantation when I was a girl, but I don't swing on grapevines much anymore and I don't really like to fish." She put down the scissors and looked around. "This big old place—is home. I couldn't leave it.''

"Being here doesn't remind you too much of—him?"

"Yes, of course it does." She went back to cutting. "I'll lose some of the pain one day, I'm told, or it will be less sharp. Someday I may even stop expecting him to call to me each time the front door opens. But, his hands touched almost every inch of this house. He walked on every floorboard. The rooms still hold his laughter—and his prayers. Even his occasional bursts of annoyance and anger. I'll never leave. I wish I could be as sure of other things as I am of that. Caroline, will you hold that corner while I cut around it, please?"

As they worked, Eliza glanced often at the nearly perfect profile of the girl who had known so much pain already, and she longed to give back even half of what Caroline had given her. Often, at night, in her room, she would try to recall the ways in which Caroline had helped, especially through those first months of shock. Even Christmas still remained to Eliza a shadowy, shapeless blur. Caroline had gone back to Knightsford to be with her grandfather, but Eliza remembered how she had waited for her to return in January. Next to Mark, Caroline had been her comfort. Too often, she was sure, Caroline and not their mother had dried the tears of the two little girls who fought so valiantly to cope with the grim finality that their papa would never come home again.

If I could, Eliza thought, as they sat down side by side to do the basting, I'd promise this lovely girl that one day she and Mark will share what Robert and I had for sixteen years. No one can do that. Mark does love her; I know he loves Caroline in some very real way, but beyond that, I just don't know.

Now and then, as they worked, she and Caroline exchanged smiles. One thing Eliza liked so much about her was that she knew how to share a comfortable silence. Undoubtedly, she and I are both thinking about Mark in vastly different ways. I know, at least, exactly how he loves me. He not only stood by my two sons at their father's funeral service, he still writes to each of them twice a week. Mark would do anything in his power for me. But then, I was thirty-nine last week. I'm a comfortable, uncomplicated age for a twenty-five-year-old to love—safely.

Caroline finished her basting first and went to get tea. Alone on the porch, Eliza tried to stop her thoughts. Thinking too much alone still depressed her, and a new fear went on gripping her. The day she most dreaded now was the day Mark would marry and move away. He had said little about his own place since Robert died, but she knew he spent many of his evenings after work now at the Davenport house, with Isaiah, in Eliza's opinion the best builder in town. Mark actually seemed drawn to the reserved, dry-humored New Englander. He greatly admired Isaiah's taste in houses, had kept Eliza informed on the progress of all three new homes Davenport had under construction in Savannah—aside from his own. "The poor man may never get his place finished," Mark had said. "If he does finish it someday, though, Miss Eliza, it will be the finest house in town."

She knew Cousin Margaret liked the much-discussed Richardson mansion on Oglethorpe Square, begun last year after the plans of a young Englishman named William Jay, a relative by marriage of bank president Richard Richardson's wife. From what Eliza heard, the Richardson house would be far grander, more ornate—a fine example of the fashionable

Regency style coveted in Savannah, certainly by those in the
financial class of the Richardsons and the Scarbroughs and the
Telfairs. To an extent, Robert had indulged a certain bent for
flamboyance, but neither he nor Eliza had ever dreamed of
leaving the rambling, generous house where belonging mattered more than ostentation.

When Caroline returned, Eliza, pins in her mouth, was smiling to herself at what Robert might say now with all the talk in
town of fine new houses.

"What's so funny?" Caroline asked, setting down the tea
tray. "What a happy surprise to come back and find you—
smiling!"

Carefully, as she'd tried to teach Eliza Anne to do, Eliza
took the pins out of her mouth before answering. "I was just
thinking about the Richardsons and the Scarbroughs and so
on. Mark tells me they're all planning new Regency mansions—hoping to knock all our eyes out, as Robert would say,
by their opulence. Mark, I'm glad to see, prefers Isaiah
Davenport's simpler, New England taste—and Mark's richer
than the whole kit and caboodle of them."

"So do I like the Davenport house better." Caroline handed
Eliza her tea. "Did Mark tell you when William Jay, the
young British architect, is coming to Savannah?"

"I didn't even know he was coming. Or, if Mark told me,
I've forgotten. But if he does come here, he just might get
rich, too, if he isn't already. Julia Scarbrough will promote
him, I'm sure."

"Mark told me that Jay isn't at all wealthy. But he's really
studied architecture and is remarkably talented for his age.
He's only twenty-one or so. Mark says Jay's plans are very
clearly drawn and, although novel in certain ways, quite easy
to build from. He's seen the Richardson house plans."

"And he's been listening to Julia's ravings about young
Jay, I have no doubt."

"No doubt. But, mainly, Mark listens to the builders'
views." She paused, sipped her tea. "I think Mark's—planning a house of his own, Miss Eliza; do you think he is?"

"He's interested, certainly." She sighed lightly. "He used
to talk of building his own place and living there as a bachelor.
He hasn't mentioned that lately. One thing I do know, and
straight from Julia Scarbrough herself, is that she fully intends
to have William Jay build a new home for her. One so large,

she won't ever again have to take down the beds in order to make room for dancing. Julia also fully intends to talk Mark into using Jay as his architect, if he ever does build his own house."

"Julia will fail at that, I can promise you. Ostentation, no matter how impressive, is not Mark's taste." Caroline stopped a moment, as though deciding, Eliza thought, whether or not to say what she was really thinking. Finally, she said lightly, "I'm glad Mrs. Scarbrough has started to visit you again. I know you like her."

"I do and Julia came to call on me as soon as she could— bear to come, Caroline. She was devoted to Robert. Do you realize that she hasn't given a party since he—went away?"

"I know. Mark says the Scarbroughs are going to London soon."

"And if William Jay doesn't get here before they leave, he'll be the first person Julia looks up over there. She will never permit the Richardsons to have the only new mansion in Savannah! I'm not gossiping. Julia told me that herself last week. The Richardson house may be finished first, but hers will be close behind."

"Do you know that you sound just like *you*—a lot of the time now?" Caroline asked, her face beaming. "Having a good talk like this with you makes me so happy!"

Eliza sighed and set down her teacup. "I'm sure it does. I've felt sorry for you and Mark so much of the time. And it's a relief having an ordinary conversation about other people's doings now and then—without working to get my breath." She patted Caroline's arm. "I'll come back entirely one day. I don't want to go on worrying all of you. I don't, Caroline. And I don't intend to, either."

# TWENTY-NINE

WITH Mackay gone, Eliza's brother, John McQueen, retained Mark as his factor. Mark had nearly doubled Jonathan Cameron's profits and told John that he longed to do equally well for him.

"Don't worry." McQueen smiled across a table at the Exchange Coffee Shop as he and Mark had breakfast one rainy summer morning. "Long ago, I stopped expecting miracles. None happened for my father. None happen for me. Just keep me from bankruptcy. Even my worldly-wise wife has acclimated herself to being poor."

"Ridiculous," Mark said, cutting a piece of thick ham. "You have good land, you're an innovative planter. Why shouldn't you be well off, John? Savannah's making a fine recovery from the war. You've formed the habit of losing, that's all. I say we break that habit."

"More power to you, if you can bring it off," John said. "I simply won't be here long enough to know about it."

"You won't be here?"

"I give myself about five or six years to live. In that time, I fully intend to do only as Margaret wants. She'll have my full attention. Far more than I'm willing to give my Causton's Bluff plantation. I waited for her too long to do otherwise."

"I'm ignoring your ludicrous prediction about dying. Eliza says that Margaret wants to visit her mother in Jamaica now. Is that why you two came to town?"

"She's at Eliza's this minute, giving her the news. We sail next week."

Mark ate in silence for a time, then said, lightly, "You'll

298

miss the excitement of William Jay's arrival from England. I also hear that the Council hopes to commission him to design our new theater."

John arched a skeptical eyebrow. "Should missing all that break my heart?"

"No," Mark laughed, "but the Richardson house won't be Jay's only triumph in our city. Unless I miss my guess, the Scarbroughs' house will be close behind the Richardsons', and there's talk of getting Jay to design not only a theater but a bank."

"I feel sure Savannah can proceed without me for a time."

"How long?"

"Not sure. A year—maybe more." He lifted a hand. "And you don't need to tell me I'll be away when my crops are sold. Yes, I will be. But you're my factor. All decisions are in your capable hands." He looked at Mark for a long moment. "I sound glib, I know. I don't feel that way. I wish I had adequate means to thank you for all you've done for my sister. Eliza *is* going to be all right, isn't she? As much as will ever be possible without Robert?"

Mark frowned. "I—think so."

"Anything wrong?"

"No. I just have to wonder sometimes if she will ever be all right again." He smiled sadly. "I even wonder if *I'll* ever learn how to be my old self without him. I know it's far harder for her. Mackay filled the worlds of so many people. He was so alive. His boys got through the funeral, I'm certain, only because they still couldn't grasp that he was—really dead. Now and then, in my office, I'm pulled up short, *sure*—absolutely sure—I've heard his laugh, his hearty shout out the office window when he needed someone down on the wharf." Mark shook his head. "Robert Mackay was the hardest of men to lose."

"Should I not be leaving Eliza?"

"Oh, I think she'll want you both to go. I wish she'd go with you. She says she doesn't dare even visit The Grange. To her, it would be almost like losing him again—to have to come back to Broughton Street without him."

John McQueen put a spoonful of sugar in his coffee and sat stirring in silence. Then, he said in his matter-of-fact voice, "Are you in love with Eliza?"

He saw Mark catch his breath, force himself to place his fork soundlessly back on the plate.

"I know that's a brash question," McQueen said, still matter-of-factly. "I like you more than you suspect, Browning. My sister, aside from Margaret, is all I have left. Maybe, just maybe, someday when she's out of her widow's weeds, more herself again, I might be able to put in a good word for you—if you do love her. I've suspected that you do for quite some time now." John waited, watching the young, tense features. Mark was frowning deeply. The frown did not come and go as John had noticed so many times before. Between the straight, dark brows, the two sharp creases deepened as the seconds ticked away. "If I'm wrong, Mark, you only have to tell me. If I'm right—and your silence tells me that I am— wouldn't it be better to have me to talk to?"

John saw Mark's shoulders heave and fall on a deep breath, but he remained silent.

"You're safe with me," John said.

When Mark finally looked at him, John saw that tears filled the deep-set gray eyes. "I've—loved her for a long time," he said simply. "I don't know when it began. But it was before Mackay died. Should I be—ashamed of myself?"

"Are you?"

"No."

"Then, that's your answer. No one has yet seen any particular deception in your makeup. You don't deceive yourself, do you?"

"I don't think so."

"If you had one even slightly tainted intention toward my sister, *she* would know it, I guarantee you that. Eliza has no idea, not the remotest idea, that you love her in any other way than you would a friend—even a mother or an older sister."

John saw the fine hands clench.

"I know. She'll never love me any other way. Never be able to think of me as more than her earnest young friend who wants to help."

"I suppose you can't finish your breakfast now."

Mark looked at the half-eaten ham and biscuits. He laughed dryly. "That's right. But she'll have a big meal waiting when I go home early this afternoon. She hasn't allowed the household routine to change one iota. A man still comes home hungry from work. Dinner is still ready."

"That makes it all the harder for you to keep—pretending, doesn't it?"

Mark stared at his plate for a long time, then said, "You know how it is, John, when you've been working for a long time or rowing a boat or riding a great distance and then you finally get a chance to rest? Only after you're resting do you realize how tired you've been all along." He smiled weakly. "That's the way I feel now, thanks to you. I didn't know how alone I'd felt in all this. How bone tired."

"No one knows? *No one?*"

"I—I think, for a reason I still can't explain, that I managed to let Mr. Mackay know the last time we were together. The night he died."

"What did he say?"

"He acted as though he hadn't really caught on."

"That sounds like him. He trusted you, didn't he? Trusted you to work your own way out of it."

Mark nodded. Then, as though the thought had just struck: "How did *you* guess?"

"I didn't guess. I sensed. After Robert died, I also wanted it to be true, for my sister's sake. You see, Browning, I trust you, too. And she *is* all I have left of my family." He thought awhile. "Can you wait—as things are now—until she's out of mourning, and longer?"

Without hesitation, Mark smiled and answered, "I can wait for as long as she needs. You see, only Eliza can send me away. I'll never go of my own accord."

"What about Miss Caroline?"

The smile vanished. "I don't know. The truth is, I care about Caroline the way I should care about Miss Eliza. I care about Eliza the way I should care about Caroline. Nothing makes much sense, does it?"

"Does it ever where love is concerned? I waited for my wife until I was almost as old as Eliza is now. Mentioning her age offends you, doesn't it?"

"Frankly, yes."

"And it wasn't very kind of me to wait until I'm about ready to leave the country to offer you a—confidant, was it?"

A slow smile brightened Mark's face. "Don't worry about that. You'll be helping me, just by knowing, all the way from

Jamaica." They stood to go. "And now I'll do more than my
best to double your profits while you're gone."

"Your reputation for compounding dollars has spread all
the way to Charleston, I understand."

Mark handed John his hat from the rack and reached for his
own. "Lucky at money, unlucky at love, eh?"

"I didn't say that; you did."


"Well aware that Judge Charlton, not I, holds the honor of
being your attorney, young man," Sheftall Sheftall said, settling himself in Mark's office in November, "I am here pri-
marily as a friend."

"Whatever the reason," Mark said, "I'm honored. What
can I do for you, sir?"

"To be blunt, you can use that intelligent head of yours and
turn down the persuasive urgings of Mr. William Scarbrough
when he comes to ask you to invest in his new oceangoing
steamship, the S.S. *Savannah*."

"I've heard about it, Mr. Sheftall, but no one has approached me. Oh, I believe Mrs. Scarbrough did call on Mrs.
Mackay not long ago—"

"Typical procedure in society-ridden Savannah. Mind you,
the Scarbroughs are among our best people. I am deeply fond
of both. They have charming daughters. None so beautiful as
their mother. But Scarbrough will be after your money. I pray
you not to invest."

"And why are you so set against Scarbrough's idea for an
oceangoing steamship?"

"Not practical."

It was evident, since he picked up his tricorn and got to his
feet, that the older man meant to give no other reasons. So
Mark thanked him, said he hoped Sheftall Sheftall would call
on Miss Eliza now that her year of mourning was ended, and
bade him good day.


"Julia was here again this afternoon," Eliza told Mark as
they sat together in the high-ceilinged parlor that night. "She
does cheer me up, but she also—as Robert used to say—mows
me down. She is barely skimming the earth these days.
William Jay arrives next week and she has already engaged
him to build what she's calling 'a dream of a house.' Mr. Scar-

brough's bought property on West Broad, and from the description of the house they've commissioned Mr. Jay to design, it will put all others in this town to shame."

Mark smiled. "At least, that's what the countess hopes." He was only half listening.

"She's very good in her heart, though," Eliza went on. "And that's rare, wouldn't you say, in a woman with her social ambitions? Of course, she's giving an enormous party in her present house for William Jay, early in December, I believe she said. You and Caroline are going to be invited. So, be prepared."

"Caroline will like that. So will I. I wish you would go, too."

"I could now, I suppose, without causing too much talk. But—" the tears welled, "you can see I'm not quite ready. Anyway, I'd be a burden to you two young people. It should be a splendid affair." When Mark didn't answer, she continued. "Julia also talked for at least a quarter of an hour about the wonders of her husband's latest progressive idea."

"The steam-powered ocean vessel?"

She reached across the space between their chairs for Mark's hand. "No one needs to give you any advice where business matters go, but do be careful when our get-rich-quick money schemes are aimed your way. People know of your wealth by now."

He grabbed her hand, but said nothing.

"Mark, is something the matter?"

He nearly turned his chair over as he jumped up, then fell to his knees before her, the small square hand pressed hard against his face.

"Mark!"

"Please don't say anything," he whispered. "I—I just needed to—to—" He forced himself to laugh, got quickly to his feet and stood above her, struggling to keep the smile on his face, to slow his breathing. "Miss Eliza, I don't—know what made me do such a thing."

The clear hazel eyes were looking up at him with such genuine concern, he could not look away.

"You're—very tired," she said. "How terribly hard you've been working this past year! Should you take the boat and go to The Grange alone for a while? You could see a lot of

Caroline and fish and take walks and—''

"No!" He gentled his voice. "I mean, I'm fine. I'm not so tired."

"You needed someone to comfort you, didn't you?" she said softly. "Every ounce of your energy has gone to smoothing the rough places for the children and—for me. I should be comforting *you,* now."

His longing to touch her again, to take her in his arms, so overwhelmed him that he felt like a man running downhill—out of control—unable to stop himself. *I must* love her even more than I want her, he thought wildly.

She was smiling up at him. " 'A nip of brandy never did a man anything but good.' Do you remember hearing him say that a hundred times? Get yourself a nip—a little wine for me. Would you, please?"

Grateful for something to do, he hurried to the cupboard where Mackay kept his good brandy and wine. The sudden desperate desire of a moment ago was waning. He poured a splash of brandy for himself, a small glass of burgundy for her. When he turned and faced Eliza, the glasses in hand, he felt almost safe again. Safe in his love for her. In whatever she could spare for him.

They sipped together in silence for a time, then Eliza asked, "Has William Scarbrough approached you yet about investing in his steam-powered sailing ship?"

"No, but Sheftall Sheftall warned me against it today."

She laughed a little. "Bless him, what did he say about a ship that will use both steam power and sails?"

" 'Not practical.' "

"That sounds like him. But you must decide for yourself, you know."

"Yes, ma'am. I've been thinking that I might invest a small amount. After all, if the maiden voyage to Europe is a success, a ship like that could mean a lot to Savannah." He changed the subject. "Eliza Anne tells me you had a letter today from Miss Margaret. How are the McQueens enjoying Jamaica?"

"They're having a wonderful time, according to her. John wrote often to our father in the old days when they were apart, but Margaret does the honors now. Have you let John know about all the money you made for him on his crops this year?" She laughed again, almost her old merry laugh. "Now, that *was* a woman question, wasn't it? Of course you've let him know."

Mark nodded.

"You didn't think he should have left his overseer in charge of loading his cotton and benne seed oil, did you?"

"Actually, I didn't. But his decision was to go with Miss Margaret."

"Mark, John has all but worshiped her since she was a little girl. He'll never change. I wouldn't want him to."

"I think it's beautiful."

"He was right to wait," she went on. "John seldom shows it, but after very restless early years, he's totally contented in his marriage. He doesn't seem to mind at all that they waited too long to have children." She lifted her glass to him with a warm smile. "Don't you wait too long, dear boy."

Once, he enjoyed her calling him dear boy. Now, it hurt.

# THIRTY

AT the Scarbrough ball given in William Jay's honor, Mark met the young British architect soon after Jay's arrival at the end of 1817. Mark's description of the much-discussed twenty-one-year-old Jay delighted Eliza.

"He's like a quite handsome bird, actually," Mark told her. "He has thick red hair that springs up from his high forehead like the crest of that woodpecker Hero calls the Lord God bird. I will say Jay is a most likable fellow, and unless I miss my guess, he'll grow wealthy in our city. The countess acts as though she thought him up. She takes full credit for him and the two will either be soul mates or enemies by the time he's finished her 'dream of a house' on West Broad. We'll never be the same in Savannah now that Jay is here," he predicted. "Wait until he begins our new theater—and our bank."

It was good having their talks at work in the yard or sitting side by side on the porch as they'd done before Mackay died. "Miss Eliza seems almost like her old self sometimes," he told Caroline on a visit to Knightsford in the spring of 1818. "I'm glad you two are such friends." Caroline seemed glad to be Eliza's friend, too. Mark was grateful. Both women were important to him in their separate ways. For right now, he was disciplining himself to live one day at a time. There was no law of church or state that said a man had to be married by the time he was twenty-six—or even thirty.

Mark had formed the habit of visiting Knightsford fairly often during the months when Caroline could not come to the city. He hated leaving Eliza alone in the house with the girls, but he also hated it that Caroline had to live long weeks at a time under the same roof with Ethel Cameron, who never addressed her husband.

"Oh, Grandfather doesn't talk to her anymore, either," Caroline said grimly as she and Mark rode along Savannah's Whitaker Street on a mild May evening. Suddenly, she turned to him, her face troubled. "Oh, Mark, I'm sorry. I love your new green gig. I should be acting as though I'm enjoying our ride. Besides, I've been in the city a whole week! Wouldn't you think I could forget Knightsford? At least, keep still about it? I know I talk too much about my home problems."

"Nothing of the kind," he said. "They're my problems, too."

"That doesn't make any sense and you know it."

"They concern you, don't they?" He let the reins go slack, allowing Handsome, his fine chestnut gelding, to set his own pace, and grinned at Caroline. "Besides, I'm your grandfather's factor. I want to be the kind of factor who really cares about everything that concerns his client. Have you guessed that I'm not very interested in going on as a merchant? I know it's usual to combine the two, but I like being a factor. It's—more personal."

"Mark, whatever you like is what you should do. Mr. Mackay always said, though, that you were smart enough to handle all kinds of business. I remember how proud I felt when he said it."

"Really? Were you proud of me way back then?"

She laid her hand on his. "That's a dumb question. Especially, when you already know the answer."

He did know. The most beguiling girl in or around Savannah cared for him—loved him more than most men dream of being loved. Not once had he been bored by Caroline's company, not once had she failed or disappointed him. He loved her laughter and it came readily most of the time. He loved her thick, dark hair. At night, in his bed, thoughts of her fragrance still haunted him. Everything about her was fragrant, clean and desirable. His desire for her was a growing ache. He kissed her too much. At every opportunity, he drank from her mouth, his hands holding her body close—caressing her sweet sides, her waist, the exquisite curve of her back. It was more and more difficult to check his senses.

Only twice had he allowed himself to imagine what it might

be like to hold Eliza as he held Caroline. Only twice had he
permitted himself even the thought of his mouth on the
strong, quiet mouth of the woman for whom he'd gladly give
up anything but his self-respect. If he lost respect for himself,
he would utterly fail Eliza. Failing her was the last thing he
meant to do—ever.

Sitting very straight beside him in the new gig, Caroline
increased the pressure on his hand. "Where were you?" she
asked.

"I was —I was hating the daylight." He covered her hand
with his.

"You're trembling, Mark."

"If it were night," he said hoarsely, "I could pull over
behind some trees and kiss you and kiss you and kiss you!"

"Dear God, help me," she breathed. "Mark . . . Mark!"

He could feel her trembling, too—eager, as always, for his
every touch. Frightened, he could tell, at the longing in her
own body. Almost puzzled by it. But she was restraining
herself. As she would, he knew, even if it were night.

Slipping the slack reins into his left hand, he caught her arm
and held it, almost consolingly. "Forgive me," he whispered.

"For what? I want to be kissing you, too . . ."

"Yes," he said solemnly. "I know."

Slowly, she withdrew her arm, moved away a little, adjusting the yellow bow that tied her straw bonnet in place. "I
wish Grandfather had come to town with me this time."
Deliberately, she was changing the subject again. "Am I silly
to worry about him out there alone—with her?"

Mark's body still ached. He struggled to even his breathing,
to help her with the change of subject. "I'm sure he's the same
as always. They've been in that big house together for more
than half a century. Anyway, we'll all be out there this time
tomorrow." At the thought of Eliza, his smile came. "I—I'm
so glad Miss Eliza finally feels she can go back to The Grange.
Do you know, it's been almost two years since she was there?"

"Mark, I've just had a marvelous idea! Do you think it
might be easier for her not to have to stay in The Grange
house? She'll miss Mr. Mackay so much there. You could stay
there with the three girls, but Miss Eliza could stay at
Knightsford. Oh, I don't mean at the big house. I wouldn't
dream of putting anyone through that. But Grandfather has a
dear little cottage down the lane from the old loom house.

You've seen it. It's all furnished; even the curtains are kept clean at the windows. No one ever uses it except Grandfather, who sometimes goes there to read. Miss Eliza would be most welcome, I'm sure."

"No servants live in that little cottage? Why, I wonder?"

"I don't know. That's one more thing I don't know. It's just always been there, so I guess I take it for granted. I tried once when I was a child to climb in a window. The place fascinated me then. Grandfather caught me up on two boxes, one leg over the open windowsill, and gave me a dreadful spanking."

"Your grandfather—spanked *you?*"

"The only time. I remember he cried afterward more than I did and he held me on his lap all evening."

At that instant, Mark knew about the cottage. Knew far more than Caroline. Jonathan Cameron's one love, Mary Cotting, had lived and died there! Without doubt, Ethel saw them in each other's arms from the very window through which little Caroline had tried to climb.

"You know what I think I'll do first thing when I get back to Knightsford, Mark? I think I'll just ask Grandfather for an explanation of that spanking."

"Oh, I wouldn't do that if I were you."

"Why not?"

"Well, it might upset him. After all, that was something he obviously hated doing or he wouldn't have cried, too."

Caroline took the reins and halted the horse. "Mark Browning, I know every time you try to gloss something over. I know every time you try to treat me as though I'm a lot more than three years younger than you. You *know* something about that cottage."

"How would I know if you don't?"

"You're doing it again."

"I'm just trying to protect your grandfather."

"Factors don't have to go that far!"

"You look far too pretty for an argument."

"Don't treat me like a—flimsy female!"

At that moment, for the first time, he remembered the promise he'd made on the day Osmund Kott had almost rammed their boat. He had promised to tell her if he ever found out anything that might explain the long-standing trouble with Osmund. "Caroline, listen to me—" he began.

Typically, when something bothered her, she was looking
straight at him. When her eyes filled with tears, he stopped
short. Her chin began to tremble. She buried her face in her
hands and sobbed.

Mark looked around them. There were people and horses
and carts everywhere. She had stopped the horse in the middle
of Abercorn Street, almost in front of the old Habersham
house, just reopened as the Savannah branch of the United
States Bank. He grabbed the reins and trotted Handsome
away from Reynolds Square toward Lincoln Street, where
there would be only old frame houses and fewer, if any,
people. Around the corner on Lincoln, he stopped.

"Now," he said, putting his arm around her, "if people
notice us, they'll think we're only having a lovers' quarrel."
She was still sobbing, helplessly, her usual control gone. Sobbing as though her heart would break.

That this was no muddled, weeping woman performance,
Mark knew very well. If ever a young lady had a reason to be
tied up in knots over *everything*—to be afraid, to give way to
crying—it was Caroline. At that moment, he made his decision. He had promised and he had also endured long enough
of the distance between them because he knew what Caroline
did not know about her grandparents—and his. Jonathan
Cameron was a fine old man. Mark had come to care about
him too, but he was being cruel to the granddaughter whom he
called the one light in his life. It may have been understandable for him to guard his dark secret as long as Caroline was a
child. She's a grown woman now, Mark reasoned, and she
deserves to know why hatred has been in the very air of the
house where she so loyally stays on, only to look after him.

"Try to contain yourself, Caroline," he ordered, starting
the horse once more.

"Where are we going?"

"Back to Broughton Street. I need to talk to you and we
need to be alone—not in the middle of a Savannah thoroughfare."

"But, Miss Eliza and the girls are—"

"Never mind. I'll handle that. All I have to do is tell Miss
Eliza that you and I need time alone. She'll scuttle the girls
right upstairs to play—or outside. Try to stop crying, please?"

*       *       *

Seated beside her on the parlor sofa, holding her hand, Mark told Caroline all Ethel Cameron had told him—every word he could remember. Especially every word that had to do with the long-ago love—however twisted and strange—which Ethel once felt toward Jonathan. He told her as much as he knew about how that love had turned to hatred. Now and then, he would stop talking and wait, just in case Caroline wanted to ask a question. She remained silent, motionless except to rub her thumb nervously back and forth on his hand as he talked.

"The cottage," she said at last, "was Mary Cotting's, wasn't it?"

"Yes. My grandmother's house."

He waited again, patting her reassuringly, as though to remind her that he'd known for a long time and that it was going to be all right with her, too, eventually.

"I despise it," she said, her voice cold, "that I am Ethel Cameron's granddaughter! I—envy you—having Mary Cotting's blood. My grandfather loved her, truly loved her, didn't he?"

"Yes. There were five years between Osmund and my mother. Five years in which Jonathan must have struggled to stay away from Mary Cotting. He failed. And my mother was born."

"Mark, could you ever learn to call him—Grandfather?"

"I've longed to many times. He hasn't told me a word. I dare not let him know that *she* did tell me."

"When you speak of him to me, now, you call him Jonathan. I know to his face, you say Mr. Cameron. But you call him Jonathan to me, don't you?"

"I guess I do."

"And do you see the young man Jonathan when you look at him?"

"Sometimes."

"A beautiful young man—like you, Mark—forced to marry —her."

"Can't you pity her just a little?"

"No!"

He took her in his arms. "There's so much to take in. Did I do the right thing to tell you?"

She made a faint little sound, resembling laughter. "Oh, if

you could see inside my heart, you'd be so proud of yourself
for having the courage to tell me! Once I've had time to—get
accustomed to the idea, I can't imagine how changed everything will be for me." Her head dropped onto his shoulder in
relief. "For the first time I'll be able to understand a little of
what's going on around me at Knightsford—not just endure
it. You did that for me, Mark. You."

He was suddenly tired, drained. He could only hold her and
smooth her hair, appreciating this desirable young woman
who loved him in the way he so longed to love her.

She pulled away just enough to look straight into his eyes.
"Mark, I want you to listen to me now; will you do that? Will
you listen without saying a word?"

"Yes."

"Good. Remember now, just listen. By telling me the truth
—the tangled, crazy, weird truth about my grandparents—
you've set me free to grow up. In fact, I think I started growing up right while you were talking. You may not believe me
yet, but you'll see. And the first proof is this: I want you to
know something, too, which only I am able to tell you. I want
it to set you free."

She was silent for a moment and he could feel her stiffen
slightly in his arms.

Then, in a barely audible voice, she said, "I know how
much you love Miss Eliza."

Mark felt as though she had struck him, but he went on
holding her.

"I know how much you love her and the way you love her."
Abruptly, she got up and walked to the mantel, her back to
him. "You love her, and maybe you've loved her for a long
time, in the way I love you." She went on. "The way you wish
with all your heart that you loved me."

"Caroline!" He stood, but did not go to her.

"Sh! You promised not to say a word. It's important to me
for you to realize, Mark, that nothing will change with us. I'll
still return your kisses in the old way because I couldn't stop! I
hope you'll go on kissing me, wanting to kiss me." She paused
only briefly. "I have—far more than kisses to give you, but
for now, I want your kisses. Oh, how I want them! Right this
minute. I want you to be kissing me, but don't you dare
move!" She turned to face him. "I'm not finished. I also want
you to know that I am truly Eliza Mackay's friend. I've

somehow been able to take her grief right into my own heart. I ache with her in that big empty bed at night. I don't think she knows how close I feel to her, but I do." She looked away, smiling. "Love *is* blind, isn't it? We're all reaching—in the wrong direction. You, Miss Eliza—I know I am. I don't have anywhere else to reach, though. It's you I love. I'm that much like Grandfather, I guess. God knows, all his life, he reached in—the wrong direction. He still does."

The lovely face, the throat, even the tilt of Caroline's head, were so like the portrait of Melissa Browning, Mark could only stare at her. He didn't move, but not because she had asked him not to. He couldn't.

"We're all going to be all right." She turned back to him. "You, Miss Eliza and me. And that isn't hokum. It's true. There isn't going to be any hatred among the three of us." Mark could see an almost imperceptible shudder. "I've had enough—hatred." She held out both hands to him.

He crossed the room in three strides and took her in his arms. For once, his passion did not tempt him. He simply held her and, after a time, gave her a long, gentle, grateful kiss.

"I'm tired of hiding in the carriage, Mark," Eliza said as they met in the front hall on a warm, autumn Sunday morning. "Would I be criticized if I just openly walked with you to church?"

"What if you are?" He smiled. "You look far too lovely not to be seen."

"Do you know I actually feel strange, wearing even this pale, pale-blue dress? Robert, I know, would be annoyed that I took so long to ease myself from black to gray—and now this. Do I really look all right?"

"I'll be the proudest gentleman at church. We'll walk, by all means. It's a glorious day." He gave her an elaborate bow. "Not even enough breeze to muss your curls under that fine matching bonnet, ma'am."

Her sensitive, appealing face turned serious. She reached to touch his arm. "Oh, Mark, Mark, what would I have done without you?"

"Don't even wonder about that. You have me."

"You've led me like a child back out into life again, haven't you? Never pushing, never hurrying me. Urging me to visit The Grange twice this past summer. I found it not only possi-

ble—I liked being there. I'll never know how to thank you for
loving my children, for handling Robert's affairs with Judge
Charlton, for buying out my share of the firm. So much, so
much. But, oh, dear boy, you have done even more—for *me*."
Her smile was radiant. How he watched for it! "For a forty-
year-old widow, today—thanks to you—I feel almost young
again. In fact, I think I do feel young."

Walking beside her toward Christ Church, Mark's heart
nearly burst. That they made a handsome couple, he had no
doubt whatever. Anyone could tell from the warmth of the
nods and bows of passing churchgoers. Eliza seemed to float
beside him, her hand resting lightly, comfortably, in the crook
of his arm. He doffed his buff-colored top hat first to the
Telfair sisters—walking also, on this perfect Sunday—then to
Mrs. Bulloch and her daughter, the progress of whose house
he was watching closely.

"Mrs. Bullock and her daughter were commenting on how
handsome you look, sir," Eliza laughed. "I could tell you
almost word for word what they said."

"Nonsense. Everyone's talking about the way you look. My
lady is going to light up the sanctuary. Just watch the minute
she walks in."

Mark thought of Mackay, of how proud he would be in
Mark's place. He smiled. "She's fine, sir," he said silently,
glancing at the embracing Savannah sky. "She's just fine.
Salute!"

# THIRTY-ONE

ON the rainy, cold night of December 4, 1818, when Jay's new theater opened its ornate doors on the first Savannah performance of Cherry's comedy, *The Soldier's Daughter,* Mark proudly escorted Eliza and Caroline. He had seen far better theater in Philadelphia, but almost anything would have pleased the audience on that festive occasion. The rain dampened only new gowns and top hats. Savannah had waited too long and excitement ran too high over Jay's splendid theater for spirits to have been dampened by anything. Once Mark and Caroline had persuaded Eliza to go with them, the two women spent hours planning their costumes. "Of course, we could both afford to have them made, Mark," Eliza had argued happily. "But Caroline and I love to sew together. We're going to make the gowns ourselves."

Seated between them—Eliza in green brocade, Caroline in blue silk—Mark found every moment of the evening entertaining. Especially, when leaning across him to exchange whispered views, the two women obviously agreed that William Jay's interior was a bit overdone. He had thought so from the moment they had been shown to their box. True, the interior was a harmonious blend of crimson, white and gold. Sixteen fluted, cast-iron columns supported the two rows of boxes, but the golden eagles painted on the box panels seemed excessive. "And that curtain," Caroline whispered. "Miss Eliza, that wildly painted curtain hurts my eyes!"

"Never mind," Mark answered, enjoying the good-natured bite to their criticism. "The Savannah Theater has given our city prestige. Whatever adds to the city, the three of us will support wholly!"

Jay's theater did add luster to the city, whose blossoming architectural wonders—new theater, banks, churches, hotels, homes—so stimulated Mark, so warmed his heart, they even toned his body. The building boom kept him walking almost every free hour. He'd never felt better exercised. In fact, he was acquiring a reputation for being a loner, almost as much a loner as Sheftall Sheftall. He walked and reveled in all that he saw. Except in extremely bad weather, he didn't rest at night unless he'd inspected the latest feature completed that day in almost every new edifice going up. His beloved city was beginning to bloom as he'd dreamed. As Mackay had dreamed. The Mackay girls teased him unmercifully, accused him of being interested in every ballast rock that went into every new foundation. He was.

And always, as he walked, he tested possible locations for the house he would build someday. He had rather liked the lots on Chippewa Square, where the theater now stood, but there were so many in other places to choose from, and the right one would eventually pass his test. The value of the land must be considered first, of course, but the location had to "feel right," he explained to Eliza.

New buildings and refurbished older ones were, after all, only a part of what charmed him about Savannah. The trees in the squares had grown in the years he'd been there, the walkways had settled, the cedar posts that held the protecting chains had aged. To Mark, Oglethorpe's shady squares were the key to Savannah's unique charm—that provincial charm his father had found so beguiling. And now the city was beginning to take on an opulent look. He remembered Mackay's smiling disgust at one point during the late war with Britain, when he read in the newspaper the financial report of the Council. "Mark, you've selected a thriving town! The Savannah city budget at this moment—with all debts paid—shows the enormous reserve of five dollars!" Mackay would be as proud now as he had been disgusted then. The city treasury was burgeoning, and all up and down Factor's Row, the merchants who had invested heavily or lightly, as had Mark, in Scarbrough's dream steamship, the S.S. *Savannah*, gossiped and planned for the future in the manner of women gathered for a quilting bee.

Mark had retained T.U.P. Charlton as his lawyer, but so far the judge had found little to do in Mark's behalf. He enjoyed planning his own investments, and even the persuasive Charlton had not been able to convince him that he should have invested more than five thousand dollars in the S.S. *Savannah*. The new ship, its components now nearing completion in New York and in Elizabethtown, New Jersey, had the financial backing of Savannah's most prominent men to the tune of two hundred thousand dollars.

"I bow to the judgment of few men," Charlton had told Mark, "but in the case of William Scarbrough, I attend to what he says. Shipping cotton by steamboat within our own country has made such a difference, think what can happen to our economy abroad should Scarbrough's Savannah Steamship Company succeed—as it surely will. Think how even partial steam power could shorten the shipping time to Liverpool! You seem to forget, Browning, that Scarbrough isn't merely a businessman with a speculative dream. He's a mechanical wizard. As brilliant, in my opinion, as he is elegant socially."

Because it came from Charlton, Mark knew that to be the highest compliment. The city buzzed with excitement over the future of trade with the world from the port of Savannah. Mark's city would go down in history, they were all sure, as the first in the world to launch a steam-powered ocean-worthy sailing vessel.

Mark fervently hoped they were right. But even Charlton could not budge him. "It is your money, Browning, and what you do with it is, of course, entirely your decision."

"Yes, sir," Mark answered. "That's right."

He hoped the other merchants and factors along the waterfront didn't think less of him, but they would all soon know. The completed S.S. *Savannah*, on her maiden voyage, was expected from the north no later than May 1 of the new year 1819.

And another Christmas with the Mackays was almost here. Investments and business, like architecture, were a part of his life. A stimulating part, to be sure, but the heart of all that held meaning for him was still in the daily life of the house on Broughton.

As Christmas approached, Mark was just about to close his countinghouse one evening when a knock came at his office door.

"I'm glad you caught me before I locked up, sir," he said,

shaking the outstretched hand of William Scarbrough. "A visit from you is always a pleasure. Please sit down. I'm honored."

"Before I get to the reason for my visit," Scarbrough said, crossing his elegantly clad legs and carefully adjusting his immaculate high collar beneath a silk Paisley cravat, "may I offer my wife's greetings to you and her fond hope that you and Miss Caroline will be joining us for our Christmas ball later in the month?"

"We wouldn't think of missing it, and do take my best wishes and thanks to Miss Julia. I enjoy her more each time we're together. I'm only sorry Miss Eliza feels she can't come too."

"Yes, but we do understand perfectly. If William Jay had managed to move the builders along at his tempo instead of theirs, our new house on West Broad might be ready in time. He didn't manage, and since we're forced to give one last ball in the old place, I can well imagine Miss Eliza being—unwilling to put herself through the sad memories she would inevitably suffer."

"That's sensitive of you to understand, sir."

"Not at all. Now, then, I'm here to let you in on what can turn out to be a historic event in our beloved city."

"Another event, aside from the S.S. *Savannah?*"

"In direct connection with it. I have just heard from the office of Secretary of War John C. Calhoun that if present plans carry, he will accompany none other than President James Monroe to our city sometime next May! The President is eager to inspect the S.S. *Savannah* himself."

Mark beamed. "Well, my congratulations to you, Mr. Scarbrough. Congratulations to—all of us in Savannah."

"I must ask you, however, until I hear for certain that the President is coming, to say nothing."

"Not even to Mrs. Mackay?"

Scarbrough thought a minute. "I see no harm in telling her." He smiled. "I've never known her to gossip, unlike my dear wife. Of course, I mean to tell Julia as soon as I'm certain. I dare not, though, until Mr. Jay assures us that the new house on Broad will be completed in time for us to entertain the presidential party."

"May I ask why you're telling me before you're sure?"

"I trust you, but my main reason is business."

Mark said nothing but began to listen more attentively. Sheftall Sheftall's two-word warning—"not practical"—stuck in his mind.

"We've heard also from Captain Moses Rogers, who greatly assisted me in the design of the S.S. *Savannah* and is, as you know, a superior engineer as well as sea captain. Rogers, whose word I take as gospel in matters such as these, informs me that we are in need of fifty thousand dollars beyond what we estimated in order to complete the *Savannah* on schedule. Of course, since the ship's arrival in our city *must* coincide with the President's visit, the urgency to raise sufficient funds only increases. I'm asking you to raise your rather modest investment by fifty thousand dollars, sir. You're the wealthiest man in Savannah at this moment, the gentleman with the most available funds. May I have your answer within two days? I'm really counting on you. The cost, as I'm sure you can imagine, of our new home on West Broad has strapped me where ready cash is concerned. Mr. Jay is brilliant, but the execution of his brilliance does not come cheaply."

Mark smiled. "I'm sure it doesn't. But he's built the theater and is contracted to build a bank, the Telfair house, your house. He also built the Richardson house. Have you thought of asking William Jay to invest?"

"Uh, yes, as a matter of fact, I have thought of it. But you see, I happen to know that the only building for which he's been paid in full so far is the theater. If he goes on as he's begun, in a year he'll be a rich young man. He isn't now. The burden of finishing the S.S. *Savannah* in time for the President's visit, then, falls on you, Mr. Browning. What do you think? May I have your answer soon?"

"Very soon, Mr. Scarbrough. Right now, in fact. My answer is no."

His visitor looked stunned. "Your answer is—no? With your pride in our city? With your ample funds, sir?"

"I'm not quite as young as Mr. Jay, and I do have the future to consider."

"Then, why not truly consider it? Shipping cotton and rice abroad by steam can put you in clover in your old age!"

"I'll have to take that chance. I've just bought out Mrs. Mackay's interest in the firm and have all but made up my mind to limit my own work to factoring. A man can earn good money if he's a skillful, attentive factor. But not as much as in shipping or merchandising. Besides, sir, I've been advised not to go too heavily into the Savannah Steamship Company."

"You've been advised? My good man, by whom? Certainly not your own lawyer, T.U.P. Charlton."

"No, he's most enthusiastic about it."

"By old Jonathan Cameron?"

"No, sir." He grinned. "I'm his factor. My job is to advise him, isn't it?"

"Then, in the name of heaven, who is spreading such ludicrous advice?"

"I'd rather not say, if you don't mind."

"But I do mind! Such talk must be stopped at once."

Still smiling, Mark said, "I doubt that this gentleman could be stopped."

Frowning, Scarbrough uncrossed his legs and then recrossed them. "Browning, I know every man of any prominence in Savannah. No one comes to mind who might even vaguely influence a bright young man such as yourself. He lives in the city proper?"

"Yes, sir. His family has been here since shortly after General Oglethorpe founded the colony of Georgia."

Mark watched Scarbrough's eyes widen. His distinguished visitor gave a short laugh, then another and another. "Old Cocked Hat Sheftall!"

"Yes, sir."

Still laughing, Scarbrough said, "But, Browning, *Cocked Hat Sheftall?*"

"I enjoy laughing—*with* Mr. Sheftall as much as anyone," Mark said, his voice pleasant but firm. "It so happens that I don't laugh *at* him. I consider him a practical and sagacious gentleman."

Scarbrough's laughter died quickly. "Well, I can see that you do and—" He took out his watch. "Dear, dear, I'm due at home this minute. My wife is having a small dinner party— but, Browning, first thing tomorrow morning, I'll be here in your office. I must set you straight immediately on the real story of our likable but foolishly patriotic son of Abraham, Cocked Hat Sheftall!" Laughing derisively again, Scarbrough went on, "I'm sure Sheftall's told you himself, in boring detail, of his heroic record in the American Revolution. He's told everyone polite enough to be trapped into listening, but let me tell you the straight of it and—"

"No," Mark interrupted. "Mr. Sheftall has never told me much about himself. We just—have a friendship."

"Good, good," Scarbrough said, at the door now, obviously nervous about getting home. "But I'll be here anytime you say tomorrow morning and—"

"Sorry, sir, but I won't be in my office tomorrow at all."

"Then, dinner tomorrow night at my home, so that I can explain about good old Cocked Hat."

"Thank you, Mr. Scarbrough, but I can't do that, either. I have an important engagement early tomorrow morning that will keep me happily occupied well into the evening. You see, I'm taking the older Mackay girls out to The Grange to gather greens for Christmas decoration."

Both halves of William Thorne Williams's bookshop door were closed when Mark walked in, jangling the tiny bell.

"I know it's late," he said to his friend Williams after they'd greeted each other, "but I need some of your vast knowledge."

Williams, in his early thirties, shorter than Mark, slightly built and beginning to go a bit bald, welcomed him. "I can't imagine a more pleasant way to end a day, Browning. Sit down. Could I brew us a pot of tea?"

"No, thank you," Mark said, seated in a worn leather easy chair beside his friend's small desk at the back. "If we make it a social occasion, I'll stay too long. So will you. Your wife and Miss Eliza will be worried. Our streets are midnight dark at six o'clock these winter days. I want you to tell me a story, and to give me your opinion of it."

Williams, never in a hurry about anything, was slowly, almost lovingly, filling his pipe. "Sounds like an interesting assignment. What's the story you want to hear?"

"Sheftall Sheftall's Revolutionary War story."

Bending over the small wood fire in a tiny grate beside his desk, Williams reached for a spile, lighted it and turned back to Mark with a quizzical expression. "Do you mean to tell me that Mr. Sheftall has never told you himself?" he asked quietly.

"That's right," Mark said. "I know when his family came. I know something of his father, Mordecai Sheftall. I know our Mr. Sheftall is a good lawyer and was a successful merchant by the time he was fifteen, that he was a hero in the War of Independence—but that's about all. Oh, except that his only legal client is my client Jonathan Cameron. I'd like to know why almost everyone in town makes fun of him, except you."

Taking his time, William Thorne Williams lighted and puffed on his pipe and sat back down. "And you, Browning. You don't make fun of him, either."

"No, but I've always thought Mr. Mackay had a lot to do with my regard for him. He made Mackay laugh—but affectionately. Tell me about the man, William. I have a good reason for wanting to know the truth about him."

"All you said is true. The Sheftalls are among our most respected families. When the Revolution broke out, old Mordecai, our Sheftall's father, was appointed deputy commissary general of issues—or some such—to the Continental troops in Georgia and South Carolina. Fifteen-year-old Sheftall became his father's deputy. But"—Williams smiled, not in sarcasm—"precocious as the young boy was, he couldn't swim a stroke. Soon, it was a troubling time for all lovers of liberty in Savannah; the British closed in on all sides. Polish General Pulaski fell in that battle. It was a bad time for lovers of liberty, be they Englishmen, Poles, Irishmen, Scots or Jews. Most Savannahians, including the Sheftalls, were trying to flee the city. Old Mordecai was able to swim Musgrove Creek. Young Sheftall could not. With the legendary devotion of the Jewish father, he stayed with his son and both were captured. For some period of time, they were prisoners of the British—on ships at sea, at nearby Sunbury, even on Antigua Island in the West Indies."

"How in the world did they get back to this country?"

"Sheftall never goes into detail there. He merely shrugs, says that they managed a parole and were permitted to sail to Philadelphia, where, after six months or so, they were exchanged for English prisoners."

Mark whistled in admiration. "Our Mr. Sheftall must have been well under twenty then. He'd already lived through more adventures than most men of thirty, hadn't he? Odd, he never told me he once lived in Philadelphia."

Williams laughed easily. "With Sheftall everything is odd and nothing is odd. You know that, Browning."

"Did he and his father ever rejoin the Continental Army, or

were they still bound by their prisoner-of-war vow not to fight the British?''

"It seems they talked their way out of that vow, too, and then—still in Philadelphia—young Sheftall set himself to recover certain monies his father had evidently advanced to the American cause. He literally badgered the bureaucrats. Even Secretary Alexander Hamilton listened respectfully to the eighteen- or nineteen-year-old Sheftall. Alas, he got only respect. The American Treasury was empty. But, through Hamilton's influence, the all-powerful Board of War gave young Sheftall an assignment. He was commissioned flag master of the sloop *Carolina Packet,* with the duty to carry money and provisions to Charleston for hungry American soldiers and prisoners.''

Mark listened intently. "That sounds like a dangerous mission to me, with the Atlantic full of British warships then.''

Williams smiled. "I want to put this in exactly the right words," he said. "It does sound dangerous. When our friend Sheftall Sheftall tells the story, it is *highly* dangerous. The truth is—I found out some time ago—that since his assignment was a mission of mercy, the enemy issued a permit that carried his little boat under a flag of truce right through the British blockade. He and his crew were in some danger—their ship overloaded, the season stormy—but the flag under which he sailed was a flag of truce.''

"I see," Mark smiled. "And I say, bless him! Why shouldn't he make a good story of it? He did have some harrowing times. Did he get to Charleston with the supplies?''

"He did, and at some point during that voyage, perhaps as he stood on the deck of the little ship, the American flag snapping above him along with his flag of truce, Sheftall Sheftall became, to himself, a kind of hero. The Revolutionary War hero he remains to this day.''

"What you're saying is that Sheftall Sheftall's good mind was caught back there in time—more than thirty-five years ago.''

"Exactly. As I see it, well into the nineteenth century, Sheftall is still a colonial gentleman. He liked everything better— back then. Is there anything so eccentric about that? There isn't a man in Savannah who knows more about what goes on in our own town today. Sheftall Sheftall's opinion is almost invariably sound, discreet and correct. He could never be called uninterested in current happenings. He just prefers to dwell on colonial times.''

Mark laughed. "Even though he fought and outsmarted the colonizers.''

"Exactly right. I took his advice when I opened my shop here back in 1805. I still take his advice. He began reading the law after the British surrendered. He's a fine lawyer.''

"Why is Jonathan Cameron his only client?" Mark asked.

"He only wants one. To serve more than one client, he declares, would take too much time from his reading. He's a student of the Talmud, the Bible, Greek and Roman history. A more widely read gentleman never darkens the door of my shop.''

Mark stood up. "You've done just what I'd hoped you'd do, William. Thank you.''

"You needed to have someone else confirm your confidence in Sheftall's good sense?''

"I needed to have *you* confirm it. Scarbrough is trying to get me to invest an extra fifty thousand in the S.S. *Savannah*. Mr. Sheftall made a special trip to my office not long ago just to warn me not to.''

"What was his reason?''

"He said it in two words—'not practical.' ''

Williams laughed, got to his feet, too. "Mr. Sheftall is a man of very few words when he means business. I think his veritable flow of words when he expounds on his own heroism is a clever subterfuge. It's a game with him. He keeps an eagle eye out for someone like you, Browning. Someone smart enough to see through his verbiage to his solid, common sense. He enjoys playing games with Savannah's merchant class. Enjoys it in the same way he enjoys wearing his tricorn and silver buckles. You're not investing the extra money?''

"No. Thanks to Sheftall Sheftall—and to you.''

They shook hands at the door. "One more question, Browning. Did you tell Scarbrough you'd think about it? Horror of horrors, did you tell him you were going to consult with me?''

Mark put his arm about his friend's shoulders. "No to both questions.''

"You're almost as smart as Sheftall Sheftall. Scarbrough is one of my best book customers, especially when it comes to buying rows and rows of handsome leather bindings for his new house. He does not think highly of me as a businessman. Few do."

Mark laughed. "But how I treasure you as a human being!"

"You won't necessarily get richer by taking Sheftall's advice," Williams said, walking to the street with Mark. "Look at me."

"I might be a lot happier, though. Look at you."

Williams's smile vanished. "Heard anything further about Osmund Kott in New York?"

"Not a word. You're still interested in him, aren't you?" Mark asked.

The smile returned to Williams's face. "William Scarbrough would slap his thigh laughing, but—I still pray for Osmund. Does that answer your question?"

# THIRTY-TWO

THE next day dawned clear and mild. When Mark checked the thermometer as Eliza and Emphie finished packing the picnic basket, it read sixty degrees. By noon, when he and Eliza Anne and Kate reached the Cameron dock, it would be even warmer. For the first time since their father died, the girls seemed almost Christmas merry. And as always, when they were going some place alone with Mark, there was high excitement.

Eliza was sending two fruitcakes and a quantity of jellies and jams to the Camerons, so they took the carriage to the waterfront, where the family schooner would be ready to sail.

Out on the river, the wind just right, Kate, now eight, sat as close as possible to Mark, who handled the rudder and sheet. Her hand lay comfortably on his knee.

Eliza Anne perched importantly on the bow, shouting directions. When Mark had caught the wind exactly as he wanted it and she had guided them safely midstream, she called, "Move over, Kate! Don't crowd him. Mark needs room to do what he's doing."

"She's fine," Mark called back. "I like her close like this. Makes it easier to keep an eye on the picnic basket."

"Just because I'm kind of chubby," Kate complained, "doesn't mean I'm a thief. Do you really think I'd snitch a piece of cake or a jam sandwich?"

He laughed. "I was teasing. Sometimes I don't think I'm very good at teasing. What do you think, Katie?"

Kate, her chin resting on her other hand, thought a minute, then said, "Well, we've talked about that. You do pretty well, but maybe you're not quite as good as Papa was. Something in his voice always told us when he was teasing or when he meant business. Do you think Papa knows in heaven that we're out here in our boat right now?"

Mark hugged her. "I'm sure he does. And he likes the whole idea."

"How do you know he knows it?"

"Well, he's with God—the same God who thought up loving in the first place. He would never have given your father so much love for both of you—for me, too—and then cut him off from even knowing about us. That wouldn't make any sense at all, would it?" He could tell Kate was thinking hard.

"I guess he knows all right," she said at last.

Mark glanced toward Eliza Anne, her dark, curly hair whipping in the wind. Her deep-brown eyes, her truly beautiful face, were solemn. She was frowning, biting her lower lip, thinking hard, too.

Finally, looking out over the water, deliberately not at Mark, she asked, "Did God give you your love for our mother?"

He jerked the sheet too hard. The boat listed to starboard, then righted itself.

"Mark? Did you hear what I said?"

"Yes, I heard you. And the answer is yes, honey."

"Then, I guess it would be all right for you to ask Mama to marry you."

Kate saved him by shouting her surprise: "Eliza Anne Mackay! That's the dumbest thing you ever said!"

"You're just too young to think of such things," her sister scoffed. "I'm not."

Mark gripped the tiller and kept silent, frantically trying to think what to say. John McQueen had sensed his love. Surely not Eliza Anne! Finally he managed to ask, "Do you really think today is the time for such serious talk? We're supposed to be on an adventure."

She surprised him completely by simply shrugging and changing the subject. "Did you buy stock in Mr. Scarbrough's steamship, the S.S. *Savannah?*"

His relief made him laugh. "Eliza Anne Mackay, you were undoubtedly born under a question mark!"

"You heard Papa tell me that all the time," she said. "I suppose it's true, but how else do you find out anything? Are you in the crowd of high-society gentlemen who will get rich when the S.S. *Savannah* crosses the Atlantic by steam?''

He gave her another surprised look. ''Who called the stockholders of the new venture a 'crowd of high-society gentlemen'?''

''Mama.''

''I didn't buy much stock, but I do own some.''

''Cocked Hat Sheftall says everybody who put up money
will live to rue the day,'' she said firmly.

''When, pray, did you discuss the S.S. *Savannah* with Mr.
Sheftall?''

''I didn't. I was waiting for some ribbon Mama wanted over
at Low's and I heard him tell Mr. Andrew Low to pocket his
pennies or put them in a bank instead.''

''He told me about the same thing, actually.''

''I certainly wish you'd listened to him,'' Eliza Anne said
gravely. ''He's smart. He's a hero, too. He won the liberty of
every American in Savannah!''

''We like him,'' Kate said, not wanting to be left out.
''When he isn't busy reading his paper, he stops and talks a lot
to children.''

''Are the people in Savannah as—rotten as Dr. Harney's
poem in his newspaper says they are?'' Eliza Anne wanted to
know.

Mark chuckled uneasily. ''Where did you read Harney's
poem? I know your mother threw our paper out as soon as
she'd read it.''

''Mothers do their best to keep things from children,'' Kate
said philosophically, ''but they don't always do it. We read it
behind our stable with the Minis girls. Every word of it! Over
and over. Eliza Anne even memorized it. Sometimes she
makes me mad getting things by heart so fast. She might be
almost as smart as Jack.''

Eliza Anne turned to face them, her gaze sweeping the river,
and began to recite:

    '' 'Farewell to Savannah! forever farewell!
       The hotbed of rogues, the terrestrial—*Hell!*' ''

''Whoa!'' Mark interrupted. ''Watch your language, young
lady.''

''That's just part of the poem,'' she said, and went on:

" 'Where Satan has fixed his headquarters on earth,
  And outlawed integrity, wisdom, and worth.
  Where villainy thrives and where honesty begs,
  Where folly is purse-proud and wisdom in rags;
  Where man is worth nothing, except in one sense,
  Which they always compute in pounds,
      shillings and pence.' "

Mark laughed. "That's a fine performance, but more than
enough! Dr. John Harney just happened to see through some
of the chicanery in our financial and political community. He
was leaving town. He simply stuck in his oar before he left."

"Does chicanery mean crooked?"

"In a way, yes. Harney was brilliant, sophisticated, and I'd
think rather bitter about life in general. Everyone in Savannah
isn't like that. Harney generalized. His way, I guess, of getting
revenge."

"For what?"

"Well, for what he saw as a mercenary society. After all,
Savannah is growing by leaps and bounds. Our merchants are
making money hand over fist. New buildings are going up. All
this can turn people's heads toward the pursuit of possessions,
money, social standing. Everyone wants to keep up with"—he
laughed—"the Scarbroughs."

"You aren't that way," Kate said, patting Mark's knee.
"You're rich, too."

"We all have everything we need. Isn't that what matters?"

"We aren't children anymore," Eliza Anne announced.
"You don't need to make careful answers like that with us,
Mark. At least not with me."

"I don't see what difference it makes anyway," Kate
mused, "whether someone is rich or not. Cocked Hat Sheftall
doesn't have much money at all."

"He could have more," Mark said. "He's a fine lawyer.
He's simply interested in other things."

"I think it's good to be just the way you are, Mark," Eliza
Anne said. "I think you really are pretty rich. You buy
anything you want for yourself, or for us. Mama says you've
handled Papa's business so we'll always have what we need.
But you hardly ever badger anybody with business talk. I
don't think Dr. Harney knew you very well, or he'd have had

to print that he wasn't writing about Mr. Mark Browning."

After a time, Kate said, "Cocked Hat Sheftall doesn't celebrate Christmas because he's a Jew and they have other holidays. I wish he did, because he'd be good to invite for Christmas dinner."

"Isn't this a rather sudden attachment to Mr. Sheftall?"

"Not really," Eliza Anne replied. "We just don't get much chance to talk to you about our friends, Mark. You and Mama always have so much to discuss and then we have to go to bed."

"Sarah and Philipa Minis, our best friends, don't celebrate Christmas, either," Kate said, still in her own thoughts. "But they're coming over anyway. Maybe Cocked Hat would come, too. Our papa thought a lot of him."

"He certainly did. Your father was the kind of man who could see through human eccentricities. In fact, I think he enjoyed them."

"In my opinion," Eliza Anne said thoughtfully, "Cocked Hat is a very kind man, too. Do you know he's the only person I ever heard say a good word for old Ethel Cameron? Even Mama, who's always telling us not to be nasty about anyone, isn't too awfully kind about her. Why does Ethel Cameron hate nice Mr. Cameron so much, Mark?"

He weighed his answer. "Well, hate is hard to explain. I can't explain it, I guess. Except to say that it's the dark, ugly reverse side of love. When we love someone, we want only good for that person, right?"

They both nodded.

"When we hate, we want only bad things to happen. Hate must be like a terrible disease. Once people are trapped in it, they seem to be helpless."

Kate sighed. "It looks like God could help people stop hating."

"Oh, He can," Mark said. "But I'm sure the person has to be willing to let Him."

"Cocked Hat must understand about all that," Eliza Anne said. "He always seems to have a good word for the old battle-ax."

"I hope we don't have to see her today." Kate shuddered. "Do you think we will have to, Mark?"

"I don't see why. The poor lady stays inside most of the time as far as I know."

"But she takes a walk every day around the empty cottage at Knightsford. You know the one I mean. Down by the old loom house."

"Yes," Mark said. "I know the one."

"I guess even she has to have a little exercise," Kate said. "But there certainly are prettier places to walk than that—cottage." She shuddered again. "It gives me a creepy feeling. Why do they keep it so cleaned up when no one lives in it?"

Mark made himself smile. "You don't honestly think I know everything, do you?"

"I wish Caroline would come to live with us," Eliza Anne said as she turned back to navigating. "How does she stay so cheerful, Mark, living under the same roof with two people who hate each other?"

"We don't know that Mr. Cameron hates Mrs. Cameron. Keep an eye out now—tide's pretty low."

"Cocked Hat says she's pathetic," Kate said.

"Look!" Eliza Anne shouted. "Look, Mark, I can see the Cameron dock. Watch out for that mudbank on this side."

"Oh, goody!" Kate clapped her hands. "I hope we find a lot of cassina berries—holly, too. When do we eat our picnic, Mark? Can Miss Caroline hunt Christmas greens with us?"

While Mark was still tying up the boat, Caroline came flying down the river path, her pink cotton skirt billowing, her arms out to the sisters and to Mark.

After warm greetings, both girls talked at once and then fell into an awesome silence as Mark stood holding Caroline's hands. "You're prettier than ever, ma'am," he said, genuinely happy to be able to look at her again. "And I insist—on demand of my crew—that you go with us to hunt Christmas greens and demolish Emphie's picnic."

"Oh, you *have* to go," Kate said intently, then in an almost reverent voice, "Mark, why don't you kiss Caroline? We don't mind."

He gave her a brief kiss on the mouth, all he dared, not wanting the old fire in him today. Instead, his heart ached at the tragedy of this high-spirited, naturally buoyant young woman forced to stay in such an isolated spot, to sleep and eat and sew and read and attempt to make a life for herself in the big, shadow-filled house where hate lived. Even today, with the sky so clear and the winter sun so dazzling, shadows hung over the tall, gabled Knightsford big house, set back under its grove of live oaks and dark magnolias. But this day belonged to Kate and Eliza Anne. Besides, Caroline was laughing with them, entering at once into their young-girl world.

"You know how glad I am to see both of you," Caroline was saying, "but I had a dream last night that made me hope maybe Jack and William might come, too."

"We hoped that, too," Kate said. "But Mark and Mama talked it over and decided it would be better if they waited till summer, when they could stay awhile. It's a long way to come down from New York."

"Oh, that must have been a hard decision for their mother," Caroline said, looking at Mark.

"It was. For me, too. They haven't been home in—"

"—in two years and three months," Eliza Anne broke in. "Our papa's been dead all that time."

"They'll be so grown up—Jack and William—we won't know them," Caroline said.

"I've felt guilty not visiting them," Mark said. "But there's been so much to do here. I don't know if you've heard, Caroline, but I'm alone at the company now. Mr. Mein and his wife finally made up their minds to move back to England for good. He's selling Coleraine."

"I know. It's almost broken Grandfather's heart. Mr. Mein wrote to him. Said he couldn't face seeing Grandfather for the last time. They didn't say good-bye."

"I guess your grandmother doesn't much care either way about the Meins or your grandfather's sorrow," Kate said.

"No, Kate," Caroline answered. "She doesn't care at all."

"Mark will do fine in the business by himself," Eliza Anne said, not about to allow her younger sister to make a more grown-up observation than she. "I don't even think he'll miss Mr. Mein, because Mark's done all the work anyway."

He gave Eliza Anne an elaborate bow of thanks. "Enough serious talk, I say. How about spreading our picnic right here by the river?"

"No better spot," Caroline said. "But, leave the hamper on board, Mark, until you've all three freshened up at the big house. Water, towels, soap are still waiting for you on the back veranda."

"Good idea," Mark said. "You girls run on ahead. I'll be along directly."

With a knowing look, Eliza Anne said, "You don't need to hurry, Mark. It could take us some little while to get clean from that dirty boat and all." Then she chased Kate up the path to the house.

Caroline made no effort to hide her joy at seeing him. Her gaze moved openly, lovingly, to his eyes, his shoulders, his hands and back to his face, as though allowing herself this one moment in which to be wholly glad.

When the girls' voices had faded entirely, Mark took her in his arms hungrily. "Oh, Caroline . . . Caroline. One real kiss, please!"

"Just—one?" she gasped, between kisses. "Mark . . . did you come only for Christmas greens?"

"You know I didn't. Why do I stay away so long? I'm starved for your nearness. When I need so to be close to you, why do I stay away? Why do I do that to—myself?"

She pulled back but touched his lips with her finger. "Why do you do it to—*me*, Mark?"

He hung his head.

"We aren't like—other people," she went on. "You know that as well as I. We're—us. I don't need to be handled carefully. Mark, I know exactly the way you love me. And even if I weren't determined not to leave poor Grandfather here with her, even if I felt free to marry you, I wouldn't. Not as long as you aren't sure. I *know* how it is with you, my darling. I know it. I'm Caroline. *I love you.* And I know how bound you are to Eliza Mackay."

He stared at her. "Oh, Caroline, forgive me."

"Nonsense. This is today. You're here where I can be with you. I'd rather kiss you, but I don't have to be kissing you. I can enjoy watching you climb trees to cut Christmas greens for the girls, too, you know."

He reached for her.

"Mark, I'll also know if you ever—love me that way."

"Caroline, I—"

"Sh! You may someday, you know. If I were free of my grandparents, I'd still want to wait. Even waiting for you is a glad thing to do." She laughed, not bitterly, almost easily. "I feel like a new woman because I've finally put it all into words."

"Caroline," he said simply. "I—love you, too."

"I know you do. Mark, I know that! Please give yourself

time. There is time. I can't leave Grandfather, but even if I could, there would still be time. All the time you need."

He reached for her hand. "I don't know what to say. I think I'm—a little crazy. I don't deserve your love."

"Pooh. Who ever does deserve love?"

Holding hands, they began to walk slowly up the river path past the small stand of woods that almost hid the old loom house and Mary Cotting's cottage.

"Is—your grandfather at the big house?" he asked.

"Yes. Giving us these moments alone. He wanted us to have at least a little time."

# THIRTY-THREE

AT her bedroom window on the second floor of the Knightsford big house, Ethel Cameron, in soft-gray crepe de chine—perfectly groomed, as always—stood watching behind the thin, flowing curtain as Mark and Caroline emerged from the river path into the clearing that led away from the cottage and toward the sweep of the carriage drive.

Her window commanded the wide curve of front lawn, newly scythed, raked clean of all but a few magnolia pods that had fallen since the people worked that morning. She could see the water, too, glistening in clear, white light, and knew, although a cypress stand along the river blocked her view of the dock, that the Mackay boat was tied there.

Melissa's son was back.

Ethel felt her throat tighten. She was growing old, but not in her mind. Her memory of the lilt and gaiety and spirit of little Melissa Cotting was as clear as though she'd seen the child yesterday. Mark Browning, though wide-shouldered and gracefully masculine, was the image of Melissa. Ethel's own granddaughter, Caroline, could never hope to do better—stuck away on a remote Savannah River plantation. At least, Mark's father had been a Northern aristocrat.

If she was truthful, Ethel did not care one way or another about her only grandchild. No point in caring. Caroline had been her grandfather's girl since the first moment she'd opened her eyes.

Oh, the day Caroline was born had been almost happy. The event had held a glimmer of hope for Ethel. She adored her son, Jon. A new child in the family could make a difference for the better. At first, Ethel tried to hope that it would, tried

335

not to allow the door of her hope to close. The fact remained
that the door had closed with firm finality at the end of
Caroline's very first month of life. It had closed on the hot,
sticky, low-hanging evening when Jon stood on the veranda
holding his baby daughter out to Ethel and saying, "Here's
your grandmother, Caroline." Something had drawn Ethel,
and her arms reached to take the infant. "Want to go to
Grandmother?" Jon had asked in his cheerful voice.

Ethel's hands had barely touched the child when Caroline
began to scream as though she'd been pinched. The hands
dropped to Ethel's sides never to reach again. Then, in less
than a minute, as though he'd watched the rejection and intended his wife still more pain, Jonathan Cameron had appeared on the veranda, his arms out to the infant, who went to
him eagerly—at only one month.

The door slammed and from that moment to this, Ethel
Cameron was interested in her granddaughter only as a necessary go-between when something simply had to be communi-
cated to Jonathan. He and his precious granddaughter,
through all the years of Caroline's life, had been as one person, having no need of her—nor she of them.

The barricade of loathing between herself and her husband
protected her mightily. To attempt a day without its shelter
would strip her of everything that made life bearable. She retained the respect of her servants, if not their devotion, but
Prince, the aging butler, became the only person for whom she
felt any concern. The obsession with hate did not prevent her
being the proper, genteel mistress of one of the truly fine
Savannah River plantations. She was never rude to her house
servants—never anything but a lady—but Ethel Cameron expected no affection. She gave none. From her parents, she had
inherited no love and only some money. She did not miss love,
and Jonathan Cameron remained a good provider. Romance,
fulfillment, sorrow, tears and joy she had found through all
her adult life between the covers of novels and biographies,
which she still ordered and devoured ten and twenty times
each. Books and Knightsford and hatred formed her world. In
them, she had found safety. She lacked nothing . . . nothing
except one supreme moment of revenge against the man who
had willfully, by breaking his marriage vows, turned her heart
to stone.

With desperate earnestness, she prayed for that moment.

Daily, she spent the first hour before sunrise with her Bible. Its pages did not comfort or soften her. As she interpreted them, they strengthened and fortified her passion for revenge. No matter where she read in the well-worn book, she never closed it for the day without turning to Romans 12:19 to read in a ritualistic whisper: " 'Dearly beloved, avenge not yourselves, but rather give place unto wrath' "—*God's wrath,* she interpolated—" 'for it is written, Vengeance is mine; I will repay, saith the Lord.' "

God, *her* God, understood the necessity for her revenge. Her one conviction lay in what to her was the fact that God's wrath had been turned upon Jonathan Cameron for all these years according to her prayers and would be turned upon him for as long as he lived on this earth to plague her. What was written before and after that one burning verse—about living in peace with each other—had no meaning. The word of God was there in that one verse, *only* to address her desperate need. Ethel's God, the God she had created in her own image, spoke to *her* through it, not to someone else. Hers was the vengeance verse. It flared into her solitary, shadow-filled days and nights —sharpening her intentions, exposing by its unwavering beam the injustice of the ugly wrong done her so long ago. She herself would need to commit no single act of vengeance. "Vengeance is *mine* . . . saith the Lord." God Himself would grant the act of vengeance in His own wisdom and in His own time. Would grant it to Ethel. She could begin her day only after she had refreshed her soul with God's promise that some day— some glorious, climactic day—He would take holy vengeance upon Jonathan. *In her behalf.*

This morning, having watched the two young people cross the lawn and vanish toward the rear veranda, she turned from the window only far enough to reach for the pages of the letter lying open on her reading table. She snatched them up and pressed them to her flat breast. This, indeed, by a way she would never have dreamed, could be the day on which she would see God's retribution at last.

A thrill of triumph surged through her body. She would have to keep watch at the window only long enough to be certain that her husband did not go with Mark and Caroline and the Mackay children on what she understood to be a Christmas greens expedition. Should Jonathan go along, even God's vengeance could be thwarted. Exactly at two o'clock this afternoon, she wanted the "beloved country gentleman," Jonathan Cameron, to be *in the big house*—in full view of the cottage. "Keep him inside, Almighty God," she prayed.

The letter, which she still held in her hands, was a direct answer to prayer. She had not laid eyes on Osmund Kott since the day her husband took him away to Bethesda Orphanage as a small boy. She despised him then wholeheartedly. She despised him now, but she shared with Mary Cotting's son the one bond by which they had, unknowingly, been bound together for nearly half a century. In Osmund's own handwriting, she now had before her—to read and reread—proof that he still hated Jonathan Cameron as devoutly as she did.

"Stay at your window, Mrs. Cameron," he had written, "and keep your eyes on my mother's cottage. I mean to carry out a plan that will devastate him. I am here, hidden in the Knightsford woods, and this day I intend to share my own vengeance with you."

Faithful Prince had slipped the letter to her with her breakfast tray. When the old servant refused to tell her where he'd gotten it, something locked her lips so that she simply took the letter and dismissed him.

All morning long, she had relived the moment when the quiet-mannered servant stood trembling in her doorway, the tray and letter held out to her. Prince was never allowed inside. No one was, except a girl for the daily dusting and the daily changing of her bed linen. This was always done during Ethel's regular walk around the cottage. This morning she admitted to a moment of near pity for Prince. The old man had been terrified. Hard to tell, of course, she thought, about the colored, but Prince's oddly thin-lipped mouth quivered and his powerful, thick hands shook as he handed her the tray. Osmund had obviously threatened him into hand-delivering the letter. Undoubtedly, she would never know the details of Prince's meeting with Kott, but she didn't care. *She had the letter.*

Keeping her attentive watch at the window, she saw them—the cheerful little Christmas group—heading single file toward the woods, Mark pushing an empty cart, Caroline and the girls with baskets on their arms. Her husband was *not* with them.

"Thank You, O God of vengeance, thank You!"

She left the window, seated herself gracefully in a high-backed spindle rocker and read again, with growing admiration and relish, Osmund's tale of his own hatred of the man whom he still called *Master* Cameron. "He was my mother's master, you know," Osmund Kott had written. "Mary Cotting had not yet worked out her indenture to him. She did not live long enough—lacking less than a year. She died, wholly owned—soul, spirit and especially *body*—by this man who has, through his heritage and charm, vamped the heart of an entire city and county and caused you and me to be despised. Oh, you *are* despised, Mrs. Cameron. As am I, and we have *Master* Cameron to thank for our outcast states. You may cringe at the word 'outcast.' I no longer cringe. I have proved to myself and to others by my successful work in New York that I can live as other men live. My trembling, panic-stricken days at Bethesda Orphanage are forever behind me. I am a man guided now by a purpose. *Master* Cameron, when at last he dies, will surely leave us both well off, but we deserve more. It is time for the act that will crucify his spirit. You may think that *Master* Cameron lives in the Knightsford big house with you. His spirit dwells still in Mary Cotting's little house—with her spirit. I beg you to keep the *Master* near the big house in view of the cottage, stay at your window after midafternoon—and wait and watch."

Ethel lifted the thin cloisonné watch that hung on a black velvet ribbon about her neck. It was nearly one o'clock. Midafternoon on a winter's day, when the dark falls early, would be just after two.

"Only one more hour, Almighty God! Only one more hour."

What Osmund intended to do, she couldn't know yet. But after so many years, one hour was nothing. She crossed the bedroom to her desk and upended the hourglass—prepared to wait.

"That one, Mark," Kate shouted up at him from the foot of a thick, gray-trunked magnolia tree. "No, not that one—*that* one!" She pointed a mittened hand at the most remote branch of glossy, dark-green leaves.

"And that's the last one," Caroline said firmly. "Mark, do be careful."

"But, Caroline, you don't think we need just a little more mistletoe?" Eliza Anne wanted to know.

"No, I do not. It will take the servants a week to clean up as it is, once Christmas is over."

Mark, perched on one foot in the crotch of two thick limbs, chopped at the branch Kate wanted. Caroline was right, of course. They already had far more than they would need to make the Mackay house festive, but he could have gone on hunting, tramping, climbing, sawing, chopping, laughing—forever. Not once all day had he thought of business. Caroline's way with the girls was a marvel. Is it really a way she has with them, he wondered, or is it Caroline—exactly as she is? No matter. She and the girls delighted him. He felt strong and agile and stimulated by far more than the merry task of searching for green leaves and red cassina and holly berries. The carefree time with his three girls was nourishing him in every way.

Even the guilt at not being able to love Caroline as she deserved seemed to lessen. He had enjoyed her too much for guilt. Perhaps she did love him with the kind of love that could endure waiting. Perhaps that was really true. Not too good to be true, but true. For him, today, she began to symbolize the kind of love God undoubtedly had in mind when He created love in the first place. Oh, Caroline was human. Very, very human at times, even weak—as weak as he—when he touched her. He supposed that she could be cruel, too. If she had ever made an effort to reach toward pathetic Ethel Cameron, Mark was unaware of it. Caroline merely seemed to tolerate the prickly woman and to worship her grandfather. She was no saint. Good, he thought, that's good. And a relief. Daring, as Mark did, to fall in love with his best friend's wife, he would be afraid of loving a saint.

Caroline, beyond anyone he had ever known, appeared to possess what seemed an almost total capacity to love. To love him, at least. More than Eliza Mackay could ever love again?

He didn't know.

All the way back out of the dense woods, they talked—mostly at once—about the sheer fun they'd had. Caroline and Kate and Eliza Anne kept allowing their heavy baskets to drag, kept dropping branches that had to be giggled over and retrieved. Mark pulled his overloaded cart with good humor and joined lustily when the girls began to sing carols.

When they came within sight of the big house, the songs and

laughter stopped. No one said, "Let's stop." They just didn't laugh or sing anymore.

After a time, Eliza Anne said, "When we begin to get close to your house, things—change, don't they, Caroline?"

"Yes," Caroline answered, her voice neither bitter nor hurt, merely factual. "They do change, honey, and I'm sorry. I change, too. After all these years, wouldn't you think I'd get so I don't notice anymore? I don't get used to it."

Mark said nothing. There was nothing to say.

"Do you suppose a lot of people hate each other the way your grandparents do?" Kate asked, kicking at a pinecone, missing it, going back to kick it again.

"I hope not."

To change the subject, Mark asked, "Could we handle just one more fine, berry-loaded holly branch? I see a dandy—and I hate the thought of leaving."

"Oh, Mark," Caroline said quickly, "You know how I hate to see you go, but it's already five after two. It gets dark so early. I'll worry about you three if I can't be sure you make it back to town while the sun's still up."

Eliza Anne dropped her basket, spilling greens everywhere. "Caroline, Mark, look!"

"What?"

"The cottage!" Mark began to run toward the clearing this side of the old loom house.

"Dear God!" Caroline gasped. "It's—on fire!"

Running, Mark called back: "Stay where you are, Kate, Eliza Anne!"

Still running, only glancing back, Mark saw the girls stop in their tracks, saw Caroline running to catch up with him—running like a frightened deer, unmindful of the briar hoops that snagged her skirts, leaping over fallen logs as though they weren't there.

Within a few hundred yards of the cottage—hopelessly engulfed now in flames—Mark stopped. In seconds, Caroline was beside him. Then, horrified, they watched Jonathan Cameron hurry on his lame leg off the big house veranda in the direction of the flames.

"Grandfather!" Caroline screamed. "Grandfather! No! No!"

Mark ran with her toward the old man, but the flames drove them back, forcing them to circle wide around the roaring cottage. Jonathan Cameron was running on a straight line. Mark could feel the heat on his own face as Caroline, running alongside him, pulled up her green cape to cover her nose and mouth. Gasping for breath, they pushed themselves to run faster toward Cameron, cutting the distance as much as they dared against the waves of roaring heat.

When Mark looked back for an instant to make sure the girls were not coming too, Caroline's scream told him what had happened. The old man, in his white suit, had plunged into the wall of solid flame.

She did not scream again, nor did she struggle against Mark's restraining arms to go after her grandfather. It was too late. Mark felt her body slump against him.

His arm steadying her, they stared helplessly at the burning cottage. His white suit and hair aflame, Jonathan ran from the building and—almost without a limp now—began to circle the cottage, the frantic motion of his body whipping the fire that engulfed him until he became a blackened, maniacally screaming torch: a fire-spitting, wildly waving human fireworks display flying about under its own power.

Her woolen cape torn away as she escaped Mark's grasp, Caroline reached her grandfather first and pulled him to the ground. Roughly dragging her back, Mark threw himself over the still-burning, half-charred body, and fighting flames that licked now at his own skin and hair, he began to roll over and over with Cameron on the stubbly earth.

The stench of hot flesh and hair sickened him. What had been the thatch of silver hair was now blackened skin and bony skull.

"Your hair, Mark!" Caroline cried, beating at the flames that still licked about her grandfather's legs. "Mark—your hair!"

He could feel the searing pain, then the quick pressure of her hands gripping and rubbing at his head. Then, the skirt of her pink dress was over his head, and with her bare hands she was smothering the fire on him. The pain seared, but when he reached to touch his own head, it was no longer burning. The flames were out. Instead of the familiar thick hair, his fingers touched a stiff, woolly mass.

The oddly dancing flames had gone out, too, on the quiet, still-smoking, twisted form on the ground. Caroline stared at what had been her grandfather's face—a blob of oily black and pink, the cooked flesh curling, splitting, stinking as no cooked animal flesh ever did.

A rising breeze whipped the fire that still leaped and crackled about the charred skeleton of Mary Cotting's little house. A towhee called from the woods where the girls waited. Mark looked at Caroline's stricken face—then back at the house, just in time to see the once pretty gabled roof slide to one side, buckle and crash to the burning floor of the room where Osmund Kott and Mark's mother had been conceived in what was called sinful love. Sinful and undying.

No one would ever know what possessed Jonathan Cameron to run straight into the burning building; no one would ever know what he meant to do. But he had plunged into it with all the drive and energy left in his aging heart. The heart that had never found solace in any other place.

Too numb to mind the pain that any contact brought, Mark took Caroline in his arms. She smelled of Jonathan Cameron's charred flesh and the heavy, black smoke that still plumed in the flames above the cottage ruins. Mark smelled of it, too.

From all the corners of Knightsford, Cameron's people had begun to assemble around the veranda steps, some with bowed heads, some with hands raised toward the smoky sky. Mark could hear nothing they were saying. There was only a low rumble of voices seeming to drift about as the smoke drifted. Caroline had seen them, too. Watching, Mark saw her hold out her arms toward them. The recognition of a bond he didn't yet understand? A plea for help? A sign that it was now too late? That nothing could be done for the master they all revered? She looked back at Mark, then buried her face in her hands. A racking sob tore from her, but only one. With what seemed superhuman strength, she lifted her head.

"We have to find the girls, Mark. They must be terrified."

Eliza Anne and Kate were standing exactly where they'd left them, motionless, their faces pinched and white.

"The cottage burned to the ground," Mark said.

"Someone set it afire," Caroline corrected.

Hoping not to show surprise at what she'd said, he took the girls by the hand.

"Mark!" Kate gasped. "Your hands are all burned!"

"A little. Caroline's, too. Come on, you two. I'll get Prince to take you to The Grange for the night. Mr. Cameron's dead.

We can't go back to town and leave Caroline.''

"But what about Mama?" Eliza Anne asked. "She'll be worried sick about us."

"One of the people can gather a crew," Caroline said firmly, "and row our plantation boat into town. We'll get word to your mother. Don't worry. If they leave within the hour, they'll be on Broughton Street about the time you would have gotten there."

Mark looked past the group of terrified servants gathered at the foot of the big house front steps—looked at the house and up to a second-floor window. A sudden movement there had caught his attention. Until now, he had not thought once of Ethel Cameron. In the front bay—the curtains drawn all the way back—she stood, her face buried in her hands.

Softly, full of mourning, the servants had begun to pray and chant. The first piercing scream from the upstairs window silenced them. And into the silence the woman who never raised her voice screamed again and again and again—a wild, wounded sound Mark would never forget. Then she vanished from the window.

*Part IV*

# 1819–1822

# THIRTY-FOUR

BY mid-April of the following year, 1819, John and Margaret McQueen returned from Jamaica. Waiting for them while their trunks were collected, at what townspeople still called the Mein and Mackay wharf, Mark decided that he would take them to his office for a short rest and a visit. They had been away almost two years, but even John, hard to impress, would be amazed at the changes in Savannah, Mark was certain. The McQueens were to spend at least one night at the Mackay house, and he meant to save most of the news of the city's progress and the presidential visit for later, when they were all together. During the brief time in his office—after he'd displayed his own remodeling at Number One Commerce Row—he planned to tell them everything about the Camerons, including his own family tie with them.

Neither McQueen could miss seeing the two new warehouses on Factor's Row. There would be time to tell them of Savannah's development at home with Miss Eliza, but he had no intention of forcing her to hear again the ugly story of Cameron's death. Besides, Caroline was at the Mackay house. He had brought her back as soon as the funeral was over.

"I put four men to the task of collecting your trunks," Mark said, ushering John and Margaret into his private office—wood-paneled now and furnished in part with the few handsome pieces he'd had sent from his old home in Philadelphia. After receiving Margaret's high praise for his taste and John's nod of approval, he said, "You are both welcome sights, believe me!"

Looking remarkably stylish and fresh after such a long sea voyage, Margaret, in a brown traveling suit and plumed hat, took what had been Aunt Nassie's comfortable armchair.

"Do sit down, gentlemen," she said. "I want to revel not only in this handsome room but in the sight of Mark Browning, the *distinguished* Mark Browning, behind his desk in his very own countinghouse!"

Seating himself, Mark grinned at her. "You're right. I'm the only old-timer left in the firm these days. It still seems strange at times that we're no longer Mein and Mackay."

John nodded. "But I'm duly impressed with your new sign: M. Browning, Factor. No longer handling imports of any kind?"

"Oh, I import my clients' needs, but I find I like the personal side of being a factor more every day."

"That's fortunate for me," John said. "Judging by my own profit these past two years, you're born to the calling."

"And I'm not alone in majoring in personal accounts. You'll see that cotton factoring is beginning to dominate the waterfront. I've been fortunate. I'm not looking for any more clients at the moment. Most important, though, Miss Eliza and the children will be all right from now on out. I expect the two of you to understand—to me, that's what matters most."

John gave him a long, probing look. "That—still is the most important thing, eh?"

"Yes," he said simply. "It still is."

"How is Eliza?" Margaret asked, unaware of the meaning of the exchange between the two men. "Oh, I know she's courageous. She's always been that way. But how is she—really, Mark?"

His small frown came and went. "All right. She stays busy caring for little Sallie. A three-year-old takes time, you know. Miss Eliza plays the pianoforte a lot. Works among the elderly and the city's poor widows, gives some time to Bethesda. I still hear her cry in the night. For us all at times, the house still reverberates with emptiness. We were hoping for something like a merry Christmas this past year, but—" He leaned toward them. "I've asked you here for a reason beyond showing off my renovations. You both need to know what's happened. Miss Eliza and I decided not to write it in a letter."

Reliving it was unexpectedly painful, but Mark told them everything he could remember about the tragic afternoon at Knightsford. He had been forced to recount parts of the story a few times before. No telling, except the first with Miss Eliza, seemed so hard as telling the McQueens. He left out nothing. It was important to him now that John and Margaret know all about his own blood-relationship with Cameron, with Osmund Kott. He even told them how Caroline's hand had become infected from the burns, how he had almost enjoyed having a Brutus haircut like Mackay's until his own hair had grown out again. He spoke of Eliza's rocklike support of both him and Caroline. He tried to describe the suddenly released pain in Ethel Cameron's screams that day. "I don't know what those screams meant," he said. "Caroline felt so strongly that the old lady wouldn't want to see us at all. We didn't see her; she stayed in her rooms." He spoke of the Mackay girls' terror. Then he described the funeral conducted two days later on the spot where Jonathan Cameron had died, by a minister brought from town by Sheftall Sheftall. It was a simple burial, at Caroline's insistence, in the bare, charred piece of ground where Mary Cotting's cottage had stood.

"Have you told Caroline that Jonathan Cameron was— your grandfather, too?" Margaret asked.

"Yes. She knew it for some time before he died. That's why she wanted to bury him there, where he'd known his only happiness."

The hardest part of all was to tell them of Caroline's almost unassuageable grief. "She's still with us here," he said. "I couldn't bear to think of her out there with Mrs. Cameron, who refused even to attend the funeral."

"She's a tough old dame," John said. "No point in Eliza or you or anyone else trying to comfort Ethel Cameron. It wouldn't be possible for her to receive comfort. She's never given any."

"Is Ethel—just out there alone in that big house now, Mark?" Margaret asked.

"Pretty much as she's always been. Caroline vows everything's the same for the old lady, except now there's no one to hate." He paused. "I feel sure Caroline will soften toward her grandmother someday. She's just so hurt by grief now."

Margaret shook her head incredulously. "Ethel Cameron— didn't even attend the funeral. Mark, didn't that break Caroline's heart?"

"I thought it would," he said slowly. "Instead, she seemed relieved." He lifted both hands in a helpless gesture. "I doubt that any of us will ever understand how Caroline has been forced to—insulate herself against her grandmother all these years. She breaks my heart now, though. You see, as long as she had her grandfather—*our* grandfather—she could cope." He half smiled. "I still don't find it easy to call him—my grandfather. I did my best for Mr. Cameron as his factor. I'll do my best to look after Caroline's interests now. You see, he wasn't able to tell me himself that I'm his grandson."

John sighed. "I doubt the old fellow could have faced telling you. After all, he kept himself financially strapped paying off Osmund Kott for keeping quiet."

"By the way, Kott's in New York," Mark said. "Doing a fine job, apparently, for James Parsons at the Browning Company."

Margaret sat straight up. "Osmund—doing a fine job?"

"I don't doubt he could," John said.

"But, *Osmund Kott?*"

"Let's drop a distasteful subject, my dear," John said firmly. "Mark? What about you? Has—anything changed for you? I mean, are you any closer to marrying Caroline Cameron?"

"John, she's in mourning!" Margaret scolded.

"I know. I'm not talking about Caroline. I want to know about Mark himself."

This, Mark knew, was John's careful, caring way of asking if he still loved Eliza. "I guess not," he answered, flushing a little. "Caroline and I are close. I suppose, closer than ever, but—"

A knock at his office door relieved him of having to say more. It was Mark's clerk to announce that the McQueens' trunks were on their way to Broughton Street and that Mark's new barouche was waiting.

It was common knowledge by now that President Monroe and his party were expected next month. In no time, after Scarbrough had urged Mark to invest more heavily in the S.S. *Savannah*, people were also talking about the fact that William Scarbrough had heavily mortgaged his city properties and his nearly completed mansion in order to finance the steam-powered ship.

Neither Eliza nor Mark mentioned Scarbrough's finances at dinner that night. The girls were not interested, of course, but they were more than interested in next month's festive plans.

Partway through the meal, Kate and Eliza Anne pushed and shoved each other verbally in their eagerness to tell John and Margaret that not only was the first steam-powered ocean-going ship in the world almost finished and due to dock in Savannah in less than two weeks, but that coming "special to inspect the S.S. *Savannah*" was President James Monroe himself, to stay for five whole days! And that the Scarbroughs' new house—"a palace, really"—on West Broad would be mainly finished just in time for the President and his party to stay there. And that William Jay was commissioned to design a huge pavilion to be erected in Johnson Square, where a ball would be given in honor of the President.

"And," Kate plunged ahead, gasping for breath, afraid Eliza Anne might get in an extra word, "you two have to come to town to stay with us for the whole tremendous blowout!"

"Kate!" her mother scolded. "What did we agree about your using that expression?"

Margaret laughed. " 'Blowout' is Julia Scarbrough's word, isn't it?"

"Sure it is," Kate said, "but I like it, too. I forgot, Mama, if we said anything about it."

Before Eliza could correct the record, Eliza Anne was launched. "They're also going to dedicate Papa's new Presbyterian Church while President Monroe's here, and we're both going to have new dresses. Maybe we'll have two or three new dresses!"

"You'll certainly need more than one," Caroline said in a mock businesslike tone. "After all, the President's staying five days and there'll be all those functions."

When Eliza went upstairs to hear the girls' prayers and to see that young Sallie was safely asleep, Mark, Caroline and the McQueens moved to the parlor for coffee.

Waiting with Mark for the ladies to be seated, before settling himself in Mackay's old chair, John said, "I want you to know, Miss Caroline, that Margaret and I consider you a—very great lady."

A typically blunt John McQueen remark, Mark thought. He watched Caroline's pale, drawn face as she recovered from her surprise. She would manage, he knew, somehow to match John's frankness. Certainly, she had tried valiantly not to allow the shadow of her grief to darken anyone else's pleasure.

At last, Caroline said, almost pertly, "Thank you, sir, but

aren't you speaking in riddles?''

"He is not speaking in riddles," Margaret said firmly. "To join in the girls' excitement over the President's visit, their new dresses—in the midst of your own sorrow—is being a great lady."

Mark saw Caroline's mouth quiver, her eyes fill with tears. She was trying so hard to smile, he longed to go to her. When Margaret did, he was relieved.

"Let me give you a hug," Margaret said. "Words are too feeble."

For an instant, Margaret's arms about her, Caroline clung for comfort, then turned briskly to pull up a small slipper chair.

"But great ladies do not wait on themselves like that." Margaret attempted to lighten the mood. "The idea of pulling up your own chair with two gentlemen present!"

"I doubt I'll ever be broken of that habit, Miss Margaret," Caroline said, her cheeks still wet with tears. "You see, Grandfather was my only gentleman at Knightsford and his legs made it hard for him to be as gallant as he felt." Abruptly, she turned to Mark. "I want these two people to—know—everything."

"They do know," he said tenderly. "I told them—in my office this afternoon."

"Thank you." She turned then to Margaret. "And, Miss Margaret, I'm so worried about Kate and Eliza Anne. They were right there! I think Mark and I kept them from—seeing—Grandfather—that day, but it was so ghastly, and they were just a way off in the woods. Is it—natural for them to seem now to be pretending it didn't happen? I mean, going back to Knightsford is the last thing I want to do, but I will do it if my being here might be forcing those two little girls to have nightmares from not mentioning it just because they don't want to make me feel bad!"

"Oh, Caroline, no," Margaret answered quickly. "This is where you belong now, with real friends."

"I'm going to be—all right someday." Caroline tried to smile. "I can't think very well yet. I don't know where I want to live or anything like that, but—"

"None of that is important now and you know it," Mark said almost sharply. "Don't even mention going back out there!"

"My sister would bar the door," John said. "Eliza wouldn't have it."

For a moment Caroline looked at the big pink rose in the parlor carpet just in front of her chair, then said quietly, "Well, I think about my grandmother in that big house by herself. But"—she lifted her eyes first to Mark, then Margaret, then John—"she's been that way most of her life." Without a trace of bitterness, she added, "She wouldn't want me there."

"You're where you belong," Mark said sternly. "Don't forget what Sheftall Sheftall told you. Your grandfather's will won't be read until next week. Sheftall has to go to Knightsford himself to get it."

"If it still exists," Caroline said.

"She fears all sorts of things and, I think, quite understandably," Mark explained. "You see, Caroline is sure someone set the cottage afire."

After a rather long silence, Margaret said, "Well, I can understand why you'd think that, Caroline. Although the cottage was quite old and almost surely built of heart pine."

"I know. I know," Caroline answered. "I know all that."

Mark watched her, fearing that she might burst into tears. Desperately, he longed to take her in his arms, to comfort her—the only way he knew how to reach Caroline these days. At this moment she appeared more alone than he'd ever seen her.

As though she'd read his thoughts, she said with a small, faint laugh, "I've been an orphan since I was one year old, but I never felt like one before. I do now. I don't belong anywhere or to—anyone."

Mark exchanged a glance with John, then looked away.

"Caroline, I have a marvelous idea?" Margaret exclaimed.

"And if it's what I think it is, brilliant wife, I'm in favor," John said with, for him, real enthusiasm.

"Come home with us," Margaret went on, "until the illustrious entourage arrives from Washington, and we'll all return to celebrate the President and the S.S. *Savannah* together!"

Caroline looked straight at Mark, her eyes questioning.

"I—we'd all miss you here," he said lamely, "but it might be a good change for you."

The room grew heavy with the painful silence.

Surprising Mark most of all, Caroline laughed her spontaneous, natural laugh, calculated to put everyone at ease. "You see, McQueens? I have been very dull company here. Mark thinks I should visit you, too." She was looking at Mark now, with her teasing smile.

"Oh, you've been an insufferable bore," he shot back, his special smile—the one that always reached her—as much, he hoped, in his voice as on his face.

She stuck out her tongue at him, and at once the atmosphere was again relaxed and comfortable.

"Well!" Margaret said lightly. "Does all this mean you will go back to Causton's Bluff with us? We're leaving tomorrow. The servants are airing the house today, cleaning up—I trust. Please say you'll go!"

"Please say you'll go—where?" Eliza demanded from the doorway.

John and Mark stood as she came into the room. "Home with us, sister, until the blowout for the President," John explained.

Eliza sat in the chair nearest Caroline.

"We'll give her all the company she needs and all the privacy she wants," Margaret said. "The woods and the marsh will be glorious—full of spring and new green. You and I can read, Caroline, and talk, walk, sleep. It's very easy to ignore my self-sufficient husband. He can sit with a pipe for hours on the front steps and think with great profit. You may even claim his company whenever you need a charming gentleman to spoil you. We want you, dear Caroline. We truly do."

Mark had not taken his eyes from Caroline's face. He glanced once at Eliza—beloved Eliza—and found in her face only concern for Caroline.

"You—mean all that, Margaret, don't you?" Caroline spoke at last, her eyes brimming again with tears.

"Try us!"

Turning to Eliza, Caroline spoke in a strained voice. "I—I feel sometimes that it might be good for Eliza Anne and Kate if I weren't around right now to remind them of—what they saw happen—at Knightsford."

Eliza went to her, her arms out. Caroline jumped up to return the embrace. *They love each other,* Mark thought, and was both comforted and disturbed by the thought.

"We don't want you to go," Eliza was saying, still holding

her. "We don't want you to leave us at all. In fact, you can't go until you promise that you'll come right back here later, to stay for as long as possible. Isn't that right, Mark?"

"I want Caroline to do what's best for her," he said.

Caroline looked straight at him. "I'm going," she said. "And don't frown so, Mark Browning. I'll get along well if no one pities me. The Mackays were here for you when you—had no home. The McQueens are here—for me."

He did his best to give her the teasing smile. "But I forbid you to stay as long as I've stayed here!"

In their room that night, readying themselves for bed, John made no effort to dodge Margaret's blunt question. In fact, he repeated it after her: " 'Why did it all seem so strained, in spite of the obvious good humor between Mark and Caroline downstairs tonight?' You asked, dear Margaret, and I'll answer. One would expect, after an appropriate period for mourning, that Mark would propose and Caroline would accept his proposal. She appears to be free at last to marry him. The town expects it. They've been seen everywhere together. She obviously loves him to distraction. The truth is, Mark does not love her that way."

"You're letting your imagination run away with you!"

"I am doing no such thing. Mark and I discussed it before we left for Jamaica. He's in love with my sister."

Starting to put on her dressing gown, Margaret let it drop to the floor. "Mark—is in love with *Eliza?* Oh, John, what a tragedy!"

"It seems so. Surely for Caroline. But it could be the most wonderful thing possible for Eliza."

"I suppose you told Mark that?"

"I did. I even pray for it when I remember to."

Slowly, her mind not on what she was doing, Margaret picked up her dressing gown and struggled into it.

"Sorry not to spring out of bed to assist you, dearest," John said.

"Don't interrupt my thoughts. I'm having difficulty sorting them out. Yes. Of course, Eliza would be cared for like a—queen for the remainder of her days. But, John, does Eliza even know how Mark feels? I don't think she does. I'm sure she does not! She acts too much like what she'll always be—Robert Mackay's widow!"

"Of course she doesn't know. That's one reason things struck you as strained downstairs this evening."

"Do not, *do not* speak in riddles!"

"Mark knew that I know. He told me tonight that Caroline now knows that it's Eliza he loves. You and Eliza did not know. The sum of those conditions equals *strain*."

"*Caroline* knows?"

John nodded.

"Now, wait a minute. Let me put this all together. Robert's been gone about two and a half years now. You think Mark may be planning to—propose marriage to Eliza?"

John shrugged. "I doubt if he knows. I think he's in love with Caroline, too."

Margaret crawled into bed beside him. "And that's quite possible," she snapped, still sitting up. "I've been in love with as many as three men at once! Including you."

"So you have and so you are better able to understand Mark than anyone else in Savannah."

"I don't think that was nasty, darling, was it?"

"No."

"Very well." She moved close to him. "Two more things and I'll blow out the candle. One, I'm going to see to it that Caroline Cameron enjoys herself at our house, and two, I loathe being kept in the dark. Why didn't you tell me that Mark loved Eliza before we went to Jamaica?"

"Blow out the candle, Margaret."

# THIRTY-FIVE

AFTER breakfast the next morning, while Margaret and Eliza helped Caroline pack for a fortnight or so at Causton's Bluff, Mark ordered his new barouche brought around from the Mackay stables in back, seemingly determined to show John Savannah's progress. As usual, John was only mildly interested in the city, but he was intensely interested in this young man who loved his sister. He meant to allow Mark to set the tone of their morning, to ask no personal questions right off. The journey about town was, to him, mainly a chance to know Mark better.

He and Mark were waiting when Hero proudly drove up in the black-and-gilt barouche, its top folded back so they might enjoy the spring sun.

"Straight to State Street on Columbia Square first," Mark instructed Hero.

"You think I ain't guessed, Mister Mark?" The big man looked back with a wide smile.

"I make this trip so often," Mark explained to John, "Hero can read my mind. I walk it when the days are long enough."

"So, the first stop will be Isaiah Davenport's new house," John said, removing his top hat and sliding comfortably down in the tufted leather seat. "Eliza tells me you're quite taken with Isaiah's work."

"And with the man himself," Mark said. "He has so many houses under construction at once, I don't always find him at his own place. I hope we're lucky. Reserved New Englander that he is, Isaiah's quite proud and excited these days. About his own work—and about the city."

"I know Davenport," John said. "Must be a fine thing to look at a great house and know you not only designed it but saw to its building—even did some of it with your own hands. Be good to see him again. He doesn't talk a man to death."

Mark laughed. "Unlike the loquacious William Jay. I'm impressed with Jay's work, though."

"He's the new Savannah obsession, I'm sure."

"Indeed he is. Our prosperous merchants are literally vying for his time and talents. And certainly, Jay has talent. I confess I prefer Isaiah's simple, good lines, but Jay is innovative. One thing I know, his stylishly shod feet seldom touch the ground these days. He thrives on it, too. What twenty-two-year-old wouldn't?"

"Eliza says he's like a runaway horse, though. Is my sister being her usual cautious self? Or is William Jay really bankrupting our vain merchant class?"

"Both, I think. Still, he's a delight to watch. Ideas seem to stream in and out of his rather impish head. The ladies adore him; the gentlemen, as Eliza says, borrow to their last line of credit to retain his services. His designs, while too ornate for my taste, have a good, solid look. Somewhat delicate at the same time." Mark laughed. "He must see Doric columns in his sleep."

"And in spite of Isaiah's lack of formal architectural education, you like his house best."

"For me, yes."

"I expect Eliza likes the Davenport house better than she likes the Richardson or the Scarbrough mansions, too," John said, giving Mark only the merest side glance.

"She does indeed."

Obviously, Mark intended to say no more about John's sister—at least not now. "Well, Isaiah's plans have always been copied from tried and true books of houses—New England and England," John mused. "Designs that have stood the test of time and taste. Dear old Mackay would surely have wanted a Jay house."

Mark smiled. "He liked ostentation, all right, but only when it gave him a laugh. That's the reason he enjoyed the countess's blowouts."

"You miss very little," John said.

They were pulling into State Street at Columbia Square. Mark asked Hero to stop across the street from the tall, imposing, red brick Davenport house—its two tall chimneys flanking each end of the steep roof, relieved only by three dormer windows. Painters were at work on the white trim around the basement windows, and slow, careful tuck-pointing—the only kind Davenport would permit—still went on above the tasteful fanlight arched over the high, simple colonial entrance.

They sat looking for a time, John nodding approval. "I see what you mean, Mark," he said finally. "It is a great house. I like it. One very similar to the house you plan to build for yourself?"

"Someday," Mark said, aware, John knew, that Hero could hear from his high driver's seat. "You—know the name of the lady for whom I hope to build it."

John gave Mark one of his rare, warm smiles. "Yes," he said. "I know her name."

Inside the house they found Isaiah at the far end of the entrance hall, on his knees beside the lower reaches of his sweeping, classical stair. He was hard at work securing one graceful mahogany banister spindle. He got to his feet, greeted his visitors and explained, as though they'd been talking together for hours, about his house.

"On the interior and the exterior," he said, "I've devised a way—my way—of signing what you might call my own signature. Here, come over here, both of you, and look up to the third floor. Do you see that one continuous, smooth line my stair and plaster design make?"

They did see and both marveled at the deceptive beauty of Davenport's simple, clean lines.

"I want my house to have what folks can recognize as—my seal. My stair is only one sign of that."

Except for the irregular sound of saws and hammers upstairs, the talk and occasional laughter of painters and tuck-pointers outside, the three men stood in silence for a time, just looking around the gracious entrance hall, which ended a few feet to the rear of where they stood in a low, wide, white door.

Pointing at the unusually low door, John grinned. "I can see a Northerner designed that door, Isaiah. Does it lead to the outside?"

Isaiah nodded. "Yep, why, McQueen?"

"Looks to me as though a true Southerner would have cut a

higher opening. You've been here long enough to know a hot Savannah summer, Isaiah."

Not bothering with one word of self-defense, Isaiah merely grunted and said, "The door suits."

Gazing up, up the smoothly curving stair again, John admired the perfect plaster work covering the structural curve that supported it at the second-floor level. "Magnificent craftsmanship."

"Much obliged, McQueen," Isaiah said. Then he turned to Mark. "You haven't said a word, Browning, about my Ionic-columned screen there, dividing the hall into front and back. The columns will be painted white. What's your opinion?"

Mark studied the somewhat heavy columns that supported Davenport's segmental arch. To John, it was plain that something about the beautifully wrought, but somewhat ostentatious, columns bothered Mark. John had known for a long time now that the young man wasn't too successful at hiding what he really thought.

When Mark waited a touch too long to respond, Isaiah cleared his throat and said, "A segmental arch is showy for my taste, too. Hate to hide my stair. My wife, Sarah, would have had a fit without those columns, though. She's seen the Richardson and Scarbrough columns Jay put in. I please her when I can."

Mark was smiling. "Thanks for getting me off that hook, Isaiah," he said. "The craftsmanship is superb, but I agree—the columns wouldn't be my choice."

"I aim to please myself in every way when I start to work designing your place, Browning. We see alike."

The three strolled into the parlor, a perfectly proportioned, elegantly turned-out room—also with columns.

"Sarah got her half columns there against the walls," Isaiah said, almost apologetically. He ran his hand over the smoothly sanded surface of a half Ionic column fastened flat against the plastered wall. "For myself, I see a parlor with good, plain surfaces to set off fine furniture. Furniture ought to decorate a parlor. There won't be any Ionic columns in your parlor, Browning. Moldings'll do it all."

"Oh, but the room is handsome," Mark said. "When do you think you can move in, sir?"

Davenport chuckled and rubbed his springy, short hair. "Depends on the weather. I work inside on my own house when I can't work outside on some other man's place."

After a leisurely tour of the entire building, including the finished third floor, where Isaiah's children would have their own rooms, Mark and John were back in the carriage on their way to the Richardson house on Abercorn. Not particularly eager for the tour of the city to last too long, John reminded Mark that he had already seen the interior of banker Richardson's Jay mansion shortly after the family moved in.

"Oh, I just thought we'd have a good look at the exterior again," Mark said, "before we go on to Jay's newest masterpiece, the Scarbrough place." He laughed. "John, I'm trying to impress you with the wonders of Savannah! To make you happy you're home again. And, frankly, I find it fascinating to see the similarities in Jay's designs. His Regency style—those heavily columned porches with sweeping stairs up each side—really make it quite easy to tell that Jay had a hand in both the Richardson and the Scarbrough houses. The Telfair entrance hall is actually even more splendid than the Richardsons'."

Looking out at the Richardson home as they passed slowly, John frowned. "A more splendid entrance hall than that one over there? Mark, if I walked into my own home between two gilt-capped Corinthian columns with baseboards painted to resemble marble, I'd feel I'd need to be in formal attire just to enter my own front door! Of course, I couldn't pay for even one of those Jay columns."

Mark laughed. "Wait till you see the countess's entrance hall! I hear it dwarfs a man."

"All I can say about that is, William Scarbrough's new steamship had better be successful."

When Hero drew the barouche up before the archaic Doric columns and heavy entablature of the Scarbrough portico on West Broad Street, John could tell that Mark was pleased to see both William Jay and Julia Scarbrough—one on each of the heavy stone stairs leading up each side to the entrance—performing. Jay was bowing to Julia. Julia was curtsying to Jay. Each would take a step up, then more bowing, more curtsying and much arm waving. John could scarcely believe what he saw. Two adults waving to each other in wild, ecstatic gestures. So intent were they, in what appeared to John to be a rehearsal, that neither had noticed the visitors.

His sardonic smile curving the corners of his mouth, John asked, "Can you explain any of that, Mark?"

Mark laughed. "Only that they're undoubtedly pretending they've just arrived at Julia's forthcoming presidential ball."

Finally, Julia spied the handsome barouche, recognized Mark, waved, picked up her skirts and hurried out to meet them. Beaming, his red cockade of hair springing, William Jay skimmed down his stair to join the group.

After warm, effusive greetings, Julia and her young, enthusiastic architect made John and Mark stand outside in the unfinished carriage drive for a moment in order to, as Julia said, "get the full, magnificent effect."

"What I was after," Jay explained in his clipped, British accent, heightened by the light, light quality of a boyish voice, "was, as dear Mrs. Scarbrough says, a 'magnificent effect' that is both monumental in character and delicate in feeling. I did it by flanking the heavy Regency portico with those delicate arched windows—there, you see?" He leaped about and pointed as he talked. "The contrast between the darkly shaded areas of the portico and the surrounding flat surfaces has been tied together into a harmonious design by the curved arches of portico, fanlight and, of course, the dear, delicate windows."

"Can you imagine how ecstatic I really am?" Julia demanded. "Just think, this young genius, William Jay, conceived such beauty on direct inspiration from Mr. Scarbrough and me! You did, didn't you, William? You said so."

"Ideas flourish in such a creative, appreciative atmosphere," Jay declared. "Savannah is the world's most delicious city! Everyone who is anyone here longs to be surrounded by beauty of form, of line, of color." He held up both slender hands. "But wait, oh, wait, gentlemen, until you see what Julia Scarbrough inspired me to on the interior of her castle!"

Julia mounted one stair on Jay's arm; Mark and John mounted the other. As they met at the spacious front door, Jay swung it open to reveal a vast, classical atrium two stories high, surrounded by a balcony supported by four more massive Doric columns—the whole after the manner of a courtyard of classical Greece or Rome.

Runted by the sheer enormity of the dramatic entrance hall, Jay, his arms extended, shouted: "Sheer, exuberant fancy!"

The high-pitched voice echoed and then the echo died away. Silence.

"Well, what do you think?" Julia demanded of them. "Don't just stand there gawking, John and Mark! What do you *think?* Don't you feel Mr. Jay has chosen exactly the right color—this warm, welcoming, clean oyster white? The floors, once they're finished and gleaming, will form the perfect contrast—and look, gentlemen, look up! Look up—as high up as you can see!"

"Yes!" Jay exclaimed. "My glorious atrium has been crowned!"

Mark and John looked to the very top of the vaulted room to find a thin, bald young man on a scaffold. Above the artist's head on a cerulean blue background, he was painting a dizzyingly lifelike night sky with a quarter moon and a scattering of the most familiar stars.

"At the moment, neither William nor I can recall his name, but the man at work up there," Julia said, "is definitely an artist of degree. That glorious dome, which will give our guests the sensation of mingling and dancing under the stars, is entirely the idea of this fabulous young Englishman! Speak, Mark. *Say* something!"

"Julia, dear lady," Mark said, "I have never, *never* seen anything like this house in all my life!"

"Nor I," John added, still staring upward at the painted image of the night sky.

"There! What did I tell you, William? When the Savannahians of *taste* see your genius, you will soar, soar, soar!"

She took Mark's arm and began to propel him toward the stair, half-hidden to the rear right so as not to mar the spaciousness of the entrance hall. "You haven't seen anything yet, gentlemen. Come along. Oh my, was any lady ever in more impressive male company?"

"I'm sorry, Julia," Mark said politely, but firmly. "John and I are expected at home. And anyway, we'll bring Miss Eliza and Miss Margaret and Caroline Cameron to see this—splendor. I promise."

Somewhat deflated, Julia said, "Oh. Well, on that promise, I will permit you to leave. But don't be long about returning. Oh, Caroline Cameron the beauteous," she explained, turning to Jay, "is Mark's intended, we all hope." The musical laughter echoed up and around her unfinished atrium. "And unless I miss my guess, this *extremely* prosperous Mr. Browning will be in need of a splendid, splendid house for his bride!"

"She was about to show us the room the townsfolk are already calling 'the history room,' " Mark said as Hero drove them briskly back to Broughton Street.

"Julia with a *history* room?"

"It's actually the dining room. The town's expecting her to make social history in it." Mark laughed. "No one can ever say William Jay does not design *for his clients.*" When John only grinned, Mark pressed him. "Say something! You left it all to me inside the house. It *is* a most impressive edifice, John. Even you have to admit that."

"I do. I do indeed admit it. Not for living, of course, but for dear Julia, entertaining is living. So, for the Scarbroughs, Jay earned his money." He stretched his long, thin legs in the carriage. "I can't wait to attend a function there, in fact. I can think of no more perfect setting for my dazzling wife."

"From what Miss Eliza has told me, Margaret's graced far more elegant surroundings in her lifetime."

John's many questions could wait no longer. "Will Eliza go with you and Caroline to the President's ball?"

Mark waited to answer. "I don't know. I feel sure she'll attend all the other civic functions for the President. She—seems to have trouble facing a blowout at Julia's. At least, that was true in the old house where Mackay was always the favorite Scarbrough guest."

"Are you going to tell my sister that you love her—while Caroline is at Causton's Bluff, Mark?"

He didn't wait this time. "Yes. Yes, I'm going to—try to tell her. But, John, do you want the whole truth?"

"If you know it and if you want to tell me."

"I've waited so long to ask Eliza to—marry me, I've grown afraid. At least, as long as I keep putting it off, I can hope. If I find out that she can never love me that way, I honestly don't know what I'll do!"

John studied the taut profile for a long time. Finally he said, "Waiting any longer is most unfair to Caroline. But then, you know that."

"Yes. If anyone in town knows it, I do."

# THIRTY-SIX

By the first of May, work was well advanced on Jay's pavilion in Johnson Square—the setting for the gala public ball to be given in President Monroe's honor at 5 P.M. Wednesday, May 12. These days, the city seemed not to quiet down until nearly midnight.

The President was now arriving a week early, so carpenters and painters worked by lamp and candlelight to finish the new Independent Presbyterian Church in time for him to attend the dedication. The entire city was being cleaned and swept. Regardless of social standing, fines were levied against those who dared litter the streets. Residents scythed their yards and trimmed their shrubbery and trees, and those who could afford scarce workmen painted their houses. Even the face of the Exchange clock had been scrubbed and painted. The S.S. *Savannah* had already put into port and lay secured at the Scarbrough wharf, awaiting her distinguished guests. Her voyage down from the north had been nearly flawless.

After Caroline and the McQueens left for Causton's Bluff, almost nightly, Mark, Eliza and the three girls, little Sallie included now, strolled to Johnson Square to inspect the progress on Jay's pavilion.

"It's huge," Eliza Anne said as they stood looking at it the evening before the presidential party was to arrive on May 8, "but not nearly big enough for everybody to dance in at once, is it?"

"Not at once, dear," her mother laughed. "People will come and go. Mostly, they'll just want to meet the President."

"Are you going to go with Mark that night, Mama?" Kate wanted to know. "Is your new gown for the public dance?"

"Are you escorting Mama *and* Caroline, Mark?" Eliza Anne asked.

"No, he is not," their mother said before Mark could answer. "Mark is escorting Caroline. We'll all attend the public dinner in the other booth they're building on Bay, but I—don't attend dances."

"Is that because my papa is dead?" three-year-old Sallie asked solemnly. "Emphie said it was."

"Yes, dear, that's the reason."

"But won't you ever dance again as long as you live?"

"Maybe, maybe not, Kate."

Mark had been listening in silence, pretending to watch two lithe young carpenters on a high scaffold as they nailed into place the framework for the vast decoration of laurel, which was a part of Jay's interior design. Mark had counted foolishly on dancing with Eliza again at the public ball. He had even dared hope that she might relent and attend the Scarbroughs' invitational ball. Of course he would escort Caroline to both events, but he had let himself hope for Eliza, too. The times when she spontaneously embraced him were so few. At the ball, at least, he could have held her while they danced.

"You're—not even going to the *public* ball?" he asked, struggling to keep his voice casual.

"No, Mark. To everything else. I'm excited about the rest of it. But, no balls. Not the public ball and not the Scarbroughs' affair."

"But, Mama, you told me Mr. Scarbrough had asked you to be his hostess, since poor Miss Julia is trapped in New York and can't get back in time now that the President is coming a week early."

"He did ask me. I'd do it if I could, for Julia's sake. Heaven knows it's going to be hard enough on her missing her own affair. The first in her new mansion. But I can't accept the honor. I suggested Charlotte Scarbrough be her father's hostess."

"Charlotte?"

"Why not? She's thirteen or fourteen by now."

"I guess I'd be too young," Eliza Anne sighed. "I'm only twelve."

"You're almost twelve," her mother corrected. "And I think it's time twelve- and nine- and three-year-old young ladies thought about heading home. Shall we, Mark? Or is there something else you want to see?"

"No, I guess not. It would take too long to walk all the way to the east end of Bay to have a look at the public dinner booth. They must be working, though, on all those roses. It's going to take bushels of roses to spell out James Monroe."

Making the usual small talk with the girls was harder than it used to be. Concealing his consuming love for Eliza had become almost impossible. Her courage through her grief had only intensified his desire to make her his wife. Tonight, if he could persuade her to return to the parlor with him after they heard the children's prayers, he meant to ask her. A week ago Eliza had started including Mark in the girls' good-night prayers. After that, his hopes had begun to soar.

"Anytime you want to go home, Miss Eliza, I'm ready," he said, taking Sallie's hand. "Do you think William Jay's pavilion is going to be fine enough for a President to dance in, Sallie?"

"I guess so," the child answered, then suddenly began to climb up Mark's legs. "I want you to carry me home, Mark!"

"Sallie!"

He swooped the child onto his shoulders and allowed her to ride in triumph back to Broughton Street.

At the house, after a supper of muffins and milk, they all trooped up the familiar wide stair. While Mark waited in his own room, Eliza saw to sponge baths and clean nightgowns.

Sitting nervously on the edge of his bed, he could think of nothing except that the time had come. *This night*, his future life—every day of it, every year—would be decided. *He was going to propose to Eliza Mackay*.

What he would say, only God knew. He rubbed the back of his neck where a dull, thudding pain had begun. He could feel his pulse through every part of his body. The longing for Eliza was so pervasive that, for once, he seemed to feel no guilt over Caroline because he had allowed her to go on hoping. Caroline, who needed him now, seemed almost remote. She would be back in Savannah with the McQueens tomorrow, but tomorrow was not tonight. Tonight, his longing for Eliza overwhelmed all else. The fact that she had turned forty-one only made her more desirable. She would know, as a younger woman could not know, how to give love to a man, how to receive his love.

Desire so engulfed him that when Sallie, clad in a long, pink nightgown, burst into his room shouting "Mama says it's time!" he could think of nothing to say to the child.

Holding Sallie's hand as they hurried down the upstairs hall, Mark could think only that—it is *past* time.

On their knees beside their mother and Mark, who also knelt, the two older girls prayed for their brothers so far away in school, for Eliza, for Mark, for Caroline, for good weather while the President was visiting in Savannah and for the life of the weakest kitten in the new litter.

When it came Sallie's turn, she reached for Mark's hand, cleared her throat so that God would be sure to understand what she was about to say, and began: "Dear Jesus, give my daddy my love and tell him that President Monroe is coming to Savannah tomorrow, and bless my brothers, Jack and William, and make them good and bless Mama and bless Mark and make me good and make Mama want to dance again with Mark. Amen."

"Well," Eliza said, "that was quite a prayer, Sallie."

Still on her knees, both eyes tightly shut, Sallie added: "Oh, and You might just as well make Mama want to dance again this week, dear Lord, because there are going to be two balls while the President is here and she has that pretty new rose-colored dress."

"I think that's enough, dear," Eliza said, getting to her feet. "Long prayers sometimes mean little girls don't want to go to bed."

"Oh, I'm going to bed, Mama," the child said with adult disgust. "But Mark is going to tuck me in tonight."

"I am?"

"Yes. Come on, Mark!"

His admirer, Sallie, had helped him, had diverted him from panic at what lay ahead if he managed to persuade Eliza to join him downstairs instead of going straight to her own room. "Wanta ride to bed?" he asked.

"Yes, yes!"

"Mark, you're spoiling Sallie rotten!"

"He certainly is," Kate offered and Eliza Anne agreed.

But Mark and Sallie were already out the door, the child riding his broad shoulders in a state of exultation.

\*     \*     \*

Mark had made quick work of tucking Sallie in so as to meet Eliza in the upstairs hall before she went to her own room. "Would you rather I didn't play with her so much, Miss Eliza?"

She laughed. "No, it's fine. You're wonderful with her. I just hope it doesn't get monotonous for you, that's all."

"Could we—could we go back down to the parlor for a short time?"

"Is something wrong?"

"No, I—I just don't feel like reading tonight. I thought maybe you—well, would you mind?"

"Not at all, dear boy. You never seem to tire of talking with me and I'm flattered." She took his arm affectionately as they started down the wide, creaking stair.

He was careful not to draw her too close. It was not easy. Every fiber in his body strained to assure his sense of the rightness of what he was about to do imbued with every step they took. They were already deep, sincere friends—the basis for any good marriage. He saw no use in her living only a half-life. If he attempted it one more day, he felt he would fail. Would fail Eliza, the children, himself. And Caroline. Had his sensuous longing for Caroline been only because he could not kiss Eliza? He truly believed that. If Eliza Mackay were not free, he gladly would have married Caroline. But Eliza was free. What he was going to do in the next few minutes was right. *Right*.

"Would you like Hannah to bring us some coffee, Mark?"

She still stood beside her favorite armchair, her soft, light-brown hair shining under the gleam of the branched candle-stand on the mantel. Her hazel eyes were green-flecked, the tiny lines at their corners hinting of both smiles and grief.

"Mark?"

He made himself smile. "Uh—no. No, thanks. I don't want a thing to drink." He was trembling so, she must see it, he thought wildly. "But, if you do—"

"No." She sat down a bit wearily and leaned her head back. "I have exactly what I want right now, some peace and quiet and my favorite chair. You wouldn't think I'd be tired just from helping arrange laurel and pine in the new church this afternoon, but I must have walked a mile or two up and down that aisle sizing up this and that vase. I missed Julia Scarbrough. Julia's not a churchgoer, but she would have loved giving us her expert advice on decorating the sanctuary for the President's visit Sunday."

Mark still stood, hating himself for not taking her in his arms before she sat down.

"I can almost see Julia pounding about in her New York hotel rooms, can't you?" Eliza was saying. "It's laughable, but ironic, too, that Mr. Monroe's visit was pushed up a week so that poor Julia was caught so far from home—shopping *for his visit!*" She shook her head. "I declare she could have a heart attack over all this. It was to be her shining moment, her greatest achievement. Entertaining the President of the United States in her breathtaking new house and for five whole days! I wouldn't want the job myself, but my heart goes out to Julia."

When he didn't answer, she sat forward in her chair, a look of genuine concern on her sensitive face. "Mark? Something is wrong. I've been babbling on about Julia and—" She stood, went to him. "Tell me, Mark."

His arms were around her and he was holding her so close against him, he felt them both sway—or was it the room? For an instant, she returned his frantic embrace, much as she would give a troubled child a hug of affection and concern, but when his arms tightened and one hand pressed her head against his shoulder, he felt her stiffen. He dared not move. She, too, stood motionless in his arms.

"Eliza," he breathed, "Eliza, I—love you. I love you!" He could feel her pulling back, trying to stand apart from him. "I've loved you, Eliza, my beautiful Eliza, for so long, so long! Let me take care of you. Please, *please* let me look after you, watch over you, love you for as long as we both live!"

Slowly, firmly, she disengaged his arms and stepped back—erect, aghast, her face pale and drawn, her lips trembling.

He heard his own voice, hoarse, barely recognizable: "Don't say it, Eliza! I beg you not to say it. You don't have to love me the way I love you. I—I won't expect that. I'd hoped, but I'll be content with the love you've always given me. I promise you. If you'll only marry me, I—I'll be content to—"

*"Mark!"* Her voice was sharp, sword-sharp. "Not another word. Do you hear me? Not another foolish word!" As swiftly as her voice turned sharp, it mellowed. "You've—paid

me the highest honor I will ever have, no matter how long I live. And—" she reached to touch his arm, "and I beg you to believe that what has always been between us from your first night under this roof *is* strong and fine and durable enough so that we can both walk on it all the way out of this—sudden notion of yours."

"It is not sudden, and it is most certainly *not* a notion!"

Her hand drew back. She rubbed her forehead briefly. "I'd as soon hurt one of my own children as hurt you. I honestly don't think I have to convince you of that, do I? But, Mark, as sensitive as you've been these past years since Robert went away, I would have sworn that you, of all people, knew that I'm one of those women who can never—love again. Part of me died with Robert. *That* part of me died with him. I can't help that. Not only because I'm so much older than you but because I couldn't be a wife to you or—anyone else. I'm—still —his wife. I'm still—Mrs. Robert Mackay."

He tried to look away from her face. He could not look away. He had heard every word, but all he could say was, "You haven't had time to think at all! You're saying things you don't really mean! Under any conditions—any conditions at all—I want you to marry me."

For a long time she stood, studying him. He would have given a decade off his life to know what her thoughts were. Her look was not withering, not cruel, not even cold. It was the look of a well-bred lady at a—stranger.

At last she straightened her shoulders, her chin lifted ever so slightly, and she said with chilling finality, "I'm going to my room now. There must be a way for us to return to our old selves. If there is, I'll find it. If not"—she looked away— "then I just don't know."

Without looking at him again, she turned and walked toward the hall stair.

"Eliza! Miss Eliza, please, don't leave me like this! I—I need you. . . ."

Steadily, without hesitation, she began to mount the stair, each light step as familiar as the sound of her laughter had been.

Wildly, he thought: Dear God, I may never hear her laughter again!

# THIRTY-SEVEN

THE city's prayer for good weather for the President's visit was answered. The next day, Saturday, May 8, dawned soft-pink and gold, with not even a white cumulus cloud in the embracing sky. Mark saw the dawn. Sleepless, crushed, somehow ashamed, he bathed and dressed early and headed for the Exchange Coffee House for breakfast, unable to face Eliza or the children in the strange new role of outcast. Outcast? That's the way she had made him feel. Eliza, of all people, had made him a stranger in the Mackay household, his home for seven years, lacking a few days.

How might she have acted had he appeared, as usual, at the breakfast table? What would she tell the girls? Sallie, he knew, would demand to know why he wasn't there. Good, he thought, striding across Johnson Square. Maybe if Sallie raises too much cain, her mother will have to—will have to—will have to what? What did he want Eliza to have to do? To lie? To have a difficult time explaining his absence? Was he angry with her for not loving him? He felt unnecessary—excess baggage in a boat that was taking water. And he did feel ashamed.

Caroline and the McQueens would be arriving in the late morning to attend the citywide celebration of the President's arrival, and the thought added to his entrapment. Caroline—who loved him as he wanted Eliza to love him—a trap? Hadn't she left him as free as a leaf in the wind since she was a girl of seventeen? Had he ever, for one moment, doubted the wholeness of her love? Could love entrap a man? Real love?

He stopped on Bay before the Exchange and looked around. The city was quiet, empty. To see Bay Street—normally bustling and cluttered with carts and wagons and carriages—so clean and empty gave him a painful sense of isolation. Increased his already painful sense of being alone.

A handsome black-and-silver carriage drove by, the bays stepping high, as any Scarbrough horses would. Mark returned the hurried, preoccupied wave of the town's merchant prince, William Scarbrough, obviously out on some last-minute errand of preparation for the President's visit to his new house. For an instant, Mark almost smiled, thinking of Julia Scarbrough stuck in New York and the President on his way that very day to *her* palatial home. He went heavily up the Exchange steps and into the big, square Coffee House. The buff-colored room was deserted, too. Tossing his top hat onto an empty rack, he took a corner table and ordered biscuits, honey and coffee.

"You working today, Mr. Browning?" the fat waiter asked incredulously.

"Uh, yes, for an hour or so," he lied. "I know Commerce Row is all closed down. I thought it would be a good, quiet time to do some concentrating."

"I expect you're right, sir. Your grub'll be right out."

The soft clatter from the kitchen made him nervous. Why isn't the Coffee House closed, too, he thought. He grew more nervous, hating the idea of conversation with anyone. Try as he might, he could not be himself with anyone in all Savannah today. He was not himself. Would never be again, no matter what Eliza had said last night: *"There must be a way for us to return to our old selves. If there is, I'll find it. If not—then I just don't know."* Is that what she'd said? Is that what she'd dared to say?

His biscuits and coffee came. He merely nodded, shutting off the possibility of more talk with the waiter. The coffee was too hot and it tasted like burned straw. He broke open a biscuit, buttered it from habit and laid it back down. He had begun to smoke. It was early for a cigar, but he clipped one—thanked the waiter for the light he rushed to him—and sat, turning the thick coffee cup round and round in its saucer, inhaling the cigar deeply and often.

"Anything wrong with the biscuits, Mr. Browning?"

"What? No. No, they're fine. Not hungry."

The front door opened and Sheftall Sheftall—his knee breeches, cocked hat, jacket and buckled shoes brushed and polished, his face, as usual, buried in a newspaper—shuffled into the room and made his way, without once looking up, to Mark's corner table.

Annoyed, but out of genuine deference, Mark stood. "Good morning, Mr. Sheftall."

Sheftall peered over his tiny glasses, calmly folded the paper, stuffed it in a pocket and sat down. "I didn't notice you at my usual table," he said. "What a morning, Mr. Browning, for a visit to our illustrious city from the President of the greatest nation on earth!" He removed his cocked hat, patted down the ancient white wig he still wore on dress occasions and waited for Mark to respond.

"Haven't you noticed the beauteous day, Browning?" Sheftall grinned broadly, exposing still another missing tooth since Mark had seen him last. He leaned nearer. "If you stood in my shoes, sir, you'd notice, all right. If your memories were a part of the country's history." Then, "I suppose you've heard that I'm to escort Mrs. Ethel Cameron."

Mark stared at him. "No! Mrs. Cameron is coming to Savannah?"

"Her first trip to the city in nearly twenty years, I believe. And, of course, you hadn't heard. Only I am aware of her plans." He tapped his stubby fingers on the table for a moment. "I observe your stare and speechless demeanor. I understand both. Only five months have passed since her husband's death. People will talk." He shrugged. "The lady wants to see the President. So be it."

"Will Mrs. Cameron spend the night in town?"

"She isn't coming until the last day, when the military and civil escort sees the President and his party a few miles along the Augusta Road as they leave the city." He wagged a finger. "She wants none of the public functions. I am simply to escort her at the President's departure to where his carriage will stop for farewell ceremonies at the edge of town. She will spend that night here at the Parker Hotel."

"I wonder if Miss Caroline knows she's coming."

"She does not. I said only I am aware of her plans. I and the desk clerk at the Parker Hotel." Sheftall cleared his throat and dropped the rhetoric abruptly. "Ethel Cameron's a very lonely old lady, Browning. I'm sure you know the girl's not been with her once since it happened."

"I do know that. I also know that Caroline is still too grief-stricken to allow herself to think of Knightsford." Then, he added, "I've thought about Mrs. Cameron every day. Found myself wondering—how deep her grief might be. I know she isn't generally liked, but somehow I feel for her."

"That's like you, I think. I feel for her, too. Most don't. It's easier to despise. Leaves people free not to bother. Ethel Cameron loved your mother, Browning."

Mark stared again at him. "You—*do* know about—my mother. About her mother, Mary Cotting."

"And about the fact that on your mother's side, Jonathan Cameron was your grandfather. I was Cameron's attorney, you know. I took a boat to Knightsford some days ago to collect his will. Ethel told me you know the whole story." He studied Mark's face. "You look hangdog, Browning. You looked hangdog when I first came in here. You've known for a long time. Does it worry you that the scandal might yet get out in town?"

"Scandal? Oh, I suppose some would still call it a scandal, even though everyone connected with it is dead."

"Everyone but Ethel Cameron."

"Of course."

"And Osmund Kott."

Mark frowned. "I guess I've tried to forget him. He's safely in New York, so far as I know."

"Osmund Kott is never safely anywhere. Aren't you curious as to why Ethel Cameron informed me that you have been told?"

"I—suppose I am, sir."

"She believes I should try, in your behalf and hers, to break Jonathan Cameron's will. With the assistance, of course, of your own attorney, Thomas Usher Pulaski Charlton."

"Why on earth would she want to break his will?"

"Because he wrote and dated a new will not a week before the poor man raced into that burning building. I have it. She swears he had been acting strangely and was not, as his actions that day proved to her, in his right mind."

"But, where do I enter any of this?"

"You don't, as I see it. But Ethel Cameron loved your mother. She feels that sooner or later you'll suffer through Kott as a consequence of her husband's past conduct and that *you* should at least have some of his property."

"I don't want it. I don't need it!"

He could feel Sheftall Sheftall's keen dark eyes on him. "Cameron left his widow nothing, Browning. No home, no property, no money, no slaves."

Mark looked at Sheftall in disbelief. "He left her no—home?"

"In that new will, drawn last year, Jonathan Cameron left everything to Miss Caroline."

"Nothing at all to help pacify Kott?"

"Nothing. And at a moment's notice, Miss Caroline can deprive her grandmother of a roof over her head. The lady is penniless."

Mark sighed heavily and slumped in his chair.

"You did indeed look hangdog when I entered the Coffee House," Sheftall commented. "You look defeated now."

"I am—defeated. I am."

"And what manner of speech is that for a prospective bridegroom?"

"Bridegroom?"

"Won't you marry Miss Caroline as soon as the proper mourning period has ended? The last time I spoke with her, she told me she loves you more than anyone else on earth. Don't look startled. It is not my practice to go about the city spreading what I've heard. If it were, do you think Miss Caroline would have confided in me?"

Mark thought a minute and then asked carefully, "Did she tell you we were to be—married?"

"No, no, no! She did not. She told me you didn't care for her in the way she cares for you. That you probably never will. But she did say that she loves you enough so that she will be content. Look here, sir, you must know by now that Miss Caroline Cameron is not a young, flirtatious strip of a girl. She is levelheaded, wise beyond her years and enormously equipped for successful marriage. I know her. She has confided in me since she was a little girl. I never made a single visit to her grandfather's plantation but that Miss Caroline and I had our private talk. The talks became a custom when she was not more than six years of age and was being used by the gracious, but weak, old gentleman as a go-between for him and his wife. Caroline loved her grandfather almost blindly. He used her all her life." Sheftall smacked the table with his palm. "It didn't damage her, though. It strengthened her. You appear too smart not to love her as she deserves, but who understands why a man does or does not love?''

Mark didn't answer. Too many thoughts were crashing about in his mind. He loved Eliza enough to be content with whatever crumbs she could offer. Caroline loved him the same way. He could almost feel his heart tighten within him—twist, tighten, reach. Toward what? Whom? By offering his love, he had caused Eliza God only knew how much torment during the hours of the night just past. He had forced a caring friend to turn and walk away because she had found herself unable to cope with his love.

With his love? For nearly seven years he had loved her well and she had thrived on that love. He had her own word for it that somehow she meant to find a way back to the comfort and safety of their old friendship. He had wounded Eliza and, in the process, Caroline. He had grown angry at Eliza for not returning his love. Angry? Wasn't he only mortally hurt? No. Here, in the presence of the brilliant, eccentric but somehow guileless little Jewish man the children called Cocked Hat, he was forced to admit to himself that Eliza *had angered* him.

"Caroline has no shred of resentment toward you, Browning," Sheftall was saying, as though he read Mark's thoughts. "Caroline understands you. In her generous nature, she has room for you as you are. In her intelligent nature. Intelligence is far more useful than mere generosity at times, you know. Mere generosity can occasion soft, sentimental traits. Caroline is not sentimental. She is strong. The Christians have a saying from their Scriptures: 'Let the mind of Christ be in you,' or words to that effect. I'm a Jew, but I sense what that means. Caroline has that kind of intelligence. It is based on love. Don't sit staring at the table. I would swear that when you've been shaken down a bit, you possess intelligence of that nature as well."

Mark tried to smile. "Look here, sir, I owe you an apology. Forgive me for not asking, but won't you join me for breakfast?"

"I don't come in here to eat. Never touch coffee. I wander in each morning to read my paper. And, yes, you owe me an apology. You are sitting at my table."

In his office a few minutes later, Mark sank wearily into the chair where Margaret McQueen had sat the afternoon she and John returned from Jamaica. He had no memory of having

ever been so tired. In need of sleep, yes, but this exhaustion
went far deeper. His heart was broken, and with it, his spirit.
For the first time since he reached Savannah, the sight of the
river from a window of Commerce Row did not cause him to
think of the day when even more ships, more and larger ships,
would dock at the Savannah wharves. Content with being a
factor, in no need of ships of his own, he had still thrilled at
the sight of the busy Savannah waterfront because Savannah
was his city. Not today.

He banged his fist on the chair.

*How did I dare?*

How did I dare think she'd ever love me? What went wrong
in my head? I loved Robert Mackay, too! I, of all people on
earth, knew how she loved him. His face buried in his hands,
he began to sob. "What do I do with this—ugly humiliation?
How can I face her again? How can I face—Caroline? What
do I do next, God?"

Dreading for the first time to enter the Broughton Street
house, he forced himself to start toward it in time for midafternoon dinner. However ashamed he felt, his love for Eliza
had not changed. In the silence of his empty countinghouse,
after he had cried out to God for help, only one thing was
clear: *the dreadful predicament into which he had thrown
Eliza.*

The children would bombard her with questions: "Mark
never misses his big meal with us; where is he?" "Mark has to
dress in his Chatham Artillery uniform, doesn't he, for the
reception at the waterfront when the President arrives?"
"Mama, does Hero have Mark's uniform ready for him?"
"He told us yesterday that he doesn't have to report at headquarters until assembly time, then march to the Strand, but
where is Mark, Mama?"

All facets of his life were so intertwined with the entire
Mackay family, he had dared to hope, to believe—married to
Eliza—they could go on as before, with only the new joy
added. The commitment on which he'd counted was, instead,
causing pain and confusion for everyone.

Halfway up the front steps, he was attacked by Sallie, then
welcomed like a returning hero by the older girls, all too relieved to see him to pursue their questions. "I simply had to
spend the morning in my office alone, without the usual inter-

ruptions,'' he explained. And that was true.

At dinner, Eliza managed to act almost as though nothing had changed, although she didn't address Mark once. She did order the children to let him go to his room shortly after they finished eating, so that he could bathe and dress. "And rest a little," Eliza added. "Mark still has a long, hard day ahead."

In his full-dress uniform, he greeted Caroline and the McQueens quickly and hurried to the Chatham Artillery headquarters. President Monroe, his Secretary of War, John C. Calhoun, and their aides were not due to arrive until sometime around six that evening. For once, Mark preferred the companionship of the members of his company. Later on, he could almost be swallowed up by the pomp and color of the military ceremony, in which other companies would also participate—the Hussars, the Republican Blues, the Fencibles and the Savannah Volunteer Guards.

Surely, he thought, as he trotted his horse, Handsome, toward Chatham headquarters, pride in his beloved company would give him back some of his self-esteem. Not once, since Mackay's death, had Mark slipped into the deep-blue coatee—a deeper blue because the men of the Chatham Artillery could afford the finest dye—without missing his friend, or without pride in the company to which they had belonged together. How deeply he still missed Robert Mackay.

Handing over his horse at his destination, he realized, with a distinct sense of irony, that he would rather have a talk with Mackay today than anyone on earth. Mackay would still be the one person who could help him work his way out of the impossible predicament he'd devised—for himself and for Eliza.

For Caroline? She was, somehow, not a part of the trouble. He had thought her even lovelier, more appealing, when she and the McQueens had reached the Mackay house only minutes before he left. The time spent at Causton's Bluff had helped her. She seemed quieter than usual, but the smile she gave Mark was the same—welcoming and vibrant.

Striding now up the stairs at Chatham Artillery headquarters, he realized that he had felt an unexpected kind of gladness when she stepped again into his arms from the carriage he'd sent to pick them up at the waterfront. Certainly, he did not understand such a feeling in the midst of such turmoil.

But then, he understood almost nothing today, beyond the fact that he could, for a time, escape into a highly regimented, impersonal, blessedly public experience. He needed to escape. Eliza had not even told him good-bye.

No company member seemed to notice his downcast face. They had all worked so hard, from the lowliest member to the captain, in preparation for this day; who cared about how Mark Browning looked? Cartridge bags for firing the special Chatham Artillery salutes had, for weeks, been fabricated at their laboratory; then the shells had been hand-filled and fuses made, also by hand. No Savannah company's work was more admired. No other company took more pride in its uniforms, equipment, precision—general merit. Today Mark was to have the honor of firing one of the two historic brass guns presented to the Chatham Artillery back in 1791 by President Washington himself.

If Eliza had not walked away from him last night, he might have resented spending most of the presidential visit at military duties. As things stood, he could only welcome the five days ahead when not one Savannah household—including the Mackays'—would be normal. Meals would not be on schedule. Able-bodied men would be drilling, hard at work at their various militia headquarters or taking part in ceremonial events. The ladies would be flying about—servants at the ready—for change after change of fashionable gowns. Different costumes would be required for each event—the citywide welcome at the waterfront, the countless public speeches, the public dinner, the two balls, the dedication service at what to Mark would always be *Mackay's* Independent Presbyterian Church. There would be smaller parties galore, even in modest homes. And blessedly little free time to think.

The welcome began with a twenty-one-gun salute from the revenue cutter *Dallas* the moment the President's boat reached Georgia waters from the South Carolina side of the river. Mark waited beside other officers in front of the long line of militia companies drawn out parallel to the river.

From five-thirty until nearly six, when the large presidential rowboat was sighted on its way across the river from South Carolina, Mark and the others waited. Then, as the oarsmen moved the President's party toward the designated wharf, T.U.P. Charlton and Mark approached the two Washington guns. First Charlton and then Mark touched linstocks to the fuses. The blasts provided the initial welcome from Savannah to the President of the United States.

In the silent instant following the discharge of Mark's big gun, he heard Sallie's shrill voice shout: "Hurray for Mark!" Then, the cheering began as the sixty-one-year-old Monroe stood in the boat to salute the volleys and to wave at the throngs lining the Strand. Mark could see the Mackays, the McQueens and Caroline. The pleasure he would have felt at Sallie's special cheer was wiped out. Eliza was not cheering. She was not even smiling.

With every ounce of his strength, he set himself to attend only to his military duties. Standing with his company at attention, he watched the President's careful review of the troops, heard the pleasant, good-natured exchange when the quiet-mannered gentleman with strangely slanting eyes politely refused the superb barouche offered him for the parade to the Scarbrough mansion. Monroe preferred the mount, also waiting.

The festive parade was led by half the Hussars, followed by the President and his party, then the Chatham Artillery and the other companies. The route chosen took them past waving, cheering crowds along Broughton Street, and at least half a dozen times, Mark glimpsed Caroline, Sallie and her sisters running beside the procession—Caroline waving her handkerchief high over her head. As she and the Mackay girls hurried past the Telfair sisters in the standing crowd, Mark saw Caroline blow him a kiss. Undoubtedly, the Telfairs also noticed. Caroline, he knew, would not mind one bit.

His heart lifted at her blown kiss, but a minute or so later, it nearly burst with happiness when—almost in front of the Mackay house—Eliza waved at him and smiled.

# THIRTY-EIGHT

ONLY Caroline and Margaret waited up for Mark that night when the welcoming ceremony and the parade were over.

"I'm sure you two would like a moment alone, at least, before you say good night," Margaret said, when they had finished cups of chocolate.

"No. Mark is going straight to bed," Caroline said firmly. "I know you've marched enough for one day, Mark, but one more march—upstairs—right now and to bed."

In his room, exhausted, he tried to figure out the new conflict he was feeling: relief that Caroline did not jump at the chance for them to be alone—but disappointment, too.

Tomorrow, Sunday, May 9, Monroe's first full day in town, would be the hardest of all for him. There would be more free time than on any other day during the celebration. Only one event was scheduled, aside from a citizens' procession. An event to which Mark and Eliza had looked forward for months—the dedication service at the splendid new Independent Presbyterian Church. For months they had talked of the day he would escort her to the first service in the magnificent, white-steepled edifice that would have made Mackay the proudest man in Savannah.

Of course, they were going. Thankfully, so were the McQueens and Caroline. He would not have to be alone with Eliza. In his bed, he tried to concentrate only on her smile and her wave as his company passed by. She did smile, he told himself. She smiled at me and waved. The concentration would not hold. Caroline and Margaret had waited up for him. Eliza had not.

For the next five days, at least, there would be little or no time alone with her. What he expected the passage of five days to accomplish, he had no idea. Eventually, his eyes grew heavy, but the fact remained: He was avoiding Eliza Mackay. Wouldn't a man, if he were really a man, simply bide his time and plead his case again? Even to himself, he could not explain why he knew with such certainty that he would never ask her a second time to marry him. Her rebuff had been absolute.

In a few days he would be twenty-seven years old. He felt sixteen and lost.

Hannah, as she had always done when Eliza was readying herself for a special occasion, helped her dress for Sunday's dedication service. The new gown was iridescent lavender grosgrain, with matching slippers and a becomingly brimmed hat adorned with one white plume that swept down to touch her cheek.

Fastening the gown at Eliza's waist, Hannah made a little melody out of her hummed approval. "Hm-m-m-m! You look prettier than when I first come to you nineteen years ago, Miss 'Liza!"

"That's nonsense and you know it," her mistress said, "but you can say it again anytime."

Hannah smiled as Eliza turned slowly before the pier glass, smoothing the skirt over her hips, lifting the long fullness for one and then two steps, testing the length. "Good thing it's right." She tried a laugh, but Hannah could see tears in her eyes. "It would be a little late to change the hem now, wouldn't it?"

"Somepin' wrong, honey?"

Eliza straightened her shoulders and preened a bit, not fooling Hannah. Then she said, "You remember who loved—this color, don't you, Hannah?"

"That good, laughin' man!" Hannah's low, caressing voice brought still more tears so that now she could see them course down her mistress's cheeks. "Miss 'Liza, they somepin' bad wrong. Worse'n just that your dress was Mausa Robert's favorite color. You gonna tell me what's wrong? Or you gonna keep cryin' till you swell up your eyes? We always git it fix when you tell me."

As though she were Sallie's age, her mistress threw herself

into Hannah's ample arms and wept. At first, the strong hand soothing her between her shoulders brought more tears. Then, Miss 'Liza jerked away, opened her eyes wide to clear them and, in a surprisingly steady voice and with few words, told Hannah that Mark wanted to marry her.

Too stunned to comment right off, Hannah simply stared at her mistress.

"Well? In the name of heaven, Hannah, don't just stand there looking at me! Say something!"

"You know I has to study for a time, Miss 'Liza. Now, look here." As though holding a skein of yarn in her fingers, she made the gesture of separating one strand from another. "Over here, we got this piece—over there, the other. Here, first, we got this happy family, even with Mausa Robert gone. Over there, we got that sweet boy, Mister Mark, with nobody on this old earth as family but us." She picked up the imaginary first strand again. "Here, we got you—knowin' in the marrow of your bones that you can't ever love no other man but Mausa Robert. *But*—how do Mister Mark know that before you tell him? The way you talk, you blame Mister Mark that he fell in love with you. Maybe you blame yourself some, too. Sh! Ain't no blame comin' your way. Ain't no blame comin' his way. What happen is natural. As natural as you cryin' yet sometimes in the night 'cause Mausa Robert ain't layin' in the bed beside you."

Seeming to Hannah to be almost annoyed at hearing the truth, Eliza Mackay turned abruptly and walked to the window. "But what can I *do*, Hannah? I told him as clearly as I could. What can I do?"

"You tol' your Cousin Margaret yet?"

"No. Oh, I've wanted to tell her, but—no. Only you."

"Then, don't tell nobody else—but the Lord."

"He already knows!"

"Course He knows! But you know of anybody else that can take all this in hand an' work it out so's nobody else gets hurt bad? So sweet Mister Mark's heart—mends?"

Hannah watched her turn slowly back to face her. "You're right. You've just told me exactly what I'd have told anyone else—in the same uncomfortable boat I'm in. I—don't always practice what I preach, do I?"

"Do anybody?"

"I don't know. I honestly don't know. Hand me my hat, Hannah, please. They'll all be waiting downstairs. I'm late."

From the bed, Hannah picked up the handsome hat as though it were made of spun glass. "Waitin' for the Lord to act can make a body mighty nervous," she said. "I tell Him sometimes I wish He'd just hand me things, the way I hand you this bonnet."

Settling the hat in place, the plume draped gracefully over her right cheek, Eliza said, "Make your answer to this short, Hannah, but do you mean that even if Mark and I happen to be alone for a few minutes, I should just say nothing? He did give me a nasty jolt, but I really want so much to ease his pain."

"There you go, honey, jumpin' smack into the Lord's slippers again! He's the *only* one to know what you ought to do and say."

Her mistress glanced again in the looking glass, pinched color into her cheeks, dried her eyes and tried to laugh. "Hannah, I don't like the way I look at all—jumping into God's slippers!"

In the jam-packed, white-walled church, people stood, even on the steps of the columned entrance outside. Mark sat between Eliza and Caroline, both sharing the hymnal and the psalmbook he held for them. The presidential party, accompanied by the mayor, members of the City Council and Savannah's top military officers, occupied the first six pews. The congregational responses were as fervent as the choral and organ music was elevating. Dr. Kollock, Mark was sure, preached a dynamic and eloquent sermon, but aside from Eliza's steady voice as she read the responses and Caroline's clear contralto when she sang, he heard nothing beyond the text from the Scriptures: "The glory of this latter house shall be greater than the former. In this place shall I give peace, saith the Lord of hosts."

*The glory of this latter house shall be greater than the former. In this place shall I give peace, saith the Lord of hosts....*

Through every remaining hour of that strange Sunday, through the citizens' procession, led by the mayor and the aldermen and the military companies, Mark marched to the rhythm of Dr. Kollock's text. Through Mayor James Wayne's interminable speech when the procession reached the Scarbrough house, through three calls Mark made with the family in his own fine carriage, riding from splendid house to splendid house of the members of the Aldermanic Welcoming Committee—T.U.P. Charlton, former Mayor Charles Harris and builder John H. Ash—Dr. Kollock's eloquent, authoritative words sounded again and again as though ordering *him*, Mark Browning, to listen . . . to believe.

"The glory of this latter house shall be greater than the former. *In this place shall I give peace. . . .*"

He had always meant to build his own house. Undoubtedly, the time had come. Maybe the peace would come, too.

There was little leisure to read the *Museum and Gazette* during those memorable five days, but Mark had noticed an advertisement that read:

> Passage for New York. The S.S. *Savannah*, Captain Rogers, will make one trip to New York, previous to her departure for Liverpool, should a sufficient number of passengers offer, and will be ready to proceed in course of this week or commencement of the next. Apply on board at Taylor's wharf, or to Scarbrough.

In spite of his strong response to Dr. Kollock's text, the next day Mark booked passage for one. Leaving town might be the kindest thing he could do for everyone, especially Eliza. He shared some of the excitement over the revolutionary new steam-powered ship and, because he was an investor, planned to make the honorary inspection run to Tybee in company with the President's party and other local stockholders. But he did not book passage out of interest in the new ship. He signed up to avoid the closeness of a home with the woman who would never love him. Once the festive week was over, he reasoned, life would return to normal. Mark now had no idea how to fit into it.

The short, ceremonial voyage to Tybee Island would be made early enough on Wednesday so that all could return to the city to dress for the public dinner that night. But first, he would have to get through two balls—the Scarbroughs' and the public ball—neither of which Eliza would attend.

The balls filled him with both relief and dread. Dread of an elegant affair at the Scarbroughs' with Caroline, the most beautiful young woman in town? Relief that Eliza would sit in the big, empty house alone while the children slept and he danced? To himself, he remained a walking contradiction.

"Wear your dress uniform to the first ball tonight, Mark," Caroline said at dinner. "Please?"

"Haven't you seen me decked out in gold and blue once too often already this week?"

"Never," Eliza exclaimed. "You're just plain grand in your uniform, Mark."

Until that moment, he and Eliza had exchanged some small talk, table talk, but for the first time since she'd turned her back and walked away from him, a hint of the old affection was in her voice. *The old, familiar affection.*

He smiled at her and it wasn't hard. Finding himself able to smile directly at her lifted such a load, he would have agreed to wear anything she asked to the public ball.

She was trying to bridge the chasm.

He must try, too. First thing in the morning, he would cancel his passage to New York on the S.S. *Savannah*'s trial run.

Margaret and John McQueen begged off attending the public ball in William Jay's specially designed pavilion. Mark's immediate response was anxiety. Since his proposal to Eliza, he and Caroline had not been alone more than a few minutes at a time.

"We only need to make an appearance for the sake of your clients who'll be there," Caroline said in the carriage as they rode toward Johnson Square, where the ball had already started. "I know how tired you must be."

"How about you?"

"Whether I stay all evening or make a brief appearance won't change a thing. I'm being criticized all over town for even going out!"

He gave her a surprised look. "Who's criticizing you?"

"People."

Caroline's old, easy manner, which seemed to have returned since she visited the McQueens, gave way to pain. It was nothing she'd said. Mark heard the pain in her voice. He took her hand. "Maybe you're imagining the criticism. It's been almost six months since—"

"Hush, Mark! Let them criticize and don't say I'm imagining it. I'm not. Neither am I going to let the talk stop me from going everywhere you want to take me." She gave him her direct, disarming look. "Something's troubling you and if we can have some good times together this week—bring you back to life—I mean to do it." When he tried to apologize for being bad company, she placed her fingers firmly over his mouth. "Sh! Not a word. I just want to be with you, if you want me." In the sunset afterglow, he could see her deliberate smile. "After all, you haven't seen my new Scarbrough ball gown. No one's seen it but Miss Eliza."

"John and Margaret were right to stay away from the public ball," Caroline said as she and Mark drew up in front of the Mackay house at nine-thirty the same evening. "Even we didn't cut any special figure trying to dance in that crowd."

"But I was lucky to be dancing with you," Mark said, handing her down from the carriage step. "Think what trouble I might have had trying to guide some of those perspiring ladies around that floor. You and Miss Eliza did yourselves proud selecting your new gown. You should wear lots of blue."

"Oh, this isn't the gown I meant," she said lightly. "I'm going to put it on now. You don't think I'd wear a gown to a public ball and wear it again the same night at the Scarbroughs', do you?"

Half an hour later Caroline, at the top of the front stair, looked down at Mark, who stood looking up at her from the hall below. Neither smiled. For a moment, she waited to begin descending the stair. God, keep me from running to him, she breathed. Keep me from doing anything or being any way that will make him feel—duty-bound. I don't want to bind him in any way. Help me just to love him. And to leave him free. I know how I look in this white gown, but please, Lord, see to it that Mark stays honest with himself. Don't let either of us do anything foolish.

In Mark's carriage, on their way to West Broad for the splendid affair already being dubbed Julia's Heartbreak, Margaret could not resist wondering how Julia Scarbrough was managing through this night of torment—"off at the North while her blowout is in progress back here."

"Most unkind," John said tersely. "Only Robert Mackay knew how to make kind jokes about poor Julia."

A block away, they could hear the music and see the night sky lit with torches, their flames waving above the double stairs that led to the handsome, heavy Scarbrough portico, visible now as Hero drove the barouche under a canopy.

Jumping down first, Mark helped Margaret and then Caroline to the newly made driveway. Margaret was stunning in gold satin, only a shade lighter than the deep-yellow plume that adorned John's chapeau. Anticipation that ran so high at the prospects of the social evening ahead seemed to affect even John McQueen, who loathed wearing his uniform anywhere. John's spirits, unusually high for him, were a good sign, Mark thought. Maybe trying to act as though nothing was changed between Caroline and him wouldn't be so hard after all.

All week he had dreaded this night. Eliza had said good-bye earlier, before the ballgoers were dressed. That helped some. What Mark had seemed to dread most was walking out the front door, leaving her alone in the empty house. Even the children were away, spending the night with the Minis girls down the block.

"I think it's marvelous that Mr. Scarbrough's hostess will be his thirteen-year-old daughter, Charlotte," Margaret was saying. "She's a beauty and should do extremely well. I thought I'd be thoroughly exhausted from socializing this week, but suddenly, standing before this gleaming castle, with the music playing, I feel like a belle again. Come along, John dear. I want to dance and dance and dance!"

After greeting William Scarbrough and his daughter, the President and his Secretary of War, Mark and Caroline waltzed easily onto the glistening new floor of the Scarbrough ballroom at the rear of the two-storied entrance hall. Julia's hand-painted stars and moon glimmered from the ceiling high above, and Caroline, her bare, straight young back cool and enticing to his touch, moved as though she were one with him. As in a vision, he only glimpsed the wide, white whirl of her skirt as they dipped and twirled and glided.

"No one needs to tell a dancer that this is an enormous house," she said, barely tilting her head so that he could see her easy smile. "Isn't it marvelous to have all this room?"

"Yes," he said, "but I'm glad we're dancing early. Once that mob has greeted the President, we won't be able to waltz. Not as you and I like it."

Now, she looked straight at him. "We're—dancers, Mark."

He managed a grin. "Yes. We're dancers."

"We should be," she said lightly. "We've had a lot of practice."

Except for one dance earlier in the evening, when the floor of Jay's public pavilion had swayed with the crowd, he and Caroline had not been truly alone since Eliza rejected him. Mark had seen to it. Until he regained his balance, he couldn't face conversation with the tender, vivid young woman who unashamedly belonged to him. Belonged to him, she had said, the way Eliza Mackay belonged—still—to Robert Mackay.

So far, even here in the almost empty ballroom, with his arm about her, Mark had not even thought of kissing her. Why? He had loved Eliza, he now knew, for years; yet the merest touch from Caroline had always set his blood racing. Would he never again be drawn to her? Was the power of his passion dead, too, along with his heart? He was certainly not uncomfortable as he whirled her nearly perfect body up and down and across the polished floor. Caroline seemed too much her old self for discomfort. He had felt guilty for agreeing that she visit the McQueens, but her revived spirit appeared strong enough to sustain him, too, tonight and he had no choice but to welcome it.

Later, after exchanging courtesy dances with the T.U.P. Charltons, with William Scarbrough and his daughter, Charlotte, with John and Margaret, with Mr. and Mrs. John Ash, they rejoined each other near the wide door that led to the Scarbrough garden in the rear. With one mind, they ducked outside for some cool air.

"Mrs. Ash is a splendid dancer," Mark said, wiping his brow with a handkerchief. "I was surprised."

"Heavy people are supposed to be good dancers, hadn't you heard? Mark, you're so warm. Should I not have insisted that you wear your uniform? That leather stock and black cravat must make you miserable."

"I'm fine, fine. Want to sit down over there on the countess's new white garden settee?"

"Poor Julia's everywhere in that house tonight, isn't she?"

"She certainly is," he said. "Poor lady." Then, with no plan whatever to do it, he heard himself telling her abruptly that her grandmother was coming to town for the President's departure and would be escorted by Sheftall Sheftall.

For a long time, she sat beside him, erect, silent. Julia's burning pine torches stained the garden the color of a sunset.

Finally, almost apologetically, he said, "I felt I owed it to you to give you a little warning."

"I—don't have anything to say about her coming, actually. It doesn't seem to concern me. I mean, I hadn't thought of attending the departure ceremonies anyway. Do you have to be there?"

"Yes. My company is to form part of the President's escort over a few miles of the road to Augusta."

"Will you—speak to my grandmother?"

"I'm not sure. Would you like me to?"

"I think so. I certainly don't feel much toward her. I think I—I might almost pity her now. Mostly, I don't know what to do about her."

"What to *do* about her?"

She nodded. "Until Grandfather's will is read, I don't know what to do about—anything, Mark." Her usually steady voice broke slightly. "I'm finding it—hard, being homeless."

"But you're not homeless! You're so welcome at—"

"I know," she broke in. "I know I'm welcome at the Mackays. I was also welcome at the McQueens."

"Would you—will you go back to Knightsford to live?"

"No."

"Just—no, eh?"

"That's right. I couldn't face that. I couldn't live under the same roof with her, now that Grandfather's gone." She gave him a childlike look. "I've never had to wonder about money or where to live before. Did Mr. Sheftall tell you when Grandfather's will would be read?"

"Next week." Mark hesitated. "He left everything to you."

There was the barest catch in her breath. Her expression did not change. *"Everything?"*

"That's right. All of Knightsford, his people, his horses, his cattle, what money there was. As his factor, I can tell you that is no small amount this year. His crops brought good prices on the foreign market. You're not poor, Caroline. Far from it."

Her eyes filled with tears, but she said nothing. Her thoughts seemed to have flown a million miles away. Mark wondered what she could possibly be thinking.

"I still can't live at Knightsford," she said at last, just above a whisper. "It's the only home she has. My grandmother will live there exactly as always, until she dies."

"But what about you? Where will you live?"

The words were scarcely spoken when he knew what he had done. Her thoughts were as plain as if she'd formed them into words: *If only you loved me enough, Mark, I'd never have to give one thought to where I'll live. We could be married. We could build our own house here in Savannah. We could be full of joy—full of joy and plans and dreams.*

He reached for her hand.

"Don't! Don't touch me, please," she whispered sharply. "And don't worry about where I'll live. There are lots of places to live, after all."

"Where?" he asked stubbornly.

"I don't know where!" She was near tears, but her eyes blazed and the color was high in her cheeks.

"Caroline," he breathed, forcing her to let him take her in his arms. "Caroline, in the name of heaven, do you *have* to be so—beautiful? So—desirable? Caroline! Don't pull away. Don't."

Her warm, fragrant body yielded. She fell against him, as though helpless. She was. He was. Helpless for different reasons or maybe for the same reason, they clung to each other like lost children.

"Someone might wander into the garden—any minute," she gasped, making no move to loosen her hold on his head, which she was pressing hard against her cheek. "We shouldn't do this. We—shouldn't. For every reason on earth, let me go, Mark!"

"I don't notice that you're letting me go."

"I'm not. Not yet. I will—I swear I will. But not yet. Oh, Mark, I've needed to be close to you."

"I've needed to be close to you, too. I always seem to need that."

Softly, softly, she began to laugh. It was the familiar, easy, freeing laugh. The one that had so many times loosed his taut nerves, reined the drive of his passion just in time. She dropped her arms and took a step away from him. Her eyes were laughing, too.

"What's so funny?" he asked.

"Us. We're really funny, you know. Look, sir, I definitely did not have this new gown made to hide myself in a garden all evening." Grabbing his hand, she pulled him along the path toward the house. "Let's dance again. When we're dancing, I *know* we're together. No couple in all that crowd of Savannah socialites has our grace, Mark. And grace, dearest, will get us very far!"

The short, festive excursion to Tybee Island on the S.S. *Savannah* was, Mark reported at breakfast the day President Monroe and his party were to leave town, a total success. Sails were used to catch the wind on the return trip, but as the flag-bedecked ship moved away from the Savannah waterfront, it moved—against the tide—by steam power alone. The noisy engine turned the big side wheel, and cheers rose from the crowds on shore and from the dignitaries on board, who rode in almost reverent awe under the impressive clouds of black smoke that poured from its slender stack.

"A sailing vessel with a paddle wheel," the President kept exclaiming. "Upon my word!"

Sheftall Sheftall had not been invited to make the short ceremonial run to Tybee, but when Mark met him at the waterfront when the *Savannah* docked sometime later, he found the older man still skeptical.

"Quite a difference between a short voyage to Tybee Island and an ocean voyage, Browning," Sheftall said. "And have you noticed that not enough Savannahians offered to book passage north to make that trial run feasible?"

At breakfast that day, when Mark recounted the gist of his brief encounter with Sheftall, John McQueen said, "It would be a joke on a lot of bigwigs in town if old Sheftall turns out to be right, wouldn't it?"

"For some it would be too tragic to joke about," Mark said.

"Mark's an investor in the S.S. *Savannah,*" Eliza Anne said. "I think you're mean, Uncle John!"

"I'm the smallest investor of the lot, Eliza Anne. But thanks anyway, for your sympathy." He got up. "You'll all have to excuse me now. For the last time this week, I have to don my uniform. When I see you again, the President will be well on his way to Augusta."

"We do excuse you, Mark," Eliza said. "I wish you didn't have to go. You must be exhausted. I know I am."

Halfway up the front stair, he heard Caroline call from the downstairs hall.

"Don't come all the way back down," she said softly. "I just want you to know that it won't be necessary for you to make any effort to speak to my grandmother when you see her this morning."

He looked down at her. "Are you sure?"

"Very sure. I've thought it over. None of it—is your problem. It's all mine."

"I may not get a chance, anyway," he said lamely.

"No matter. What is there to say, if you do?"

At the point on the Augusta Road where the town fathers were to take their leave of Monroe and his party, Mark, with the others making up the military escort, sat his horse at attention and waited through the brief exchange of farewell speeches. At every opportunity he had glanced about the small crowd, looking for Sheftall Sheftall and Ethel Cameron. There had been no sign of them. From the corner of his eye, his head held rigid under the weight of his chapeau, he saw one after another distinguished Savannahian bow, then shake the President's hand and return to their carriages. The morning air was soft and moist; almost no breeze stirred the thick strands of gray moss that hung from the oaks lining the Augusta Road. There was not much loud talking among the well-wishers. Everyone seemed tired, including the President. Mark could hear only the low hum of voices, the tinhorn call of a pileated woodpecker somewhere in the woods nearby. As he waited at attention, his back and his shoulders ached. What, he wondered, could anyone have left to say? Surely, the President and his party longed to be en route. To stop talking.

And then, the light clatter of a gig and one horse came within hearing, slowed, stopped, and Mark saw Sheftall Sheftall assist Ethel Cameron to the ground and walk with her to a vantage point where she could see the President.

The late arrivals had walked no more than ten or fifteen yards, when gentlemen and the four or five wives present began to whisper and nudge one another. How, Mark wondered, did they recognize the aging woman when she hadn't set foot in the city for so many years? Mark would have given almost anything to know what Sheftall was saying to her. All he could tell was that Sheftall Sheftall seemed most attentive, yet as casual as though it were a daily occurrence for him to escort the widow of Jonathan Cameron to a public function.

Neither made any effort to approach President Monroe, but stood to one side for what Mark estimated was a matter of only thirty or forty seconds, turned, walked quickly back to the gig and rode away.

One week after Monroe's party left the city, the S.S. *Savannah,* amid still more fanfare, moved under her own steam from the port of Savannah and headed for Liverpool.

For one long month, nothing was known of the success or failure of the first sea voyage by steam. Then, word came that the *Savannah* had indeed reached Liverpool, astounding the British as "with wheels plying to the utmost and all sails set, she went into the Mersey, proud as any princess going to her crowning, the spectators absolutely astounded at her appearance."

From Liverpool, after another month for viewing by the public, the S.S. *Savannah*—on the same day the Mackay boys came home—made her way to St. Petersburg in Russia. Then, on November 20, with Jack and William, Mark, Caroline, Eliza and the girls in the crowd on the Strand, she steamed once more into her home port.

"Now what will old Cocked Hat Sheftall have to say?" fourteen-year-old Jack wanted to know. "He was so sure the *Savannah* would be a failure. Let's go find him and watch him climb down the limb!"

"Not so fast," Eliza stopped him. "Mr. Sheftall *seems* wrong lots of the time. He often is proved right in the end."

"That's right, Jack," Mark said. "The old fellow didn't say the *Savannah* couldn't make it over and back across the Atlantic. He just said it wasn't a practical commercial investment."

"If it got over and back, Mark, doesn't that mean it's good?" William asked.

"But it carried no cargo and no passengers," Caroline said. "It seems to me, we'd better gather a few facts before we do more than cheer the *Savannah* for being so beautiful."

"You surely do know a lot for a young lady," William said admiringly.

"Speak of the devil," Jack blurted. "Look who's coming our way in the crowd. Old Cocked Hat!"

"Watch your language," Eliza whispered.

"Because I said 'speak of the devil'? Just an expression, Mother dear. Just an expression."

"Not very respectful of an older gentleman."

Both boys greeted Sheftall warmly and their greeting was returned. Doffing his tricorn, Sheftall bowed to Eliza and to Caroline. Then, after patting the younger girls' heads, he pronounced the boys exceedingly mature and declared that he himself felt ten years older than he'd felt that morning, just seeing how both Mackay sons had shot up. Finished with that, he turned to Mark. "Come with me, Mr. Browning?"

"Sir?"

"You understand English, I believe. I asked you to come with me. Excuse us, ladies, young gentlemen?"

Off to one side of the cheering throng, Sheftall reached up to whisper in Mark's ear: "Osmund Kott is in the crowd!"

"What?"

"Your hearing going bad, sir? I said Osmund Kott is here for the welcoming of the *Savannah*."

"Are you sure?"

"If you'll turn about thirty degrees to the east and cast your eyes halfway down the bluff, you'll see for yourself. Dressed fit to kill—there, in that expensive brown top hat, seated on a bench, alone."

Mark was too stunned to answer, but he saw his uncle and felt a wave of near nausea when Kott turned to look back at him, lifted his top hat, then waved it in a friendly, gentlemanly fashion.

"Speechless, eh?" Sheftall chuckled. "If my memory serves, I told you he was never safely anywhere."

"Yes. Yes, you did, sir. And I am speechless, I guess, except to wonder what he's up to—here!"

# THIRTY-NINE

WHEN the excitement died down in the city, following the return of the S.S. *Savannah*, all the Mackays went to Causton's Bluff for a holiday. Since the McQueens' bedrooms would be filled and because she could not respectably stay in the Mackay house alone with Mark, Caroline accepted Julia Scarbrough's warm invitation to visit her in the handsome new mansion on West Broad.

"You're a very foolish young lady," Julia declared as they worked their separate frames of embroidery on a bright December morning in the pretty family sitting room on the second floor. "Not only would my house be the perfect place to announce your engagement to Mark Browning, who would do it more splendidly than I?"

"No one, of course," Caroline said. She was being pushed on the subject that caused her the greatest heartache, but Julia's insistence did amuse her. "I know you think I'm being coy, Miss Julia. I'm not. There just aren't any prospects of my marrying Mark. Please, believe that and let's talk about something else."

"Of course there are prospects! There are always prospects when a beautiful young woman sees as much of a gorgeous young man as you see of Mark. Now, let's be serious. Your dear grandfather's been gone a year. We can use a Christmas motif—cedar garlands dipped in lime to simulate snow, mistletoe, holly wreaths, swags and swags and swags of pine, hundreds of yards of wide red ribbon and—"

Caroline gave her fancywork a vicious needle punch and stood up. "We're going to change the subject, Miss Julia, or I'm going to my room."

Julia blinked. "You mean that, don't you?"

"Yes, I mean it. Rude as it may sound, coming from a guest in your house. If you can't forgive me, I can always accept the Minis girls' invitation to visit with them."

"Oh, they're so much younger! You'd be bored in no time."

"Perhaps. But your generosity and your foolish insistence do make me feel rude."

"I'm going to ignore 'foolish insistence,' but how am I being generous?"

Caroline went to the tall window before answering. "Just— by having me here with you now, when I don't have a home."

"But you *do* have a home. You're the mistress of one of the most prosperous plantations on the Savannah River and—"

"I know, I know!" She ran back to Julia and knelt beside her, the violet-blue eyes pleading for understanding. "I didn't mean to sound cross. I feel anything but cross. You told me yesterday that you understand why I can't live at Knightsford with—her."

Stroking Caroline's hair, Julia answered in as soothing a voice as she could muster. "I do understand. Poor, poor Ethel Cameron. I also understand and admire your not forcing her —at her age—out of the only home she ever had as an adult. You know William and I want you here for as long as you'll delight us with your presence, Caroline, my dear. What I can't seem to absorb is—why you and Mark don't get married! That would solve everything. You would have your *own* home."

Caroline got slowly to her feet. "I'm sorry I can't talk about that, Miss Julia."

"You think me a gossip, too, don't you? Well, I suppose I am. If your reason for not marrying him is something you want kept a secret, I wouldn't advise your telling me. I really wouldn't. How lonely Mark must be at the Mackay house in all that silence! Shall we invite him for dinner tonight?"

"You did invite him for dinner tonight."

"So I did. Will the Mackays be back in town for Christmas? Surely, they will."

"Oh, yes. We're all having Christmas together. The Mc-Queens, too. Jack and William go back north to school in January. We're going to have the kind of Christmas neither boy will ever forget. As for me, I'll be all right, *if* no one pushes me faster than I—can go."

* * *

On an unusually cold winter afternoon, January 10, 1820, the largest family group at the waterfront for the departure of Mackay's old ship, the *Eliza* (now owned by Habersham and renamed the *Valiant*), comprised all the Mackays, including little Sallie, and, of course, Mark and Caroline. The younger girls jumped up and down, not from delight—they were saying good-bye to their brothers, Jack and William, for at least another year or more—but to keep warm as a cutting wind off the water brought tears to everyone's eyes.

Eliza embraced one and then the other of her sons, over and over, admonishing Jack not to dare risky things and William to get plenty of rest, telling first one and then the other of her love, of how proud she was of them, of how good it would be when their schooling ended and they were all back together to stay.

While the family said their personal farewells, Mark and Caroline stood a bit to one side, Mark's high fur collar up against the wind, Caroline in a thick alpaca cape, her hands thrust deep into a fur muff. Mark watched Eliza in particular. Not only because he hated anything that caused her pain, but with a new realization that motherhood was now the ruling emotion in her life. She had already spoken of how wonderful it would be for her when the children began to give her grandchildren. No one else loved Eliza's children more than Mark did, but without quite understanding why, he invariably changed the subject when she began to talk of her grandchildren. William was already fifteen, Jack fourteen, and Eliza Anne past twelve. Within a few years Mark's Eliza would be a grandmother. The thought, today, in the biting wind, chilled him more than the cold did. Mark's Eliza? Who *was* his Eliza? What manner of woman? Who was the *real woman?* Had he given his heart to a romantic idealization of the middle-aged little lady hugging first one and then another of her sons, keeping an eye somehow on all three daughters at once because the wharf was such a rough place?

"Miss Eliza is never more beautiful than when she's giving her full attention to the children, is she?" Caroline asked.

"Hm? Oh, do you think so?"

"Yes. Look at her. She doesn't seem to mind this ghastly wind one bit. Nothing matters but the children. And not just

Jack and William—all of them. She's a beautiful lady, Mark. Really beautiful.''

Eliza turned from the children at that moment and smiled at the two. "Don't stand way over there, Mark, Caroline. The boys want to say good-bye to both of you, too."

Mark's heart warmed as though there were no icy wind. "Yes," he said to Caroline. "You're right, she is a beautiful lady."

In his bed that night, sometime after the watchman in the Exchange Tower had called out "Twelve of the clock and all's well," Mark lay in the dark beneath a stack of heavy covers and thought about why Caroline had mentioned Eliza's beauty with the children. Had any other woman mentioned it —any other woman in love with him—he would have considered it trickery. Tonight he was beginning to see that the best way to return to a comfortable friendship with Eliza Mackay was to try to see her, not as a woman whose beauty stopped his heart, but as one who would always be a mother and a grandmother and never Mark's Eliza. Any fool could see that Caroline was right, that she saw Eliza as she really was and would always be—the devoted mother of Robert Mackay's children. Was Caroline trying to help him see her that way?

Caroline Cameron would not resort to feminine wiles, although reminding himself that she was certainly no saint still helped. It helped, he knew, because he'd feel like a boor devouring the mouth of a saint!

The thought of Caroline's mouth lingered. He changed positions in bed. Could he ever, even if she were willing, kiss Eliza as he kissed Caroline? Would the memory of Robert Mackay, his friend, stop him? Had he allowed his imagination to propel him to dream the impossible?

Only one door away down the hall, Caroline lay this minute —also alone—her body warm and eager, also curled beneath Eliza Mackay's quilts and blankets.

Only two doors in the other direction lay Eliza. He clenched his fists. The wind seemed about to tear the shutters from their hinges.

Then, with a painful mixture of anxiety and relief, he faced the irrevocable fact that now, this minute, at almost 1 A.M. of the black, cold, windy early morning of January 11, it was

Caroline for whom he longed—this time with far more than desire.

The house cracked and groaned in the battering cold. Mark groaned, too. If only he could settle inside himself the kind of love he felt for Eliza Mackay, he could put an end to the loneliness. Put an end to loving Eliza? What was it she had said that ugly night when he'd begged her to marry him? *"There must be a way for us to return to our old selves. If there is, I'll find it. . . ."*

"Why can't *I* think of a way?" He repeated the question in a hoarse voice, aloud in the icy room. *"Why can't I think of a way?"*

His body was restless, his mouth hungry, his arms aching, his heart reaching, his spirit—alone.

The clang of the fire bell was so sudden, so loud, he was out of the bed and into the upstairs hall in his nightshirt before he managed to recognize what it was. Eliza appeared first, then Caroline, then the two older girls.

"Go back to your room until we call you," Eliza ordered the girls. "Keep Sallie in bed!"

Caroline, hugging herself in the cold, gasped, "Mark!"

"The fire alarm bells," he said stupidly. Without a thought of a robe, he ran down the stairs and out into the front yard.

Hurrying toward him from his own house a few doors away, Mr. Minis shouted: "Fire, Browning! Looks from my second floor to be over toward Market Square. Get on some warm clothes. We'll have to help!"

"Right, sir. Won't take me a minute."

"I've been yelling my head off for new fire-fighting equipment in this town," Minis called back, his voice fading as he ran toward his own house. "Savannah's got nothing to fight with! Grab all the buckets you can find, Browning!"

Before the two men could reach the actual fire, they heard the death screams of the horses trapped inside Boone's livery stable on Baptist Square at Jefferson.

"Dear God," Mark gasped, his lungs and legs cramping from the long run, "I wonder if Boone got my horse, Handsome, out?"

"What? You keep your horse with Boone?"

"Yes, sir." He lengthened his steps, spurted ahead of Minis

and reached the burning stable first. The wide, low shape of the wooden building loomed black and intact, but inside, flames roared. Rearing, its front feet pawing, only one horse was silhouetted against the glare. Rooted in the street, helpless, Mark saw the final plunge and struggle, saw the pawing form vanish into the crimson roar as the roof of the building crumbled almost soundlessly into a blaze of flesh and beams and clapboard.

The livery stable had stood beside a row of wooden houses, some two-storied—a few cottages still there from Oglethorpe's settling of the city. The first two flimsy houses had already begun to burn. Windblown flames reached eagerly and easily across the fifteen feet or so that separated the row from where the stable had stood. No longer the familiar, dirty, paintless wood tone, the old houses pulsated now—hellish red.

The streets around the fire—Jefferson, St. Julian, Congress —and the market itself on Market Square glowed in reflection, as did the faces of disorganized clots of men swarming the streets. Here and there a few—Mark and Minis among them—had begun a bucket brigade, but the tiny splashes of water arcing from the useless buckets steamed for a few seconds and were devoured.

"Never realized we had so many wooden houses over here," Minis yelled, passing a leather bucket to Mark to be refilled from a tank of water someone had carted from the nearest pump.

"Looks like they're all wood," Mark shouted back, heaving the bucket to the man next to him, who was—quite suddenly and out of nowhere—Sheftall Sheftall. "Mr. Sheftall! You don't think this is too strenuous?"

Sheftall straightened his cocked hat and answered by spitting disgust.

Frantic, seemingly futile, muscle-tearing, skin-searing labor went on hour after hour as wind-driven flames rollicked toward Market Square, blackening, then collapsing every structure in their widening path.

Once, for only an instant, Mark saw William Jay standing alone, his eyes wide with horror. The fire had not reached a Jay house yet, but the reason for the young architect's horror was plain. Cinders and shingles and boards sailed on the west-northwest wind, which blew stronger and more steadily throughout the night. "That infernal wind!" Mark could hear scraps of talk, repeated again and again. "That infernal wind and the drought!" "No rain in months!" "Everything's going up like a tinderbox." "Dear God, dear God, where will it end?"

After a few hours, Mark realized that somewhere in the roar and confusion, he had lost Sheftall and Minis. He prayed for them both and for himself. His hands were black and blistered, and by the time dawn began to streak the eastern sky, he was dazedly reaching for every bucket passed to him without much sense of what he was doing. A bucket in his hands, he either released it if a pair of hands reached out, or tossed its contents in the general direction of the nearest lick of flame.

It helped immeasurably when another man—any man—ordered him to hand on the bucket or empty it. He was beyond thinking. Finally, he caught a glimpse of the man whose strong, sooty hand had been reaching steadily, firmly, for bucket after bucket for the past hour, working so efficiently that almost no water was lost. Mark's eyes burned so that his vision blurred, but he squinted in the eerie red light at the face above those inexhaustible, capable hands and recognized Osmund Kott.

Mark stood staring at him. He was too exhausted to speak, too stunned at the sight of Kott pouring out his strength and energy for the sake of other men's property. Mark tried to smile.

His uncle smiled back and handed Mark still another leather bucket of water that felt like lead.

With the help of Emphie, who was able to make Sallie mind, and Hannah, whose authority was never questioned by the two older girls, Eliza was able to maneuver her daughters back to their rooms upstairs. Before Hero left to help the city fire brigade, of which he was a member, he built a good fire in the parlor for Eliza and Caroline. Through the night, until dawn had almost brought color back to the trees in the yard, they sat alone before Hero's fire—adding occasional logs, praying, talking to keep themselves sane, waiting.

"I knew I cared for Mark from the moment my husband brought him home that day, but oh, Caroline, I love that young man now as though he were my very own son!"

Caroline smiled weakly. "Excuse me, but you've told me that, Miss Eliza, about twenty times tonight."

"I know. I know I have. Could I make more tea?"

"If we drink one more cup of tea, we'll float away." Caroline began to pace the floor. "If anything happens to Mark out there tonight, Miss Eliza, I won't have any reason to go on living."

"He's all right. Mark's a very levelheaded young man."

"I don't care how levelheaded he is—I want to see him. I want to know he's safe! Please, please let me try to find him!"

Eliza went to her. "My dear, we've been through all this before too. You simply can't run right into God knows what kind of danger out there."

"I wouldn't go far. I wouldn't have to go very far. Look! I can see more than that awful red glow now! I can see—the flames!"

"Dear God!"

"I think the whole city could burn, Miss Eliza. I do! And I'm warning you—as soon as full daylight comes, I'm going, so don't try to stop me."

One and then a second heavy explosion shook the house so that Eliza's delicate French mantel clock fell to the brick hearth and shattered.

"What are those explosions?" she gasped.

"I don't know what they were, but I'm going to find out—right now!"

"Caroline, no! Come back!"

Still fastening her cloak, her head bare, Caroline ran toward the flames, west on Broughton, across Drayton and Bull, her heart pounding in her ears above the shouts and screams and clatter and crash of collapsing buildings. She had dressed earlier, during the first attempted flight from Eliza, but this time had forgotten her warm hood on the bench in the front hall. Mark, she knew, would be in the thick of the fire, working somewhere this side of Market Square, which was still a towering mass of flames. Again and again as she ran, she begged God to watch over him, to keep him safe. "He's all I have left! Don't let what happened to Grandfather happen to Mark!"

The flames had not reached Broughton. Running along the wide, sandy street all the way west, Caroline was aware that Broughton was dark, even in the coming daylight. In contrast to the wildly lighted city to the north toward Bay, it was dark. Her legs hurt so, she stumbled and fell. Back on her feet, catching her breath, she saw that she was at the corner of Broughton and Whitaker and that she had lost a slipper. Her legs were so numb with cold, she hadn't noticed until she stopped running.

The dawn sky lightened, but it brought no hope. The smoky air was thick with shouts and screams—a woman's scream as her home fell heavily into itself, the precious belongings inside. Then a child began to wail.

Moving again over the smoldering, wet debris, Caroline hurried out Whitaker in the direction of Congress. Looking back once, she could see that Christ Church in Johnson Square still stood, untouched, plainly visible in the eerie, wavering light. That was good. She tried to run faster.

A tiny woman, carrying too heavy iron skillets and a three-year-old child, stumbled past, weeping. The child's soundless terror struck Caroline's heart; the child was Caroline herself, staring in horror at the sight of her grandfather's leaping, flaming body.

Plodding on in the direction of the fire fighting, where the crash of buildings roared, she could still see the child's face, white under the soot streaks. It had become her own.

At St. Julian, her shoeless foot bleeding, she stopped to search the faces of the blackened, half-soaked figures of men futilely attempting to wet down a house not yet consumed. The corner of Whitaker and St. Julian seemed deserted. She twisted and rubbed her cold-reddened, stiff fingers. The street corner was not deserted. Somewhere just behind her, she could hear weeping. Then she saw a man—sitting down—sobbing. Caroline went to him. It was William Jay, his face streaked with soot, his hands blistered, his sobs cruel.

"Mr. Jay," she said, touching his shoulder, "Mr. Jay, it's Caroline Cameron. Are you hurt?"

A flare of ugly red lighted his tortured eyes. He could not speak. He could only shake his head no and point to the wild scene about them.

"Pray! Pray that none of your beautiful houses burns.

Don't be ashamed of your tears. Just pray.''

He nodded, looking directly at her for the first time.

"Have you seen—Mark Browning? Have you seen him at all tonight?''

He nodded again and pointed toward the inferno that had been the market.

"Oh, my God," she gasped. "But was he—all right? Did you talk to him?''

"Yes," Jay panted, choking on a gust of acrid smoke that seemed driven directly at them. "Yes, Miss—Cameron. Don't go—any farther. I—beg you . . .''

"Was he this side of the market when you saw him?''

He nodded.

"Is he—part of a bucket brigade, Mr. Jay?''

Another nod.

"Thank you. Oh, thank you. And, please be all right. Please pray!''

She began to run again, west on St. Julian. Her eyes streamed tears from the heat, her nose burned, her face felt like fire itself, but she kept moving until—in what had been the entrance to someone's home—she saw a man on the ground. He was trapped. A heavy charred beam lay across his leg. Both arms flailed in pain, but the man was silent. It was Mark! An older man was struggling to lift the beam and free him.

"Mark!" she screamed. *"Mark!"*

On her knees beside him, she fought to keep back her own sobs. Nothing must add to the agony in that black-streaked, tortured, beautiful face.

"Go—home—Caroline," he gasped. "In the name of God, what are you doing here?''

The man trying to move the heavy beam grunted and swore. It would not budge. Leaping to her feet, Caroline grabbed one end and lifted with all her might. Mark screamed.

"Stop!" the strange man shouted. "I'll have to get something to use as a lever. You tend to him. I'll be right back.''

On her knees beside Mark, as gently as her numb hands could manage, she tried to wipe his face with her handkerchief. Skin—the young, firm skin she'd kissed—sluffed away. Caroline stifled a cry.

From behind, heavy, running footsteps. The stranger was

back with a piece of charred two-by-four. Without a word, he began to push it under the huge beam that trapped Mark's leg; then, straightening his back, the man heaved mightily. Praying, her eyes riveted on the two-by-four and the ugly beam, Caroline held her breath. Slowly, the beam began to move. If it rolled to the right, Mark could be crushed.

After what seemed an eternity, it rolled—to the left.

The stranger collapsed to the ground, the two-by-four still in his hand. Mark groaned, tried to move his freed leg. The dear bloodshot eyes looked up at Caroline. "I—I can't move it," he whispered.

"But, is the pain—some less? Tell me it is!"

He nodded his head. "Some." He tried valiantly to smile. "No, lots. Lots—better. But—I've got to get out of here, Caroline. I'm in the way!"

"Listen to me, Mark. Listen carefully." As she began to explain her plan, a building crashed nearby, and for the next several minutes she badly burned her own hands beating out and knocking away embers that fell on Mark and the prostrate, kind gentleman who had helped him. Kneeling again beside Mark, she went right on: "Are you listening? I'm going to run to the Mackays, hitch their pair to your carriage and come back for you. Will you try to be patient?"

"I'll watch over him," the stranger said, pulling himself up slowly. "I promise you, Miss Caroline."

At the sound of her name, she looked up into the face of Osmund Kott. *"You,"* she gasped, struggling to her feet, refusing his offer of assistance. "I—didn't recognize you!"

"I know," he said gently. Nodding down toward Mark, he added, "Neither did he—for a long time. I doubt he knows who pulled the beam away now. But, it doesn't matter. I will see to him while you're gone. I'd go for the carriage in your place, ma'am, but I don't expect Mrs. Mackay would let me have it."

"No," Caroline said stiffly. "Neither do I." She looked from Kott to Mark and back at Kott. "I—have no choice but to believe that you'll see to him," she said. "I—do thank you for what you've already done."

Without another word, she turned and began the long trip back to Broughton Street.

* * *

With Hero away fighting the fire, Eliza helped her hitch the Mackay pair to Mark's barouche and promised to pray through every minute until Caroline had him safely home.

Galloping the horses along Broughton toward the still-raging fire, Caroline prayed, too. When she pulled the carriage as close as possible to where Mark lay on St. Julian, she helped Osmund Kott lift him, struggling against groans and cries of pain, onto the carriage floor.

"He'll be all right there," Kott said, adjusting Caroline's rolled-up cloak under Mark's head. "Too bad you didn't think to bring a pillow. You'll be half-frozen by the time you get him to the Mackay house."

"I'll be fine," she answered tersely, scrambling up into the high driver's seat.

"Sure you don't want me to go along to help you get him in the house?"

In answer, she snapped the reins on the horses' rumps and began to drive through the rubble away from the flames and toward Broughton. Every few yards, she looked back to be sure Mark was all right. Once, he raised his hand in brief assurance. But before they reached Bull Street, she could tell he'd fainted.

Nearing the house at last, the sight of Eliza, Emphie and strong, big-shouldered Hannah waiting by the front gate was like a gift from God. Together, they struggled to lift the deadweight of his unconscious body from the carriage floor; to carry it up the front walk and into the house. He roused and began to moan just as they eased him onto the narrow bed in the first-floor spare room.

Hannah forced brandy between his blackened, dry lips, and Caroline kept poultices—clean cloths dipped in cold linseed oil—on his scorched face and forehead. She could tell that he was conscious, but he did not speak. He simply lay there, hurt and exhausted, bearing his pain, his eyes closed. After a time, his eyes fluttered open and he looked through swollen lids at the ceiling.

"Miss—Eliza?" he whispered.

Eliza's name on his lips struck Caroline's heart. She dropped the oil-soaked cloth in the basin and turned away.

"Yes, Mark," Eliza said. "We're all here with you. You're home now. Eliza Anne is at the Minises' to get someone to go with her for Dr. Waring. You're safe, Mark. Everything will be all right soon.''

Suddenly frantic, he tried to pull himself up on his elbow. ''Caroline! Miss Eliza, Caroline is still—at—the fire!'' Helpless tears began to roll down his face as he struggled to get out of bed.

''No, Mark!'' Eliza said. ''Caroline is right here—just on the other side of the room. Caroline brought you home in your own carriage!''

''Caroline?'' he whispered.

In an instant, she was on her knees beside him. ''Mark, oh, Mark, I'm here! It's Caroline. Can't you see me?''

He shook his head, tears still falling onto the pillow.

''Miss Eliza, he—he can't see!''

''All that smoke an' soot,'' Emphie mumbled. ''Ain't no wonder.''

''Yes,'' Eliza said, ''I'm sure you're right, Emphie.''

''Be the first time if she is,'' Hannah grumbled. ''Lemme go get some witch hazel to bathe them eyes.''

''Shouldn't we wait till the doctor gets here?'' Caroline asked. ''We don't want to do the wrong thing.''

''A lotion of weak witch hazel be the best thing,'' Hannah said sharply. ''You done think I ain't took care of a hundred burnin' eyes, chile? Move over, Miss 'Liza. Lemme pass.''

In less than an hour, by what Eliza called a miracle because there were so many injured in the city, Dr. Waring and his son were there—alone with Mark—setting the broken leg. In the parlor Eliza and Caroline gripped each other's hands and tried to pray above their own anguish at Mark's cries.

When, finally, the screams stopped and Dr. Waring hurried away to tend other injured Savannahians, Hannah ordered them both to bed.

''Dr. Waring, he say Mister Mark'll sleep till late this afternoon,'' Hannah said, in full charge. ''Ain't nothin' you two can do but get in my way. When Mister Mark wakes up, you'll know. First, I bathe his eyes again with weak witch hazel—'' In a superior fashion, she added, *''on* doctor's orders.''

As they climbed the wide stair together, Eliza asked, ''How was Mark's leg broken?''

''A big, heavy beam from a collapsing building fell on

him—pinned him to the ground for God knows how long.'' At the door of her room, Caroline added, "Osmund Kott pried the beam off him, Miss Eliza.''

*"Osmund?* Osmund Kott is in Savannah?"

"He most certainly is. He might well have saved Mark's life. The other men had all they could do to fight the fire—try to save children and old people. Yes, Osmund is back. It terrifies me that he is, but he was kind to Mark. I don't know why, but he was."

"Caroline! Your hands are burned!"

In a flat voice, she asked, "Are they? Osmund and I tried to lift the beam first. I—guess it was still burning on the end I grabbed."

"You poor girl. Let me help you undress. I'll tend those burns."

"No! I just want—to be alone. Miss Eliza? Did you see that some of Mark's hair is burned away?" She began to weep. "That's almost the worst part!" Her eyes grew wide. She was staring again. "I *saw* my grandfather's hair—*on fire!* It—all burned—all of it!"

"Caroline!"

"He was running round and round, trying to get away from the flames, and all his beautiful hair burned right off. . . ." Abruptly, she looked at Eliza. "We've got to lie down, I guess. But we dare not sleep. The fire is burning this way. We have to be ready—at any time—to move Mark."

# FORTY

No one knew for certain, but sometime between noon and one o'clock the next day, the fire burned itself out or, as some claimed, was finally extinguished. There was no doubt anywhere that the men of Savannah—slave, free, Negro, white— had exerted themselves beyond human effort to control it. There was also no doubt that Savannah was no more equipped to handle this devastation in 1820 than it had been twenty-four years earlier when another conflagration had brought so much suffering to the city.

The flames had died out just short of Broughton. All morning long, once they received word of the needs in the burned-out section of town, Caroline and Eliza, after no more than an hour's rest, had scoured the house for extra linens, food, blankets and clothing. Hero made countless trips distributing their collections.

"Mister Brasch down at the bakery, he givin' away bread," Hero reported, and this was just the beginning of a regional outpouring of generosity to the city. Planters in the area, through Mayor Wayne and the aldermen, donated enormous amounts of rice and corn. The St. Andrew's Society, of which Mackay had been a member, lived up to its motto, "Relieve the distressed." Advertisements ran in the local newspaper offering free grain and beef, given by other landowners. Monies, foodstuffs and clothing arrived also from Northern and other Southern states. No one had been killed, although many, like Mark, were injured. And no one starved, but nothing could alleviate the suffering of loss. Ninety-four city lots, between Bay on the north, Jefferson on the west, Broughton on the south and Abercorn on the east, were left without livable houses and tenements. Three hundred and twenty-one wooden buildings—many double tenements—and thirty-five brick buildings were totally destroyed.

"Still the most pitiful sights are the poor squares," Caroline told Eliza two weeks after the fire. She had just returned from the newly built market on the green at South Broad Street. "I hope you don't see them for a while. They're piled with everything from burned mattresses to broken chairs to cradles. It's horrible! All those personal things strewn out in the open for —everyone to see."

"Our squares, I suppose, were the only available open space that ghastly night, weren't they? The only places where one burning building wasn't going to set the next one afire. Caroline, aren't we blessed?"

"I still hope you don't see the city for a while, but until you do, I don't think you'll realize how blessed we are, Miss Eliza. The fire burned right *to* Broughton Street! And to Abercorn. Right up to this house!"

"The Lord, He protect us," Hannah stated flatly. "The good Lord, He stop the fire just before it burn our home."

Eliza sighed. "I wonder about things like that, Hannah."

"Go on an' wonder, honey, but you gotta thank."

"Oh, I do thank Him. But, far better Christians than I lost everything—homes, furniture, clothing—everything. Keepsakes, family portraits, things no amount of money could replace. I know the Lord doesn't have favorites. I—wish I understood better."

"Best to leave room for what they calls 'mystery,' " Hannah warned, pulling a large basket out of the cupboard. "If I don't cut them camellias in the yard, there won't be no more bloom."

"Eliza Anne and Kate should be doing that, Hannah. Where are they?"

"Swingin' in the big oak swing, I s'pect," she called back on her way outside.

"They should be in here, for that matter, Caroline, offering to help shell these lovely peas you found at the market."

Caroline dumped the pea pods into a bowl and sat down beside Eliza at the kitchen table. "I know the girls aren't to go out on the streets alone until all the vandalism and confusion have died down, but I saw them on my way to the apothecary to get salve for Mark's burns."

"Where in the world were they?"

"On Bay, one on each side of Mr. Sheftall Sheftall. Kate was reading his newspaper aloud to him. His eyes were burned, too, you know. I was proud of your daughters."

"Yes." Eliza's eyes laughed. "But Mrs. Minis says his eyes are healed. She says Mr. Sheftall can see again. Those girls are the limit. You're right, though, I am proud of them for being kind to him. And, oh, Caroline, how wonderful that Mark can see again!"

Caroline bit her lip. "How wonderful that he's—alive. Most of the time I can't think of anything else. Miss Eliza, that beam could have struck him in the head!"

"But it didn't. He's going to get entirely well. Maybe a tiny scar under his jawline on one side from the burn, Dr. Waring said today. Nothing more."

Tossing her sewing aside, Caroline jumped up. "Oh, has Dr. Waring already been here?"

"While you were at the market. I should have told you."

Caroline flushed, then smiled. "I try not to tire Mark out with too many visits before Dr. Waring gets here every day. But I'm going up now."

"Good, because he asked for you first thing when I took the doctor to his room. I never saw anyone happier to be back in a room than Mark is to be—"

"Mark asked for me in front of Dr. Waring?" Caroline interrupted.

"Yes. Why not?"

"I'm just—glad he did. I'll be back down to help you shell these peas."

"Take your time. Make the boy happy."

She knocked softly on Mark's door and waited.

"Caroline?" His voice sounded almost normal.

She opened the door and flew to him, dropping, as she always did, to a tomboyish squat on the floor beside his big chair. "Hello, sir!"

"Where have you been? You're late!"

"I didn't know I had a definite appointment with your highness. Did I?"

"No, I guess not. But it must be almost noon. I've been lonely."

"I brought you breakfast; the girls have all been here, I'm sure. Miss Eliza came, she just told me, with Dr. Waring. I think you've been busy."

He was smiling at her with the smile that still made her weak with joy. "Tad Lewis from my office was here for over an hour, too, but those people weren't—you." He reached for her hand and kissed it. "You're pretty today, Miss Cameron. Could you possibly stand up and kiss me, since I can't bend that far yet?"

Leaning over the chair, she took his face in her hands and kissed him tenderly, gently, afraid of hurting the burned places. They hadn't kissed since the fire. In an instant, his arms were around her and he had pulled her down onto his lap. Almost with his old strength, but with a new, somehow different hunger, he began to kiss her. She responded far more eagerly than she meant to, but as always, could not help herself.

"Only God knows how I've longed to be close to you," he breathed, caressing her back and shoulders, kissing her between words now. "Caroline, I am grateful—that you—probably saved my life—but can we forget that? I don't want you to—misinterpret—anything—as mere gratitude. This"—he kissed her eyes and cheeks and forehead—*"isn't"* gratitude. It's good for a man to brush death. It brings him to his senses."

"Oh, Mark . . . don't say a word you don't mean!"

"I love you, Caroline! With all my heart, I love you. I want you. I need you." Abruptly, almost roughly, he held her away so their eyes could meet. "Before you leave this room, I beg you to tell me you'll marry me. Even if I have to hobble down the aisle at Christ Church on the crutches Dr. Waring promised to bring me tomorrow, I want to marry you—just as soon as possible!"

She struggled to stand up. He was holding her too tightly.

"Mark, Mark, please—"

"Please, what?"

"You've been awfully ill. You might be just—imagining this!"

He released her. She stood up, but still close.

"Caroline," he began, his voice somehow older, more

mature—to her, even more musical than before. "I've had lots
of time since the fire. Lots of time alone to let the truth soak
into me. It has, finally. I—I had some kind of boyish dream
about Miss Eliza. She and Mr. Mackay were my idols. When
he died, it just suddenly seemed exactly right for me to step in
and—take care of her. I let it build up in my mind at night,
here alone in my room, until it built itself all out of proportion
to what was really—true. I'm glad you knew what I was going
through because of you. You did know, didn't you?"

"I certainly did."

"I'm glad, because there must never be any falseness or
pretending between us. Not ever."

"I can't pretend, Mark. It isn't goodness in me; it's just that
I have to be—exactly as I am and I'm not comfortable with
anyone who isn't. That's why I broke all the rules of proper
flirtation with you. I've loved you since the first night I met
you and I'd have felt silly not letting you know."

"Then, why can't you say you'll marry me, now that I've
finally come to my senses?"

"I don't know! Isn't it as plain as the nose on your face that
I—don't know?"

He reached for her again. This time, she did not resist.

"It's probably only the fact that you're a woman and I'm a
man," he said. "Women are mysterious. Men are right out in
the open."

"Ha! *Who* has been—right out in the open? Of the two of
us, who has?" She was trying to talk while returning his
kisses, trying to delay just a little—and failing. "O God, help
me! Mark, how I love you!"

"It's time for us, Caroline," he breathed. "It's time!"

"Mark, be careful of your leg. I'm too heavy to be on your
lap!"

"Christ Church is still standing," he whispered hoarsely.
"The fire didn't burn Christ Church, Caroline. We can get
married just as soon as I get my crutches! Can't we? Can't
we?"

She pulled away.

"No," she said firmly. "No, we can't get married just as
soon as you have your crutches. It takes longer than that for a
woman to get ready. There isn't a seamstress in this town who
could make the kind of wedding dress I want in one day. Dr.

Waring's bringing those crutches tomorrow, you said. You'll just have to wait because—'' She backed away from him, a serious, almost childlike look in her eyes. "Because I mean to be wearing the most exquisite gown in the world the day I marry—the most beautiful man in the world!''

Eliza Anne, who had been eavesdropping in the hall outside Mark's door, turned and ran down the stairs, back through the first-floor hallway and burst into the kitchen, where her mother and Emphie were shelling peas.

"Mama, I'm going to die!''

"You're—what?'' Eliza looked up from her work, smiling unconcernedly.

"I said I'm going to die—any minute!''

"I heard you, dear. But there must be a reason.''

Emphie shook her birdlike head and dismissed Eliza Anne's high drama with a wave of her hand.

"It's *going* to happen! I heard it with my own ears. I know I was eavesdropping, but I meant only to be paying Mark a visit, and oh, Mama, Mama, my heart is about to burst with excitement!''

"You have us both on the edges of our chairs now,'' Eliza said calmly, "so what's your secret? And you know what I think of eavesdropping.''

"Mark and Caroline are going to be—*married.*'' The word "married'' almost overcame her. Instead of shouting it as she fully intended, her voice cracked. "Mark's in a big hurry, but Caroline has to have the most gorgeous wedding dress in the world made first and they'll be married in Christ Church because it didn't burn down in the fire and, oh, Mama, do you think Caroline will ask me to be a bridesmaid? After all, she doesn't have a sister and she's been here with us so much lately, I'm about exactly like a sister!''

Eliza looked at Emphie, wishing she were Hannah, since Hannah knew that Mark had also asked her to marry him. Emphie was Emphie, though, and Eliza dared not let her true feelings show. There was no better cook, but Emphie definitely was not one to be trusted with confidences. Weak with relief, Eliza let a handful of unshelled peas fall back into the bowl before her on the table. "You have really brought us news, dear,'' she said, her voice strangely quiet after such an announcement. "But you must let them tell us. I forbid you to mention what you wrongly overheard to anyone else. Is that clear?"

"Oh, yes! I wouldn't tell anyone but Kate and the Minis girls, anyway. Sallie's far too young."

"Well, just don't tell anyone. Telling everybody will be part of the happiness for Caroline and Mark. You must not rob them of that."

"Was that true when Papa asked you to marry him all those years ago?"

"Yes, it was."

"Oh, Mama, please don't let tears come—not today!"

Eliza Anne kissed her mother's hair. "I still cry for Papa sometimes, too. That is why you're about to cry now, isn't it?"

"Partly, yes. I'm also inclined to weep a little when I'm very happy—and relieved. I'm both happy and relieved over Mark and Caroline." And praying, she added in her thoughts, that Mark is not being hasty. The President's visit had helped. Even the ghastly fire had distracted everyone's thoughts from personal problems, but Eliza had suffered over Mark.

Hannah, starched white apron swishing, bustled into the kitchen, carrying her basket filled with camellias. "Lord have mercy," she boomed, "I done took this basket of flowers up to show Mister Mark before I fix 'em for his room an', Miss 'Liza, the Lord He done answer our prayers in jig time!"

"Hannah," Eliza Anne moaned. "Did—they tell *you?*"

The broad, brown face glowed. "What did who tell me?"

"Mark and Caroline! They're going to be married!"

"Eliza Anne," her mother scolded. "Didn't I just warn you not to mention this to anyone?"

Lap full of basket and flowers, Hannah sank to a straight chair, crushed. "You mean Miss Caroline an' Mister Mark they done tol' this chile *first?* Both of 'em swore to me that *I* was the first to know!"

"No," Eliza said firmly. "They did *not* tell her first. She eavesdropped in the hall outside Mark's room. You're the very first to know—from them, Hannah. And I'm going to have to find a way to stop my daughter's ears and tongue."

"No, you won't, Mama. I didn't mean to tell Hannah just now. Honestly, I didn't. It's just that—my heart runneth over!"

"I'm sure it does, but growing up means that even hearts that runneth over can be controlled until the time is right."

"It do mean that," Hannah declared. "Take your mama here, she done do herself a job of controllin' her own heart."

"You did, Mama? When?"

"That's enough, Hannah, and that's enough, Eliza Anne. Emphie's the only person in this room doing what she's supposed to be doing—shelling peas and keeping her mouth shut."

"She must be sick," Hannah mumbled, pulling herself and her basket out of the chair. "Here, lemme git these flowers fix for that sweet Mister Mark." Dumping the camellias—white, pink, red—on the dry sink, pounding into the pantry in search of a proper bowl, Hannah went on talking to herself: "Ain't no wonder I caught myself pickin' so many camellias! Somepin' musta told me they was big things takin' place in this house. Thank ya, Jesus! Somepin' done warn me for sure."

At Caroline's suggestion, Mark was the one to tell Eliza. In fact, Caroline was his messenger to Eliza that he wanted to see her right away in his room.

"Except for Caroline," he said, when Eliza had taken a small rocker near his big chair, "I don't think I'd have the courage to be as—frank as I'm going to be. Would you hold my hand while I tell you what I have to say, Miss Eliza?"

"Of course! And I already know it's something good. I can tell by your face."

He grinned a little. "It shows, eh? But I'll be able to enjoy it even more once I know—how you feel."

Eliza longed to help him, but perhaps he needed to handle this himself. She waited, his hand in both of hers.

"When I—asked you to marry me," he began nervously, "I meant every word of it. It wasn't any sudden impulse. I think I was in love with you before Mr. Mackay died. In fact, the last time we had dinner together, the night before he died, I all but told him."

"Mark!"

"I know that's a shock to you. But, Miss Eliza, he was that kind of man, wasn't he? He always, always gave everyone room to be truthful. He was—like Caroline that way. They're really a lot alike, actually."

Her voice unsteady, apprehensive, Eliza asked, *"Did* you—

tell him, Mark? I—really need to know that."

"Not exactly. It was a fine moment. You know how he was always playing Cupid with Caroline and me; well, I—told him that night that I didn't think there was another Eliza Mackay in the world. That I loved you so much, I didn't think I could ever love another woman."

"What on earth did Robert say to that?"

"He laughed in that fine, understanding way he had. He simply agreed that there wasn't another woman like you—anywhere. That was what he said, as nearly as I remember now." He gripped her hand. "You've got to believe that he—that he and I experienced a rare, close moment of friendship. I see now that he knew exactly how I love you. Not the way I imagined, but the way I really loved you then. The way I love you now."

"There will never be anyone like him, Mark."

"I know that. I desperately want you to know that I now know and accept, too, that you can never love another man. Not *any* other man—ever."

"That not only satisfies me, it makes me feel very close to you. I have always felt close to you, Mark." She could feel her face redden. "That's probably why I handled your addressing me that night—so poorly. Oh, I was very poor at it. I hurt you unnecessarily by just walking out of the room, but I—felt so helpless. I was—scared, too."

"Maybe," he began, "I can make some of it up to you now. We need you. Caroline and I are going to need you in so many ways. We're getting married." He laughed softly. "I feel sure Hannah told you. We were both too happy not to blurt it all out to her when she heaved into the room with a big basket of camellias."

"She told us down in the kitchen. You made her really happy by letting her be the first to know. You've made me happy, too. You see, I've come to love Caroline, to admire her courage, her honesty. And I do see why you say she's quite like Robert. She has a lot of his natural buoyancy, even though life has bruised her time and time again." She held his hand to her cheek. "She's—almost fine enough for you. And very, very wise. Only a wise young woman would have insisted that you and I have this talk—right now. Not a minute later."

He pulled her to him and kissed her forehead. "Dr. Waring

is bringing my crutches tomorrow," he beamed. "If I'm not too weak from all this loafing around, maybe I can make it downstairs to the table for dinner. We can all celebrate together. For as long as I live, Miss Eliza, I want you to be right there with me when everything happens—good or bad."

She brushed back a short lock of his singed hair. "There's no way on earth I won't always be with you in everything. Even when I'm—with Robert again, even when I die, Mark, I'll still be right with you."

He couldn't handle the stairs the next day, but a week later, after hours of practice with Caroline beside him, up and down the upstairs hall, he did manage. His young muscles strengthened quickly. The heavy wooden crutches, which he would have to use for two months, grew lighter by the day. His hair, which Hero had cut, was growing out. By March, a month and a half after the fire, he was able at last to go with Caroline in the carriage to inspect the heartbreaking destruction in his city.

"We mustn't stay out too long," she warned as she snuggled beside him under a fur rug. "The wind's cold. I can't have you getting a chill just when your leg's getting well." She called out to Hero up front in the driver's seat: "Let's stay on Broughton for a while."

"Good idea," big Hero grinned back at them. "Broughton Street look the same as ever."

Holding Mark's hand under the rug, Caroline said, "I'm glad you didn't see Savannah the day after the fire—especially the afternoon they finally put it out while everything was still collapsing and smoldering and smoking."

"I'm sorry you saw it," he said. "I'd have spared you that, if I hadn't been so full of Dr. Waring's laudanum."

"But, Savannah means so much to *you*. Even after almost two months, it's still—pitiful. Last week, anyway, Mrs. Distil was still coming every day to where her little cottage had been on St. Julian to sit on the front steps and cry. You'll see; the squares nearest where the fire raged are still cluttered with unclaimed belongings. I really think some of the older folk will never get over their heartbreak."

"I've tried to picture it," he said hoarsely. "I must have read the account in the *Georgian* a hundred times. It's still more than I can take in. Now they say four hundred and sixty-three buildings gone, not counting outbuildings. Caroline, think how many people felt sheltered in those houses, think how much laughter and contentment and sorrow and sickness and romance went on behind those poor walls." He took a deep breath, tightened his grip on her hand. "Why do I love this city so much?"

"I'm beginning to love it, too, because you do. I loved Knightsford when I was a little girl. Then I loathed it, lovely as it is."

"That could change."

"Maybe. But I'm beginning to belong to Savannah. Your Savannah. You don't give me any choice, you know."

"Caroline, I'm so devoted to the town, right now I'm scared to look when Hero turns that corner onto Jefferson, where it all began."

"It isn't pretty, darling. It's ghastly. Do you think it will help that I'm—with you?"

In answer, he slipped his arm around her and held her close.

"I be going to turn now," Hero warned gently.

Slowly, the carriage rolled beside the blackened ruins of the livery stable, where Mark's fine horse had burned to death, and along Jefferson past lone chimney after chimney, standing gaunt and useless on the black, rubble-strewn ground of what had been house after house, tenement after tenement, shop after shop after shop. Mark looked in silence. Almost no walls stood, so that when he noticed a thin, wooden one bravely standing, its flowered paper barely scorched, tears began to roll down his cheeks. I can't help the tears, he thought. Even those nearly worthless wooden buildings were a living part of Savannah when I found her. A wave of regret swept over him because for years he had walked along Jefferson, wondering how, without causing too much heartache and inconvenience for those of modest means who owned or rented the unpainted frame houses, they could be torn down to make room for new, handsomer structures. He shuddered. He had been right, of course, from the standpoint of local economy and progress. Heaven knew, most of the houses along Jefferson were ugly, uncared for, even rickety. Now, the carriage wheels slipping unsteadily in and out of ruts in the soft, sandy street, he longed to stop and weep for every lost cottage.

Caroline was quiet, too. He knew why. She, of all people, sensed his grief. At each devastated site, he felt her pat his hand under the fur rug, sharing his sorrow over the destruction of places even he hadn't known he loved.

Across the landscape of stark chimneys and scattered debris on the now vacant lots that separated Jefferson from the old square where the market had stood, he could see only a wasted expanse. Nothing remained to block the view. The two explosions, when the fire had reached the store where gunpowder had been illegally kept, had all but wiped out the market buildings. Traditionalist that he was, Mark was certainly going to fight on the side of those who were enraged that the city fathers had moved the market to the South Broad Street green. If enough Savannahians protested, it would surely· be moved back where it belonged.

As they crossed St. Julian, the lots around the squares were so empty he could see all the way to Johnson Square, where, indeed, Christ Church still stood. In the burned-out area, only Christ Church, the Planters' Bank, Washington Hall and a few brick buildings had been spared.

"I don't think we should try to cover the whole burned-out section from Jefferson to Abercorn—"

"—from Bay to Broughton," he finished for her on a sigh. "No. Not today. I think we'd better go back now." He swiped at the tears. "I—can't look at much more of it."

Caroline instructed Hero and fell silent again, waiting, Mark knew, for him to say something—or nothing. He was sitting up by then, very straight on the carriage seat, no longer holding her hand—looking, looking in spite of himself, at every ruin they passed, tears wetting his cravat. She made no effort to hold his hand again, but finally, as they turned off Bull Street onto Broughton, where the city was the same as ever, she whispered, "Beauty *can* come from ashes, Mark. Remember that."

He fell back against the carriage seat and reached for her hand. "I will remember. Caroline, you and I are going to help create some of that beauty. You'll see. I'm all right now, and the very next time we're out, we'll begin to look for a place to build our house. Maybe we'll look for the very saddest, most damaged piece of ground." He brightened. "Would you like that?"

She held his hand to her breast. "Mark, yes! I'm already

fairly practiced at making—beauty from ashes."

"How did I ever manage to find a woman like you?"

"You didn't. I simply had sense enough to wait for you to figure out what a wonderful wife I'll be."

When William wrote that he and Jack would be home late in May to stay, they set the wedding date—June 1, 1820—allowing only one week for Mark's tailor to make new suits for William, who would be Mark's sole supporter at the Christ Church ceremony, and for Jack, his official greeter.

"You couldn't do a more meaningful thing for William," Eliza told Mark the day she accompanied him to Low's to select gifts for William and Jack, for Sallie, as flower maiden, and for Eliza Anne and Kate, who would be maids of honor to Caroline.

"I hope Jack isn't hurt that I chose William," he said. "You know how I feel about them both, but somehow William and I have always been close."

"You handled it just right. Jack feels very important as your head greeter at the Washington Hall reception afterward." She laughed. "Of course, Jack never feels much less than important, anyway."

"He's a charmer. And hasn't William turned into a fine-looking young man? Some Savannah girl is going to be swooning over him any day now."

"Oh, I think he already has his eye on the Bryan girl, Virginia. I just hope she's old enough to know that William is always terribly serious about everything he feels. Jack can cope with the most flirtatious girls, not William."

"Virginia Bryan impresses me as an unusual little person. Hard to believe, since she's only twelve. Caroline is very fond of her."

Eliza took his arm as they crossed Johnson Square. "This is a happy shopping trip, isn't it?"

"Yes," he said, smiling down at her. "And it could have been impossible, if you weren't exactly as you are. Caroline and I couldn't have managed this fancy wedding without you. We don't have anyone but you, Miss Eliza."

# FORTY-ONE

THREE days before the wedding, Mark and Caroline walked under a full moon, hung like a great gold coin in the embracing Savannah sky. How can a mere ceremony bring us any closer? he wondered. She seemed always a thought ahead of him. Her laughter matched his. Even her gratitude that he loved her, which she expressed often, did not embarrass him. It was too genuine. She did not worship him. He felt secure in that. Worship of another human being could only stifle in the end, or destroy. People were created to worship God. Aunt Nassie always said that only God could handle worship. Caroline simply loved him with all her intelligent, noble being. Long before he knew he loved her, the word "noble" came to his mind often for Caroline. She enjoyed some of her most infectious laughs over his use of the word. He loved her laughter. He loved her body, her mind, her spirit. Mark loved Caroline Cameron for herself and eased daily more deeply into the sheer comfort of her presence.

She held his arm as they strolled now along the Strand. He smiled down at her. The smile she returned seemed almost the smile of a child. A trusting, not a dependent, child.

I welcome even her fears, he thought, pressing her arm to his side. Lord knows, she has helped me deal with mine. His happiness was so complete at this moment, no fears of any kind came to mind. Caroline, by being Caroline, had put them in proper perspective. Her one overriding fear, he knew, was Osmund Kott. Not her grandmother but Osmund—Mark's own uncle. He feared him, too, he supposed, in a way, although not so helplessly. Actually, she did not seem any longer to despise Kott—only to fear him.

Soon after the fire, while he was still bedfast, Mark had wanted to send Kott a note of thanks by Sheftall Sheftall, who always knew where to find anyone in town. Kott had shown true heroism during the long hours in which the fire had raged. Mark had learned from T.U.P. Charlton that hours after Osmund had saved Mark's leg, he had also rescued two children and their mother from a burning house on Abercorn.

While he was writing the note of gratitude, Caroline had come into Mark's room. When he showed it to her, she had turned and fled without a word. Later, when he'd tried to convince her that it was only a note of gratitude, she begged him not to send it.

"I'll agree to whatever you ask of me for as long as I live," she vowed, "except—any kind of contact with that man. He killed my grandfather!"

"Caroline, you don't know that! So far as anyone knows, he only came to town the day the S.S. *Savannah* returned to port."

"I can't prove it, but I know it. Oh, Mark, I beg you, for the sake of our marriage, not to have anything at all to do with him. He's poison. He doesn't have blood in his veins, he has poison! He killed my grandfather because he was so sure he'd been remembered in that will."

"But, darling, your grandfather ran into the burning house himself."

"And Osmund knew he'd do it!" She had begun to weep. "Don't you see? All his life he ruled my poor grandfather. He was still ruling him—in death."

Mark had held her very close that day and prayed that she was ridding herself of *all* the bottled-up childhood tears.

To this moment, he had never thanked Kott for what he did during the fire. When Caroline had stopped crying, Mark had slowly torn the note into tiny fragments and handed them to her.

In the moonlight, beside her now—three days before their wedding—he could still remember the look of relief on her face.

"You must be thinking very hard, Mr. Browning," she said as they crossed Bay in the direction of home. "I can hear your brain whirring."

"Can you read my thoughts?"

"Most of the time."

He laughed. "How true."

A half block or so from the Mackay house, Mark noticed a tall man waiting in the street in front of the gate, his back to them. "Look," he said. "I wonder who that is. He's too tall for either one of the boys and too old. It might be the new dock supervisor I hired last week. Awfully well dressed, though."

"Mark! I'm *afraid*."

"Nonsense. Hello!" Mark called as they came closer. The man turned to face them.

"Good evening." Osmund Kott bowed to Caroline and held out his hand to Mark.

"No," she whispered quickly. "Please don't—touch his hand, Mark!"

"Miss Caroline holds a grudge against me, I know," Kott said in his soft, gentlemanly voice, addressing Mark as though Caroline were not present. "I can't say that I blame her, but her reasons for hating me are now all so long ago. I—I hoped to be able to ask a favor this evening, of both of you."

Too fast for Mark to stop her, Caroline ran up the front walk and into the house.

"I apologize, Browning. I certainly didn't intend to upset your young lady."

"What is it you want?"

"A very small thing, actually. I may surprise you with this piece of news, although by now, I doubt it. You see, you are my only living relative. My nephew. Your mother was my sister. I find myself wanting very much to attend your wedding."

Mark studied the once handsome, still interesting face for a long time before answering. "Under the circumstances, I find it hard to believe, sir, that you'd expect Miss Caroline to agree to—"

"I merely hope for it. I also have a second favor to ask of you, if I may. When you're no longer living with the Mackays —once you're in your own house—I beg you to let me come sometime just to look at the portrait of my little sister, Melissa. I was only able to glance at it the night I visited your aunt, Natalie Browning, in Philadelphia—more years ago than I care to remember."

Mark stared at him.

"Yes, Browning, I was the man who tried unsuccessfully to—reason with your aunt. She was a woman of towering rage. I managed only a glimpse of my sister's portrait. I long for time to study the picture, to memorize Melissa's face—as she was at the end. Painfully beautiful, as I recall."

"Look here, Kott, I am deeply grateful to you for rescuing me during the fire. You well may have saved my life, but—"

"Allowing me to be present at your wedding," Osmund interrupted, "offering me the pleasure of seeing my little sister's portrait, would be the most effective ways of showing your gratitude."

Mark weakened for just an instant. "I—I suppose so," he said. "But you do upset Miss Caroline and I don't intend to allow that. We might as well be frank with each other, Kott. Since Caroline has been old enough to recognize such things, she's known how you tormented her grandfather."

"Your grandfather, too," Kott said evenly.

"I know."

"By the way, who told you?"

"Mrs. Cameron. But none of that concerns you, sir. Miss Caroline loved her grandfather with all her heart." Mark took a deep breath. "She's so upset by it all that she even believes that you had a hand in his death."

Kott chuckled easily. "I can tell how absurd you think that to be. It is, of course. Stop the hand that fed me for so long? Does Miss Caroline also believe me to be a fool?"

"Why did you leave Parsons's firm in New York? What are you doing here?"

"Roots. Roots hold a man, if he has any sense of tradition and family. By the way, why did you call your own firm in New York—Parsons's firm a moment ago?"

"That's my affair. But I'm sure if you did your work well for him, I could help get your old job back."

Osmund laughed pleasantly. "Anything to get me out of Savannah again, eh? No, thank you, Mr. Browning—Mark. I believe uncles do have the privilege of calling nephews by their Christian names. No, thank you, Mark. I'm staying here. I'm a native Savannahian. I intend to find work here—perhaps in your factorage. I shan't be a burden. I feel certain, although no one has notified me, that my father, Jonathan Cameron, remembered me amply in his will. Oh, not from devotion, but to save Miss Caroline further trouble."

"I can tell you that he did *not* remember you." Mark could have bitten off his own tongue. He had no right to tell this man anything about the will.

Shocked at what Mark had told him, Kott recovered quickly. "He—left me nothing, eh? Then, I *will* need a position in your firm. You will do well to see to it. I want only peace for you and Miss Caroline. A good paying post would bring with it my guarantee of that peace."

Feeling trapped, Mark waited before he said anything else for which he would be sorry. Parsons had written to Mackay that Kott had indeed done good work at the New York headquarters, but having Kott in their lives could make Caroline ill.

Mark stood there in the street helpless under the cool, courteous gaze. Why hadn't he followed Caroline into the house? He felt himself waver again. Kott's silent waiting drove harder than the threatening words.

William Thorne Williams still believed that time and decent treatment could change his uncle. If Kott could be helped, time might also lessen Caroline's fear. A surge of pity for the lonely, despised man before him rolled over Mark like a giant wave, leaving him weak, angry, wanting to help, but more aware than ever of why Caroline feared this man.

"I'm not a bad person," Kott was saying. "I'm rather a lost person. I need your help, Mark. You're all I have, you know. Even God has cast me off."

Aunt Nassie's remembered words came in a rush: "God casts off no repentant heart, Kott," he heard himself say. "I know you need help, but so far I haven't noticed a single sign of a repentant heart in you."

In the flat, white light of the full moon, Mark saw him look suddenly down at the ground. Once, twice, Kott kicked at a pinecone, as a nervous small boy might do.

"Did you hear what I said?" Mark asked. "You're too smart not to see how much you need to let God change you. But I see no signs that you want to be changed. I can tell you now, though, that I can't be blackmailed into a job."

"I heard what you said." Kott's voice was low, husky, with a strong hint of real—or faked—tears. "Indeed, I did hear you. And, well, I'm—stymied.''

"Stymied?''

"It's as though you've struck me in the face—a second time.''

"I felt no hostility toward you that night at the Scarbrough house," Mark said in what he hoped was a firm voice. "I feel none now, but there is no room for you in my life with Miss Caroline, and I have no notion of how I could help you. Only God would have the slightest idea of how to go about such a thing. That isn't sarcasm. It's a statement of fact.''

"You make me think of my old Savannah employer at the bookstore, Mr. William Thorne Williams," Kott said sadly. "He and I had long theological discussions in those days. Mr. Williams is the only man in Savannah ever to treat me with trust and kindness.''

Perhaps Thorne Williams could help him think of a way out of all this, Mark thought, grasping at straws. No. Williams would try, but Osmund Kott was no longer the gentle bookseller's problem. He was Mark's problem. "I wasn't thinking in terms of abstract theological discussions," he heard himself say. "I was thinking of you—and God—squaring off together.''

"You're a devout churchgoer, I know.''

"I don't enter into this one way or another. I was merely taught, and still believe, that God can change *anyone* who wants to be changed.'' Mark's bad leg was trembling. He was beginning to tremble all over.

"Even—Osmund Kott? Do you honestly believe, Mark, that God—if He exists at all—can change a man like me?''

Desperately, Mark wanted to get away, to hurry into the house. Something in Kott's voice held him.

"I beg you to answer me, nephew," Kott pleaded earnestly. "Do you honestly believe that God—can change a man like me?''

"Yes. I have no choice but to believe that.''

"No choice?''

"No choice.''

"Please, Mark, could you explain what you mean by that?''

"Well, I—I know how much trouble and sorrow and torment you've caused, at least for one kind old gentleman. I know only too well how you terrify Miss Caroline. I love her with all my heart. There is no way to blot out her fear of you, Kott, except for you—in time—to show her, to show me, that you have truly asked God to forgive you and have allowed Him to change you. As you are, there is no hope of anything."

Kott turned to stare into the empty street. For what seemed an endless time, he said nothing. Finally, still not looking at Mark, he said brokenly, "Do you suppose Mr. William Thorne Williams might give me back my old job?"

For purely selfish reasons, Mark's hopes rose a little. If William Thorne Williams, a man of true intellect and faith, had tried once to help Kott, he might indeed be willing to try again. Remembering his long-ago first visit to the bookshop on Bay with Mackay, he remembered also how well Kott had conducted himself, how knowledgeable he was about books. A perfect gentleman. Thorne Williams had told Mark later, after Kott had left the city, that he'd never had a more satisfactory employee. Had Thorne Williams, a devout man, ever mentioned to Mark that only God could change Osmund Kott? Was that why Mark had thought to bring repentance into this odd, moonlit encounter? He honestly couldn't remember. But, after a moment, he said, "I'll be glad to speak to Williams about you."

"No, oh, no," Kott protested. "I wouldn't want to trouble you. Williams is a gentleman. A man of the spirit as well as the intellect. Even though I left him rather abruptly to go north, I wouldn't hesitate at all to speak for myself." He held out his hand. "You've—struck me again, Mark. But somehow this time, for my good. I promise you I won't embarrass you at your wedding next week. I won't be there. I wish you would shake hands, though."

Mark held out his hand. His uncle's grip was firm and warm.

"Thank you," Kott said. "You've given me more to think about these past few minutes than I've had in all my fifty-three years. I'm deeply grateful."

Mark stood watching as the solitary man walked away, west on Broughton, into the shadows and out of sight. Then he went inside to reassure Caroline that Osmund Kott would not make trouble.

Reassuring her might help convince himself.

# FORTY-TWO

THE wedding took place without a hitch, except that Sallie, in her eagerness to keep pace with the bride as they moved down the aisle of Christ Church, stepped on the floating veil and ripped it. "But such a tiny rip," Caroline said later. "Who noticed? I felt it rip, but honestly, Sallie, I just wanted to giggle."

Because Mark had lost so much time from his counting-house while his leg healed, they postponed a wedding trip until September, when the weather would be cooler.

"But, you must go somewhere now," Eliza urged, when they were all home from the Washington Hall reception that night. "It just isn't right for us not to see you off—in some direction. What about a week at The Grange? The two of you?"

The old dread of being so near Knightsford flashed only briefly in Caroline's eyes. Eliza and Mark both noticed the look, but they also saw it leave. Two days after the wedding, the bride and groom set out in Mark's spanking new roomy sailboat—Mark handling the sails, Caroline at the helm.

They reached the Knightsford dock just before noon and were surprised to see Prince waiting.

"This is kind of you, Prince," Caroline said, her voice guarded, even with the servant who had looked after her all her life, "but how did you know we were coming?"

"Miss Eliza Mackay, she done sent a letter to Miss Ethel." He beamed. "Miss Ethel, she send many happy returns."

Caroline, stepping onto the dock before Mark could help,

432

narrowed her eyes at Prince. "You don't exactly lie, Prince, but you always make everything sound far better than it really is. What did my grandmother really say when she found out we were married—and that we were on our way to The Grange?"

Mark saw the old servant lower his eyes, clasp and unclasp his big hands. "She—Miss Ethel—she say that you—do well to get—Mister Mark Browning."

Caroline laughed. "Mark, that's a good omen. My grandmother and I *never* agree on anything. This is the very first time in my entire life. And"—she took his arm—"I do agree with her. Oh, how I agree!"

"Yes, ma'am!" Prince echoed.

Mark bowed. "You did indeed do well," he said with a grin, "almost as well as I."

"Yes, sir," Prince said, relieved and happy that they were both laughing. "Ain't nobody like Miss Caroline anywhere in the worl'."

"Can you believe I'm on my honeymoon, Prince?"

"No, ma'am! Seem like you oughta still be goin' fishin' with me."

The merest hint of uneasiness clouded her face when she said, "We—had hoped to slip in without anyone knowing."

"Oh, ain't nobody gonna come anywhere near The Grange," Prince announced, squaring his shoulders. "I see to it. Miss Ethel, she don't see nobody no time." He lifted their one small trunk from the boat and hoisted it to his shoulder. "Miss Ethel, she the same as ever."

"But, is she all right?" Caroline asked hesitantly.

"Same as ever. She be glad you marry Mister Mark."

"I'm sure she is. It must comfort her to know that I'll be living in Savannah from now on."

Plodding ahead of them up the river path toward the carriage Mark gave the Mackays so long ago, Prince called back: "Miss Ethel, she tell me nearly every day not to worry. When you say she have to leave Knightsford, she promise to take me with her to Baltimore, where she can stay with her niece, her dead sister's daughter."

Mark glanced quickly at Caroline. She was frowning, but since she did not return his look, he couldn't tell whether she was touched or annoyed.

"This Baltimore idea is all news to me," she said. "But, you may tell her, Prince, that she's welcome to stay on at Knightsford for as long as she lives. I have no plans for the place whatever. Grandfather did leave it to me, as I'm sure she's told you. My husband will continue as its factor, but she is welcome to stay. Will you give her that message for me?"

"Oh, yes, ma'am! I give it to her for sure!"

"Exactly as I've told you, Prince? None of your embroidery to make it sound better to her?"

When they reached the carriage at the head of the path, Mark saw Caroline look in the direction of the old cottage yard where Jonathan Cameron was buried.

"I tends his grave," Prince said softly, depositing the trunk in the carriage. "I tends it regular."

"Thank you," she said, then turned her attention busily to checking the boxes and bundles she and Mark had carried up from the river. That done, she went to Prince, shook his hand and thanked him again. "It's good to see you, Prince." Then, she gave him her sunny smile. "I'm one of the two happiest people in the world. The other one is my husband."

After Eliza's house servant, Grange Annie, served their dinner, Mark and Caroline went across the stubbly front yard of the modest cottage and down the path to sit awhile under their favorite oak by the river.

"Did you know Miss Eliza was writing to my grandmother, Mark?"

"No. I guess she felt it was only right to tell her about us."

"It was, I'm sure. We could have chosen a happier place for me this week. But I'm going to be fine. I promise." She sighed. "There is one thing I have to do, though, early tomorrow morning."

"Visit your grandfather's grave."

"Yes."

"You won't mind taking the chance that we might meet Mrs. Cameron on her morning walk?"

"Yes, I mind. But I have to go. I—want to tell him myself—about us." She had not looked at Mark since they sat down. Her eyes were still on the river. "Where do you suppose she walks now that the cottage is gone? For some stubborn rea-

son, she always circled it. Do you suppose she now circles—
his grave?''

Mark took her hand. "I hope—oh, I hope we haven't made
a mistake coming here, darling. If we left right now, we'd have
time to get back to town yet today."

"Don't pamper me! I'll be all right after I've visited Grandfather."

"Then why don't we go over there now? Annie's Solomon
can saddle the two Mackay horses for us. We can take our old
shortcut."

She looked at him, her eyes beaming with gratitude. "I do
want to go now, but let's go bareback!"

As the two horses pounded over the narrow road toward
Knightsford, Mark's thoughts flew back to the terror-filled
afternoon of Mackay's attack, when he and Caroline had ridden hard from Knightsford to The Grange. He could still
almost feel his own fear that day of losing his friend, his
desperation over Eliza. Then he found himself smiling at the
thought that Mackay, wherever he was this afternoon, would
surely be triumphant because Mark and Caroline were married
at last. The cheerful man had tried so hard to play Cupid.
Every remembrance of Robert Mackay was still good, buoyant, comforting.

Nearing the Knightsford road, they slowed, and suddenly,
Mark's thoughts of his friend shifted from mere memory to a
quiet certainty that at this moment—as they headed toward
the grave of Jonathan Cameron—Mackay knew. Knew how
far they would ride before reaching the grave, knew the
whereabouts this minute of the isolated old lady who would
undoubtedly be watching their every move from her high,
front window behind the upstairs porch.

At the edge of the mowed section of lawn nearest the old
loom house, which still stood—weather-gray and rickety—
they dismounted. Hand in hand, they walked slowly toward
the grassy clearing where the lone, graceful marble marker
stood, adorned by two pots of Prince's red geraniums.

Still hand in hand, they stood beside the now sunken spot of
ground where the charred body of Jonathan Cameron had
been placed. Caroline's grandfather—his grandfather—had

been tall and straight. The sunken area seemed incredibly small.

The marker was not new to Caroline. She had designed and ordered it herself and had it sent out from town:

JONATHAN CAMERON, Esquire
Master of Knightsford
1743–1818
". . . whosoever liveth and believeth
in me shall never die."

Mark, still unable to kneel because of his injured leg, stood close beside her as she knelt, bowed her head and closed her eyes. For a long, long time, she did not move a muscle. From the burned-off stump of the old pecan tree that had shaded Mary Cotting's house, a mockingbird experimented up and down the scale and finished with a quiet, low trill. Then, only silence filled the almost windless afternoon. Plantations were usually noisy places—dogs barked, roosters crowed, hammers rang, people laughed or shouted, babies cried from down at the quarters. Oddly, a silence had come. Silence that was not heavy, merely pervasive, broken only now and then by the ticking sound of a nearby cardinal and a light rattle of palmetto fronds somewhere behind them in the direction of the big house.

Was Ethel Cameron watching?

Caroline, still kneeling, reached for his hand. He grasped hers. She said nothing. The gesture had seemed for his sake, an endearing, small assurance for him that she was somehow making progress in her attempt to close this last door to her painful early life.

Irresistibly, Mark's gaze was drawn again toward the big white country house—straight to the window on the right corner of its second story, where he had heard Ethel Cameron's screams the day her husband burned to death. His eyes picked out the merest glint of movement at the window. He strained against the sun to see more clearly. Had a single beam of sunlight picked out the enormous diamond he had seen her wear? He was sure of it. He kept his eyes fixed on the window, wanting Ethel Cameron to know that he, at least, was remembering her, too.

With his free hand, he waved briefly. Perhaps she saw, perhaps not. At least he had waved.

In a while, Caroline got lightly to her feet. She was smiling. Tears wet her cheeks, but Mark knew that she had closed the door—perhaps even on her grief. Neither spoke as they mounted for the ride back to The Grange. No words were needed.

# FORTY-THREE

BACK in Savannah, after an idyllic week at The Grange, Mark worked in the yard with Eliza one late June evening while Caroline and the girls painted.

"Do your distinguished colleagues on Commerce Row knows that the successful Mr. Mark Browning spends so many evenings digging in the dirt with me?" Eliza asked.

He grinned. "I manage to get my fingernails quite clean by morning."

Mark pressed the soil down around the last leggy cosmos plant and stood up to survey what they'd done.

"If these don't fill out and bloom," Eliza said, half to herself, "it will definitely be our fault. We waited too long to set them out."

"Afraid so," he said, looking at the straggly plants.

Eliza stooped again to smooth the fresh soil with her fingertips. "I'm ashamed to be so late, but for such a long time after the fire, I had no heart for anything. Now, I'm too busy with community work to tend to my yard." Standing again, she gave Mark a rueful smile. "Those poor, burned-out folk, Mark. Life isn't fair, is it? We weren't even touched by the fire."

"Your heart was certainly touched," he said. "Are you sure you aren't working too hard remaking clothes, going house to house hunting the people in need? I worry about you, Miss Eliza."

"Don't, dear boy. Trying to be useful to other people is a widow's salvation." She glanced toward Mackay's porch chair. "I still miss him so much. People don't mention the word 'sympathy' to me anymore, of course—as they shouldn't. But it's like—yesterday to me sometimes. Those are the times when, if I didn't find something to do in a hurry, I'd sink up to my chin in self-pity." She brushed a damp lock of hair back from her forehead. "Don't waste one minute of your life with Caroline, Mark. Two people who love each other never, never have enough time at best. She's so happy, so radiant these days. I wonder how you can bear to leave her long enough to run your business."

He beamed. "It isn't easy. I just wish I could give you happiness, too."

"You do give me happiness! You both do. And someday, you'll have a child and my life will be just as enriched by it as it will be with my own first grandchild." She laid her hand on his forearm. "You've helped me make the bridge. You and Caroline. By the way, have you decided where you'll go on your real wedding trip? I know where Caroline longs to go."

"Philadelphia." He shrugged. "Not my notion of an ideal choice, but she's convinced me that she'd rather see the city where I grew up than take a trip to Europe or the West Indies or any other place. Needless to say, we're going to Philadelphia." On his knees again, he began to trowel fresh holes for another bucket of plants she handed him. "Is that row straight enough, ma'am?"

"Perfect," she said. After a brief silence, while he worked, she asked, "Any more word from Osmund?"

Still working, he said, "No. I'm thankful to say. He kept his promise about the wedding, anyway. He didn't come."

"Oh, Mark, I shouldn't have brought him up. But he is in the picture again, I'm afraid. The worst part about poor Osmund to me is that he's like trying to pick up a blob of quicksilver. You never know whether he's going to shoot—this way or that. Where do you suppose he's living?"

"I haven't the slightest idea. I've even asked around Factor's Row. No one seems to know."

"Why do you think you bothered to ask if anyone knew his whereabouts?"

He sat back on his heels. "Your quicksilver analogy, I guess. He doesn't seem to frighten me, but he does make me nervous."

"I can't imagine what I could ever do about Osmund, but

I'm always here—for you and Caroline—longing to help."

He smiled up at her. "Please, always be here, Miss Eliza."


On the fifth of September a vessel docked in Savannah from the West Indies, and within a day and a half, word had spread about the city like wildfire that five of the West Indian sailors had died and three more were desperately ill with yellow fever. Before the week was out, the killing disease had become an epidemic in the poor east end of town near abandoned Fort Wayne.

Townsfolk who had relatives elsewhere or plantations or money to get away began to leave the city in droves. When Mayor James M. Wayne had resigned in July for personal reasons, Mark's attorney, Judge Charlton, had once more given himself to the duties of managing the city. Now, while many aldermen took their families and fled the steadily spreading disease, T.U.P. Charlton stayed.

Mark and Caroline had booked passage for Philadelphia on September 15, but before they left, they saw Eliza and her children safely to The Grange to stay until the epidemic ended.

"Should I visit your grandmother while I'm out here?" Eliza asked Caroline as the Mackays said good-bye to the newlyweds at the Knightsford dock. "I confess I'm apprehensive about it, but I'll do what you want me to do, Caroline."

When she saw the change in Caroline's face, Eliza could have smacked herself for asking.

"Do as you like," Caroline said. "I've never had a suitable idea for—anything that has to do with my grandmother."

"I'm sure Mrs. Cameron's lonely," Mark offered.

"I expect I'll visit her," Eliza said, almost to herself. "I expect I'll—have to go."

"No need to give her any warning." Caroline's voice was curt. "She'll be dressed to the hilt already."


On board the *Valiant*, the Habershams' new name for Mackay's old schooner, the *Eliza*, the Brownings booked the same stateroom where Robert Mackay had cared for Mark more than eight years ago.

Lying in his arms on their third night at sea, Caroline, obviously still troubled at having been short with Eliza, said, "I have to thank you again for making me go back to give Miss

Eliza another hug the day we left them all at Grandfather's dock.''

"Are you still fretting over that little incident, darling? You know Eliza Mackay thought nothing of it.''

She pressed closer to him. "And, we are leaving all of Savannah behind, aren't we? Every minute the ship is in motion, we're moving farther and farther away from—everything back there.'' Suddenly playful, she tapped the end of his nose. "Can you—just for our wedding trip—put even Savannah behind you?''

"Yes, ma'am,'' he said and began to brush her mouth with his lips. "At least, I'll try. . . .''

Returning his kisses, she murmured, "I'm jealous of Savannah, I think.''

"You want to know the truth?'' he whispered, his hands and mouth caressing her. "The truth is that you make it difficult—for me to—concentrate on—anything—but you, when we're this close. . . .''

She held him to her. "Mark . . . oh, Mark! No one, no one in all the world is kissing you now—but me! Do you realize that? Only I'm here—only I'm here, kissing you, loving you. . . .''

The schooner dove and rose among the heavy waves of the sea, but in no time they were unaware of the ship's diving and rising. They were sweeping each other along—oblivious of all else—in the restless drive of their own free, wholly natural passion. The passion that had melded them—even against Mark's wishes—for so long.

"Each time I love you, I feel as though I've—come home,'' he breathed, when at last they again became conscious of the sea beyond them.

"You felt that way about Savannah, too,'' she teased.

He kissed her shoulder, her arm. "That's right. I did.''

"I am jealous of Savannah.''

Sighing contentedly, he rolled on his back. "You may have good reason to be.''

Caroline surprised him with a quick, hard kiss on the mouth. "Let Savannah try to kiss you like that!''

During the remainder of the voyage north, Mark talked to her freely about his early life, which seemed now almost to belong to someone else. In the privacy of their cabin, or on deck in the sunshine, he retold the tales he'd told Mackay of the good times as a boy with his childhood friends, but mostly, he spoke of the merry, always spontaneous times with Aunt Nassie.

"I wish she could be there waiting for us," Caroline said.

"So do I. But had she lived, I might never have come to Savannah."

"Do you believe that?"

"I guess not. Thanks to my father, I was in love with Savannah before I was ten years old."

After breakfast one morning, stretched on their stateroom bed while Caroline sat in the one comfortable chair, Mark was quiet for a time as he looked up once more at the dark-varnished ceiling of what so long ago had been Mackay's stateroom. How much had happened since then! How much had changed and yet how much was still the same, he thought. Lying on the same bed, staring up at the same ceiling, he marveled that on his first voyage down, he already loved Savannah, already felt so certain he had made the right decision. Mackay had called his complete break with his youth and home city—daring. It didn't seem daring to Mark then and certainly not now.

He looked at Caroline and smiled. "I love you," he said. Her eyes answered: *With all my heart, I love you.* Mark sighed contentedly and looked up again at the dark tongue-and-groove pattern overhead, his thoughts leaping to the new house he dreamed of building.

After a while, she asked, "Do you wish you could talk to Mr. Mackay about those two lots we like on Reynolds Square?"

Swinging his legs over the side of the bed, he sat up. "I think you do read my mind sometimes! I was thinking about our new house. Yes, I wish almost every day that I could talk things over with Mr. Mackay. But I have you now. We haven't mentioned the two lots we like so much for a whole day. Any new ideas? Do you still think we should settle on that spot?"

"I've never had any doubts about it. I like living close to the Mackays, and just think how fulfilling it will be to build our own beauty right where the charred ruins of those old burned-out houses are standing yet."

He gave her his sunny smile. "Still thinking of beauty from ashes, eh? Well, so am I. In fact, last night after you'd gone to sleep, I had a brand new idea. Miss Eliza says to this day there are so many poor people in town who have no means of buying or building or even renting homes for themselves. Their old homes are gone; they're crowded in with relatives or friends, many now sick with yellow fever. What would you say if we built a row of good, modest houses for a few of those folk? I'll give you the pleasure of deciding where. What do you think?"

She sat up straight. "I think it's the most wonderful idea even you have ever had! But how can they pay you if they don't have funds?"

"Some of them have enough to pay very low rentals, Miss Eliza says, but the low-rental properties are burned down—almost all of them. We'll keep our rentals at a bare minimum. The people who live in our row of houses wouldn't even know we own them. Judge Charlton can handle that part of it." He wasn't smiling now. "Caroline, you and I have always had plenty; we never wanted for material things. But my grandmother was an indentured servant. I don't forget that. I think we'd both enjoy our new house far more if, at night when we go to sleep, we could know that at least some of those homeless folk have their own places, too. At rents only high enough to protect their dignity."

She went quickly to sit beside him on the bed. "I knew it! I wasn't going to ask, but I knew you weren't thinking of a profit-making venture."

He looked surprised. "Oh, no. It—it would be something to —enjoy. For us, and I hope for them. We might tell Miss Eliza, but I don't see any reason why we have to let it be known at all."

"People would find out, though."

He shrugged. "Maybe not for a while. I guess we would need to tell Miss Eliza. You'll need her help in selecting the families really in need. Don't you think we'll be happier in our own new place—if we do that?"

She put her arms around him and whispered, "Yes, yes, I do." And then she began to laugh softly.

"What's so funny?"

"You."

"Why?"

"You seemed to be having such a good time talking about your own early life—your father, Aunt Nassie, your Philadelphia friends—and now look! Savannah is right back in the center of our conversation again."

He was laughing, too, returning her hugs.

"Tell me about Mr. Woodrow Woolsey. After all, we're staying in his house—if we ever get to Philadelphia."

"Oh, I think I've told you all there is to tell about old Woolsey. He's a proper Philadelphian. He reeks with dignity and aplomb. He thinks I'm entirely foolish to have signed three fourths of the company over to Parsons. But I like him and I'll be so proud to have him meet my wife."

"Does Mr. Woolsey have a wife?"

"Yes," he said uncertainly. "Aunt Nassie thought a lot of her. I confess I don't remember her too well. A shy lady."

"If there's nothing else to tell me about Mr. Woolsey, talk to me more about your father. I wish I remembered mine."

"You would have adored my father," he said. "I did. I wish I were as good to look at, for your sake."

She hit him. "Hush! I couldn't bear it if you were one scintilla handsomer than you are. Lean over—let me kiss your gorgeous, straight nose."

"Thank you, ma'am. I seem always to remember Father being perfectly tanned by the sun. He spent so much of his life on board ships."

"Trying to get over his broken heart."

"He never did."

"Darling, does it still seem strange and unreal to you that your mother—the woman this fascinating Browning man could never forget—was Osmund Kott's sister?"

"I don't think I've ever managed to take it in."

She thought a minute. "Osmund, repulsive as he is, wouldn't be such a problem if I could bear the sight of him. I can't help it. He scares me! I stop being me when I see him. I'm someone else!"

"I know, I know. But why do we have to talk about him today?"

"I guess I keep hoping that here, all alone on this ship, we can somehow untangle all the mixed-up things in our families that—could hurt us later."

He looked at her adoringly, tenderly. "Do you think that even *we* can untangle Osmund Kott or what to do about your grandmother in the few days we have left at sea?"

She got up abruptly. "We have no problem with her! I mean simply to let her live out her life at Knightsford and that's the end of it. We don't even have to see her."

"You're ignoring the fact that your husband is the Knightsford factor. I'll have to go there, often."

Caroline grabbed his hand and headed them both for the stateroom door, out into the narrow hall, up the stairs and onto the sunlit deck.

"That was sudden," he said as they went to the railing to look out over the ocean swells. When she said nothing, he added, "I think this is almost the exact spot where I was standing when that big wave knocked me flat—the day Mackay rescued me."

Ignoring that, she said, "Just talking about Osmund and my grandmother smothers me. I couldn't stand to be inside a minute longer."

"Caroline, do they know each other?"

"She must have known Osmund when he was a child. Before Grandfather took him to Bethesda to live. I don't think I've ever thought about whether they know each other or not. You forget that you knew the whole eerie story long before I did." Then, "Mark, why do you suppose Grandfather knuckled under to him all that time? Why was he so afraid of Osmund? My grandmother already knew about his illegitimate son and daughter."

"The old fellow was afraid of the city, I guess. No one there did know, evidently."

"Why did you ask me just now if Grandmother and Osmund know each other?"

"There's something I haven't told you," he said carefully. "Now, please don't be upset. Shortly after your grandfather died, Pos, his white overseer, quit."

"Pos *quit*?"

"With no notice. In fact, he'd been gone for nearly two months before I knew it. Matthew, your grandfather's driver, has been doing Pos's work. If Matthew could read and write, I'd keep him on—with your permission. He can't keep records, so I have to find an overseer. Outside the Mackay house that night, Osmund begged me for a job. James Parsons wrote that he'd done his work as supervisor of the vast Browning docks in New York almost flawlessly."

"I don't believe that!"

"Well, I do."

"Why?"

"Because I trust Parsons's word. He made a rich man of me. I trust his business sense completely."

"And you're thinking of asking my permission to make Osmund overseer at Knightsford." Surprisingly, the tone of her voice told him nothing.

"Yes, I am. But you don't have to decide today. We'll talk to Parsons together when we get to New York. That's a long time away. Philadelphia first. You're not to worry about any of this now."

"If you want to make Osmund Kott overseer at Knightsford, that's entirely your decision."

He turned her toward him. "You don't have anything at all to say about it?"

"Only that if he and my grandmother hate each other, it will serve them both right to be thrown together."

Mark, stunned by the intensity of her ill will, fell silent. Finally, he said, "That didn't sound like you."

"I know. It just came out. I doubt that I really feel that way, but, Mark, neither am I sure I don't. Those two people *tear me into little pieces.*"

"How about a walk around the deck?"

Her smile came slowly. But, it did come. Marking time as might a Chatham Artillery officer in full dress, she saluted him. Unlike Chatham Artillery officers, they held hands and marched around the deck, the wind blowing her dark, thick hair—and his.

# FORTY-FOUR

THE schooner was delayed by heavy Delaware River traffic when they attempted to dock in Philadelphia on the afternoon of September 21, but Woodrow Woolsey, lean, sandy-haired, bespectacled and fastidiously attired, was waiting with three servants as Mark and Caroline finally disembarked.

Woodrow Woolsey had always been "old Woolsey" to Mark—stuffy, impeccable, proper, well-bred, difficult to impress. Mark's dockside welcome back to his home city was enjoyable, if for no other reason than that for the first time, he saw something akin to awe on Woolsey's patrician face. The sight of Caroline, dressed from plumed hat to kid slippers in soft brown, brought the first stammer Mark had ever heard from the articulate lips of the senior partner of the venerated law firm of Woolsey, Capstan, Barlow and O'Brien.

"Wh-wh-what an altogether pleasant surprise, meeting—Mark's wife!" Bowing over Caroline's hand, he added, "I am simply delighted, Mrs. Browning. Simply *delighted*."

"Your pleasure is most evident, sir," Mark said with a proud smile as he and Woolsey shook hands.

Dinner in the high-ceilinged, richly appointed Woolsey dining room was epicurean, and, of course, Caroline charmed demure, petite Mrs. Woolsey, a wisp of a woman who seemed comfortable only when deferring to her husband.

Woodrow Woolsey had contributed to the financial needs of Savannah after the fire and seemed intent upon Mark's finding out what he could do to help now that the catastrophe-stricken city was in the deadly grip of yellow fever.

"Men are dying of it," Mark said. "I'm sure money to help in the support of their widows and children would be much appreciated."

"I know the Woolseys would be interested to hear about your new project, Mark," Caroline said, not looking at him, he knew, for fear he'd stop her. "So many of our poorer citizens lost their homes in the fire, you know," she explained, "and my husband told me on the voyage up of his marvelous plan to build easily affordable housing for some of them."

Mark caught Woolsey's uneasy glance. "Why don't we change the subject away from our poor city's difficulties?" he asked.

"Nonsense, dear. I'm sure the Woolseys will be deeply touched by what you mean to do."

Woolsey smiled benignly in Mark's direction. "Do tell us, Browning. After all, I'm no longer your financial adviser. Not that you ever took my advice anyway."

Mark laughed. "I doubt that you would approve my plan, sir. But, my wife and I are going to find at least two tithings of city lots and build a row of houses—sturdy but modest—for those who lost their homes in the fire."

"I suspected some such—"

"Foolishly benevolent gesture?" Mark teased.

"Yes. I suppose you will refuse even to collect proper rents," Woolsey muttered. "Or if you sell these houses, you'll make no profit."

"That's exactly right, Mr. Woolsey," Caroline said, smiling her most enchanting smile. "You know my husband quite well, don't you?"

"Too well," Mark laughed.

"To each his own," Woolsey said. "I see nothing ungenerous about seeing that your investment is returned, however."

"Oh, Mark will charge minimal rents. After all, we wouldn't want to embarrass those who need housing."

"Of course not," Woolsey said, clearing his throat.

A grin on his face, Mark looked directly at his host. "You see, sir, I'm still not a very shrewd businessman. But, things have worked out well, in spite of me."

"Because of you, I'd say," Woolsey sputtered. "If what I've learned of your success as a factor is true. But why stick only to factoring, Browning? Wasn't your Mr. Mackay a merchant, too?"

"Yes, sir. A fine one."

"More money in combining factoring and merchandising."

"Excuse me, sir," Caroline said, "but my husband just happens to like being a factor. He enjoys the personal aspect of caring for his clients beyond their business needs."

Woolsey cleared his throat again. "I'm sure he does."

"He really does so many fine things for his planters—so many things beyond marketing their crops. He looks after them all the way from lending them money to finding schools for their children in other cities—with places to board as nearly like home as possible." She paused. "You see, he was my—late grandfather's factor at the end of his life. I know firsthand of his skills."

"Yes, yes. I'm sure you do. I must say, Browning, I'm glad to see you with such a spirited wife."

"She is that, sir. The somewhat scared, nervous young man who left Philadelphia some eight years ago certainly needed spirit."

"You may have been scared," Woolsey said dryly, "but you were also stubborn. Still, any man needs a spirited wife."

Out of politeness, no one looked at shy little Mrs. Woolsey.

That night, just before they drifted off to sleep in the high, canopied bed in the Woolseys' guest suite, Caroline whispered, "I'm going to make a point of paying lots of attention to poor, overshadowed Mrs. Woolsey. I could weep over her! She just sits there and—cringes."

"Aunt Nassie worried a lot about her, too. Outside of me, I doubt that anyone mourned Aunt Nassie's death more than Mrs. Woolsey did. My aunt even made an Abolitionist of her!"

"Mrs. Woolsey—a radical Abolitionist?"

"I didn't consider Aunt Nassie radical."

After a long silence, she asked, "Mark, are you—an Abolitionist?"

He laughed. "I wasn't a member of Aunt Nassie's society, if that's what you mean. But I can't bring myself to own anyone, Caroline. Is that going to bother you?"

"How can we keep up Knightsford?"

"Your grandfather owned—and now you own—a hundred and forty-five people. Knightsford will go right on."

"But what about our house in the city? How does one run a household without servants? Mark, I can't even cook! I can do needlepoint, but I can't sew on a button. Miss Eliza taught me how to cut out little girls' dresses, but how can we run a house without servants?"

He snuggled against her in the bed beside him. "I thought we were both sleepy after all that sea air. I know I am," he said on a big yawn.

"Just answer my question about running a house without servants, please. I simply want to know—_how_."

"Didn't you think our dinner today was well prepared and served? Didn't that little Scottish lass do an expert job unpacking your trunks? You said she did."

"Yes, but we don't have many white servants in Georgia!"

"We have more and more immigrants—from Ireland, Scotland, Germany—every year. They're the poor folk who are right now plagued by yellow fever. There are free Negroes, too."

"I know, but wouldn't people think it awfully strange if we—Mark, I don't even know what I'm trying to ask you. I'm not upset. I'm just—mixed up."

He turned her over and snuggled to her back, spoon fashion. "One of us with a clear mind is enough for tonight. I'm very clear about loving you with all my heart and I'm very clear about being sleepy. Good night, Mrs. Browning. Happy honeymoon. . . ."

He felt her body soften and fit into his. "Good night, Mr. Browning. I hope I can wait to see you in the morning."

Keeping her promise to herself, Caroline spent most of the first day in Philadelphia with timid, nervous Myrtle Woolsey, who seemed never to lose her surprise that Caroline appeared to enjoy her company. Their husbands went into the city for the day and, of course, became the ladies' main topic of conversation.

"They've spent the morning, I'm sure, renewing old acquaintances of Mr. Browning's at my husband's firm," Myrtle said as she and Caroline sipped tea at the end of their luncheon of chicken sandwiches and watercress, beautifully served by the Woolseys' German butler, Johann. "They spent at least three hours at the Philosophical Society, where they dined. My husband is more at home at the Philosophical Society than here in his own house. He's most brainy, you know."

"But what are your interests, Mrs. Woolsey? What do you enjoy doing the very most of anything—aside from managing your servants, planning menus and so on."

"Oh, Mr. Woolsey manages the servants. He's such a good hand at it. He spends half an hour, by the clock, each morning with cook, and they plan what we'll eat. Cook does the shopping. Our cook is a Negro and it seems Negroes are most particular, especially about the quality of fresh produce."

"Excuse me if I ask a personal question, but do you pay your cook a regular salary and does she live here?"

"Yes, oh, yes. Woodrow pays the servants. He handles all that. And, yes, Marie has a large room on our third floor."

"I see."

"Now, Johann, our butler, has his own small house. Very nice, I understand, some distance away where rents are cheaper, of course. Susan, the Scottish girl who unpacked for you, lives in also. But, my goodness, why am I belaboring you with all this household talk? I'm talking so much!"

"I'm interested in your household—and in you."

She felt Myrtle studying her for a moment. "You honestly seem to be, Mrs. Browning," she said. "You really seem to be—interested. I'm just ever so glad you and your beautiful husband are here."

Caroline placed her teacup on a side table, went to Myrtle Woolsey and hugged her. "I'm glad we're here, too. And I quite agree—my husband is beautiful!"

The hug almost overwhelmed the frail, anxious lady. "My goodness," she gasped. "Thank you. I mean, I'm sure I shouldn't have used the word 'beautiful' to describe such a manly young—"

"Oh, no! You're absolutely right. I tell him to his face how —beautiful he is."

The thin mouth flew open. "Think of that! Just—think of *telling* him."

The next day, feeling they'd both shown their respect and

gratitude by spending the first full day with their host and
hostess, Mark and Caroline left, after breakfast, for their own
look at Mark's native city.

"This is what you've been waiting for," he said, taking her
arm and hurrying her down the Woolsey drive onto Third
Street. "You chose Philadelphia out of all the world, Mrs.
Browning, so let's go."

'Wait, Mark. Not so fast."

"I thought sure you'd want a full explanation of all the sites
in the cradle of liberty—right off."

"Oh, I do, but first, I need just to stand here on a famous
Philadelphia street and—feel. My own heart's love was a little
boy on this street!"

He laughed. "Well, your heart's love was a little boy on a
lot of Philadelphia streets, but he was born not quite two
blocks from here."

"Where? Oh, where?"

"We'll work our way toward the old Browning house on
Locust. That's Walnut Street there." He pointed a few doors
south where Walnut crossed Third. 

"How odd to give streets numbers for names when there are
such lovely words available."

"I suppose, but like Savannah, Philadelphia has a definite
plan."

He explained that the town had been laid out like a grid;
that the heart of the city formed where Market, running east
and west, bisected Broad and that streets bearing names ran
parallel with Market, numbered streets with Broad. He spoke
of Philadelphia's two rivers, the Schuylkill and the Delaware,
which led to the sea.

Looking around her at the handsome houses, she said,
"This little country girl will never be the same, will she? Will I
actually get to see Independence Hall and the house where you
were born, Mark?"

He laughed. "I'm glad you put them in that order."

They began to walk, Mark telling her what he remembered
of the owners and the history of certain old residences they
passed, of how he and Aunt Nassie, when Mark was four or
five, used to walk past the oldest bank in the nation and watch
as the handsome stone pediment was set in place. "It's a
private bank now, owned by a rich merchant and ship owner

named Stephen Girard. So far as I know, it's still called the Girard National Bank." He smiled down at her. "Do you wish I had a bank named for me?"

"I do not. *I'm* now named for you and that's fine with me."

They turned onto Walnut, where Caroline decided that the splendid mansion beside a small corner garden—the Bishop White house—was too large and too overwhelming for her taste.

"I think all these places are magnificent," she said, "but I honestly don't see any I'd like for us. I love Philadelphia, but some of these houses do overwhelm me."

"Good," he said. "I'm influencing you."

"Mark? Do we dare picture Savannah being—this way someday? Beautiful, sedate, prosperous, with lots of other people besides the Scarbroughs and the Davenports and the Richardsons and the Telfairs living in fine houses? Do we dare believe that even those who aren't very well-to-do will have good homes? So that Savannah will make a visitor feel its spirit—its history—the way I feel Philadelphia's right this minute?"

"That's one of my dreams," he said simply.

For a long, long time, when they reached Independence Square, Caroline stood looking at Independence Hall, its stately tower white in the autumn sunlight that glinted from the multipaned colonial windows. Mark waited.

"I'm—in awe of it. Just think, Mark, our country began here. They signed both the Declaration of Independence and the Constitution—right here!"

"It was built as the Pennsylvania Statehouse," he explained. "People here still call it that, but it's Independence Hall to me. I've often meant to ask Isaiah Davenport if he's ever seen it. I'm sure he has."

"He told us about Carpenters' Hall once," she said. "He must have seen this, too."

"You don't forget much, do you?"

"Not if it has anything at all to do with you—or where you were born. Mark, do you remember the toast Mr. Davenport made—the last toast of the long evening when President Monroe was in Savannah?"

He looked surprised. "Yes. Yes, I do. But no ladies were

present. How did you know about it?''

"You told Miss Margaret and me that night when you got home. I can even repeat the toast." Her eyes on Independence Hall, she solemnly quoted Isaiah Davenport: " 'To the union of our country. May the last trump alone dissolve it!' "

"Isaiah's a man of few words, but they ring true, don't they?"

"Have you ever thought what a short time ago our country was born? Miss Eliza was two years old when Independence came and she certainly doesn't seem old to me. All this is—so exciting! Take me to the house where you lived—right now."

All the way along Locust to the corner where the Browning mansion stood far back under its huge trees—farther back from the street than any of its wealthy neighboring houses—Caroline was quiet. When at last Mark stopped walking and said, "Well, there it is," she still said nothing.

They had been holding hands. She disengaged her hand and went slowly up to the tall, ornate iron fence that surrounded what must have been three to four acres of choice city property. Slowly, she reached toward the artistically forged spindles in the fence and began to move her hand along them one by one as she walked alone all the way to the last ornamental post beside the winding drive that led back to the great house itself. To Mark, the twenty-room brick mansion had always been—just home. He had never thought much one way or another whether he liked or disliked its vastness, its almost fortresslike dimensions—dark-red brick, the fourth story hidden in the autumn-dipped foliage of maples and oaks that stood around it. Houses were uppermost in his mind now and he studied it—the place where Brownings had lived for more than seventy years. The house his Grandfather Browning had built, never suspecting that he would sire only one son, who would lose his wife before he could perpetuate the name beyond Mark himself.

He glanced at Caroline, who, having touched every spindle in the long fence, was slowly walking back now to where he stood. She seemed unable to tear her gaze from the great house.

He smiled at her. "I like Independence Hall much better."

She hurried to him. "Oh, Mark, I thought Knightsford was a big house. Weren't you—scared, living here?"

"I don't remember it if I was."

"And did you used to go along as I just did, touching every spindle in that iron fence when you were little?"

They were standing in a public street. He could only touch her arm. "I might have. I don't remember now."

"We're—not going inside, are we?"

"I didn't inform the present owners."

"I wish we were on our way back to Savannah, do you?"

He gave her what he hoped was a reassuring smile. "Savannah's our place to be—for always." He gestured sweepingly, taking in the vastness of the Browning mansion and its winding drive. "This is all like something I—dreamed once, long ago."

That night, after Mark and Woolsey's somewhat disturbing talk of the financial panic that seemed to be imminent in the country, Caroline asked, when they'd gone to their own suite, "I wonder why Mr. Woolsey didn't use his gloomy financial forecasts to try to talk you out of building your row of Savannah houses for our poor people? He obviously doesn't approve."

Mark helped her unfasten the sapphire necklace that had belonged to the mother Caroline could not remember. "Woolsey just never approved of *me*. Come to think of it, he made no mention of the poor economy at all, did he, when he scoffed at the idea of our row houses."

"No, and you haven't said a word about the panic to me, either. Did you know about it before we left Savannah?"

"Oh, yes. There's been talk of financial trouble for weeks. I'd know about it, if for no other reason, because the price of cotton on the Liverpool market is down."

"What does it all mean?"

"Fewer jobs for those who need them most. Probably a somewhat lower return on Knightsford, for next year at least. I might get a few thousand less from the Browning Company if shipping drops, but we'll be fine, darling. Are you worried about it? Somehow I didn't expect you to worry."

"I was thinking about the McQueens. They just barely get by. And what about Miss Eliza? The Grange really isn't very productive yet, is it?"

"They're going to be all right, and I see no reason why we

can't go ahead and buy the city lots for our place and for the row houses—just as soon as we get back." His tiny frown deepened. "I confess I don't feel that confident about William Scarbrough, though. If the panic spreads, he could be wiped out. I wouldn't mention that to anyone but you."

"Oh, poor Miss Julia! I hate to think what bankruptcy might do to her."

He shook his head. "It's poor Miss Julia's taste and social ambition that have helped to bring down her husband."

She knelt before him and began to remove his boots.

"Say, I can do that, ma'am!"

"Hush. I feel so equal when I kneel before you, sir." She hauled off one boot and then the other. Without getting up, she asked, "Mark, did the S.S. *Savannah* ruin Mr. Scarbrough?"

"Like Julia, it helped. Sheftall was right. The whole idea was ahead of its time. There just isn't room aboard that ship for enough fuel to take it by steam across the Atlantic. Woolsey doesn't seem to think the *Savannah* was more than a rather colorful disaster, as far as profit is concerned. But with the price of cotton down to eight cents a pound, how can Scarbrough recoup his losses? Not only from the *Savannah*, but look at all the city lots he bought after the fire. I'm sure he intended to pay for those from the profits on houses he'd build to sell. How can he build houses if his credit is gone?"

She got up slowly and began to brush her thick, dark hair at the dressing table. "Oh, darling, women aren't supposed to be, I know, but I'm so interested in the whole financial world. Business is really—terribly important, isn't it? I mean, it not only has to do with vague things like Liverpool markets and banks and loans—it has to do with *people*. If Mr. Scarbrough has to take bankruptcy, Miss Julia might—have a seizure of some kind!"

"I hope he isn't close to anything so drastic," Mark said, watching her in the looking glass. "I do know the house Jay built cost Scarbrough over seventy-five thousand, about twice what he'd planned. Neither of them can resist owning the best."

She turned to look at him. "Do we only *think* we don't love possessions? Do you suppose you and I feel a little superior because we believe we care first about love and beauty and people? How do we really know that, Mark? We've never been tested at all. We've both always had so much of everything. When you showed me the Browning house today, all I could think was—Mark was born in a storybook castle!"

He thought a minute. "It's always been just—our house to me. What do you call the big Knightsford house? How does it seem to you?"

"Just—Grandfather's house."

"I'm glad you didn't seem to want to see inside the old place on Locust Street. I like my memories of it, just the way they are."

She sighed. "I wish I liked my memories of Knightsford. Oh, I do like remembering all the happy times I spent in Grandfather's room, but if he weren't buried there, I'd be in favor of selling it right out of the family when—she dies."

# FORTY-FIVE

AT The Grange about sundown, Jack answered a knock at the Mackay cottage door, open to the clear, early October weather.

"Good evening," Osmund Kott said cordially, his spotless white linen shirt open at the throat. "You're Jack Mackay?"

"That's right, sir." Jack was instantly sorry he'd called him "sir." "What do you want, Kott?"

"I'd be much obliged if I could see your mother."

"State your business."

"A pleasant visit is all. I'm stopping for a few days at Knightsford. It's a fine evening and I thought—"

"Just a minute." Jack closed the door and hurried to the small parlor, where Eliza had been reading aloud from Jane Austen's novel *Pride and Prejudice*.

"Who's at the door, dear?"

"It's that Kott fellow, Mama," Jack whispered. "He wants to have a 'pleasant visit' with you, so he says. What'll I tell him?"

A frown creased her forehead. "Tell him I'll receive him here in just a minute. All of you scoot." She addressed the children. "Only Jack and William will please stay nearby—in the kitchen will be fine." As they all filed out silently, she smoothed her skirt, took off her glasses and laid aside the book.

In no time, his hair well groomed, his lean face cleanly shaved, Osmund Kott stood in the parlor doorway. He bowed.

"Please come in," she said.

"Thank you, Mrs. Mackay. May I take this chair?" He pointed to Mackay's old tapestry armchair.

"I suppose so, yes. What may I do for you?"

"I need your help."

She stiffened. "I fail to see how I'm in any position to help you, Mr. Kott."

"I remember you always called me by my first name, what few times we've spoken over the years, Mrs. Mackay." He glanced down at his informal, but neat, clothes. "I guess my having worked at a good position in New York for a time, returning decently attired, does make a difference."

Eliza gave him a penetrating look. "Most sincerely, I hope *you* are different, Osmund."

"That's really why I'm here. You see, I'm working again, for the present at least, with that splendid Christian gentleman Mr. William Thorne Williams."

"I'm glad to hear that, but I fail to see—"

"Your—boarder, Mr. Mark Browning—"

"Mr. Browning is not a boarder. He's been like a member of our family for many years."

"I understand. At any rate, I talked with him out in front of your town house one night not too long ago and he—meaning only to be cutting me down to size, I'm sure—informed me that only God could help me. But he added that God could do just that."

"I—see." Eliza prayed silently for insight and, above all, wisdom. Osmund was clever and would as soon distort Mark's words as to sit there giving her that earnest look.

"You do see?" he asked eagerly. "Do you know what Mr. Browning meant by that?"

"Yes. I believe I do. God can—does—change us."

"I've not had a happy life. I've known only trouble through almost every year of it."

"You've—also made trouble."

"Yes. I most certainly have. But after more than six years in a responsible supervisory position in New York, Mrs. Mackay, I see the folly of my old ways. I like responsible living now." He held out his slender, well-shaped hands. "I truly want to be different, from now on. Mr. Browning suggested that I speak with Mr. Williams at the bookshop. I did that and now have my old job back. But after so many years in a better position at the North, I long to find a more fruitful work than Williams can offer me in his small establishment.''

"I don't see where I enter the picture."

"Only as a—spiritual guide."

Eliza gave him a severe look, one in which she was sure both her mistrust of him and her pity showed. Carefully, she asked, "A—spiritual guide?"

"Yes, ma'am, if you please. I so much want to become a communicant of Christ Church. Browning's church. Mr. Williams's church. Our best church, in my opinion."

"And what does Mr. Williams say about your—desire to enter the Church?"

"He urges me to go on with my study of the Bible, to pray, to learn more about the things of God for one year and then let my desire to become a communicant be known."

"I—can't think of any better advice."

"But you can promise to pray for me. You're known in the city as a genuine Christian, Mrs. Mackay. Not one who hides behind her piety, but who lives lovingly. If any man on this old earth ever needed prayer, I'm that man. Have you ever—prayed for me, ma'am?"

Stunned, Eliza cleared her throat, waited a moment, then answered truthfully: "No, I have—never prayed for you. I've known for most of my life of your—troubles, but I've never prayed for you. I certainly don't understand you. I probably never shall, but God does. I will pray for you from now on."

It had been dark for nearly half an hour when Osmund Kott rode up the oyster-shell drive under the great trees to the front door of Knightsford, dismounted and knocked firmly.

The door swung back and Prince admitted him without expression.

"Miss Ethel, she be waitin' for you in the parlor."

"*Sir,*" Osmund corrected.

"Sir," Prince said.

"Thank you, Prince. I'll go right in."

From her usual place on the edge of the black-and-gilt settee, Ethel Cameron greeted him with: "How did she receive you?"

"With courtesy, of course," he said. "We didn't expect less of Eliza Mackay, did we? May I sit down?"

She waved one thin, jeweled hand absently toward a cane-backed chair. It was no surprise to Kott that Ethel Cameron preferred no one to be truly comfortable in her presence. He took the chair.

"Exactly what did you ask of Mrs. Mackay?"

"That she pray for me."

He saw a faint smile work at the corners of her mouth. "And will she?"

"I have her promise and, of course, a valid reason now to call on her again before the Brownings return from the North."

"When are they expected?"

"Rumor has it in late November, if the yellow fever has subsided in town." He smiled. "So, you see, dear lady, we have ample time for God to do His work."

She did not smile. "It would be well for you to remember, Osmund Kott, that I, too, read my Bible and pray twice a day. It is well for you to remember also that no man dare attempt to—fool God. It matters not at all about fooling Eliza Mackay or Mark Browning. God? No."

"My dear lady—"

"My name is Mrs. Cameron."

"Mrs. Cameron," he began earnestly, "I am serious about my pursuit of God. I mean to be the Knightsford overseer, an enormous responsibility, the dispatch of which can be carried out only by a steady gentleman." He smiled again. "One who is not only capable, but who has excellent connections for disposing of portions of the Knightsford crops in Charleston. I have even arranged for loading our stolen portions of the crops under the cover of darkness. I will, of course, once Browning has put me in charge, handle the packing of bales, so that a good heavy ballast rock at the center of each bale will—"

"Enough! I don't want to know any details concerning your—chicanery, *Cotting*. I care only about my share of what you manage to make for yourself!"

He had never given her the pleasure of knowing that he'd long ago caught on that when particularly irritated with him, she called him by his mother's real name, Cotting. He ignored it now. "You can leave all details in my hands, Mrs. Cameron."

"I intend to do just that." She bit off her words. "I have no choice. My selfish granddaughter owns Knightsford. Only God knows what she really means to do with the plantation —with me. I know what she claims, but what reason have I to believe her?"

"Unlike me, she's partly *your* own flesh and blood," he said evenly.

She stood. "That's enough! You will never again make reference to such a thing in my presence. Is that clear?"

Standing, too, Kott bowed. "Very clear, Mrs. Cameron."

"Watch yourself with Eliza Mackay. She's no fool. By the time the Brownings return, she must be deeply interested in your spiritual welfare. I don't care a fig for it, Kott, but I do need you here as overseer. You need to be here. In war, allies don't always share devotion—only need of each other."

"Mrs. Cameron, if you heard even a little of the talk in town about the financial panic ahead in the whole nation, you'd be still more convinced that we need each other. The panic could even depress young Browning's vast wealth. Your granddaughter worships him. We need to act on my Charleston connection at once. She'd sell Knightsford out from under you at the snap of a finger if Browning needed money."

"Dear God," she breathed. "It's worse than I thought. *If* you're not lying."

"I swear to you I'm not. And, we both hold excellent blackmail hands with each other," Osmund went on, only his lips smiling. "You still have my letter, delivered the day the cottage burned. That's your hold over me. I wrote the letter; you kept it all this time. That's my hold over you. Dear Mrs. Cameron, we can both sleep soundly tonight and every night until I move safely into your overseer's cottage."

After a dinner of roast rack of lamb, English peas and countless other harvest vegetables, heavyset, affable James Parsons, his deeply lined face nearly always intent, sat with Caroline and Mark in the torchlit formal garden at the rear of his New York town house. For over an hour, Caroline had perched on the edge of a wrought-iron chair, listening to the business talk with total attention.

"From my extensive travels," Parsons was saying, "I believe I have a wider view of the world economy—of our own national economy, for that matter. I see the current depressed state as temporary. Perhaps a year or two and then things should improve."

"For the sake of planters in the South," Mark said, "I certainly hope so. You haven't been south, sir. Those with limited cash, in the face of such high shipping costs, are on shaky ground. Many of them can't wait a year or two for things to improve."

Parsons chuckled. "Always the fault of the hard-nosed Northerner, isn't it, Browning? Always the fault of the infernal opportunist who owns the ships—your grandfather, your father, now you, me." He leaned toward Mark. "Are we Northerners really so bad? Our costs are going up. As industry expands up here, machines must be bought. You'd never believe the money the Browning Company spent last year alone on new winches. Ships cost three times what they once did because wages rise and tools grow dearer. We're at the start of an industrial age. Industry will eventually lower costs, but not yet."

"And, the South is still agrarian."

"It will always be agrarian," Caroline put in firmly.

"You may be right, Mrs. Browning, for this century at least," Parsons said, not at all annoyed at her touch of defiance. "That fact divides us as a nation, too, in a way. And that's unfortunate."

"We dare not let anything divide us," Mark said. "And yet, I can give you an example of how devastating your Northern shipping charges are to a Southern planter. As this planter's factor, what happened to him the past year nearly broke my heart."

Parsons grinned. "Broken hearts and business don't mix, Browning."

"But, human beings are still involved, sir. This client, who owns cypress timberland, makes excellent hand-hewn shingles. For a long time I've had the unpleasant task of reporting that his shipping charges to the North were costing from twelve to twenty percent of his gross sale. But last year, when I arranged shipment for seventy-four thousand shingles, which sold for two hundred forty-three dollars and thirty-one cents, the shipping cost him one hundred seventy-one dollars and sixteen cents—leaving him a mere seventy-two dollars and fifteen cents profit for the year!"

"I sympathize, but that undoubtedly helped you and me.

Those shingles may well have traveled north on a Browning boat."

"They did, sir."

"Excuse me, Mr. Parsons," Caroline said, "but what's a Southern businessman to do? We have a friend who's overextended his credit—a brilliant, normally successful merchant who would, under ordinary circumstances, recoup with the next crop, but—"

"You inadvertently answered your own question, Mrs. Browning. He overextended his credit." Parsons smiled. "That isn't your husband you speak of, is it?"

Mark laughed. "No, sir. In fact, I've been accused of being too cautious. You may not believe this, but I've invested only five thousand dollars of all the money you've sent me so far."

"Was your investment a good one?"

"We don't know yet, but I'm doubtful. I was one of the smaller investors in the steam-powered S.S. *Savannah*."

"Sorry to hear that," Parsons said. "But glad your loss will be minimal. Scarbrough had a progressive idea, but just not feasible yet. I've kept up on the whole thing. They went only a small part of the way across the Atlantic on steam. Just no way worked out yet to carry enough fuel for such a distance. Too bad. More coffee, Mrs. Browning?"

"No, thank you. My husband and I did a lot of walking around New York today. I think we should get back to our hotel."

"One question before we go," Mark said. "One very direct question. Please answer me freely. My wife knows the whole story. Did you have any trouble with Osmund Kott when he worked for the firm here?"

"Not in the least! I expected it, too, after the problems he tried to cause your father—long before you went to Yale, Browning. I took Kott on, frankly, hoping to save you trouble —or embarrassment—with him in Savannah." He turned to Caroline. "Your husband, as I'm sure you know, has been more than generous with me. I took Kott on as a stevedore. Within a year, he was my dock supervisor."

"And you didn't have—any trouble with him?" Caroline asked, her eyes wide with disbelief.

"None whatever. Not a minute's trouble—until one day early this year, he just left town. I hope he isn't in Savannah now." When neither answered immediately, Parsons said, "I gather he's there."

"Yes, sir," Mark answered. "He is."

"Working for you, Browning?"

"No," Caroline said sharply. "Excuse me, Mark. I know Mr. Parsons asked you, but—" She looked at Parsons. "He's —after my husband for a position," she explained, her voice tense, uneven. "My husband wants to make him overseer of the plantation my late grandfather left to me. Frankly, I'm afraid of him, sir. My husband doesn't seem to be, but I am!"

Holding up one pudgy hand, Parsons said, "I have no intention of interfering where I don't belong, but you did ask my opinion, Browning. I can tell you both that while Kott was here, he was far more than satisfactory. I don't like him, but I believe he could do almost anything he set his mind to."

Mark stood and helped Caroline to her feet. "We won't forget your kindness to us, Mr. Parsons. I owe you a great deal. If you're ever in Savannah, we'll want so much to return your hospitality."

"My pleasure." Parsons stood, too. "So, you're off to Newport tomorrow?"

"That's right," Mark said. "For a month at least. We'd hoped for a letter while we were here saying Savannah's yellow fever epidemic is over. None came. Perhaps there'll be one at Newport."

"You may hear yet. Your boat doesn't sail until right after noon tomorrow. There's a good chance your letter could arrive first thing in the morning. We're expecting three ships from Savannah before one o'clock."

The next day just at noon, Mark escorted Caroline to their stateroom on the Newport schooner, then went ashore to make sure that their extra trunk—filled with gifts—had been put aboard. On his way back to the boat, he was paged and a clerk from Parsons's office handed him a letter. It was from Eliza.

The Grange
13 October, 1820

Dear Mark and Caroline,

Except for an unexpected visit from Osmund Kott,

our days pass uneventfully. The children are all well,
thank God, and William and Jack, now so grown up,
appear content to spend their days with the girls.
William seems especially content since pretty little
Virginia Sarah Bryan is visiting Eliza Anne and Kate.
Virginia is so young, but in spite of William's shyness,
I detect his awareness of her unusual delicacy and
beauty. Some of this is difficult for Jack, who insists
that he needs his brother to handle the boat for
his fishing and finds him too often more interested in
gathering flowers with his sisters and their house guest,
Virginia. I am all right and give thanks to God every
night that my wonderful husband bought The Grange.
We know the land is not making much money, but the
soil needs years of reworking still. The best factor in
the world is a member of my family, so I do not really
worry.

I am sure you are both on needles and pins to know
about my visit from Osmund Kott. He reported, Mark,
that you had told him that only God could change him
from his nefarious ways. I was stunned when he stated
that he had come for one purpose only—*to ask me to
pray for him.* He is either quite sincere or up to his old
tricks again. God forgive me if I judge the man
wrongly. He said that he is staying at Knightsford, but
where, I cannot imagine. I may have to pay that visit,
Caroline, to your grandmother, and God will have to
forgive me again because now I'm sure my motives are
mixed. Osmund wants very much to become overseer at
Knightsford. *What will he think of next?* I am praying
much for God's guidance, should Osmund visit me
again. I want to feel justly toward him, but he
makes me shake like a leaf.

Your new young clerk, John Johnston, brought supplies last week, Mark, and reports that he had written a
letter to you concerning your business, which is, in
spite of the fall in cotton prices, satisfactory. He also
brought much news of happenings in the city. The poor
foreigners and locals are still dying from yellow fever.
Your clerk says that of over seven thousand people in
town, fewer than two thousand remain and that over

three hundred houses stand empty—as does our dear home. I am so glad to have all our people here at The Grange with us in safety. Savannah was hit by a severe storm on 1 October, and the next day Mayor Charlton was asked to deliver a spirited address urging everyone still in town to collect leaves and berries fallen in the storm and to carry them to the common for burning. It is believed that the fever lurks in these fallen leaves and berries. Judge Charlton and a few aldermen remain to help in every way. Your clerk also tells me that the new synagogue is well along and that Mr. Sheftall is busy with that. William Jay stays in the city, devoted to his architectural calling. The Telfair mansion progresses, as does the Bulloch house. William Jay and Alderman Isaiah Davenport have been bickering both privately and in Council meetings. It seems Jay does not always keep the streets clear of his building materials or some such. The Davenports have moved at last into their splendid new home on State, and I long for the pestilence to end so that I may visit.

I also long to see both of you again. When you return, we will have to attend Robert's Presbyterian Church because a most talented young man named Lowell Mason has been named church organist. He is also a fine composer.

We are eager for your return, but beg you to wait for word that the fever has run its course. I know you are happy. I pray you are both well and we all send love.

As ever,
ELIZA MACKAY

# FORTY-SIX

THE narrow streets and colonial houses rising steeply from the blue harbor at Newport enchanted Caroline. Their hotel, which overlooked Narragansett Bay, was comfortable and well located for long walks about the quaint town and convenient for the extensive shopping they planned. Taking gifts to all the Mackays and their people from each place they stopped had all along been their goal. If they selected carefully in Newport, the new trunk might hold everything.

Caroline was especially delighted when Mark found the old toy shop still run by the same aging gentleman who had sold him and Aunt Nassie a cherished red cart with iron horses when Mark was a small boy.

"It's almost as though you were a child back there with me," he told her one bright blue morning as they sat on the wide hotel porch. "We've seen Philadelphia and New York together—now Newport—I'll never have to come back again."

She looked up from a letter she was writing to Cousin Margaret. "But I want to come back—often!"

"We will, don't worry. I wasn't saying anything profound or mysterious. It's simply as though you've joined me now, all the way back to my childhood. You've gathered up all the loose threads and worked them into a fine new pattern that has to do only with us." He reached for her hand. "Everything is of a piece now—the past, the present, the future. I hope I can do that for you someday at Knightsford."

For a moment, she looked out over the sparkling bay. Then, a little wistfully, she said, "I hope so, too."

On the delayed wedding trip, Mark had had ample time to

think—to look back, to look ahead. Caroline, thank heaven, allowed a man time for his own thoughts. With her, he'd never felt obliged to keep up a lively conversation. He remembered telling Mackay on the first voyage to Savannah that he didn't yet know himself. He smiled a bit at the memory. Today, under the clear, high Newport sky, two years away from his thirtieth birthday, he realized that undoubtedly he had merely been like every other young man entering his twenties, tending to dramatize his dreams a bit, to puzzle with far too much seriousness over his so-called real self.

Had he, indeed, now found himself? Did he understand himself any better? He felt no pressing need to find answers, and that undoubtedly meant he had matured. There were certainly some constants in his life. He had known, before his twentieth birthday, that a strange, still unseen, coastal Georgia city was to be his city. Savannah remained a constant. Rising in his family's important shipping firm had never been a goal. That had not changed. He was content, even fascinated, with factoring. Thanks to Robert Mackay, he had learned how to be a friend, how to be a living part of an honest-to-goodness family. Needing, wanting a family of his own had been a constant. He and Aunt Nassie had done their best for each other, but Mark had always pictured himself, at the end of a workday, climbing the steps of his own home, eager to see his own wife and his own children.

Looking back now, he wondered why it had taken him a whole year alone in the vast, dark Browning mansion to make up his mind to head for Savannah and his own life. Only this morning, in the sun on the hotel porch, did he remember that he had once posed the same question to Jonathan Cameron. "Grief, my boy," the gentle voice had responded without a moment's hesitation, "paralyzes a man for a time. It's like being stuck in the sand. Then, slowly, we begin to move again, to act."

He looked at Caroline, intent upon her letter to Margaret McQueen, and wondered if he should tell her what her beloved grandparent had said. A wave of lingering guilt swept the thought aside. Mark, so stubbornly in love with Eliza Mackay while Caroline had been working her way through those first paralyzing weeks of grief, had not helped her at all. He had been relieved, in fact, when this tender, almost unbearably lovely girl had fled to Causton's Bluff so as not to cast the shadow of her sorrow over him, Eliza, the children. Today, for the first time, he thought to ask God to forgive him for having failed Caroline when she needed him most. He had never even thanked the McQueens for giving Caroline love and shelter. He asked forgiveness for that, too, and vowed to do it once they were back in Savannah.

Savannah. Does God really care where on a map we live? Had God freed him to make what Mackay called the daring move to the city his father had loved so passionately? Surely, it would have taken an act of God to keep Mark away from Savannah, once the sharp edge had worn off his grief. Today, he also seemed to understand why Mackay had thought it strange that he did not press the search for his mother's family soon after he reached Savannah. Learning the facts from Ethel Cameron had stunned him—had brought what had always been the fantasy of a lovely face in a portrait to stark reality—but he had been able to place it all where it belonged, in the irrevocable past. And out of it, there was Caroline.

He looked at her for a long time and then the thought struck: Perhaps what was required of him now was to help her lose her dread of Knightsford and put the ugly, dark past of Knightsford in her past. What she faced was far harder than grief over the dead. There was a clean finality about death. Her difficult grandmother still lived. Somehow, he meant to help. Mark himself had begun to love Knightsford, although he had spent so little time there. Its history held part of his own roots. He was no less a Browning, but he was Jonathan Cameron's grandson. Caroline had become a Browning and he had become a Cameron. They were one. Mark was enjoying their visit to Newport as much as she, but—he smiled to himself—only a few more days and they'd be heading *home*. To his city. Maybe, after all, being himself, in his own place, mattered far more than being either a Browning or a Cameron.

His thoughts had just turned to lonely, isolated Ethel Cameron—who apparently loved no one, whom no one loved—when Caroline began to fold the pages of her finished letter.

"A kiss for your thoughts, sir," she said with a smile. "Although I really can't pay you out here in broad daylight."

"I'll make a note of your indebtedness, ma'am. Do you

really want me to tell you what I was thinking?"

"Of course."

"My mind had just gone to—your grandmother, all alone out there by the river."

Her smile vanished. "It's just as well that I interrupted," she said in the clipped, almost cross voice she invariably used when Ethel Cameron was mentioned. "The best, the only way to contend with Grandmother is—not to think about her at all."

"I don't honestly believe either of us can do that. Doesn't the poor old woman haunt you now and then?"

"Of course she does! Knightsford haunts me, too. I don't know why you had to bring it up."

"Isn't there some way we can learn how to—discuss Knightsford and Mrs. Cameron without—"

She jumped to her feet. "Without causing me to begin to snap like a turtle?"

Mark went to her, took her hand.

"I *do* snap when you bring her up. And, Mark, I know, once we get back to Savannah, she and Knightsford both have to be dredged up and dredged up! I know that. You're the Knightsford factor. We own it. There are decisions we both have to make. I wish I didn't snap. I'd give anything to be able to stop!"

"I promise we won't think of one other thing for months— but our new house."

"You can't promise that."

"Yes, I can. At least until planting time, we'll concentrate only on our master builder, Isaiah Davenport, and"—he smiled—"beauty from ashes."

She laid her hand on his. "I'm really going to try to be— better."

"I know that," he said gently. "With all my heart, I count on you—being *you*."

"Oh, Mark," she whispered, "what if I'm—just not enough?"

At the start of the second week in November, Mark's clerk, Johnston, came in person to The Grange with the good news that Eliza and the children could safely return to Savannah. There had been no new cases of yellow fever in more than a fortnight. On the day before they were to leave, the children —not at all glad to leave the carefree outdoor life at The Grange—were fishing for the last time. Back in the city, Jack and William would have to find work and the girls would be held more strictly to lessons.

Eliza, Hannah and Emphie spent the last full morning in the kitchen mending and packing clothes as fast as Grange Annie brought them, sweet-smelling, from out back. Hannah and Emphie, condescending in their status as town house servants, made no effort to hide their triumph that they were at last returning to what they called "society." Both women sang at their work, stopping only now and then to praise the Lord that their time in the country was almost over. Flaunting their privileged positions over Annie only made her every entrance with a stack of clean laundry haughtier than the one before. She, too, felt superior. After all, as she declared to Eliza, as though the other two women weren't in the kitchen at all, "Anybody trusted to be in full charge when the mistress is away most of the time is high up!" Her last load deposited on the big kitchen table, Annie looked down her aquiline nose at Hannah and Emphie. "*Some* folks needs a mistress on top of 'em every minute!"

"Some folks wouldn't know how to behave in town," Hannah declared. "Some folks 'bout have to be kep' in the country!"

A knock on the front door relieved Eliza of having to attempt to soothe prickled feelings. She hurried along the center hall to answer it herself.

"Good morning, Mrs. Mackay," Ethel Cameron said, smoothing an imaginary wrinkle from the long, full skirt of her ribbed bottle-green silk. "I hope I'm not intruding."

"Please come in," Eliza said, leading her into the small, somewhat crowded parlor. "You won't believe this, but I had planned to visit you this very afternoon!"

"Interesting."

Touching Ethel Cameron's silk-clad elbow, she directed her to the more comfortable of two old chairs.

"We're leaving first thing tomorrow," Eliza explained, taking the other chair, "and—well, I was hoping to pay a call on you today."

"So you said."

"I—I'm ashamed that I've stayed so busy that I haven't called on you long ago. I—"

"Never mind thinking of an excuse, Mrs. Mackay. When a woman has been shunned for as many years as I—even by normally warmhearted people such as yourself—no explanation is necessary." She motioned in protest. "And no, I don't care for tea. I don't make social calls, as I'm sure you know. I've made no calls at all since the last time I was here, in fact. The day I brought the little volume of Shakespeare sonnets for young Mr. Browning. I trust he received it safely."

"You didn't hear from him? That isn't like Mark at all. He's the soul of courtesy."

"Undoubtedly he wrote, thanking me. Mr. Cameron was still alive then. I'm sure the note was deliberately destroyed before it could reach me."

"I see."

"I doubt that you do, but that is no longer important."

After an awkward silence during which Ethel Cameron kept her eyes steadily fixed on the river outside, Eliza said, "Mark and Caroline have had a splendid trip. I expect them back in Savannah by the end of the month. Mr. Davenport's promised to have plans for their new house ready when they return. He also promised to begin building just as soon as Mark has purchased the lots."

"They do intend, then, to—live in the city."

Eliza sensed something like relief in the dry, brittle voice. "Yes, Mrs. Cameron. I supposed you knew that."

A powdery, yet grating, sound—a laugh—escaped the ancient throat. "I have not seen my granddaughter since the day she left Knightsford after the burial of my husband." She glanced briefly at the carpet. "Well, that isn't quite true. From my bedroom window, I saw the two of them at—his grave one morning. I understand that was soon after their marriage."

Eliza's sudden pity for this isolated woman kept her from answering immediately, and Ethel Cameron filled the silence.

"I do wish you'd stop pretending you think that Caroline and I have what people would call a natural relationship. You know perfectly well that we do not. We've never had it. She has—tolerated me for all the years of her life because of—him. Now, stop your sympathetic frowning. I need no sympathy. I merely need you to use your influence with Mr. Browning."

"In what way?" ·

"Knightsford is without an overseer. The driver, Matthew, a capable but illiterate Negro, is running the entire operation now. To allow such a condition to continue on land as rich and productive as Knightsford is, to say the least, slovenly business. A kind of carelessness I frankly wouldn't have expected from Mr. Browning."

"I'm not conversant with any of these problems," Eliza said firmly, "but I'm sure Mark is not neglecting your plantation, Mrs. Cameron."

Eliza plainly saw the thin, nearly white lips tremble. "Knightsford once belonged to my family—half of it, at least. Not one blade of grass nor one grain of rice nor one boll of cotton now belongs to me. Knightsford is the property of my granddaughter, who loathes me!"

"That's not true! Caroline is—"

"Don't tell me what she is. I know her. Even as a child, she turned that bewitching beauty on me and for a time, I succumbed to it. I—had a kind of unexpressed affection for her as a child. After all, she is the daughter of *my* son and his lovely wife. Caroline is *my* own flesh and blood. But for all her years on earth, she was *his* tool. He used her to placate, to manipulate me to his liking. She is, sadly for her, *his* flesh and blood, too. She loathes me now. She's loathed me for years. What I might want or need would be just exactly what she would refuse to do now that she owns Knightsford."

Eliza kept silent. Tears, foreign to that expressionless, enigmatic face, were coursing down the heavily powdered, wrinkled cheeks. Ethel Cameron with tears on her face left Eliza dumb. She waited.

"I notice you have nothing to say," Ethel Cameron whispered hoarsely, swiping at her wet cheeks with a fine linen handkerchief. "What could you say, after all?"

"I—wish I knew what it is—you want of me."

"I've told you. Your influence on the young man in my behalf. Caroline has sent word to me by Mr. Sheftall and Prince that I am free to live out my life at Knightsford." The bony, veined hands reached helplessly toward Eliza. "How? Under what circumstances? Who will buy my supplies? Who will oversee the planting, the harvests, the fields? *Under what circumstances?* Begging every dollar from her? Notifying *her* when I need a new gown? A cloak? A pair of gloves? I've lived my life at his mercy! Through Caroline, once he and I no longer addressed each other face to face, I had to plead for every jewel, every gown, every pair of slippers. Am I to spend my old age—begging from her?" The thin hands twisted in her silken lap. "I see you are appraising my jewels, Mrs. Mackay —my rings, my gold bracelet, my necklace." Her chin lifted proudly. "Any beautiful woman—and I was—*needs* a few gems. Her soul needs them. This belonged to my mother." One hand flew to the necklace and rested on it. "This necklace, this glorious emerald piece, is the only valued possession I own that did *not* come—through Caroline—from him!" She struck the necklace with her open hand. "This—is—mine. I am here asking, perhaps begging, you to help me. If you will not, I will sell the necklace and leave Knightsford forever."

"Mrs. Cameron! Not your mother's necklace!"

"My mother's necklace, yes. With the money, I can live out what time is left to me in a room at my niece's house in Maryland." She shuddered. "Doing that would be—suicide. I have never known peace. I have never known love. *But I have been the mistress of Knightsford.* If she makes my staying there impossible, if I do have to leave, it will kill me. Literally. But, my emeralds are my security. If she forces me to go into servitude to her, I will sell them." Her hand still lay over the green, cool stones, a throat pulse throbbing visibly above them.

"But, what do you want of me?" Eliza repeated as calmly as she could manage.

"I want you to plead my case for me with Mr. Browning. I believe him to be a—quality young man. I didn't expect to like him, I confess. I do. But, I have no influence with him. You have. Beg him for me, *please*, to retain Mr. Osmund Kott as overseer at Knightsford." She lifted a warning hand again. "Now, don't gasp, Mrs. Mackay. I *do* mean—Osmund Kott. God knows he's suffered, too, all his life. No one controls the circumstances of one's birth. I rather despise him as a person. I'm sure he despises me. But we manage, having lived in servitude to my husband, to understand each other."

"Mrs. Cameron," Eliza began carefully, "how well do

you—know Osmund Kott? Am I presumptuous to want to find out how it is that he's staying at Knightsford?"

"He was born at Knightsford."

"I know. But what made him think that you would receive him into your home at all?"

"I don't know the answer to that. Mr. Kott and I do not indulge in idle questions or answers. I don't even know where he sleeps. Let us say that—circumstances make a wary relationship possible. You can help with those circumstances. Osmund Kott would see to my well-being were he the overseer at Knightsford."

"How do you know that he would?"

"Circumstances."

"Do you believe that—Osmund is changing?"

" 'Judge not that ye be not judged.' "

Eliza struggled to control her voice. "I, too, know that Scripture passage!" Her voice sounded sharp-edged, even to her own ears. I must not allow myself to be sarcastic with this poor woman, she told herself. "Osmund was here some time ago—to ask me to pray for him," she said with all the care she could muster. "He came again to assure me that—"

"I know."

"He told you that he visited me—asking for prayer?"

"Yes. And as a Christian, I fail to see how you dare under-estimate the power of God, Mrs. Mackay."

Suddenly, Eliza stood to end the visit. "I'm afraid I can promise you nothing," she said curtly. "I happen to trust both Mark and Caroline to do the right thing by you in all ways. I will go on praying for Osmund Kott because he asked me to—because I suppose no one is beyond God's grace. More than that, I can promise nothing. I hope you'll excuse me now, Mrs. Cameron. We're in the midst of packing."

# FORTY-SEVEN

DURING the busy Christmas holiday back in Savannah, Mark and Eliza had only one chance to discuss Ethel Cameron's desperate visit to The Grange and her unfathomable request that Osmund Kott be made the Knightsford overseer. Mark listened attentively as Eliza tried to recapture the visit, and he understood perfectly that Ethel Cameron's words and manner had utterly frustrated Eliza.

"I failed completely to be—even civil with her at the end," she confessed. "I understand, oh, how well I understand, how the woman affects Caroline!"

"My beloved needs a lot of healing in that area," Mark said with a sad smile. "Actually, I'd already thought of making Kott overseer. I even mentioned it to Caroline. Somehow, I can't turn my back on Kott. Not only because he's my uncle, but because if a man asks for prayer, I don't think he should be ignored. I doubt that he tolerates being ignored anyway. Miss Eliza, I mean to do all I can for both him and Mrs. Cameron, but I have to consider Caroline, too."

"Does anything have to be done right away?" Eliza asked.

"No. Regardless of what Ethel Cameron told you, there's no rush about hiring a new overseer. This is still December. I won't need to have an overseer until just before planting time next year."

Through the early months of the new year 1821, Mark, except at night when Caroline fell asleep first, tried not to allow himself to think much about either Osmund Kott or Ethel Cameron. Eliza had suggested that a talk with William Thorne Williams might help where Osmund was concerned, but Mark,

although he and Williams were friends, put that off, too. The
Knightsford people would be sharpening tools, repairing har-
nesses, patching barns, stables, sheds—the usual winter jobs.
The plantation was not being harmed by his waiting until
spring to act.

Within a week after their return, Mark owned the two city
lots on Reynolds Square on the corner of Abercorn and
Bryan. The sometimes mild, sometimes chilly days of January
and February seemed to sail by as, daily, he and Caroline bent
over Isaiah Davenport's house plans spread on Eliza's parlor
floor. Davenport had, in an almost miraculous way, brought
their dreams to reality—on paper, at least. From a book of
tried and true plans—before the wedding trip—they had
selected ideas. Even their dreams for the new house matched.
Both still admired William Jay's brilliantly conceived, columned, solid Regency mansions; both thought Jay's new
bank as grand as any they'd seen in Philadelphia or New
York, merely smaller. They admitted to being overwhelmed by
the splendor of Jay's houses, and the skillful classical forms
awed them.

"But I much prefer Isaiah's plans," Caroline said. "I don't
want to live in a house that awes and overwhelms me. I want
to *live* in our house. I don't care, Mark—I just don't care a fig
about outshining anyone in Savannah. I want our home to be
tasteful, welcoming. *Ours.* I want it to speak to our friends
when they come inside. I don't want to make them feel small
or insignificant by comparison."

Although they both agreed not to have one single Doric column, except flanking the entrance, they seriously considered
asking Davenport to duplicate the freestanding stair in his own
house on Columbia Square. They visited the Davenports often
these days. Both Mark and Caroline would stand for minutes
at a time, looking up at Isaiah's simple, thin-spindled stair,
whose continuous flowing curve lifted both eye and spirit.

"It's the kind of line any architect might well hope to
achieve just once in his lifetime," Mark said one day when
Isaiah was standing beside them in the entrance hall by the
stair.

In his terse New England manner, Isaiah answered, "I
would hope it might remain—one of a kind."

Mark glanced quickly at Caroline, who patted Davenport's

shoulder and said with a smile, "All right, sir. We won't ask you to duplicate it for us. You're right. It should be and will remain—one of a kind."

"Your husband knows all about my spindles, though," Isaiah said, in as nearly comforting a voice as he ever managed. "Told him all about each one as I put it in. Every tenth spindle is iron. Feel it, Miss Caroline. Cold to the touch. I can give you these spindles—graceful to look at, but strong. I'll just turn your stair a bit more sharply. You'll both like it. I guarantee you will."

Their house, like Davenport's, would be four stories, counting the ground-floor kitchen, pantry and wine cellar. Mark liked the idea of finishing the top floor as private quarters for the children they hoped for. The roofline would not be quite so steep; neither Mark nor Caroline cared much for Isaiah's expanse of tin roof exposed to the street. Tin kept out heat. They would therefore have a tin roof, but it would not be so visible.

Also like Isaiah's house, theirs would be built of English bond brick, the exterior trim white, their only two slender Doric columns adorning the entrance. Unlike Isaiah's double front stairs of wrought iron, Caroline and Mark wanted only one stair, with wrought-iron railings, to lead straight to their door from the street.

Julia Scarbrough, still hiding the fact, if indeed she had been told, that her husband was near bankruptcy, informed them that Jay insisted, "Federal houses such as Davenport's are going quickly out of style." They didn't care. They liked what some of Davenport's plan books described as transitional—Georgian to Federal. Stylish or not, they knew what they wanted.

The first-floor plan was not unlike that of the Davenport house. A large formal drawing room to the right as one entered, a smaller drawing room to the left, behind which was the dining room, connected by two doors to a stair leading to the ground floor. On the second floor front, overlooking Reynolds Square and the tops of city trees, would be their master bedroom. On the same floor, three other rooms would be there for the McQueens, for the Mackays, for anyone who wanted or needed the blessing of love and comfort and quiet beauty for a time.

Mark had also bought a block of other lots, near the old market, on which Isaiah would build six modest row houses as the start of their dream of helping those who still lacked homes because of the fire.

"Give me at least three years to finish it all," Isaiah said and stuck to it despite Caroline's pleadings for two years at most. "Takes time," he insisted. "With the row houses going up, too, I can't put a whole crew on your big house. That plaster ceiling medallion you want in your drawing room, Miss Caroline, the carved wooden molding—all take time. Get another builder if you're in a hurry. I want it done right. My men work at their own pace, but they work like artisans—colored and white. We don't rush. We build."

Davenport's abrupt, concise speeches only endeared him to them both. "I even like the way his hair sticks up," Caroline said. "Have you noticed, Isaiah's hair is always wet down first thing in the morning? But in an hour, he might just as well have two curry brushes strapped to his head! I hope Mrs. Davenport appreciates him enough."

Mark was sure the Davenports were compatible. After all, Isaiah hadn't particularly wanted to put up those columns in the hall or to decorate his formal drawing room with pilasters flat against the walls. Mrs. Davenport had won in both instances.

Caroline and Mark liked the Davenports more all the time, thought their children interesting. The early winter weeks passed quickly, happily, with never enough hours in the days.

Mark and Eliza found time for one of their rare talks alone one afternoon in late February when he came home early from Commerce Row and found that Caroline and the Mackay children were visiting the Bryans.

"I can picture William about now," Mark said as he built a fire in the parlor fireplace. "I think you're right about his feelings for little Virginia Bryan, Miss Eliza."

"She's awfully young yet." She sighed, not unhappily. "But then, William isn't like other boys. He can wait—and enjoy it somehow."

Sitting in Mackay's old leather chair, Mark said, "We haven't talked like this for a long time, have we?"

"Far too long," she said. "But your life is so exciting, so

full now, I don't know how you keep up as well as you do. Caroline tells me the two of you are going back to the North in the spring to buy furniture and china and silver and carpets for the entire house. You have nothing usable from the old Browning home?''

"Oh, there are those few pieces not being used now in my office. Still in storage in my warehouse down on River Street," he said. "Most of our Philadelphia furniture was heavy and dark. Queen Anne or William and Mary, as I remember, although I'm no expert on such things."

"But you do know what you like," she said. "You made me think so often of Robert, who always wrote of his ignorance of women's dresses, scarves, jewelry, and then arrived home with the most exquisite things. He certainly had his own opinions. So do you."

As always, such remarks pleased Mark. "Miss Eliza? We haven't mentioned Ethel Cameron and Osmund Kott for a long time. I sent a boatload of supplies out there to her today, and when my clerk and stevedores came back this evening, they told me Kott had been right there at the dock to receive everything." He shook his head. "I wish I knew what's going on with those two."

"How on earth can we find out? Should I bundle up the children and take them for an early holiday at The Grange? They love being in the country this time of year. So do I. My corn should be coming up soon, too."

Mark sighed. "I'm the one who needs to go," he said. "I—I can't put it off much longer: I don't neglect my other clients. In another week, I'll be just plain neglecting the Knightsford account and that client is the light of my life! I don't make sense, do I? I neglect Caroline's affairs so as not to upset her. But hasn't she seemed better lately? Almost like herself again. Do you agree?"

"I do and she may surprise you. Have you asked her about a trip to Knightsford? You and Caroline are more than welcome to stay at our cottage if she can't face the big house with her grandmother. Have you mentioned it at all, Mark?"

"No," he said simply. "I promised her while we were still in Newport that I wouldn't bring up Knightsford for two months after we came home. Keeping the promise hasn't been nobility on my part. Just cowardice. It's been longer than two months.

I can't bear to see that look on her face. The way her voice changes. As she says, she 'snaps.' ''

"Snaps?"

He nodded. "She does. Even the mention of Knightsford frightens her."

"Mark, would it help at all if I went with Caroline to the North to buy your furniture and carpets for the new house? Oh, I know she'd be terribly disappointed not to have you, but could you somehow work things out at Knightsford while she and I were gone?"

For a long time, he looked at her wonderingly. "You'd really do that, wouldn't you? The voyage alone is tiring, even dangerous at this time of year. Scouring Philadelphia and New York for house furnishings isn't an easy job either."

"Nonsense."

"Actually, with the national economy what it is, I shouldn't leave my accounts for the month or six weeks it would take. But, Miss Eliza, be sure you really want to do it before you mention it to Caroline."

"Oh, I'm not the one to tell her. That's your job, young man. And I think you have the perfect reason—your business. She'd never doubt you in a million years if you told her you shouldn't leave now."

"As far as the economy is concerned, there's nothing to doubt. Things are bad North and South. Sometimes I'm almost embarrassed that I have funds to build a row of rental properties, a new house for Caroline and me—and buy furnishings. I don't take the financial panic lightly, though. I really shouldn't leave."

"Then don't. I'm more than glad to go with Caroline."

"I'll give it some thought, if you're sure."

"I'm very sure. I've—never even seen Robert's grave, you know."

At the end of the month, when word came from Jamaica that Margaret McQueen's mother, Mary Cowper, had died, Mark made up his mind about the New York shopping trip. He broached the subject to Caroline as she lay on his shoulder in their bed the same night they learned of Margaret's loss.

"Not only is it unwise, maybe risky, for me to be away right now with the cotton market so low," he explained, "shipping costs have forced me to think of buying a ship of my own. A schooner I've liked for a long time will dock here three weeks from now. I'd like to inspect it myself." When she lay motionless, silent, he went on. "Besides, I can't think of anything that would help Cousin Margaret more now than a trip with you and Miss Eliza. Margaret adored her mother. It's hard to lose a parent when you're so far apart. Too, seeing Mackay's grave in New York will certainly help Miss Eliza. I remember how I felt when suddenly I knew I'd never have any contact with my father again. No burial service to attend, no grave to visit anywhere in the world. The trip could help them both. Spring is a hard time to be sad."

There was another long silence, broken finally by Caroline, her voice controlled, but obviously with difficulty. "And—spring is planting time at Knightsford. You mean to hire Osmund Kott while I'm gone—to spare me having to talk about it." She pulled herself up on her elbow and looked straight down into his face in the dim, wavering light from the hall candle that burned each night until Eliza came up to bed. "Mark, I love you so much, whatever you decide is all right. I hate going to shop for our furnishings without you, but God knows, I'm devoted to those two women. They're my rescuers. I know you trust my taste—" her voice broke. "And I—trust you to do the right thing about—a new overseer."

She had agreed so easily to go without him that Mark couldn't think of anything to say.

Abruptly, Caroline kissed him. "I do get so tired waiting for you to kiss me! You kiss me so seldom."

They laughed at her joke, but when Mark began to make love to her, she was crying.

"Dearest," he said helplessly. "Dearest Caroline, what's wrong?"

Sobbing as though her heart would break, she buried her face in the pillow to keep the Mackays from hearing. Mark held her, waiting. When she quieted, he waited also for her to speak first, to give him some clue as to why she had wept.

"I'm—sorry," she said at last. "Not sorry I cried. I had to, but, darling, I'm empty now. I can't—love you back tonight."

"Don't even think of that. Are you all right?"

"No. I'm not all right. I'm full of panic."

"I know. I wish I never had to mention Knightsford again."

Her voice still uneven, she said, "When I was a little girl, I thought Knightsford was such a—noble name."

"You will again. You'll think that again, because it's true. And, Caroline, *you* are true, too. Not many people are. Never act with me in a way you don't feel. Good or bad. Panic or joy."

"Can you really settle everything while I'm away? Is there really a way to—settle it once and for all?"

"I don't know, but I promise to try. I care about your grandmother. I—even seem to care about Osmund in some way." He went on quickly, before she could voice her fear again. "I understand your anxiety about them both. I'll find a way to handle it all and I'll also always do my best to free you of—everything out there. That's what I want more than anything now—for you to be free of whatever frightens you. It may take time, but I'm hopeful, darling."

"Should I be ashamed of myself?"

"No."

"All right," she said. "Then, I won't be."


The day Caroline, Margaret and Eliza left for Philadelphia and New York, Mark went straight from the dock where he had waved them off to Sheftall Sheftall's home on West Broughton Street.

Seated together on a narrow porch that ran along the second story of the square frame house, Mark tried unobtrusively to keep his overcoat well closed against what to him was a day far too chilly to be outside.

"Glad you kept your coat on," Sheftall said in a matter-of-fact voice. "I get as much fresh air as possible myself. Offer it to my friends, too. What's on your mind, Browning? The Knightsford overseer?"

"That's right, sir. You relieve me by coming directly to the point."

"The fields should be prepared right now for planting. Are they prepared?"

Mark looked out over the quiet, tree-lined street. "I don't know. I haven't been out there in months."

"Uncharacteristic of you. Well, I have been."

"You've been to Knightsford recently?"

Sheftall nodded, polishing the lenses of his tiny round spectacles between folds of a worn jacket. "You're still the Knightsford factor, I'm still the Knightsford attorney. You've been busy with plans for a new home and attempting to keep your clients afloat against the plunging cotton prices on the Liverpool market. I went."

Mark leaned toward him. "What did you find? Tell me exactly how things are, with Mrs. Cameron, with—"

"With Osmund Kott?"

"Yes, sir. Is he still there?"

"He is and seemingly in full charge. I was pleasantly surprised. You would be, too, if you saw the order, the bustling activity—not only in the fields but over the entire plantation. Are you paying Kott for all his work?"

"Why, no, sir. I haven't even—hired him!"

"Someone has. Matthew obeys him as overseer, relieved to be doing so, I might add. Mrs. Cameron informed me of Kott's new status herself. Obviously, she hired the man."

"But, does she have the legal right to do that, sir?"

"No, of course not. Few things stop Ethel Cameron, though, if her mind is made up. And, you have been remiss."

"That's right. I have."

"Uncharacteristic of you, Browning," Sheftall said again. "There must be a reason beyond the business of marriage and the start of a new house and a nationwide financial crisis."

"There is a reason. My wife seems to go to pieces at the mere mention of Knightsford. I promised her I wouldn't do anything, not even bring up the subject for two months after we returned from our wedding trip."

"It's been over three months."

"That's right. And I feel guilty."

"In this case, wasted energy."

"Perhaps. Mr. Sheftall, you know more about Osmund Kott than any other man in Savannah. Should he be the overseer at Knightsford?"

"If you want efficiency, improvement in the productivity of the land, yes. The man's abilities astound me, I'm frank to say. I've known him boy and man as a waterfront bum, a troublemaker, the gentle-voiced lover of books under William Thorne Williams, the persecutor of Jonathan Cameron. I've known Kott as a gentleman and a derelict. Irresponsible and trustworthy. Our brainy friend, Thorne Williams, says his establishment never runs so smoothly as when Osmund is helping him. Business is so bad, our merchant class is now reading more than ever. Of course, they have no cash with which to pay Williams for the books they buy. He was amazed at Kott's cunning in extracting money from the pockets of otherwise financially embarrassed gentlemen. Even Scarbrough, who appears on the verge of bankruptcy after the obvious failure of the S.S. *Savannah*, reached right into his pocket and paid for seven volumes of English books. Thorne Williams is bereft, though, at what Kott did to him."

"What did he do?"

"Left the store one evening and never returned. Went straight to Knightsford and took charge. There won't be any seed to plant until you send it out to him, but Kott has the fields ready."

"Mr. Sheftall, can you tell me what the relationship between Ethel Cameron and Kott really is? If I knew that, I—I might be able to think my way through this mess."

"It is a puzzling mess, in a way. In another, the Knightsford land, with the cooperation of the Almighty's weather, could be one of the most productive plantations on the Savannah River this year—thanks to Osmund. As for Ethel Cameron, I think she despises him. I also think he rather despises her. But they have enormous respect for each other. They both succeeded in making almost every waking hour in the life of my friend and client, Jonathan Cameron, wretched. Mutually, they take pride in that."

"And that's—the bond between them?"

"If there is one, yes."

"Where does that leave Caroline?"

"In as ugly a dilemma as any lovely young lady could find herself. Your wife is still being used as a tool. All her life, she's been a tool. Ethel used her to influence Jonathan to give her the luxury she feels life owes her. Jonathan used Caroline as his only means of communication with the peculiar lady he married. Had it not been for the child Caroline, had husband and wife been forced into direct encounter, Jonathan Cameron might have been driven to murder."

"Murder?"

"Such an act would have crushed him, of course. By nature, there wasn't a violent bone in the man's body. But he was mortally afraid that his past sins would become known through a divorce suit—scandal enough in its own way. Except for Caroline's pathetic role as intercessor, I think he might have murdered Ethel before he would have divorced her. Jonathan could have withstood a murder trial far more easily than the criticism of Savannah society over a divorce. He was not a brave man. What you must understand, Browning, is that those two folk truly hated each other."

Mark thought for a time, frowning deeply. "Can you—conceive true hatred, Mr. Sheftall?"

"After my years as Cameron's lawyer, yes, I can."

"Did they ever show civility toward each other?"

"Oh, always civility. And they did have one child, Caroline's father." Sheftall shrugged. "I suppose it's possible that they might have endured in a reasonably compatible marriage, had poor Jonathan not purchased the indenture of—Mary Cotting."

"Kott was the first visible symbol of her husband's love for Mary Cotting," Mark said. "Doesn't it stand to reason that Mrs. Cameron would hate Kott?"

"She may, she may." Sheftall's voice was calm, musing. "That really has nothing to do with today's predicament, though. You see, Ethel has lived with hatred for most of her seventy-odd years. It's her native air. She no longer minds it."

"And you think she wants Kott there as overseer?"

"Evidently she does. She seems to believe that she can force him to see that Caroline and you treat her fairly. She's terrified of—poverty."

"But we both want her life to go right on as it's always—'"

"I know, I know," Sheftall interrupted. "I know that. I also know of no means by which you or I could follow the twists and turns of two such hate-filled minds. We waste our energies in attempting to find logic anywhere at Knightsford right now."

Mark stood. "Mr. Sheftall, what do you think I should do?"

"Act on facts as we know them. Allow Kott, because of what he has already done so successfully, to continue as overseer. Every penny of profit from your sales of Knightsford rice and cotton belongs to your wife and to you. Look out for your own interests. Pay Kott the going wage as overseer, see that

Ethel continues to live in the style to which she is accustomed, and, by all means, keep her and Caroline apart. At least, for the present."

Mark laughed dryly. "That won't be hard."

"Except for an occasional business call at Knightsford, you won't have to see Kott, either. To the relief of us all, you will be keeping him out of the city. With the help of Jehovah, things may eventually work out."

"I suppose what bothers me is just knowing that such an ugly situation exists. I don't handle bad feelings of any kind very well."

"Only God does."

Mark smiled a little. "Knightsford is such a beautiful place. I dream of my wife's enjoying it again, of being able to take our children there. Caroline is mortally afraid of Kott. Do you suppose that will ever change, sir?"

Sheftall Sheftall got up slowly, adjusted his faded jacket and his cocked hat. "You're rushing ahead, of course. The wise Solomon declared that there is a time to be born and a time to die. There is also a time—right now—in between birth and death for you to feel your way through. Browning."

With a deep, heavy sigh, Mark said, "Yes, sir. Kott makes me so angry, too. I dread trying to deal with him even in a business way. I also pity him."

"Still, his having taken over at Knightsford has saved you from a hard decision, has it not? He's there working well and with Ethel Cameron's consent. You've been saved some trouble, at least. Why not give it a try, especially since the wise Solomon would agree that there is also a time to plant."

They shook hands. "Thank you, sir. A talk with you always helps clear my head."

"Make all the money you can make at Knightsford, Browning. We've had so-called financial panics before. They end. Success in Savannah in the past has been in the pockets of the merchant class. It will be again, but look at some of them today. Many have allowed their plantations to go to ruin. The coastal economy, my thinking tells me, may be shifting toward planters in the future. You're blessed—not only with an inherited income of considerable size, with a fine factorage firm, but now, with one of the richest plantations on the river. Give God the thanks." The little man, caught, as people supposed, in the futile web of past heroism, raised his hand as though in blessing: " 'O give thanks unto the Lord; for He is good: for His mercy endureth forever.' Forever, Browning, includes the time to be born, the time to die and—everything in between."

# FORTY-EIGHT

PERHAPS it was due to his own high spirits because of his happiness with Caroline, but the faces gathered about public bonfires in the squares that Christmas of 1821 seemed to Mark to be more cheerful than last year, when the financial crisis first became known. Caroline, Eliza and Margaret had been back from a most successful shopping trip at the North since July. Daily, Mark signed for their purchases of oriental carpets, furniture, silver and china as they arrived, one after another, at his dock. The Browning warehouse was piled high.

Margaret had reveled in the entire journey, and Eliza told Mark that although she had wept at Robert's grave in Trinity Churchyard, she now felt a deeper acceptance, which seemed, somehow, to free her. Caroline was lyrical over the new furnishings. Almost nightly, she insisted that Mark take her to the warehouse so that she could try again to explain to him exactly what was inside each wooden crate and barrel. Mark's profits at the countinghouse were down, but not those from the Browning Company. His only foolish investment had been with Scarbrough in the S.S. *Savannah*, now pronounced a failure even by Scarbrough, who was desperately trying to borrow money in town. Mark had found it extremely hard to refuse Julia's husband the twenty thousand he begged to borrow—"just until this infernal financial panic ends"—but knowing a loan would not help, he had refused.

"Letting him have the money wouldn't really have changed anything in the long run," Mark told Eliza as, once more, they worked side by side in the Mackay yard preparing the flower beds for winter planting early in the new year 1822.

490

"I'm desperately sorry for both Julia and her husband," Eliza said, stopping to crumble the earth that Mark had just turned. "Being without funds hurts them more than it ever hurt me." She laughed. "Robert and I had good times, some that were not so good, but I grew up knowing what it is *not* to have money. My dear, optimistic father's dreams gobbled up what money we had the way Jack eats popcorn."

"I can't help comparing Miss Margaret with Julia Scarbrough. Both are such socially adept ladies—glorious dancers, sparkling conversationalists. Both have traveled, lived luxurious lives. But there the similarities seem to end."

"Cousin Margaret was even more successful socially," Eliza said. "The belle of three continents. And then, she married my dear, not very successful brother."

"And lived happily ever after." Mark grinned. "Do you think Miss Julia could do that?"

"I don't know. Her life has revolved around her social standing all the years I've known her. Maybe she'll surprise us. Maybe this awful crisis will end. I'm sure William and Julia care deeply for each other when they take time to realize it."

"I think that's the reason Margaret does so well with limited funds. She loves your brother."

"Yes." Eliza stood up, wiped her hands on a smudged apron tied around her old winter coat. "Heaven knows it took forever to find out that she loved him, but she knows it now. Mark, is John going to have any profit at all this year? I know he's more than fourteen thousand dollars in debt on Causton's Bluff."

Mark finished raking the newly spaded bed before he answered. "I'm certainly doing all I can for him. Cotton has gone up, but only by one cent. John experimented a bit too long with his benne seed oil, I think. If he hadn't, he'd be a rich man now. Before I took over his account, he was almost giving the oil away. I've raised the price for him just about all I can in the face of the general crisis. I think he'll be able to pay off some of his indebtedness, though."

She laid her hand on his arm. "Listen to me. Don't do anything generous with John, please. He's not the world's best businessman, but he is awfully smart. He'll work his way out of it."

Mark grinned and patted her little square hand. "I promise. I know how proud John is, too." He thrust the spade into the sandy soil, pushed it with his toe and turned over a shovelful. "I'll tell you one plantation heading for a good year, in spite of everything. Knightsford. Miss Eliza, Osmund Kott is a born planter. Caroline's people respect him, work for him, obey him."

"Is he kind to them?"

"He's fair, I think. All business. I wouldn't swear that they like him, but they work steadily and quietly. More bags have been picked a day than ever before."

"Osmund is a great tragedy, isn't he?" she asked.

"I suppose he is. Had he been born in any other circumstances, he'd be a rich man now. I'm sure he knows that. I'm sure he dwells on it a lot. I guess I've become somewhat interested in him—as a human being."

"Do you like him now, Mark?"

"I couldn't go that far. Do you—still pray for him, Miss Eliza?"

"Almost every day. I mean to every day. Does Ethel Cameron speak of Osmund when you're out there on your inspection trips?"

He thought a moment. "Not that I remember. No, I'm sure she hasn't mentioned his name once."

"What do you and Ethel talk about when you call on her?"

He shrugged. "The weather, the crops, her needs. She gives me an order for staples—flour, salt, tea, coffee. This time she ordered several yards of fine silks and cottons. I imagine she's having dresses made."

Eliza smiled. "With Ethel it would be *gowns,* not dresses. I smile, but I could weep over that woman."

"Kott seldom mentions her to me, either," he said. "If you were to judge the talks I have with him, you would conclude that he and I had simply enjoyed a purely business relationship for years. There is never a personal word spoken."

"No one mentions Caroline, the real owner of Knightsford?"

"Never. When I come back here after trips out there, Caroline also acts as though I'd merely been at my counting-house all day."

"Give her more time, Mark. This time next year, the baby

will be here, you'll be living in your fine new town house.
Caroline will, for the first time in her life, be at home, in her
own place. That's going to make such a difference."

He beamed. "Oh, I hope so. Miss Eliza, you will stay close
to her now that we're sure our baby's on the way? Will you
please stay close to Caroline—and to me?"

She looked at him for a long time. Then, she said, "Mark, I
wouldn't know how *not* to stay close to you both. Once you've
left here to move into your own home, I imagine you'll have to
bar your door to keep me away. Oh, I'll miss you—so much!"

He took a step toward her, still holding the spade. "We'll
visit you—every day."

"You'll do no such thing! That would be a terrible burden.
But, dear God in heaven, seeing you leave my house will
be—almost like losing Robert all over again. . . ."

From the first day Isaiah Davenport had given instructions
for clearing the lots Mark had purchased on Reynolds Square,
Jack Mackay had been involved. Not only with his fertile, enthusiastic mind, but with his muscles as well. It was he who
knocked down the two old chimneys, cleaned and stacked the
good English bricks that frugal Isaiah said could be used as a
garden path once the house was completed. It was Jack who
bossed the crew of Davenport's Negroes who did the actual
clearing of the weeds, stumps and blackened rubble. And
because Isaiah saw at once that Jack had a bent for engineering, he hired him as his assistant draftsman and personal
helper. When Davenport had to be away supervising another
house, Jack was on hand to see that every procedure went just
right—especially the careful bonding of the brick basement
and the precise locking together of the heavy broad-axed foundation beams. By the time the sturdily braced frame began to
go up, Jack was more than enthusiastic.

"If Mr. Davenport still has him on his payroll, I hope Jack
will be half as interested in the finishing process," Eliza told
Caroline one spring morning at breakfast after Mark had gone
to work.

"What do you mean by wondering if he'll be as excited over
the finishing? That's going to be my favorite time!"

"It would be for me, too, but Jack talks incessantly of how
much he enjoys the engineering of a house. He knows Isaiah

Davenport is a fine builder, but Jack declares him to be an engineering genius.''

"Engineering? I thought Jack was determined to be a professional soldier. Has he given up on West Point?''

"Not at all, I'm sorry to say. He still wants to be a soldier and, of course, I hate the whole idea. But he now thinks he's going to try to get into the Department of Engineers.''

"Oh, I see. Well, I predict he'll get into whatever he wants. That boy is a charmer, Miss Eliza. At seventeen, he's almost as handsome as his father. And Mark is amazed at the responsibility Mr. Davenport's entrusted to him. It looks to me as though Jack's practically the boss when the boss is away for a few hours. You should hear him barking orders to the workmen. They listen and obey him, too. But he's very reasonable about it all. He laughs a lot. The men laugh more than New Englander Davenport likes, I think, but Isaiah's fair, too. He knows Jack does get them to work.''

They sipped their coffee in a comfortable silence for a time; then Eliza said, "Dear William is just as happy working with Mark. How that boy has adored your husband from the day his father first brought Mark to this house. I can't believe that was almost ten years ago.''

"William is—is fine-looking, isn't he?''

"To me, he is, although I've always considered him quite a plain little fellow.'' She laughed at herself. "He'd love my calling him a 'little fellow' at eighteen, wouldn't he? Maybe you're right about his looks. He's so tall now—taller than Jack; his shoulders have filled out some. His face has matured. Perhaps William is growing up to be—rather handsome. But, oh my, if I had met Mark only recently, I believe I'd have to declare him—almost perfect in looks. He was attractive at twenty, of course. But even though I doubt he'll ever lose that boyish charm, especially when he smiles, now, nearing thirty, he's really striking. Most important, he's beautiful *inside*. His heart and spirit are still almost too good. I wonder if he isn't being overly generous in the way he's building those row houses? He's as fussy over their quality as with your own place.''

"I knew he would be, didn't you? He seems pleased with the people you've picked out to live in them. He means it, you know, when he insists that he wants to remain anonymous to his tenants. Miss Eliza, I don't think Mark gives much thought to the impression he makes on other people. He really doesn't want to be thanked. He's just not particularly conscious of himself that way."

"We'd all be better off like that." Eliza laughed.

"I'm serious. Did you ever see Mark strut?"

"Strut?" Eliza laughed again. "Well, yes, I think I have. The first time he marched with the Chatham Artillery in a parade, he strutted. Why not? He does take your breath away in that uniform. I know what you mean about his seeming to ignore himself, though. I call it—being natural. Men know as well as women when they're irresistible. Have you ever watched some of them make sweeping, striding entrances into Julia Scarbrough's atrium? Their heads are so high, they barely make it under her two-storied ceiling!"

"Sometimes I wish Mark would strut a little," Caroline mused. "I'm always so proud of him, but he only laughs at me when I tell him. I can just see a few of his Chatham Artillery comrades if they had Mark's wealth and even half his good looks."

"Actually, I think Jack struts. I hope not too much. Of course, he is only seventeen. Savannah girls contribute to a young man's strutting. They're already spoiling Jack. William has eyes, still, only for Virginia Sarah Bryan, though. I pray a lot about that, actually."

"You do?"

"Yes, because she seems almost too right for William. The Bryans are such a fine family. Virginia's late father was loved by just about everyone except those he rightly opposed when he served in Congress from Georgia. To me, Joseph Bryan was a man with a rare capacity for living. He had a sense of humor, too. When he retired from public life and married Virginia's mother, Delia Forman, from Maryland, he named their lovely home on Whitmarsh Island 'Nonchalance.' Robert always got a chuckle out of that. Mr. Bryan was a brilliant lawyer, but he loved his plantation. I don't think Mark had a chance to meet him. He died in the fall of the year Mark came to Savannah. Our families have been close. It does seem so right. I'd feel safe about William if someday Virginia returned his love."

"You really believe he's serious about her, don't you?"

"I'm sure of it. William never, never gives his love lightly."
She sighed. "That's one of the many reasons I pray. Ever
since he was a little boy, I've watched William protect his
heart. I don't think he's really as shy as people think. He's
just—careful. But when he loves, all of William goes into it.
I've been thankful so often that Mark—is Mark. The boy
idolizes him."

Eliza, deep in her reverie, jumped when the front door
banged.

"What on earth?" she gasped.

"Mama! Mama!"

William burst into the dining room, followed by his three
sisters, their faces as white as ghosts.

"William! What's wrong?"

"It's—Uncle John," Eliza Anne managed, just above a
whisper.

"Yes, Mama, it's Uncle John." William walked directly to
his mother and laid his hand on her shoulder. "His Jim just
rowed to Mark's wharf with word that—Uncle John is dead."

"Dear God," Eliza breathed, half in shock, half in prayer.
"Poor, poor Cousin Margaret! Her mother—now John." She
grasped William's hand and held it to her face. "William,
William, what must we do?" An almost childlike helplessness
on her face, she stared up at him. "Tell me what to do,
William!"

"We'll go to Causton's Bluff right away in Mark's boat,"
Caroline said, taking charge. "If you're up to it, Miss Eliza, I
know Margaret needs you."

"Yes," Eliza said. "Yes, we'll go."

"Get your mother's cape, Katie." Caroline was giving quiet
orders now. "Sallie, tell Emphie to bring hot tea right away.
You must drink some strong tea before you go, Miss Eliza.
Eliza Anne, run up to my room, please, and fetch my blue
cloak. I'm going with your mother."

# FORTY-NINE

EVERY day through rainy, flower-filled April and the greener, gentler month of May, Margaret, with William beside her, walked the block south on Abercorn, across Oglethorpe Square, to the old Colonial Cemetery to visit John's grave. Depending on her state of mind, the two made the journey just after dawn, before breakfast or when William came home in the late afternoon from work at Mark's countinghouse.

"You are so dear, William, to do this," Margaret said day after day as they walked, often in silence, along the familiar streets, only now and then commenting when a late azalea bloomed or a mockingbird sang from a fire thorn, its clumps of tiny berries still green. More often than not, William only squeezed her hand and said nothing. "I know I shouldn't have stayed on here in Savannah with your family. I know I should have gone right back to Causton's Bluff. When I do go back, it will be like—John has died again. But I can't go. Isn't it crazy how foolish we can be—all the time knowing it so well?"

"You also know how welcome you are here, Cousin Margaret. We all feel better about you. After you do go home, I'm going to hate it every night when I try to go to sleep. I'll lie there and imagine how empty that big house will be for you. I can feel your pain already and you haven't even gone back yet. Mark's looking after your fields; why can't you stay all summer with us?"

"Oh, William, they are *my* fields now, aren't they? How can I ever think of them as anything but—John's fields? And what would I do without Mark? What would I do without you to go with me to the grave every day? Dear God, William, don't we all need each other? Don't we *need* each other? And isn't that a ridiculous thing for me to say when I'm the one who's doing all the needing? What am I doing for any of you?"

"A lot for me," he said without a moment's hesitation.

"What? What am I doing for you?"

"You're letting me be your friend. Not just your—cousin."

Angling across the old cemetery, she stopped, as she always did, a few feet away from the still settling mound of earth where John's body lay. Each new day seemed to require a fresh gathering of courage to move closer.

"It—might help," she said on a warm June afternoon, "once his marker is in place. I don't know why, but I'm hoping it will help—some. It seemed to help your mother just to see your father's stone." When she began to weep, William took her in his arms. "I haven't—really let John go yet," she sobbed. "I'm trying, but so much of the time, I don't understand why he's—lying there!"

"Mama's going to be so lonesome after Mark and Caroline move away; please stay with her this summer. Stay till after Christmas with all of us. Please? Don't you want to be here when Mark's new baby comes? That'll be September. I think seeing a new life born might—well, it might help some."

"You're a most persuasive gentleman, William Mackay," she said as they started back toward Broughton Street. "And I'm weak as water right now. I'm—afraid to go back to Causton's Bluff, if I'm truthful. It's hard not to be truthful with you. Do you really think Isaiah Davenport will finish at least the master bedroom so Caroline's first child can be born in the new house? I can't picture that meticulous Rhode Islander allowing anyone to rush him."

"All he tells Mark is that he'll do his best."

"William, I have to go to Causton's Bluff for some clothes. I must look in on how the servants are doing. Be sure no one's ill or shirking just because I'm not there. Go with me, will you?"

"You know I'll go, Cousin Margaret. Anytime you say."

"And wouldn't you like to take that lovely little Virginia Bryan? It would be perfectly proper with me as chaperone. We could stay over one night. Or, if I can't face that, make a one-day trip of it. With Virginia along, my breeding will keep me from blubbering my head off the first time I walk in the house. I know she's only fourteen, but I'm sure her mother would let her go with us."

"Oh, so am I! Miss Delia is a very warmhearted lady." William's enthusiasm was instant. "She already knows I'm going to wait for Virginia."

Margaret stopped walking to stare at him. "What? What did you say?"

Looking at the dusty street, William blushed. "I haven't even told Mama yet. But I've known for quite a long time that I want Virginia Bryan to be my wife someday." Looking straight at Margaret, he said, "I'm so sure, that waiting for her to grow up and for me to be able to support her will not be hard at all." He sighed his relief. "I'm glad I told you. I didn't mean to, but I'm glad I did."

"Is it a secret?"

He shrugged. "No. I told you her mother already knows it. She didn't say anything much when I explained it to her, but she did give me a kind of warm, encouraging smile."

"And have you told Virginia?"

"Oh, no. I guess she's too young. But she smiles at me a lot. We trade books. I walk her home from church."

Taking his arm again as they strolled slowly across Oglethorpe Square, Margaret asked, "What do you want to do with your life, William? Jack, who never lacks for words, has made it quite plain that he intends to go to West Point—"

*"If* he can get an appointment."

"Oh, I'm sure that will not be an obstacle. He explained at length to me the other day that several of his father's Chatham Artillery friends have offered to help with the necessary recommendations. He means to graduate from West Point and become an army engineer. That way he figures he can build at least five hundred forts before his career ends. I adore Jack, but it's your plans I'm interested in now. What kind of work appeals to you? Business—perhaps with Mark?"

"Working with Mark suits me," he said, "but I don't think I'd be very good at business on my own. I do fine as his clerk—one of his clerks—but what I really want to do deep down is to be a planter like Uncle John."

"I see. Did you ever know that your Uncle John didn't much care for being a planter? Oh, he worked very hard at it, but he 'endured' much of the time."

Crossing the street, William was silent. Then, slowly, thoughtfully, he said, "Well, I think I can look back and kind of understand what you mean about Uncle John. He was always so good to be with, but he was more or less firm-jawed about some things. I mean, he made fine jokes and I always wished I could have thought of witty things the way he did, but—I do see what you're trying to tell me."

"And I had no ulterior motive whatever in telling you. Being a planter is not only sometimes profitable—even for dear John, who seemed to have an aversion to profit—it's also an important profession."

"Oh, you didn't discourage me," he said. "My mind's pretty much made up about that, too. I'm saving all I can of what Mark pays me. I thought next year I might move out to The Grange and see what I could do to help raise Mama's income a little from her land there. Get some planting experience."

"Listen to me, William," she said with more enthusiasm than she'd shown since John's death. "I have an idea. Let's say right now we'll stay overnight at Causton's Bluff. That way, you can ride over some of the fields and give me your opinion of what needs to be done next."

Grinning broadly, William said, "I can't think of anything I'd like to do more—that is, if you think I know enough about it."

The day before the new baby was due on September 1, the strong arms of both Hero and Mark were needed to get Caroline into the carriage for the ride from Broughton to the almost finished house on Reynolds Square in time for the child to be born there.

Half sitting, half lying between Mark and Eliza on the cushioned carriage seat, Caroline held tightly to both their hands. The baby had kicked unmercifully for so long, her body was so distended, so off-balance, she had vowed to herself that she'd never, never go through such an ordeal again. Today, jolting along in Mark's well-sprung carriage over the rutted, rain-puddled streets, she all but spoke her vow aloud.

"What a wonderful moment for you, Caroline," Eliza was saying. "Just think, you're on your way to spend your first night in your new home and at the same time you're on your way to a woman's crowning experience." When Caroline only stared blankly at her, she went on, "Try to put the discomfort to one side. From now until the baby's here, you'll have to push that fine mind of yours to the utmost—mind over matter. Mind over matter. What you think while the baby is being born is as important as anything else. Maybe more so."

"I—can't—think at all, right now," Caroline gasped, glancing at Mark, hoping that he was all right. That he didn't hate her for perspiring and looking so out of shape, for being cross. He was white as a sheet and also perspiring. "Oh, Mark," she whispered. "Will it ever be over?"

"Of course it will be, dearest," he said, his voice unsteady.

"Who's going to stay with you? Miss—Eliza—promised to be—in the room with me. Who's going to—be with you?"

"William," he said. "He and Cousin Margaret will be back from Causton's Bluff first thing tomorrow. Maybe yet this evening. I'm counting on William."

"Don't forget to count—on God—too," Caroline whispered. "Pray for me, Mark. I don't—want—to die!"

"Never in my life have I heard such nonsense." Eliza's voice was firm. "It's perfectly normal for the two of you to be scared half out of your wits. This is your first child, but you're fine, Caroline. All the signs are good. You and the baby will be all right. Mark, I'm speaking to you, too. You look as though you're about to face a hangman's noose!"

At high noon the next day, rain pouring down, the bell of the Exchange Tower tolled twelve as Eliza, a blanketed bundle in her arms, came out of the master bedroom and walked carefully along the tool-strewn upstairs hall to where Mark stood as though rooted to the unfinished floorboards. Glancing down at the bundle and then up at him, Eliza smiled. "She's here, Mark. Your daughter is here."

"Caroline?"

"She's going to be fine. It was very hard on her taking that carriage ride so close to her time. I'm sorry she screamed so. I know how that terrified you."

"But, she is—all right? She's going to live—and everything?"

Eliza smiled. "Yes, dear boy. She's going to live and

*everything.* The trouble was, your new daughter entered the world feet first. That's terrible for the mother. But, she's here." As Eliza held her out to Mark, with no hint at first of an infant's whimper, the child broke into what sounded like an angry protest. "Baby!" Eliza patted the tiny blanketed rump. "Baby, for goodness' sake, what kind of an announcement was that? Is that a ladylike way to greet your father?" The screaming went on. "Hush! Hush that noise. This is your father. . . ."

A crash of thunder shook the house and a blinding bolt of lightning snapped. The screaming stopped abruptly.

Mark tried to laugh. "It—took a lot to stop her, didn't it?" He touched one bright pink cheek. "Hello," he said, almost timidly. "Your mother said your name was to be a surprise to me—if you turned out to be a girl. You're a girl, all right. What's your name, baby?"

"I'm to inform you that your new daughter's name is—Natalie."

"How like Caroline to name her for Aunt Nassie!" He beamed at Eliza, his pleasure too deep for mere words. Then, "Could—could I hold her for a minute?"

Carefully, Eliza gave him the baby, placed his hand in the right position to support the tiny head and whispered—not to Mark—to Natalie: "He hasn't even noticed! Can you believe your papa's so excited, he hasn't even noticed that you have red hair?"

*"Red hair?"*

"You have a titian-haired daughter on your hands, sir. Even Caroline, weak as she is, was flabbergasted. She knows of no one in her family with red hair. Was it in your family?"

"No, but it is now!" He smoothed the silky, damp, coppery wisps, ever so gently, brushing them back, then forward. "What do you know about that, Miss Eliza? I hadn't even noticed! She's so—red all over, I guess I thought—" His laughter came a touch more easily now. "I guess I thought she was—just a bald-headed baby." For a moment, he looked at the child, shaking his head. "Natalie? Why did you have to treat your mother that way? Was it important for some reason to come into the world feet first? You're—beautiful, though." Glancing up at Eliza, he repeated himself, his delight mounting. "Look! She *is* beautiful, Miss Eliza! Does Caroline think she is?"

"Caroline's still too weak to make judgments. All she managed to say was—'red hair, Miss Eliza! She has red hair.'"

"When can I go in to her?"

"Dr. Jones wants her to sleep for at least an hour. Natalie's entrance into this old world was an ordeal. Mark, look at your daughter! She hasn't been here but a few minutes and she's already sizing you up."

The tiny eyelids parted just enough for them both to glimpse two deep-blue eyes.

"Is she really—peering around or does it just seem that way?"

Eliza laughed. "With this one, I'm just not at all sure. Mark, where's William?"

"I didn't want him to go out in this rain, but he insisted that I deserved a pot of Hannah's coffee. He'll be back soon. Oh, he's bringing Cousin Margaret, too."

"She's become quite dependent on William, hasn't she?"

"So have I. Quiet William is an important young man in all the ways that count. May I keep Natalie until William and Margaret get here?"

"Of course not. Even Miss Briggledy needs some sleep." She held out her arms and Mark deposited the baby as though she were made of glass. "She won't break, Mark. Certainly not if her performance up to now is any sign!"

*Part V*

# 1822–1825

# FIFTY

THROUGH every day of the first months of his daughter's life, Mark could see new beauty and new strength in Caroline. For the first few weeks, she insisted upon caring for the baby herself, which, of course, kept the Brownings at home most of the time. Unwilling, still, to buy servants, Mark scoured the city for a competent nurse, not an easy task because none of the gentlemen with whom he worked on Commerce Row understood his insistence upon paid domestic help.

He went on with his queries just the same, and in the course of conversations with his colleagues, he felt that he also could sense a new optimism rising in the city. Local merchants, threatened with financial disaster at the height of the panic, had regained at least tenuous footholds. Even William Scarbrough was still holding on. He had lost his outlying properties and a number of city lots, but his mercantile firm continued and he and the countess still entertained lavishly in their mansion on West Broad.

Toward the end of summer, Mark found Gerta Schultze, a Savannah-born German woman, and hired her as Natalie's nurse. Earlier he had retained Maureen O'Toole, an Irish girl, as cook, and a free Negro houseman-driver named Jupiter Taylor. The fine new house on Reynolds Square was run with comparative ease, thanks to Caroline's able planning. They were now free to renew their social life by attending the round of autumn parties and balls. Proudly, they entertained Mark's associates, family friends and relatives in their own home.

"I'm quite amazed, really," Julia Scarbrough prattled at Mark as they danced together one November night across the polished floors of his large formal drawing room. "I didn't think Isaiah Davenport had so much beauty in him! Oh, he's a dear man. I meant nothing personal, of course, but I was truly worried about you and Caroline. William and I could not see your choosing Isaiah over our own William Jay. Isaiah wasn't a bit kind to the poor boy, you know, before Jay left for Charleston."

Sensing a ticklish turn in the conversation and aware that Isaiah Davenport's wife was dancing nearby with Jack Mackay, Mark swept Julia across the floor and into a corner of the room. "I don't think Davenport and Jay had more than the expected problems," he said. "William Jay was a bit careless about piling his building materials in the city streets. Isaiah, as alderman, did what he felt was his duty. He fined him. They parted friends, I believe. Is Jay still in Charleston?"

"Very clever of you, Mark dear, to end your defense of Mr. Davenport with a question. I'll be kind and step into the trap. Yes. Jay is still in Charleston, but as superior as Charlestonians feel to us here in Savannah, they don't appear to have our superb judgment. I hear he isn't doing well at all there. My heart breaks for him."

"You do like our house, though, don't you, m'lady?"

"I adore it. You and Caroline brought out the very best in Mr. Davenport. And the furniture! Mark, the furnishings—from carpets to draperies—all superb! The Brownings do have magnificent taste."

He propelled her out into the entrance hall. "Have you seen our taste in daughters?"

"Little Natalie, the titian seductress? I do declare that child is menacingly lovely! Everyone expected you and Caroline to have a pretty child, but who could have dreamed up Natalie? When she grows up, sir, you must be on guard."

They finished the dance and Mark escorted her back toward the large dining room, where William Scarbrough had been waltzing with Caroline. Seconds before they reached them, Julia blurted: "I have heard surprisingly little criticism of you, Mark, for refusing to *own* your servants. Some, of course. But I thought you'd be relieved to know—not much. I'm so fond of you, I take it all as a mere eccentricity of yours."

Mark bowed. "Thank you, Miss Julia."

"I suppose that tenderhearted Eliza Mackay is staying in with poor Margaret McQueen through her mourning time. What a pity! Such a lovely evening to miss." They were approaching Caroline and Scarbrough now and Julia caroled, "William dear, don't you wish one of our daughters had been old enough to capture this enchanting Mr. Browning? I understand, Caroline darling, that poor Mary Savage, considered our current belle, is still grieving that she was born too late."

Mark winked at Caroline, who replied pleasantly, "Miss Julia, I wouldn't blame every woman in Savannah for hating me."

"By the way, Browning," Scarbrough changed the subject smoothly. "I ran into Savannah's once troublesome Mr. Kott the other day when I was making a business call out on the Savannah River."

Carefully avoiding Caroline's eyes, Mark answered only, "Oh?"

"I was at Coleraine Plantation when Kott rode in, accompanying a wagonload of pine logs he was delivering. The man was exemplary in his manners and offered the good news that Knightsford is prospering under his care. I suppose my own business has kept me too busy, but I simply hadn't heard that Kott was back on the scene—much less working for you."

"He's doing a more than satisfactory job, sir."

"So I gathered. He looked quite presentable, in fact. An eerie sort of fellow, I always thought, but the proof is in the pudding, eh?"

"That's right, Mr. Scarbrough."

"Julia and I aren't much for churchgoing, although we live by Christian principles, I should hope, but Kott also informed me that he's a changed man. Some sort of religious conversion, I believe. At least, he spoke freely and almost embarrassingly of what he called the power of God."

"Mark," Caroline interrupted, the old look of panic in her eyes, "I promised Gerta we'd slip away to kiss Natalie good night. We're quite late doing it." To the Scarbroughs, she added, "Excuse us if we vanish from our own party for a few moments?"

They looked in on their child; then, halfway down the stair

that led from Natalie's third-floor rooms, Caroline stopped.
"Mark, was I too rude downstairs a while ago with the Scarbroughs? I still can't—hear Osmund's name mentioned
without my face freezing. I know what that look does to you,
and none of it's your fault."

"You were fine, darling. There's nothing to worry about."

"Don't talk to me as though I'm a silly child! I know I am,
but I don't want you to treat me that way."

His hand under her chin, he turned her face up to him so
that he could look squarely into her eyes. "What upsets you,
upsets me, too. But Osmund and I get along. We operate on a
strictly business basis. Oh, now and then, he tries to talk to me
about his new, changed character, about what God has done
for him, but—"

"What do you say to him when he does that? Mark, what
on earth do you say?"

"Very little. I merely listen. And hope it's true. Miss Eliza
says I underestimate God. She may be right."

"Does Miss Eliza think he's changed? Does she really think
he's telling the truth?"

"In my opinion, she's just about where I am with the whole
thing. When she reminds me that God is all-powerful, she's
also reminding herself."

"I know we have to go back down to our guests, but if I
don't tell you this right now, I might never tell you. At the
Presbyterian Church last Sunday afternoon during Mr. Lowell
Mason's *Oratorio,* I—thought a lot about God."

"That doesn't surprise me. I won't forget that music,
either."

"I—oh, this is such a crazy time to be telling you, in the
midst of a party, but—well, for your sake and for Natalie's
sake, I—tried to give myself to God while I listened to Mr.
Mason play. Suddenly, I just felt so sure that I *needed* to do
that. I've talked to Him all my life, even as a little girl, but,
Mark, there isn't a woman alive good enough for you. Maybe
if I live very close to God, I can be—almost good enough. I'm
also really scared of being Natalie's mother."

"Scared?"

She nodded. "Scared that I'll never quite know *how* to
be—her mother. Do all parents think their child is—different?
I know that's a stupid question. Don't even try to answer it.

But I'm with her all day long. She is—different. She's already given us both so much joy, but she's just beginning her life, dearest. We don't have any idea what she may be like later.''

Margaret McQueen, learning ever so slowly to live at Causton's Bluff alone, spent less and less time in Savannah but asked more often that William be allowed to visit her. William loved the rich Causton's Bluff land, and Mark was amazed, when he tallied Margaret's accounts in November 1824, to find her profits up. They were not up drastically because the national economy still lagged, but enough so that Mark could make her payment of three thousand dollars against the nearly fourteen thousand John McQueen died owing on his land.

For still another year the city had passed through the summer and fall without an epidemic. The Council's conversion of wet rice culture to dry had undoubtedly helped, as had new and more frequent sanitation inspections. Financial losses had forced a few men to leave town. Richard Richardson, the bank president, who had borrowed so heavily from his own bank in order to build the first William Jay mansion in the city, had moved away. The United States Bank now owned the Richardson house. The Boltons were also gone, but Mackay's dear friend, the Frenchman Petit de Villers, was again earning a modest profit as a merchant. Mark liked Mackay's old friend and had secretly thrown considerable business de Villers's way, but he was surprised when Eliza admitted knowing it.

"You're often foolish," Eliza said. "But how good of you."

"Life is good to me," Mark answered as Jupiter Taylor drove them toward Mark's house on a windy November evening. "The least I can do is try to show a little gratitude. Monsieur de Villers lied to me, though," he grinned. "He promised not to tell anyone."

"I'm his son's godmother, don't forget. He tells me everything. I'm so glad he's back in society again. How such a naturally outgoing, merry-hearted man lived through all those years of seclusion and grief, I'll never know."

"His wife's been dead for over a decade, hasn't she?"

"Yes. Poor, poor man had a long and painful time of it." Eliza turned toward him on the carriage seat. "Now, sir, you said you had big news for Caroline and me this evening, I have some for you right now. Monsieur Petit de Villers and Cousin Margaret have been to the theater together twice lately!''

"Good! Do you suppose they might get seriously interested in each other?''

She shook her head. "No, not the way you mean. I could be wrong, but I don't think either of those two will ever marry again. They do lend each other support, though. Petit can certainly understand Margaret's battle with her grief. I had them over the other night and there was actually more laughter in the house than I've heard since you and Caroline left us. I noticed William talked to Petit far more than he usually talks to anyone but you or Margaret.''

"Miss Eliza, I'm just thinking aloud, but, William has done so well supervising Margaret's land at Causton's Bluff with only weekly trips out there. Margaret and Petit are friends now. Since William likes him, why doesn't Cousin Margaret transfer her accounts and business to de Villers?''

Eliza smacked his knee. "I imagine because she's perfectly satisfied with Mark Browning, her present factor.''

"Seriously, it might help all around. Petit is close to the Bryans, William is waiting ever so patiently to marry little Virginia Bryan, Margaret and de Villers see each other. Petit always needs a bit more income.''

"What am I going to do with you, Mark?''

He kissed her hand. "Keep me. Just keep me, Miss Eliza.''

Jupiter Taylor pulled the carriage onto Bryan Street and slowed as they reached the house. "Not one, but two ladies will be waiting to greet you," Mark said, helping Eliza down from the high step. "My two-year-old daughter set up such a howl when Caroline and Gerta tried to put her to bed before your arrival, we both succumbed. Natalie is still up waiting for you.''

"Waiting to pull my hair, I have no doubt.''

"That's her stock-in-trade. I know she's a holy terror, but so pretty—so strangely pretty. Remember how dark blue her eyes were the first time I saw her? To me, they're even more arresting now that they've turned such a light, pale blue.''

"Spoiling her is like a game for you now, Mark, while she's so young," Eliza warned, stopping to examine the growth of an azalea bush she'd helped Mark set out in the narrow strip of ground in front of the town house. "No matter how captivating those pale-blue eyes, don't overdo the spoiling. You'll make life harder for Natalie later on."

Taking her arm as they mounted the wide front steps, Mark laughed. "I know that. Caroline knows it, too. But you don't live with the little rascal—we do. And we never know where we stand with her. Sometimes she doesn't even seem to like us. I can hold out my arms to her and she might just laugh, narrow those eyes and run away. She runs, in fact, all day long. We have to put everything breakable out of her reach when she's downstairs."

"Nothing so unusual about that for a two-year-old. She's discovering her own world—outside the two of you."

"But it doesn't even scare her when she sends a crystal bowl crashing to the floor. She laughs! I thought only boys were destructive."

"Fiddle. Just plain fiddle."

"Did Eliza Anne and Kate hit you in the face? I don't remember that Sallie did."

"Kate hit me sometimes, but it always made her cry if she thought she'd hurt me."

"Not Natalie Browning," he said, opening the door. "She laughs. And if she's a mind to, hits you again."

At dinner in the softly lighted dining room, after Natalie was finally put to bed, Eliza, seated on the long side of the damask-covered table, looked from Mark to Caroline, in their places at either end. The moving light from a tall silver candelabrum shone on their faces—Caroline, more serene than Eliza could remember, her thick, dark hair lost in the shadow, the glow in her violet-blue eyes melting. The same light picked out Mark's sensitive features—the evenly formed mouth, the straight nose, the place between his dark brows where his characteristic little frown came and went. How deeply she loved them. How she longed for Robert to see the Brownings —exactly as they were this moment, mature enough, yet still youthfully vibrant, in their places at the head and foot of their own table, in their own home.

The young Irish woman, Maureen, who insisted upon serving what she cooked herself, removed their plates.

"A delicious veal roast, Maureen," Eliza said, smiling at

the woman. "And your squash soufflé was perfect."

"Thank you, Mrs. Mackay. My sainted mother's recipe."

After dessert of Maureen's pecan pie, Eliza said in a half whisper, "She'd never admit it in a million years, but I think even Hannah would agree that Maureen is a marvelous cook."

"Oh, that reminds me," Mark said, laughing. "Maureen told me this morning that your Hannah put her in her place in Market Square yesterday."

"What in the world did Hannah say to her?"

"Well, they exchanged a few pleasant words first about how glad they both were that the market had been moved back to its old place in Market Square—"

"I'm glad it's back where it belongs, too," Caroline interrupted, "but it's been back there a long time now. Why were our two cooks sparring?"

"Because they're experts," Mark said. "Hannah won, I feel sure, but she made Maureen furious in the process."

"Oh, dear, I'll have to speak to Hannah," Eliza said.

"No, no, no, Miss Eliza. Really fine cooks enjoy sparring with each other." He laughed. "It seems Hannah kept shadowing Maureen—first over the green vegetables, where she informed her that 'Mister Mark' didn't like collards, and then over the squash, where Hannah let it be known that 'Mister Mark' preferred pie squash to crookneck squash."

Laughing, Caroline asked, "What kind of squash do you think Maureen used in her soufflé tonight, Miss Eliza?"

"Crookneck, I'm sure. You don't think she'd take Hannah's nosy advice, do you?"

"The last rapier thrust good old Hannah made—and the one I imagine hit home—was to say, 'Good day, miss. It does my heart good to see a *white* woman with sense about a market.'"

"Mark, Hannah shouldn't have done that," Eliza said. "It's certainly no secret to me that she feels superior to your cook—and that stands to reason, since Hannah's never known many white women who knew how to cook—but she went too far."

"Oh, she went much further," Mark continued. "She mumbled—quite loudly, I take it—as she walked away that she did hope 'Mister Mark' wouldn't keep on losing so much weight!"

"You haven't lost weight, have you?" Caroline asked.

"If anything, I've put on a few pounds."

Eliza folded her napkin and took a deep, resigned breath. "All I can say is that it's more than poor Hannah can bear that someone else—especially a *white* cook—has the privilege of trying to please you, Mr. Beloved Browning."

Suddenly serious, Caroline asked, "Are we talked about in town—for paying our servants, Miss Eliza?"

"A little. It's just that folk aren't used to it. Any change that surprises causes tongues to wag."

"Am I being stubborn to insist upon hiring our help?" Mark asked openly, with no hint of self-defense.

"You will always do what you believe in, Mark," Eliza said, turning her thin china cup round and round in its saucer. "No one can be faulted for that. You aren't trapped in our economic system. You're free to follow your convictions. That's what you should do. Maureen and Gerta—and your free colored man—have to live, too. My Grandfather Smith hated owning other human beings."

"But he must have been good to his people," Caroline put in.

"Oh, he was. And he owned over a hundred at one time, counting his house servants. They'd always owned their help, their fathers and grandfathers owned theirs—it's the way we all live."

"I'm not trying to prove anything," Mark said thoughtfully. "And God knows I don't feel—more Christian than anyone else. It's just that I was brought up believing that slavery is—" He gave Eliza a loving smile and stopped abruptly.

"You were brought up to believe that slavery is wrong, an abomination. I don't even like the word. I don't use it, actually. And I expect it *is*—very wrong. Only God has the right to be anyone's master." Eliza smiled a sad little smile. "I—would be totally helpless to try to change my way of living now. As you of all people know, Mark, I don't have any money for wages. Even tiny ones."

"I know that."

"Miss Eliza?"

"What is it, Caroline?"

"Your house people are like members of the family. Hannah and Emphie and Hero are—well, I lived there with you long enough to know that you confide in Hannah as you would your own sister."

"That's right." Eliza glanced at Mark. He was frowning, watching Caroline intently. "I've told Hannah—although not Emphie—things I haven't told another living soul."

Caroline's lovely features contorted with what Eliza guessed was a confused rather than a troubled thought. "I—I could never, *never*—confide in Maureen or Gerta," Caroline said haltingly. "I'd feel strange even to think about it. Do I feel that way only because they're both—white—like me? I always told Grandfather's Prince everything."

Eliza saw Mark look at her for an answer.

She smiled, thought a moment and said, "Caroline dear, I just don't know. I've had Hannah all my married life—and since. Maureen and Gerta have been with you for less than two years."

"But that's a long time! I found myself telling Hannah personal things when I'd lived at your house only a week or so."

"I don't think we're solving this question," Eliza said cheerfully. "What was that big news you've made us wait to hear, Mark? Dinner's over. We're both on the edges of our chairs."

Noticeably relieved, Eliza thought, Mark said, "Oh, oh, yes. My big news." He leaned toward them eagerly. "I went by Mr. Davenport's house today to pay off the last of the supply bills he received from the North and found him just home from a City Council meeting. You'll never guess who's agreed to visit us in Savannah—and be celebrated at least as lavishly as was President Monroe."

"The Marquis de Lafayette!" Caroline guessed.

Mark nodded proudly.

"Is that true?" Eliza asked. "I knew he was in the United States, but I didn't dream we'd get him to Savannah."

"When, darling? When?"

"They're hoping for next spring."

"Oh, dear," Caroline moaned. "And this is only November!"

"But think of the preparation we'll have to make. We're fortunate, I guess, to be squeezed into an already crowded itinerary; we'd better be thankful he'll come at all. Now that

Mrs. Maxwell rents the Richardson house from the bank; present plans are for the marquis and his party to stay there. I certainly know of no more elegant accommodations for such a revered visitor."

A lady on each arm, Mark escorted them into the small parlor, where all the chairs were comfortable, though not as lavish as in the formal dining room. After he'd seated Eliza and Caroline, Mark took a chair and rested his head against the high back. "Outside of President Washington, we don't have a more beloved man anywhere in American history than General Lafayette. Aunt Nassie just might be pacing about heaven right now at the mere thought that I'm going to get to look at her magnificent hero—face to face."

"And my—grandmother," Caroline said, still unable to mention her without a chill in her voice. "I wish I had a handful of pennies for every time she told me about the crippled old Philadelphia lady who remembered Lafayette from when he was helping us fight our Revolution. I never asked whether or not Grandmother knew the lady, or where she even heard the story, but she loved telling it. It seems that when the marquis passed by in a Philadelphia parade, the normally helpless old lady pushed her beloved family aside, shouting, 'Let me pass, children, that I may again see that good young marquis!' "

Eliza could see Mark trying to cover the relief he felt that Caroline had mentioned Ethel Cameron almost casually. He laughed, perhaps a bit too heartily, and said, "My Aunt Nassie loved Lafayette enough to push anyone aside for one tiny glimpse."

"I wonder how long he'll be remembered by our children's children for all he did to help us win our independence," Eliza mused. "All the way up to the twentieth century, do you suppose?"

Eliza's question required no immediate answer. They were quiet for a time, as friends can be, thinking their own thoughts.

Then, abruptly, Caroline sat straight up. "Miss Eliza, Mark, for days I've been asking God to help me overcome my—revulsion at even mentioning my grandmother. Mind you, I don't think I really want to overcome it. I'd like it much better if I could just—pretend she isn't related to me at all." Caroline was twisting the tip of the corner of her lace shawl.

"I don't like what I'm going to say, but—" She jumped up, hurried to the window, her back to them. "But, I have to say it. And it's all General Lafayette's fault!"

Going to her, Mark asked gently, "What's his fault, darling?"

"He made me think of her! When I was probably six or seven, I remember how my grandparents argued over who was the greater man—Washington or Lafayette. That was back when they were still speaking to each other."

"Your grandfather favored Washington, I suppose," Eliza said as calmly as possible, encouraging Caroline's response, she hoped.

"That's right, he did."

"And the marquis himself would have agreed with your grandfather," Mark said, following Eliza's lead. "Lafayette loved General Washington so much, he named his son for him."

"Grandmother thought Lafayette was the nobler of the two," Caroline went on doggedly, "because he had to leave his home and family and come to a foreign country to fight with us. Washington, according to her, deserved far less credit. He was already an American. It was his battle to fight."

"Your grandmother had a point, of course," Mark said carefully.

"What difference does it make if she had a point or not?" Caroline demanded.

Mark shot a quick glance at Eliza, who shook her head, urging him to wait.

Slowly, Caroline turned to face them. "Forgive me. I—snapped."

Not touching her, Mark said softly, "You can be any way you need to be with Miss Eliza and me."

After a deep breath, she said, "I'm just going to tell you both right out. I think I'll have to make some kind of move toward—my grandmother. Maybe it's God or maybe I'm crazy, but if it's all right with you, Mark, I'd like to take Natalie and visit Knightsford this weekend." When neither Eliza nor Mark spoke, Caroline plunged on. "Don't you see, I can use her admiration for the marquis as my excuse for visiting her—after all this time. She'll—really like knowing that he's—coming. . . ." Her voice trailed off.

Firmly, Mark said, "You don't need an excuse for trying to be a peacemaker, darling."

"I need an excuse for *myself*. Sometimes you're almost —dense about my grandmother!" She looked from one to the other, her face flushed. "There's no way either of you could know what happens inside me even yet, when her name is mentioned!" She threw herself into Mark's arms, weeping. "Help me, Mark, help me!"

The pain in Mark's face as he held her told Eliza how deeply Caroline's hurt had eaten into him. This was a moment when they needed to be alone. As close as we are, she thought, I am still a third person. "Mark, I have to get home."

"Not now, Miss Eliza," he begged. "Please, not now!"

"Jupiter can take me. I'll be perfectly all right."

Abruptly, Caroline pulled away from Mark, dried her eyes and said, "That was exactly what I needed to put an end to my—tantrum."

"My dear," Eliza said, "you are *not* a tantrum thrower!"

Making herself smile, tears still coursing down her cheeks, Caroline said, "I inherit it from Natalie. Mark and I will both ride home with you. I'm all right. I just got scared for a minute at what I said I was going to do." She straightened her slender shoulders. "I've known, ever since Mr. Mason's *Oratorio,* that I had to try to make peace with Grandmother. I still hate the idea, but I'm willing. It has to be this weekend. If we wait, I might back down."

"I'll be right there with you when you see her again," Mark said simply.

"You, too, Miss Eliza. Please, I want you and all the Mackays with me! Please?"

"All right, we'll go. But someone else will be there with you, too," Eliza said. "God."

"I know." Caroline's tears had stopped. "I know. . . . But wouldn't it be so much easier—wouldn't everything be so much easier—if we could *see* Him?"

# FIFTY-ONE

A misty rain was falling from the dark, low sky when Hero brought the carriage around to the front of the Mackay house on Friday. The air was far from warm, but there was no chill in it as the entire family piled in—Jack and William on the front seat with Hero, little Sallie on Jack's lap. Room had to be left for Virginia Bryan, who would be waiting to join them at the Bryans' house in town.

"I wish I were in love," Jack said as they stopped for Virginia. "Look, old William is so smitten, he doesn't even have sense enough to get under the stoop. Look at him—standing right out in the rain. What a day for a trip—anywhere!"

"Rain or no rain," Eliza said firmly, "this is when Caroline needs to go. She wants us with her, so we're going. We won't melt in a little rain."

"I think it's going to stop," Eliza Anne said. "I have one of my feelings. I get them just the way Papa always did."

Sallie, eight, said, mainly to herself, "I wish I knew why it's so important for Caroline to talk to cross old Mrs. Cameron."

"Never mind," her mother said. "It is important."

The girl sighed deeply. "Sometimes I wish I'd never grow up. Grown-ups are so peculiar."

"Sallie, sometimes you sound as though you don't care whether we answer you or not," fifteen-year-old Kate remarked, pushing Eliza Anne to make more room for her own widening sitter. "You say things and just let them hang there in the air. I suppose it's because you're so young."

"Maybe," Jack called back, "she just likes the sound of her

own voice. I like the sound of mine."

The front door of the Bryan house opened and they all saw Virginia in the wide entrance, dressed in teal-blue traveling clothes with a brimmed hat to match. No one in the carriage spoke as William hurriedly grabbed her valise, his angular body bending to make it easy for Virginia to take his arm. As though not a drop of rain were falling, he led her slowly down the steps and along the walkway, his eyes never leaving her face.

"They make a fine couple," Eliza whispered. "Doesn't William look tall? And isn't she lovely in that outfit?"

"I wish I had her light, curly hair," Eliza Anne whispered.

"I wish I had her big, brown eyes," Kate said. "Mama, why didn't I inherit Papa's eyes?"

In the driver's seat, from her perch on Jack's knee, Sallie told herself that she wished she had Virginia's pretty nose.

"Hush, every one of you," their mother whispered. "They're here."

After greetings all around, Virginia, in her young, serious manner, spoke to Eliza. "You're kind to invite me, Mrs. Mackay. I wasn't sure up until the last minute, though, that I could come. Mama isn't well at all today. Do you think she'll be all right while I'm away?" Before Eliza could answer, Virginia laughed shyly. "I don't know what made me ask you that. How would you know? I—I just wanted so terribly to come along." With the merest glance at William, she added, "Never in all my life have I wanted so much to go anywhere!"

The rain had almost stopped when they met Mark and Caroline and Natalie at Mark's wharf for the trip to the Knightsford dock. Even the inclement weather went nearly unnoticed because everyone marveled most of the way at Natalie's wild delight in her first river ride. Jack and William handled the boat, so when the active child became more than her mother could manage, Mark took Natalie on his lap. He did keep her from falling overboard, but not once did she stop chattering and screaming her delight at the water.

That night, Natalie finally asleep and everyone in dry clothes after the showery trip up the river, Eliza played the old Grange pianoforte while they all sang. Then, after a half-hearted attempt at a game of charades, one and then another went to their beds or makeshift pallets. The last to go were Mark and Caroline.

"I'm proud of you," he said as he banked the parlor fire against the damp night chill.

"I don't see why."

"Because you were able to sing and then to perform that fine Nefertiti charade." He hung the small shovel back on its iron hook and sat down on the settee beside her. "I know how nervous you must be about tomorrow morning."

"We're definitely going in the morning—first thing," she said grimly. "Grandmother gets up early. She'll be dressed to receive by nine at the latest. Eight wouldn't surprise me."

"Let's go to bed, sweetheart. I want you to have a good night's sleep."

"Mark, you won't just take me there—and wait outside, will you?"

He gave her his warmest smile. "Caroline, if you, for any reason, want to get rid of me, you'll have to send up a flare or fire a cannon."

"You do think it's best not to take Natalie on this first visit, don't you?"

"That has to be your decision. I want whatever makes you more comfortable."

She laughed a brittle half laugh. "I've never been comfortable with my grandmother in my life! I—I just thought how excitable Natalie is, how it might frighten her if I forgot and raised my voice or—"

"Dearest," he said, pulling her to her feet. "Please stop fidgeting. Natalie isn't excitable unless she's trying to get her own way. I don't think it would harm her at all to go, but maybe your mind will be freer without her. What if she broke one of your grandmother's treasures right off?"

When Solomon, Grange Annie's husband, brought the old Mackay carriage around at eight-thirty the next morning, the clouds were still low and heavy, but it was not raining. Mark settled a basket on the carriage floor before helping Caroline up the carriage steps and onto the driver's seat.

"What's in the basket?" she asked. "I don't think she'd like it at all if—after all this time—we brought her a present. She hates getting presents."

Hopping up beside her, he said, "It isn't for your grandmother. It's for us." He nodded his thanks to Solomon and started the horses. "We're going to be so relieved, we'll be ready for a celebration when this visit is over. Grange Annie made us a picnic."

Caroline grasped his arm and moved closer. "Oh, Mark, if I—if I say the wrong thing, please stop me!"

"You won't, you won't."

"Even if I snap at you for stopping me, do it anyway." She sighed heavily. "Oh, I wish it were a sunny day."

William and Virginia were strolling hand in hand along the narrow, sandy road when the old Mackay carriage passed, heading toward Knightsford. The younger people waved, the Brownings waved back, but the carriage kept right on.

"I guess they knew we didn't want a ride," William said.

"More than that, Miss Caroline is in no mood for small talk. You don't seem to realize how nervous she is about seeing her grandmother for the first time since—since her grandfather burned up."

"I do realize," he said, watching her earnest young face as they walked along. "Don't forget I'm a close friend of Mark's. He talks to me. Sometimes he asks my advice."

"He does?"

"Yesterday when we were going over some bills of lading in his office, he wanted to know if I thought they should bring little Natalie so her grandmother could see her today, or wait for their second visit."

"Mr. Browning asked you that? He must think highly of you!"

William's shy smile lifted the lines on each side of his mouth. "He makes me feel pretty important at times. Virginia, could I ask you something?"

"Anything!"

"Do you think I'm foolish to want to be a planter more than anything else?"

"Why would I think that?"

He shrugged self-consciously. "Well, I haven't told even my mother, but Mark wants to make me his dock supervisor. He's bought a new ship. It'll be in Savannah sometime early next year. Four more planters signed up with him this month. He could have had six, if he hadn't shunted two of them to Monsieur de Villers. Mark doesn't seem interested in getting any richer. But being his dock supervisor could lead to bigger things for me.''

"Do you want to be rich, William?''

He laughed. "Me? No. I just want to own some good land, care for it, have somebody I can trust like Mark to handle my marketing—'' He glanced at her, saw she was not looking at him and dared to add: "I want my own home—a wife, children. The Grange isn't a big plantation—only about five hundred acres, I guess—but when I save enough money, I might buy it from Mama.''

In the cool November air, he felt his face grow hot when she stopped, took his arm and turned him to her. "William Mackay? Don't you ever let anything stand in the way of your becoming a planter, do you hear me?''

"Yes, ma'am. I—I was hoping you'd say that.'' He rolled a big slash pinecone under one boot, back and forth, then said, "But waiting till I can own land anywhere might take a long time, Virginia. Did—you think about that?''

She nodded, her sweet, intelligent face upturned to his.

"I guess you come only to my shoulder, don't you?'' he said. "You have to hold your head back, even to look at me, don't you?''

She went on looking up at him and for the first time, William kissed her on the mouth, his hand holding one of hers. The kiss was a mere touch of his lips, but it was long enough, he told himself. He dared not frighten her. Then, helpless to stop himself, he took her in his arms, certain that he could never live very long without being close to Virginia.

A few sprinkles began to fall. They both laughed, but he did not let her go.

Her arms tightly around his neck, she breathed, "I can wait, William. I won't mind waiting at all.''

He kissed her again, then again. "I'll—mind,'' he said hoarsely. "I'll mind waiting—a lot. But I vow I won't ask you to marry me until I own my own land.''

"Why can't you ask me now, and then we can wait—together?''

A sudden noise in the woods that fenced the narrow road startled her.

"Don't worry," he said. "That was probably only a squirrel landing in a pile of underbrush."

"Why can't you ask me now?" she repeated.

His mouth felt dry, but afraid to lose the moment, he blurted, "Virginia, when I've worked enough years so I can get some land, will you—marry me?"

He was hoping for her arms about his neck again. Instead, her hands dropped to her sides, and tears filled the soft, brown eyes that now looked not at him but toward the sandy curve in the road that led to Knightsford. It was as though she'd gone into some familiar, secret place of her own to realize the miracle. After a moment, she looked back at him and nodded and nodded—yes. Yes.

"I'll try hard to hurry things up," he said. "I love you, the way Mark loves Caroline."

She took his hand and they walked on slowly. "Just think," she said, "you'll stay by me if my mother dies, the way Mark is staying by Caroline—today when she sees her grandmother. I've heard about Ethel Cameron all my life. I've never met her, but she has always—scared me from afar."

"I met her. I think she's just a lonely, bitter old woman. She might even be scared a lot of the time, too."

"William, you're so understanding and wise."

"I'm just—myself."

"Isn't it romantic that we have Mark and Caroline as our —dream lovers?"

He laughed. "We do?"

"Oh, yes. Ever since I was a little girl, they've been my ideals."

"They've only been married four years."

"Four years ago I was only twelve, don't forget."

"I fell in love with you even before then," he said.

She stopped walking. "Then, you've waited already—all those years!"

"That's right."

"My mama's getting sicker all the time. I know she is. But I don't think I'll be nearly as—afraid now that I know we're going to get married. Do you think Caroline is less frightened of her grandmother this morning because Mark is there beside her? They must be at Knightsford by now, don't you think they are?"

*    *    *

On the Knightsford veranda, Mark knocked at the wide front door and they waited.

When Prince finally opened it, the old servant could only gasp, "Why—Miss Caroline!"

"Good morning, Prince," Mark said. "I hope we're not too early to see Mrs. Cameron."

Prince went on staring at Caroline. "You—a stranger, ma'am. You the last person I 'spect to open our door to!"

"I know, I know," she said, her voice strained. "Tell my grandmother we're here, please. We can talk later, Prince."

"I see is she dressed yet, ma'am."

"She's been dressed for more than an hour and you know it!"

"If you will, please," Mark said, hoping to cover her agitation, "just tell Mrs. Cameron we're here—and in no hurry. We don't want to rush her."

Prince bowed. "Yes, sir."

"It is raining out here, Prince," Caroline said. "I assume it's all right if we step inside?"

"Oh, scuse me, ma'am. Yes, ma'am." He closed the door softly behind them and disappeared around the curve up the wide stair.

Caroline whispered, "Mark, if I don't sit down, I think I might faint."

He steadied her. "But, darling, he didn't invite us to sit down. Try to be calm. Let's don't do anything that might upset her."

Looking around at the polished console table flanked by its familiar tall chairs, then up at the crystal chandelier, she said, her voice still tight, "I've spent my *life* trying not to upset her."

"I know. One more time, darling. She might surprise us. She might just be glad to see us. This could be the last time you'll have to be so careful."

Prince's footsteps descending the stair were quiet and slow. He must be older than Ethel Cameron, Mark thought. Years of trying to anticipate her would age anyone. "What did she say, Prince?"

A finger to his lips, Prince led them into the small parlor where Mark had drunk tea with Ethel Cameron so long ago.

Remembering on which end of the settee she had sat that day, he touched Caroline's elbow, directing her to a velvet Gainsborough chair.

"I know not to sit on that settee," she said.

He gave her a cheerful smile. "Let's try to keep a sense of humor. Where we sit—where anyone sits—is only ludicrous, after all."

Caroline tried to smile, too. "I'll do my best."

Safely in the parlor, Prince spoke in the softest voice. "Miss Ethel, she be down in a few minutes."

"Still reading her Bible?" Caroline asked.

"I seen it open beside her, miss."

"That means she still has to pray, Mark."

"We're in no hurry," he said, trying to sound calm. "Have you been well, Prince?"

The old servant smiled for the first time. "For a man older than the river, yes, sir. 'Ceptin' for my gimpy leg. But Miss Ethel, she been havin' dizzy spells."

"Sorry to hear that," Mark said. "Does she have them often?"

"Seem like it to me she do, and she have another one if she come down them stairs and find me still here." He bowed to them both and left for the back of the house.

"How old is your grandmother?"

"About seventy-four or -five, I'd think," she said nervously. "Grandfather would be well past eighty."

"I hope those dizzy spells don't mean anything serious is wrong."

"Women like my grandmother outlive everyone." Then, "Mark, listen!"

"What?"

"I heard her door open!"

"That's all right, dearest. We're here to talk to her. The sooner the better."

Light, unhurried footsteps moved along the bare floor of the upstairs hall and stopped. Mark stood, hesitated only a moment and went to the entrance hall to be on hand to greet Ethel Cameron. The first wide rise of stairs was empty. He saw no one and heard nothing. For what seemed a long time, he stood looking up to where the stair curved sharply, his heart pounding. How must Caroline feel? he thought. This

.was, in a way, worse than fear. How, indeed, must the strange, lonely woman feel—waiting, as she so obviously was, for the courage? the will? the strength? to descend the stair. For an instant, he remembered her standing in the high front window screaming the day Jonathan Cameron died.

What was she like now—today? Had six years changed anything? They would soon know. He heard three, four, then five steps, and Ethel Cameron stood on the landing where the stair curved, one hand on the polished mahogany railing, the other clasping her forehead.

If a dizzy spell should strike her now—Mark bounded up the steps toward her.

The look she gave him told him nothing at all. The hand that had clutched her head was now primly at her waist. As always, she was immaculately groomed, her thin, crepelike skin whiter than he remembered, undoubtedly accentuated by her lavender gown.

Mark bowed and took her arm. "I hope we haven't disturbed you, Mrs. Cameron," he said. "Caroline is with me."

"So Prince said." She pushed his hand away. "Please remember, Mr. Browning, that I live here. I go up and down these steps at will."

"Of course." He stepped aside for her to pass, to begin the descent that would bring her face to face with Caroline for the first time in six long years.

In the downstairs hall, she clapped her hands sharply. When Prince appeared, she ordered tea, dismissed him with a wave and walked resolutely into the small parlor.

"Good morning, Caroline," she said, extending her hand. Both the voice and the gesture were as though they had casually parted yesterday.

"Grandmother." Caroline's voice was shaky. She hesitated only a moment, though, before offering her own hand. "You look well."

"Thanks to your—charity." Ethel Cameron bit off the word. "I've ordered tea. Please sit down—both of you."

"We could have some more rain," Mark said lamely, taking a chair as soon as the ladies were seated. "The last time I was here, Kott was hoping for rain. This has been a good, steady kind. Fine for the crops and the woods. Things have been hazardously dry lately."

"I quite agree, Mr. Browning. But I'm more interested, I must confess, in why—after six years—you're both here this morning."

"To—make peace," Caroline blurted, her eyes wide, hopeful.

Until that moment, Ethel Cameron had been looking only at Mark. Now, slowly, she turned to her granddaughter.

"Peace? There is as much peace in this house as there ever was," she said coldly. "The peace of God has been in my heart through all these long years in which you've chosen to live—away. It is still there. Perhaps I should cancel our tea. If that's why you came, there is simply no new peace to be made. I am already—peaceful."

"Oh, we came to see you for yourself," Mark said, hoping it wasn't the wrong thing. "We brought Natalie along, too. She's at The Grange. Caroline felt that she wanted you to know your great-granddaughter." He forced a smile. "Our little girl is one of a kind, believe me."

"Grandmother, please—forgive me. Please forgive me," Caroline begged.

Mark ached to go to her, to whisper how proud she was making him this minute. To tell her he knew how hard it was.

Ethel Cameron stood. "Begging forgiveness does not become you, Caroline. After six years, I didn't expect you back, if that's what you mean." She clapped her hands and when Prince came, she canceled tea. "Obviously, I didn't expect you—ever again. You've left me my—dignity. That's quite enough. You've always loathed me—"

"No!" Caroline broke in.

"Please don't interrupt. Perhaps worse, you've tolerated me because I—had the misfortune to be married to—him."

"Grandmother, please!"

"I am grateful for your—charity." The thin, bent shoulders straightened. "In a life that has amounted to almost a—cipher —you have at least allowed me to continue as mistress of Knightsford. That's all I've ever had and by God's mercy, it has been enough. Along with your grandfather, you deprived me of love and affection for all the years of my life. It's gracious of you not to have deprived me of Knightsford for my remaining years. I see no reason whatever for reconciliation. My faith sustains me and—"

"Stop it!" Caroline shouted. "I'm a woman now, Grand-mother. I see a lot of things I just couldn't—see while I was still so young."

"I see, too," Ethel said, her voice suddenly choked. "Today I see that the one thing you might have done that—would have helped, you—*refused* to do!"

"What, Miss Ethel?" Mark asked eagerly. "I beg you not to send us away like this. What could we have done? What did we leave undone?"

A stifled sob escaped the taut, corded throat before Ethel managed to say, "You—did not bring—my great-grandchild with you *today!*" The hooded old eyes blazed. "The one thing you might have done, you did not do. Now, will you go, please? At once?"

Caroline ran from the room, down the hall and outside. Mark could not follow because Ethel Cameron, grabbing her head, began to sway. He caught her, led her to a chair and did not let go of her hand as he said, "Mrs. Cameron, I'll get Prince and one of your women to help you. But, I have to say this first. We almost brought Natalie. We made this trip so that you could meet our little girl. We are going to bring her here. We just thought everything might be easier for you and Caroline if, after all this time, you met alone first."

Her head lay against the damask back of the high tapestry chair to which he'd led her. Her eyes were closed, but her voice was quite strong again. "Please, get out."

On the veranda he found Caroline hugging a weathered white post, sobbing. It did not lessen until he'd picked her up, lifted her into the carriage, got in beside her and held her for a long time. When she finally grew quiet, he said as firmly as he could, "I'm bringing Natalie to see her tomorrow. But, *I* am bringing her, dearest. Whatever happens, Natalie is young enough to forget. Don't ask me to let you come, too. You're not going through that again. Is that clear?"

"Yes, Mark," she whispered thickly. "Yes. I'm—still too—hard for her."

# FIFTY-TWO

THAT night in the small room he and Caroline shared at The Grange, Mark slept little. Caroline's dread of Ethel Cameron had become his dread, too. When the old Mackay clock on the parlor mantel struck two, he noticed with relief that Caroline had finally stopped tossing and was apparently asleep. Desperately, he tried to keep his own body quiet, so as not to disturb her as over and over he relived the cruel, brief minutes at Knightsford.

Shortly after they had blown out the bedside candle, Caroline had cried again, sick that she had allowed her grandmother to so distract her that she forgot to tell her about the visit of the Marquis de Lafayette. Pathetically, she had counted on that news to soften the old lady.

"She's always done that to me," he recalled her telling him in the dark last night. "Why do I go on letting her make a blank out of my mind?"

"You didn't let her do that," he'd insisted. "You went to make peace with her and you didn't deviate once."

"I was going to use Lafayette's visit as a way to—break the ice. I dived right in without even giving myself a chance!"

"I promise I'll tell her tomorrow when I take Natalie over. Our little girl might do wonders."

"Don't hope for that," Caroline had said flatly. "Just—don't hope for that, Mark."

He did hope, though. When he roused from a short sleep as the clock struck five, he was still hopeful. The fact that one could never anticipate whether Natalie would awaken from her afternoon nap full of smiles or pulling hair had kept him from taking the child back to Knightsford yesterday afternoon. He dared hope for the best because he'd seen the old woman's face when she spit out her disappointment that they hadn't brought Natalie on the first visit. He had seen the pain in her eyes, and the more he thought about it, the more hopeful he became. He meant to take his daughter to meet her great-grandmother as early in the morning as Caroline and Eliza could get the child ready.

Natalie would be ready the minute her eyes flew open. He'd never known her to refuse a ride anywhere. And morning was her most amenable time of the day.

At Caroline's insistence, William went along. Natalie's love affair with the outside world could be dangerous without an adult to restrain her. She had always seemed to turn herself inside out in a carriage or a buggy. The air, the sunlight, the sudden vastness of what she could see, never failed to send her into a delirium of motion. William was the perfect choice. Watching over Natalie made Jack nervous, but William could be firm while smiling, could, at times, even hold her in his arms without eliciting a howl.

Driving the carriage, Mark kept an eye on his two passengers by frequent glances over his shoulder. Most of the time, Natalie's peals of laughter told him that all was well with her and William. Once, though, when he looked back, his own heart squeezed with envy. For weeks his daughter had struggled to free herself every time he hugged her for longer than an instant. Her mother, too, was learning that she dared not act on impulse to take the adorable-looking child into her arms. They had both settled for holding Natalie's hand. Now, there she was on this bright, crisp autumn morning, bouncing along, not only clinging to William, whose arms enfolded her, but laughing up at him.

"Where are we going?" Mark called back.

"To Dram Cam's!" Natalie shouted.

"Where? What did she say, William?"

"I think she said 'to Dram Cam's,' " William answered. "Is that what you said, Natalie? *Dram Cam's?*"

The child's answer was a piercing, bell-like laugh and a big wiggle of her whole body. Then she began to shout: "Dram Cam! Dram Cam! Dram Cam!"

When Mark caught on that she was shouting her version of Grandmother Cameron, he was so proud, he longed to bury his face in her fat little stomach and make his "growly noise," which she loved. He had explained to her before they left that they would be visiting Grandmother Cameron, and Natalie had remembered! "What's the matter, William?" he joked. "Can't you understand plain English? She's going to see her Grandmother Cameron—Dram Cam."

William mussed the golden-red curls, held her up in the air and said, "You're pretty smart, young lady. You're pretty smart."

"Me pity," she screamed, laughing. "Me pity!"

"That's right," Mark heard William say. "You are pretty. But don't forget, pretty is as pretty does. Ouch! Stop pulling my hair!"

When Mark drew the carriage up before the entrance of the Knightsford big house, sun slanting off the tall windows and gleaming along the bare, brown wisteria vines that twisted about one end of the veranda, Prince was polishing the front-door brass. At first sight of Natalie's bright head and her heart-stopping smile when William lifted her to the ground, the aging man's face lit up like a sunflower. For several minutes, after Natalie had grabbed Prince's thick, brown fingers, there was no understanding what the old man and his chattering little friend were saying to each other. Whatever it was, there was joy in it, and knowing how little joy Prince had experienced through his long years of service to the Camerons, Mark sat for a time in the driver's seat, hating to interrupt.

He had no sooner jumped from the carriage, though, when the front door opened from the inside and Ethel Cameron herself appeared—a look of wonder and something akin to ecstasy on her face. Mark bowed to her, as did William. She made no sign of having seen them. Prince, still stooped on his gimpy leg so that his grizzled brown face was at eye level with the child, had not seen his mistress.

But Natalie had seen her! With a burst of energy, she broke away from the surprised Prince, ran on her dimpled legs to the front steps and before Mark could reach her, was climbing them on hands and knees. Gesturing for William to leave Natalie alone, Mark stood still—watching as, jabbering delightedly, Natalie reached the veranda level. Regaining her

balance momentarily and pitching forward in her haste, she
ran straight into her great-grandmother's outstretched arms.

Mark and William exchanged looks and waited. Ethel
Cameron still seemed unaware that they were standing there.
For longer than Mark believed possible, knowing his wiggly
daughter, he watched the woman enfold the child, her jeweled
hand stroking, stroking the back of Natalie's curly red hair.
When he heard Natalie grunt, he knew that she was hugging
her great-grandmother, too.

After a time, her eyes on the child only, Ethel Cameron
stood up, took Natalie's willing hand in hers and vanished
with her inside the front door.

"Lord, have mercy," Prince breathed. "You the papa of—
a angel, Mister Mark!"

Mark tried to laugh. "I agree, Prince—sometimes. What do
you think, William? Should we leave them alone for a while?"

"That's why we brought Natalie," William said.

"We could drive out and find Osmund Kott, check the yield
from the south fields. I need those figures."

"I'll drive," William said, pulling himself onto the high
front seat.

"Tell Mrs. Cameron we'll be back in an hour or so," Mark
told Prince and climbed up beside William.

Osmund Kott saw the carriage bumping toward him over
the pocked road, swung quickly onto his horse and galloped
in the direction of the south fields, where the carriage was
headed. Although he'd schooled himself not to admit to any
kind of pleasure, he couldn't restrain a smile as he recognized
Mark Browning. Kott was doing a superb piece of work at
Knightsford. He knew it. He had been wise to have slipped
almost unnoticed into the position of overseer. Browning had
no choice but to hire him. His sister's son was paying him well
and he was saving almost every penny of it. The bigger the cotton yield, the more rice he produced, the more he was paid by
Mark Browning. Few men were fool enough to pay an overseer on a profit basis, but his nephew was obviously a fool.
Osmund meant to go on working hard, increasing yields, saving his earnings, and one day to take full advantage of what he
had long recognized as foolish generosity in Mark Browning.
One day Kott fully intended to offer to buy a portion of the

Knightsford land. That would be the day when, unless his generally accurate perception of human nature failed him, Browning's generosity would prevail.

As an adjunct to this well-thought-out plan, Osmund had been able to slip larger and larger portions of the Knightsford crops up the river to Charleston for sale at his private outlet there. Except for 10 percent to Mrs. Cameron, all monies from those transactions belonged to him. Not once had young Browning appeared suspicious of a single bale of Knightsford cotton or a single bag of Knightsford rice. Obviously, the yields had been shipped abroad without inspection. It had required some skill to steal enough ballast rock under cover of night from the Savannah waterfront, but the pile from the last haul would be more than he needed for this year's crops. Only one heavy stone per bale or bag brought up the weight so that the stealthy shipments to Charleston were not missed.

Long ago, he had discarded the idea of attempting to blackmail his nephew. That had worked with Osmund's weak, frightened father, Jonathan Cameron, because of his past life. It would not have worked with Browning and, indeed, wasn't needed. The generosity plan was working just fine. It also offered diversion for Kott and far less strain. With his present employer, he meant to perform so efficiently that the plan would remain foolproof. Browning would never become suspicious so long as yields continued to increase. Browning was a fair man. Kott counted heavily on that.

When Ethel Cameron died at last, Browning would undoubtedly sell all of Knightsford. He and Miss Caroline were plainly city folk. A position in the highly successful factorage on Commerce Row could well be in the cards for Osmund, too—later, when he was too old to ride the fields. His nephew made it all almost too easy. Actually, the only thing a man had to do was—work, remain pleasant and wait.

Waving, he galloped toward the oncoming carriage.

Standing at the edge of the south fields with Kott, Mark asked detailed questions about yields from the first picking and for estimates of the second-picking yield. Kott answered promptly and satisfactorily. When they had finished their business talk, the two walked leisurely back to the carriage, where William waited.

"We have a little time to kill," Mark said. "Join us, William. You're more interested in planting than anything else in the world." As William climbed down from the driver's seat, Mark added, "Looking over these fields will give you a fine picture of high yield."

Kott beamed his pleasure as the three strolled toward a stand of woods nearby, picked out a fallen log in full sunshine and sat down.

"Mr. Mackay and I brought my little daughter over to see Mrs. Cameron this morning," Mark explained. "They seem to have taken such a liking to each other, we decided to leave them alone for a time and find you. How are things going in the upper fields? The picking almost finished for this round?"

"Oh, it is finished," Kott said proudly. "A crew of twelve nigras picked the last acre yesterday. Shouldn't take long to give it the final picking early in December. No doubt this rain we've had will bring it to bloom by then."

Mark was looking out over the partially picked west fields some distance from where they sat, the unpicked cotton a blanket of white over the flat, sandy earth. Here and there, moving steadily from place to place, cotton bags dragging behind them, straw hats and colored bandanas bobbed slowly up and down.

"The Knightsford people have done a splendid job, haven't they, Kott? I had no idea they'd have picked over the entire south fields before the end of this month. Good work."

"Thank you, sir. I try. They work as well as any nigras if they know I'm on a horse watching their every move." He grinned pleasantly. "The good Lord understood about nigras and cotton. If cotton grew any taller, they could hide in it. Knightsford nigras keep marching all day long, I'm happy to say. Our full-grown hands pick from a hundred fifty to two hundred pounds a day of seed cotton."

Mark frowned. "I wish someone would find a way to develop a mechanical picker. Picking cotton, I hear, is hard on the fingers."

"You one of those Northern Abolitionists, Mark?" Kott asked evenly.

"Not exactly."

Osmund spit. "Well," he went on in his most pleasant voice, "cotton just doesn't ripen all at the same time. Any overseer, if he's worth his money, has to keep his people everlastingly at it.''

"Yes," Mark said noncommittally. He got to his feet and extended his hand. "Well, you've done your usual fine job. Do you think I can offer us out on the market at five hundred pounds an acre—ginned?''

"Oh, yes, sir," Kott said, pumping Mark's hand. "If the weather cooperates, a little more than that.''

"I suppose our new gin is still working well?''

Osmund laughed. "Listen, I take care of that gin like it was a little child.''

"That reminds me, William, you and I had better get back to the big house. My little child and her great-grandmother might be tiring of each other.''

As the three walked toward the carriage, Kott said earnestly, "You're a prince of a man to bring your daughter over to see that poor old lady. She's very lonely these days. Sometimes she even invites me for a talk." He grinned. "A woman with her breeding inviting the overseer? Of course, at other times she pretends she isn't at home when I go. But, I do go. Every day.''

"You do?''

"That's the very least any human being could do, it seems to me. For the Lord's sake," Osmund said. " 'Whatsoever ye do unto the least of these, ye do also unto me.' ''

"Uh—that's right," Mark said warily. "Prince tells me she's been having some dizzy spells. Do you know about that?''

"First I've heard. Of course, even the high and mighty Prince can't be sure about her. Sometimes she's as nice as pie. Other times, she's downright hateful. I don't take offense. I consider her painful solitude.''

"I see. Well, I'll be back next month. From what I gather from the Liverpool market, cotton's gone up to all of nine cents. Nothing like before the war, but some improvement. I'm hopeful for the future.''

"Oh, Mark, I'm also very hopeful. Very hopeful indeed.''

On the way back to Knightsford, Mark asked, "What do you think of Kott these days, William? You didn't open your mouth once while we were with him.''

"I didn't happen to think of anything to say to him.''

Mark, beside William on the driver's seat, threw an arm around the young man's shoulders. "A few more honest men like you, my friend, and we'd have a better city." When William only smiled back, Mark asked, "I'm going to repeat my first question—what do you think of Kott these days? Not the fine job he's doing. The man."

He waited while William thought a minute. "I think—two ways about him. Both good and bad. He strikes me as being—both good and bad at the same time."

Now it was Mark's turn to ponder. Finally, he said, "I wonder if we wouldn't all have a far more peaceful time of it if we could bring ourselves to accept the fact that everyone is both good and bad. Wouldn't we get hurt less often if we stopped expecting those we love to be only—good?"

"The Bible says we're all both good and bad at the same time," William said.

"It does?"

"I'm not very quick at getting things by heart, but I memorized one verse that says: 'For the good that I would, I do not; but the evil which I would not, that I do.' I always felt so sorry for doing something bad when I was a boy, and Mama made me memorize that verse so I could learn to forgive myself."

"You make it hard for me to believe that we've all got some evil in us, William. I don't see it in you."

"You're not God."

As always, when they were alone, Mark was—at some point—mystified by William's wisdom. "I can't argue with you there. And from now on, thanks to you, I'm going to try to see Kott as a strong mixture of good and evil. Whatever he does certainly has a strong effect. What he says or does that's good comes out with such force, it throws me off-balance. I tend to believe the best of the man. On the other hand, we've all seen his bad side often enough to know the power it can have over him. Over anyone who gets in his way. None of this is easy, is it?"

"Nope. Thinking things through is never easy."

William had slowed the horses at the sweeping curve in the Knightsford drive. They could see Natalie and Ethel Cameron sitting side by side on the top front step.

"They seem to be waiting for us," Mark said with some apprehension. "I hope we weren't gone too long."

When Mark jumped to the ground and walked toward them, Ethel Cameron stood, Natalie clinging to her hand. "Thank you, Mr. Browning," the old lady said, as though he'd done a business favor. "I'm deeply grateful to you."

"You're more than welcome," Mark told her, bowing. "Caroline and I thought it best for you and Natalie to get acquainted—just the two of you." He was making conversation and it sounded like it.

Natalie made no move toward her father, and when he looked closely, he saw her pale-blue eyes narrow. She was angry with him for being there. He forced a laugh. "My daughter doesn't seem particularly glad to see me. I don't think she wants to say good-bye to you yet."

Ethel Cameron made no comment, but stooped to pick up a linen towel filled with the fragments of what appeared to have been a fragile blue Chinese bowl. "You will kindly give these to Caroline," she said. "She always wanted it in her room."

Obviously, Natalie had broken the bowl during one of her roughneck romps around the house. Mark began an effusive apology. Ethel stopped him. "Simply do as I say, Mr. Browning. And tell Caroline that Natalie is welcome to break anything she pleases in my house."

When Mark and William returned to The Grange with Natalie, Caroline was waiting on the narrow front porch. With a gallant smile, she waved William off to the stable with the carriage, embraced Mark, then picked up Natalie. The child was flushed and beaming now, delighting her mother—anxious as Caroline was about what Mark might have to tell her—because she did not wiggle to be put down.

"Mark? What happened?"

"Your grandmother and Natalie fell into each other's arms as though they'd been waiting for years to meet each other."

Caroline frowned. "They have been. At least Grandmother has been. What else? What did she say? Did she—mention me at all?"

He handed her the towel full of fragments. "She said to give these to you. I'm sure Natalie broke it."

Caroline stared at the fragile pieces of the pretty Chinese bowl for which she had begged as a child. It was her bowl.

Grandfather had brought it to her from New York when she
was five. A dreadful fuss had ensued because the bowl was
rare and valuable—Ethel Cameron insisting that no child
should own such a treasure. As always, Grandfather had given
in and the lustrous blue bowl had remained locked in the high
china closet, in plain view through the glass door but always
out of reach of young hands. "I wish you'd break it," she
remembered telling Grandfather in tears and rage. "I'd rather
see it broken than always out of my reach."

"Why—did she send these—pieces to me, Mark?"

"I don't know. She said to tell you Natalie is free to break
anything she pleases."

"She—*gave it to Natalie to play with?*"

He shrugged. "She must have. I wasn't invited in the house
this time. I'm sure that was best, anyway, on their first meeting."

"But—what am I supposed to do with it?"

"She simply said that as a child, you always wanted it in
your room."

Caroline's hurt was too deep to express, even to Mark.
Natalie began to laugh merrily and to fight her mother's arms.
Caroline put her down. Promptly, she ran to Mark and began
to pound him.

"I don't know what this means," he said, shaken by
Caroline's obvious pain, "but our wild little charmer is a different child with her great-grandmother. She was sitting beside
her on the steps as quietly as you please when William and I
drove up to get her. Caroline, Natalie could be just the key
we've been looking for."

"I wonder if I'm really looking. I—feel swept along, most
of the time against my will. Mark, did she really tell you that I
always wanted that blue bowl?"

"How else would I have known, darling?"

"What did she say when you told her about the marquis's
visit?"

He smacked himself on the forehead. "Can you believe I
completely forgot to tell her?"

"I certainly can believe it. She's an expert at confusion. If
you weren't invited in, you must be starved. Annie has something ready." To Natalie, she said, "Annie has something
good for you, too, you ravishing little minx. *After* your vegetables—a sugar cookie!"

Natalie raced for the kitchen, jabbering her delight.

"Your grandmother adored her," he said.

Caroline's short, mirthless laugh showed both pleasure and helplessness. "I think I'm glad about that. I know we have to go home to the city tomorrow, but, Mark, please make me come back soon! I know what I have to do where she's concerned, but it doesn't get any easier." She slipped both arms around his neck. "I'm glad you forgot about Lafayette. When we get back, I'll have that, at least, to tell her. A reason for inviting her to Savannah."

He held her. "Do you have to have a reason?"

"Yes. Yes, I still have to use a crutch of some kind with her, or I'll fall flat."

At Eliza's urging, Mark and Caroline took the child and returned the following weekend alone to The Grange. "Invite her to dinner at the cottage while you're there," Eliza insisted. "She may refuse, but do it anyway. And, by all means, ask her to spend Christmas with you in town. Since she is so drawn to Natalie, she just might accept."

When Natalie was finally asleep on their first night back at The Grange, Mark and Caroline sat alone before the Mackays' large fireplace. Hot flames boiled out the sap from green live oak logs so that they sizzled and sang.

For a long time, neither spoke. Thankful that silence could hold them as close as conversation, Mark waited for her to break it. As he waited, he held one of her hands. Now and then, he glanced at her face—almost mystical in the firelight. As his mother's face was, shrouded in its secrets.

"Could Miss Eliza be right?" she spoke at last. "About asking Grandmother to visit us for Christmas? At least, when Lafayette visits, there'll be lots of public affairs to attend. But, Christmas? Shut up with us in—our house? She's fled to her own rooms at Knightsford for so many years, what would she do in a strange house?"

"Darling, listen to me. Christmas is three weeks away yet."

"But we've planned a party! She hasn't been around people in so long. She's a recluse. Mightn't it be unfair to her?"

"If it will be too much for her, she'll refuse. But we'll have done our part. And"—he pulled her closer—"tonight is— tonight. We don't have to decide about Christmas or the marquis's visit right now."

"Mark, she isn't—evil, is she? My grandmother is just a bitter, lost old lady, isn't she?"

"Yes, and our baby daughter is going to melt that bitterness. I've decided to count on that. What can we lose by counting on it?"

She kissed both his hands. "Does it ever overwhelm you that I'm the one who actually *captured* you?"

He laughed. "When you begin to talk good nonsense like that, then I know my girl's in charge. The poised, courageous, light-hand-on-the-rein girl I love so much."

"I'm not poised and not one bit courageous about her."

"No one forced you to make that first move."

"You're wrong. I think—God forced me to do it."

"I don't believe He forces us to do anything."

"All right. I won't quibble. But He made me—willing—in church right in the middle of Mr. Mason's music. I wish we hadn't gone that Sunday!"

He was laughing again. "And I wish that I were half as honest as you."

"That's silly. With you, I just blurt out whatever I'm thinking." She buried her face in his shoulder. "And, Mark, I'm scared to see her tomorrow. I'm going, but I dread it, I dread it, I dread it!"

# FIFTY-THREE

WHEN they went to Knightsford the next day, Ethel Cameron, Natalie on her lap, listened politely while Mark invited her to spend Christmas with them in Savannah. Hoping to interest her, he went into some detail about the house Isaiah Davenport had built for them on Reynolds Square—the arrangement of the rooms—accenting the privacy she would have at all times. Now and then, he paused, hoping Caroline would join in. She was perched uncomfortably on the edge of her chair in the Knightsford parlor, her face flushed and, Mark thought, touchingly eager. At one point she did leap a bit awkwardly into his invitation by describing Natalie's own quarters on the third floor, assuring her grandmother that the little girl would revel in serving her from her own tiny tea set.

Except that she glanced down at the contented child on her lap now and then, Mark saw not one change of expression on Ethel Cameron's face. She remained silent. Nothing to do, he decided, but plunge into the second invitation to visit them when Lafayette would be due in the spring. He explained in detail the city's plans to receive the marquis on March 19 of the new year 1825. He told her that Georgia Governor George M. Troup would be there representing the people of the state, that the Council had appointed not only a military committee to welcome the distinguished visitor but a citizens' and an aldermanic committee as well. Caroline supplied the news that the general and his son, George Washington Lafayette, would be entertained at the Richardson mansion, now Mrs. Maxwell's lovely boardinghouse, on Oglethorpe Square and that Lafayette would lay the cornerstones to monuments planned

in memory of General Nathanael Greene and Polish General
Casimir Pulaski, who fought with Lafayette for American
liberty.

When Ethel still said nothing and showed no particular interest beyond courteous attention as they talked, Mark tried to
remember other details that might impress her.

"I know you'll be happy to learn that your friend Mr. Sheftall Sheftall, because of his own illustrious Revolutionary War
record, is not only serving on the citizens' committee, but will
be among the few Savannahians to greet General Lafayette
personally when he steps onto Georgia soil."

She spoke for the first time. "That is the very least they
could do for Mr. Sheftall."

"Oh, I quite agree," Mark said.

Still on the edge of her chair, Caroline said, "Mr. Sheftall
remembers actually meeting the marquis in Philadelphia during the war."

"So he's told me often," her grandmother said curtly.
"Now, if you'll both excuse us, it's time for Natalie and me to
spend the remainder of the morning together in my rooms."

Standing, Mark said, "Of course, Mrs. Cameron."

Natalie, who had jumped down, was holding Ethel Cameron's hand, jabbering happily as the two walked toward the
hall.

"Natalie," Caroline called helplessly, "please don't break
anything!"

When the great-grandmother and the child were out of sight
up the wide stair, Caroline whispered, "What are we supposed
to do?"

Mark hoped his smile was reassuring. "Be together. Isn't
that what we do best?"

Tears filled her eyes. "Mark, I don't ever remember that
she—held me on her lap—ever."

"I'm sure you were just too young to remember."

"I'm not sure of that at all."

"Would you like to look around the plantation while we
wait?"

"If you don't think we'll run into Osmund."

"I can't guarantee that. He's everywhere. But he's the
reason for the profit. My other clients are already in debt to
me on next year's crop." He smiled. "You're not, Mrs.

Browning. Osmund has changed. If we happen to see him, I don't think you'll mind nearly as much as you believe."

"You always think the best of everyone."

"Let's go prove me right."

Caroline stopped in the front hall. "Mark, should we just—leave—Natalie here with her?"

"Darling, she's our daughter's great-grandmother."

So the carriage would not pass Jonathan Cameron's grave, Mark took the road to the north fields. Caroline sat silently beside him on the driver's seat, but at least she'd agreed to go, to risk seeing Osmund Kott. It was important, Mark thought, for her to find an interest in Knightsford as it was today—her plantation—no longer her grandfather's. No longer a place to avoid. He had never known Natalie to respond to anyone as she had to Ethel Cameron. As the child grew older, she would want to visit Knightsford often. Caroline, if he could help her involve herself again in the shadow-and-sun-dappled beauty of the plantation, would find their visits far easier.

As an outsider, Mark had admired the Knightsford big house and its rolling green lawns, its dark magnolias and gnarled oaks, from his first sight of it. In a sense, he was still enough of an outsider to see the old place as it could be in the future—a happy spot to visit, no longer haunted by Caroline's memories of growing up there. That she had been happy with her grandfather all her life, no one could doubt. In the midst of his own tragedy, Jonathan Cameron had managed to create a positive atmosphere for her, some of the time, at least. Mark longed to do as much.

Perhaps, he thought, God means us all to be little creators. We are, in a sense.

As her husband, he was certainly responsible for the atmosphere he created around Caroline day in and day out. In a way, he had the responsibility to create the mood of the world in which she lived, just as God had taken on Himself the responsibility to create the physical world in which humankind lived. Except for her times of terror and dread of her grandmother, no one created a more livable world for a man than Caroline for Mark. He glanced at her nearly perfect profile. She was looking straight ahead, her hands clasped together tightly in her lap.

After a few moments, when he looked at her again, she sensed it and smiled at him. "I'm—trying, darling," she said. "I'm trying."

Making it as interesting as possible, he explained the yields of cotton as they rode past the north and east fields, fully aware that he was showing her nothing new, that she had taken the same ride many times with her grandfather. He spoke of the changes Osmund had made in the diking system in the rice fields off in the distance toward the river. She understood it all, of course, and seemed interested. At least she asked a few questions and commented that it was ironic that Kott had so increased the yield of both rice and cotton.

"How carefully do you examine the cotton bales and rice bags he sends into the city, Mark?"

"No more than those from other plantations," he said, frowning. "Why?"

"He isn't above weighting both bales and bags. Grandfather told me of other planters who had ballast rocks packed into the center of their cotton bales and their bags of rice. If only the outside was checked, they appeared normal. Osmund isn't above doing that."

Mark laughed. "Maybe not, but don't forget, he's planting more land than your grandfather ever planted. He's getting more work, somehow, out of the people."

Over the jolt and rattle of the carriage, Mark heard a horse galloping at some distance behind them.

"Oh, Mark, he's coming! How did he know we were here?"

"Who can answer that?" He spoke as casually as possible, forcing himself to smile at her. He reached for her hand and held it firmly, giving her all the strength he knew how to give.

"I'll try, Mark. I promise you, I'll try."

As he rode up behind them and then alongside, Osmund slowed his horse to a trot. Still moving along beside them, he bowed from the waist and doffed his cap to Caroline. "What a pleasant surprise," he said. "Not bad weather to be so close to Christmas, is it? Out to examine the last picking?"

"Not exactly," Mark said, stopping the carriage team. "Our daughter's with her great-grandmother for the morning. We're just looking around. Not much white left along here. The people have done extremely well."

"Treat them well, you reap the reward of their labor. By the way, we've begun something new at Knightsford that will interest you, I'm sure, Miss Caroline. Each morning, I meet for prayer with the field hands before they tie on their sacks for the day. It seems to have worked wonders."

Mark saw Caroline look straight at Kott for the first time. "You do *what?*" she demanded.

"Have a short time of prayer with the field hands and—"

"I heard you," she snapped. "I just don't believe it!"

Hoping to smooth things over, Mark said, "Whatever you're doing, it's working. You did have good hands to begin with, though. Mr. Cameron always treated his people right."

"I fully expect us to be entirely finished with the picking well before Christmas," Kott went on, as though Caroline had not challenged him. "Do I have your permission, sir, to reward them extra come Christmas?"

"Of course," Mark said, glancing at Caroline. "I'm sure you'd be in favor of that, wouldn't you, dear?"

"You know I would," she said, looking out over the reddish-brown fields, her struggle to control herself plainly in her voice. "I intend to find out about that prayer meeting, though."

Osmund's laugh was entirely pleasant. "Oh, I don't blame you one bit, ma'am," he said. "Your past experience with me has been anything but—prayerful. If anyone understands that, I do. How did you find your grandmother this morning?"

For an instant, Caroline did not move a muscle. Then, slowly, she turned to look at Kott. "Very well. Why do you ask?"

"I hear the old lady's been having dizzy spells lately. I go by to see her every day, you know."

"You—visit my grandmother every day? Does she—converse with you?"

He laughed softly. "Oh, yes. She seems to welcome civilized conversation. Knightsford can be a lonely old place. Only the workers don't get lonely out here."

"By the way, that nine cents a pound went up to ten on the Liverpool market," Mark said, hoping to change the subject. "I can't be sure the last of your cotton will bring ten cents, but I'm hopeful."

"That's good news, sir." Osmund looked at the pale-lemon

winter sun. "I have a lot of work to do yet today." He bowed
again to Caroline, still holding his work cap. "I'm sure you
want to ride on. But before I go, is there any chance that you
might be bringing your little girl out to Knightsford for
Christmas?"

"Why, no," Mark said. "We have no such plans. Why do
you ask?"

"No reason except that Christmas does have a way of
making lonely folks—lonelier. Good day to you both." He
galloped off.

"Mark, only Osmund Kott would dare lie about praying
with my grandfather's people!"

Mark sighed. "I admit that did stretch my credulity."

"Drive me back to the big house, *now*. Prince will know.
I'm just plain going to ask him to tell me the truth."

"Will he? He has to live here with Osmund, you know."

"Yes. I wouldn't swear to it about anyone else, but Prince
and I have been friends since I was a little girl like Natalie."

"She's up in her rooms with my child," Caroline told
Prince as she met him in the backyard on his way to the well.
"Please don't be nervous. Please, be my friend. I want you to
tell me something. If you still care about me, Prince, you'll tell
me the truth."

His eyes on the house, the thick, brown fingers moving anx-
iously over the bail of the bucket he carried, Prince whispered,
"Yes, ma'am. I sure do care about my little Miss Caroline."

"Just shake your head yes or no. Does Osmund Kott, the
overseer, have prayer with the field hands each morning
before they go to work?"

For the first time, Prince looked straight at her, then at the
ground.

"Prince! You don't have to look away as you were taught to
do when you speak to a white lady—not with me. I want you
to *look at me.*"

When he did, his frightened eyes told her everything.

"Osmund Kott lied, didn't he? He knew the field hands
would lie to protect him if my husband or I asked. But your
eyes are not lying, are they? Don't be frightened. He'll never
know I asked you. My husband—a Northerner—might have
gone straight to a field hand. I know better. Prince, just shake
your head yes or no. *Does he pray with the field hands?*"

The white-thatched old head moved firmly from side to side. "He—lied, Miss Caroline," Prince whispered. "He—foolin'—her, too." He jerked his head back toward the big house.

"My grandmother?"

Nodding his head yes, Prince turned quickly and limped off toward the well without looking back.

"Prince!" she called as loudly as she dared. "What does he lie to her about?"

The old man kept walking—around the corner of the kitchen storeroom and out of sight.

Still standing alone in the backyard path, Caroline began to weep. Dear God, help me, she cried out in her heart. If it weren't for Osmund, Mark and I might find a way to—be with Grandmother. But, God, You know Prince wouldn't lie to me!

When she made her way slowly back around to the front of the big house, she saw Mark examining a deep-pink camellia blooming on the old bush at the south end of the veranda. He hadn't seen her. Caroline stopped to watch him reach for still another full-petaled flower. Something like fury surged through her. Mark Browning should not be dragged through such ugly, nerve-racking uncertainty just because of her!

If Eliza Mackay had married him, his life would be good. Ethel Cameron and Osmund Kott could cast no dark shadows over Eliza's life. Mark would have had someone free to help him, someone who wouldn't always be crying out for him to help her. She began to walk slowly toward him. Somehow, she vowed, somehow, I'll find a way to—to stop dragging him down.

A twig snapped under her foot and Mark turned quickly, ran to her and took her in his arms.

"Did you find Prince?" he asked.

"Yes. There are no prayer meetings with the people."

"You're sure, I suppose."

Caroline tightened her arms about him. "As sure as that—I love you."

He took her hand and they walked toward the Knightsford front steps. "If you're that sure, then I'll be more careful with Kott. I promise. Do you think the man just has flights of fancy?"

"That's a nice way of putting it. Let's go in the house.

Maybe they're back downstairs by now." She shuddered. "Osmund scares me so much, I—suddenly want to beg Grandmother to visit us at Christmas. She didn't say no. She didn't answer either way—about Christmas or next spring when the marquis comes."

"I've almost gotten so I don't expect a direct answer from her," Mark said.

Holding hands, they climbed the wooden steps, Mark bouncing his weight a little on one sagging tread. "Kott will have to see to that step," he said. "In fact, they all need to be replaced."

She didn't answer. At the front door, Mark knocked. They waited while Prince shuffled out of the kitchen and down the hall to let them in.

"It still seem funny that you knock on this door, Miss Caroline," Prince said softly, then added in a barely audible whisper, "I know it be your house now."

"Let's forget about that," she said. "Is my daughter still upstairs?"

"Yes, ma'am. I ain't heard a peep outa the two of 'em."

Mark laughed. "Unusual for Natalie, I must say."

"What do you suppose they do up there, Mark?"

He shrugged. "Aunt Nassie and I could spend hours over one book of maps or pictures."

"I 'spect Miss Ethel, she be cuttin' out her fancy paper dolls," Prince said.

"Paper dolls?" Caroline asked in complete surprise.

"Oh, yes, ma'am, she be a real artist with a pair of scissors and some paper." He held an imaginary scissors against an imaginary piece of paper, snipping as he talked. "She fold the paper just so and then she begin to cut—an' cut an' cut—an' the chillurn's eyes, they pop right out they heads."

"What children?"

"The quarters chillurn. Miss Ethel, she cut and cut upstairs there by herself, then she send me down to give 'em the dolls. The dolls sure are purty, too. All fastened together like they was doin' a ring dance."

"My grandmother makes dolls for—the quarters children? I—I never remember her doing that—*not once*, Mark."

"No, ma'am," Prince said, "you wouldn't 'member. She only been doin' it since—since—" He stopped, his eyes on the floor.

In a whisper, Caroline said, "—since my grandfather died."

Prince nodded.

Then, from upstairs she heard the brassy click of the latch on her grandmother's door, and Natalie laughed and shouted, "Dram Cam! We go down."

"That's exactly right, you pretty child, 'we go down.' Dram Cam doesn't want to, but I suppose we must. They're back."

"Mama? My mama? Papa?"

"Yes." The yes was icy.

Their footsteps, Ethel's light and steady, Natalie's romping, moved along the bare upstairs hall and stopped suddenly. She's embracing my child, Caroline thought, and hated the flicker of revulsion she felt. Poor woman! Oh, my poor, poor grandmother! Caroline managed a smile as she and Mark stood waiting, looking up from the downstairs hall as the two descended the stair.

When Prince left as hurriedly as he could, Caroline whispered, "Mark, I hope Natalie hugged her back, don't you?"

He smiled. "She did. Don't worry, she did."

Natalie chattered all the way down the stairs, Ethel holding firmly to her hand. When the child jumped the last two steps into Mark's arms, Ethel stopped. Then she said politely, "Thank you. Thank you, both."

"Oh, Grandmother," Caroline's words tumbled out, "don't thank us for time with your very own great-granddaughter! We want you to have lots more time with her. Grandmother, please, we do so want you to visit us for the holidays in Savannah. We'd be so happy if you'd agree right now to come."

"Happy and honored, Miss Ethel," Mark added, "to have you for as long as you'd like to stay—as a part of our family. Will you come? I'll send my boat for you, or better still, we'll come for you ourselves."

"I'm planning to ask Mr. Sheftall to escort me into the city when the marquis arrives in the spring. Otherwise, I never leave the house except for my daily constitutional, weather permitting."

"Grandmother, think about it, *please?*"

"Good day to both of you. I should hope you won't wait so long to visit Knightsford again." Ethel turned to start back upstairs, then looked down at Caroline. "And, naturally, should you like, you are welcome to stay—here."

"Bye-bye, Dram Cam!" Natalie shouted. "Bye, bye, bye!"

Caroline saw the merest hint of a smile pull at her grandmother's mouth. "Yes," Ethel said, "yes, Dram Cam—loves you, beautiful child." She wiggled her jeweled fingers. "Bye, bye, bye . . ."

# FIFTY-FOUR

ELIZA Mackay sat alone in her parlor two weeks before Christmas, working to finish a needlepoint cover for the cushion she meant to give Jack for his room at West Point. He would leave the day after New Year's, 1825. A fancywork pillow might seem a strange Christmas gift for a dashing, witty young cadet, but Jack would treasure it. The design, drawn by Eliza Anne, was of the rambling old Mackay house, complete with the actual trees and shrubbery under which the children had played.

Jack, she mused, was as unlike his quiet, introspective brother, William, as two sons could be, but so like his father. He had grown fond of Shakespeare, of music, of art—perhaps a bit fonder than Robert had been—but his humor, his love of dancing, even his appearance, made her think of her beloved.

Both boys and the three girls were with Mark and Caroline today at The Grange, once more gathering greens to decorate the old house for the girls' Christmas dance four days from now.

William had persuaded Cousin Margaret to go along. Those two shared a friendship that excluded no one, but which, Eliza was glad to see, served to sustain them both. She had a hunch that Margaret had done the actual persuading, not William. Virginia Bryan's mother had died in September, and William had seemed as crushed as the heartbroken girl who would someday be Mrs. William Mackay. Unlike faithful William, Jack, the hunter, the dancer, the flirt, appeared to love every girl he met, and would have been far easier for his father to understand.

How Eliza would miss Jack! His appointment to West Point had come through rapidly, and his eagerness to be gone was so evident that Eliza had trouble balancing her happiness for him and her dread of letting him go. His interests were as wide as the sky, but they focused in his love for engineering. West Point had been his dream even before Isaiah Davenport hired him to help with Mark's house four years ago. Jack had gone on working for Davenport in order to help his mother financially, but she had seen growing restlessness in him this past year. He had no desire to become a builder of anything but bridges and forts for the Army.

Jack wanted to be a military engineer as much as William wanted to be a planter. "So much to think about," she said aloud to herself, smoothing the stitches over her knee. If only she could talk things over with Robert. For the children's sake, she seldom mentioned the ongoing pain of missing him but after more than eight years, it was there.

Mark, so grown up now, so mature in his judgments, so successful, had confessed not long ago that he, too, still missed Robert. "I seldom make a business decision or give anyone advice on any subject without first trying to decide what Mr. Mackay might have done."

Mark. Eliza's "dear boy." She could smile now at that awkward, painful night when he had proposed. For months afterward, the memory had been all pain and humiliation because she had handled it so poorly. Mark had always seemed, if not a son, a younger brother. Now that her own brother was gone, too, Mark was even dearer.

I am blessed, she thought. I am blessed. When I think of poor Cousin Margaret out there at Causton's Bluff alone —even when I think of pathetic old Mrs. Cameron rattling around in her big house—I know I am blessed to have the children, to have Mark and Caroline so close by.

As she threaded the needle to work in a darker green for the magnolia trees, she was frowning. Eliza always frowned when Ethel Cameron came to mind. Somehow I should be able to help with her, she told herself for the hundredth time. I owe it to Mark and Caroline, but how does anyone but God reach Ethel Cameron? They should all be overjoyed that Mark's irresistible child, Natalie, had seemed to captivate her. Why, she wondered, were they not overjoyed? Why had she and

Caroline and Mark admitted a kind of uneasiness? Oh, she could see Mark's trying to think creatively about the old lady's obvious obsession with the child—the child's with her, for that matter—but privately, to Eliza, he had admitted anxiety.

How it would simplify everything if poor Ethel could die! The thought shocked Eliza and she asked immediate forgiveness.

With a deep sigh, she put away her needles and thread, folded the pillow cover and went to the high front window. Robert, she knew, would say, "Don't take that unsolvable problem onto your own lovely shoulders, dear Eliza. No one's ever been able to touch Ethel Cameron!"

Well, she'd never agreed with Robert on absolutely everything. She didn't agree now, but neither did she have a solution. Perhaps there is none, she thought. Perhaps it isn't wicked, after all, simply to wait for Ethel to die, for Ethel to escape her own misery.

Only half attentive at first, she saw a well-dressed man walk into sight past her enormous old crepe myrtle tree. The tall, slightly stooped but energetic man slowed, looked both ways on Broughton Street, then opened her gate and started up the walk. It was Osmund Kott.

"I was in the city," he explained when she opened the front door, "and I thought I'd drop by to thank you for your prayers in my behalf, Mrs. Mackay. I'm deeply grateful."

"I—well, I'm grateful, too, if they helped, Osmund. Have you been in town long? The Brownings and my family are at The Grange."

"I know. I saw them about ten this morning, cutting holly and pine branches on both plantations."

Eliza said nothing. She had not asked him to sit down. They still stood in the front hall.

"You see," he went on, ignoring her lack of courtesy, "I'm here on a mission of mercy in behalf of Mrs. Cameron."

"Oh?"

"She isn't well these days. At her age, I'm sure she spends much of her time dwelling on the past. Perhaps, even as I do, she feels some guilt for her abuse of others."

"This is something of a coincidence, Osmund," Eliza said carefully. "I was thinking of Mrs. Cameron only a few moments ago, wishing I could help." She paused. "You certainly seem to be—interested in her."

"I understand the symptoms of the disease of—isolation, loneliness. I've been alone all my life. I'm fifty-seven years old, Mrs. Mackay. Oddly, in view of the fact that I am no blood kin to her, Mrs. Cameron—living on the same plantation as we do—is the closest I've ever come to having a family."

"Why, Osmund—I suppose that's true, isn't it?"

"You're not the only one who's never given it any thought, but, yes, it is true. I visit her every day now. She doesn't always choose to see me, but when she does, we have fairly pleasant talks."

"I wonder how often she's had pleasant talks—with anyone."

"Seldom, I'd say, in the past half century."

Eliza rubbed her forehead, trying to absorb it all. Fifty years, she thought . . . that's four years longer than I've been on earth.

"I have quite pleasant relations with Mr. Browning," Osmund was saying. "He never mentions it, but by his trust, he does rather treat me as his uncle. When I imply that he trusts me, I mean where my work is concerned. As a man, to him, I merely exist."

"What does Mark have to do with your reason for being here?"

"Quite a lot, actually. As I said, I am here on a mission of mercy in behalf of Mrs. Cameron. Browning holds the key. Browning and his wife and their little girl."

"I don't follow you."

"I'll try to be plainer. They have invited Mrs. Cameron to spend Christmas with them here in the city. She can't do that."

"Why not?"

"She just can't, that's all. She would be a nervous wreck after a social holiday in Savannah. The woman is a recluse. Mentally, she could crack under the strain."

"Osmund, what are you trying to say?"

"Yesterday Mrs. Cameron asked me to set some of the young hands to gathering greens—Christmas greens for her at Knightsford! She tells me that the big house hasn't been decorated for Christmas since Miss Caroline was a child. Not since her parents died in the epidemic, in fact. Mrs. Cameron wants Knightsford decorated this year so that, if her prayers are answered, as she says, the house will be cheerful and happy for the child. She worships the Browning child.''

Eliza stared at him. "She—she's been praying they'll decide —out of the blue, without an invitation—to leave their own home and spend Christmas with her?''

"Yes, ma'am. I'm here to beg you to use your influence on the Brownings. To beg them to surprise the old lady—as a Christmas gift.''

"That, as nearly as I can remember, is the gist of my conversation with Osmund Kott," Eliza told Mark and Caroline in the Brownings' informal drawing room that evening. "I know you're both tired after all that tramping around in the woods today, but I thought you should know as soon as possible.''

"But, Miss Eliza," Caroline said nervously, "we're giving an enormous dinner party here in town on Christmas Eve! How can we cancel at this late date?''

"We can, darling," Mark said. "We'd cancel it if there were sickness in the family, wouldn't we?''

"Well, yes, but—''

"Osmund says Mrs. Cameron is having frequent dizzy spells these days.''

"Oh, I know; Prince told me that, too. But she's always had dizzy spells—when she wants her way.''

"Don't say anything you'll be sorry for, Caroline.'' Eliza spoke gently. "I do hate to upset you, but I thought perhaps—''

Caroline whirled on her. "You thought perhaps I might— give in to her again? Miss Eliza, I've spent my life giving in to that old woman!''

When no one spoke, Caroline looked from Eliza to Mark, then whispered, "Forgive me.''

"It will be simple to send Jupiter around town with notes of apology, dearest," Mark said gently. "We can change the date for our dinner party to early next year.''

"I don't want to change the date! I want her to accept our invitation to come here. I do want her, Mark; I really do. I'm guilty of shutting her out for Grandfather. I know that. He

was so easy to love. Miss Eliza, she told Mark that she even
loved his mother when she was a little girl. Now, my grandmother adores Natalie. I'm sure she loved my father."
Caroline's eyes filled with tears. "She—skipped my generation. I remember *begging* her to let me wear the little signet
ring Papa wore as a child. She'd—show it to me in its velvet
box. I longed for it, but I was never allowed to wear it." Her
hands were stretched toward them, beseechingly. "I can't tell
you how I wanted to wear that tiny ring! And both of you stop
looking at me with so much pity because I can't help crying.
Stop it! I really don't know why I cry, so don't feel sorry for
me."

Eliza stood, Mark with her. "Hero is waiting to drive me
home. I think you two need to discuss this alone."

"Don't go," Caroline begged. "Please don't go! What
business is all of this to Osmund Kott? Do you think she might
have sent him in to—sway you, Miss Eliza?"

Eliza thought a minute. "I—don't know. That hadn't occurred to me. He seemed sincere enough."

"He seemed sincere enough when he told Mark and me he
prayed with the people before they went to pick in the fields,
too. I found out he was lying!"

"Oh, dear," Eliza said on a sigh. "Now, I don't know what
to think."

Caroline got up, her eyes pleading. "Mark, help me! Help
me be calm and sensible!"

"What comes to me right now," he said softly, "is that we
all need time to weigh everything."

"Christmas is only two weeks away!"

"I know, darling. But one more day won't matter. Can't we
wait at least until tomorrow?" He slipped his arm around
Caroline.

"Mark's right, my dear. Give yourself a night to sleep on
the whole matter."

Caroline disengaged Mark's arm and hurried to the window
alone. After a strained silence, she said, "I don't need to sleep
on it. I already know what we have to do. We'll go to Knightsford. Why I always give in fighting, I don't know. But I am—
giving in. I know she's old. I want to do something for her. I
know Natalie holds the key to whatever's left for Grandmother and me. We'll go, Mark. I'll write the notes to our

guests." She turned to face them. "But, oh, we've got to pray that none of this will in any way harm Natalie!"

Eliza frowned in surprise. "Caroline, how could it possibly harm Natalie?"

"I don't know, Miss Eliza. I—don't know."

# FIFTY-FIVE

ON December 23, after two days of rain, the nor'easter winds went on blowing. Rough waters forced Mark to take Caroline and Natalie to Knightsford by carriage. The trip overland, always hard, was slow and miserable because of the muddy, deeply rutted road. With Jupiter driving, Mark, seated between Natalie and Caroline, let his thoughts run back to other Christmases with the Mackays. He would miss them all this year. Jack would be gone when they returned from Knightsford. Mark had told him good-bye yesterday when he stopped at the Broughton Street house to leave the Mackays' presents. "This trip to Knightsford," he'd told Eliza, "can work wonders—or it can shatter Caroline. Think about us."

Jolting along in the carriage now, his mind went to Mackay himself, to the still vivid memory of how Robert Mackay had kept his distance from Jonathan Cameron and all his strange troubles. He smiled grimly to himself in the dark. Here I am, riding into the middle of it, he thought.

He had lost count of how many times Mackay had refused to become Cameron's factor. Well, Mackay had a right to refuse. Jonathan Cameron was Mark's grandfather, not Mackay's. Mark's own blood-relationship with Cameron still seemed remote. Even now, he had to prod himself at times to realize that Osmund Kott was his uncle. How quickly he'd been able to put the whole eerie saga behind him! Oh, not in his actions, necessarily, but in his private thoughts. How much he had been influenced by blood ties to hire Kott, he wasn't sure. Undoubtedly some. Mark wasn't a rebel against the

560

mores of society, and people normally favored family members. Undoubtedly, he had accepted his grandfather as a client for that reason. In part, at least.

How much did blood ties truly matter, he wondered? Aunt Nassie used to talk at length of his responsibilities as a Browning. Would he, Mark, be any different had he been born into a family of poor or modest means? Would he have been less or more lonely as a child had his father been a penniless, instead of a rich, drifter? Of course it was good to have money to fulfill his dreams, to build new houses for Savannah's poor. He and Caroline had taken Christmas dinner to all the families now living in the row houses built last year. The visits had meant much to them both. But, aside from the fortune, was there a special, singular feeling about being a Browning? A Cameron? A Mackay? A Charlton? A Sheftall? A Minis? A Habersham? A Kott? Did it matter deep inside that he was indeed the nephew of the unpredictable man whose mother had been named Cotting? Cotting shortened to Kott had briefly intrigued Mark when he first realized that Osmund was his mother's brother. He seldom thought of it now. Osmund Kott was—Osmund Kott. His strange, clever, often charming personality had stamped identifiable content into the name Kott. The name didn't make Osmund what he was. Circumstances did that, not Mary Cotting's blood. Not Jonathan Cameron's blood.

Most of what Aunt Nassie had taught Mark continued to help. He had simply never entirely agreed with her concept of blood and family name. A man was what he believed about himself, about God, about his fellow human beings. Mark was, on this windy, rainy, cold coastal night, only himself. As Caroline, her head on his shoulder, was herself.

She stirred. "Where are we?"

"I think we're nearly there. I can't see, but I think I felt us slipping and sliding through some water where the creek below Knightsford sometimes washes over the road. Are you all right?"

She sighed. "Yes. But only because I'm sitting beside Mr. Goodness and Mercy."

"Flattery will get you anywhere you want to go," he teased.

"Oh, Mark, I hope we're doing the right thing. Don't fret. I'm not agitating. But, what if Osmund was lying again? What if she didn't decorate the house or even want us? What if she hates having us?"

"You are agitating, I think," he said gently. "Try not to. We're almost there. The carriage is loaded with gifts and food and wine. And, do you realize that our normally rambunctious daughter is still sleeping like an angel? Couldn't that be a good omen?"

She pressed her head against his shoulder. "If I'd had you to handle me all my life, I wouldn't be struggling so now."

Rain was beginning to fall again when the mud-spattered carriage rolled up the drive at Knightsford, its passengers stiff with cold, Natalie awake and screaming her protest at the darkness.

"Grandmother loathes crying children," Caroline said, the old nervousness in her voice. "Try to get her to hush, Mark."

"Look, Caroline—look, Natalie! Bright lights at all the windows in the big house!"

Natalie responded with an even more piercing complaint.

"Mark, I can't believe it," Caroline gasped. "I've never seen lights all over that house—not ever! She _is_ expecting us. She is hoping we'll come. . . ." Her voice sharpened. "Natalie, that's enough screaming!"

Holding Natalie up so that she could see out the carriage window, Mark said, "Look, baby! Those bright lights are all for you! Can you see them?"

Natalie only raised the level of her wail.

"They're Dram Cam's lights," Mark persisted. "Dram Cam lit each candle just for—you!"

"Oh, Mark, do you have to call my grandmother by that dreadful name?"

"Dram Cam?"

"It's so silly."

"Not to Natalie, it isn't. Is it, baby? You're going to see Dram Cam. Do you remember Dram Cam?"

The wailing stopped. There were no tears and no nose to blow. The screaming had been pure protest. "Dram Cam?" the child asked.

"Yes. Dram Cam's waiting for you right inside that big house."

A veritable stream of Natalie jabbering ensued, all delighted.

"It is a silly name," Mark said to Caroline, a smile in his voice, "but it works."

"Yes. Thank heaven."

The wide front door burst open, sending a shaft of yellow light across the dark veranda. Prince stood in the doorway. They could see his hands raised in jubilation above his white head.

When they entered the open door and walked into the big front hall, Caroline could only gasp: "Mark, look! It's—really true. She—did expect us. Look at the vases of magnolia and the cedar garlands. She did decorate for us. . . ."

"It's going to be a good Christmas," he said, holding Natalie in his arms. "Did you have a hand in all these fine decorations, Prince?"

"Yes, sir! We all did."

Caroline had not expected anyone but Prince to be there to greet them. The entrance of the Knightsford big house had always been used by her grandmother only as a place to pass through, coming and going on her daily walk. For years, Caroline and her grandfather had eaten alone in the spacious dining room. She was not disappointed to be greeted only by Prince, but they were both puzzled when he made no move to obey Mark's instructions to bring everything in the carriage to their room—wherever they were to sleep in the huge, empty house.

Prince neither responded with his usual yes, sir, and yes, ma'am, nor moved from where he stood to one side of the cheerful hall when Caroline asked where they would be sleeping. A big smile on his face, he stood instead looking toward the back of the hall. Then Caroline saw her, as did Mark, the minute Natalie began struggling to get down. In the shadows at the very end of the long hall stood Ethel Cameron, in dark-plum silk, her hands clasped nervously at her waist, waiting in silence for someone else to make the first move.

"Grandmother!" Caroline gasped, her voice scarcely audible over Natalie's happy chatter.

Relieved, she saw Mark hurry toward the old lady with Natalie, his free hand extended. Ignoring Mark's outstretched hand, her grandmother reached for the little girl, and for a long, suspended moment, old woman and child clung to each other. Finally, Natalie planted a noisy kiss on the dry, lined cheek.

"We guessed right, didn't we?" Mark asked pleasantly. "You were hoping we'd come, weren't you, Mrs. Cameron?"

Slowly, Caroline watched her grandmother lower the child to the floor, still holding on to her hand. "I wanted the child," the elderly woman said evenly. A stiff smile creased her face as she looked adoringly down at Natalie, who was jumping up and down. "I think the child wanted to spend Christmas with me." Then, looking at Mark, not Caroline, she asked, "How did you know, Mr. Browning?"

Caroline watched Mark's face. He would not lie, but what might the mention of Osmund Kott do to her grandmother?

"Frankly, we did have a hint that you might want us," he said simply.

With no change in voice or expression, Ethel said, "Osmund Kott, I have no doubt. I had forbidden him to mention it to anyone but I'm glad he disobeyed. You must all be exhausted from that dreadful ride. Prince will take you to your room—your grandfather's old room, Caroline, here on the first floor."

"No!" This from Caroline, involuntarily. "I mean—thank you, Grandmother. We are tired—and cold."

"The room should be warm," Ethel said. "Prince laid a fire this morning. I've eaten. Prince, give them a chance to freshen up, then inform Lettie when to serve their food. Tell her not to forget the boiled custard for—my little angel." Her hand lay on Natalie's head as she spoke. To Mark and Caroline, she added tersely, "Put her to bed as soon as you've fed her. I'll expect her in my rooms bright and early tomorrow morning."

"Of course, Grandmother," Caroline said helplessly— stupidly, she thought.

When Ethel started up the wide stair, Natalie set up such a howl that Mark was able to quiet her only by promising that she'd see Dram Cam just as soon as she slept.

Her heart thumping, her legs like wood, Caroline followed Prince down the hall to her grandfather's room, dreading the sight of the place where the only love she'd ever known, until Mark, had been shared. She hadn't been in that once safe, happy room since his death. Had she dreamed that her grand-mother would put them there, she could not have faced the trip.

In the doorway, Prince, Mark and the baby behind her, Caroline stopped. The dark four-postered bed, its canopy bird print unchanged, brought back one of her earliest memories—the sound of his gentle laughter as her grandfather bounced her on that same bed. The long-plumed birds on the coverlet still matched those in the canopy. They had "camped out" on that bed, in a tent improvised from the coverlet. Her eyes darted around the room. She was dreading fresh pain at the sight of each familiar object—especially his books on the shelves. Two volumes still lay on the table beside his big chair, where Caroline had sat blissfully on his lap hour after hour through long, rainy afternoons. On the bedside table the prized porcelain statue of Ben Franklin still stood, and the brass candlestick. On the far wall his military jackets and sword hung near the dark bulk of the familiar clothespress. That his clothes were still inside, she had no doubt.

Behind her, holding Natalie, Mark waited, giving her time, she knew. He was holding their daughter, or Caroline would have run into his arms as she longed to do. You're a grown woman, she scolded herself, the mother of a little girl who needs you to behave like a mother. Abruptly, she took Natalie in her own arms. The child's body felt warm and soft and comforting. For a brief moment, Natalie hugged her back and pressed her firm, smooth cheek against her mother's. The irony that she could not show this irresistible child to her grandfather almost overwhelmed her.

"Shall I take off her damp clothes, darling, and put on her nightgown?" Mark asked, his voice easing her ever so gently back into the moment.

"Please," she said, handing him the baby. "Prince? Are—*his* clothes still here?"

The old man bowed his head. "Yes, ma'am. They all be here."

"Is it—out of the question for you to put us in another room? There are seven bedrooms in this house!"

"She say this one, Miss Caroline. I try to tell her. She bit my head off. Time you get used to it, she say. Time you learn how to come here—to see *her*."

Caroline stared at the old servant. "Mark? Did you hear that? Grandmother wants me to—learn how to come to see *her!*"

"That's good news," he said, smoothing Natalie's long flannel nightgown after she'd jerked it down over her own head. "We have more good news, too. Natalie put on her own nightgown. I think she needs a word of praise from her mama."

"Yes," Caroline said, trying to respond to the child. "That's wonderful, Natalie. You're getting so grown up. In no time you'll be able to dress yourself.'

In response, Natalie reach d for the small porcelain figure of Benjamin Franklin and hurled it to the floor. The shattered pieces rattled across the bare boards. Her control shattered, too, Caroline began to weep.

Prince stooped to pick up the fragments and Natalie laughed merrily.

Mark buried his face in his hands.

# FIFTY-SIX

CHRISTMAS dinner, though simple, showed careful planning. There was wild stuffed turkey, ham, bowls and bowls of vegetables, yams, biscuits—and plum pudding for dessert.

Mark, seated at the opposite end of the long table from Ethel Cameron, made a mental note to share later with Caroline his amazement at how well the Cameron servants performed after six years of no dining in the large, elegantly furnished room. At the last minute, Ethel Cameron, without any warning, had sent for Osmund Kott to dine with them. Mark had to discipline himself not to glance too often at Caroline, seated straight across the table from Kott. She had managed, he noticed, to eat a little of almost everything, but not once had he seen her look at Osmund.

Doing his best to keep at least a thread of conversation going, Mark marveled at Ethel Cameron, who ate slowly, showing no hint of being ill at ease, but uttering not a word. Pleasant, easy talk, he was sure, would be far harder for her than what to him seemed an almost unbearable agony of near silence. Without Kott, in fact, the time spent at the table would have been unendurable. Off and on, the two men conversed with each other about national politics and the difference steamboats had made in transporting cotton and rice.

They were all there, though, Mark kept reminding himself, and most important, Ethel Cameron had joined them.

When the meal ended at last, Caroline, as though she'd spent the time firming her resolve, went straight to the old ebony-and-gilt pianoforte and began to play the poignant melody of the new hymn "When I Survey the Wondrous

Cross." Bless her, Mark thought, for trying, but why wasn't she playing Christmas carols or at least something a bit more lively? He loved Lowell Mason's new hymn—Caroline played it often for him at home—but surely, this group needed a bit of cheering up. He wouldn't say anything to her for the world, and perhaps the Mason music helped Caroline in some way. It had been during Lowell Mason's concert at Mackay's church, after all, that she had first felt the need to make peace with her grandmother.

Osmund Kott stood beside the pianoforte, absorbed in the music. Ethel, on the edge of her settee, listened, her face expressionless. She had sent word to Lettie to bring Natalie as soon as her nap ended. One way or another, Natalie would liven things up. As Caroline went on playing the haunting music, Mark stood, his back to the fire. Now and then, he smiled at Ethel Cameron, hoping for a smile in return. She seemed not to notice him or Caroline or Kott. Her eyes darted often toward the hall, watching, he knew, for Natalie to come bounding in.

When Caroline touched the last note, Ethel Cameron said, "Don't be surprised that the pianoforte is so out of tune. It's been years since anyone has touched it."

Mark had been moved all day long by the enormous, seemingly fruitless effort Caroline was making toward the old lady. Now, turning from the keyboard, she asked hopefully, "Did you like that melody, Grandmother?"

"Well enough."

"The words are beautiful, too," Caroline went on. Then, as on impulse, she began not to sing but to speak the opening lyrics of the hymn: " 'When I survey the wondrous cross, on which the Prince of Glory died, my richest gain I count but loss, and pour contempt on all my pride.' "

"You used to sing, Caroline," her grandmother said. It was more an accusation, Mark thought, than a request.

"Oh, she still sings," he offered. "How about some Christmas music, dear? Do you have a favorite Christmas song, Mrs. Cameron?"

"I believe not, Mr. Browning."

He smiled at her. "Can't you call me Mark? I am in the family now."

She barely nodded.

"I wish you'd play more, Miss Caroline," Osmund Kott said eagerly. "I haven't heard music of any kind for so long."

Without looking at Kott, Caroline said, quite cheerfully, "I'm sure Christmas music would be more appropriate," and went brightly into the familiar French carol "Angels We Have Heard on High."

Immediately, Mark saw Osmund begin to tap his fingers on the pianoforte case in time with the rhythm. Throughout the verse and the "Gloria in excelsis Deo," Kott seemed transported. I hope it's real, Mark thought, and felt a bit con-science-stricken at his own skepticism. Christmas should be a time of love, not skepticism. He felt himself beginning to hope that Osmund Kott was enjoying himself as much as he seemed to be.

When Caroline began the carol again, Mark was startled to hear Osmund sing. He not only knew every word, his tenor voice, though untrained, was oddly beautiful. The elevating Gloria refrain, Kott singing lustily, resounded through the house and brought Lettie, Prince and their daughter, Mina, out of the kitchen to listen from the hallway.

The music still rang out when Natalie appeared by herself —nightgown, stocking feet, eyes bright, face alight with smiles—and headed for the parlor. Lettie reached for her, but missed, as the child passed her in the hall and went directly to Osmund, chubby arms out to hug the legs of the man she'd never seen. Mark saw Osmund smile down at her and place one hand on her shiny head.

He finished the song with Natalie looking up at him, en-tranced. Mark and Caroline applauded, joined by the servants in the hallway. Everyone was laughing but Ethel Cameron, who did not move a muscle or change her expression.

"Hello, little girl," Osmund said, stooping to Natalie's eye level. "What's your name?"

"Natalie Browning."

"Mark!" Caroline exclaimed. "She said it correctly! Did you hear? She said Natalie with an *l*—not Natawee."

"Nata*wee!* Nata*wee!*" the child yelled.

"All right, honey, don't spoil it," Mark laughed.

"Dram Cam!" Natalie shouted and ran to throw herself onto Ethel Cameron's lap.

After a somewhat determined keyboard improvisation, as

though she were collecting herself again, Caroline began to play Mark's favorite, "Drink to Me Only with Thine Eyes." This time, Osmund Kott wisely did not sing and Ethel Cameron, with eyes for Natalie only, began to pat the child's hands together in time to the music. Except when Lettie hurried silently in with Natalie's warm robe, the old woman and the child went on patting time together. Mark sighed with relief. From that moment, the evening went far better than he had dared hope.

As soon as Caroline stopped playing, Osmund took his discreet leave. Mark managed to remove a sleeping Natalie from her great-grandmother's arms without rousing her, and after polite good nights, he and Caroline went gratefully to their room.

"It wasn't too bad, after all, was it?" Caroline said, when they had tucked Natalie into the old cherrywood cradle where her father, then she, had slept as infants.

"Thanks to you, my darling," Mark whispered. "I've never been as proud of you as I am tonight."

"I'm trying. I'm really trying. For Natalie's sake—for yours."

"And for your grandmother's, too?"

She hit him Natalie fashion on the shoulder, then kissed him. "Yes. For her sake, too."

Ethel Cameron, as always, stayed in her rooms the next morning, waiting for Natalie to be sent to her. For two hours she played paper dolls and pat-a-cake with the child, then sent her away with Lettie and dressed for her walk.

Her daily pattern was to circle the cleared area where the cottage had stood. She would walk around it once or twice, depending on the weather, then return to her rooms. Today she passed the cleared area and the grave of her husband, but did not complete the circle. Instead, she headed for the overseer's cottage a quarter of a mile away. When Osmund opened the door to her light tap, she marched inside and, without being invited, sat on a straight chair.

"You'll find that cushioned chair more comfortable," he said casually, as though she called on him every day.

"I'm not here for comfort. I want you to leave Knightsford."

"Such a request is impossible," he said calmly. "I take my orders from Mr. Browning."

She felt her whole body begin to tremble. Struggling to keep her face a mask, she asked bluntly, "Why did you burn the cottage?"

He laughed, as at a child's whim. "Isn't it a bit late to ask, ma'am? That's ancient history."

"Not to me. *Why?*"

"I hated my father."

"So did I."

"Of course you hated him. I wouldn't have written telling you my plans otherwise."

"Why *did* you write that letter to me?"

"I needed someone to hate with me. I was lonely. So were you. It is all ancient history, though, I don't hate anymore. The thought of what happened that day sickens me now."

"That's a lie."

"It isn't, but I'm sure I can't convince you. I've done all I know to show you kindness. I've been genuinely concerned about your dizzy spells. I've kept watch over you—"

She shrieked: "Shut your evil mouth!"

A smile spread slowly across his face. "Undoubtedly, a lady of your standing has never—never before raised her voice in such a *common* scream. I'm sure you're terribly embarrassed by it. You sounded rather like the wife of my old friend the fishmonger at Yamacraw."

Ethel gripped the seat of the hard chair with both hands. "Why—did you—write me your plans—to do—what you did?"

"I had no intention of acting alone. We both knew what he'd do. We both knew he'd be driven to try to put out the fire."

"I was not involved!"

"Oh, yes, you were—by your silence then—and you are involved now by your continued silence. You've kept my letter as proof that I set the fire. But, Mrs. Cameron, you can't do a thing with your proof since it also proves you an accomplice. I should have known he wouldn't leave me money, but I wanted at least a place at Knightsford. *I was born here!* I needed you at a disadvantage in order to have my place. You would have been agitating to be rid of me except for that letter. We had each other trapped, m'lady. We make good trap-fellows.''

Her head began to swim. "How—did you—know he'd run into—the fire that day?''

"Simple. As a child, I was right outside the window, hiding in her oleander bushes, the day your husband weakened and came into my mother again more than four years after I was born. The day Mark Browning's mother was conceived. I was a small boy, but I listened and I heard—I *saw* how he loved her! My mother had your husband's very life wrapped around her heart. She loved him as much as he loved her. I've never forgotten that day. I knew—I knew that even after she'd been dead for all those years, the sight of her cottage burning would send him out of his mind with panic. That squat, thick-walled tabby cottage was all he had left of her! He still loved her so much, he thought he could put the fire out with his bare hands.''

Ethel was sobbing now. Hating it, but sobbing, out of control.

"You loathed him, too," Kott said. .

She nodded helplessly. "Yes—but not that much. I didn't hate Jonathan—*that much*." She jerked her shoulders back. "Jealousy isn't hate!''

"One follows the other.''

"Not with me. I'm—a Christian!''

He smiled. "You forget, dear lady. I'm a Christian, too, now. Hate does follow jealousy. You saw the little Browning girl run to me first as I stood singing last night. Your monster, jealousy, sent you here today to order me off the place. It won't work. Browning is among the most successful factors in Savannah. He's told me that Knightsford is one of the few plantations making a profit. I'm here because I'm needed.'' He leaned down; his eyes looked defiantly into hers. "You're here, Mrs. Cameron, only by the charity of your grand-daughter.''

With all her might, she slapped him across the face. Stunned, he stood for a moment, staring at her; then a kindly smile softened his features. He reached for another straight chair, set it near hers, straddled it and began to explain as though she were six years old:

"My father dribbled funds out to me all my life. He saw to a decent home and a Christian upbringing for Melissa. He dumped me into an orphanage, and until the day he died, he kept me dangling on his line like a poor, hooked trout, with just enough money to keep me reasonably quiet."

"You blackmailed him!"

"Yes, or I'd have gotten nothing. He's gone now and I'm here, earning my way at the place where I was born. Browning needs me. You need me, dear lady."

"Nothing of the kind!"

"When they're gone again—back to their own world in Savannah—I'll once more be your only human tie. I'm the one who got them to come this time. You need me to keep you in touch with the living."

She rubbed her forehead as though trying to clear her mind. "I can always burn the letter and tell them I saw you set fire to the cottage."

"Good. That would free me forever from any whiff of suspicion. No one would believe you because as far as anyone else knew, I was still in New York." He laughed quietly. "I'm not worried. I *am* a changed man, Mrs. Cameron. God has done a real work of grace in me."

She drew back from him, tried to get to her feet. Her dizziness wouldn't permit it.

"That's right, rest a bit longer, old lady. I'll be kind to you, don't worry. None of this upsets me."

"Osmund . . ." Her voice came out almost as a wail. She could hear it, but could not change it. "Osmund," she began again, pulling as far away from him as she could, "why—don't—you—kill me, too?"

He smiled. "I told you, ma'am. I'm a Christian now. You forget that I didn't kill my father. He—killed himself."

Slowly, she struggled to her feet. When Osmund tried to help her, she pushed him away and by some means managed to reach the door of his cottage before the pain struck her head—struck her head—and seemed to knock it free of her body.


"How did Osmund know to find us at The Grange this morning?" Caroline asked as she held on during the wild carriage ride to Osmund's cottage.

"Who knows?" Mark answered, urging the horses. "I suppose he saw us pass. He said your grandmother seemed all

right when she reached his house. Why do you think she went
in the first place?"

"I only know it scares me having him pounding along
behind us now!"

"I'll need him to help me get her in the carriage. We've got
to take her home."

"Oh, Mark, what if she's—dying?"

To Caroline, the carriage ride back to Knightsford, her
grandmother's motionless body in her arms, seemed endless.
It did end, though, and she walked helplessly behind Osmund
and Mark as they carried the limp form up the front steps and
into the big house.

"Shouldn't she be on the first floor?" Mark gasped, out of
breath.

"No. There's only one bedroom down here," Caroline said.
"She would be in a terrible state if she came to—in Grandfather's room. Take her upstairs, please! Take her to her own
rooms. She'll feel safe there."

Through the long night, Caroline didn't leave her grandmother's bedside, although Mark begged her to let him stay.
"She might wake up and want me. I'm all right, Mark. My
fear of her—is gone. Stay close to Natalie. I'm all right."

About noon the next day, Osmund returned by boat from
Savannah with Dr. Jones. Caroline, numb for lack of sleep,
was waiting with Mark in Ethel's room when Dr. Jones joined
them.

"She's had a stroke," Jones said, after he examined the still
form in the bed. "She seems to have no use of her right side.
No response when I prick her. Of course, she is unconscious.
Try to keep her comfortable. She may or may not come to
again."

"There's—nothing you can do for her?" Caroline whispered. "Nothing?"

Jones shook his head, patted Caroline's arm and went
downstairs with Mark.

From the hall outside her grandmother's room, where she'd
gone to try to compose herself before returning to the sick
bed, Caroline heard Mark say from downstairs, "A glass of
brandy before you go back to town, Doctor?"

"Sounds good, Browning. I'm not as young as I once was,

either. By the way, that Kott fellow seems to be working out all right for you here."

"I don't see how he could do better," she heard Mark answer.

"Well, he can certainly handle a sailboat. Magnificent!"

"Sit down, sir," Mark said. "I'll get your brandy and send for Kott to take you back to the city."

Weak and stiff with exhaustion, Caroline returned to her grandmother's room, opened the door—a thing she'd never done before without knocking—and sat down again at the bedside.

Except for a barely perceptible rising and falling of the withered breasts, there was no movement whatever. She looks almost young, Caroline thought. How pretty she must have been then. "Grandmother," she whispered, "forgive me. Forgive Grandfather. Please, please, forgive *him*. His loving heart—" She fell silent. Her head against the back of the rocker where she sat, she thought—no. Grandmother didn't know about his loving heart. Only Mary Cotting and I knew about that. Only Mary Cotting and I and—Mark's mother, little Melissa. I know he loved Melissa. Maybe he even loved Osmund once.

She sat up, ashamed that her thoughts had flown so naturally away from the still, pale, lonely form on the bed—straight to her grandfather.

Leaning now toward the bed, she picked up the bony-thin hand. "Grandmother, I love you, too, now. Can you hear me? Please come back. Please, please come back and let me prove it. Come back for Natalie's sake! She's too young to understand about—dying."

The front door closed softly downstairs and Caroline knew the doctor had gone. Mark would undoubtedly walk with him to the dock. Instant alarm and fear seized her. Not fear of the helpless old woman in the bed, but of being alone in the big house without Mark—even for a short time. Trembling violently, she rushed out into the hall and down a few steps—to find Mark on the landing. He hurried to her. "You didn't go to the dock," she gasped, and fell into his arms.

"No, no, dearest, I'm right here. Osmund was waiting on the veranda. He'll take good care of Dr. Jones." Mark looked at her, "You're white as a ghost! Is she worse?"

Caroline shook her head. "Just the same. But I—I was terrified—in this house—when I thought you'd gone out even for
a minute."

"You're so tired," he said, holding her. "You're asleep on
your feet. Tonight, I'm sitting with your grandmother."

"No! I can't sleep in Grandfather's room by myself!" She
hid her face on his shoulder. "I'm really all right, except
that—I'm afraid. I'm afraid in—a new way. I couldn't sleep
—where he slept. Not without you." She clung to him.

"Listen to me, Caroline. Listen carefully. What you're feeling now has just been mostly pushed down inside you all these
years. There isn't anything new to be afraid of. There isn't."

She nodded. "I know, but I'm even scared I might—see my
grandfather's ghost in his room. That's how mixed up and
rattled I am, Mark. I hurt for Grandmother because it might
be too late for her ever to know she's—loved now. I hurt for
*him!*"

Her sobs brought Prince tiptoeing from the kitchen.

"Miss Caroline will be all right," Mark told him. "Get
some tea and bring it along with fresh linens to the first room
at the top of the stair. Bring the baby's cradle. Tell Lettie to
make up the bed, then light a fire, please. Miss Caroline is
sleeping upstairs tonight."

"Thank—you," she sobbed as he led her the rest of the way
up the stair. "Thank you."

# FIFTY-SEVEN

For the remainder of the day, Caroline agreed that Lettie would sit with Grandmother Cameron so that Mark could spend more time with Natalie.

"We should have brought Gerta along," she said as they went for a short walk in the late afternoon while the child napped. "I confess I was afraid a—white servant would upset my grandmother."

Mark was smiling at her. She could feel it. "Might make her think you're married to an Abolitionist?"

"Oh, I don't know. Something like that, I suppose. You're so patient. How can you stand me? You not only have one infant, some days you have two! Natalie isn't very happy with poor Mina looking after her. I was stupid not to bring her own nurse."

"I can send Osmund back to town tomorrow for Gerta, if it will ease your mind."

"I think it would, but I hate asking another favor of him."

"Actually, Osmund's offered to spend time with Natalie. She seems to like him."

"*What?*"

"Caroline, the man isn't all bad. He's been kind to your grandmother."

"I don't know that he isn't all bad. And no—he can't look after Natalie. None of this must harm her in any way." She stopped walking to look at him. "I honestly believe you'd trust our little girl to that—man!"

After a moment, he smiled at her again and said quietly, "Yes, I would. But not if it upsets you."

"No, Mark!" she shouted. "No! No! No!" A kind of self-anger swept through her, and the more she heard herself shout at Mark, the angrier she became. "I'm tired of letting your soft heart make me feel as though I'm—a *witch!* I'm sick and tired of your trusting people as though everyone were as—as good as you insist upon being!" When he tried to calm her, she fought like a child in a rage, pounding him on the chest with her fists. "Let go of me—stop pampering Osmund Kott —and act like a *man!*" She was crying now, pounding Mark again because she wanted so to pound herself. "Stop it, do you hear me? Stop it! Stop it, Mark!"

His arms at his sides, he said, "Caroline, I love you."

"I love you, too, idiot!" Her voice broke. "You are an idiot or you wouldn't love me. Mark? Mark, please make me stop—" In his arms now, she cried until her head ached. Blessedly, he kept quiet. If he'd spoken one kind, loving word, she might have slapped him.

Then, she stopped crying. For what could have been a full minute, or five minutes, she stood apart from him in the Knightsford lane, her face buried in her hands. The fury she'd felt took time to drain away. Finally, she found the voice to say, "I—don't care—how disgraceful divorces are. If I were you, I'd divorce me! I—didn't mean any of what I said to you. . . ."

Back in the upstairs room he'd had prepared so that she could get some rest, Caroline stood with Mark beside the cherrywood cradle and looked at their sleeping child. Mark had not said a word since her helpless attempt at humor about a divorce, her helpless apology. Humor had almost always rescued them. She was sure he must be punishing her this time. They had exchanged not one word, nor had their eyes met. His gaze was fixed now on the sleeping little girl. Only once or twice had Caroline failed to sense at least the mood of what he was thinking. Even when Grandfather died, she had not felt this—*lost*.

"Do you really think Osmund Kott could—harm her?" he asked quietly.

"I don't know, Mark!" She'd be sure to wake Natalie if she raised her voice like that again. "I'm not much of a mother right now. I'm just—me and I'm afraid, I'm deathly afraid, of being shut out so far away from you. Come back to me. Please!''

He was looking at her now, his eyes neither cold nor angry. Not even hurt. Puzzled? Was she so—unlike herself at Knightsford that she puzzled even Mark?

"May I help you get undressed?" he asked, his voice still telling her nothing. "I'd like very much to bring you a tray from the kitchen and put you safely to bed before I take Natalie down to have her supper."

He didn't caress her once, but his hands were gentle as he unhooked her dress, helped her out of it, out of her petticoats and drawers and into a nightgown. Neither spoke. Neither seemed ready for the drastic adjustment they'd have to make should their talking rouse Natalie. Slowly, so the headboard wouldn't creak too much, Caroline eased herself into bed. Mark covered her and removed a pillow because he knew she liked to sleep with her head flat on the mattress.

"Even a short nap will help," he said. "You could catch twenty winks, I'll bet, while I'm down in the kitchen."

Lettie had offered herself again or Prince to sit with Ethel Cameron that night, but Mark thought Caroline would sleep better knowing that he was there. Settled in a fairly comfortable large rocker, brought from an unoccupied room, he began the long vigil. He thought Ethel Cameron's color was a bit more natural. Once, after half an hour or so, he was sure the thin eyelids flickered, ever so slightly. He spoke her name. There was no response.

His thoughts went quickly back to Caroline. She had shrieked at him, but they had not quarreled. He couldn't have endured that. Anger, bad feelings, had always made him ill. A quarrel with Caroline was more than he could comprehend. And yet, he knew he had frightened her by the merest suggestion that he might trust Kott with Natalie. She was simply in such a state that anything he might have added could only have made matters worse. He had gambled on silence. He now knew—now saw so clearly—that she had tried too hard to bring a quick end to her grief over Jonathan Cameron. Had tried too hard, for Mark's sake.

He, of all people, should have better understood the depth of her grief. Not only had he lost the two people dearest to

him, pain still shot through his heart like a bullet when
Mackay came to mind. He still missed his friend. Especially
when he was dressed in his officer's uniform and was marching with the Chatham Artillery through the streets of Savannah, the memory of Mackay's pleasure in that uniform never
failed to rush over Mark. At this minute, he could almost hear
Mackay's buoyant explanation of why they marched, sleeves
touching, in ranks that formed a human wall. "Because our
cannons are so heavy that they have to be carted, we often
march like infantrymen. Infantrymen can be attacked by
cavalry. A horse won't jump over a wall too high for him.
He'll turn back. If we're forming a high man-sized human
wall, we're safe."

Mark longed to form a wall for Caroline until her heart
could find peace again. He frowned, rubbed his forehead to
blot out the sound of her voice screaming: "Stop pampering
Osmund Kott—and act like a *man!*"

A man-sized wall. The shriek, so unlike Caroline, did not
linger. He longed to tell her right now that it would not. She
had screamed at him from helplessness. He had once felt
helpless before Eliza Mackay that long-ago night when he
foolishly asked her to marry him. There was no comparison,
of course. Caroline's trouble ran so much deeper, but the
humiliation, the helpless shame, were similar. He knew even
as she shouted the words that she did not mean one of them.
Anyone can lose control when pain is sharp enough. Caroline
had spoiled him. Through so much, she had remained so confident, so brave. Loving him, she had kept control of her emotions even through his immature adoration of Eliza Mackay. I
wrong her, he thought, when I expect her never to crack.
Maybe I'm growing impatient with her fear of her grandmother, of Osmund Kott. Maybe I've never really understood
it.

He got up and went to the window. There was only black
outside; nothing had shape or color. But something distinct
was beginning to form in his mind as he stared into the night.
Almost like the gradual coming of dawn, he was slowly beginning to see that without realizing it, *he* had remained safely
outside the Cameron trouble. Oh, he had made himself accept
the strange circumstances of his mother's early life, but Mark
Browning had reached his majority before he had a hint that a

man named Jonathan Cameron lived anywhere on the earth. Perhaps he had seemed to accept it so well because—until this moment—he *had* been able to stand *outside* the tragedy, looking in, trying to help, offering advice, but not once feeling the bondage.

Wouldn't he have been better prepared to help Caroline now, he wondered, if he'd allowed himself to move inside her pain? To understand Cameron better? Had he rather looked down on Jonathan Cameron as being weak? Too weak to stand up to Osmund Kott? To risk town gossip? With all his charm and gentleness, too selfish ever to have given Ethel Cameron a chance? Had Mark perhaps resented Cameron's use of Caroline as a go-between? Had this given him the convenient excuse not to dwell on his own grandfather's suffering?

Something like guilt had begun to gnaw at his mind, but he quickly refused it. Undoubtedly, had he not stood outside the trouble, he could have helped Caroline more, but to feel guilt was probably a kind of arrogance. He was not "all good" as people thought of him now and then. He was human. As selfconcerned and as faulty as any other man. As any woman. He and Caroline were in the human predicament together. For the first time, he realized how comforting a truth that could be.

Back in his chair beside Ethel Cameron's bed, he dozed, then seemed to awaken on the thought that once Ethel died, Caroline would be free of both Camerons. Fully awake, he knew that would not be true at all. Caroline could only be freed by the chance for her and her grandmother to experience peace together before it was too late.

He sat studying the immobile, fine-boned face. If you could bring yourself to give her that tiny ring she wanted so much as a little girl, he thought, you could wipe out all those ugly years by that one gesture, Mrs. Cameron. He glanced about the large, well-furnished room, wondering idly where the old lady kept the small gold signet ring.

Surprisingly, the thought of the child's ring he had never seen turned his thoughts to Osmund Kott, child of Bethesda Orphanage, who had grown into the man no one trusted. But wasn't Osmund a child of Knightsford, too? The reality of that also seemed to strike for the first time. Kott, like Caroline, had been born at Knightsford. He sighed. If ever a man had been born to trouble, it was Kott. Like a lightning flash, Mark remembered his own boyhood terror when Osmund Kott had driven Aunt Nassie to scream, out of control with anger. The man had a knack for making the world shriek back at him. And yet, he was born of the same parents as Mark's mother, who had left behind only fragrance and beauty.

The nearly soundless breathing from the big bed changed to gasps and groans as Ethel Cameron opened her eyes. "Who's —there?" she whispered, her words slurred.

"It's Mark, Mrs. Cameron. How wonderful to see you open your eyes! I—almost can't believe it. You're looking right at me, aren't you? You *know* me!"

"You're—married—to my granddaughter. Why—not?"

Not wanting to overwhelm her with either talk or motion, Mark waited while she moved the fingers on her left hand, fluttering them ever so slightly, like a tiny bird restless in the nest. Then, she frowned and turned her head to look at her limp right hand lying open on the blue silk counterpane. Her frown deepened. She groaned with the struggle. The limp fingers did not move. Her dim eyes turned to Mark, beseeching him.

"Don't worry too much," he said. "Dr. Jones wasn't even sure you'd wake up. Since you have, and since you can speak, I'm sure you'll get back the use of your right side."

Her eyes darted toward her legs. The left pushed up the covers, the right lay motionless.

"Where is my leg—it's gone!" she whispered. Tears squeezed from her eyes.

"You are temporarily paralyzed," he said. "I'm sure it's only for a time."

There was so much agony of spirit, so much pain in her face, Mark tried to look away. He couldn't. She deserved someone to watch with her, to try to feel with her while she pushed her way through the stark realization of sudden helplessness. The left side of her body—her left hand, the left corner of her thin, dry mouth—twitched. For the first time, Mark saw that one side of her face was paralyzed, too. He reached for her able hand. She jerked it back. He waited.

Mark hadn't noticed the ticking of the small porcelain clock on her dressing table. He heard it now.

"I want so much to help," he said.

The good hand flipped at him, as though to say: *No one can.*

The clock ticked. The minutes marched away. Finally, she looked at him again, her left hand clenched into a thin, bony fist. "I—need to—take my walks," she said hoarsely. "I—need to—to cut—my dolls. I—need to—dress *every day.*" Her head moved from side to side, slowly, as though she wondered, even marveled, at her own despair. "I—don't—have anything else—to live for."

"You have—Caroline," he ventured.

The good hand gestured again. "She—loathes—me."

"You're wrong," he said evenly and, he hoped, convincingly. "You're wrong about that. She's been so troubled all these years. She needs you to love her now."

The gray head turned away. "It's—late," she whispered. "It's—late, Mark."

Somehow her first use of his Christian name gave him hope. "It's never too late for love, Mrs. Cameron. Caroline knows how to love you now. You can take my word for that. She'll be overjoyed to know you're awake and talking."

"Why isn't—she here—then?"

"Because she sat with you all last night and part of the day. I made her go to bed. She was crying so hard, I—just made her rest."

"Why—was she—crying?"

"Worry over you in the main."

The hand flipped again.

"I wouldn't lie to you," he said.

"No, Caroline—is—blessed. Go, please, over—there to my —dressing table. In the top—left-hand drawer—a tiny velvet box. Bring it." She lifted her good hand, adding, "Then, go to the table by the—front window—bring my Bible."

Mark picked up the single candle, did as she asked and came back to her. "Which do you want first?"

"The box, please. Open it."

When he lifted the curved lid, a small gold circlet lay on the deep-blue velvet lining. "It's the baby ring Caroline always longed for you to give her," he said. "Oh, Mrs. Cameron, if you give it to her now, everything will be all right. Do you know that very thought came to me while you were still asleep?"

Her look was piercing. "For Natalie. Natalie—is my—joy. *You* give it—to—your little daughter."

Mark frowned. "That's kind of you, so kind of you, but I beg you to ask Caroline to give it to the baby. Please, Mrs. Cameron."

After a long silence, she said rather clearly, "I like you, Mark, but—I owe you—nothing. It is—my wish that *you* give —the ring—to—my darling Natalie."

"Wouldn't it be more meaningful if you gave it to her yourself? You know she adores you."

Ignoring him, her speech thickening, she instructed him to lift the cover of her Bible, to remove the letter he'd find there addressed to her. *"Do not* unfold the letter, *do not* read it. Burn it. Before—my eyes, please. Burn—every—shred. . . ."

Careful not to examine it, Mark took the letter and stood where she could see his every move. "Are you sure?" he asked.

"Burn it!"

"You're absolutely certain?" he asked again.

"Yes!" She choked, coughed, then barked in a raspy voice: "Burn it!"

Still careful to let her see him, Mark did as she asked, standing to one side of the fireplace so she could watch until the last black curl vanished into ash.

Back beside her again, he took her good hand. This time she permitted it. Ever so slightly, he felt her dry, weak fingers tighten over his. Mark smoothed the damp hair back from her forehead. "Caroline and I love you," he said simply. "Please don't turn us away."

One side of her mouth twitched.

"Can you rest awhile now?" he asked. "I'll be right here. Then, first thing in the morning, I'll bring Caroline and Natalie to visit you. If you can't give Caroline the little ring for Natalie, I promise I'll do it for you."

Her lined, papery cheeks were wet. She nodded, then closed her eyes.

The next morning, Mark waited in the upstairs hall while Caroline and Natalie went in to her. For half an hour or so, he could hear Caroline's low voice, Natalie's surprisingly subdued talk, her baby laughter, the rasp of Ethel Cameron's slow, labored speech.

Suddenly, Natalie's voice, strangely tight and scared, cried: "Mama! *Mama?*"

Then, silence.

After what seemed a long, long time, the door opened softly and Caroline, holding the velvet ring box in one hand, Natalie by the other, fell into Mark's arms and wept.

Beyond the open door as he held her, he could see the frail, flat form covered over entirely by the blue silk counterpane.

# FIFTY-EIGHT

AT Sheftall Sheftall's urging, they buried Ethel beside Jonathan at the site where Mary Cotting's house had stood. Aside from the rector of Christ Church, the Reverend Abiel Carter, the only Savannahians to attend the funeral were Eliza —in spite of Jack's departure for West Point—Cousin Margaret and Sheftall.

"You were right to persuade Caroline to bury her there," Eliza said to Sheftall Sheftall two days later as she and Margaret waited with him on the dock for Osmund Kott to ready the bigger Cameron boat for their return to Savannah. "You're a good and wise friend. Mark and Caroline need you."

Eliza noticed Margaret glancing up the river path, along which the Brownings, arm in arm, were coming to say good-bye. "Before they are within hearing distance, Mr. Sheftall," she said, "you're a peacemaker. I'm sure seeing her grandparents united in death will help heal Caroline's wounds."

Sheftall nodded sagely. "I felt so, Mrs. McQueen." He looked out over the river, but Eliza could see that behind the round spectacles, his eyes had filled with tears. "I—I was devoted to both Camerons. Odd, most people thought. But then, most people think me odd."

Eliza hurried along the dock to embrace Caroline and Mark. "Are you two sure you shouldn't be going back to town with us? I know how disappointed William and the girls will be. William was so nervous about being left in charge of your affairs, Mark,"

"We're coming back tomorrow," Caroline said. "We both

586

think it's best for Natalie to stay here, at least through another night and day."

"She's disturbed." Mark frowned. "We left her just now, Lettie in pursuit. She's still hunting her great-grandmother. Natalie needs a little more time to adjust to Knightsford without her."

"Just know we'll all be thinking about you," Eliza said. "Have dinner with us when you get back to the city tomorrow, please?"

"Of course we will—gladly," Caroline said. "We should be in town a little after noon."

Eliza nodded to the Reverend Abiel Carter, who now followed Prince down the river path to join them for the boat trip home. "I'd like to thank you, Reverend Carter, for your many kindnesses to us all."

Caroline and Mark thanked him again, too, as they shook hands once more. "My coming may have been providential," the rector whispered to Mark and Caroline. "I had no chance to tell you last night, Browning, but Mr. Kott informed me yesterday that he wants to become a communicant of Christ Church soon. He feels he's ready spiritually."

Eliza saw Caroline's dismay. She also saw her quick recovery when Mark gave his wife an anxious glance.

"Yes," Mark said carefully. "Kott has also spoken to me about it. I'm—willing to sponsor him, Reverend Carter."

"I see. Well, he did behave as a perfect gentleman when he brought us here from town. In fact, he spoke most earnestly of his faith."

"Thank you for telling me, sir," Mark said. "I'll drop by the rectory for a talk within the next week or so."

Good-byes were said hastily, because on the quiet, clear winter morning, everyone could hear Natalie crying all the way from the big house. Back with the child, Mark tried and Caroline tried. Even Prince attempted to distract her from her demands to see Dram Cam by riding her on his shoulders as he used to ride Caroline. Nothing worked.

Natalie slept, finally, for two fitful hours in the afternoon, then woke up screaming her protest—still angry because her mother and father could not produce Dram Cam.

Caroline did manage to feed her a few bites of custard, but

in no time Natalie threw it up all over her mother's last clean housedress. The crying began again and went on until nearly dark, when Osmund Kott, back from Savannah, stopped by to tell them that William had met Eliza and Margaret. Kott had personally seen the Reverend Carter to his house.

"Is the little girl ill?" Kott asked, standing with the Brownings on the veranda because they had not invited him in.

"No," Caroline said quickly. "Well, I don't think she's really ill. She's—"

"She's terribly upset that she can't find her great-grandmother," Mark offered. "It will take time. She doesn't realize what's happened."

A fresh burst of wailing came nearer as Natalie's uneven footsteps pounded toward them along the entrance hall.

"Oh, dear," Caroline said, "she's gotten away from Lettie again!"

"I'll go to her," Mark said. "Thank you, Kott. See you tomorrow before we go."

Mark reached for the child, who jerked past him and ran straight to Osmund.

"Natalie!" Caroline gasped.

"It's all right, Miss Caroline," Kott said, kneeling to embrace the distraught child. "It's all right, isn't it, Natalie? Everything's going to be—just fine, from now on."

Mark and Caroline stood staring at their daughter—no longer wailing, snuggling into Kott's arms, beginning to make almost happy little singing sounds.

Still kneeling, Kott held the child away from him so he could look right into her red, swollen eyes. "Listen, Natalie," he said confidentially, "I have to go to my own house and get some sleep now. Just the way you'll be in your bed in no time, sleeping, too. We'll both sleep and then, before you know it, I'll be back to see you."

The child gave a short, delighted laugh. "Like Dram Cam?"

"That's right," Kott said. "Like—Dram Cam."

When, at high tide, Prince pushed Caroline, Natalie and Mark away from the Knightsford dock in the Mackays' old sailboat about ten the next morning, the air was mild and there was just enough wind to fill the sails. Neither Mark nor Caro-

line could face the return trip by land. Two of the Knightsford
people would drive their carriage back to town later in the
week. Anyway, Natalie loved sailing on the river.

"We'll think of lots of things to do, honey," Mark told his
daughter, who sat bright-eyed, now seemingly content, on the
stern seat beside Caroline. "Right now, by sitting very still,
you'll be helping Mama steer the boat."

The child laughed.

"I hate to admit it," Caroline said, after they'd glided along
for a time past the winter-bare sweet gums, the shadowy oaks
and the myrtles along the shore, "but he helped us out last
night and this morning, didn't he?"

"Osmund? Yes, he did. Our daughter seems to feel about
him exactly the way she felt about Mrs. Cameron."

"I know," Caroline said and fell silent.

After a moment, Mark smiled. "I couldn't translate the
meaning of that 'I know,' Mrs. Browning. Was it—relieved?
Or was it—anxious?"

"It was just plain worried. I don't like it, Mark. I don't like
her to be close to him at all."

"Remember what Miss Eliza said. Children her age go
through phases. A month later, they may not even recognize
someone whom they once adored. We were helped past a bad
time last night and again this morning. I'm just going to be
thankful."

Caroline hugged Natalie to her and returned Mark's smile.
"All right, dearest. Me, too." Then she took such a deep
breath and exhaled so noisily that Natalie began imitating her.
"That's enough, Natalie," Caroline laughed. "Mama won't
do that again. Neither of us had better breathe so hard again
or we'll get whirly in the head."

This made Natalie laugh loudly, and then she began to
shout "pat-a-cake, pat-a-cake, baker's man" at the top of her
voice. They let her go on for a time, and when she shouted
"Dram Cam!" in the same happy, carefree way, they exchanged vastly relieved looks.

"Maybe the bad time is really over," Mark said.

"Oh, darling, I wish we weren't in a boat! I wish I were
where I could put my arms around you and tell you and tell
you that—yes, yes, the bad time could be over!" She beamed
at him. "Maybe it *is* over—really over. Not only for our red-

head, for her mother, too. What a patient, loving father our daughter has."

Mark smiled back at her, kept smiling. "Dear Caroline, if Natalie's mother is all right at last, then her father's world is perfect."

"You're not at all worried about Osmund, are you?" she asked, after a time.

"Do you want the truth?"

"Of course I want the truth!"

"No. And I'm not going to worry about him. The worst thing he can do to me is—torment you."

"I really have made some progress, haven't I?"

He blew her a kiss. "And I'm proud. Welcome back to— *our* world, darling."

Natalie had stopped jabbering. Mark thought she actually looked sleepy. "Can you let her catch a few winks on your lap and still keep us in the middle of the river?" he asked.

"Watch me."

Mark tugged at the sheet. "We barely have enough wind. I wish I could make this boat go faster."

"Are you longing to kiss me, too?"

"Longing is not a strong enough word, ma'am."

"She's already sound asleep."

He looked adoringly at the child. "What an incredibly beautiful little girl you gave me, Caroline. With all my heart, I wish Mackay could see her."

"I wish Grandfather could see her—our parents, too, yours and mine. And oh, I do wish Aunt Nassie could see her name-sake!"

"Our little minx gave your grandmother real happiness, didn't she?"

Caroline's eyes glowed. "And, Mark, Grandmother and I made peace! That's the miracle." After a time, she asked lightly, "Why do you suppose you thought of Mr. Mackay a minute ago? I know you still miss him, but what was it that brought him to your mind—right then?"

He grinned. "Moving along in a boat, I guess, on my way again to my one place to be."

"Savannah."

Mark's whole heart sang in his response: "That's right, dearest. Savannah . . ."

# *AFTERWORD*

BECAUSE she lived eighty-four years, Eliza Mackay will go on being an integral part of the lives of Mark and Caroline Browning through a second novel to follow *Savannah*—a sequel on which research is already under way. I became attached to Eliza and Robert Mackay in writing her father's story, *Don Juan McQueen*, and felt strongly that the Mackays were exactly the kind of cultivated but down-to-earth people with whom Mark Browning would form a permanent attachment. The Camerons and the Brownings are—difficult as it is for the author to believe after having "lived" with them for most of two years—fictitious, although soundly based on study of the social history of their period and the contents of old letters.

The Mackays, of course, were real people, and many other actual names of early Savannahians have been used. Once more I am indebted to my late beloved friend, historian Walter C. Hartridge, for the superb material in his books *The Letters of Robert Mackay* and *The Letters of Don Juan McQueen to His Family*. It should be noted here that for simplification for both author and reader, three children of the Robert Mackay family were not used in the novel: Mary Anne, later Mrs. Benjamin Stiles; Margaret, later Mrs. Ralph Emms Elliott; and a second son named Robert.

Robert Mackay's grave may be found in New York, not far from Broadway, beneath Trinity Church's Gothic spire. The flat stone reads simply:

In Memory of
Robert Mackay, Esquire

591

of Georgia,
died 6th. October 1816,
aged 44 years.

Eliza, because Savannah's old Colonial Cemetery (now called Colonial Park) was overcrowded, is buried in lot 486 at Laurel Grove Cemetery, one of Savannah's most picturesque settings. With her lie her children William, Catherine (Kate), Sarah (Sallie) and Eliza Anne's husband, William Henry Stiles. Eliza Anne, probably because of the Civil War, is buried at one of the Stiles plantations, Etowah Cliff, in Cartersville, Georgia. John Mackay (Jack) is with his mother's grandparents, Mr. and Mrs. John Smith, her mother, Anne McQueen, and her brother, John McQueen, in the old Colonial Cemetery, near the monument marking the grave of Button Gwinnett, a Georgia signer of the Declaration of Independence.

Sheftall Sheftall was indeed a very real character, who baffled and charmed Savannahians through a long and curiously respected life. Mr. Sheftall's grave is in the Old Jewish Cemetery in ground given to the highly regarded Jewish community by his father, Mordecai Sheftall, in the eighteenth century. B. H. Levy, whose hospitality and invaluable help were offered unstintingly in my research for *Savannah*, is, with his wife, in possession to this day of Sheftall Sheftall's brown leather cocked hat.

The Robert Mackay home, which stood at what would now be 75 East Broughton, was torn down some years ago to make room for a business district, but other landmark houses are open to the public. The Owens-Thomas House, considered a fine example of English Regency in America, is an experience in the reflected talent and fancy of the young British architect William Jay himself. In fact, I gained enormous insight into Jay's innovative mind from studying this house, presented in the book as the Richardson House, later Mrs. Maxwell's boardinghouse. I gained still more insight into young William Jay by "experiencing" the Scarbrough House at 41 West Broad Street, now the headquarters for the famous Historic Savannah Foundation and open to the public. Julia Scarbrough's night sky, painted by her "artist of degree," is no longer there, but Historic Savannah has restored the impressive house, and your imagination, if you look up upon entering, will have no trouble "seeing" it. Another magnificent Jay creation may be seen by a visit to Savannah's splendid Telfair Academy of Arts and Sciences at 121 Barnard Street. William Jay's handsome bank unfortunately fell to what is still relentlessly called progress.

The lot selected as the site of Mark Browning's house on Reynolds Square at the corner of Abercorn and Bryan are today occupied by the Army Corps of Engineers, but should you dine at The Olde Pink House across the square, you will be in "Mark's neighborhood" and in the oldest residence in town—built by the Habersham family.

On the northwest corner of State and Habersham you will find *my favorite* Savannah house—the Davenport House prominent in the novel. Built by Savannah's master builder, New Englander Isaiah Davenport, the great house escaped the demolition ball in 1955 when the Historic Savannah Foundation saved it. My cherished friend Mary Harty, an authentic Savannahian in all ways, is in charge on weekends of what, to me, is Isaiah Davenport's masterpiece. In a drawing room Mary will show you the handsome oil portrait that is my concept of Mark Browning as a young man. Loving thanks to Mary Harty for productive hours spend with her "learning" the house and Isaiah himself.

Savannah is one of the richest American cities for historic exploration, and there are too many building preserved, including the city's beautiful churches, for mention here. But a leisurely walk through Colonial Park Cemetery, in downtown Savannah, and Laurel Grove Cemetery will fascinate the reader who revels in searching out a book's characters. Any walk or drive through and around Savannah's shadow-and-sun-filled streets and squares and along Factor's Walk can keep a perceptive reader happy for days.

I must also thank Dr. John Bonner, of Camden, South Carolina; Mr. and Mrs. Hugh H. Gordon, of Bluffton, South Carolina; David P. Lawson, Rita Trotz, William Samuel, Gordan Grant, Malcolm Bell, Walter C. Hartridge II, Richard M. Raines, Gordon B. Smith and Remer Lane, of Savannah; for specialized help and guidance. I urge a visit to Fort Jackson and the old building most haunted by the author— Hodgson Hall—home of the superior Georgia Historical

Society at 501 Whitaker Street. To Anthony Dees, director, to his staff, Susan Murphy, Lisa Fore, Karen Osvald and especially to Barbara Bennett, my heart-deep thanks for patience and expertise—by long distance and in person. I also thank Henry Green, of St. Simons Island, who answered as only the expert can the odd questions only a novelist can ask. Thanks also to James Darby, director of the Public Library in Brunswick, Georgia, and to Marsha Hodges and Dorothy Hauseald for their always prompt and accurate assistance.

Mary L. Morrison, author and editor of *Historic Savannah*, the excellent survey of old Savannah houses, not only shared insights and research knowledge; more than once she offered the special easy grace of her hospitality—as did my longtime meaningful friend Susan Hartridge.

Author-playwright Constance O'Hara, of Philadelphia, shared her knowledge of both old Savannah and old Philadelphia. Without Scott W. Smith, director of Fort Jackson, and his wife, Frances Smith, I certainly would have confused the military portions of the book and the history of Fort Jackson. To my friends Frances Pitts, Jimmie Harnsberger, Reba Spann, Sarah Bell Edmond, Agnes Holt, Theo Hotch and Elsie Goodwillie, my love and thanks for so much.

I have yet to learn of an author who dared try a book about Savannah without the singular guidance of Lilla M. Hawes, retired director of the Georgia Historical Society. Lilla not only freely helped throughout the research, she checked the enormous manuscript and confirmed the confidence I had newly placed in a young lady named Brenda Williams Lock. Brenda not only handled my entire historical chronology for *Savannah*, she handled my every peculiar need and whim throughout the long months of research and writing and has already begun research for the sequel to *Savannah*.

As always, words fail in any adequate expression of thanks to my closest friend and fellow author, Joyce Blackburn, who edited an extremely rough version of the entire novel and successfully lived under the same roof with me throughout. With the same inadequacy, I thank Nancy Goshorn, my mother's best friend—more my sister than were we related. Mother died at the exact hour in which the huge manuscript went to my editor, Carolyn Blakemore, at Doubleday. Of thirty-one books, this is the first book Mother did not read in manuscript, but she goes on, with even more energy now, making me believe that I can always write another. Supporting us all and deserving of more than thanks is Mother's neighbor Mary Jane Goshorn, of my hometown, Charleston, West Virginia. In this deeply felt paragraph I want to thank my superb assistant, Eileen Humphlett, of St. Simons Island, who not only typed at high speed through the entire 922 pages of manuscript after coping with her regular workday, but helped with my mail and always with my peace of mind. Eileen's calm intelligence never fails to shrink my most insurmountable mountains. I also thank her husband, Jimmy Humphlett, and her three children, Mark, Jay and Beth, who "played house" so that Eileen could be free to type. All the way from Chicago, my friend Lorrie Carlson went on faithfully lightening the mail load.

Along with Carolyn Blakemore, the one editor I've wanted for so long, I thank her assistants, Peter Schneider and Robert Frese, my expert copyeditor, Janet W. Falcone, and designer, Paul Randall Mize.

I have waited to dedicate just the right book to a cherished friend, who in a singular way has encouraged me to go on lifting my sights as a writer—Easter Straker, of WIMA-TV, Lima, Ohio. We have been friends since before the mountains were in place, and although I now know my reach does not equal your dream for me, here, Easter, is *Savannah*. If it falls short, at least it has been my favorite endeavor to date.

EUGENIA PRICE
St. Simons Island, Georgia

# Eugenia Price

### ❧ ❧ ❧

Hailed as one of the United States' greatest
writers of historical fiction, Eugenia Price
presents the stirring events and everyday
happenings of Georgia's St. Simons Island.

Enjoy all the books in this
stunning trilogy...

**BRIGHT CAPTIVITY**
_____    95968-0  $6.99 U.S./$7.99 CAN.

**WHERE SHADOWS GO**
_____    95969-9  $6.99 U.S./$7.99 CAN.

**BEAUTY FROM ASHES**
_____    95917-6  $6.99 U.S./$7.99 CAN.

Against the backdrop of an elegant Cornwall mansion before World War II and a vast continent-spanning canvas during the turbulent war years, Rosamunde Pilcher's most eagerly-awaited novel is the story of an extraordinary young woman's coming of age, coming to grips with love and sadness, and in every sense of the term, coming home...

# *Rosamunde Pilcher*

The #1 *New York Times* Bestselling Author of *The Shell Seekers* and *September*

# COMING HOME

"Rosamunde Pilcher's most satisfying story since *The Shell Seekers.*"

— *Chicago Tribune*

"Captivating...The best sort of book to come home to...Readers will undoubtedly hope Pilcher comes home to the typewriter again soon."

— *New York Daily News*

## TODAY JOANNA HAS THE LIFE SHE'D ALWAYS DREAMED OF...

Joanna Jones, the successful host of *Fabulous Homes*, a New York-based TV show, seems to have it all. Blessed with great looks, she has a successful lover and a job that gives her fame and money, while allowing her to indulge her passion for beautiful homes.

## TOMORROW SHE MIGHT LOSE IT ALL...

Suddenly and shockingly, Joanna will discover what she doesn't have: a committed relationship she can depend on. Now she faces a stunning discovery alone and makes the tough decision to leave her glittering life for an old Nantucket house on the ocean, new friends, and unexpected enemies. The choices ahead will test her courage; the surprising twists of fate will challenge her faith as she faces a day of ashes, a time of sorrow, and one extraordinary new chance for love, happiness and....

# ~ *Belonging* ~

## BY NANCY THAYER

**"Nancy Thayer has a rare talent for conveying the complexity and richness of women."**
**—*Publishers Weekly***